Shadow Falls: The Beginning

Born at Midnight

and

Awake at Dawn

c. c. hunter

🦅 ST. MARTIN'S GRIFFIN 🐾 NEW YORK

SHADOW FALLS: THE BEGINNING: BORN AT MIDNIGHT Copyright © 2011 by C. C. Hunter and AWAKE AT DAWN Copyright © 2011 by C. C. Hunter. All rights reserved. Printed in the United States of America. For information, address St. Martin's Press, 175 Fifth Avenue, New York, N.Y. 10010.

www.stmartins.com

Design by Kelly S. Too

ISBN 978-1-250-03682-7 (trade paperback)

First Edition: March 2013

10 9 8 7 6 5

Born at Midnight

To Lilly Dale Makepeace.
Just looking at your smile reminds that magic
is alive and thriving in this big old world.

Acknowledgments

They say it takes a village to raise a child; well, it also takes one to get a spark of an idea and turn it into a book. First I want to acknowledge my editor, Rose Hilliard. Your faith in me means more than you'll ever know. And here's to my other village people: My husband for being supportive to the point of perfection. I'll love you forever, baby! My agent, Kim Lionetti, who takes my dreams and helps them become a reality. What's next, Kim? My village angels who are my critique partners and writing family: Faye Hughes, Jody Payne, Suzan Harden, and Teri Thackston. Girls, thank you for the support, but mostly, thank you for the friendship.

Chapter One

"This isn't funny!" her father yelled.

No, it wasn't, Kylie Galen thought as she leaned into the refrigerator to find something to drink. In fact, it was so not funny she wished she could crawl in beside the mustard and moldy hot dogs, shut the door, and not hear the angry voices spewing from the living room.

Her parents were at it again.

Not that it would go on much longer, she thought as the mist of the fridge seeped out the door.

Today was the day.

Kylie's throat tightened. She swallowed a lump of raw emotion and refused to cry.

Today had to be the suckiest day of her life. And she'd had some pretty sucky days lately, too. Acquiring a stalker, Trey breaking up with her, and her parents announcing their divorce—yup, sucky pretty much covered it. It was no wonder her night terrors had returned full force.

"What have you done with my underwear?" Her father's

growl spilled into the kitchen, snuck under the refrigerator door, and bounced around the hot dogs.

His underwear? Kylie pressed a cold diet soda can to her forehead.

"Why would I do anything with your underwear?" her mother asked in her oh-so-nonchalant voice. That was her mom all right, nonchalant. Cold as ice.

Kylie's gaze shot out the kitchen window to the patio where she'd seen her mom earlier. There, a pair of her dad's tighty-whities dangled half out of the smoldering grill.

Just great. Her mother had barbecued her father's shorts. That's it. Kylie was never eating anything cooked on that grill again.

Fighting tears, she shoved the diet soda back on the rack, shut the fridge, and moved into the doorway. Maybe if they saw her, they'd stop acting like juveniles and let her be the kid again.

Her dad stood in the middle of the room, a pair of underwear clutched in his fist. Her mom sat on the sofa, calmly sipping hot tea.

"You need psychological help," her father yelled at her mom.

Two points for her dad, Kylie thought. Her mom did need help. So why was Kylie the one who had to sit on a shrink's sofa two days a week?

Why was her dad—the man everyone swore Kylie had wrapped around her little finger—going to move out today and leave her behind?

She didn't blame her dad for wanting to leave her mom, aka

the Ice Queen. But why wasn't he taking Kylie with him? Another lump rose in her throat.

Dad swung around and saw her, then shot back into the bedroom, obviously to pack the rest of his things—minus his underwear, which at this moment sent up smoke signals from the backyard grill.

Kylie stood there, staring at her mom, who sat reading over work files as if it were any other day.

The framed photographs of Kylie and her father that hung over the sofa caught her attention and tears stung her eyes. The pictures had been taken on their annual father and daughter trips.

"You've got to do something," Kylie pleaded.

"Do what?" her mom asked.

"Change his mind. Tell him you're sorry you grilled his shorts." *That you're sorry you've got ice water running through your veins.* "I don't give a flip what you do, just don't let him go."

"You don't understand." And just like that, her mom, void of any emotion, shifted her attention back to her papers.

Right then, her dad, suitcase in his hand, shot through the living room. Kylie went after him and followed him out the door into Houston's stifling afternoon heat.

"Take me with you," she begged, not caring if he saw her tears. Maybe the tears would help. There'd been a time when crying got her whatever she wanted from him. "I don't eat much," she sniffled, giving humor a shot.

He shook his head but, unlike her mom, at least he had emotion in his eyes. "You don't understand."

You don't understand. "Why do y'all always say that? I'm sixteen years old. If I don't understand, then explain it to me. Tell me the big secret and get it over with."

He stared down at his feet as if this were a test and he'd penned the answers on the toes of his shoes. Sighing, he looked up. "Your mom . . . she needs you."

"Needs me? Are you kidding? She doesn't even want me." *And neither do you.* The realization caused Kylie's breath to catch in her lungs. He really didn't want her.

She wiped a tear from her cheek and that's when she saw him again. Not her dad, but Soldier Dude, aka her very own stalker. Standing across the street, he wore the same army duds as before. He looked as if he'd just walked out of one of those Gulf War movies her mom loved. Only instead of shooting at things or being blown up, he stood frozen in one spot and stared right at Kylie with sad, yet very scary eyes.

She'd noticed him stalking her a few weeks ago. He'd never spoken to her and she hadn't spoken to him. But the day she pointed him out to her mom, and Mom hadn't seen him . . . well, that's when Kylie's world slid off its axis. Her mom thought she was making it up to get attention, or worse. With the worse being that Kylie was losing her grip on reality. Sure, the night terrors that had tormented her when she was a kid had returned, worse than ever. Her mom said the shrink could help her work through them, but how could she do that when Kylie didn't even remember them? She only knew they were bad. Bad enough to have her wake up screaming.

Kylie wanted to scream now. Wanted to scream for her dad to turn around and look—to prove that she hadn't lost her mind.

At the very least, maybe if her dad actually saw her stalker, her parents would let her off from seeing the shrink. It wasn't fair.

But life wasn't fair, as her mom had reminded her more than once.

Nevertheless, when Kylie looked back, he was gone. Not Soldier Dude, but her dad. She turned toward the driveway and saw him shoving his suitcase in the backseat of his red convertible Mustang. Mom had never liked that car, but Dad loved it.

Kylie ran to the car. "I'll make Grandma talk to Mom. She'll fix . . ." No sooner had the words escaped Kylie's lips than she remembered the other major sucky event she'd had plopped into her life.

She couldn't run to Grandma to fix her problems anymore. Because Grandma was dead. Gone. The vision of Nana lying cold in the casket filled Kylie's head and another lump crawled up her throat.

Her dad's expression morphed into parental concern, the same look that had landed Kylie at the shrink's office three weeks ago.

"I'm fine. I just forgot." Because remembering hurt too much. She felt a lone tear roll down her cheek.

Dad moved in and hugged her. The embrace lasted even longer than his usual hugs, but it ended too soon. How could she let him go? How could he leave her?

His arm dropped from around her and he physically set her back. "I'm just a phone call away, Pumpkin."

Swiping at her tears, hating her watery weakness, she watched her dad's red convertible get smaller as it buzzed down the street. Wanting to be alone in her room, she started to run inside. Then she remembered and looked back across the street to see if Soldier Dude had pulled his usual disappearing act.

Nope. He was still there, staring, stalking. Scaring the bejeebies out of her and making her angry at the same time. He was the reason she had to see a shrink.

Then Mrs. Baker, her elderly neighbor, toddled out to get her mail. She smiled at Kylie but not once did the old librarian glance at Soldier Dude taking up residence on her front lawn, even when he stood less than two feet from her.

Weird.

So weird it sent an unnatural chill tiptoeing down Kylie's spine, the same kind of chill Kylie had gotten at Nana's funeral.

What the hell was going on?

Chapter Two

An hour later, Kylie walked down the stairs with her backpack and purse over her shoulder.

Her mom met her in the entryway. "Are you okay?"

How could I be okay? "I'll live," Kylie answered. More than she could say about Grandma. Right then, Kylie had a vision of the bright purple lipstick the funeral home had put on her grandmother. *Why didn't you take that off of me?* Kylie could almost hear Nana asking.

Weirded out by the thought, Kylie looked back at her mother.

Her mom stared at Kylie's backpack and her worry wrinkle appeared between her eyes. "Where are you going?" she asked.

"You said I could spend the night with Sara. Or were you too busy grilling Dad's shorts to remember?"

Her mom ignored the grilled-shorts comment. "What are you two going to do tonight?"

"Mark Jameson is having an end-of-school party." Not that

Kylie felt like celebrating the event. Thanks to Trey dumping her and her parents divorcing, Kylie's whole summer was headed for the toilet. And the way things were going, someone was going to walk by and flush it.

"Are his parents going to be there?" Mom raised one dark eyebrow.

Kylie flinched emotionally, but physically didn't blink. "Aren't they always?"

Okay, so she lied. Normally she didn't go to Mark Jameson's parties for that very reason, but blast it, look where being good had gotten her. She deserved to have some fun, didn't she?

Besides, hadn't her mom lied when her dad asked about his underwear?

"What if you have another dream?" Her mom touched Kylie's arm.

A quick touch. That's all Kylie ever got from her mom these days. No long hugs like her dad gave. No mother/daughter trips. Just aloofness and quick touches. Even when Nana, her mom's mom, died, Kylie's mom hadn't hugged her and Kylie had really needed a hug then. But it had been her dad who'd pulled her into his arms and let her smear mascara on his suit coat. And now Dad and all his suit coats were gone.

Drawing in a gulp of oxygen, Kylie clutched her purse. "I warned Sara I might wake up screaming bloody murder. She said she'd stake me in the heart with a wooden cross and make me go back to bed."

"Maybe you should hide the stakes before you go to sleep." Her mother attempted to smile.

"I will." For one brief second, Kylie worried about leaving her mom alone on the day her dad had left. But who was she kidding? Her mom would be fine. Nothing ever bothered the Ice Queen.

Before walking out, Kylie peered out the window to make sure she wouldn't be assaulted by a guy wearing army duds.

Deeming the yard to be free of stalkers, Kylie ran out the door, hoping that tonight's party would help her forget just how badly her life sucked.

"Here. You don't have to drink it, just hold it." Sara Jetton pushed a beer into Kylie's hands and ran off.

Sharing elbow room with at least thirty kids, all packed into Mark Jameson's living room and talking at once, Kylie clutched the ice-cold bottle. Glancing around at the crowd, she recognized most of them from school. The doorbell rang again. Obviously, this was the place to be tonight. And according to every other kid at her high school, it was. Jameson, a senior whose parents never seemed to care what he did, held some of the wildest parties in town.

Ten minutes later, Sara still MIA, the party shifted into full swing. Too bad Kylie didn't feel like swinging along with them. She frowned at the bottle in her hand.

Someone bumped into her shoulder, causing the beer to splash on her chest and run down in the V of her white blouse. "Crap."

"Oh, I'm so sorry," the responsible bumper said.

Kylie looked up into John's soft brown eyes and tried to smile. Hey, being nice to a cute guy, who'd been asking about her at school made trying to smile easy. But the fact that John had been friends with Trey kept the thrill down to a minimum.

"It's okay," she said.

"I'll get you another." As if nervous, he shot off.

"It's really okay," Kylie called after him, but between the music and the hum of voices, he didn't hear her.

The doorbell rang again. A few kids shifted around and gave Kylie a view of the door. More specifically, the shift gave her a view of Trey walking inside. Beside him—or she should say plastered against him—sashayed his new slutty girlfriend.

"Great." She swung around, wishing she could teleport herself to Tahiti, or back home would be even better—especially if her dad would be there.

Through a back window, she spotted Sara on the patio and Kylie darted outside to join her.

Sara looked up. She must have read the panic on Kylie's face, because she came running over to her. "What happened?"

"Trey and his screw toy are here."

Sara frowned. "So, you look hot. Go flirt with some guys and make him sorry."

Kylie rolled her eyes. "I don't want to stay here and watch Trey and what's her name making out."

"Were they already making out?" Sara asked.

"Not yet, but get one beer in Trey and all he'll think about is getting into a girl's panties. I know because I used to be the girl in the panties."

"Chill." Sara pointed back at the table. "Gary brought margaritas. Have one and you'll feel fine."

Kylie bit her lip to keep from screaming that she wouldn't feel fine. Her life had toilet-bound stamped all over it.

"Hey." Sara nudged her. "We both know all you'd have to do to get Trey back is to grab him and take him upstairs. He's still crazy about you. He found me before I left school today and asked about you."

"Did you know he was going to be here?" Betrayal started unraveling the little sanity she had left.

"Not for sure. But chill."

Chill? Kylie stared at her best friend and realized how different they'd become these last six months. It wasn't just Sara's need to party or the fact that she'd given up virginhood. Okay, so maybe it was those two things, but it seemed like more.

More as in Kylie had a sneaking suspicion that Sara longed to rush Kylie to join the partying-non-virgin ranks. Could Kylie help it if beer tasted like dog piss to her? Or if the idea of having sex didn't appeal?

Okay, that was a lie, sex appealed to her. When she and Trey had made out, Kylie had been tempted, really tempted, but then Kylie remembered her and Sara talking about how the first time should be special.

Then she recalled how Sara had given in to Brad's "needs"— Brad who was the love of Sara's life—yet, within two weeks of giving in, the love of Sara's life had dumped her. What was so special about that?

Since then, Sara had dated four other guys, and she'd slept

with two of them. Now, Sara had stopped talking about sex being special.

"Look, I know you're worried about your parents," Sara said. "But that's why you need to just let loose and have some fun." Sara tucked her long, brown hair behind her ear. "I'm getting you a margarita and you're going to love it."

Sara darted off to the table by the group of people. Kylie started to follow but her gaze slapped against Soldier Dude, looking as scary and weird as ever, standing by the group of margarita drinkers.

Kylie shot around, prepared to bolt, but she smacked right into a guy's chest, and darn it if more beer didn't jump out of the bottle and fall right between her boobs. "Great. My boobs are going to smell like a brewery."

"Every guy's dream," the husky male voice said. "But I'm sorry."

She recognized Trey's voice before she did his broad shoulders or his unique masculine scent. Preparing herself for the pain that seeing him would cause, she raised her gaze. "It's okay, John's already done it once."

She tried not to stare at the way Trey's sandy brown hair fell against his brow, or the way his green eyes seemed to lure her closer, or the way his mouth tempted her to lean in and press her lips to his.

"So it's true." He frowned.

"What's true?" she asked.

"That you and John have hooked up."

Kylie considered lying. The thought that it would hurt him appealed to her. It appealed to her so much that it reminded her of the stupid games her parents played lately. Oh, no, she would not stoop to their "grown-up" level.

"I haven't hooked up with anyone." She turned to leave.

He caught her. His touch, the feel of his warm hand on her elbow, sent waves of pain right to her heart. And standing this close, his clean, masculine scent filled her airways. Oh God, she loved his smell.

"I heard about your grandma," he said. "And Sara told me about your parents getting a divorce. I'm so sorry, Kylie."

Tears threatened to crawl up her throat. Kylie was seconds away from falling against his warm chest and begging him to hold her. Nothing ever felt better than Trey's arms around her, but then she saw the girl, Trey's screw toy, walk outside, carrying two beers. In less than five minutes, Trey would be trying to get in her panties. And from the too-low-cut blouse and too-short skirt the girl wore, it appeared he wouldn't have to try too hard.

"Thanks," Kylie muttered, and went to join Sara. Luckily, Soldier Dude had decided margaritas weren't his thing after all and left.

"Here." Sara took the beer from Kylie's hand and replaced it with a margarita.

The frosty glass felt unnaturally cold. Kylie leaned in and whispered, "Did you see a strange guy here a minute ago? Dressed in some funky army outfit?"

Sara's eyebrows did their wild, wiggly thing. "How much of that beer did you drink?" Her laughter filled the night air.

Kylie wrapped her hands tighter around the cold glass, worried she seriously might be losing her mind. Adding alcohol to the situation didn't seem like a good idea.

An hour later, when three Houston cops walked into the backyard and had everyone line up at the back gate, Kylie still had the same untouched margarita clutched in her hands.

"Come on, kids," one of the cops said. "The sooner we move you to the precinct, the sooner we can get your parents to come get you." That was when Kylie knew for certain that her life really had been toilet-bound—and someone had just flushed.

"Where's Dad?" Kylie asked her mom when she stepped into the room at the police station. "I called Dad."

I'm a phone call away, Pumpkin. Hadn't he told her that? So why wasn't he here to get Pumpkin?

Her mom's green eyes tightened. "He called me."

"I wanted Dad," Kylie insisted. No, she needed her dad, she thought, and her vision clouded with tears. She needed a hug, needed someone who would understand.

"You don't get what you want, especially when . . . my God, Kylie, how could you do this?"

Kylie swiped the tears from her face. "I didn't do anything. Didn't they tell you? I walked a straight line. Touched my nose and even said my ABCs backwards. I didn't do anything."

"They found drugs there," her mother snapped.

"I wasn't doing drugs."

"But do you know what they didn't find there, young lady?" Her mother pointed a finger at her. "Any parents. You lied to me."

"Maybe I'm just too much like you," Kylie said, still reeling at the thought that her dad hadn't shown up. He'd known how upset she'd been. Why hadn't he come?

"What does that mean, Kylie?"

"You told dad you didn't know what happened to his underwear. But you'd just flame-broiled his shorts on the grill."

Guilt filled her mother's eyes and she shook her head. "Dr. Day is right."

"What does my shrink have to do with tonight?" Kylie asked. "Don't tell me you called her. God, Mom, if you dare bring her down here where all my friends—"

"No, she's not here. But it's not just about tonight." She inhaled. "I can't do this alone."

"Do what alone?" Kylie asked, and she got this bad feeling in her stomach.

"I'm signing you up for a summer camp."

"What summer camp?" Kylie clutched her purse to her chest. "No, I don't want to go to any camp."

"It's not about what you want." Her mom motioned for Kylie to walk out the door. "It's about what you need. It's a camp for kids with problems."

"Problems? Are you freaking nuts? I don't have any problems," Kylie insisted. Well, not any a camp could fix. Somehow she suspected going to camp wouldn't bring Dad home, it wouldn't make Soldier Dude disappear, and it wouldn't win Trey back.

"No problems? Really, then why am I at the police station at almost midnight picking up my sixteen-year-old daughter? You're going to the camp. I'm signing you up tomorrow. This isn't up for debate."

I'm not going. She kept telling herself that as they walked out of the police station.

Her mother might be bat-shit crazy, but not her dad. He simply wouldn't let her mom send her off to a camp filled with a bunch of juvenile delinquents. He wouldn't.

Would he?

Chapter Three

Three days later, Kylie, suitcase in hand, stood in the YMCA parking lot where several of the camp buses picked up the juvenile delinquents. She freaking couldn't believe she was here.

Her mom was really doing it.

And her dad was really letting her mom do it.

Kylie, who'd never drunk more than two sips of beer, who'd never really smoked one cigarette, let alone any pot, was about to be shipped off to some camp for troubled kids.

Her mom reached out and touched Kylie's arm. "I think they're calling you."

Could her mom get rid of her any faster? Kylie pulled away from her touch, so angry, so hurt she didn't know how to act anymore. She'd begged, she'd pleaded, and she'd cried, but nothing worked. She was about to head off to camp. She hated it but there was nothing she could do.

Not offering her mom one word, and swearing not to cry in front of the dozens of other kids, Kylie stiffened her back and took off to the bus behind the woman holding the sign that read SHADOW FALLS CAMP.

Jeez. What kind of hell hole was she being sent to?

When Kylie stepped on the bus, the eight or nine kids already there raised their heads and stared at her. She felt an odd kind of stirring in her chest and she got those weird chills again. Never, not in all sixteen years of her life, had she wanted to turn and run away as much as she did now.

She forced herself not to bolt, then she met the gazes of . . . *oh, Lordie, can you say freaks?*

One girl had her hair dyed three different colors—pink, lime green, and jet black. Another girl wore nothing but black—black lipstick, black eye shadow, black pants, and a black long-sleeve shirt. Hadn't the goth look gone out of style? Where was this girl getting her fashion tips? Hadn't she read that colors were in? That blue was the new black?

And then there was the boy sitting almost at the front of the bus. He had both his eyebrows pierced. Kylie leaned down to peer out the window to see if she could still see her mother. Surely, if her mom took a look at these guys, she'd know Kylie didn't belong here.

"Take your seat," someone said, and stepped behind her.

Kylie turned around and saw the bus driver. While Kylie hadn't noticed it earlier, she realized even the bus driver looked a little freakish. Her purple-tinted gray hair sat high on her head like a football helmet. Not that Kylie could blame her for teasing her hair up a few inches. The woman was short. Elf short. Kylie glanced down at her feet, half expecting to see a pair of pointed green boots. No green shoes.

Then her gaze shot to the front to the bus. How was the woman going to drive the bus?

"Come on," the woman said. "I have to have you kids there by lunch, so move it along."

Since everyone but Kylie had taken their seats, she supposed the woman meant her. She took a step farther into the bus, feeling as if her life would never, ever be the same.

"You can sit by me," someone said. The boy had curly blond hair, even blonder than Kylie's, but his eyes peering at her were so dark they looked black. He patted the empty seat beside him. Kylie tried not to stare, but something about the dark/light combination felt off. Then he wiggled his eyebrows, as if . . . as if her sitting beside him meant they might make out or something.

"That's okay." Kylie took a few steps, pulling her suitcase behind her. Her luggage caught on the row of seats where the blond boy sat and Kylie looked back to free it.

Her gaze met his and her breath caught. Blond boy now had . . . green eyes. Bright, very bright green eyes. How was that even possible?

She swallowed and looked at his hands, thinking that maybe he had a contact case out and had changed his lenses. No case.

He wiggled his brows again, and when she realized she was staring at him, she yanked her suitcase free.

Shaking off the chill, she moved on to the row of seats she'd chosen as her own. Before she turned to sit down, she noticed another boy in the back. Sitting by himself, he had light brown hair, parted to the side and hanging just above his dark brows and green eyes. Normal green eyes, but the dusty blue T-shirt he wore made them more noticeable.

He nodded at her. Nothing too weird, thank God. At least there was one normal person on the bus besides her.

Sitting down, she gave blond guy another glance. But he wasn't looking at her, so she couldn't see if his eye color had gone weird again. But that's when she noticed the girl with three different hair colors had something in her hands.

Kylie's breath caught again. The girl had a toad. Not a frog—a frog she could have probably handled—but a toad. A huge honking toad. What kind of a girl dyed her hair three different colors and carried a toad with her to camp? God, maybe it was one of those drug toads, the ones people licked to get high. She'd heard about them on some stupid crime show on TV but had always thought they'd made it up. She didn't know which was worse: licking a toad to get high or carrying a toad around just to be weird.

Pulling her suitcase up on the seat next to her just so no one would feel the need to join her, Kylie let out a deep sigh and looked out the window. The bus was moving, although Kylie still didn't see how the bus driver managed to reach the gas pedals.

"Do you know what they call us?" The voice came from the seat where toad girl sat.

Kylie didn't think she was talking to her, but she turned her head that way, anyway. Because the girl looked directly at her, Kylie figured she might be wrong.

"Who calls us?" Kylie asked, trying not to sound too friendly or too bitchy. The last thing she wanted was to piss these freaks off.

"The kids who go to the other camps. There's like six camps in the three-mile radius in Fallen." Using both hands she pulled her multicolored hair back and held it there for a few seconds.

That's when Kylie noticed the girl had lost her toad. And Kylie didn't see a cage or anything where she could have tucked it away.

Great. She would probably have some freak's humongous drug toad hopping into her lap before she knew it. Not that toads totally scared her or anything. She just didn't want it jumping on her.

"They call us boneheads," the girl said.

"Why?" Kylie pulled her feet up in the seat just in case a toad hopped by.

"The camp used to be called Bone Creek Camp," the girl answered. "Because of the dinosaur bones found there."

"Ha," said the blond boy. "They also call us boners."

A few laughs echoed from the other seats. "Why is that funny?" the girl wearing all black asked in a tone so deadly serious that Kylie shivered.

"You don't know what a boner is?" Blond Boy asked. "If you'll come sit beside me, I'll show you." When he turned around, Kylie got another look at his eyes. Holy mother of pearls. They were gold. A striking feline gold. Contacts, Kylie realized. He had to be wearing some kind of weird contacts that were doing that.

Goth Girl stood up as if to join the blond guy.

"Don't do it," Toad Girl, without her toad, said and stood up. Moving out into the aisle, she whispered something in Goth Girl's ear.

"Gross." Goth Girl slammed back in her seat. Then she looked over at the blond boy and pointed a black-painted fingernail at him. "You don't want to piss me off. I eat things bigger than you in the dead of night."

"Did someone say something about the dead of night?" a voice came from the back of the bus.

Kylie turned to see who'd spoken.

Another girl, one Kylie hadn't known was there, popped up from the seat. She had jet black hair and wore sunglasses almost the same color as her hair. What made her look so abnormal was her complexion. Pasty. As in pasty white.

"Do you know why they renamed the camp Shadow Falls?" Toad Girl asked.

"No," someone answered from the front of the bus.

"Because of the Native American legend that says at dusk, if you stand beneath the falls on the property, you can see the shadows of death angels dancing."

Dancing death angels? What was wrong with these people?

Kylie swung around in her seat. Was this some nightmare? Maybe part of her night terrors? She pushed deeper in her cushioned seat and tried to focus on waking herself up from the dreams the way Dr. Day had shown her.

Focus. Focus. She took in deep breaths, in through the nose, out the mouth—all the while silently chanting, *It's just a dream, it isn't real, it isn't real.*

Either she wasn't asleep or her focus had gotten on the wrong bus, and darn if she didn't wish she'd followed it onto a different bus. Still not wanting to believe her eyes, she gazed around at the others. Blond Boy looked at her, and his eyes were black again.

Creepy. Was none of this coming across completely off the normal chart to anyone else in the bus?

Turning in her seat again, she looked back at the boy she'd dubbed the most normal. His soft green eyes, eyes that reminded her of Trey's, met hers, and he shrugged. She didn't exactly know what the shrug meant, but he didn't appear all that weirded out by everything. Which in some small way made him as weird as the others.

Kylie swung back around and grabbed her phone from her purse and started texting Sara. *Help! Stuck on a bus with freaks. Total, complete freaks.*

Kylie got a text message back from Sara almost immediately. *No, you help me. I think I'm pregnant.*

Chapter Four

"Oh, shit." Kylie stared at the text message thinking it would disappear, or that she'd see a "just joking" magically appear at the bottom. Nope. Nothing disappeared or appeared. This was no joke.

But please. Sara couldn't be pregnant. That didn't happen to girls like them. Smart girls . . . girls that . . . Oh, hell. What was she thinking? It happened to everyone and anyone having unprotected sex. Or sex with a faulty condom.

How could she forget that little film at school, the one Mom had to sign for her to see? Or the pamphlets Mom had brought home and unceremoniously left on Kylie's pillow like a bedtime snack?

Talk about a mood killer. She'd arrived home from one of the hottest dates she'd had with Trey, wanting to enjoy the high from his hot kisses and bold caresses, only to find the statistics of unwanted pregnancies and equally unwanted sexually transmitted diseases waiting for her. And her mother knew Kylie always had to read herself to sleep. No sweet dreams that night.

"Bad news?" someone asked.

Kylie looked up to see Toad Girl sitting in the aisle seat across from her, her legs pulled up to her chest and her chin propped onto her knees.

"Uhh. Yeah . . . no. I mean . . ." What she meant was it was none of her damn business, but being that blunt or rude never came easy for Kylie—well, not unless the person really pushed the wrong buttons—buttons that her mom seemed to know so well. Sara called Kylie's unwillingness to state her mind the "too nice" disease. Her mom would have called it manners, but because her mom excelled at hitting Kylie's buttons, her mom considered Kylie lacking in the manners department.

Kylie pulled her phone closed just in case Toad Girl might have super twenty-twenty eyesight. Then again, she guessed the person she should worry about having super eyesight was the blond guy, with his . . . She cut her gaze to where he sat and found him staring at her with . . . blue eyes. O . . . kay, at least one thing was clear, it couldn't get any weirder.

"It's nothing really," she said, forcing herself to look back at the Toad Girl and not stare at her multicolored hair. The bus came to a quick stop and Kylie's suitcase dropped to the floor. Aware that the blond guy still stared, and afraid he might take the empty seat as an invitation to come sit beside her, she moved over.

"My name's Miranda," the girl said, and smiled, and Kylie realized that other than her hair and her pet toad, the girl looked pretty normal.

Kylie introduced herself, giving the floor a quick check to confirm the toad hadn't decided to visit.

"Is this your first time at Shadow Falls?" Miranda asked.

Kylie nodded. "Yours?" she asked out of politeness, then she looked down at her phone, still clutched to her stomach. She needed to text Sara back and say . . . oh heck, what was she going to say to Sara? What did you say to your best friend who just told you that she might be . . .

"My second time." Miranda pulled her hair up and bunched it on top of her head. "Though I don't know why they want me to come back, it's not like it helped me the first time."

Kylie stopped trying to mentally write the text and met the girl's hazel eyes—eyes that hadn't changed colors once—and curiosity had Kylie almost stuttering. "What . . . what's it like? The camp, I mean. Tell me it's not too bad."

"It's not terrible." She released her hair and it fell into waves of black, lime green, and pink around her head. Then she glanced to the back of the bus where the pale chick now sat up and leaned forward as if listening. "If you don't mind the sight of blood," she whispered.

Kylie chuckled, hoping beyond hope that Miranda would, too. But nope. Miranda didn't even smile.

"You're joking, right?" Kylie's heart did a cartwheel in her chest.

"No," she said in a completely unjoking manner. "But I'm probably exaggerating."

A loud clearing of a throat echoed in the bus. Kylie looked up to the front to where the bus driver stared into the big mirror. Oddly, Kylie felt as if she stared right at Miranda and her.

"Stop that," Miranda hissed in a low voice, and clapped her hands over her ears. "I didn't invite you in."

"Stop what?" Kylie asked, but the girl's odd behavior had Kylie shifting farther away. "Invite me where?"

Miranda didn't answer; she frowned up at the front of the bus and then bounced back into her seat.

That's when Kylie realized she'd been wrong. Wrong about the fact that it couldn't get any weirder.

It could, and it did.

Not terrible. If you don't mind the sight of blood. Miranda's words played like scary music in Kylie's head. Okay, the girl admitted to exaggerating things, but come on, losing even a little blood was too much. *What kind of hellhole had her mother sent her to?* she asked herself for what was probably the hundredth time since she'd gotten on the bus.

Right then Kylie's phone buzzed with an incoming text. Sara again. *Please don't tell me . . . u told me so.*

Kylie pushed her own problems aside to think about her best friend. They may have had a rough few months, but they had been best friends since fifth grade. Sara needed her.

Kylie started texting. *OMG, wouldn't say that. Don't no what 2 say. R U OK?? Do ur parents no? Do you no who the father is?* Kylie deleted the last question. Of course Sara knew who the father was. It had to be one of three guys, right? Unless Sara hadn't been honest about what she'd done on the dates with her two last guys.

Oh, God, Kylie's heart went out to her best friend. Even considering Kylie's terrible circumstances of her parents' divorce, Nana's death, and being sent to "bloody" Shadow Falls Camp with some very strange people, Sara had it worse.

In two months, no matter how bad things were, Kylie would

go home. By then, she'd hopefully have gotten over the shock of losing her dad, and Nana. And maybe over the summer, Soldier Dude would lose interest in her and disappear permanently. But in two months, Sara would have a belly the size of a basketball.

Right then, Kylie wondered if Sara would even go back to school. God, Sara would be so embarrassed. To Sara, fitting in was . . . everything. If blue eye shadow was the rave, you can bet Sara would have blue eye shadow before the week was out. Heck, she'd missed nearly a week of school when she got a big pimple on the end of her nose. Not that Kylie liked going to school with a big zit, but duh, everyone got a pimple every now and then.

But not everyone got pregnant.

Kylie could only imagine what Sara was going through.

Kylie reread her text, added a little heart, and hit send. As she waited for Sara to text back, Kylie realized she'd never been happier than right now that she hadn't given in to Trey.

"Ten minutes for bathroom breaks," the bus driver said.

Kylie looked up from the phone to the convenience store. She didn't have to go, but considering she wasn't exactly sure how much longer the ride would be, she dropped her phone in her purse and stood up in the aisle to follow the others off the bus.

She'd taken two steps when someone wrapped a hand around her arm. A very cold hand. Kylie jumped and swung around.

The pale girl stared at her. Or at least she assumed she stared at her. With her almost-black sunglasses, Kylie couldn't be sure.

"You're warm," she said as if surprised.

Kylie pulled her arm away. "And you're cold."

"Nine minutes," said the bus driver firmly, and motioned Kylie forward.

She turned around and walked out of the bus, but she felt Pale Girl's stare bore into the back of her. Freaks. She was stuck with freaks all summer. Cold freaks. She touched her arm where the girl had held her and could swear she still felt the chill.

Five minutes later, bladder empty, she started back to the bus and saw a couple of the other kids paying for drinks. Goth Girl looked over at her from the front of the line. Then the boy with all the piercing who'd sat at the front of the bus walked past Kylie without saying a word. Deciding to grab some gum, she found her favorite grape flavor and went to stand in line. When she felt someone step behind her, she looked back to see if it was Pale Girl again. Nope, it was the boy from the back of the bus, the one with soft green eyes and brown hair. The one who reminded her of Trey.

Their gazes met.

And held.

She wasn't sure why he reminded her of Trey. Sure, their eyes were similar but it was more than that. Maybe it was the way his shirt fit across his shoulders, and the certain air of . . . distance. Trey hadn't been the easiest person to get to know. If they hadn't been assigned as lab partners in science class, she didn't know if they'd ever have gone out.

Yup, something about this guy seemed hard to get to know, too. Especially when he didn't even speak. She started to swing back around when he raised his eyebrows in some kind of weak greeting. Taking his lead, she raised her own brows at him and *then* turned around.

When she faced forward, she saw Miranda and Pale Girl talking by the door and they were both looking right at her.

So, they were now ganging up on her, were they?

"Great," she muttered.

"They're just curious," the deep voice whispered so close to her ear that she felt the warmth of his words against her neck.

She looked over her shoulder at him. This close, she could really see his eyes, and she realized she'd been wrong. These weren't Trey's eyes. This guy had flecks of gold around his pupils.

"About what?" she asked, trying not to stare.

"You, they're curious about you. Maybe if you opened up a little . . ."

"Open up?" Okay, that annoyed her. She'd been giving him the benefit of the doubt about being the normal one, but not if he was going to start acting as if she was being the unfriendly one. "The only ones who spoke to me were the blond guy and Miranda, and the other one, and I talked to all of them."

He quirked the other eyebrow at her. And for some reason that pushed her button. "Do you have a nervous twitch or something?" she asked, and then bit her tongue. Maybe she was overcoming the too-nice disease. Sara would be proud. Her mom . . . well, not so much.

Her mom.

Just like that, the image of her mom standing there in that parking lot filled Kylie's mind.

"You don't know . . . do you?" the boy asked, and his eyes widened, his gold flecks seemed to sparkle.

"Know what?" she asked, but her mind seemed stuck on her mom. On the fact that she hadn't even hugged her good-bye.

Why had Mom done this to her? Why had her parents decided to split? Why did any of this have to happen? The familiar knot, the need-to-cry knot, formed in her throat.

He looked over at the door and when Kylie followed his gaze, Miranda and Pale Girl were still there. Had all three of them gone to the camp before and they were like buddies and she was the new kid on the block? The new kid they'd decided to pick on?

The lady behind the counter spoke up. "Hey, you wanna pay for that gum?"

Kylie looked back at the cashier. She dropped a couple of bucks on the counter and left without getting her change. She brushed past Miranda and the other girl with her chin held high and without blinking. She dared not blink for fear the flutter of her eyelashes would bring on tears.

Not that their snotty attitudes made her want to cry. It was her mom, her dad, Nana, Trey, Soldier Dude, and now even her concern for Sara. Kylie couldn't care less if these weirdoes liked her or not.

Chapter Five

An hour later, the bus pulled into a parking lot. Kylie had seen the Shadow Falls Camp sign posted in front. A wiggle of fear stirred in her stomach. She shifted her gaze around, almost surprised the place didn't have a high fence and a locked gate. They were, after all, considered to be "troubled" teens.

Kylie heard the bus engine rumble to a stop. The bus driver jumped down from the seat and stretched her little chubby arms up over her head. Kylie *still* didn't know how she reached the gas pedals.

"We're the last bus to arrive, guys," she said. "Everyone is waiting in the mess hall. Leave your things in the bus and someone will bring them to your cabins later."

Kylie looked at her suitcase. She hadn't put a tag on it. How would they know it was her suitcase? Easy—they wouldn't. Great, she could take the luggage with her and risk getting in trouble for not following the rules, or leave it and risk losing all her clothes.

She was not going to lose her clothes. She reached for her suitcase. "They'll bring it to you," Miranda said.

"It doesn't have my name on it," Kylie replied, trying to keep the sharpness from her tone.

"They'll figure it out. I promise," she said as if trying to be nice.

But was Kylie going to believe her? *No.*

Suddenly, the green-eyed Trey lookalike moved into the aisle. "Believe her," he said.

Kylie looked at him. While she didn't trust Miranda, there was something about this guy she believed. While standing there, he reached in his pocket and pulled out some money and dropped it in her hands.

"Excuse me," Goth Girl, said, and pushed past Miranda.

Kylie stared at the dollar and few coins.

"It's your change from the store." He motioned for her to step into the aisle.

She dropped the money into her purse and started out. His footsteps dogged hers. She felt him behind her. Felt him lean in a little closer, his shoulder brushing against her back.

"My name's Derek, by the way."

Caught up in listening to his deep voice and feeling Derek behind her, she didn't see Blond Boy jump out into the aisle. In mid-step motion, Kylie had one of two choices. Plow into Blondie or fall back into Derek. An easy decision. Derek's hands caught her by the upper forearms. His fingers pressed against her bare skin where her sleeves ended.

She looked up over her shoulder and their gazes met.

He smiled. "You okay?"

Amazing smile. Like Trey's. Her heart did a little jump. God, she missed Trey.

"Yeah." She pulled away, but not before noting Derek's warm touch. Why that seemed important she didn't know, but the pale girl's coldness had left an equally odd impression.

They moved out of the bus and made their way into a large cabin-like structure. Right before Kylie entered the door, she heard a strange kind of roar. Like a lion. She paused to see if she heard it again, and Derek bumped into her. "We'd better move inside," he whispered.

Kylie's stomach fluttered with fear. As she took that first step over the threshold, she somehow sensed her life would forever be changed.

About fifty or sixty people filled the huge dining hall that had large picnic tables running parallel to each other, and the air smelled like pork-n-beans and grilled hamburgers. Some of the kids were sitting, others were standing.

Something felt off, odd. It took her a minute to realize what it was. Silence. No one spoke. If this was the school's lunch room, she probably wouldn't be able to hear herself think. And that's what everyone appeared to be doing right now. Thinking.

A quick sweep of the crowd had Kylie once again feeling as if she didn't belong here. There was a large amount of what Kylie's mom would call "rebellion evidence." Sure, Kylie rebelled. But she guessed she did her thing in less noticeable ways, not so much with her clothes and such, but in her surroundings. Like the time she and Sara had painted her room purple without permission. Her mom had freaked.

These kids, they didn't just paint their rooms, they wore their rebellion boldly. Like Miranda's hair or that other kid on the bus who had nose rings and piercings. As Kylie's gaze shifted around, she noticed a couple of kids had tattoos or shaved heads. And there were tons more goth-dressed kids. Black obviously had not gone out of style with troubled kids.

Uneasiness started crawling on Kylie's skin. Maybe she had hung out with Sara too long, but it seemed evident that she didn't fit in. But unlike Sara, Kylie wasn't so eager to become one with this crowd.

Two months. Two months. She repeated the words like a litany in her head. In two months, she'd be out of here.

Kylie followed Blond Boy to an empty table in the back. And when she got there, she realized all her bus companions had hung together. Not that she felt as if she belonged with them, she hadn't even had eye contact with some of them, but face it, a known freak was better than an unknown one.

Suddenly, Kylie started feeling people turn and look at her. Or were they looking at all of them? The new kids were on display. The crowd's gazes became a collage of cold stares with different-colored eyes, but similar expressions and a lot of eyebrow twitching.

Weirded out to the max, she looked at Derek, then Miranda and even Pale Girl and Blond Boy, and damn it if they were doing it, too. The eyebrow thing. It wasn't cartoonish, and not as noticeable as Sara's whole roll your eyes and pucker your brows kind of thing, but just a little twitch.

Like Derek had done back at the convenience store.

What was it with the eyebrows?

Looking back into the crowd, fighting the urge to look

down at her shoes, she forced herself to hold their gazes. Face it, she didn't want to be the chicken of the bunch. The one everyone picked on. And if that made her like Sara, so be it.

"Looks as if we are all here," a female voice said from the front.

Kylie tried to find the face behind the voice, but her gaze clashed with another stare—a cold, bright blue-eyed stare that somehow stood out from the rest. Pulling her attention away from just the eyes, Kylie noticed the boy's jet-black hair. And just like that, she remembered.

She remembered him.

She remembered . . . her cat.

"It can't be," she muttered under her breath.

"What can't be?" Derek asked.

"Nothing." Kylie forced her gaze to the front where the woman spoke in a singsong type of voice.

"Welcome to Shadow Falls Camp. We are . . ."

The woman, probably mid-twenties, had long red hair that hung almost to her waist. She wore jeans and a bright yellow T-shirt. Standing beside her was another woman about the same age, but good God, she wore goth. All black, even her eyes appeared black. Somebody really needed to subscribe to a fashion magazine or two.

Kylie looked over at Goth Girl who'd been on her bus. The girl stared at the woman with a sense of admiration.

"My name is Holiday Brandon and this is Sky Peacemaker."

Right then the cabin door opened and a couple of men walked in. They looked like lawyers, or some other serious type of profession that demanded they wear matching black suits.

Kylie watched the two women up front shift their gazes to the visitors and frown. She got the feeling the two men weren't expected. That they were even unwelcome.

Sky, the goth leader, walked over and led the men outside and Holiday continued. "Okay," the singsong voice said. "First we're breaking down into newbies and returnees. Everyone who has been here before will move outside. You'll find some helpers out there with your schedules and cabin assignments. As always, the rules of this place are posted in your cabins. We expect you to read them. And let me make something clear right now, we're not going to rearrange cabin assignments. You are here to get along, and get along you will. If a serious problem arises, bring it to the attention of either myself or Sky and we'll discuss it, but not until after twenty-four hours. Any questions?"

Someone in the front raised a hand. "Yeah," the female voice echoed in the room. "I have a question."

Kylie leaned to the right to see the girl. The girl, another goth-dressed individual, turned around. "It doesn't have anything to do with the rules, but . . . I want to know, who the hell is she?"

The girl pointed—pointed right at the table where Kylie stood. Or was she pointing right at Kylie? No, she couldn't be.

Oh, damn. She was. She was pointing *at* Kylie. "Crap," she muttered when about sixty pair of eyes all turned and focused directly on her.

Chapter Six

"Relax," Derek said in a voice so low she was certain no one else heard it. And she could barely hear him thanks to the thumping of her own heart.

"Introductions will happen over lunch," a female voice said. Kylie thought it was Holiday again, but she couldn't be sure. They all continued to stare. Stare at her. Her mind raced and her heart pounded. Gushing sounds echoed in her ears.

Tearing her gaze away, she eyed the door and fought the urge to run. Run fast and run hard. But face it, she'd never been a good runner, and too many freaks stood between her and the door. Then, oddly, she remembered something she'd learned about wild animals. If you run, they think you're dinner and will chase you.

Oh, double crap. Okay, deep breath. Then another one. Her lungs expanded. These weren't wild animals, just weird-ass teenagers.

Right then, Kylie's phone beeped with another incoming text. Probably Sara. Kylie ignored it. And for the first time, Kylie decided she possibly could have been wrong about Sara's situation being more difficult than her own. She wasn't a hundred percent certain of that, but something deep in her gut said this wasn't just about her going to Mark Jameson's party.

But what else could it be about?

And why? Why of all the freaks in the room had she been singled out? Was it because she didn't twitch her eyebrows? Oh, she could twitch her brows as good as the next person. And darn if she wouldn't be practicing that as soon as she got alone. Problem was, she just didn't understand the whole twitching thing. Was it the Shadow Falls Camp version of a secret handshake?

"Come on. Let's get things moving," the singsong voice said again. "Returnees, outside. Newbies, hang right here."

Kylie experienced the tiniest bit of relief when the crowd stopped staring and started shuffling around, reaching for purses and backpacks. Or at least most of them stopped staring. Kylie looked over to the right and saw the black-haired boy with bright blue eyes standing there, his gaze locked on her. *Lucas Parker.* She recalled his name, even though it had been a long time since she'd seen him.

I'm glad they left, she recalled her dad saying. *Take my word on it, that kid is going to grow up to be a serial killer.* Kylie felt a fist wrap around her heart and squeeze. Was she really at a camp with a possible serial killer?

Could it really be him? Of course, she could be wrong. It had been, gosh, over ten years. Chills tiptoed up her spine, and then he turned and moved into the flow of other returnees out the door.

Kylie saw Miranda take a few steps. She stopped in front

of Kylie and said, "Good luck." Kylie couldn't tell if the girl was being a smartass or serious, so she just nodded.

The blond boy stepped behind Miranda and grinned at Kylie. "Wouldn't want to be you," he said as if joking, then he followed Miranda out.

Knees locked so she wouldn't crumble, Kylie came to her senses long enough to realize that at least half the crowd had gone. And of her bus buddies, the only ones remaining were Pale Girl, Goth Girl, Derek, and the guy with all the piercings.

"Okay," Holiday said. "Now, what I want is for all of you who know why you're here, to move to the far left. All of you who don't, move to the far right."

Kylie remembered her feeling that this was about more than her trip to the police station and started to move to the right, but she noticed everyone shifting to the left. Not wanting to be singled out any more than she already had been, she went to stand beside Derek.

He shot her a look of disbelief. Deciding to practice the whole eyebrow thing, she crinkled her forehead.

When she looked over, only four people stood on the right side of the room. One of them was the pierced boy from her bus.

Holiday looked at both groups and Sky walked in and stood beside the redheaded leader. "Okay, righties, come with me. Sky is going to talk to everyone else." Holiday started out, then stopped and glanced back over her shoulder. Her gaze slapped right into Kylie. "Come with us, Kylie."

Shocked the women knew her name, she shook her head. "I know why I'm here," she lied.

"Really?" asked Holiday.

Deciding to take a stab at it, she said, "I got caught at a party where drugs were found."

A few snickers filled Kylie's ears.

Holiday frowned at the snickerers and motioned Kylie forward.

"Is it because my parents are getting a divorce?" she asked, feeling desperate.

Holiday didn't say anything, but then she didn't have to. The look she shot Kylie reminded her of her mom's don't-go-there stare. And the one time Kylie had gone there, she'd been grounded for a month. So Kylie followed Holiday and the four others out of the dining hall.

When they walked past the crowd standing outside, Kylie felt all the eyes turn toward her. Miranda nodded and mouthed the words "good luck." For some reason, Kylie suspected the girl's intentions were genuine.

Then Kylie spotted Lucas Parker standing beside the goth girl who'd raised her hand and asked about Kylie in the big meeting. They had their heads together, whispering, and they both stared at Kylie as if she didn't belong there. And damn if Kylie didn't agree with them. That's when Kylie realized that Lucas was dressed goth, too. Or at least he wore a black T-shirt. Of course, he looked really good in that shirt. It fit his upper torso—his very lean yet muscular upper torso—like a glove. So unfair, how guys didn't have to follow any fashion guidelines to look good.

Realizing she was staring at the guy's abs, and that the goth chick was smirking at her, Kylie turned away and pretended she hadn't noticed the girl's rude expression. Now if she could just pretend none of this was happening. Right then the pierced guy fell into step beside Kylie. She glanced at him and tried to smile. They might be strangers, but at least they'd ridden the same bus and he seemed just as clueless as she was.

He leaned in. "You wouldn't have brought any drugs with you, would you?"

Kylie's jaw dropped open in shock and mortification. *Just shoot me now.* Friggin' great. Thanks to her little slip in the dining room, everyone now considered her a druggie.

Holiday, her red hair flowing down her back, led them into a smaller cabin with a tin roof, located right behind the dining hall. From the wooden-plank porch hung a sign that read CAMP OFFICE. Kylie and the other four followed her to a back room that looked like a classroom.

"Have a seat, guys." Holiday leaned against the desk in the front as she waited for everyone to settle in.

Kylie felt the woman's gaze on her every few seconds as if she thought Kylie might try to bolt. Much to Holiday's credit, the idea had crossed Kylie's mind more than once. Hence the reason she chose the desk closest to the door.

Yet something kept Kylie from running, something besides the fact that she had never excelled at the fifty-yard dash. Something more than fear of being caught trying to escape.

Curiosity.

For an unknown reason, Kylie sensed that whatever Holiday had to say, it was going to explain things. And Kylie desperately wanted an explanation.

"Okay," Holiday said, and offered everyone what appeared to be a relax-everything-is-cool kind of a smile. Nevertheless, it was going take more than a smile to convince Kylie.

"What I have to say is going to be a relief to most of you, because deep down you've known that something was . . . different. Some of you have known it all your life, some of you have only recently come upon your destiny, but either way, this is probably going to be a shock." Holiday's gaze shifted to Kylie. "You guys are here because you are special. Gifted."

Holiday paused and Kylie waited for someone to ask the question, and when no one did, she blurted it out. "Define special."

"We've all read about the supernaturals, thing of legends, and from childhood, we're taught that they don't exist. The truth is that they do exist. Not everyone in the world is alike. And some of us are a lot more different than others. Some of us were born like this, some of us were changed. But no matter how this happened to you, if you are here it is because this is your destiny. It was chosen for you."

"Wait a minute," Kylie said before she could stop herself. "What are . . . I mean, are you saying that . . . that things like . . . like—"

"Vampires exist?" Pierced Guy asked. "Oh, shit. I knew I wasn't crazy. That's why I got really sick."

Kylie had to swallow to keep from laughing. She'd been about to say things like angels, but this was . . . it was stupid. The boy had obviously done too many drugs. Everyone knew that . . . that vampires and crap like that didn't exist.

She waited for Holiday to correct the guy. And then waited

some more. During that second delay, Kylie remembered how cold Pale Girl's touch had been. She remembered Blond Boy's ever changing eye color, she remembered Miranda's disappearing toad. No. She refused to let herself start to . . .

"That's right, Jonathon," Holiday said. "They exist. And yes, you were turned last week."

"I knew they weren't just dreams," said the other girl. "The wolf I dreamed of. It was real."

Holiday nodded.

"No." Kylie held up her hand and shook her head so hard that blond hair brushed back and forth across her face. "I'm not going to believe this."

Holiday met Kylie's gaze. "I'm not surprised that it's you, Kylie, who finds this the hardest to believe."

"What am I?" blurted out the other sandy-haired girl.

What am I? The girl's question vibrated in Kylie's head. Not that she had the least bit of desire to ask it herself. She didn't believe in this crap. *I do not believe.*

Holiday smiled at the girl and gave her a soft accepting look. "Your birth mother was fairy. You have healing gifts. And I know you have suspected this."

The girl's eyes widened with what appeared to be relief. "I healed my little sister, didn't I? My parents thought I was crazy," she said. "But I knew I'd done it. I felt it when it happened."

Holiday gazed at her with sympathy. "That is sometimes the hardest part of this. Knowing what we know and not being able to share it with others. But very few ordinary humans can accept us for who we are. This is part of the reason you are here—to learn how to deal with your gifts and how to live in a normal world."

Kylie's mind raced. She recalled the strange things that had been happening—the return of her night terrors and . . . Soldier Dude, the stalker that only Kylie seemed able to see. Panic started to unravel her logic. She closed her eyes and desperately tried to wake herself up. It had to be a dream.

"Kylie?" Holiday's voice had her opening her eyes. "I know this is hard for you to accept."

"It isn't just hard. It's impossible. I don't believe—"

"But you are scared to ask, aren't you? Scared to ask the reasons you are here, because deep down, you know you belong here."

I know that neither my mom or dad want me. That's why I'm here. "I shouldn't be here," Kylie snapped. "I haven't been having dreams of wolves. I have night terrors. I'm hardly able to remember my dreams. I haven't been bitten by a bat, and I haven't healed anyone."

"Vampires and werewolves are not the only supernaturals that exist." Holiday paused and then pressed her palms together in front of her. "What do you want, Kylie? Proof?"

Chapter Seven

"Yeah, proof would be good," Kylie said, unable to keep the sarcasm from her voice. "But now you are going to tell me that you can't give me that, right? You're going to tell me some little speech about how I have to believe in it anyway, right?"

"No, actually, I planned on giving you the proof." Holiday's voice held an odd kind of calm that made Kylie take a deep breath. It also scared the bejeebies out of her. What if Holiday was telling the truth? What if . . . Kylie recalled how cold the pale girl was on the bus. No way. She was not going to believe in this. Vampires and werewolves existed in fiction, not in real life.

The woman pulled a cell phone from her jeans and made a call. "Can you send Perry into the office classroom? Thanks."

She placed the cell back in her pocket. "Now, all of you are welcome to stay and see this. Or if you'd like to go on out, each of you have a mentor waiting out front. They are here to answer your questions."

Kylie watched them look among themselves and they all

agreed to stay. It made her feel better knowing she wasn't the only one having doubts about any of this.

After a few minutes, long minutes during which silence penetrated the room like a fog, she heard the sound of footsteps in the front of the cabin. The door opened, and the blond boy from her bus, the one with weird eyes, walked into the room.

"Hi, Perry. It's good to see you again," Holiday said with sincerity.

"It's good to be back." His gaze met Kylie's and her breath caught when she found herself staring at eyes so dark that they didn't appear human. Right then, his creepiness level moved up in leaps and bounds.

"It would make me very happy if you'd do the honor of showing us your special gift."

Those non-human eyes didn't shift from Kylie. Perry grinned. "So you have some non-believers, do you?" Turning his head, he focused on Holiday. "What would you like to see?"

"Why don't we let Kylie decide?" Holiday looked at her. "Kylie, this is Perry Gomez, he's a very gifted shape-shifter, one of the most powerful ones there are. He can probably become anything you can imagine. So why don't you tell him what you'd like to see him become?"

Kylie kept moving her gaze between Holiday and Perry. Realizing they waited for her to say something, she forced herself speak. "A . . . unicorn."

"Unicorns don't exist," Perry said, his expression seeming to say he felt insulted by her choice.

"They used to," Holiday added, as if coming to Kylie's defense.

"No shit?" Perry asked. "They really existed?"

"No shit," Holiday repeated. "But we should work on our language." She smiled. "Just think of a horse with a horn. I know you can do it."

He nodded, then he pressed his palms together and Kylie saw his black eyes roll back into his head. The air in the room suddenly felt weak, as if something had sucked the oxygen out of it. Kylie stared at Perry even when everything inside her said not to. Right then her curiosity, her need to know evaporated into the not-so-breathable air. She'd never understood that saying, "Ignorance is bliss," until this moment. She wanted to remain ignorant. She didn't want to see, didn't want to believe.

But she did see.

She saw sparkles forming around his body—sparkles as if a bucket of floating glitter had been spilled around him, as if a thousand lights came on and reflected each miniscule piece of glitter. The hundreds of diamond-shaped twinkles swirled around him. Slowly the sparkles fell to the floor and left standing where Perry had once stood was a huge honking white unicorn with a pink horn in the middle of its forehead.

Chapter Eight

The unicorn, aka Perry, swatted its tail back and forth, as if strutting its stuff, then swung around in Kylie's direction. The beast took two steps toward her, close enough she could have touched it if she'd been so inclined. But no inclination existed.

It reared its head, made a neighing noise, then one of its deep dark black eyes winked at her.

"Shit!"

"Damn!"

"Oh my God!"

"Holy cow!"

"Mo fo!"

Kylie wasn't sure who said what, one may have even leaked out of her mouth, for all five responses had shot through her addled brain. Taking in another gasp of air, she looked at Holiday, who stared at her with soft green eyes.

"It's okay," Holiday said. "Perry, change back now."

Kylie dropped her forehead against the flat, cool surface of her desk top and concentrated on breathing and *not* thinking. If she let herself think, she'd cry and the last thing she wanted to do in front of these people was show any sign of weakness. Hell, these freaks probably fed on weak people.

"You guys should leave now," Holiday's voice, now with an authoritarian tone, seemed to echo in the room, bouncing inside Kylie's head.

She counted to ten and then somehow managed to sit up. The desks around her stood empty. Perry, back to his human form, and the others shuffled out of the room. Perry gave her a quick glance over his shoulder. His brown eyes, normal-looking eyes this time, almost appeared apologetic.

Remembering Holiday's order about leaving, Kylie forced herself to stand. If she could just get out of here, she might be able to find a secluded place where she could freak out in private. Where she could cry, and attempt to come to terms with . . . No. Don't think yet. Not yet. She swallowed the few tears crawling up her throat and her sinuses stung.

"Where are you going?" Holiday asked.

Kylie looked back her. It hurt to talk around the knot of emotion lodged between her tonsils. "You said we should leave."

"They should leave. *You* need to stay."

"Why?" A watery film coated her vision and hopelessly, Kylie realized she couldn't stop it. The tears had arrived. *Why?* The one-word question plowed through her confused mind and morphed into dozens of questions. Why was any of this happening? Why was she being singled out again? Why did her mother not love her? Why did her dad turn his back on her? Why couldn't Trey give her a little more time? Why did all these freakish kids act as if she were the weirdo here?

She blinked back a few tears and dropped back into the seat. "Why?" she asked again. "Why am I here?"

Holiday sat in the desk beside her. "You're gifted, Kylie."

She shook her head. "I don't want to be special. I just want to be me—normal me. And . . . and to be completely honest with you, I think there's been some huge mistake made here. You see, I'm not . . . gifted. I . . . I certainly can't turn myself into anything. I don't suck at anything, except maybe algebra. But I've never been great at things, either. Sports are so not my thing, and I'm not super talented or even the extra smart type. And believe it or not, I'm okay with that. I don't mind being just average . . . or normal."

Holiday laughed. "There is no mistake, Kylie. However, I know exactly how you feel. I felt just like that when I was your age and especially when I realized the truth."

Kylie swiped at her face to hide the evidence of her tears and then forced herself to ask the question she'd been trying not to think about since the whole thing started. "What am I?"

Chapter Nine

"Can you handle the truth?" Holiday asked softly, her eyes filled with empathy.

Handle it? I just saw a boy turn himself into a unicorn. Can it get any worse?

Seconds after Kylie asked herself that, she got a chill. What if it could get worse? She recalled Holiday saying there were other types of supernaturals besides vampires and werewolves, which in Kylie's mind had to be the worst kind of supernatural, not that she had expertise in the field or anything, but what if Holiday had only said that to calm her down? Would she have lied?

"Yes, I can handle it," Kylie said, sounding braver than she felt.

But when Holiday opened her mouth to speak, Kylie blurted out, "No." She dropped her face into her hands, then removed them and stared again at the redheaded camp leader. "I don't know if I can handle it."

How could she when it was just too much?

Kylie bit down on her bottom lip so hard it hurt. "I mean, if you are about to tell me something like I'm dead, that I need to start acquiring a taste for blood and I can't even eat sushi, I won't be able to handle it. Or if you're going to tell me that I'm going to start howling at the moon, eating people's cats, and will spend the rest of my life having to get waxed if I want to wear a bathing suit, then I don't think I can handle it, either. I like cats and I tried waxing once, and that hurt like a son of a gun." She dropped her hand between her legs, remembering.

Holiday laughed, but Kylie had been as serious as a heart attack. Waxing had really hurt and she hadn't let Sara talk her into anything like that since.

"Do you think I can handle it?" Kylie asked, afraid of the answer.

"Honestly, I don't know you very well yet, but I trust Dr. Day's assessment of you."

Kylie blinked. "What does my shrink have to do with this?"

"Your shrink—as you call her—is the one who recommended you to us. She recognized your gifts, she's half fairy, you know."

Kylie tried to process that information. "I'm here because of her? That woman is . . ." Kylie leaned closer, almost as if whispering might make it less of an insult. "She's a few fries short of a Happy Meal." Kylie dropped her hands on the desk. "I wouldn't lie to you. She's a flake."

Holiday frowned. "Unfortunately, all supernaturals come off a bit flaky when viewed from the normal prospective. She spoke very highly of you."

Kylie felt a little guilty then, which she suspected had been the camp leader's intent.

Holiday dropped her palms on top of Kylie's hands. "I won't

lie to you, either, Kylie. The truth . . . the truth is, we don't know what you are."

Kylie sat up a little straighter, chewing on that bit of information, and Holiday sat quietly as if allowing Kylie the time to adjust. Not that Kylie was adjusting. Oh, hell no. She was working on finding a positive slant to all of this. "Don't you see? That's because I'm not anything. I'm just me. Normal me."

The woman shook her head. "You have gifts, Kylie. Those gifts could have come from various supernatural forms and almost always they are hereditary."

"Hereditary? Neither of my parents are . . . supernaturals."

Holiday didn't look convinced. "In rare cases, it could skip a generation. It could be fairy, it could be you are a descendent of one of the gods. It could be—"

"Gods? Gifts? What gifts?"

Holiday cleared her throat, and her eyes met Kylie's with empathy. "You can talk to the dead—sometimes in your sleep. Other times when you're awake."

Warmth spread into the top of Kylie's hands, but cold spread into her heart. "The dead?" Her mind started filtering though images, all of them Soldier Dude, since she couldn't recall anything from her night terrors.

"No, you're wrong. I never talked to them. Never, ever. Not one word. Mom taught me to never talk to strangers, and I've lived by that."

"But you've seen them, right?"

Tears welled up in Kylie's eyes again. "Just one. And I'm not sure he's a ghost. Sure, my mom didn't seen him, but my mom . . . she's always in her own little world." But then there was her neighbor, the way she had walked right past Soldier Dude and never even glanced at him. *Oh damn. Damn.*

"It's scary, I know," Holiday said. "I remember when I first started experiencing it."

Kylie pulled her hands out from under Holiday's grasp. "You . . . you have the same . . . talent?"

Holiday nodded and looked over to the left.

Kylie gave the room a visual sweep. "But none are here now, right?"

Instantly, Kylie felt it. That cold . . . the eerie in-the-bones kind of cold that she'd experienced so often lately.

"They are always here, Kylie. You're just turning your mind off."

"Can I do that?" Kylie asked. "Can I just turn my mind off permanently?"

Holiday hesitated. "Some people can, but this is a gift, Kylie. To not use this gift is a waste."

"A waste? Oh no, I didn't ask for this gift." Her own words echoed inside her head and she realized she'd practically admitted that this was real. She didn't want it to be real. Didn't want to accept it or believe it. "I'm not sure I have this gift. I mean, I hear about normal people seeing ghosts all the time."

Holiday nodded. "It's true. Some ghosts accumulate enough energy that even a normal has been able to see them."

"Then that's what's happening to me. I'm just dealing with a super-charged ghost. That's it. Because I'm just normal."

"The evidence says different."

Her breath caught. "What evidence?"

Holiday stood up and motioned for Kylie to follow. Her

knees felt weak when she stood, but she followed. Holiday spoke as she walked. "First, there's the fact that you are unreadable."

"Unreadable?" Kylie asked as they walked into a small office.

"All supernaturals have the ability to get a sneak peek into other minds. When reading a human, we see a similar pattern with everyone. When reading other supernaturals, we can generally sense what they are. Unless they are purposely blocking us out. Which most don't do as a sort of courtesy to others."

"Is that the eyebrow-twitching thing?" Kylie asked.

"You don't miss much, do you?" Holiday smiled. "And the thing is that people with the gift of ghost whispering are often slow at reading others and are very difficult to read. We're not being rude, but our minds function on a different plane than everyone else's does. With practice, however, we can train ourselves to open up enough so that we aren't coming off as holier than thou. Your pattern, and the fact that you are unreadable tells me that you are more than human. And then there's this evidence." The camp leader pulled out a file drawer. She drew a piece of paper out of a file with Kylie's name on it and placed that paper in Kylie's hands.

Kylie looked at the copy of her birth certificate. Nowhere on the document did it say anything about her being supernatural or about her seeing ghosts. She glanced up at Holiday with questions running through her mind.

Holiday must have either read her thoughts, or her expression, because she answered, "You were born at midnight, Kylie."

"So? Why is that supposed to mean something?"

Holiday ran her finger over all the files. "Everyone here was born at midnight."

Kylie's heart thumped a little harder. She watched Holiday's red-painted fingernail move over the file tabs where the names appeared in bold type. None of the names meant anything to Kylie until her gaze found one that did.

Lucas Parker.

Not that he mattered. His name only leapt out at her because it was one of the few familiar things here. Another sweep of icy emotion tiptoed up her spine.

Kylie swung around and her breath caught when she saw him. Not Lucas, but Soldier Dude. And he just stood there, closer than ever before, and stared at her with his cold, dead eyes.

Less than ten minutes later, Kylie sat at a lunch table.

Alone.

Only her, Holiday, the other camp leader, and the two men, occupied the dining hall.

Every few minutes, Kylie's mind would try to wrap around everything that had happened—everything from the unicorn to her not being human. But her mind wasn't in a wrapping mood.

Deny it. Deny it. The words played like a song in her head.

The sound of the voices in the front of the dining hall brought Kylie's gaze up. Holiday had received a call from Sky, and because it was almost lunch time anyway, Holiday had told Kylie to just come with her and she'd show her to her cabin after lunch.

Holiday's gaze shifted to Kylie. Kylie stared at her phone, pretending she didn't feel uncomfortable, while Holiday and the other camp leader, Sky, stood at the front with the two black suits who had dropped in earlier.

Kylie couldn't hear the conversation, but whatever it was, she could tell it wasn't good. She peered up between her lashes again. Holiday and Sky were frowning. Holiday seemed the most anxious of the two, tapping her foot and twirling her hair in a tight rope.

Then one of the men raised his hands in the air and spit out, "I'm not pointing fingers, but I'm telling you like it is. Get to the bottom of this and make it stop or I swear, higher-ups are going to shut the camp down."

Shut the camp down? Kylie lowered her gaze and pretended not to hear, but she couldn't stop the hope from building in her chest. Ever since Holiday had left her alone at the table, Kylie had been tempted to call her parents and beg them to come get her.

Ah, but what would she tell them? *Hey, Mom, Dad, guess what? You sent me to camp with real freaks, a bunch of bloodsuckers and cat killers. And oh, I'm a freak, too, but they don't know what kind yet.*

Kylie's stomach clenched at the thought of how that conversation would turn out. Chances were her mom would yank her out of the camp and commit her to a psycho ward. Not that it would be worse than what she was in now.

Staring at her hands, Kylie remembered what Holiday had said about her gift being hereditary. Did her mom or dad see ghosts? Not her mom, otherwise she wouldn't have brought in the mental doctor the first time Kylie brought up Soldier Dude.

And her dad would have told her if he had any special abilities, wouldn't he?

Not that Kylie had accepted that she had any gifts. It was still highly probable that Holiday was wrong about her being one of them. Maybe Soldier Dude was just a high-powered ghost, like Holiday said could happen. And surely there were normal people who were born at midnight, right?

Nevertheless, the idea of trying to tell her parents any of this seemed absurd. Seemed absurd? Who was she kidding? It was over-the-top completely one hundred percent crazy, and if she hadn't seen Perry change himself into a unicorn, she wouldn't have believed it, either.

The conversation up front got a little louder, but not as loud as before, not loud enough for Kylie to distinguish words. So she stared at her phone and pretended to read Sara's last text, but in truth, she'd already read it.

Her friend hadn't told her parents about her missed period, and as soon as Sara's mom left for her lunch appointment, Sara was going to the store to buy a pregnancy test. Some time this afternoon, Sara would know if she was pregnant.

Kylie hadn't asked Sara about the father, she hadn't even asked Sara if she would consider an abortion. For some reason, Kylie didn't see Sara doing that. But six months ago, Kylie would have sworn that Sara would never find herself pregnant, either.

Kylie let herself worry about Sara for a minute before she shifted back to her own issues. Like how she was going to survive the next two months. And by survive, she didn't mean just mentally. Vampires and werewolves killed people.

Only the bad ones, Holiday had explained on the walk over

here when Kylie had almost jumped out of her skin anytime someone came close. Was Holiday certain that no bad ones were at the camp? Some of them had looked pretty grim to Kylie. Not that she considered herself an expert at distinguishing bad supernaturals from good ones. But in a way it sort of compared to how Kylie felt about snakes and spiders—there were good ones, and there were bad ones. But for safety's sake, she avoided all of them.

God, Kylie hoped she didn't get stuck rooming with any of them. Surely Holiday wouldn't expect her to sleep in a cabin with someone who . . . who might be tempted to kill her while she slept. Then again . . . Great, that meant she'd probably be sleeping with one eye open the entire two months.

The conversation between the two black-suited guys and the camp leaders came to an end and the two men started to leave. But one of them, the taller of the two, turned around and looked right at Kylie. And then he did it. He twitched his brows at her.

Kylie looked away, but she sensed him standing there in that same spot, still staring and twitching. She felt her cheeks heat up.

The door to the dining hall shut, but then she heard it open again. Kylie looked up and saw the other teens start to filter into the room. As each one entered, Kylie found herself guessing— fairy, witch, werewolf, vampire, or shape-shifter. Were there other kinds of supernaturals? She'd have to ask Holiday about the different types, like what "descended from the gods" meant.

Kylie started trying to put the types she did know into one of two groups: supernaturals who wouldn't consider a human a part of the food chain, and those who did.

Derek walked through that door and Kylie found herself

curious about what type of supernatural he was. He stopped a few feet in the room and looked around. The moment his eyes lit on her, she knew he'd found what he'd been looking for. He'd been looking for her. Even not knowing what he was, or exactly what group he belonged to, the thought that he liked her enough to look for her made her feel less lonely.

As he moved toward her, a very small smile appeared in his eyes, and she thought again about how he reminded her of Trey. Was that why she liked him, or at least liked him better than everyone else? Because he did look like Trey a little?

She'd have to be careful, she told herself, not to confuse familiarity for something more.

"Hey," he said as he sat down beside her. When she looked up at him, she realized her shoulder barely came to his mid-forearm. Which meant he was taller than Trey—probably by a couple of inches.

Kylie nodded and dropped her phone in her purse.

"So . . . ?" he asked.

Kylie met his green eyes with flecks of gold. She knew exactly what that one-word question asked. He wanted to know what she was. She started to answer him, to tell him she didn't know what she was, just her gift, but she suddenly found she wasn't ready to say it aloud. To say it aloud meant she believed it. And she didn't, not yet.

"It's been a crazy morning," she said instead.

"I can imagine," he answered, and she sensed a bit of disappointment in him. He'd wanted her to trust him.

Good luck with that, Kylie thought. Between people dying on her—meaning Nana—people divorcing on her—meaning her parents—and people breaking up with her because she wouldn't put out—meaning Trey—her ability to trust anyone had taken a dive off some very high cliff. And it had landed on the bottom of some gully, a mangled mess, right beside her heart.

Miranda dropped down in the seat on the other side of Derek. "Hey . . ." She leaned over and looked at Kylie. "We're rooming together. Isn't that cool?"

"Yeah." Kylie quickly tried to figure out exactly what Miranda was. She remembered the toad and for some reason guessed her to be a witch.

"I'm in with you guys, too," someone else said, and sat down on the other side of Kylie.

Kylie turned and found herself staring at her own reflection in Pale Girl's dark shades.

Chills ran up Kylie's spine. Kylie didn't know if she was a werewolf or a vampire, but something told her she was one of the two. Which basically meant, she fell into the humans-are-on-the-food-chain group.

The girl lowered her glasses, and Kylie got a look at her eyes for the first time. They were black and slightly slanted, exotic, as if she was part Asian. "My name's Della . . . Della Tsang."

"Uh . . . Kylie Galen," she managed to say, hoping her hesitation didn't come off as fear. But it was fear and Kylie couldn't deny that.

"So Kylie," Della said, pulling her glasses down another inch, "do tell. Exactly *what* are you?"

Was it her imagination that at least a dozen other teens turned and looked toward their table? Did they have super hearing? Kylie's phone buzzed. "Uh, I should . . . take this."

She grabbed her phone from her purse, stood up, and went to stand in the corner, away from everyone.

Glancing at the screen to see who to throw handfuls of praise to for calling at the right moment, Kylie's heart did a tug. She'd expected it to be Sara, maybe her mom or dad. She hadn't expected it to be Trey.

Chapter Ten

"Hello?" she answered hesitantly, and her chest immediately filled with a familiar kind of missing-Trey achiness that until she saw him at the party had almost disappeared. Almost.

"Kylie?" The deep sound of his voice did another pull on her emotions.

She swallowed a knot down her throat and visualized him in her mind—his green eyes staring at her like he did when they made out. "Yes?"

"It's Trey."

"I know," she answered, and closed her eyes. "Why are you calling me?"

"Do I need a reason?"

Since you're sleeping with some other girl, you do. "We're not together anymore, Trey."

"And maybe that's a mistake," he said. "I can't stop thinking about you since I saw you at the party."

She'd bet he stopped thinking about her when he got his new bang toy alone that night. Lucky for them, they'd left about fifteen minutes before the cops had arrived. So while Kylie had been sitting at the police station, Trey had probably been expanding on his luck by getting lucky with his new girlfriend.

"Sara told me that you were at some camp in Fallen," he said when she didn't say anything. "She said your mom sent you there because of the party."

"Yeah," she answered, even though she realized it wasn't the whole truth. But she couldn't tell Trey the truth. Not even part of the truth. That's when it hit her, how many lies she'd have to tell everyone she knew. That's when she realized something else. Her mom hadn't been lying when she'd said Dr. Day had convinced her that Kylie needed to come here. Maybe her mom hadn't wanted to get rid of Kylie as badly as she thought. That should have made her feel better, but the achiness in her chest grew.

She missed her mom. She missed her dad. She wanted to go home. The gonna-cry knot formed in her throat and she swallowed it.

"Are you allowed to get phone calls?" Trey asked, his voice bringing her back to the moment and away from her thoughts.

Allowed? Kylie hadn't considered that. "I think so. No one's told me I couldn't." But she hadn't read the rules that were supposed to be posted in her cabin, either. Not that it was her fault; she hadn't been allowed to go to her cabin yet.

She looked up to see if anyone else was on a phone. She spotted two people talking and two more texting. One of the texting kids was Jonathon, aka Piercing Guy, who stood with two other guys. Beside them stood Goth Girl, who hung with a crowd of other goths.

Kylie also spotted Lucas Parker. Not on the phone but talking to a group of girls that looked like his personal fan club. He was smiling at something someone said. And she could see the girls holding on to his every word, practically swooning all over him. Let them laugh and swoon, Kylie thought. He hadn't killed their cat.

"I'm going to a soccer camp in Fallen next week," Trey said, bringing her back to the conversation. "I thought maybe we could . . . maybe we could find a way to get together. To talk. I miss you, Kylie."

"I thought you were with that girl, Shannon."

"We weren't ever really going out. But we're not seeing each other anymore. I could never talk to her."

But I'll bet you did other things. It hurt to remember how the girl had hung all over him at the party.

"Say you'll at least meet me," he said. "Please. I really miss you."

Her chest grew heavier. "I don't know if I can . . . I mean, I don't know how things are run here yet."

"I think our camps are just a mile or so apart. It wouldn't be hard for us to meet."

She closed her eyes and thought how good it would be to see Trey. To see anyone she knew wasn't a freak, but especially Trey. He had always been her go-to person when things bothered her. Which was why his breaking up with her had broken her heart.

"I can't make any promises, not until I figure things out here." Kylie looked up.

Holiday and Sky were moving to the front of the room.

"Lunch is ready," Sky said. "Let's let the new people start first. And then we'll jump into introductions."

Introductions? The thought of having to talk to the group had butterflies nosediving in her stomach.

Kylie saw Derek turn and look at her as if wondering if she wanted to get in line together. She kind of liked the idea of standing beside him, instead of standing alone.

"I have to go, Trey," she said.

"But Kylie—"

She hung up. She hadn't done it to be mean, but the idea that he might feel a bit rejected didn't bother her too much. Payback could be hell.

Derek stood up and waved her over. Yup, Derek was taller than Trey. Moving Derek's way, Kylie tried not to flinch when Della joined them, and the three of them walked to the line together.

Della ended up behind Goth Girl from their bus and they started talking.

Derek turned and focused on Kylie.

"Boyfriend?" he asked.

"Huh?"

"The phone call?"

"Oh." She shook her head. "Ex." Instantly she remembered how several of the other kids had looked at her when Della had asked what she was. She leaned closer to Derek. "Could you hear me on the phone?" She lowered her voice. "Could everyone hear me?"

"I couldn't. It was just . . . your body language." He seemed to note how she looked out in the crowd. "But yes, some of the others have super hearing."

"But not you?" She hoped he would tell her what she wanted to know. That he'd tell her what he was.

"Not me," he said, and they moved a few steps forward. His arm brushed up against hers and for a second, she didn't know if she wanted to back away or lean closer. The fact that he wasn't cold seemed to make closer an option. When her arm met his again, something so comforting spread through her.

"So what are you?" she asked, and then bit her tongue. It wasn't fair for her to be asking questions that she herself didn't want to answer. "That's okay, you don't have to answer that."

She looked away, embarrassed, and listened to the chatter of the crowd. Unlike earlier, when silence had reigned, now if she tried really hard, she might convince herself that she was in a room filled with regular teens.

And that's when Kylie knew that she'd stopped trying to deny it.

Laughter along with a few of the more feminine squeals filled her ears. She should have found the "regular" thought comforting, but she couldn't push away the truth. The truth was none of these people were regular or normal.

Not even her.

That thought shot a wave of panic into her stomach and she wondered how in the hell she would manage to eat anything now.

"I'm half Fae." Derek's voice came close to her ear. The tickle of his breath sent flutters to her stomach. Not the kind that stemmed from fear, but something different. Pushing that aside, she tried to concentrate on what he said.

Fae? The synonym search in her brain started spinning through files until she recalled reading once that Fae was French for *fairy*.

Her mind started spitting out data. Holiday was fairy. Holiday had said Kylie might be fairy.

She turned and met his green eyes. In a voice so low it barely came out a whisper she asked, "Do you . . . do you see ghosts?"

"Ghosts?" His eyes widened as if the question were unbelievable. But duh, how could that seem crazy when . . . when . . .

Her train of thought came to an abrupt halt when Kylie felt someone behind her. Her heart raced to a fast song and she feared it would be Soldier Dude. But the cold, the one she'd suddenly realized always came when he was near, didn't seem to be present. She watched Derek's gaze rise over her shoulder. He nodded.

She turned her head and her breath caught when she found herself staring into the light blue eyes of Lucas Parker.

"I think you lost this." His voice reminded her of a radio announcer—deep with a rumbling quality that made it unique—memorable. A quality that made him sound older than he appeared.

Aware that she stared, she jerked her gaze to his hands where he held out her Coach billfold that her grandmother had splurged to get her last Christmas.

Immediately, Kylie looked back at the table where she'd left her purse. It sat on top just as she'd left it. How had he gotten her billfold?

She took her wallet from his hands and fought the temptation to make sure her mom's credit card was still tucked safely inside. Her mom would be so pissed if she lost it.

Torn between doing the socially acceptable thing of saying thank you or questioning him on how he'd gotten his feline-
murdering hands on her possession, her mind spun. Then because
she mostly always did the socially acceptable thing, the two simple words, "thank you," formed on her tongue, but she couldn't
spit them out.

She couldn't help wondering if he remembered her. She
couldn't help noticing how his blue eyes seemed to look inside
her, just as they had all those years ago. They hadn't been friends,
but neighbors for a very short time. He hadn't even been in her
grade. But they had to walk the same three blocks home from
school every day, and she could remember that walk being the
best part of her day. From the first time she'd seen him riding his
bike on her street, he had fascinated her in a mysterious kind of
way.

And just like that, she remembered with clarity the last time
she'd seen him. The sense of fascination shattered, leaving in its
place a cold wind of fear.

She'd been sitting on a swing with her new kitten in her
hands—the kitten her parents had given her because Socks had
come up missing. Lucas's head had popped over the fence,
and his blue eyes met hers. The kitten had hissed and scratched
her, trying to run for cover. The boy stared and then said, *Be
sure to take the kitten in the house at night. Or what happened to
your other cat will happen to it.*

She'd run to her mother crying. That night her dad and
mom had gone to talk to Lucas's parents.

Her parents hadn't told her what happened, but she recalled
her daddy looking angry when they'd returned from the visit.

Not that it mattered, because the next day Lucas Parker and his parents were gone.

"You're welcome," Lucas said, his deep rumble now slightly laced with sarcasm. Then he turned and walked away.

Oh, great. All she needed was to start making enemies of one of the humans-are-on-the food-chain gang—especially one she knew was capable of doing despicable things. But face it, being nice to Lucas Parker was going to be hard. After all, he had killed her cat and threatened to do the same to her kitten.

Chapter Eleven

During lunch, the introductions proved to be as embarrassing as Kylie thought they would be. Everyone had said their name and "what" they were, but when her time came, she'd only offered her name. The silence in the room had felt suffocating in the seconds afterward. Holiday had jumped in and explained that the origin of Kylie's powers was still being deciphered and that her "close-mindedness" was not intentional, but a product of her gifts.

If anyone in the room doubted that she was the freak of all the freaks, they had now been informed of the fact by the camp leader. Oh, Kylie suspected Holiday had been trying to help, but Kylie could have really done without it. Luckily, she had already managed to force down half a turkey sandwich because after that, there was no way she could swallow another bite.

Right after her embarrassing moment in the spotlight, Kylie's phone rang. She saw her mom's number on the call screen and turned the phone off. The last thing she wanted was for her conversation with her mom overheard by the super-hearing individuals.

As soon as the official lunch meeting ended, Kylie found Holiday to get her cabin directions. Dinner was set at six and until then, the afternoon was free. During downtime, mingling and getting to know your camp companions and cabin roomies was encouraged.

Instead, Kylie spent the four hours mingling with her emotional turmoil and hidden away in her closet of a bedroom. Hey, she understood the difference between "encouraged" and "required."

Sitting up on the bed, she noticed again the size of her room. Not that she was complaining. The fact that she had her own room made the size a non-issue. Considering the night terrors that plagued her three or four nights a week, the privacy was much appreciated. She just hoped the walls were thick enough to contain what her mother called "bloodcurdling screams." The walls at home sure as heck weren't.

Biting down on her lip, Kylie wondered again how her mom could do this to her. Send her here when only a week ago, her mom had suggested she not spend the night off anywhere because it would be embarrassing for her to let others see her in a sleep-dazed terror.

Shaking off thoughts of her mom, Kylie looked around the room again. Her afternoon hadn't been a total waste. She'd unpacked her things, called her mom—aka, the Ice Queen—back, tried to get in touch with a MIA Sara—who still hadn't called or texted—read the camp rules, and indulged in a good ol' fashioned meltdown with lots of tears.

A much-deserved meltdown.

For sixteen years she'd tried to figure out who she was. And while she'd always known she'd had a ways to go, she'd felt pretty confident in her discoveries. But today she realized not only was she wrong about who she was, but she didn't even know *what* she was.

Talk about an identity crisis.

Her phone buzzed again. She looked at the caller ID and saw her dad's name.

Her dad who'd left her.

Her dad who hadn't picked her up at the police station.

Her dad who hadn't visited her before she'd been forcibly shipped off to camp.

Her dad who obviously didn't love her near as much as she'd thought he did.

Her dad who in spite of everything, Kylie missed with all her heart.

If that made her a daddy's girl, so be it. Besides it was probably just a temporary condition. Sooner or later she'd give up loving him so much like he'd given up on her. Right?

Her throat locked up. The temptation to answer and beg him to come get her was so strong that she tossed the phone onto the foot of the bed. She listened to the buzz and knew if she answered that call she'd tell him about supernaturals and about her being one of them—about running into Lucas Parker the potential serial killer.

Keeping secrets from her mom had always felt easy, because it seemed her mom kept her own secrets; but keeping things from her dad was algebra—damn hard.

So instead of taking the call, she plopped her head on the pillow and gave in to another bout of tears. When someone knocked on her bedroom door, Kylie still wore the watery evidence of tears on her cheeks.

Before Kylie could decide what to do, the door opened and a nose peeked through the crack. "Are you awake?"

Since Kylie sat up on the bed and saw Miranda's eyes right above the nose, Kylie didn't lie. "Yes."

Miranda stepped in—uninvited.

"Hey, I just . . ." Miranda's hazel gaze lit on Kylie's face and the girl's mouth dropped open.

Kylie knew exactly what had the little witch gaping. Kylie envied the girls who could cry and barely smear their mascara, but she lacked that particular skill. When Kylie cried, her fair skin broke out in big red dots and her eyes swelled so much that she didn't look human.

Wait. According to Holiday, Kylie wasn't human. Who knew?

"Are you okay?" Miranda asked.

"Fine." Kylie forced cheeriness into her voice. "Allergies."

"Should you go see a nurse? Seriously, you look terrible."

Thanks. "No. I'm fine. It'll go away in a bit."

"It's not contagious, is it?" Miranda stopped a few feet into the room.

"I sure as heck hope not," said a voice at the door. A voice that belonged to Della, who still wore her dark shades, and who Kylie had learned during the introductions was a vampire. Yup. A real vampire.

"I'm not contagious," Kylie said, and realized she should have said yes so they'd leave her alone.

Miranda moved in and sat on the foot of the twin bed, and

Della followed her but didn't sit down. Instead, the girl removed her sunglasses and eyeballed Kylie up and down. Her dark expression reminded Kylie of a how a person on a diet stared at a Girl Scout cookie right before it became mouth mush.

Kylie's skin crawled at the thought of becoming mush in anyone's mouth.

"You are coming to dinner and the campfire, aren't you?" Miranda asked.

"Is . . . is it mandatory?" Kylie asked, hoping her reaction to Della didn't show.

"Are you scared of me?" Della blurted out, axing all of Kylie's hopes of hiding the fact that Della scared the pee out of her.

"Why . . . why would I be scared of you?"

"Because I have sharp teeth?" She opened her mouth and exposed her pearly whites that did indeed showcase two sharp canines. "Because I might suck your blood out?"

It took effort not to cringe at Della's words, especially when the girl ran her tongue over her lips.

"Quit teasing her." Miranda laughed and rolled her eyes.

"That's just it." Della waved at Kylie. "Her heart is racing and her pulse is running off the chart. Look at the vein in her neck, it's throbbing. I don't think she knows I'm teasing."

The fact that Della mentioned Kylie's veins had her blood pumping harder. "Of course I do," Kylie lied. "Holiday said everyone here was good . . . people."

"And you believed her?" Della's black eyes accused Kylie of being dishonest.

Kylie decided right then that Della's ability to read her vital signs surpassed her ability to lie. "I want to believe her. But I'll admit it, I'm still trying to wrap my mind around the fact that . . . that supernaturals exist."

"But you're a supernatural," Miranda said. "How could you not know—"

"Holiday *thinks* I'm a supernatural." Yeah, somewhere in the last few minutes Kylie had gone back to hoping Holiday's analysis was meritless.

"You are a supernatural," both Miranda and Della said at the same time, both their eyebrows twitching ever so slightly.

"Or at least, you aren't all human," Della said. "We can tell that by looking at your brain pattern."

"And you guys are never wrong?" Kylie clutched her knees tighter to her chest.

"Everyone's wrong once in a while," Miranda said.

"But not very often," Della added.

Nevertheless, their answer spurred Kylie's hope. "But it does happen. Right?" The heaviness in her chest lightened.

"Yeah, there are the people with brain tumors," Della added.

Kylie dropped her forehead on her knees. She was either a supernatural or dying of a brain tumor; she didn't know which was worse.

"And a few whose brains are just loopy," Miranda added.

Kylie raised her head. "Loopy?"

"Yeah, like a frog's hair from being loco."

"Then maybe I'm just loopy. I've been accused of that before."

"No, wait," Miranda said. "Didn't Holiday mention you had gifts?" Miranda and Della both raised inquisitive eyebrows.

Kylie shrugged. "Yeah, but that could just be because I'm dealing with a super-charged ghost."

"Ghost?" Miranda and Della said in unison.

Kylie could be wrong, but both girls looked appalled and scared. Their shock reminded her of Derek's reaction earlier when she'd asked if he could see ghosts.

"You can see the dead?" Della stepped back from the bed. "Oh, hell. I do not want to room with someone who has ghosts hanging around. That's too freaky."

Even Miranda popped up off the foot of the bed. Kylie stared at them, completely befuddled. "You're joking right? You two are scared of me? You're a witch." She pointed at Miranda. "And you're a vampire." She wagged her finger at Della. "And ya'll are calling me"—she poked herself in the chest—"freaky?"

Miranda and Della exchanged a look, but neither girl denied what Kylie had just said.

"Fine, forget it then," Kylie said, hurt by their attitude. "But just for the record, I don't talk to them." Then she realized that both girls were looking at her the same way she'd been looking at them all day. The bitterness of tasting her own medicine had Kylie turning things over in her mind.

"So they just hang around you?" Della started eyeballing the room. "Please tell me there's not any here right now."

"There's not," Kylie snapped, but her anger wasn't directed at her, just the situation. Because dad-blast it, if she'd heard someone could see ghosts, she'd probably be afraid of them, too.

"Good." Miranda reclaimed her spot at the foot of the bed.

Della continued to glance around. "Nope. Too weird. I don't want to room with you."

"I'm not any weirder than you are." Kylie stared at the vampire and for some reason wanted Della to accept her.

"She has a point," Miranda said to Della. "We're probably pretty scary to her, too. I say, let's try to make this work. You know, be buds."

Della let out a deep breath. "Okay, but you'll tell us when you see a ghost hanging around?"

Kylie nodded, but quickly realized how hard that request was going to be to keep, because the familiar icy feeling of a ghostly presence hit right then. The saving grace was that she didn't "see" the ghost. Not that she looked hard, but who could blame her not wanting to clash gazes with a dead person?

Kylie hadn't thought she could eat, but when the warm, spicy scent of pizza hit her nose, she realized how little she'd eaten all day. She'd managed to down one slice of thin pepperoni and cheese and eat half her salad before she started feeling self-conscious from the occasional twitching stares. Some of the campers were still trying to figure her out. Well, good luck with that. She took another bite of salad and hoped that if they managed to do it, they'd let her in on the secret.

As Kylie moved her gaze around the room, she found Derek sitting at another table. There was a red-haired girl sitting next to him, and from her body language she found Derek more interesting than her pizza. The girl leaned so close to Derek that her left breast brushed against his arm and from the way Derek leaned into the girl, Kylie figured he enjoyed the girl's attention.

The tiniest bit of jealousy echoed in her chest, but Kylie pushed it back. It was just because he looked like Trey. Biting down on her lip and her emotions, she knew she'd have to be careful where Derek was concerned. It would be easy to confuse her feelings for him.

Right then the half-fairy looked over his shoulder at her. Their gazes met and held. The flutter, the good one, started happening again in the pit of her stomach.

"I think he likes you," Miranda whispered.

Realizing she and Derek had drawn attention, she glanced away. "He's probably just curious about me like everyone else," she whispered back.

"Nope. He's hot for you," Della said, reminding Kylie of the supernatural hearing of some of the campers. "When he was sitting by you at lunch, he oozed so much testosterone that it was hard to breathe. He wants your body," Della teased.

"Well, he's not getting it," Kylie said.

"So you don't like him?" Miranda asked, sounding thrilled.

"Not like that, I don't." It felt like a lie, but she ignored it, because she knew any feeling she might have stemmed from his looking like Trey. She had enough stuff going on in her life right now. She sure as heck didn't need to start falling face-first into another relationship, especially one based on a lie. Derek wasn't Trey.

And Trey wanted her back. Or at least he'd insinuated that on the phone earlier. With all the other stuff she'd been zapped with today, she hadn't had time to consider how his confession made her feel. Happy? Sad? Angry? Maybe a little of all three?

Trying to prevent emotional overload, Kylie reached for her glass of diet soda and watched Della pull the pepperoni off the pizza and pop it in her mouth. The very tips of her sharp canines caught Kylie's attention and her thoughts skipped past Trey issues and landed on living-with-a-vampire issues.

As another piece of pepperoni disappeared down Della's throat, Kylie realized that the girl was eating. From the fictional books she'd read, she'd assumed vampires didn't eat. They only drank . . . Kylie's gaze slammed against Della's glass filled with some red, thick liquid.

"Oh crap." Kylie's stomach heaved, and she placed a hand over her mouth.

"What?" Della asked.

"Is that . . . blood?" she muttered, and looked around the dining hall, noticing the glasses filled with the red substance that were occupying the tables in the room.

Miranda leaned in. "It's gross, isn't it?"

"Hanging out with toads is gross." Della's voice came edged with anger.

"I don't hang out with toads," Miranda snapped, her hazel eyes grew bright with what appeared to be embarrassment. "I put a spell on this guy. He deserved it, of course, but now I can't seem to reverse it so whenever he misbehaves, he automatically turns into a toad and pops in to see me."

Desperation echoed in Miranda's voice, but Kylie barely paid it any heed. For some reason the fact that Miranda could turn people into toads didn't bother Kylie near as much as the fact that Della was drinking blood. But holy hell. What kind of blood was it?

Della looked at Kylie and read her disgust. "Seeing dead people is gross, too. This"—she picked up her glass and took a big gulp—"is not gross."

When Della pulled the glass away, a couple of red drops beaded right below her bottom lip. Della's pink tongue shot out and caught the droplets.

Kylie's stomach knotted and the pizza, now a lump in the bottom of her gut, wanted to find its way up.

"Of course"—Della's smile came off wicked—"you guys will find that out when you have to try it."

"I tried it last summer and it was gross," Miranda said. "It tastes like a dirty penny smells."

"What?" Kylie swallowed hard. "I have to drink blood? I'm not doing it. Nope. Not me." She put her hand over her mouth and concentrated on not barfing.

"Not drink it, just taste it," Miranda said. "We all have to learn about each other's cultures toward the end of the summer. We, the witches, put on a ceremony and show some of our magic; the werewolves, last time we actually saw Lucas Parker transform himself. It was scary. Whatever you do, don't piss off a werewolf."

Kylie's mind stopped fixating on drinking blood and fixed on Lucas Parker transforming into a wolf. Then she remembered their little meet-up during lunch. The one where she'd probably pissed him off.

Of course, she didn't need to hear Miranda's warning. She knew firsthand what he was capable of doing. Then for some crazy reason, she found herself trying to find him in the crowd. He either wasn't there, or had his back to her.

"Werewolves aren't as badass as vampires," Della said, defending her species with enthusiasm. "Werewolves only have full power once a month. Vampires—we're a hundred percent twenty-four/seven. It's *my* kind that you don't want to piss off."

Kylie sat there trying to digest the conversation while her shaky stomach worked on digesting the pizza.

"And then the shape-shifters—that was weird, but not scary," Miranda continued.

"What did the Fae do?" The question came from a deep, obviously male voice.

Kylie recognized Derek's voice before her eyes found him. And when she did find him, she realized he'd found her, too. He stared right at her.

Her already knotted stomach knotted some more. Only these knots, like the flutters, weren't all unpleasant. Yup, she was going to have to be extra careful with Derek where her emotions were concerned.

"Well," Miranda said, her tone a little higher pitched than normal. "Because fairies have different gifts, each one did a short presentation." Miranda gave her hair a twirl and smiled extra wide.

"What's your gift?" Della asked Derek as she pulled another piece of pepperoni off the pizza and slipped it between her lips. Lips that had just drunk blood.

A long pause followed the question. Derek's posture stiffened. "Who said I even have gifts?" His tone implied he didn't like to be questioned. Or could he be like her, and wasn't too thrilled to have his gift?

"One of the fairies last year could read people's thoughts," Miranda continued, obviously not picking up on Derek's mood. "Can you read my mind now?" She bit down on her lip and sent him a sultry look.

Kylie's gaze shot back to Derek. Could he read minds? No, she didn't think he could, because he'd asked earlier what she was. Or was he just making conversation?

She recalled thinking some private thoughts about his body, comparing it to Trey. Oh, great. How embarrassing would that be if he knew she'd imagined him without his shirt? Then she realized she was doing it again. Kylie felt her face flush and Derek, still staring, didn't miss a thing.

"Another fairy could move objects with his mind," Miranda said louder as if trying to get Derek's attention on her. "Of course, witches can do that, too."

"Really?" Della sounded honestly amazed. "Do it now. Move my plate." She leaned back as if to give Miranda room.

Miranda's gaze shot to Della and she frowned. "I can't. It's against the rules."

"Rules? Screw the rules," Della said. "Do it. No one is going to know but us."

"I can't." Miranda's cheeks turned pink, almost as pink as the streaks in her hair. It was good to know Kylie wasn't the only one who suffered from blushing.

"Why not?" Della argued. "Just because of some stupid rule?"

Miranda glared at Della. "Why don't you just go drown

yourself in blood?" Miranda glanced at Derek, who she'd obviously wanted to impress, and turned pinker.

"Oh, stake me!" Della snapped.

"Be careful, or I might," Miranda shot back, her expression passing embarrassment and going straight to anger.

Kylie's gaze shifted from Miranda to Della as they took turns slamming each other with insults.

Great. Now her two roommates were going to be trying to kill each other.

"You two should chill," Derek said, as if he'd read her mind.

"I'm already as chilled as I can get," Della said, and focused on Miranda. "Somebody's got a chip on her shoulder. And you'd best be careful, because I'd be more than happy to knock it off for you." She jumped up and before Kylie could focus on her, she was gone.

"Cool," a new voice in the crowd said.

Perry, aka Weird-Eyed Boy who'd turned himself into the unicorn, stood beside Derek. Kylie stared at his black eyes, and her heart raced to the tune of panic.

"Hey," Perry said to Miranda. "I'd love to watch you two go at it and rip each other's clothes off."

"In your dreams," Miranda said.

"Yeah." Perry chuckled. "Especially the clothes off part."

"Grow up." Miranda grabbed both hers and Kylie's trays and shot off to drop them off.

"Thanks," Kylie said to her, but looked from Derek to Perry, not sure which one made her more nervous—Derek who made her feel things she didn't want to feel, or Perry who just plain freaked her out. Her phone buzzed. She pulled her cell from her purse, hoping it was Sara with not-pregnant news and not her dad. A sigh escaped her lips when she saw Sara's number.

"Later," Kylie said to the guys. Then, eager to escape, she took off outside where she could have a private conversation. Though who the heck knew how far she'd have to go so the super-hearing supernaturals couldn't listen in?

Chapter Twelve

"Just don't panic," Kylie told Sara thirty minutes into their conversation. "It'll probably be fine." Kylie couldn't say that with a huge amount of enthusiasm, but she gave it a shot. That's what friends did. Yet deep down, Kylie knew if Sara was pregnant, and there seemed to be a good chance she was, it wouldn't be fine.

"Thanks, Kylie," Sara said. "What am I going to do without you all summer?"

"Survive," Kylie said. "That's all I'm planning to do, too."

Kylie had spent the entire conversation hiding behind the office, sitting on the ground, leaning against a tree and trying to calm Sara down.

Sara's mom had canceled her lunch and insisted her daughter spend the day with her, going to the art museum and then shopping. The Museum of Fine Arts in Houston was great and Sara actually liked art. As for the shopping, who wouldn't love that? But not with your mom while you're afraid you were pregnant.

"I totally can't believe this is happening," Sara continued. She hadn't even picked up a pregnancy test yet. She was too freaked.

Not that Kylie wasn't up to her eyebrows in her own issues, but talking to Sara about her problems helped Kylie not to focus on her own. Plus, focusing on Sara was pretty much the norm for them. Face it, when Sara was upset, and sometimes even when she wasn't, Sara tended to be a tad self-absorbed. Kylie never minded. She'd always preferred listening to other people's problems than blabbering about her own.

Good thing, Kylie supposed, since right now she couldn't talk about what was going on. Well, not to any normal person, anyway.

"Well, I should go," Sara said.

One of the last sprays of the day's sun shot a golden glow around the green scenery. With dusk closing in, the heat index no longer felt so suffocating.

"Call me when you get the test," Kylie said.

"I will. And thanks."

Kylie closed the phone and her eyes. Leaning her head against the tree, she recalled her newfound hope that maybe Holiday was wrong about Kylie being a supernatural. She also remembered the two black-suited guys saying the camp could be closed down if "it" didn't stop—not that Kylie had any idea what "it" was. But if both of those hopes came true, Kylie could almost see her life being tolerable.

Or at least somewhat tolerable. The issues of her parents, Nana, and Trey almost felt manageable now. Amazing how one's perspective altered after learning you might not be human.

Holiday's voice played through Kylie's mind: *The truth . . . the truth is we don't know what you are. It could be fairy, it could be you are a descendent of one of the gods. It could be—*

Kylie recalled interrupting the camp leader, and now she wished she'd hadn't. Even though she hadn't given up on being normal, she couldn't help but wonder what else she might be.

Trying to stop the emotional jitters from making her stomach twitch, she concentrated on not thinking and just listening. A late-afternoon breeze stirred the leaves of the tree, crickets warmed up for their night song, a baby bird called to its mama. Kylie remembered the hiking trips she'd taken with her dad. Should she call her dad back now?

Later, she told herself. Maybe then she would know what to say to him about why he hadn't come to get her at the police station when she called him. For now, she was just going to sit there and absorb nature and almost relax. She closed her eyes and slowly the tension faded.

Kylie wasn't sure how long it had been, ten minutes or an hour, but something jarred her awake. Her eyes sprang open to darkness. She sat very still, listening. Not even the crickets breathed. Fighting the fear of the unknown, she remembered real monsters existed.

A deep, sinister roaring, like a lion, filled the dark silence, and then came the howling of dogs . . . or were they wolves? She glanced up at the black sky. The moon, not a full moon, looked blurry from the smear of clouds crawling past it. The sudden need to go somewhere where she felt safer shot through her. Before she moved, she heard a twig snap.

She wasn't alone.

Her heart raced and she considered her options—scream or run. Maybe both. Before she could do either someone spoke up.

"Still afraid of me, huh?"

She recognized Della's voice and her heart stopped most of the racing. Most of it. "Not as much as before." Kylie looked up. The vampire loomed over her.

Della laughed. "I like the way you mostly tell the truth."

"You can really tell when people are lying?" Kylie asked.

"Not everyone. Depends on how good of a liar they are. The good ones can control their pulse enough so I don't hear it. Then there's the people for who lying is so second nature it doesn't affect them."

Kylie stood and dusted the grass and twigs off the butt of her jeans. She'd have to be careful and not lie to Della. Or either get better at it.

"Holiday sent me to sniff you out."

"Sniff me out?" In the dark, Kylie could barely make out Della's expression, but she could tell the girl was smiling. Her white teeth seemed to almost glow in the night.

"You can smell me?" Kylie brought her arm up to her nose.

As if Kylie was a communal sniffing project, Della leaned in and sniffed. An appreciative moan left the girl's lips.

The tips of Della's sharp canines appeared at the corners of her mouth and Kylie jerked her arm back. Della's smile faded. Kylie got the odd impression that the vampire honestly didn't want Kylie to be afraid of her. So vampires had feelings, too. Somehow, realizing that made the girl more human and less scary.

"Everyone is at the campfire." Della started walking.

Kylie moved in step with her, not an easy task since Della's pace wasn't for wimps. "Do I really smell good to you?"

Della didn't look at her. "Do you want me to lie so you'll feel better? Or do you want the truth?"

"The truth . . . I think."

Della stopped and her tone came out huffy. "There's blood in your veins, I really like blood, so yes, you smell yummy. But it doesn't mean . . . Let me put it like this. Imagine you're hungry and you go into a hamburger joint. Every table is filled with people and their plates of big juicy hamburgers and greasy fries. The smell is ambrosia. So . . . what do you do?"

"Hurry and order," Kylie answered, not getting the point.

"You mean you wouldn't go steal any food off anyone's plate?"

"No," Kylie said.

"Okay, so if stealing someone's lunch is bad, you can imagine stealing a few pints of blood might create a tad more of an issue than swiping a Big Mac. I'd have to be really starving. Or really angry before I'd do that."

The girl came off pretty dang angry. Kylie asked, "Do you get *really* angry a lot? Have you ever got that mad?"

Della let out another exasperated huff. "I've never killed anyone that I can remember. Is that what you want to hear me say?"

"Yeah." Kylie smiled. "So vampires really aren't a threat to humans?"

"I didn't say that," Della said.

"Meaning?" Kylie asked.

"Meaning just like there's good and bad humans, there are good and bad vampires. And really bad vampires who belong to gangs and purposely try to cause havoc everywhere they go."

"What kind of havoc?" Kylie asked.

"Let's just say they'd steal your Big Mac. Or worse."

"Okay," Kylie said, pretty sure she knew what "worse" meant, and she didn't like it one bit.

"Then there are the betweeners," Della continued.

"Betweeners?"

"Like humans who have been known to get into some trouble, but aren't totally bad. Vampires can be like that, too."

Kylie nodded. They started walking again and her curiosity grew. "What are your gifts? If . . . you don't mind me asking?"

"Heightened senses. Heightened strength. And—oh, shit! I just remembered your gifts." She came to an abrupt halt. "There aren't any ghosts around here, are they?"

Kylie did a quick check for coldness. "Nope. But seriously, I don't think I'm really gifted."

"You don't want to be gifted, do you?" Della asked.

"No," Kylie answered, coming close to lying. Then she remembered Della was a human—make that a "nonhuman"—lie detector.

Kylie realized they were heading into the woods; a spray of clouds passed over the moon and darkness cloaked the area. That's when Kylie heard it again, the deep roar of what sounded like a jungle cat.

"Did you hear that?" she asked.

"You mean the white tiger?"

"The what?" Kylie reached out and grasped Della by the elbow. The coldness of her skin had Kylie letting her go even quicker than she grabbed her. The roaring stopped but the temperature of Della's skin sent a chill up her arm. Were vampires really dead? She didn't think she could ask that question.

Della looked back at her as if she knew the coldness repulsed her. Kylie looked down and tried to pull free a twig that had clung to her jeans, hoping to keep Della from seeing too much.

When Della started moving again, Kylie remembered what they'd been talking about. "This is Texas. We don't have white tigers."

"You do at wildlife parks. There's one a few miles from here. It's both a refuge and a park. Like a zoo. Visitors can drive through and even feed the tamer animals."

"I went to one once," Kylie said. "I just didn't know there was one here."

"Yup." Della raised her nose in the air and sniffed. "And most of the animals need their litter boxes cleaned. Stuff stinks. Especially the elephants' crap."

Kylie inhaled, fearing the stench, but only the scent of the woods, of moist earth and green vegetation filled her nose. She supposed having a heightened sense of smell wasn't always a good thing.

Each step took them deeper into the woods. Thorn bushes caught on her jeans. She had to speed walk to keep up.

"Where is the bonfire?" Kylie asked, feeling winded.

"About a fourth of mile. A little farther than our cabin."

"Why didn't we take the trail?"

"It's quicker this way."

Maybe for a vampire. They continued on for another three or four minutes without talking. Kylie thought of all the questions she'd like to ask Della, but didn't know if she would be offended.

Concentrating on the ground to avoid the largest thorn bushes and stumps, Kylie plowed right into the back of Della.

"Sorry—"

Della swung around so fast, Kylie only saw a blur, but there was no mistaking the girl's cold hand pressing over Kylie's mouth. "Shh." Della's fierce expression added a menacing touch to her warning. Then she swung back around, her head tilted as if listening.

Kylie tuned her own ears to hear. But like earlier, when Kylie had just awakened, only silence filled the woods—no insects, no birds. Even the trees held their breath.

Why?

A blast of cold air shot past as if something had flown by. But nothing was there. Then Della made a low guttural growl.

Kylie looked up. The girl's eyes were glowing, and a lime green color beamed from her face, making her look anything but human. Fear took up residence in Kylie's chest, crowding out her heart and lungs.

The whisk of wind passed again. Kylie looked back over her shoulder, and when she looked back around, she saw him. He stood far too close—taking up half of her personal space. Blinking, she took in his jet-black hair and Asian eyes. Eyes similar to Della's, but his eyes glowed gold not green.

His surreal stare focused on Della. "Hey, Cuz."

He cut his cold, gold gaze back to Kylie and leaned in. His nostrils flared. "I see you brought us a snack."

Chapter Thirteen

Before Kylie could think to react, Della jumped in front of her. "What are you doing?" Della demanded. "You can't . . . you can't be here."

"Don't worry, Cuz," he said. "They can't hear or smell me this far away. I know their limitations."

"Forget their limitations. *You* aren't supposed to be here," Della snarled.

"So I can't come see my favorite cousin?"

"Not here." She waved her hand. "Now leave before you get my ass in all kinds of trouble."

"You're not going to introduce me to this yummy-smelling individual." In a flash, he moved to stand in front of Kylie again. This time even closer. She could see an ugly scar running alongside his chin. The smell of his breath wafted up her nose. It smelled like the grocery store when you got too close to the meat department. Raw meat.

One word echoed in her panicked brain. *Run!*

Fear kept her from obeying.

Della growled and less than a second later, her vampire roomie had sandwiched herself between Kylie and the scar-faced cousin. "Leave her alone, Chan. You're scaring her."

He took a step back. "I'm just joking. I had my dinner." He ran his hand down his shirt—a light colored shirt that Kylie noted had stains down the front. Stains that could very well be . . .

Fear froze her lungs as the coppery scent of blood filled her nose. A noise escaped her lips. She took a step backward and almost tripped on her own feet.

Della shot her a quick glance, then refocused on Chan. "Go home. I'll see you when camp's over."

"So you're going to join us when you get out of this joint?" he asked.

"I don't know what I'm doing when this is over. That's why I'm here, to figure that out."

"Your parents will never accept you. You can't live in that world anymore," Chan said.

"You don't know that," Della said, pain sounding in her tone.

"I do know. I tried it. Save yourself and them the heartache and just come and live with us. We're your new family."

"I told you I'll make my decision when I leave here."

"This place is going to feed you a pack of lies. They want to change us . . . all of us. It's a ploy by the government."

"They aren't feeding me anything. They made it clear, it's my choice. Now go away before you get me thrown out of here."

"Trouble is my middle name, Cuz."

"Chan." Della made that low snarling sound again.

"You are no fun," he said, and then took off, moving so fast he left only a cold wake of fear behind.

Kylie found a tree to lean against. Della stood there, head tilted as if listening and staring off in the direction Chan had disappeared, no doubt making sure he'd left.

Slowly, she turned to Kylie. Her eyes had faded back to her own shade of black. The moon found its way from the clouds, allowing Kylie to read the emotions in Della's face.

"I'm sorry," Della said, and her expression matched her words.

Kylie couldn't answer; she hadn't even gotten her breathing under control. Back still against the tree, she wrapped her arms around herself to fight off the chill that had nothing to do with the temperature.

"He wouldn't have hurt you," Della said.

"He called me a snack," Kylie insisted, managing to eke the words out from her shaking lungs.

"He enjoys scaring people. He wouldn't have done anything."

Kylie arched a brow in disbelief. "Is he . . . does he belong to one of those gangs that harm humans?"

"No, he just likes to act out sometimes."

"Is that why you kept getting between us?"

"I did that because I could smell how afraid you were."

While Kylie couldn't totally buy into Della's words, she sensed Della believed it. Or at least she wanted to believe it.

The normal noises of the woods returned. A few insects chirped in the distance. Della stood there almost fidgeting. "Can I ask you a big favor?"

"What?" Kylie asked.

"Don't mention this to anyone? Other supernaturals aren't supposed to visit." The pleading in Della's voice seemed to cost her.

"What if he comes back?" Kylie could almost smell the scent of raw meat that had lingered on his breath.

"He won't. I'll make sure of it." Pausing, Della studied Kylie's face. "Please. If they find out, I could be sent home and I really need to be here right now."

Kylie remembered how Della had protected her and for reasons Kylie didn't quite understand, she trusted the vampire to protect her again. But did she trust her enough to put her life in her hands? Probably not, but her gut instinct made the decision for her.

"Just make sure he doesn't come back. I don't want to become another blood spatter on his shirt." Saying the words sent another chill down Kylie's back.

When the chill hung on longer than it should, she wondered if the cold stemmed from her panic or was it from something else? Was someone else here? Someone other than . . .

"Thanks." Della smiled. "I knew I liked you. Come on—let's get to the bonfire before they send someone after us."

They started walking again, but every other step had Kylie looking over her shoulder. What frightened her more—finding a ghost or Della's cousin—she wasn't sure.

The smell of wood smoke grew stronger as they made their way through the woods. The half moon shifted in and out behind clouds, shrouding them either in moon shadows or complete darkness. The strange animal sounds kept playing in the distance—lions, elephants, and even wolves. But thankfully, the cold faded into the darkness.

Della never seemed to lose her way so Kylie stayed close, ignoring the feel of thorns and bushes catching on her jeans. Finally, a reddish glow appeared between the trees.

Able to think clearly at last, Kylie took advantage of their last few minutes alone to ask Della a few questions. "Is . . . your cousin the one who did this to you?"

Della looked over her shoulder. "Did what to me?"

"Turned you into a vampire."

"Oh. No. I was born with the virus. But yes, it was probably the contact with him that activated it."

"I thought you became a vampire by getting bit? Or is that just a myth? I mean, I realize there's a lot of myths about supernaturals. I saw you could eat pizza. And you were in the sun."

Della smiled. "The sun and I don't get along, but sunscreen mostly takes care of that. I can eat—not like I used to. I mostly need blood. And yes, some humans can be turned by being . . . bit. There are parts of the myths that are true. However, most of us are born with the virus. But it takes being exposed to another vampire before the virus is activated."

Kylie tried to understand. "So you knew you were a vampire all your life?"

Della chuckled. "Hardly. The virus runs in my family but we never knew anything about it because it only affects one in fifty family members, and even then it may not be the active virus. Everybody thought Chan died in a car accident when he was in France. Then one night I saw him, at this party. Freaked me out."

"I can imagine." A lot of this was freaking her out.

"Anyway, he of course could sense that I had the gene and having come in contact with him, he knew I'd turn and get sicker than hell. He showed up to help me. He told me that I was a vampire. It was a big friggin' shock to my system. Sort of like what you're going through right now."

"Yeah, but I haven't been sick. We're not sure if I'm anything."

"Yeah, denial is a big part of it," Della said. "I remember. I swore I just had a bad case of the swine flu."

Kylie bit back another denial and let Della continue. "I went through it all. Of course with vampires it's worse. The change is damn painful." She moved a few branches out the way and held them back for Kylie to pass.

"So your parents don't know?" Kylie asked.

"You kidding?" Della asked. "They would freak."

They kept walking and Della continued. "I got really sick at first. The doctors didn't understand it, either. Chan explained everything to me. He hid in my bedroom and took care of me for almost two weeks. I owe him big for that."

"Enough to leave your family for him?" Kylie asked, remembering what Della and her cousin had argued about. Then Kylie recalled her own family drama and sympathized with Della's plight. Losing someone you loved hurt like hell. An image of her father flashed in Kylie's mind and her chest tightened.

Emotion made Della's eyes bright. "There's a community of vampires who live in Pennsylvania. Chan thinks it's best if I go there and live. It's hard to live with family and keep this from them. I just . . . I don't know what's right. We . . . my family and

I, used to be so close. Well, Dad's always been a hard ass, but I know he loves me. Mom was my best friend and I have a little sister and I can't imagine leaving her."

"Would your mom let you go if you asked her?" Kylie asked.

"No. I'd have to run away and I know that would break their hearts. Which is why most young vampires fake their deaths, so the family moves on. I don't want to do that, but . . . I'm pretty much breaking their hearts now anyway. It's like a war zone at home."

Della's voice shook and Kylie didn't look but she figured there were tears in her roommate's eyes. Then again, Kylie wasn't sure if vampires could cry. But tears or no tears, she could hear the pain in Della's voice.

"It's hard," Della continued. "I had to go out at night to get blood. It's not as if I can keep a supply in the fridge. I'm basically nocturnal now, so staying awake at school during a boring class was almost impossible. The school convinced my mom I was either doing drugs or depressed. My parents, even my mom, were riding me and accusing me of all sorts of shit. All we did was fight, and I couldn't make it stop. So Chan may be right."

Kylie struggled for something to say. Staring straight ahead she spotted the red and orange flickers from the bonfire. The voices of the campers who were standing around a fire filled the night. She glanced at Della and offered her the only thing she could. "If it makes you feel any better, my home life sucks right now, too."

They walked out from the last line of trees into the clearing and they almost collided with a dark figure that leapt out of the trees, landing with almost a silent thud. Della growled. A startled yelp filled Kylie's throat, but then she recognized the dark figure with very blue eyes.

Lucas Parker.

"That's a good way to get hurt," Della snarled.

His gaze stayed fixed on them, harsh, accusing.

Kylie froze under his intense stare, but Della, unaffected by his ominous presence, gave Kylie a cold nudge to continue walking.

Lucas fell in step beside her and his deep voice came out as little more than a whisper. "If he comes here again, I won't sit by and do nothing." With that, Lucas took off.

"Shit," Della muttered.

Ditto.

Kylie watched Lucas move into a circle of other campers, and all of them greeted him as if he was some kind of leader. Before Kylie could look away, the girl who always seemed attached to Lucas's hip glanced back and her eyes turned greenish gold as she stared daggers at Kylie.

"Someone's jealous," Della snapped.

While the idea was laughable, Kylie could swear she did see jealousy in that girl's eyes.

A short time later, Kylie found herself alone, staring at the fire and listening to the strange animal sounds in the distance. Her gaze followed the trail of smoke that seemed to snake up to where the half moon hung in the sky. Breathing in the scent of burning wood and charred marshmallows from the sticks of several campers, Kylie fought emotional overload. Then, gazing at the flickering fire, she found herself missing Sara like she'd never missed her before.

At first, Kylie didn't understand the upheaval of feelings for her best friend, but when she glanced around the crowd the reasons became clear. Blindingly clear.

Welcome to the world of cliques.

School had always been about the cliques. Among the many, there'd been the cheerleader/popular clique, the school band clique, and then the smart/college-focused clique—completely different from the geek clique—and the art club clique. Then there was the one Kylie and Sara belonged to, the cliqueless clique.

Not that it was the worst one to belong to. In truth, it wasn't even a clique at all; they just belonged to the group that was considered floaters. They hung—not really belonged to, but just hung—with one group for a while, then they'd move to another. Thankfully, people didn't dislike them or poke fun at them like they did some of the unpopular groups. How could they poke fun at them when people hardly knew they existed? Or at least that's how Kylie had always felt at school. Not really disliked, or mistreated, just invisible.

And the reason for missing Sara right now, well, that was a no-brainer. Kylie might have been a floater, but she'd never had to float alone. Since fifth grade, she and Sara had been a team. And Sara had definitely been the head floater—the role naturally taken on since she was the one who worried the most about fitting in.

Inhaling another gulp of smoke, Kylie moved to escape the

path of the wind. As her gaze moved from one group to another, one of Nana's old sayings filled her head, birds of a feather flock together.

The flocks, or cliques, were different at camp than in high school. She spotted Della and the pierced boy, Jonathon, crowding around a group of kids, all vampires, no doubt.

Standing close to the fire, roasting marshmallows, was Perry, the shape-shifter, and with him were two other guys and a girl. Kylie wondered if they could all turn into unicorns.

Derek stood to the side of another crowd, as if he wasn't so sure he wanted to belong. She assumed these must be the fairies, or Fae as he called them. Not that she blamed him for using the different version. No straight guy would want to be called a fairy. Not that anyone could mistake Derek for gay. Something about the way he walked and carried himself was overtly female-loving male—like Trey.

Staring under her lashes, she let herself admire Derek's overtly male body. The wide shoulders, the square jaw, the way he filled out his jeans. That's when she realized she was doing it again—comparing Derek to Trey. She really, really didn't want to get caught up in that emotional storm, so she looked away.

Luck would have it that her gaze shot straight to another hard male body among a different flock of campers. Lucas. His warning about Della's cousin echoed in her head as she let her gaze move over his tall frame. Not that she planned to allow herself to appreciate the view for long. The fact that she appreciated it at all annoyed her. She owed her cat more loyalty than that. Right?

Before she could force her gaze away from his solid torso

wrapped in the black T-shirt, she noticed his goth-dressed girl-friend standing next to him. Her body was pressed so close, that nobody would dare come between them.

Lucas turned around as if he'd sensed her staring. Kylie attempted to look away, but his gaze locked on hers. She felt caught. Then the strangest thing happened. A forgotten memory surfaced. She'd been walking home from school, and a few of the older boys had started picking on her. One of the bullies had picked up a rock and slung it at her, but Lucas appeared out of nowhere and caught the rock. Like some kind of pro baseball player, he slung it back at the kid and hit the bully right between his legs.

The boy fell in the street moaning. Lucas had walked beside her the rest of the way home—as if to protect her. Those bullies never bothered her again.

Realizing she continued to stare at Lucas during her memory recall, she swung around. She noticed Miranda chatting with an artsy-looking crowd—obviously the witches of the group. Still feeling the tingle of Lucas's gaze, and needing something to get her mind off both him and her ex-boyfriend's lookalike, she started moving toward Miranda.

Hopefully, Kylie had learned enough floater skills from Sara to get her through the next few months. Because face it, why should camp be any different than high school? Belonging to a group and fitting in just wasn't in her cards.

Kylie's pillow didn't smell right—didn't feel right, either. Nothing felt right. She'd been the first to leave the campfire. When

Holiday stopped her on her way out to ask how she was doing, Kylie had been tempted to hit the leader with a deluge of questions. *Couldn't I just be a bit loony instead of gifted? And if I'm truly gifted, how do I find out what I am? And . . . What's the real chance that camp could be closed down by those black-suited dudes? Oh, and can I do anything to make sure that happens?* Okay, she wouldn't have asked the last two questions, but not from a lack of wanting.

More than anything in the world, Kylie wanted to go home—back to her own miserable life, back to her own miserable world.

Nevertheless, standing in front of Holiday, Kylie recalled the supersonic hearing of some of her campmates and put her questions on hold. According to her schedule, which had been handed out at the campfire, she'd have an hour counseling session with Holiday before lunch tomorrow.

Before that, right after breakfast, Kylie was to show up for the daily activity of Meet Your Campmates Hour. Supposedly each camper was to be paired up with someone for an hour to get to know a little about each other, their gifts, and the culture of their species.

Now, wouldn't that be fun? Not.

Sure she was curious, yet it would be kind of be nice to figure out what she was, or hopefully what she "wasn't" before investing in what everyone else was. And if she could prove she wasn't anything but human maybe she could go home.

She rolled over for about the hundredth time, knowing part of the reason she couldn't sleep was the fear that she'd have another night terror. Good God, she didn't want to have to explain that to her cabin mates.

The sound of her stomach grumbling filled the lonely darkness. Was there anything to eat in the fridge? Slipping out of bed, wearing a pair of navy boxers with hearts and a pink tank top, she moved to the door.

The door creaked when she stepped out of her room. The eeriness seemed to bounce against the log walls. Kylie gazed at the two closed doors leading into the other bedrooms. She'd heard Della and Miranda come in and listened to see if the two of them were still planning to kill each other. Hey, if she was going to have to wake up to a bloody mess, she wanted to be prepared.

Fortunately, the two of them had exchanged a non-combative conversation. It seemed all Miranda wanted to talk about were the boys. Derek included. Not that Kylie minded, of course.

A couple more steps and Kylie looked again at the bedroom doors. Hopefully, they were now both dead asleep. Okay, maybe *dead* wasn't the best word. Especially considering she didn't know if vampires were dead or not. Did they even sleep? And for that matter, were they immortal like the books said they were?

Kylie's bare feet pressing against the plank boards brought on a moan-like sound from the old wood. She recalled the visit from Della's cousin. Then she remembered the vampire gangs. Clutching handfuls of her tank top in both fists, she debated skipping a snack, for fear of becoming one.

And then the boards creaked again.

Chapter Fourteen

Kylie took one backwards step closer to her bedroom door. Then another noise made her stop short. She listened, recalling the wild animal sounds from earlier that night. This sound wasn't so wild, though. Breath held, she tuned her ears to pick up the noise. She heard it again, a very faint mewing. A soft, gentle sound.

A movement at the window caught her eye. Kylie swung around. Fear entered her chest first, but melted as soon as she saw the orange kitten perched on the outside window ledge. Startled by her sudden movement, the kitten fell from the ledge. "Don't go," Kylie muttered, at first not understanding her sudden concern for the kitten. Then understanding hit. What if Lucas or one of the werewolves happened by?

Kylie hurried to the door and opened it. She knelt down at the threshold and made the squeaky little noise that she knew cats loved.

"Come here, baby. I'll take care of you," she cooed. Her words were met by a rustling in the bushes. "Trust me." A few seconds later, the little yellow fur ball came swaying over.

"What a cutie," she whispered, and with a gentle finger stroked its white chin. The kitten turned on its purring machine, moved in, and started rubbing itself against her bare calves. She scooped up the creature and stared into the gold eyes, snuggling the purring little animal against her breasts, and then carried it inside.

The cat meowed and tried to escape from her arms, as if it didn't want to be shut inside, but Kylie held it tight. "No, no," she cooed. "There are monsters out there. You're safe here."

The animal seemed to relax as she passed her fingers softly over the back of its ear. "You hungry?" She butted her nose against the top of the kitten's head and cradled it closer against her chest.

She walked to the fridge, opened it to see what she could munch on, as well as offer the poor kitten.

A door creaked open behind her, and Kylie turned and watched Miranda, wearing a large yellow T-shirt and a pair of long pajama bottoms with smiley faces printed on them walk out of her room. Her tri-colored hair was a tad mussed and Kylie noticed she looked younger without her normal makeup.

"Hey," Kylie said.

"I thought I heard . . ." Miranda stopped and her eyes grew round. "What's that?"

"A kitten. Isn't she . . . or he adorable?" She held the animal up to check its sex. The kitten started twisting, even hissed, but Kylie held it tight. "It's a boy. *He* was peering in our window." She cradled him against her chest again and glanced back at the fridge. "I think he's hungry."

"Oh, no." The annoyance level in Miranda's tone had Kylie turning back around.

"What?" Kylie asked, genuinely confused. "Are you allergic to cats?"

"Same old trick, huh?" Miranda said, but Kylie didn't think her roommate was talking to her.

Instead, Miranda pointed a finger at the kitten and started wiggling her pinky finger back and forth. "Roses are red, violets are blue, show your true self or I'll put a hex on you."

"Stop. I'm changing back." The words spewed from the kitten.

Kylie stood frozen. *Words.* Oh, what the hell! Was she dreaming? Cats couldn't . . . talk. She looked at Miranda, not completely ready to toss the kitten across the room, but close. "Did I imagine . . . ?"

Miranda looked at Kylie and her lips twitched almost in a smile, but she held it back, and directed her gaze back to the kitten. "Do it now, Perry!"

Perry.

Kylie looked down at the kitten cozied up against her breasts. Sparkles, diamond-shaped sparkles floated around the red tabby. Then *poof.* Perry appeared, standing in front of Kylie, his head plastered against her breasts.

Kylie screamed.

Della shot into the kitchen. "What's . . . ?" She blinked. "Do you guys want to be alone?" She snickered and motioned to Kylie and Perry.

Snapping out of her stupor, Kylie grabbed the little twerp by the ear and yanked him off her chest. "He's leaving now."

"Ouch. Ouch," Perry muttered as Kylie dragged him past the kitchen table. "Let go of my ear!" he ordered in a roar that sounded like some kind of angry beast.

But Kylie wasn't feeling up to taking orders and she was too mad to be scared of him. Holding on to his ear like a tick to a dog, she dragged Perry past the small coffee table, yanked open the door with her free hand, and then shoved the pervert out the door with such force that he landed on his ass.

But she wasn't finished with him yet.

She pointed a finger at him. "You come anywhere near my breasts again and it won't be your ear I drag you out by next time. And in case you don't know what body part I'm referring to, let's just say the next time you turn yourself into a kitten, you'll find you've been *neutered*." She slammed the door with a loud *whack*.

"Creep." Kylie swung around, clenching and unclenching her fists.

Both Della and Miranda stood there, eyes wide and mouths hanging open in a kind of warped shock.

Miranda giggled first. "Sorry," she muttered. "But that was so freaking funny."

"Was not," Kylie snapped, still fuming, her throat tightening with anger.

"Oh, yes it was." Della started laughing so hard that she fell against the table. "You have spunk hidden behind your innocent face. I *like* it."

"Either that or she's stupid," Miranda said, and then snorted. "Do you realize what Perry is? He's like the most powerful shape-shifter in the world right now. Everyone knows you don't piss off a shape-shifter. They have terrible tempers."

"I . . . he . . . he tricked me into letting him snuggle up against my breasts." She recalled hearing the twerp's voice morph into a very threatening roar.

Okay, so maybe her actions had been a tad stupid, but nothing, nothing made her blood boil more than someone making a fool out of her, and that's what he'd done.

Fighting the tears, because she always cried when she was mad, she spotted the fridge still open and marched over to shut it. The cold blast from the white box hit her face the same time as she remembered . . . "Gross, I checked out his privates."

Behind her, both Della and Miranda spewed more laughter. Then for some off-the-wall reason, what hadn't seemed funny suddenly did. Kylie leaned into the closed fridge and started laughing. For the next five minutes, they sat at the kitchen table, giggling until they had tears in their eyes. It reminded Kylie of what she and Sara would so often do.

Or had until everything had changed.

"You should have seen his expression when you were pulling him by the ear," Della said. "I wish I'd had a camera."

"I almost felt sorry for him," Miranda said.

"Sorry for him?" Kylie asked.

"Yeah, he's kind of cute in that boyish kind of way. Don't you think?"

"Cute? Oh, heck. He's a freak," Kylie insisted.

"Aren't we all?" asked Della, her humor fading just a notch.

Not sure I am, Kylie thought, and almost said as much, but something plopped down on the table. Kylie screamed when she saw the toad.

Miranda rolled her eyes and snatched up the creature.

"Being bad again, Mr. Pepper?" she seethed at the amphibian, holding the beast a foot from her face, his toad legs dangling almost to the table.

"What did he do for you to put a spell on him?" Della asked, studying the toad in disgust.

"Like our friend Perry, he's a member of the pervert club." Miranda gave the toad a little shake. "He's my piano teacher and he tried to start playing something besides the piano, if you know what I mean."

Della snarled at the toad. "Why don't we just make him a midnight snack and be done with it? Do toad legs taste as good as frogs?"

"Hmm. Don't know." Miranda glanced at Della. "But I'm willing to find out," she said, and eyed the toad.

Kylie could be mistaken, but she could swear the toad's eyes grew large with fear.

Miranda laughed. "If only I was that type of witch."

"What kind of witch are you?" Kylie asked, somewhat relieved.

"A screwed-up witch." Miranda frowned and then scowled at the toad. "You know the drill, Mr. Pepper, stop thinking bad thoughts and you'll go back to normal."

The toad wiggled his legs and then vanished into thin air.

"What kind of curse did you put on him?" Della asked.

Miranda moaned in frustration. "If I knew that, I could stop it."

"You mean, you don't remember?" Della asked.

Miranda lowered her gaze. "I remember what I thought I said, but I'm . . . I'm dyslexic and I get my spells wrong sometimes, and I have to know exactly what I said to make it stop. So until then, every time that pervert thinks about an underage girl, he's transformed into a toad and pops in for a visit."

Kylie leaned in. "While it sucks for you, it sounds like he deserves it."

"Yeah, *he* does. But he's like a constant reminder that I'm a screw-up."

"True," Della said. "But on the positive side, you're keeping him from doing anything wrong. I hate perverts. I had an old neighbor who would stand at his window, empty lotion in his hand, and whack off in front of me or other girls."

"That's disgusting," Miranda said.

"Yeah, but what I hated was that a girl down the street had already told me he did it to her, too. She told her parents, the parents called the police. The police came back and said that he's a deacon of the church and it was basically my neighbor's word against his and they believed him."

"That's why I did the whole curse thing," Miranda said.

"But I handled it." Della grinned.

"What did you do?" Kylie was almost too scared to ask.

"I broke into his house and replaced his lotion with some really bad-ass superglue that my dad uses at his lab at work. You should have seen the look on his face when he couldn't get his hand off his dick. Then I made an anonymous call to the police and reported him. I mean, how could he deny doing it? His hand was stuck to the crime scene."

They all burst out laughing. Wiping the tears of laughter from her eyes, Kylie looked at Della and Miranda and she could have sworn they were just normal teenage girls.

Well, she could have sworn until the blast of cold snuck up on her from behind. Kylie glanced over her shoulder hoping beyond hope nothing was there.

But hopes were often futile.

Soldier Dude stood only a few feet from her. Too close. Closer than he'd ever been. The chill from his presence sent an icy fear climbing her spine.

"Kylie?"

She heard Miranda call her name—or was that Della? Kylie couldn't tell because it sounded as if it came from another world. A world in which ghosts didn't exist. A world Kylie wanted to get back to, but couldn't.

The dead guy kept his eyes on Kylie while he slowly reached up and removed his helmet. Blood, bright red blood, gushed down his forehead. Kylie's breath caught as she watched the blood trickle down his face. Then everything went into slow motion. Kylie stood up, wanting to escape.

Drip. Drip. Drip.

Blood droplets splattered onto the floor and left tiny speckles of red on the top of her bare feet. The drops kept coming. The specks of blood kept landing on her feet and then they started forming letters and then a word. *Help* . . .

Kylie tried to inhale, but her lungs refused to take in the frigid air. Letting go of the oxygen trapped in her mouth, she saw a cloud of cold air float up from her own lips.

"What's wrong?" Miranda's voice seemed to float in Kylie's mind.

Good question, Kylie thought.

Too bad she didn't have a freaking clue.

"Do you guys smell that?" Della's voice registered in Kylie's awareness but in a distant kind of way, like background music in a movie. "Something smells yummy."

"I don't smell anything." Miranda's words followed. Their conversation continued but suddenly it rang like a distant echo. "Oh shit . . . shit . . . shit. Kylie's aura is turning black. Black . . . black . . . black. I think there's a ghost. Ghost . . . ghost . . . ghost."

"Damn," Della said. "I hate this shit." Footsteps sounded, her friends were running away. A door slammed. Kylie wanted to run, too, but she couldn't. She couldn't move. The blood continued to spatter on her feet, but she refused to look to read the words.

"Wait." Della's tight voice sounded through walls. "She stopped breathing. Kylie's stopped breathing. We have to do something."

Kylie heard the door swing open. Heard her name being called. But that's when everything went black and her body slumped to the floor.

Chapter Fifteen

Coolness whisked across Kylie's brow and stirred her into a semi-alert state. One that brought on all the "w" questions: Who, What, When, Why, and Where. The musty smell of the pillow answered the Where question.

Camp. Still at camp.

The emotional overload from the last few days filled her chest. She forced her eyes open. Holiday sat on the edge of the bed. Her red hair hung free over her shoulders and concern appeared on her face and shined from her bright green eyes.

"Is she awake?" The hauntingly familiar masculine voice filled her ears and Kylie could hear echoes bouncing around her head. She shifted her gaze to the left.

Holy crap.

Holiday moved the damp cloth across Kylie's brow again. "Hey, you with us now?"

Kylie wasn't listening, or looking at the camp leader. She gazed at . . . Lucas Parker—cat killer extraordinaire.

And protector from bullies, Kylie's subconscious pointed out.

Though why her subconscious wanted to defend him was be-yond Kylie.

What was going on?

Lucas leaned down as if to touch her. Kylie shot up, pushed the cloth from her face. "What happened?" And then, just like that, it all came back at once.

The ghost.

The blood. So much blood.

Then she was hit by another mind-boggling piece of infor-mation. She must have passed out. How geeky was that?

"You fainted," Lucas said, his big voice filling the small room and making it feel even smaller.

Did he have to point out the obvious? And why was he here anyway? Wasn't there some of kind of "no boys in the bedroom" rule? If not, Kylie needed to see about getting it added.

She glanced over at Holiday.

"It happens sometimes," Holiday said. "When the ghosts start getting closer."

"I'm fine now." She lunged out of bed and doggone if the room didn't start spinning on its axis. Round and round. Lucas caught her elbow.

His touch was tight, but not enough to hurt.

His touch was warm and somehow warm tingles danced up her arm and made her even more light-headed. But at least things quit spinning.

Her first impulse was to jerk away, but afraid that would be too telling, she forced herself to appear calm. Of course, if he could read her heart rate like Della, she was pretty much screwed.

And speaking of Della, where were . . . Kylie shifted her focus to the doorway. Della and Miranda stood there, shoulder against shoulder, peering in as if Kylie was the nightly entertainment. Oh damn, how embarrassing. She could just imagine them running from their hiding spot—because she had the vague memory of hearing running footsteps—and them finding her on the floor. But how had she gotten in the bed?

Kylie glanced away from her roommates to Lucas. Had he picked her up? Held her in his arms? Her heart rate started climbing again. That's when she realized that he was still touching her.

"I'm fine." She gave her arm a quick jerk.

He released her, one finger at a time, as if afraid she might fall on her face again. Right before his last finger let go, she noticed his gaze sweep downward. While her pajamas weren't indecent, she became instantly aware of how thin her top was—and even more aware of how the scoop neck of the tank scooped lower than most of her tops. Or as Sara would say, her girls were trying to peer out and say howdy a little more than usual.

Kylie took a step back and crossed her arms over her chest.

"Why don't you let me talk to Kylie alone," Holiday said to Lucas, who still hadn't stopped staring, though his gaze had shifted from her chest to her face with a cold indifference.

He nodded, but she saw his dark brows twitch ever so lightly. So he was still trying to read her, was he? Right now, she was relieved knowing that he wouldn't get anything.

And just like that, another memory from the past surfaced and she remembered Lucas Parker doing the eyebrow thing when she was young. Had he tried to read her then? That thought brought up the question that had been bouncing around her head since she'd first spotted him. Did Lucas remember her?

"We can finish our discussion tomorrow," Holiday said to Lucas as if dismissing him.

"Okay," he said, offering Holiday a smile. Then he walked out.

Della and Miranda moved away from the doorway to let him pass. Kylie didn't miss the unfriendly way Della and Lucas exchanged glances. Was Della worried that Lucas had told Holiday about her cousin Chan's surprise appearance at camp? Probably.

"Shut the door," Holiday added as Lucas was almost out.

Kylie looked back at the camp leader, feeling as if she was about to be chastised for . . . for what? Fainting? Or had Lucas told her about Chan and now Kylie was in trouble for not speaking up?

"You don't have to be afraid of Lucas," Holiday said.

Kylie studied her. "Can you hear my heartbeat, too?"

Holiday grinned. "I read emotions, not heartbeats, but I also read your fear from the way you turned white as a sheet when you saw him."

Kylie almost blurted out what she knew about Lucas, but she didn't. It felt too much like tattling. Instead, she asked a question. "Why was he here?"

"He was in the office when Miranda came to get me."

Kylie looked at the clock; it was almost one in the morning. She couldn't help but wonder exactly what Lucas and Holiday were doing at that hour. Sure, the camp leader was older, but not by many years.

"Are you and he . . . close?"

"Depends on what you mean by close." Holiday arched a brow. "This is his third time here. He's assisting us with some things and even training to work with us next year. But that's all." Then she asked, "What happened tonight?"

Kylie swallowed, stalling. How much should she tell?

"The ghost appeared again, didn't he?" Holiday asked in the beat of the indecisive silence.

Kylie nodded, yet more than anything, she wanted to deny it. "Yes, but Miranda and Della said that people who are a little loony sometimes give off the same mental image of not being human. So maybe I'm not gifted and maybe the ghost is just a powerful one, like you said sometimes happens. Or I could even have a brain tumor."

Holiday sighed. "The chances of either one of those are very slim, Kylie. Don't you think?"

"Maybe, but the chance exists," Kylie insisted. "I mean, you said most of the time ghost whispering stems from . . . a condition that's hereditary. That one of my parents had to have been gifted, too."

"Neither of your parents ever . . . showed any signs of being different?"

"No. Never." Yet even as she answered, she reconsidered her mother's cold nature. Could that qualify as "different"?

"I also told you that in rare situations it can skip a generation."

"But I knew my grandparents on both sides. Don't most people know if . . . if they're not human?"

"Most people do, but . . ." Holiday stared at her as if disappointed, and then she folded her hands in her lap. "I suppose that's what you should work on while you're here."

"Work on?"

Holiday stood up. "Everyone here has a quest. Something they're seeking answers for. I suppose your quest is to discover if you are, or are not, completely human. And if, as I suspect, you are one of us, then you must also decide if you'll embrace your gifts to help others, or turn your back on them."

Kylie tried to wrap her mind around the possibility that one of her parents wasn't human, that they might understand what Kylie was going through. Wouldn't they have said something to her?

Holiday placed a hand on Kylie's shoulder. "You should try to get some sleep. We have a busy day tomorrow."

She nodded and watched Holiday almost make it out the door before the question popped out. "How . . . how do I find the answers? I can't go to my parents and ask them if they see ghosts. They'd think I was crazy."

Holiday turned around. "Or maybe one of them would confess the truth to you."

Kylie shook her head. "But if all this is a mistake, then all of that would be for nothing. They already have me seeing a shrink. If I start talking about ghosts, they might have me committed."

"It's your quest, Kylie. Only you can decide how you want to do this."

The next morning Kylie and Miranda walked to breakfast together. Della had already taken off by the time Kylie got up. When Kylie asked about Della, Miranda informed her that vampires often held before dawn meetings where they performed rituals.

"What kind of rituals?" Kylie asked.

"Don't know exactly, but my guess is it has to do with feed-ing on blood."

Kylie pressed a hand to her stomach, sorry that she'd asked. Of course, her sickly feeling could partly be due to the fact that she'd hardly slept. Then on second thought, nope, it was for sure the blood. The idea repulsed her in a big way. Seeing the red stuff in those glasses during dinner last night had been too much. If nothing else, at least Kylie might lose a few pounds over the summer.

They walked the next few minutes in silence. "How did you sleep last night?" Miranda finally asked, although Kylie knew what her roommate really meant. Namely, was Kylie okay and what the hell had happened to make her faint?

Kylie decided to ignore the subtext and answered the ques-tion as asked.

"Fine." Kylie lied, aware the white lies might work with Mi-randa, just not Della.

In truth, Kylie had stared holes in the ceiling considering what Holiday had said about Kylie's quest. No matter how Kylie looked at the problem, she couldn't think of a way to ask her parents if they were not all human.

But she could think of a lot of questions she'd like to ask someone about herself. Questions like: if I am a supernatural what other kind of species could I be? And if I'm not one of you, do I have some kind of a brain tumor? Kylie didn't know which was worse.

Then the revelation hit. Maybe getting answers to those

questions would help her rule out the possibility of being anything but human. It wasn't the best plan, but it was a start. And she had to start somewhere.

"You didn't look fine last night," Miranda said.

She hadn't been. When Kylie finally went to sleep, she'd dreamed. Crazy, weird dreams that involved Lucas Parker and her. They were swimming. He hadn't been wearing a shirt and neither had she. She'd woken up, feeling out of breath, and tingly. Tingly the way Trey had made her feel when they'd kissed for a long time. How could her body betray her and actually find Lucas Parker desirable? Not that she would let her body win this one. If there was anything she knew about herself, it was that she could control her desire. She'd gotten really good at stopping Trey, even when stopping had been the last thing she'd wanted.

So that gave her a new goal. Not only would she try and find out if she was human, she was also going to make darn sure she didn't get close to Lucas.

"I did okay," Kylie lied again.

"I don't believe you, but let's let that slide for now." Miranda looked away. "Cute vampire dude on the left," she whispered, totally changing the conversation.

"What?"

"The blond wearing a football jersey," Miranda whispered again. "What I wouldn't give to hook up with him."

"I thought you didn't like vampires."

"I never said that. And if I did, it wouldn't apply to the male vampires, anyway."

Kylie couldn't have cared less about a cute vampire, and the last place she wanted her mind to go right now was to thoughts about hooking up with any guy, but her gaze moved to the left on its own accord. No one was there. "Where?"

"Over there." Miranda nodded in the opposite direction.

"You mean right," Kylie corrected. "Not left."

"Right, left. I always get them messed up. I'm dyslexic, remember? But he's a cutie. Maybe I'll get his name in the Meet Your Campmates session today."

The blond guy stood chatting with a group of other boys. Kylie remembered seeing him, but couldn't remember his name. His stature and overall appearance reminded her of Perry, who was not Kylie's type. Especially after what happened last night.

"Are you really okay?" Miranda asked after they passed the group of boys. "You looked out of it last night. Your aura went all freaky."

"I'm fine." And then because she didn't want to talk about last night, she asked, "Are you really dyslexic?"

Miranda didn't answer right away. "Yeah. And according to my family, you'd think it's something I asked for." Her tone had lost the giddiness that seemed constant in her voice.

"So is your family all witches?"

"Yeah, but my mom can be a bitch, as well."

"Aren't all moms?" Kylie asked.

"Maybe." Miranda sighed. "Not that I really blame her. I've sort of let the family down, big time."

"How's that?" Kylie asked.

"I was destined to be the High Priestess next in line. But before I can be given the title, I have to pass some tests. And tests and I just don't get along. So my family could lose their place in the coven if I can't come through."

"Why does it have to be you? Why can't one of them step up to the plate?"

Miranda sighed. "It doesn't work that way. It's me or the honor goes to Britney Jones."

"Wow, talk about keeping up with the Joneses." Kylie gave the joke a stab, hoping to make Miranda feel better.

"Yeah." Miranda's tone implied the joke fell short.

"Sorry," Kylie said. "So what would it take for you to pass the tests?"

"Only to overcome dyslexia. Which is basically impossible," Miranda said. "Ohh, ohh, look to your left—I mean your right. Your purring breast-loving kitten is here. And he's blushing. You know, it has to be terrible on his ego to have been tossed out on his ass by you."

"I hope so." Kylie spotted Perry, and he did appear rather red-faced.

Good.

"You didn't tell Holiday about him, did you?" Miranda sounded concerned. The girl obviously had a soft spot for the twerp.

"No." Kylie frowned. "But I might if he does it again." She didn't know if Perry had super hearing, but she hoped so.

They were almost to the dining hall, just past the camp office, when the two black suits from yesterday came barreling out of the door.

Kylie slowed down and studied their body language. They weren't happy. Watching them hotfoot it to the parking lot,

Kylie couldn't help but hope that their little visit today had to do with the closing of the camp.

Right then, the bigger of the guys stopped and swung around. He stood frozen in one spot, staring and twitching his brows at her.

He leaned down and whispered something to the other man and then they started forward. Right toward Kylie.

Crappers.

Chapter Sixteen

Kylie felt like a trapped animal in the Black Suit's snare.

Dad-blast it. Why was everyone picking on her?

Better question, what in Hades could they want with her? She wasn't even a card-carrying supernatural person yet. And she hoped she got tossed out of the club before she got rubber-stamped.

Lucky for her, at about twenty feet away, the big guy's phone rang. He paused and answered it. Then he turned to his partner and said something and they both shot off.

She let out a held breath. "Thank God."

"What?" Miranda asked, and studied her in confusion.

Remembering that Miranda wasn't a first-timer, she asked, "Who are they?" She nodded to the retreating black-suited men who were now getting into a black sedan.

"Who?" Miranda asked, staring at another group of boys.

"The Black Suits?" Kylie asked.

"Gross, they are way too old for you." Miranda pulled a hair band from her pocket and put her multicolored hair up in a ponytail.

Kylie shot her roommate a glance. *Honestly, were boys the only things Miranda ever thought about?*

"I'm not interested in hooking up," Kylie said, and started walking again. "I'm just curious."

"Oh. They're from the FRU." Miranda fell into step beside her.

"And who are they?" Kylie asked.

"It stands for the Fallen Research Unit. You know, like Fallen, Texas? The city we passed through to get here? The FRU is basically a part of the FBI. The part that deals with supernaturals."

"What?" Kylie stopped and grabbed Miranda by the arm. "You mean, the government knows about vampires and such?"

Miranda made a face. "Of course they do. Who do you think funds the camp?"

"I thought our parents did." Kylie started moving again when she noticed a couple of people staring at them.

"Well, they pay some, but it takes a lot more to keep this place up."

"But why is the government behind this?"

"Well, that depends on who you ask. The camp has caused a lot of controversy in the supernatural community. Mostly just a lot of bigots mouthing off, if you ask me."

"What do you mean?"

"Some of the elders in each species, mostly old farts who don't believe in interracial relationships, claim the camp encourages it and they want the camp closed down. To their way of thinking, each species should stick to their own kind. To me, it's the same thing as race. They say we should maintain the purity of the species, but that's a bunch of bull. The species have been crossing since the beginning of time."

Kylie tried to digest it. "So the government has the camp because they want the species to get married?"

Miranda laughed. "I don't think the government cares who we hook up with. They're doing it to try to promote peace between the species so we don't go bat-shit crazy one day and try to wipe each other off the face of the planet. Humans included."

"Are there problems between the species?"

Miranda looked surprised. "You really are ignorant to all this, aren't you?"

"Yes," Kylie admitted, and didn't even feel bad about it. She hadn't even known other species existed when she'd climbed on board the bus. How could she be informed?

"Okay, here's a quick history slash political lesson," Miranda said. "Vampires and werewolves have been waging war against each other for, like, forever. What do you think the Civil War was really about?" She hesitated. "My own ancestors aren't much better. The Black Plague was set off because they wanted to annihilate fairies."

"You're kidding me, right?" Kylie asked. And to think she'd listened to her history teacher when he'd said it had been spread by infected rodents.

"Serious as a heart attack. However, in defense of my own kind, witches are the species who are succeeding best at conforming into the human world. There're less covens that actually live in groups. But of course, that's also because our lifestyles are easier to blend with the human lifestyle. We also aren't involved in near as many gangs, causing problems for the humans."

"Gangs? You mean like the vampire gang?"

"So you've heard of the Blood Brothers?" Miranda asked.

Not wanting to mention Della's cousin, Kylie shrugged. "Della just mentioned that gangs exist."

"Exist? Oh, yeah. Of all the gangs, the Blood Brothers are probably the worst. They're into everything, all kinds of crimes. A good mix of everything. Murder, robbery."

Stealing Big Macs. The concept rolled around Kylie's brain. "But how come we don't hear about these gangs or crimes on the nightly news?"

"You do. You just don't know they're not human. The crimes are always explained by serial killers, just murders, then there's the missing people. Haven't you heard how many people go missing every year?"

"I guess so." Kylie felt a chill straight through to her bones. She wrapped her arms around her chest and shivered.

"To rogue vampires or werewolves, the rest of us are food," Miranda said.

Kylie thought about Della's cousin calling her a snack and wondered if he was rogue. Then she thought about Della's blending issues and concerns about leaving her family. "This is so screwed up."

"Not any less screwed up than the human race," Miranda said.

"I guess not," Kylie admitted, remembering she had her own human issues happening at home.

Right then she remembered another and more immediate

problem she had to contend with. "What's the Meet Your Camp-mates Hour really about?"

"Oh, it's kind of cool." Miranda grew animated again. "Half of us write our names on a piece of paper and the other half draws. We are paired together and spend an hour getting to know each other. Of course, it's always better if you get a hot guy."

Great, with Kylie's luck, she'd get stuck with Perry. She felt her face grow red when she remembered she'd checked his genitals.

After breakfast, Kylie stepped out of the dining hall to talk to Sara who'd gone to the drugstore to buy a pregnancy test earlier that morning. Unfortunately, she'd bumped into her mom's best friend at the checkout counter. Sara had been able to ditch the test before the woman noticed it, but the whole encounter had brought her right back to where she started—with no idea if she was pregnant or not.

"How's it going at the camp?" Sara asked.

"Just peachy," Kylie answered. She would have loved to have talked to her best friend about everything that had happened but she knew better. No way would Sara understand when Kylie herself didn't.

"That bad, huh?" Sara replied. "Aren't there any cute guys?"

"A few," Kylie answered, and then she changed the subject back to Sara, and they talked for another ten minutes about Sara's dilemma.

Kylie still had her phone in her hand when her mom called a second after she'd ended her conversation with Sara.

"How was your first night?" her mom asked.

"Okay," Kylie lied, still undecided how to deal with her mom and her questions.

"No night terrors?" her mom asked.

"No," Kylie answered. *No, as in I didn't wake up screaming bloody murder. I just passed out when a bloody ghost showed up for a visit. After a visit from a shape-shifting kitten and a perverted toad.*

"That's good," her mom said. "So what all are you doing today?" Her mom's voice had that fake cheeriness that Kylie always hated because she knew it wasn't real.

"I have meetings with one of the camp leaders, a meet-and-greet hour where you meet one-on-one with another camper, and then I think there's some kind of art program and a hike this afternoon."

"Sounds like a full day," her mom answered.

"Sounds boring," Kylie retorted.

Her mom ignored her remark. "Have you spoken with your dad?"

Kylie hesitated. "He called and left a message, but I haven't had a chance to call him back." Another lie. She'd had a chance, she just didn't know if she could lie as well to him as she did to her mom.

"Well, when you do, check and see if he plans to come up Sunday for parents day. If so, I'll wait until next week."

"You two can't even be in the same room together now?" Kylie asked, not trying to hide her feelings. Her throat tightened with emotion. "Couldn't you two have at least stayed together until I left for college?"

"It's difficult, Kylie," her mom said.

"Yeah, on everyone." The emotion grew in her throat, but when she looked up she saw Della walking toward her and she fought back the need to cry. "I've gotta go."

"Okay," her mom said. "Have a good day and call me tonight, okay?"

"Yeah." Kylie closed the phone just as Della stepped up beside her.

"Hey," Kylie said. "I looked for you during breakfast."

"I ate earlier." She rubbed her stomach and Kylie tried not to think about what Miranda said about the vampire rituals. But the thought was already there, making the half of the Danish she'd consumed feel heavy in the pit of her stomach.

"You'll get used to it." Della grinned as if she knew what had caused Kylie's frown.

"Maybe," Kylie said. Then, remembering to be honest with Della, she added, "But I doubt it."

Della chuckled, then her smile faded. "Sorry about your parents. How long have they been separated?"

"Do you make it a habit of eavesdropping?" Kylie slid her phone in her pocket.

"I wasn't trying to listen in." Resentment rang in Della's voice. "It just, you know, happened."

Kylie bit down on her lower lip and let go of her frustration when she remembered that Della had confided in her about her own family issues. "I'm sorry. It's just hard. It happened last week."

"I can imagine." Sincerity creased Della's forehead. Then her expression changed. "Oh, I almost forgot what I came to tell you. Remember I told you Derek had a little thing for you? I was wrong. It's not little. It's a big thing."

"Why do you say that?"

"Because Brian, the blond vampire, just drew your name for the Meet Your Campmates Hour and Derek asked him to swap."

Kylie compared spending an hour with a strange vampire to spending an hour with Derek, who made her miss Trey, and she didn't know which was worse. "What did Brian say?" she asked, unable to stop herself.

"He said no . . . unless Derek was willing to pay for it."

"No way. Tell me he didn't give him cash to get my name."

"Okay. He didn't give cash to get your name." Della laughed and leaned in as if she had some juicy secret to tell. "He's paying in blood, Kylie. A pint, to be exact."

"Blood?" Kylie stood there shocked. The shock quickly turned into disgust. "He can't do that," she said.

"He can and he did. They made a deal. And believe me, you never go back on a blood deal with a vampire."

Kylie shot off to the dining hall to find Derek.

She could not, would not, let him do this.

Chapter Seventeen

Derek came through the door just as Kylie rushed in to find him. "Hey, I was coming to look for you." He held up a tiny strip of paper. "I got your name." He smiled.

His smile came off so warm, that if Kylie wasn't so furious, and disgusted, she could have gotten lost in it.

"Yeah, I know. I heard." She squinted at him in disapproval.

He studied her and then cautiously added, "I thought we'd take a walk. I found a great spot when I went hiking yesterday."

"Look, I'm flattered but you can't do this, Derek," she snapped.

"Do what?" A frown replaced his smile.

"I know what you did to get my name. And I can't let you do that."

"It's nothing." He started walking away from the door, and then looked back at her when she didn't follow. "You coming?"

"It's blood," she seethed, and closed the two steps separating them and grabbed him by the forearm. "Come on, I'm gonna make this right." She gave him a tug, but he didn't budge. That's when she noticed how solid his arm felt under her hand.

He leaned in. "It's done, Kylie. Let's just go spend our hour together, okay?" His scent—a combination of spicy men's soap and Derek—wafted over her.

"You've already . . . done it?" Her gaze shot to his neck.

"No, but the deal's done."

"I'll undo it," she said, trying to ignore his scent and how much she liked it . . . and how much she liked him. Realizing she still held his arms, she let go. Touching him caused her to recall how she used to touch Trey. How much she liked Trey, missed Trey.

Derek's frown tightened. "You can't undo it. So just come on. Please."

She stood there staring at him. "At least let me try."

He closed his eyes for a second, and then he lowered his head closer and whispered, "Please trust me on this, Kylie. There is nothing you can do to change it."

Something about his voice seemed to reach deep inside her and scramble her thoughts. Or perhaps it was how his breath whispered against her jaw line, the soft, sweet tickle right below her ear that made it impossible to think.

Impossible to tell him no.

"Okay." But even as she cratered to his wishes, she told herself she had to be careful. Derek, for whatever reasons, had some kind of power over her and that could be dangerous.

His green eyes focused right on her baby blue ones and he smiled again. "Let's go."

He held out his hand. She almost took it, but managed to refrain at the last second.

"I'll follow." She stuck her hands in her pockets.

Disappointment weakened his smile, but he nodded and started walking. And she did what she told him she'd do. She followed.

They didn't talk for the first five minutes as they started up a trail. Then he turned off the trail and led her up through a thick patch of trees and bushes. Between yesterday with Della and now this, it would be a miracle if she didn't come down with poison oak. Or worse, chiggers.

Just when she was about to say something, she heard the soft sound of running water, as if they were about to come across a small stream.

"It's right here." He glanced back at her, his eyes carrying a smile even when his lips didn't.

She followed him for a few more feet and then stopped and stared at the stream and the humongous boulder, about the size of a twin-size bed, perched on the edge overlooking the trickling water. The morning sun streamed through the trees, making everything seem so green, so lush. So alive.

Kylie inhaled the air, which smelled just like everything looked—fresh, verdant, and wet. In the distance she could hear what she thought was a waterfall—Shadow Falls. It had to be. The sound of cascading water filled the silence and somehow seemed to call out to her.

"Is there a waterfall around here?" she asked.

"Yeah, but it's prettier here." Derek hopped up on the rock. "Come on." Once settled, he held out his hand to help her up.

She moved in but before she took his hand, the question popped out. "Why did you do it?"

He looked down at her. "Do what?"

"You know what," she accused.

"Are we still stuck on that?" He shook his head. "It's not a big deal, Kylie. Now come up and sit down. This place is even more amazing when you look at it from this angle."

She took his hand and with hardly any effort he pulled her up. Letting go as soon as she had her footing, she found her spot, careful not to sit too close.

Not that it helped all that much.

Feeling his gaze on her, she looked out at the stream and tried to refocus. "Wow," she muttered. "You're right. It's prettier from up here." And it was. The extra height offered a better view of the flowing water. The streams of light sneaking from the trees hit the water and made it twinkle. From this angle, the whole place seemed to be bathed in a mixture of shadows and light, and it reminded her of something she might have seen in fairy-tale book. Almost . . . magical.

"Why?" she asked again without looking at him.

"I was curious about you. I've been curious ever since I saw you standing by your mom before you got on the bus. You were so sad and . . ."

She remembered Miranda saying that some fairies could read your thoughts and before he could continue, she spoke up. "Can you read my mind?" Turning to him, she felt her face heat at some of the more embarrassing thoughts she'd had about him.

"No." He smiled and in this light, his green eyes with golden flecks literally sparkled. "Why are you blushing? What have you been thinking about me?" He leaned a tad closer until his forehead rested against hers. Her heart did a flip and her next breath tasted sweeter. Realizing she was staring, she remembered what he'd asked.

She didn't answer his question, just asked another one. "Then how did you know I was so sad?"

He hesitated and his smile faded. "I can't read thoughts, but I can read some basic emotions."

She looked at him and sensed he was telling her the truth.

"For some reason I cause a mixture of emotions in you. Some positive, some not so positive, but I'm not sure why."

He was being honest, and Kylie felt she owed him the same in return. "You . . . you remind me of someone I know."

He picked a twig off of a tree and studied it. "A good someone, or a bad someone?"

"Both. He's my ex-boyfriend."

"I see." He waited for a minute and then asked, "What happened between you two?"

"He broke up with me."

"Why?" he asked.

She'd offered him some of the truth, but not about this. "You'd have to ask him." It was a lame answer and she knew it the moment the words spilled.

"But he's not here and you are." He took the twig and brushed the leaves across her cheek. Then he followed the path with his finger. He was coming on to her and she didn't exactly know how to stop it.

In truth, she didn't know if she wanted to stop it. Unlike what had been going on lately, these feeling were not so foreign to her. Not that she needed to get caught up in something else right now.

She looked away and tried to clear her head. "What's it like being fairy . . . Fae?"

"Half," he said.

She glanced back at him and remembered thinking that, just like her, he didn't sound too thrilled by the idea of being a supernatural. She also realized this might be her opportunity to learn something about the whole fairy species. After all, according to Holiday, Kylie could be part fairy.

"So what's it like being half fairy?"

"It could be worse, I guess." He stared at the twig.

"Who did you inherit it from?"

He cut his eyes to her again. "For someone who doesn't like to answer any questions, you ask a lot."

He had a point.

"Okay, I'll tell you about me, but then you tell me about you? Deal?"

He arched an eyebrow and actually seemed to consider it. "Okay." He leaned back on his arms and studied her.

The position made his chest seem extra wide. She found herself comparing him again to Trey. And sorry, Trey, she thought, but Derek won the best body award. Then again, it wasn't just his body. She studied his face. His features were . . . more masculine. More chiseled.

Chasing that thought out of her head before she started emitting emotion he might read, she started talking. "I don't know what I am. I think I'm just human but—"

"You're not human," he said, and looked at her in that odd way everyone did here.

She rolled her eyes. "Yeah, I know I don't have a normal brain reading, or whatever it is that you guys read. But I found out that normal humans can give off this same reading if they're a little off, like halfway crazy. And sometimes I'm pretty sure I'm crazy. Or," she admitted with less enthusiasm, "the other option is that I could have a brain tumor. And I've had lots of headaches lately, too."

His expression said he was horrified by the idea. "Have you been checked?"

"No." And until she saw the concern in his eyes, she hadn't allowed herself to honestly be worried about it. But God, what if she really did have a brain tumor? What if . . .

His brow pinched as if confused. "But . . . what about seeing ghosts?"

"How did you know . . . ?" She recalled asking him if he saw ghosts. "Some humans can see ghosts. Even Holiday said so."

He tilted his head in a very disbelieving way. "So you really believe you're just human?"

His question brought a swell of emotion to her chest. "Yeah." She paused and then added, "Okay, the truth is, I don't know what I believe."

And without warning, tears filled her eyes.

"Oh, damn. Don't do that." He reached over and brushed a tear from her lashes. His touch was so warm, so comforting, she almost reached for his hand and held it to her face.

Instead, she moved his hand back and wiped her own eyes. "I'm just so confused. I mean, these last few months have been hell. My boyfriend breaks up with me, my grandmother dies, my parents are getting a divorce, and then I start seeing this dead soldier guy. Now I'm being told that I'm not human and . . ."

He pulled her against him and she didn't fight it. She rested her head on the nice spot between his shoulder and chest and just breathed in his scent. Amazingly comfortable, she closed her eyes. Somehow just being like this made the knot of emotion crowding out her heart go away.

"I'm sorry." She pulled away. "I know guys hate it when girls do this."

"Do they?"

"Trey did," she answered.

"I'm not Trey." Then Derek added, "Actually, it wasn't so bad." He smiled and touched her check. "Besides, your nose is kind of cute when it turns red like that."

She swatted his hand and grinned. She wasn't sure, but it felt like the first real smile she'd had in weeks. "Okay, now it's your turn. Tell me about you."

The playfulness vanished from his eyes. Leaning back a little, he pressed his palms against the rock to hold himself up. And sitting there, his muscles in his arms flexed, his eyes all serious, he looked good. Really good.

"But you are so much more interesting," he said, his voice low as if he could read her emotions and knew the reaction she was having to his presence.

"You promised. Besides, I told you everything."

His tilted his head forward and looked up at her through his dark lashes. "You haven't told me everything." His voice held the slightest hint of an accusing tone. "As a matter of fact, there's the thing I'm the most curious about."

"What thing? What else is there?" she asked, and tried not to get caught up in enjoying the view again.

"What's up between you and—"

"I'm not talking about Trey and me. That's . . . too personal."

"Okay, but I wasn't going to say Trey. I meant what's going on between you and the werewolf?"

Chapter Eighteen

Kylie pushed her hair behind her ear. *Deny it. Deny that anything is up.*

"What . . . werewolf?" she asked, but darn if her voice didn't lack conviction.

Derek's eyes stared right at her. His gaze reminded her of Della's when she knew Kylie had lied.

"Don't deny it," he said. "Your emotions were all over the place every time you glanced at him. Kind of like when you look at me, only . . . more. You either really like him, or . . . he scares you."

"I thought you could read emotions?"

He sat up and crossed his arms over his chest. "Passion and fear read almost the same."

"Well, trust me, it's definitely the latter," she answered, but after last night's dream she knew the truth could have been summed up better with one word. *Both.* But she hadn't admitted that to herself yet. She sure as heck didn't plan on admitting it to Derek.

"So where do you know him from?" he asked.

"Who says—"

Derek held up his hand to stop her. "It's not normal to be that scared of people we don't know."

She glanced down at her clutched hands. "He lived beside me when I was young. Let's just say I knew something was off with him then. I just didn't know what it was . . . the whole werewolf thing."

"Did he—"

"No more." It was her turn to offer him the determined stare. "I've given you all I'm going to. It's your turn."

He looked at the stream and she sensed he disliked talking about himself as much she did. "What do you want to know?" he asked.

"Only everything," she said with a certain amount of teasing in her voice, hoping to put him at ease.

"My father was Fae. My mother's human."

"Was?" she asked. "You said your father *was* Fae. Did he pass away?"

He picked another twig from the bush and twirled it around with his fingers. "Don't know. Don't care. He left when I was eight. A real deadbeat dad, if you know what I mean."

"I'm sorry." Kylie sensed he cared a lot more than he wanted her to believe.

"Did you know he was Fae?" She brushed an ant from her arm.

"Yeah, I don't remember ever not knowing. But after he left, we didn't really talk about it or him a lot. Mom was crushed that he walked out."

His mom hadn't been the only one crushed. Kylie saw sadness in his eyes that he tried to hide. Her own chest felt heavy—heavy for him, and perhaps a little for herself. Her own father issues hadn't disappeared. They waited in line with everything else she had to fret over and sort out. Then she remembered that this was Derek's time. He'd listened to her and she owed him the same.

"Sorry," she said.

"Why? I'm not. If he didn't want me, I sure as hell didn't want him."

He couldn't lie any better than she could, Kylie thought. "Did you know you were gifted all your life?"

He stared at the piece of stem with a few leaves still attached to it that he had in his hand. "No. I mean, I knew I could read people better than most, but I wasn't even sure it was . . . because of being Fae. It wasn't until about a year ago that tapping into people's emotions got stronger. And then . . . I finally realized I was different."

"How are you different?" She felt her eyes moving to his chest, remembering how good it had felt to rest against him. The craziest thought hit. What would it feel like to kiss him?

He tilted his head to the right and studied her. "How much do I look like your old boyfriend?"

Were her emotions so readable, she wondered, feeling her face flush. "Not that much, but . . . enough that . . ."

"That you're attracted to me?"

Feeling her face heat to a nice shade of red, she looked back at the stream. "I wouldn't go that far."

"Why not?" His breath was on her cheek again. Warm.

Soft. Tempting. When had he gotten this close? Uncomfortable with how near his mouth was to hers, and how tempted she was to let it get even closer, she jumped down from the rock.

"Stop!" he said.

"What?" She turned around to look at him. "I think we—"

"Don't move," he said in low, very serious voice.

"Why? I—"

Something rustled in the bushes beside her. Kylie looked down and saw a huge snake slinking out from the thick underbrush. A huge grayish black snake with a pointed nose, the kind of nose her father made her aware of so she would know the difference between a nonpoisonous and a poisonous snake when she went on their camping trips.

Panic built as she recognized the species. A water moccasin, which just so happened to be the most aggressive snake found in Texas.

And one of the most poisonous, too.

The snake moved in tight S-like patterns—patterns that brought it closer to Kylie. Fear swelled inside her. A scream crawled up her throat. Logic said that she couldn't move away from the snake fast enough to avoid getting bitten. Logic said she needed to stay very still, but . . . the hell with logic—she wanted that thing away from her.

Derek's hand tightened on her shoulder. "It's okay." His voice was so low, so soft. "It's just passing by. Stay very still. Let it go. I'm here. Nothing is going to happen."

His hand grew warmer, unnaturally warm, and just like that, her fear vanished. Her heart stopped racing and the clutching in her stomach eased. She watched the snake's fat, chubby body slither across the tip of her Reeboks as if it were a butterfly passing by. Something in her brain told her that the calm she now felt, the absence of fear, wasn't normal; that somehow Derek had done this to her. She wasn't even afraid of that right now. It was as if Derek's touch had removed her ability to experience fear, leaving only curiosity in its place.

Curiosity about the snake.

About how it moved like that.

Curiosity about Derek. How had he changed her emotions? What would it feel like to lose herself in his kisses? Would he make her feel the way Trey had? Maybe even better?

"You're doing good. It's almost gone," he whispered.

And then it was gone. Its round body slipped into the stream, causing only the slightest of ripples as it sank down and moved with the water's current.

Derek kept his hand on her shoulder as she watched the creature disappear among the rocks. Then, slowly, he lifted his palm away. The storm of emotion hit her so hard that she screamed. When screaming alone wasn't enough, she swung around, and started climbing the rock. Her heart pumped in her chest, as if it might burst, and her stomach felt as if it knotted all the way around her backbone.

Derek caught her as she ascended, but she didn't stop moving, thinking only about getting away from the slithering snake.

"It's all right," he said, laughing, and fell back on the huge rock, carrying her with him. She landed half on top of him. His arms came around her, but not too tightly. His hands gently rested on her back.

Blinking, she felt her panic evaporate, and she met his green eyes. This close, the flecks of gold seemed brighter. Her gaze lowered to his mouth, to his lips that appeared so soft, so inviting.

The warmth of his body melted against hers. His natural scent worked its way into her senses. She caught her breath.

"You okay now?" he asked, his voice deeper.

"Yeah." When he stole her panic, had he taken her willpower, too, because she really wanted Derek to kiss her. Or she could just kiss him. It sounded like a damn good idea to her. She inched a bit nearer until his lips were so close to hers she could feel their heat.

"Let her go!" a dark male voice boomed from behind them.

Chapter Nineteen

"Let her go, now!"

The deeply serious voice rang a few familiar bells, but quicker than she could wrap her brain around it, Derek shot up with a force that sent Kylie rolling right to the edge of the rock.

Right before Kylie fell, Derek caught her. As soon as she felt secure, she raised her head. Lucas leered at them from the edge of the stream. The flickering of sun and shadows surrounded him, adding to his intimidating presence. His light blue eyes pierced into them with the harshest of stares.

"She's fine," Derek said, his tone matching his stern expression.

Feeling suddenly foolish, she felt the need to explain. "I saw a snake."

Lucas inhaled. He looked around on the ground. "A water moccasin."

"I know," she said. "That's why I screamed."

"It's gone," Derek said, and his words implied that Lucas should be gone as well.

"I heard her scream," Lucas said, as if he, too, felt the need to explain his behavior.

The two guys stared at each other, neither saying a word. Kylie got the distinct feeling they didn't get along. She wondered if fairies and werewolves also had bad blood between them. Heck, for all she knew, World War II could . . .

"She's not screaming anymore," Derek said.

"I'm fine." She jumped down from the rock—after giving the ground a quick check for snakes first.

When she looked up, Lucas had turned his disapproving gaze on her. "If you're that scared of snakes, maybe you should stay out of the woods."

"I'm not that scared, it just—"

"I took care of her," Derek said. His tone was dark, almost angry.

"Yeah, I saw how you were doing that."

Derek sat up higher on the rock as if he was ready to leap down. "Look, if you have a problem—"

Lucas apparently didn't care to hear what Derek had to say because he swung around and in less than a second, he was gone.

Kylie blushed, realizing how the situation must have appeared to Lucas. Then seeing the unhappy expression on Derek's face, she said, "I'm sorry. I shouldn't have screamed, it was just—"

"You didn't do anything wrong." Derek offered her his hand to pull her back up. "He was being a jerk and overreacting. He didn't have to come here. I wouldn't have let anything happen to you."

She stared at Derek's hand and remembered how her fear had subsided with his intense touch.

"What happened just now?" she asked.

"He just overreacted—"

"No. Not with Lucas. With your touch . . ."

"What do you mean? My touch?"

Other questions started buzzing around like bees gone wild. "How did you know the snake was here?"

The look, the one that said he didn't like talking about himself, returned but she wasn't about to let him off this hook. Not this time.

"Wait. Did you make that snake come here?" she asked.

He frowned. "Do you think I'd put you in danger just for kicks?"

Did she believe that? "No. I don't. But you knew it was here. You knew it was here before it showed itself."

"I only knew a second before. If I had known earlier, I'd have stopped you from getting down."

The sun sprayed a new bright stream of light through the trees and it hit her eyes, making it hard to see. "How? How did you know?"

He jumped from the rock, landing solid on his feet beside her. "It's part of my gift," he said, but he didn't sound happy about it.

"You can predict the future?" she asked.

"I wish."

"Then what?"

"I can read the emotions of animals and creatures." He tucked the tips of his fingers into his pockets.

"Wow." She attempted to wrap her mind around it. "That's . . ."

"Weird, I know," he growled. "Like I'm Tarzan or something. Holiday says I can shut it off, and that's why I'm here. To learn how. But Holiday's not thrilled about my quest. She thinks I'm going to be letting down some Fae god if I turn my back on my gift. But the Fae god can just go to hell. I didn't ask for this. The only Fae in my life left me and Mom. Why the hell would I want to be like him?"

Kylie heard the pain in his voice and related in a big way. "You wouldn't. I'm sorry."

She meant it, too. Not just because she understood all about parental resentment right now, but because like him, if she turned out to be supernatural, she'd be shipping the gift back to sender. While Derek's plight contained a lot of emotional baggage, Kylie's contained a heck of a lot of questions. And the unknown brought on its own emotional issues. While she knew the truth could prove to be painful, she needed answers.

And standing in the middle of the woods, with the mixture of sun and shadows, feeling submersed in the supernatural world, she became determined to find those answers.

She met Derek's gaze again. "Communicating with animals can't be nearly as bad as . . . some other things."

He kicked a rock into the stream. It splashed and seemed to blend in with the other woodsy noises. "Like seeing ghosts?" he asked, understanding more than she wanted him to.

"Among other things," she said honestly. "I can't imagine waking up and realizing I have to drink . . . blood." Just the mention of the word reminded her of what Derek had done to get her name for this hour chat.

And she couldn't let him do it. She didn't know how to stop it, but she had to try.

She looked at her watch. "We should probably be heading back."

Reaching over, he took her hand in his and turned her wrist over so he could see the time. The feel of his hand sent a sweet electrical current up her arm and it reminded her how close she had come to letting Derek kiss her. Or had she almost kissed him?

"We have a half hour," he said, holding her hand.

She pulled away, recalling how his touch had controlled her emotions when she'd seen the snake. He'd probably saved her life, but that wasn't the point. She didn't like the thought of anyone trying to control her. Or manipulate her, either. "Yeah," she said, "but we still need to see about how we're going to get you out of giving blood."

His expression darkened. "The deal's already made, there's no going back. And besides, it's not an issue."

"What if he turns you into a vampire?"

His eyes widened. "Oh, hell, you think I'm going to let him bite me? No way. It's too risky and way too gay."

She blushed, feeling ignorant. "Then how do you plan to do it?"

"The same way you give blood at a blood drive. With a sterile needle and an IV bag."

She stood there staring at him, questions coming quicker than she could line them up to ask. "You're going to a doctor's office to get it done? How will—"

"No." He laughed. "Most vampires carry their own supplies. They're better than most nurses at finding veins. It's one of the first things a vampire is taught. How to get blood without killing the donor."

Had Della brought her own blood-draining equipment? "How do you know how vampires . . . ?"

"Feed? I've done it a couple of times." His smile made her feel even more ignorant.

"You've given blood to a vampire before?"

He nodded. "Like I've been saying, it's not a big deal."

"Who? And how did you even know vampires existed?"

"Her name's Ellie. We go to school together. And you're forgetting that all supernaturals recognize each other."

Yes, she had forgotten the whole eyebrow wiggling thing. And for a darn good reason, too. She didn't "read" supernaturals, which gave her a little more hope that she wasn't one of them. Then she wondered if she had any supernaturals in her school back home. Besides Lucas for that short time.

"How many are there?" she asked, even though she was afraid to hear the answer. "How many supernaturals are there compared to humans?"

"I think the consensus puts us a little less than one percent, but growing. Why?"

"Just wondering if I went to school with any."

"You could have," he said. "But not likely. Most supernaturals go to private schools or are home-schooled. For obvious reasons."

"What reasons?" she asked.

"Species issues mostly. Most believe that they need to learn a different history. And most of them can afford it since they use their gifts to become financially well off."

They? Kylie noticed that Derek didn't completely view himself as one of them, either. "So you went to a private school?"

He shook his head. "Dad bailed, remember?"

"Yeah." She sifted through her other questions. "What about the girl you know? Ellie, right? She went to your school?"

"She's a recently turned vampire," he said. "She hasn't gone to live with her kind yet."

Kylie thought about Della. "Do they all have to go live with their kind?"

"Not from what Ellie said. But I know it isn't easy for her to blend in with the normals."

Kylie heard the sense of caring in his voice and her curiosities took a U-turn away from Della's problems, away from the whole supernatural business to a more personal business.

"Are you and Ellie close?" Embarrassed at how she almost sounded jealous, Kylie shook her head, but she couldn't stop from continuing. "Duh, you gave her your blood. Of course you're close."

He arched his brows and another one of those almost smiles tickled his lips and made his eyes brighter. "Is this your way of asking if we're still together?" The green twinkle in his eye said he liked her interest.

"No." At least she didn't think it was, but oh heck, she wasn't completely sure.

"We broke up about six months ago."

"Why?" she asked, and then just as quickly wished she could take it back.

"She met a werewolf." Resentment laced his voice.

"Not Lucas?" Kylie asked.

"No, not him."

Kylie remembered. "I didn't think vampires and werewolves got along."

"Neither did the Hatfields and the McCoys."

A soft wind blew and a strand of her hair whipped across her face and caught between her lips.

He brushed it back. The tips of his fingers whispered over her cheek, causing all sorts of tingles to run down her neck. She caught his hand, felt the tingles intensify, and then released it just as fast.

"What happened earlier?" she asked before she lost her nerve. "When you touched me."

He stuck both his hands into his jeans pockets, as if he were trying to fight his temptation to touch her again.

"I don't know what you mean," he said, but she could tell he was lying.

She shook her head. "Don't lie to me, Derek. When you touched me, you changed how I felt and we both know it."

He looked shocked that she'd figured that out. "I just stopped you from being afraid so you wouldn't do something stupid and get bit."

"So when you touch someone, you can control their emotions?"

"Yeah," he said as if wasn't a big deal.

But it was a big deal, to her anyway. How much of the whole attraction she felt for him was even real? How much of it was because he made her feel it?

Something cold and hard wrapped itself around her heart. "Did you do it before?"

"Do what before?" He looked truly confused now, or was he just faking it?

"Mess with my emotions."

He studied her. "Why are you getting angry?"

"Did you do this, Derek? Did you make me feel the way I feel about you?"

He looked insulted. "No," he said with conviction, but she wasn't convinced.

She poked him in his chest. "So help me, Derek, if—"

He caught her hand and she flinched.

"What? Now you're afraid of me?" He shook his head. "First you justified what you feel for me because I look like your old boyfriend. And now you think I'm messing with your emotions. Why is it so hard to think that you could just like me?"

"Because you have the power to do it, don't you? You have the power to make me like you." She took a deep breath and continued. "Have you ever used this to convince a girl to do things she normally wouldn't?"

His eyes tightened. "Wow," he said in an accusing tone. "You are just looking for a reason to dislike me, aren't you? That boyfriend of yours really did a number on you."

Maybe. But that was beside the point. She was almost certain that her feelings now had more to do with Derek than Trey. The simple truth was that liking Derek was going to complicate the next few months. She had enough crap on her plate, and she didn't need this, too.

"You didn't answer my question," she said, standing a little straighter. "Have you ever used this power on a girl to get what you wanted from her?"

His frown grew almost angry, but she could swear she spotted a bit of guilt in his eyes, too. He looked away.

"If you don't answer me, I'll assume the worst," she said.

"Fine." He faced her. "I've used it to get a girl's attention, but I've never used it to get her to sleep with me. That would be rape. And I don't care how much you want to dislike me, Kylie, I won't pretend I'm something bad just to make you feel better." He waved back to the path through which they'd come. "I think we should probably get back."

She heard the hurt in his voice. Instant embarrassment shot through her and she realized what a cold bitch she was being. God, maybe she was just like her mom after all.

He started walking. She followed. They walked in silence. "Hey," she finally said, unable to hold it back any longer.

"What?" He didn't look at her and kept on moving down the trail.

"I didn't mean to imply that you were some kind of rapist."

"Then what were you trying to imply?" He still didn't look at her.

She tried to think how to put what she needed to say. She hated reaching for the old cliché but it was all she could come up with on short notice. "I like you, Derek, I do. But I'm thinking we should just be friends."

He laughed but the sound had no humor. "So you're going to deny that you feel anything." His pace picked up. "You're going to deny that you almost kissed me back there. That you wanted to kiss me."

Increasing the pace of her own footsteps, she wanted to deny it, and almost did, but caught herself before she lied. "No, I'm not denying it, but I can't trust how I feel right now."

He swung around. "Because you think I'm messing with your emotions?"

"No. Yes. Okay, maybe that's a part of it, but it's also because you remind me so much of Trey. Look, I have all this other stuff happening to me right now." Emotion tightened her voice. "Things at home are crazy. I'm seeing ghosts. I have people telling me I'm not all human, and I'm halfway hoping I find out that I'm just crazy or that I have a brain tumor." She blinked and refused to cry again. "I don't need *this*, too." She waved a hand between them. "But I really need a friend."

He sent her a look of resignation. "Okay. If friendship is all you're offering, then I'll take it. Don't like it, but I'll take it."

"Thank you," she said, meaning it.

He nodded and studied her as if reading her emotions again. Heck, maybe he could read them and then tell her what it all meant, because right now she felt like a scrambled mess.

"It's going to be okay," he said.

"Is it?" She paused. "I just don't know where to start to find the answers."

Derek drew a deep breath and then looked around as though he was afraid they might be overheard although there wasn't anyone else in sight. He leaned in closer.

"I don't have all the answers," he said, dropping his voice to just above a whisper. "And I don't even think this is an issue, but . . . there's one thing you might try."

Chapter Twenty

"Tell me," Kylie said, eager for any help she could get. "I'm willing to try anything at this point."

Well, almost anything.

"There's a girl here," Derek said. "She's Fae, too. Her name's Helen."

"I met her," Kylie said. "She was in the group with me when Holiday explained why we were here."

"Yeah. Her gift is healing. But when she was telling us about herself she said that even before her sister's tumor was found, she could see it. Personally, I don't think you have a tumor, but if you're concerned about it, maybe Helen can check you out. At least you'd stop worrying about it."

"That's an excellent idea." Kylie almost hugged him, but decided at the last moment it wasn't wise. She really didn't want to encourage Derek that they could be more than friends. At least not now, a little voice inside her whispered—the little voice that really liked how it felt to be close to him, the same little voice that had wanted her to kiss him earlier. "Thank you," she said.

"You're welcome." He brushed the back of his hand down her cheek and you can bet her little voice liked that, too. "By the way . . ."

"By the way what?" she asked.

He smiled and the gold in his eyes seemed to glow hotter. "Back there. You weren't the only one who . . . I mean, I wanted you to kiss me, too."

"But we're just friends," she said, wishing she could say it with more conviction.

"Yeah." And he didn't say it with a heck of a lot of conviction either.

When they got back to the camp, it was almost time to meet Holiday. Kylie wanted to call Sara, so she decided to go behind the office to the little hiding spot she'd discovered yesterday.

She made it around the building when she realized she wasn't the only one who'd discovered the hiding spot. Kylie shifted herself in reverse, but not quickly enough. Lucas and his attached to-the-hip girlfriend swung around. Lucas grimaced and Goth Girl smiled. Then she reached up and made a show of buttoning her blouse.

"Sorry," Kylie muttered, and shot off. But she felt a pair of light blue eyes burning into her back as she went.

She made it around the front, only to find Miranda and Della standing near the office yelling at each other.

Kylie's first thought was to leave them be, but when she spotted Sky, the other camp leader stepping out of the dining hall, Kylie marched over to break the two up before they got in trouble.

"I swear, if you wave that little pinky finger at me one more time, I'm gonna break it." Della leaned in. "And you know I can do it."

"Stop it," Kylie said, stepping between them. Miranda shuffled back in front of Kylie and bumped noses with Della.

"You lay one bloodsucking finger on me and I'll hex you with the worse case of pimples you've ever seen."

"You can't hex me," Della spouted out. "Your hexes are retarded."

"Stop it." Kylie spotted Sky looking over at them. "We've got company."

"Giving pimples is one hex I got down." Miranda stepped back, but Della moved in.

She obviously didn't like pimples. "Look, if I get one zit, I'll drain your blood while you're asleep and sell it on eBay."

"Would you guys put a sock in it," Kylie snapped, but it was too late. Sky was on the move.

"Is everything okay?" the tall, goth-dressed camp leader asked.

Sky was also a werewolf, or so Kylie had heard. She still couldn't identify the supernaturals just by looking at them.

Miranda pasted a smile on her face. Della attempted to do the same, although Della's smile looked more like a snarl.

"It's fine," they said in unison. "We're just—"

"Arguing?" Sky's eyebrows tightened in accusation.

"Having a little disagreement," Miranda said.

"Over?" Sky asked.

Della spoke up. "She purposely spilled my blood that was in the fridge."

"I didn't purposely spill it. It fell out when I opened the door."

"There's blood in our fridge?" Kylie frowned.

Sky rolled her eyes. "You have to learn to get along." Sky's dark eyes shot to Miranda. "You are a returnee, Miranda, we expect better from you."

"Yeah, well, get in line with the be-disappointed-by-Miranda crowd." Miranda shot off in a huff.

Sky watched her leave and then looked back at Kylie and Della. "Solve your own problems at your cabins, not in public, or Holiday and I will have to get involved. And trust me, you don't want us involved." She turned and left.

Kylie glanced back at a smiling Della who appeared unaffected by Sky's warning.

"So what happened with you and fairy guy?" Della asked.

"Forget that. You and Miranda gotta stop this."

"Stop what?" Della shrugged.

"Stop threatening to do bodily harm to each other." Right then, Kylie spotted Lucas's girlfriend walking toward them. The girl's eyes narrowed in fury and her lips tightened as she zeroed in on Kylie. If looks could kill, Kylie would be a hair away from decomposing. Then the pissed-off werewolf stormed on past.

With the thought of death hanging on, Kylie noticed a slight headache, a consistent throbbing in her left temple. The idea that she actually might have a brain tumor had her catching her breath.

"Threatening isn't doing," Della said. "So spill it. What did you and Derek do? Did you at least get to first base?"

"We didn't do anything." Kylie pressed a hand against her temple. "Look, I like you and Miranda, so both of you need to pull your big girl panties up and stop fighting before they separate us and I get stuck with a different roommate." Someone like Lucas's girlfriend.

"That wasn't a fight. We were just having a tiff."

"You threatened to sell her blood on eBay," Kylie said. "Where I come from, that qualifies as a fight."

"Yeah, but you're not in your world anymore."

Della's statement hit hard like only the truth could. Nothing was the same anymore. A boy had just given a pint of his blood to get to spend an hour with her. She'd seen toads who were really perverts hopping on her kitchen table, and she'd checked a kitten's privates only to have him end up not being a kitten. And don't forget, she was being haunted by Soldier Dude. Her head throbbed harder.

"Besides, I'd never sell her blood. I'd savor every drop of it. Witches' blood is sweet."

Sweet. Kylie held up her hand. "Stop right there. I can't handle this." She looked at her watch. Crap. No time to call Sara. "I have to go meet Holiday," she said. *And figure out my life, because like Dorothy, I'm simply not in Kansas anymore.* Kylie turned to leave.

Della caught her by the arm. "Oh, I meant to tell you—"

"Wait." Kylie held up her hand. "Does it have anything to do with blood?" She couldn't deal with blood talk, period.

Della's eyes tightened. "No," she said, sarcasm in her tone.

"Then you can tell me."

"Or not." Della crossed her arms. "Maybe I should let you be waylaid for being a smarty pants." Della walked off.

Waylaid? That didn't sound good. "Della, wait," Kylie said.

Della turned back around. "If I tell you, will you put a stop to all the 'blood is gross' remarks?"

It was gross. "I'll try."

"Trying is for sissies," Della shot off. Kylie glanced at her watch again. She needed to meet Holiday, but Della's warning about being waylaid . . .

"Della." Kylie caught up with her. "Okay, no more remarks. Now tell me. How am I going to be waylaid?"

Della let go with a huff. "You know those men in the black suits? I'm told they are FBI."

"What about them?"

Della cocked her head. "They're planning on interrogating you."

"Me?" Kylie asked. "Why?"

"Don't know."

The only thing Kylie could think this could be about was . . . "Wait. Is this about your cousin? Are you sure he doesn't belong to one of those gangs?"

"No." Della frowned. "They'd be talking to me if it was. Besides, they didn't say anything about visitors. They said they thought you could be hiding something because you don't let anyone read you."

Kylie tried to wrap her hurting head around the facts, but she just couldn't do it. "Are you sure they said me?"

"Yup. Holiday wasn't happy about it. Yet supposedly they are like the head honchos around here. What they say goes. But I can tell you that Holiday stood up for you. She told them that you were innocent, but they just said they'd find out for themselves."

And exactly how did they plan to do that? Was it the CIA or FBI who were accused of torturing? Oh damn, she already had a headache—she didn't want to add "get tortured" to today's to-do list.

Della's gaze shifted up over Kylie's shoulder. "Uh, don't look now, but I think Holiday's looking for you. And . . . I think she's found you."

A second later, Kylie felt someone beside her. Only it wasn't Holiday. The cold slammed against her side and Kylie knew "he" was back.

She drew in a deep breath, determined not to pass out, but barely managed to get the cold air down her throat. Forcing herself to move, she shifted her eyes ever so slowly, praying she wouldn't see him this time.

Someone wasn't listening to prayers today. But at the least there was no blood this time. Soldier Dude just stood there staring at her with his big blue eyes. Eyes that seemed to want to tell her something. But what? What could he want? She recalled the word *help* splattered in blood the last time she'd seen him. Just what kind of help could he need from her?

The idea of asking him crossed her mind, but somehow she sensed that if she spoke to him, it would bring him closer. She closed her eyes and mentally pleaded for him to go away.

"And here she is." Della's voice registered ever so slightly in Kylie's awareness. Opening her eyes, she saw Holiday move in between her and Soldier Dude.

"You ready?" the camp leader asked.

The cold faded and the goose bumps on Kylie's arms melted back into normal skin. Even the frigid air in her lungs warmed. A wave of relief washed over her.

"Oh," Holiday said, and took a step back. "Did I interrupt something?"

Kylie knew the camp leader didn't mean her and Della. Blinking, Kylie gazed at Holiday and tried to focus. "Can't you tell him to leave me alone?"

"Doesn't work like that," Holiday said.

"What doesn't work like that?" Della asked.

"Ready?" Holiday said again to Kylie.

"For what?" Kylie asked. Why did the FRU want to talk to her?

"Our meeting," Holiday said.

"Can I come?" Della asked.

Kylie looked at her roommate and saw in her gaze that she was trying to help. An effort that Kylie appreciated more than her roomie could know.

"Can she?" Kylie asked.

"Afraid not." Holiday eyed Della. "I think the vampires are holding a group session. You should be there." The camp leader's gaze shifted back to Kylie. "Come on." Holiday put her hand on Kylie's back and led her away.

But just what the hell Holiday was leading Kylie to was yet to be seen.

Chapter Twenty-one

"There're a couple of people who want to meet you." Holiday moved Kylie toward the main office.

"Who?" she asked, hoping that Della was wrong.

"They're from the FRU."

She'd heard the acronym several times since arriving at Shadow Falls Camp. This time, however, when the three letters formed in Kylie mind, a new thought hit. *Freaks-R-Us.*

"They're the people who support the camp," Holiday added as she guided Kylie up the steps.

"Why?" she asked, and stopped at the door. "Why do they want to meet me?" She wasn't even sure she was a freak.

Holiday's gaze softened. "Mostly curiosity. They've never met anyone they couldn't read."

"I thought you said this was common with people who could see ghosts?"

Holiday appeared to be debating what to say. "It's not just because they can't read you, Kylie. It's because what they can see of your brain pattern isn't common."

Kylie's headache resumed its pounding. And the fear that she really could have a tumor stirred in her chest. She envisioned herself with her head shaved and big ugly scars running across her skull. It was horrible.

But so was admitting that she was as much of a freak as the rest of them.

"You're special, and they sense this. So come on. It'll only take a minute and then we can have our meeting."

Holiday's hand on Kylie's back grew warm. Immediately, Kylie knew the camp leader had emotion-controlling abilities similar to Derek's. All Kylie's reservations about having a brain tumor and about meeting the Freaks-R-Us squad dissolved as the warmth of Holiday's hand flowed inside her.

"Why are you doing that?" Kylie stepped away.

"Doing what?" Holiday asked.

"Trying to take away my fear?" She shifted out of Holiday's reach.

Holiday's eyes grew round. "Wow. You can sense this? That's amazing." She touched Kylie again. "That means—"

"Stop doing it." Kylie backed away again. She didn't care about amazing, or what it meant, at least not now. She cared about what waited for her on the other side of the door and about possibly having a brain tumor. "It makes me think maybe I should be afraid."

Holiday shook her head. "You don't have anything to be afraid of." She reached out again and Kylie looked at her hand.

Holiday held up her palms. "Trust me."

"Sorry," Kylie said. "But I have a hard time trusting people who can manipulate my emotions." And yes, in a small way she meant Derek, too.

Holiday sighed. "Believe it or not, Kylie, I respect that. But right now, I need you to meet these two men. Nothing bad is going to happen. I give you my word."

While Kylie still wasn't convinced, with another look into Holiday's expression, most of Kylie's concerns faded. Only this time it seemed to be from her own intuition rather than Holiday's influence. For some reason, Kylie's gut told her she could trust Holiday. Then again, it could just be because she didn't have a choice. In more ways than not, Kylie was a prisoner at this camp.

The introductions were as awkward as Kylie expected. The two men did their share of eyebrow twitching, which only made Kylie feel more uncomfortable. She wanted to tell them they were wasting their time trying to twitch info from her. She didn't, of course. The too-nice disease again. So instead, she sat at a table and tried not to fidget under their intense stares.

The bigger man with darker hair was named Burnett James and the other was Austin Pearson. Up close, Kylie couldn't help but notice how *GQ* perfect the two men were. Not that she was into old guys—or she should say "older" because they looked about ten years older than her—but she could still appreciate perfection.

Kylie also noticed how Burnett kept stealing glances at Holiday when she wasn't looking. He obviously had the hots for her.

Not that Holiday seemed aware of his interest. If anything, Kylie got the feeling the camp leader found both men annoying. Especially Burnett.

"So . . ." Burnett turned a chair around, straddled it, and sat down.

Holiday watched the man and frowned as if disapproving of his sitting position.

"This is your first time to Shadow Falls Camp, huh?" Burnett asked.

Kylie nodded. Then recalling her mother's belief that answering without words showed disrespect, she followed up with, "Yes . . . sir." The "sir" part of the sentence slipped out as an afterthought and she wished she hadn't done it, because it came out sounding sarcastic. Not that she meant it like that, but her interrogators might not realize that.

Burnett placed his elbows on the back of the chair, laced his fingers together, and studied her. After very slow passing seconds, he tilted his head slightly as if listening—listening for something that no one else in the room could hear. Like the sound of Kylie's heartbeat. Just what kind of supernaturals were these two? Were they, like Della, human lie detectors? Somehow Kylie suspected that Burnett had that ability. Which meant Kylie would have to be careful not to get caught in a white lie.

"What brought you to Shadow Falls, Miss Galen?"

Holiday stepped closer. "She was sent here by—"

Burnett held a hand up at Holiday and frowned. "I'd like Miss Galen to answer." While his words could be construed as non-hostile, Kylie noticed his edgy tone.

Holiday must have noticed it, too. She shot the man a glare

that no doubt contained language she probably couldn't use in the presence of the campers. Kylie got the feeling that this wasn't the first time these two had bumped heads. Heck, for all Kylie knew, they might have bumped more than just heads. They could be old lovers.

Austin cleared his throat as if hoping to clear the tension in the room.

"Go ahead, Kylie," Holiday said, then everyone looked back at Kylie.

She sat up a little straighter and tried not to wince. "I was told . . . by Holiday, that my shrink is the one who got me signed up. I think she convinced my mom that this was a camp for troubled teens."

"And are you?" Burnett tossed out the question.

"Am I what?" Kylie asked.

"A troubled teen?" His tone rang with accusations.

"Of course she's not," Holiday insisted.

Burnett shot a frown back at the camp leader. "As a courtesy, I allowed you to be present, but if you keep interrupting—"

"Bite my ass, Mr. James," Holiday snapped, obviously mad enough not to care about Kylie hearing the PG-13 language.

"Don't tempt me," Burnett retorted.

"Tempting you hasn't crossed my mind," Holiday shot back. "You've been a class-A jerk since you came to see me."

Kylie bit her cheek to keep from smiling. The tension between these two could be cut and served up with hot fudge. It was the kind of tension one saw in a romantic flick.

"Maybe it's the icy reception you've given me for no damn

good reason. If I didn't know better I'd think you have a preju-
dice against vampires."

So he was a vampire. Kylie actually felt proud of herself for
figuring it out.

"Don't fool yourself." Holiday squared her shoulders. "It's
not vampires I have a problem with. It's men who think something as inconsequential as a badge gives them the right to in-
timidate others. From the moment you walked into my camp
you've acted as if we should bow down to you. And if that's not
bad enough, you're now accusing my kids of—"

Austin cleared his throat again, louder than before. "I think
we should get back to Miss Galen here."

Or not. Kylie would like to know what it was the FRU was
accusing the campers of doing, exactly. However, her curiosity
faded rather quickly when everyone's gaze shot back to her and
she recalled Burnett's question.

"No, I do not consider myself a troubled teen."

Burnett's right brow arched. "Have you ever belonged to a
gang?"

"No," she answered, and wondered if he was referring to the
Blood Brothers. "I've never really gotten into any trouble."

"Really. Weren't you just hauled down to the police station
during a drug raid?"

Kylie suddenly understood Holiday's dislike for Mr. Tall
Dark and Handsome. He did have a way of making people feel
small.

Maybe it was Holiday's nerve of standing up to the vampire
that gave Kylie courage. Or perhaps it was just that with all the

other crap slung at her today, Kylie's ability to play nice had played out. Then again, maybe she had a brain tumor provoking her to do things she normally wouldn't do.

Tilting her chin up, she let the words roll off her tongue without remorse. "You'd think if you were able to get your hands on that report, that you'd have at least read it. Because I'm sure it stated that I was not doing drugs or drinking."

Burnett's eyes tightened in the corners. But Kylie preferred to focus on Holiday's pleased smile.

"Are you finished now?" the camp leader asked.

"Just a few more questions." Burnett's piercing gaze never shifted from Kylie. "How do you feel about our camp, Miss Galen?"

"It's great." Kylie's heart sputtered when she remembered she couldn't lie. "At least everyone else I've met here seems to like it."

"And you don't?"

Don't lie. "I'd rather be at home."

"And why is that?" Burnett's eyes darkened to black.

"Everything is so . . . new to me."

"What's new?"

"The fact that people like you even exist." It was the truth. However, she didn't mean it to sound so . . . derogatory.

"Like me? As in vampires?" he asked, clearly offended.

"Supernaturals," Kylie corrected.

"And what do you think you are?" he asked smugly.

"I'm not sure," she answered truthfully. "But I'm hoping I'm nothing. Just me." *With a brain tumor.* She pushed that thought aside to chew on later.

He stared harder and Kylie's courage winced. He shook his head and his brows tightened. "Why are you being so close-minded?"

"I'm not. Believing in all this . . ." It occurred to her that he wasn't talking about her ability to accept all this, but rather, his inability to read her mind.

"She can't help it." Holiday stepped forward. "It's a condition of one of her gifts. She's a ghost whisperer."

Kylie nodded as if to say ditto. Both men's eyes widened.

"Ghost whisperer?" Austin said, and turned to Holiday, but before he shifted, Kylie spotted something that looked like fear cross his expression.

"Like you?" Burnett glanced at the camp leader.

"You've read my file?" Holiday asked.

"It's my job to know who I'm working with."

"Funny, you didn't offer your file to me," she responded. "And you expect me to work—"

"I'll have it sent over. If it really interests you," he countered, his voice dripping with sarcasm.

"On second thought, don't bother," she clipped out. "But to respond to your earlier comment, yes, Kylie's a ghost whisperer just like me." While Holiday's tone lacked the earlier attitude, the brief smile that flashed on her lips contained attitude plus.

"You, too?" Austin shuddered. "I hate ghosts."

"Is she fairy?" Burnett asked, staring and twitching again at Kylie as if attempting to read her once more.

"We're still trying to decipher that," Holiday answered.

"So her parents are not registered as supernaturals?" Burnett questioned.

"No," Holiday replied.

"They could be rogues."

"Be what?" Kylie asked.

"They would have never sent her here if they were," Holiday answered Burnett, leaving Kylie's question hanging.

Kylie's phone buzzed, but she ignored it, not wanting to miss out on any conversation that centered on her.

"Or maybe that's why she's here." Burnett's harsh glare focused on Kylie again. "Were you sent here with a purpose, Miss Galen?"

"No, and my parents didn't do anything wrong," Kylie insisted.

Holiday took a step closer. "If your hearing isn't off, you should be able to tell she spoke the truth."

Burnett nodded. He stood and then focused on Holiday. "You're right. She doesn't seem involved. But I want to be updated on her condition."

Holiday's expression hardened. "I don't see why that is necessary."

"Neither do I," Kylie blurted out, not liking how they discussed her as if she wasn't here.

Burnett ignored Kylie and focused only on Holiday. "You'll comply with my wishes, Miss Brandon, or I'll see to it that my boss finds a camp leader who will."

For the first time, Holiday flinched, telling Kylie the camp leader cared more about her job than she did her pride. "I'm simply curious as to why you're interested in her."

"In addition to watching over this project, I'm in charge of tracking any anomalies in our alliance. Miss Galen qualifies."

"I'm an anomaly?" Kylie blurted out in disbelief.

"Okay, I'll update you," Holiday said, still paying Kylie no heed.

Burnett looked a tad smug, as if he knew he'd won. Then he glanced back at Kylie. "You may go now."

Kylie gazed up at Holiday. "I thought—"

Holiday interrupted. "We have a meeting. I'd appreciate if you two could let yourselves out."

Burnett crossed his arms over his wide chest. "Your meeting will have to be rescheduled. I need you to go through the files with me. Since it appears that Miss Galen is not our suspect, we need to find out who is."

"And you just assume that it's one of my kids," Holiday seethed. "Have you even considered that—"

"Yes, I do assume that. All the evidence points here," Burnett snapped.

Evidence of what? The question lay on the tip of Kylie's tongue, but something warned her not to push it.

Holiday's lips tightened before she turned to Kylie. "We'll meet after lunch. Is that okay?"

Kylie nodded, disappointed all her questions would have to wait, but it didn't mean she couldn't start getting other answers. Standing up, she nodded good-bye, then walked out of the meeting room with purpose. She had things to do. Things to figure out. And first on her list was to find a certain fairy and get her brain scanned for tumors.

· · ·

Kylie stepped out of the office, not sure how to go about finding Helen the healer. Her phone buzzed again and she pulled it from her jeans. It was a text from Sara. One word appeared on the screen.

"Negative," Kylie said aloud, and smiled in relief for Sara. She started punching in Sara's number when someone moved beside her. A tall and wide frame cast a tall and wide shadow.

Before Kylie looked up, she somehow knew the owner of that shadow would have jet black hair and light blue eyes. Taking a deep breath, she slowly looked up.

Damn, she hated being right.

Chapter Twenty-two

"Can we talk?"

Lucas Parker's voice sent almost as many chills through her as the slight pressure of his hand against her back. Almost. But not quite.

She fought against the urge to shiver as he nudged her away from the group of kids standing about fifty feet to their left. While his words lent itself to a question, the fact that he was moving, and taking her with him, implied she didn't have a choice.

The warm feel of his hand on the small of her back took her back to last night's dream—the one where they were swimming together. That thought reminded her that she'd interrupted Lucas and his girlfriend earlier today. Kylie blinked, praying she wouldn't break out in a full-blown blush.

"What do you want to talk about?" she managed to ask, but she guessed he meant Derek and her. He'd seemed plenty angry when he'd caught them on the rock—she just didn't know why. She tried to stop walking, but he kept moving her along. Unless she wanted to trip and land on her face, she had no option but to put one foot in front of the other.

Kylie's Reeboks rushed to meet his pace. Then she saw the line of thick trees in front of her and no way was she going in the woods with him. Nope.

"Stop!" She jerked away from his hand and tripped, losing her grip on her phone. It landed with a thud on the grass. And Kylie almost joined it.

He caught her by her forearm and lifted her with complete ease. Catching her breath, she realized the back of his hand rested against her breast.

She stared at his hand, against the swell of tingling flesh, her heart racing—racing from fear and from something else. That something else having everything to do with the dream she'd had last night and where his hand was now. "Let me go," she seethed.

He released her and held his palms out. "I wouldn't hurt you, Kylie."

"How would I know that?" She took a step back and waited to see if he'd say something about knowing her before. Maybe even remind her that he'd saved her from a bunch of bullies. At which time she'd have to remind him that he'd still killed her cat.

But he said nothing. He just stared at her and the expression in his eyes appeared hurt. Like he had that right.

God, did he even remember her? Or Socks?

He passed a hand over his face and asked, "What was that all about?"

What was what all about? Then she thought she knew.

"Derek drew my name. We were just talking." *Unlike what you and your sidekick were doing. And not that it was any of your business, anyway.*

In the bright sunlight, Kylie noticed Lucas's beard stubble, something most seventeen-year-olds didn't have. Then she recalled he was a werewolf and wondered if that explained it. Or was he just one of those guys who matured early, who had a full beard by the time they graduated high school?

"I saw how you two were talking, but that's not what I'm asking about."

"In that case, I'm sorry I interrupted you and that girl." She reached down and picked up her phone.

When she stood back up, he was frowning, but to his credit he didn't try to claim she hadn't interrupted anything.

She couldn't explain why that almost upset her. But damn it. What was wrong with her? An hour ago, she'd wanted Derek to kiss her and now she was having the hots for the guy who killed her cat?

Stress, she decided. Stress obviously brought on the hook-up hormones. Or did a brain tumor do that?

Lucas let out a sigh. "I didn't mean that, either. I meant what did the FRU want with you?"

Kylie pressed a hand to her left temple to assuage the ache and tried to think how to explain it. Then she wasn't even sure she should explain it.

"I don't know." She didn't know enough about what the FRU suspected to make sense of it herself, let alone to explain it to anyone else.

His eyes tightened. "What do you mean, you don't know?"

"I mean, I don't know. Nothing is making sense to me these days."

Skepticism filled his expression and insisted she give him more. But why was he asking? Could he be behind whatever it was the FRU suspected her of doing? Her own suspicion started to build.

"Why do you want to know?" she asked.

"They've been hanging around and I can tell Holiday is upset. I asked her about it, but she said I didn't have to worry. If something's going on, I want to help her."

Kylie remembered Holiday had brought Lucas with her last night when she'd had the dream. Maybe the two of them were friends, but if Holiday chose not to tell him anything, far be it from Kylie to interfere.

"They wanted to talk to me because they think I'm an anomaly. They're trying to figure me out like everyone else is."

The disbelief in his gaze lessened. "Did they do it? Figure you out?"

She shook her head. "Apparently I'm a real puzzler."

"Girls generally are," he said, and smiled. And holy crap, if his smile wasn't one of those that made a girl's heart fall over on itself.

She caught herself from being lured into his smile and mentally slammed on the brakes. Then, because she didn't want to stand there while her heart did somersaults, because she needed to find Helen and see if she could detect a tumor in Kylie's brain, Kylie held up her phone. "I have to make a call."

· · ·

It took Kylie twenty minutes to find Helen. During that time, she'd texted Sara a bunch of smiley faces, but had foregone calling her. Now that Sara's trauma was over, Kylie felt justified in concentrating on her own. And the first order of business was to get her brain scanned by a certain half fairy.

Moving across the dining hall, she studied Helen who was sitting at the table, her nose in a book. The girl came across as the quiet but really smart type—the kind who never had to study in school, but wasn't really proud of it.

"Hi," Kylie said when Helen didn't notice her.

Startled, Helen jerked her attention up. A strand of sandy blond hair fell across her face and she brushed it back. "Hi."

Kylie opened her mouth to speak, only to realize she didn't have a clue how to ask if she would check her for a brain tumor. The silence hung heavy and Kylie forced herself to start taking. "I . . . I just . . ."

Noise from the other side of the room erupted and Kylie looked at the other campers. "I'm Kylie Galen. You and I were in the group—"

"I remember," she said in a mellow voice. Kylie didn't know Helen, but she instantly identified with her. She was another cliqueless wonder. A loner. Kylie couldn't help but hope that the girl had someone like Sara who made her life easier.

"Can we talk?" Kylie asked. "Somewhere else?"

Helen glanced over at the other campers, and then picked up her book and backpack.

When they stepped out of the dining hall, Kylie noticed several groups of hungry teens congregating near the building.

She headed away from them, and tried again to find the words to ask Helen. "I was wondering if . . . I sort of—"

"Derek told me," Helen said.

"He did?" Kylie's chest pinched at the thought of Derek trying to help. Behind that pinch came guilt at still not being able to trust him. Was she wrong to be unsure of her feelings for someone who could control them as easily as he could breathe?

"There's a quiet spot behind the office," Helen said.

"Not there." While Kylie didn't think Lucas would already be hooking up again, she didn't want to chance it.

She saw the path back to her cabin was mostly unpopulated, so Kylie headed that way.

They passed a group of kids, laughing at something one of them said. In the midst of the group, she spotted Lucas's girlfriend, and before Kylie could look away, the girl met her gaze and snarled. Why did the she-wolf hate her so much?

Trying not to focus on Lucas or his girlfriend, Kylie glanced at Helen. "Do you think you can help me?"

Helen shrugged and everything from her expression to her posture appeared uncertain. "I've only done it with my sister. I'll try, but . . ."

"But what?" Kylie asked as they continued down the path.

"Aren't you scared?" Helen asked.

Kylie stopped walking. "Should I be?"

Helen did another one of her insecure shrugs. "Maybe. I don't know. All I know is that I'm scared."

Oh, just great. Kylie swallowed the nervous tickle down her

throat. "Is it going to hurt or something?" When Helen didn't immediately answer, Kylie asked, "Did it hurt your sister?"

"No," Helen admitted.

A sigh left Kylie's throat. Second thoughts started building, but then she remembered how badly she wanted to get to the bottom of everything. "I need to know."

Helen motioned Kylie to move behind a row of large oak trees. The girl tossed down her backpack and then looked at Kylie.

"How do we do it?" Kylie asked, her stomach knotting.

"Honestly, I don't know. With my sister I just . . . We were fighting. She had stolen my diary. And then all of the sudden . . ." She let out a breath.

"So we have to start fighting?" Kylie asked, unsure what Helen was getting at.

"No." She shook her head. "It was almost like . . . You know how we can peek into everyone's mind?"

"No, I don't know," Kylie answered, frustration tightening her tone as her headache returned with a new vengeance.

Surprise registered on Helen's face. "You really can't see people's brain patterns? But I thought we all could do that."

"I can't," Kylie answered. "Which is why I don't think I'm one of you guys." She clasped her hands together to keep them from shaking. Her heart lurched at the thought that she honestly might have a tumor. Then her mind went back to the idea of reading brains. "Have you always been able to do it? Always?"

"Sort of. I mean . . . I could do it, but I didn't know *what* I was doing. I just thought it was like closing your eyes real tight and seeing the different splotches of red. But now that I know what it is, it's so much clearer."

Their gazes met and Helen twitched her eyebrows.

"What do you see?" Kylie asked, her heart racing.

"Just your pattern." Helen continued to stare, unfocused like when Kylie looked at one of those posters where if she stared at it long enough, she might see a hidden image. "You aren't like . . . normal people. They have these even waves. Yours is . . . up and down and then you have some weird kind of scribbles. But you aren't letting me read you."

"I don't know how to let you read me." Kylie bit down on her lip and tried to stare at Helen, unfocused to see if she could see anything. Nothing happened, but her eyes crossed.

Blinking, Kylie asked, "Do I have to let you read me before you can see if I have a tumor?"

"No, but . . ." Helen refocused her eyes.

"But what?"

The girl let go of a sigh. "Like I told you, I don't know how it works. With my sister, I had my hands . . ." Helen raised her hands on each side of Kylie's head. "I was . . . holding her head." She hesitated. "Do you want me to try?"

Kylie nodded, even though doing it made her pulse race. Helen placed a hand on each side of Kylie's head. Kylie watched the girl close her eyes. Her smooth forehead wrinkled and her mouth tightened in concentration. Kylie stood there staring and hoped no one stumbled upon them. She could hear the rumors now. Kylie and Helen were making out behind the trees. Right.

Several seconds ticked by, and with each increment of time, Kylie felt more awkward. She was about to call it quits when her head began tingling. The tingles turned to heat. All at once, a comforting warmth radiated from Helen's palms.

"I'm doing it." Excitement rang in Helen's voice. "It's working."

The heat from Helen's hands eased inside Kylie's head. Kylie continued to stare at Helen, trying to read her expression. What was the girl seeing? Should Kylie be calling her mom and having her go out and start shopping for wigs? No way was Kylie walking around bald.

Slowly, the hold Helen had on her head lessened. The fairy dropped her hands to her sides. After two deep breaths, she opened her eyes.

"And?" Kylie blurted out. "Do I have a tumor? Do I?"

Chapter Twenty-three

"Hey, where have you been?" Miranda asked as Kylie dropped down on the bench beside her and Della in the dining hall fifteen minutes later.

"Talking to Helen." Kylie brushed a strand of blond hair behind her ear, her nerves still jumpy.

"Who's Helen?" Della held her glass of "juice"—that's what Kylie had decided to think of it as—to her mouth.

"Helen Jones." Kylie motioned to the quiet girl who had just sat down at another lunch table. While Kylie had invited Helen to join them, she'd declined, saying she'd promised to sit at the fairy table today.

Kylie watched Helen sit next to Derek and lean in to whisper something in his ear. Kylie didn't need super hearing to know Helen had shared the no-tumor verdict. As if to prove Kylie right, Derek met Kylie's gaze and smiled.

Kylie returned the gesture. While she was comforted that Helen hadn't seen any black dots in her brain as she'd spotted in her sister's, the answer moved Kylie closer to accepting that she was . . . well, not all human. And that was not comforting at all.

Della leaned forward and whispered, "How did your interrogation go? Did you find out what they suspected you of?"

"What interrogation?" Miranda's eyes grew round.

Kylie looked around at the crowd. "I'll tell y'all later."

Miranda nodded. "Oh, did you hear we're getting a computer? They're putting one in every cabin."

"Cool," Kylie said, only half listening. Instead her mind chewed on the possibility of insanity explaining her odd brain pattern. For sure, there'd been times she felt crazy—these last few weeks topping the list.

"You'd better get your lunch before they stop serving," Della said.

Kylie noticed that several of the campers were already stacking their trays and leaving. The tumor scan had taken longer than Kylie had thought.

"Yeah." Kylie stood up.

"Oh," Miranda said. "Perry was trying to find you earlier."

Kylie frowned and leaned down. "What did he want?"

"Maybe for you to check his sex again." Della snickered.

Kylie groaned.

Miranda chuckled and then got serious. "I think it was to apologize. He told me that he even tried to get away from you, that you were the one to bring him inside."

Kylie recalled that the kitten, aka Perry in disguise, did try to resist when she brought him in. As he did when she pried his hind legs apart. "He still shouldn't have been peeking in our windows."

"True," Miranda said. "But at least he's willing to apologize. It takes a big person to do that."

"Or a little twerp who's afraid I'll tell Holiday on him," Kylie said.

"She has a point," Della said.

Kylie walked to the lunch pickup window. The elf who had driven the bus stood behind the counter—all three feet of her, the tip of her head barely hitting the countertop. She cocked her head back and looked at Kylie, her brows twitching. "Have we figured out what you are yet?" The elf slid a food tray at Kylie.

"Not yet," Kylie muttered, not liking the fact that everyone at the camp knew about her identity crisis.

"Does your friend need anything to eat?" the little woman asked, frowning.

"What friend?"

The cold brushed down Kylie's right side—his presence as noticeable and as welcome as a paper cut. "You can see him, too?" A wisp of steam left her lips with the words.

"Nah, just feel him. Don't like it, either." The elf backed away from the counter.

Go away. Go away. Closing her eyes, Kylie willed Soldier Dude to leave. When the chill faded as quickly as it had come, she wondered if it was really as easy as just wishing him away. One more thing she needed to talk to Holiday about. Nevertheless, the small victory offered Kylie a tiny sense of control. Real tiny.

Picking up her tray, she went back to join Miranda and Della. Admittedly, she didn't search the room for any guys wearing army garb. Why look for trouble?

"Bad day?" Miranda asked when Kylie dropped her tray rather discontentedly on the table.

"Bad month." Kylie picked up the sandwich and sniffed. "I hate tuna." She felt her throat tighten and swallowed the knot of emotion, swearing she wouldn't cry.

"You like peanut butter and jelly?" Miranda asked.

"Yeah." Kylie looked at Miranda, thinking she was offering to swap. Instead, she was holding out her pinky and waving it at Kylie's sandwich.

The sandwich in Kylie's hand moved. Kylie looked at it, and her mouth fell open. Peanut butter and red jam oozed over the crusty edges of the bread. "Holy crap." Kylie dropped the sandwich back on the tray.

"Wow." Della leaned over. "Can you zap me up a second glass of blood? Oh, make it O negative. I hear that's the best."

Miranda made a face. "I do *not* do blood."

"Why am I not surprised?" Della huffed.

Kylie shut out all talk of blood and shifted her gaze from her transformed sandwich back to the sandwich transformer. "I thought you said you couldn't do magic?"

Miranda made a funny face. "That's hardly enough to call magic. I've been replacing my lunch with peanut butter and jelly sandwiches since I was two. My mom tried force-feeding me liverwurst. Who in God's name eats that stuff?"

"I'd bet I would love it now," Della said.

Kylie's stomach growled and she pulled back the bread to give the sandwich a quick check. "Is it . . . safe to eat?"

"You think I'd poison you?" Miranda asked, clearly offended.

"No, but it could be radioactive or something. I don't know what happens to food when it's . . . zapped here."

"I've eaten my sandwiches all my life," Miranda said.

"Yeah, we see what it did to you, too," Della added, her tone sounding more and more annoyed.

"Go suck a vein," Miranda snapped.

"You got one?" Della countered, and bared her teeth.

"Please." Kylie looked from one roommate to the other. "I beg you, don't start this again." Only when they both seemed resigned to stop bickering did Kylie revisit the idea of eating. Amazingly, she was starved. Getting one's brain scanned must increase one's appetite. Or maybe it was that her headache had finally taken a hike. Either way, she was hungry enough to take a chance and eat a sandwich that had been conjured up by Miranda's pinky finger.

Picking up the sandwich, Kylie sank her teeth into the soft white bread. "It's good," she told Miranda, as she moved the bite around in her mouth, and tried to keep the peanut butter from sticking to the roof of her mouth. "Thank you."

"You're welcome," Miranda said. "And in return, all I'd like is for you to put in a good word for me with Derek—since you don't like him."

Della made a snorting sound. "You are so blind. Kylie's crazy about him."

Miranda's mouth fell open and she looked at Kylie as if waiting for her to rebuke Della's claim. But the peanut butter got caught on the roof of her mouth and Kylie couldn't have spoken even if she wanted to. Not that she was overtly ready to speak up. She didn't know how to answer.

Frustrated at Kylie's silence, Miranda addressed Della. "She said she didn't like him."

"She lied." Della shrugged.

Miranda snapped her head around to Kylie. "Do you like him? If so, just tell me you like him."

"Who does Miss Don't-know-what-I-am like?" Lucas's girl-friend plopped down on the opposite side of the table.

Kylie's gaze shot to the werewolf. Strange. She couldn't ever remember having so much anger or dislike being lopped on her in one cold stare.

She managed to push the lump of sandwich she'd pried off the roof of her mouth to her cheek. "No one," she said, but it came out muffled.

"Really?" The werewolf's lips turned up in something that might have been considered a smile if the smirk accompanying it wasn't so evil. "By the way, my name's Fredericka. I thought you'd like to know the name of the girl who will kick your ass if you even try—"

"Ha. That's funny," Miranda said.

Funny? Kylie shot a look at Miranda and right then the blob of bread, peanut butter, and jam slid halfway down Kylie's throat. She covered her mouth and coughed, which only made the situation worse, because as the golf ball–sized lump of food tried to come up, it lodged between her tonsils. She gasped for air, but got none. Zilch.

"What's funny?" Fredericka's cold stare now focused on Miranda, which might have concerned Kylie if she wasn't slightly preoccupied about not being able to breathe. She started thumping her chest.

Can't breathe.

"You kicking her ass," Miranda shot back.

Hey. I can't breathe here. Kylie reached for her throat, the universal sign of choking.

"I mean, with all the help Kylie would have stopping you and all."

Seriously, I can't breathe. Oh, friggin' great, she was at a camp full of bloodsucking, meat-eating creatures, and she was about to die of asphyxiation from a peanut butter and jelly sandwich.

Fredericka leaned forward, getting closer to Miranda. "You think I'm scared of your scrawny little butt?"

Still can't breathe here, guys.

Finally, Della—you gotta love an attentive vampire— reached around Miranda's shoulders and gave Kylie one extra hard thump between her shoulder blades. The clump of food dislodged from her windpipe. While it hurt going down, at least oxygen started passing.

"Me?" Miranda's voice came out squeaky. "You thought . . . I meant . . . No, no. I didn't mean help from me." Miranda pointed a finger at Della. "She might take you on. She's got this whole vampire combative attitude going, but I didn't mean her, either."

"But she's right," Della said, half her attention on Kylie and the other half on Fredericka. "I'd help Kylie kick your ass in a heartbeat." She curled her lips at the werewolf, showing off her canines.

Fredericka didn't appear concerned. Not that Kylie was certain of anything; she was still working on getting the needed oxygen to her brain, while giving the drama playing out in front of her a wee bit of attention. Hey, if she was about to get ripped apart by a werewolf, she wanted to know the reasons why.

"Then who are you talking about?" Fredericka leaned across the table and a low growl escaped her throat.

"I mean Kylie's ghosts." Miranda said. "She's got like a dozen or so hanging around, or hadn't you heard?"

What? Kylie coughed—good thing the lump of bread had gone down and not up because she would have choked on it again.

"I don't know about you, but I'm not messing with the dead. Don't you remember last year when Holiday talked about the death angels?"

Death angels? Kylie recalled Miranda talking about the legend of dancing death angels at the falls on the bus ride to the camp. She gave up one more cough and then held up her hand. But right before she started talking, she noticed the fear in Fredericka's expression.

Not wanting to come off like a scared rabbit confronting a hungry wolf—even though that pretty much described exactly how Kylie felt—she looked Fredericka directly in the eyes. "Stop." Cough. "I don't want to fight you." Cough. "I don't even know why you'd want to fight me. Or my ghosts."

Hey, Kylie was no fool. She fully intended to take advantage of the fear she spotted in the girl's eyes.

"Just stay away from Lucas," Fredericka warned, but her voice lacked its earlier confidence.

"Me?" All the crappiness of the day, of the last few weeks, zeroed in on this high and mighty B with an itch, and the scared-rabbit feeling faded.

"You know what?" Kylie snapped. "Maybe you should go tighten the leash you have around your so-called boyfriend's neck, because every time I've spoken to him was because he came up to me. Not the other way around."

"You'd better watch your back," Fredericka said.

"She doesn't have to," Della said. "Her ghosts do that for her. Didn't you hear about the little incident that happened at our cabin last night?"

Fredericka shot up and took off.

Kylie pressed a hand to the table and stared after her. "What a bitch."

"Yeah, she was like that last year, too. But we did good," Miranda said, and placed her hand on top of Kylie's.

"We rocked," Della said, and put hers on top of Miranda's.

"Thank you," Kylie said, and looked from one roommate to the other. "Y'all didn't have to stick up for me, and I appreciate it."

"Hey, we're friends," Miranda said. "And that's what friends do."

Smiling at her two new friends, Kylie realized that coming to camp wasn't going to be *all* bad.

Then, letting go of a heartfelt sigh and feeling her bravado kick down a notch, she met Miranda's gaze. "Do death angels really exist?"

Chapter Twenty-four

"And oh, do death angels really exist?"

It was probably the seventh or eighth question Kylie had pitched at Holiday during their meeting thirty minutes later. The moment Kylie's foot had stepped inside the office, the questions just started flowing.

"That's . . . a lot of questions." Holiday smiled and motioned for Kylie to sit down.

Kylie set her phone down on Holiday's desk and took a chair. When she'd left the dining hall, she spent the last five minutes talking to Sara, celebrating the fact that her pregnancy test was negative, but now Kylie was back to focusing on her own mission of finding answers.

"Yeah, and I'm only getting started," she said. "I also want to know what else I could be. The other day you said—"

"Really?" Holiday's brow arched. "So you've accepted that you're one of us?"

The question bounced around Kylie's head. "No. I just want to be prepared if . . . that's what I discover."

The camp leader brushed her long ponytail of red hair behind her shoulder. "I heard you had Helen check you for a tumor."

"Who told you?" Kylie asked, imagining the whole camp teasing her about it. Or even worse, teasing Helen. The girl seemed even shyer than Kylie and the last thing Kylie wanted was for her to get hell because of something Kylie had talked her into doing.

Holiday shook her head. "It wasn't like that. Helen was excited that she discovered how it worked and wanted to share it with me."

Kylie nodded. She understood how Helen felt and didn't begrudge her sharing the news with Holiday.

"But you still aren't a believer, are you?" Holiday asked, meeting Kylie's gaze.

"I could still be . . ."

"Crazy or schizophrenic."

"Right," Kylie said, relieved that Holiday understood.

Holiday sighed as if exasperated and Kylie's relief evaporated.

"It's just I don't think either of my parents are gifted. And you said this is most likely hereditary. Plus, I can't see into people's head and see any patterns. Helen said she could always do it."

"That's Helen. Most of us with ghost whispering powers—it just appears one day." Holiday sighed. "And there could be a hundred reasons why your mom or dad hasn't shared this with you. You . . ." She held up her hands. "What am I doing? My job isn't to convince you. It's to help you find your own answers."

Kylie almost apologized for disappointing Holiday because

she honestly liked her, but how could Kylie just believe this without some proof?

"Let's get back to your questions." Holiday paused as if recalling the list. "Do death angels really exist? I'm assuming you heard about the legend of the name Shadow Falls."

"Yeah," Kylie said. "Is it true?"

"I've never seen the shadows. Of course, it wasn't quite dusk when I was there."

"I mean the death angels?"

"Well, I haven't ever seen a death angel either. But I know several people who claim they have. Some think they exist only in the legends, but since all supernaturals are considered legends, it's hard to say they don't exist."

"Are they known to be evil?" Kylie asked, her curiosity stemming from both Fredericka's fear and Miranda's hesitancy to talk about them later.

"Not necessarily evil. They are thought of as powerful ghosts who are . . . avengers. It's believed that they right the wrongs of the supernaturals. And stand judgment of them."

"Is that why everyone seems so scared of ghosts?"

"Yup, that would be the reason." A smile twitched Holiday's lips. "Frankly, we scare the bejeebies out of most supernaturals. Remember the FRU?"

Kylie nodded and inwardly admitted it scared the bejeebies out of her, too.

Holiday placed her right elbow on the table and then rested her chin in her open palm. "To be honest with you Kylie, death angels per se may not exist, but I see all my ghosts as being a lot like we think death angels are. I mean, I've actually had several protect me in different ways. Sure some of them need something from us, but more times than not they are here to either help us, or to help us help someone else. As scary as this all seems to you, you should know that it's a special calling. Very few supernaturals have this gift. It's said that it is bestowed on only those with worthy spirits, good hearts, and courage."

"But I'm not those things," Kylie said, pleading her case. "On Halloween, I wouldn't even go into the haunted houses."

Holiday chuckled. "I didn't say you were perfect, Kylie. Heaven knows that I have my faults as well. But our hearts want the good to win. We're still afraid, we still make mistakes, but if we listen to what our hearts want, we will find the right way." She rested her left hand on top of Kylie's.

Kylie looked at their hands joined together on the table. "Is being a ghost whisperer a common gift for fairies? And elves?" Kylie remembered the bus driver sensing when Soldier Dude had dropped by for a visit. "At lunch, the elf, the one who drove the bus that brought us here, she knew the ghost was there."

"Yes, there have been studies that say it is more common with fairies and elves. But it's not unheard of for others to have this ability. While certain gifts are bestowed to different species, each being can have less or more, depending on their spirits or their links to the gods and goddesses."

"So what else could I be?"

"This morning when I touched you and you sensed that I was trying to calm you . . . the fact that you could feel that is . . . well, unusual. Generally speaking, another fairy, depending on their level of power, may be able to sense it, but . . . honestly, I've never heard of anyone sensing it through touch."

"So assuming I'm not human, I'm also not fairy?"

"I didn't say that. What I can say is that whatever species your gifts stem from, your lineage to the gods is closer than most. I think you are just coming into your powers and who knows what all awaits you."

Kylie just stared. Holiday acted as though her words were supposed to make her feel better. "But do we know—if I *am* one of you—that I'm not like a vampire or werewolf?" Kylie held her breath as she waited for Holiday to answer.

Holiday shrugged. "I'm guessing if you were of that species, we would have seen some of the normal characteristics that are linked to them. However, there are a few of all species that are what we refer to as atypical. Their heritage is with one species and yet they lack certain characteristics, and are often gifted in other ways. The studies seem to conclude that, perhaps, these individuals are the very few that have combined genetics of two or more species. Not that it has really been proven."

Oh, great. She could be a hybrid. Just like her sociology teacher's car.

"So . . . normally, you really don't have half of one species and half of another? I thought Miranda said they've been mixing forever."

Holiday smiled. "Yes. But generally, the species with the closer lineage to the gods is the one passed on in the DNA. Here again, the gifts of the child may vary, but the basic characteristics seem to remain true for each species, such as the transformation into a wolf, or the need for blood to survive—if the virus is active."

Kylie's mind was trying to wrap around all this information. "Isn't there some blood test that could tell if I'm anything at all?"

"Regrettably, no. Oh, they are still trying, believe me. However, it's legend that the gods made our blood the same as humans, and unidentifiable as a matter of survival. If normals, or even one form of a supernatural, could test for certain species, they might be able to eradicate certain types."

Kylie conceded that point. If she'd found out two weeks ago that vampires and such existed, she'd have been all for trying to eradicate them. But now, after knowing Della, Miranda, Derek, Holiday, Helen, and even Perry—the little twerp—Kylie would never agree to it.

Then she remembered she wasn't the only one who didn't know why she was here. "Is there any kind of supernatural that isn't hereditary?"

"Well, as I mentioned earlier, in rare incidences it has been known to skip generations. Especially in the instances of vampirism. Then there are humans who are simply turned by either vampires or werewolves, but it's suspected that even in those cases, the victims who survive being turned have been touched in some way by the gods. Or demons."

Demons? Okay, Kylie wasn't ready to deal with them just yet. "But you don't think I'm a vampire or a werewolf, right?"

"I think it's unlikely."

Which basically meant, if Kylie wanted to get to the bottom of this, she'd have to go to her parents. And just how in the heck was she going to do that, assuming her parents were as clueless about this as she was? Knowing her mom, if Kylie started asking questions, she'd get herself pulled out of camp and stuck in a loony bin.

During the art hour later that afternoon, Kylie was paired up with Helen and Jonathon. The teen had removed all his piercings except his left earring. Kylie also noticed the way he carried himself, as if somehow becoming a vampire had given him a double shot of confidence. Even Helen seemed quicker to smile and totally comfortable with her new role as fairy/healer.

Kylie remembered Holiday saying how the camp would make most of them feel relieved because they always sensed they were different. Kylie saw that relief in Helen and Jonathon—it was as if they'd finally discovered who they really were. It was just one of a dozen or more things that made her different from everyone else here at camp. She couldn't help but wonder if this failure to identify with her supernatural self wasn't another sign of her not being anything but human.

Their art assignment was to take a walk as a group of three, find a spot, and then sit and sketch the same thing. Kylie, her mind still stuck on seeing the falls, suggested that they take a walk to the waterfalls. She felt pretty sure she could find her way back to where Derek had taken her and then follow the sounds from there. Face it, she was curious, but both Helen and Jonathon refused to go, saying only that they preferred to stay away from that place. Instead, they walked down one of the trails and found an old tree that had been split in two from what she assumed had been lightning.

While Helen and Jonathon got into the whole sketch-a-tree

thing, Kylie spent most her time trying to figure out how to approach her parents. Her mother already thought she was nuts because of Soldier Dude. What would she say when Kylie asked, point-blank, if her mom had any fairy ancestors, saw ghosts, or could transform herself into a unicorn.

Later, when Kylie met up with her hiking crowd, she almost bailed when she found out Lucas was leading the group. Then, afraid ditching would get her into trouble with Holiday, Kylie plastered a cordial look on her face that she didn't really feel, and swore to ignore him. Fifteen minutes into the hike, she realized she didn't have to ignore Lucas because he did a championship-winning job of ignoring her. Half an hour into the hike, and not once had he addressed her personally or even glanced her way. Not that she cared.

It was a downright shame Fredericka wasn't around to see how unimpressed the two of them were with each other. Okay, the truth was, Kylie counted her blessings that she and Fredericka hadn't crossed paths again. Somehow Kylie had to muster up some courage, or at least learn to fake some. Because sooner or later they were bound to come face-to-face again. Kylie's hands began to sweat just from considering it.

And to think Holiday thought she had courage. Ha.

In the beginning of the hike through the woods, Kylie mostly hung with Miranda, when her roommate wasn't chatting it up with the five or six male hikers. Honestly, when it came to the opposite sex, Miranda reminded Kylie a bit of Sara. A little too out there. Then again, it might be Kylie was a tad jealous at how easily both of them could flirt.

Even though Kylie didn't consider herself unattractive,

playing that whole giggly role didn't come easy for her. She was fortunate that Trey hadn't been turned off by her more subdued style.

Thinking about Trey reminded Kylie that he'd called again during art class. He'd left a message, too, but she hadn't listened to it yet. Hey, he'd have to get in line. She had her own issues to deal with. But even as she tried to push thoughts of him away, she remembered him saying in their first conversation, *I just want to see you. I miss you.*

Her chest tightened, because damn it. She missed him, too.

Kylie felt Miranda nudge her with her elbow.

"This is Kylie. We're rooming together," Miranda said.

Waving at the group of guys walking on the other side of Miranda, Kylie quickly went back to checking the trails for water moccasins and pretending she wasn't listening to Lucas's spiel about the camp.

According to him, real dinosaur bones were actually found here back in the 1960s. After a few more minutes, Kylie forgot about feigning disinterest and like the rest of the group—minus a few of the boys and Miranda—hung on Lucas's every word.

Lucas took them up to a creek bed where an archeologist had roped off some prehistoric footprints. Kylie found the whole story fascinating. And it had nothing to do with the fact that Lucas's deep voice sounded hypnotic. She'd always found archaeology intriguing.

"So, are they still excavating the site?" Kylie asked. "Couldn't there be even more dinosaur bones here?"

Lucas turned to her. "Not on camp property, they're not." His tone lost its earlier enthusiasm and his focus shifted back to the others so fast Kylie had no doubt that her being here annoyed the hell out of him. Surely he knew she hadn't chosen to be on his little adventure.

If Kylie had any reservations about his attitude being a figment of her imagination, it died when Miranda whispered, "I don't see why that bitch Fredericka thinks he's into you. From what I can see, he barely tolerates you."

"I know," Kylie muttered, but even as the words left her lips, she recalled how he'd looked at her last night in her PJs.

"I've been thinking about Fredericka and I swear, she's so evil," Miranda whispered. "I'll betcha she wasn't born at midnight. Some supernaturals lie . . ."

Kylie nodded, only half listening, and that's when it hit. "Oh my God, that's how I can do it. Thank you." Kylie gave Miranda's arm a good squeeze, and for the first time she felt as if uncovering the truth was in her reach.

Chapter Twenty-five

That evening, Kylie stayed behind at the cabin when Miranda and Della went to the music get-together at the dining hall. Supposedly, some of the guys were going to sing and had brought guitars, and then, a little later, Holiday and Sky were bringing out some music CDs to play so everyone could dance. Kylie wasn't feeling in the mood to dance. Or even to listen to music. She had far more important things to do. Sitting at the small desk off the kitchen, she reread the e-mail she'd just written, wondering if she should click send or delete the whole thing.

> Hi Mom,
> We got computers in our cabin, so I thought I'd e-mail you instead of call.

Truth was, she figured she could lie better in an e-mail than over the phone.

You know how you are always fussing about me going over
my minutes. Anyway, I'm doing okay.

Another lie. Nothing felt okay. Well, except her friendship
with Miranda and Della.

I have a question. We're doing some crazy horoscope read-
ings and it's partly done by comparing your time of birth to
that of your parents.

And that was the lie that Kylie had been worrying about
saying out loud, but she still felt it was clever.

Can you tell me what time you and Dad were born? And is
there any way I could check and see when Nana and Papa
were born? What about Grandma and Grandpa Galen? Don't
we have like that family tree thing that Grandma filled out?
Did she put the time of their births on it?
Thanks for your help.
Kylie

Kylie's finger hovered over the send button. She almost added,
"please hurry," but decided not to push her luck. If she acted
too anxious about it, her mom would start to ask questions.
Best to play it cool.

Taking a deep breath, she hit send. Excitement shot through
her. If this worked, she'd have her answer. Or at least, she'd be
closer to knowing the truth.

She'd asked Miranda to clarify the whole midnight-born rule, and according to her, there were some humans who were born at midnight. And then there were some supernaturals who were not born at midnight. However, the latter were known as the untouchables—demons, born of the devil.

And while Kylie considered her mom cold, she didn't consider her evil. If one of her parents were part demon, she would have known. Right?

Then there was the whole probability that it had skipped a generation. Which was why Kylie had asked for her grandparents' times of birth. She knew she was dreaming that her mom would have that info at her fingertips, but hey, Kylie wanted answers.

And she wanted them now.

Thirty minutes later, Kylie stood guard over the computer, obsessively clicking NEW MAIL, when her phone buzzed. She ran to the bedroom to find it. As she hurried through the door, she remembered she hadn't listened to Trey's messages yet. He'd called again during dinner, and she hadn't answered then, either.

She told herself it was because she was surrounded by people who could listen in, but she could have walked outside and taken the call.

She could have, but she hadn't.

Deep down she knew that meant something. She just wasn't sure what it meant.

Snatching her phone from the bed, she eyed the screen. Frowning, she took the call.

"Hello, Mom." Kylie fell on top of the mattress. "Didn't you get my—"

"E-mail? Yes, but I don't want to get an e-mail or text. I want to talk to you."

"Okay." Kylie listened as the silence filled the line. See, that was the problem with her and her mom. They really had nothing to talk about.

"Did you have a good day?" her mom asked.

"It was okay." Another awkward moment. "Did you read my e-mail?"

"Yes," her mom said.

"Can you tell me what time you were born?"

"It was late."

Kylie's heart stopped. "How late?"

"I don't know the exact time. Are they feeding you well?"

Kylie closed her eyes. "It's camp food, only slightly better than the school cafeteria. Do you have your birth certificate? That should have the exact time."

"I think it was around eleven. Just say eleven."

"I need the exact time, Mom," Kylie muttered. "I told you. It's for a camp project."

"My birth certificate is in the closet in that box with all those other important papers and old pictures. It would take me forever to find it."

"Please?"

"Why is this important? You don't even believe in horoscopes."

There were a lot of things I used to not to believe in. "Like I said, it's for a camp project. All the kids are doing it." *Can't you do that much for me?* "Do you have Dad's birth certificate?"

"Have you spoken with him?" her mom asked, lowering her voice.

"No," Kylie answered, and the feeling of abandonment swelled in her chest.

"You're not angry at him, are you?" her mom asked.

Hell, yes. He left me to live with you. "Honestly, I don't know what I'm feeling."

"It's not good for you to be angry, Kylie."

Why not? You stay angry at him. Right then, Kylie realized something she should have realized long ago. Her mom was forever angry at her dad. Kylie just didn't understand why.

Her mom sighed. "I need to know if he's coming on Sunday."

"Why are y'all doing this?" It was a question Kylie had never asked. She'd always assumed her mom, being her mom, had one of her temper tantrums and told him to get his stuff and leave. She'd even heard her mom tell him to get out a couple of years ago when she'd walked in on them fighting.

"Doing what?" Her mom asked as if she seriously didn't have a friggin' clue.

"The divorce. That's what."

Silence. "Kylie, that's between your dad and me."

"Like it doesn't affect me? How can you even think this wouldn't affect me?" Tears filled her eyes.

"I'm sorry this is hurting you, Kylie." Her mom's tone came out hoarse. "I never wanted it to hurt you."

Was the Ice Queen crying?

Kylie closed her eyes and felt a few tears slip down her

cheeks. "Will you *please* look for your birth certificates?" she asked, trying to hold back the tears.

"Fine," her mom said. "I'll see if I can find them and I'll e-mail the information to you. If not tonight, tomorrow."

"Tonight would be better." Kylie pulled one of her knees to her chest.

"I'll see," her mom said. Which meant Kylie could expect it to happen tomorrow. "Promise me you'll call your dad about Sunday."

"Bye," Kylie said.

"Kylie. Promise me."

The knot tightened in her throat. "Promise."

Kylie hung up and stared at her phone. What was she going to say to her dad? Oh, hell, why not just do it and get it over with. She started punching in his number, only to realize she'd accidently punched in Nana's old number.

And just like that, it hit. The swell of grief. She missed her grandmother so much. Missed calling her whenever she had some crazy problem with her mom. Missed the way Nana would pat Kylie's cheek and say, "It's all gonna be okay."

A knock sounded at her bedroom door. "Kylie?" Della's voice echoed on the other side.

Kylie closed her phone and wiped her tears from her face. "I'm on the phone," she said. "Can't visit now."

"But, I . . . I have a surprise for you," Della said.

"I don't want a surprise." Couldn't they just leave her alone? For once?

"I'm opening the door. I hope you're dressed."

The bedroom door opened. "I said I . . ." Kylie's words evaporated from the tip of her tongue, or maybe they crawled down
the back her throat. That might explain her inability to speak.
Then again, it was probably just the shock of seeing who stood
beside Della.

Chapter Twenty-six

"I found him sneaking into the camp. Better me, I suppose, than one of the others." Della stared at Kylie. "Do you want to see him?" She gave Trey the up and down look. "He's kind of cute. If you like his type."

Kylie opened her mouth to speak but nothing came out. So she just sat there with her mouth hanging open like an idiot, staring at Trey.

"Hey." He pushed Della aside and moved into her bedroom.

"Not so fast!" Della yanked him back a good three feet and looked at Kylie. "You wanna keep him, or should I toss him to the wolves? I heard they're hungry."

Trey, looking stunned that Della—only an inch or so over five feet—could move him so easily, rubbed his arm where she'd latched on to him and stared down at her.

"It's okay," Kylie managed to say.

"Thanks," Trey said, cutting Della an odd look, and Kylie wasn't sure who he was thanking. Her for agreeing to see him, or Della for bringing him here.

"Okie dokie. Later." Della leaned in. "By the way, no one knows he's here but me. So you're gonna have to sneak him out." Della waved and then stepped out and shut the door.

Trey rubbed his arm one more time and stared at the door before he turned back to her. "That is one weird and strong bitch."

Kylie's shot her gaze to the door, afraid Della would storm back in and defend herself. "She's not a bitch. She's my friend. What are you . . . doing here?"

"What do you think I'm doing? I came to see you."

Kylie shook her head. "You said it would be next week."

"Yeah, but I have a cousin who lives a couple of miles from here. I talked Mom into letting me come up early so I could see you." His gaze shot to the phone in her hands. "I called you at least twice and left messages. Didn't you get them?"

Realizing what he'd done to see her, Kylie felt guilty for not taking his calls or even checking his messages. "I . . . it's been crazy." A few lingering tears slipped from her lashes. She blinked them away and just stared at him. His sandy brown hair hung just a little longer than before and his bangs brushed against his eyebrows. He wore a dark green T-shirt and jeans. Her gaze lowered to his chest. The place she always loved to rest against. Oddly, she remembered him as being buffer. Or was she remembering Derek?

"You're crying." He moved in and concern, honest to goodness concern, filled his green eyes. "Are you okay?"

The compassion in his gaze sent a wave of emotion through her. She stopped caring about what he looked like and just wanted to feel loved. She nodded yes, but the truth slipped from her lips. "No. Everything in my life is falling apart."

Trey moved in and before Kylie could stop him, he was doing what Trey did best, holding her. He'd joined her on the twin bed. Her cheek rested against his chest, and she listened to the steady pounding of his heart. Inhaling his familiar scent, she closed her eyes. She'd give in for a moment. Just a moment. Then she'd push him away.

"Is this about your parents' divorce?" His hands moved tenderly against her back. His touch felt good. Familiar. Normal. Life the way it should be. Like the way it was less than a month ago.

"That and everything else," she said, accepting that she couldn't tell him about the camp and what was happening to her.

"You mean your grandma?" he asked. "I know you two were close."

"Yeah." She pulled back, wiped her eyes, and stared at him stretched out beside her on the tiny twin bed. Silence and sudden physical awareness vibrated in the small room. They were alone. They were in a bed.

It wasn't as if they hadn't been in bed together before. He'd visited her several times when her parents hadn't been home. And they had met at Sara's house a couple of times when her parents hadn't been there. It was just . . . those were the times that things usually went too far. When telling him to stop had made him mad.

"My camp is right next to yours," he said.

She nodded and then blurted out what she needed to say to him before she lost her nerve. "You shouldn't have come here, Trey. I have no idea what kind of trouble I'll get into if we're caught." She did know the number one rule posted: no normals allowed on camp property without permission. And here she was with one stretched out in her bed. It felt wrong. But it still felt right.

"I miss you, Kylie," he said, ignoring what she'd said to him. "Really miss you." He reached up and tucked a strand of her hair behind her ear.

She swallowed. "I miss you, too, but—"

He leaned in and placed a soft kiss beside her lips. Whatever she was about to say got lost in her head. She closed her eyes and even while a little voice inside her told her to stop him, she didn't want to stop this. She wanted him to kiss her, to make her forget.

Oh, yes, she wanted to forget.

His mouth touched hers, slow at first, as if making sure she wanted it, and then he slipped his tongue into her mouth. She loved it when he kissed her like that.

The next thing Kylie knew, Trey had his hand up the back of her shirt and if she didn't stop him, she knew what came next. He would undo her bra. He would touch her breasts, and it always felt so good when he touched her. There was even that one time that she'd let him take her shirt off.

She felt his hands on her bra hook. He deepened the kiss, as if to distract her. She decided to let him do it, too.

But then what? The question bounced around her head. She would stop him, right? She always stopped him. That was the reason he'd dumped her, the reason he'd hooked up with that other girl.

That was when he'd broken her heart.

Opening her eyes, Kylie broke the kiss.

His eyelids fluttered open and she stared at his eyes, searching for a reason *not* to stop him this time. She wanted to lose herself in his eyes . . . to see the gold flecks sparkle.

Oh crap! Trey didn't have gold flecks in his green eyes. Derek had the eyes that pulled her in. Shocked, she put a hand on Trey's chest and recalled how good it had felt to lean against Derek's chest just this morning—how she had felt safe and accepted. "I . . . maybe we shouldn't—"

"Shh. Please don't say it." He put his finger over her lips. "This feels so good, Kylie. And I want to hold you like this, I want to touch you." His hand shifted around to her front and softly passed over her bra, making her breast feel tight. "What's wrong with us being together if we love each other? And you know that's how I feel, don't you? I love you."

I love you. Those three little words played like a slow song in her head. He moved in again for another kiss. She wanted to be loved so badly. And it did feel good, Kylie admitted to herself. It helped her forget.

She let herself become lost in his kisses again. Lost in how his hands moved over her naked skin over her back up to the bra latch. Unlike before, he had her bra unclasped in seconds.

Probably because he'd had practice. Okay, that thought put an end to the warm emotions swirling inside her. Or was it the cold that suddenly invaded the room? Oh, gawd, Soldier Dude was back.

Here.

Now.

Watching her make out with Trey.

"Okay, sorry. I can't do this." She pulled away and stood beside the bed, not looking anywhere but at Trey. *Go away,* she told the coldness, and squeezed her eyes closed.

When she opened her eyes, she felt the chill fade. She focused again on Trey, stretched out on the bed frowning at the ceiling.

"Not again," Trey muttered, and he sounded angry. He always got a little mad when she first stopped him. One time, he even dropped her off at her house without speaking to her.

Without wanting to, she found herself comparing him to Derek. Not just his body, in that Derek won hands down, but his attitude. For some reason, she didn't think Derek would pressure her so hard to give it up.

And then pout like a spoiled brat when she refused.

A tiny ribbon of anger swirled around her other emotions, overpowering passion and hunger and even her fear. "Who do you think you are, Trey? You can't just come into camp and expect me to have sex with you, especially after everything that's happened."

He sat up and brushed a hand over his face. "I didn't come here expecting to have sex." He let go of a deep gush of air. "I came to talk. Fine . . . yeah, I want sex, too. And I don't understand why you keep—"

"You want it enough that you'd break up with me and find someone who would give it to you?" Why she'd asked that she didn't know, because it had already happened.

He frowned.

"Did you sleep with her?" Kylie asked. In her heart she already knew the answer, but for some reason she needed it confirmed.

He didn't say a word. He didn't have to. The confirmation was all over his face.

"Did you tell her you loved her, too?" The thought stung like a paper cut right across the heart.

Even more guilt filled his eyes, and then he shook his head and fell face-first into denial. "No, I didn't sleep with her. And why would I tell her I love her, when I love you?"

Kylie didn't have Della's super lie-detecting skill, but she knew he'd just lied to her. Knew it with certainty and she wanted to throw something at him. "Don't lie, Derek."

"Derek?" He sat up in bed. "Who the hell is Derek?"

"Trey," she snapped.

"Who's Derek?" Trey asked again.

She shook her head. "It doesn't matter. We . . . you and I aren't together anymore."

"So you're together with him?"

She shook her head. Then, realizing what a mistake this had been, she faced the fact that this was partly her fault. "I'm sorry. I should have just told you no when you asked if I would see you. I can't see you now or next week."

He looked so hurt. Just as she'd known he'd been lying about sleeping with that girl, Kylie knew the hurt on his face was real. Trey did care about her. He'd just cared about having sex more.

"Are you seeing someone else? Is that who Derek is?" He

jumped off the bed and stopped right in front of her. "I know I screwed up, Kylie. But . . . please, give me another chance. I really miss you." He reached out to touch her.

She pushed his hand back. "I believe you miss me, Trey. I do. But I can't do this now."

"We don't have to have sex. We can just talk, okay? I'll wait until you're ready, I swear. Let me take you out for a pizza or something. I drove my dad's truck and—"

"I already ate dinner. Where did you park the truck?"

"At the front gate, but please . . ."

"I can't," she said.

"Don't tell me you don't care about me anymore. We dated for almost a year."

"I don't know what I feel." She reached back under her shirt and rehooked her bra. "I'm confused about everything right now . . . except that I know you hurt me, Trey. When school starts up, maybe we can . . . talk. But right now I have to get you out of this camp before something bad happens."

"Like what?" he asked. Something close to disgust crossed his face. "Is it true what they say about this place?"

"What who says?" she asked.

"My cousin and the other campers from last year. They say that all the kids who attend here are juvenile delinquents who were into really weird crap. Real freaks."

Only a few days ago, she would have totally agreed with him, but now . . . "Don't believe everything you hear." She reached down and found her phone on the bed. "Just trust me on this, okay? You've got to go." She gave him a nudge toward the door.

She took him through the woods, staying a few feet from the trail back to the dining hall. Once there, she peered around a tree to make sure the coast was clear. The muscles in her gut relaxed a little when no one was hanging outside. She hurried Trey past the entrance and breathed a sigh of relief when they moved behind the gate to his truck.

He looked down at her. "I do love you," he said.

She only nodded and motioned for him to go.

He reached out and she let him hug her. She even returned the embrace. Her emotions started zipping all over the place again. Deep down, she admitted that while she didn't think she'd ever forgive Trey for dumping her, a small part of her still cared about him. And who knew, maybe by the time school started up again, she'd feel differently. But as for now . . .

As he drove away, Kylie stayed in the parking lot until his taillights faded into the darkness. Standing there, she hated how alone she felt.

When she turned around, she realized she'd been wrong. She wasn't alone. Just friggin' great. Someone stood by the gate, watching her. Kylie couldn't make out who it was, but she prayed it wasn't Holiday or Sky. As she got closer, she recognized her lone watcher.

It wasn't Sky or Holiday.

It was worse.

Fredericka.

Determined not to show any fear, Kylie walked right past her. She got almost to the dining hall when the girl whizzed by and came to a sudden stop in front of Kylie.

She managed to stop right before slamming into the she-wolf.

"So, Ghost Girl had company, huh?" Fredericka said in a condescending voice. "What have you been doing? Screwing in your cabin?"

Kylie wondered if being turned into a werewolf explained the girl being such a bitch, or if she had always been this mean.

"If I was, at least I did it in a bed and not in the woods like some people I could mention."

Fredericka's eyes went from black to a deep burgundy in a nanosecond. Kylie wasn't up on werewolf color trivia, but she could guess that meant anger. That's when she realized that pissing the werewolf off probably hadn't been the best thing to do. Then again, Kylie also knew people like Fredericka preyed on the weak. She couldn't let the girl know how much she really frightened her.

The she-wolf growled. "Do Holiday and Sky know you've been entertaining guests? Maybe I should I fill them in?" Her voice seemed to vibrate from her solar plexus.

Right then, Kylie saw Holiday step outside the dining hall. As badly as she hated the idea of Holiday knowing Trey had been here, Kylie refused to let this B with an itch have something to hang over her head.

Kylie hot-footed it past the she-wolf and stopped in front of Holiday. "Hi. I just had a friend stop by uninvited. I realize it's against camp policy. I wasn't aware he was coming, so I escorted him out and it won't happen again."

Holiday frowned and it looked as if she was about to read

Kylie the riot act. Then her gaze shifted over Kylie's shoulder. When her focus returned to Kylie, the look of anger faded. "Thank you for telling me. Make sure it doesn't happen again. We only allow visitors on parents day. We can't have normals poking their noses around here uninvited."

Kylie nodded. "I understand." And then she took off to her cabin, praying Fredericka didn't follow.

By nine o'clock that night, Kylie had kept her promise to her mom and called her dad. It had been short, to the point, and hurt like a toothache. She didn't mention he hadn't come to see her before she'd been shipped off to the camp. She didn't mention that he hadn't come to get her at the police station, either.

And neither did he.

Basically, he told Kylie he loved her, he missed her, and he would see her Sunday on parents day at ten o'clock sharp. Oh, and he had to go, because he was out with a client.

Hanging up from the sixty-second call, Kylie remembered her mom always accusing her dad of putting his job before family. Kylie thought hell would be announcing a snow day before she agreed with anything her mom said. But right now, Kylie wondered how many inches they were predicting. Going into her bedroom, she dropped on the bed and hugged her musty-smelling pillow, but she didn't cry this time.

Maybe she was cried out, or just too angry at Fredericka. Maybe she was still in some kind of aftershock from her little make-out session with Trey—who she'd accidentally called Derek. Dang it, here she was afraid to like Derek, in case she only liked him because he looked like Trey. Now she was with Trey, and Derek came popping in her head. And don't forget the attraction/fear she held for a certain blue-eyed werewolf. Just how messed up could she possibly get?

Kylie heard the door to the cabin open and slam shut. She had her feet on the floor to go greet Della and Miranda when she heard the tone of the words being slung back and forth between her roommates.

"I called the computer first," Miranda yelled.

"I beat your little witch butt fair and square," Della responded.

"Listen here, you good-for-nothing vamp!"

Kylie stormed into the room. Della sat at the computer, her canines showing and growling. Miranda stood, chin held high, with her pinky finger held out in the air wiggling while her voice spewed something about zits.

"Stop it! I'm sick of this," Kylie yelled. "Can't you two fight like normal people?"

Miranda shot her gaze to Kylie. "Why would we fight like normals?"

"We're not normals," Della retorted. "Neither are you, and the sooner you accept that, the better off you'll be."

"You don't know that," Kylie snapped. "Fine, you two go ahead and kill each other. Just don't leave a mess, because I don't want to get stuck cleaning up any body parts." She swung around to go back to the bedroom when she recalled the reason she'd come out in the first place. She did another about-face. "By the way, if you hear me screaming bloody murder in the middle of the night, don't worry, I'm just having a night terror." She started back to her room.

Della called out. "Stop right there, Miss Smarty Pants! Don't you think for one minute that you're going to go into that bedroom without explaining first?"

Kylie swung back around. "I did explain it. They are just bad dreams."

"Not that. I mean the hot guy sneaking into the camp looking for you. Or did you forget about the little present I delivered earlier?"

Kylie wished she could forget. Seeing the questions in both her roommates' eyes, and knowing that Della could have gotten in a lot of trouble for delivering Trey, Kylie figured they both deserved something. She went to the kitchen table and dropped in a chair. "His name is Trey and he's old news."

"How hot was he?" Miranda asked, and sat beside Kylie.

"On a scale of one to ten, he was an eight," Della answered Miranda, and then looked back at Kylie. "Why is he old news?" She moved away from the computer and dropped in a chair across from them.

"Because he left me for some slut who would put out, that's why."

"Jerk," Miranda said.

"That piece of human shit," Della piped in. "You should have told me, I'd have roughed him up a bit."

Silence fell and the three of them sat there looking at each other. Miranda stretched her hands out on the table. "So if he left you for someone who would . . . put out, does that mean that you've never . . . you know?"

"*You know* what?" Della snapped. "What are you asking her?"

"I want to know if she's done it," Miranda said. "Are you a virgin, Kylie?"

Chapter Twenty-seven

Kylie looked at her new friends and wondered if she should share something so personal. While still a little perturbed at their "normal" remark, she felt a bond with these two. A bond she'd shared only with Sara.

"Yes, I mean, no. I haven't ever done . . . you know. Guess that means I'm not only a freak, but a virgin freak." Kylie stared at her hands a minute and then added, "It just never felt right, okay?"

Miranda leaned forward. "Don't be hard on yourself. I haven't gotten there, either. Hey, don't get me wrong. I came close, but as my uncle would say, this isn't horseshoes, right?"

Both Kylie and Miranda turned to Della, who looked paler than usual.

Miranda slapped her palm on the table. "Spill it, Vamp. We did."

Kylie gave Miranda a light nudge with her elbow. "Della doesn't have to spill anything if she doesn't want to." Kylie leaned back in her chair and decided a change of subject was needed. "Fredericka caught me saying good-bye to Trey."

"Oh, crap," Della said, some of her color returning. "What did she do?"

"She basically threatened to tattle on me, and then Holiday stepped out of the dining hall right then."

"Did she tell her?" Della asked.

"No, I decided to do it myself and not give that bitch the pleasure."

"What?" Miranda asked. "You told Holiday you brought a normal into camp without permission? Did Holiday come unglued?"

"No. She told me not to do it again," Kylie said.

Della cleared her throat. "Did you tell her I was the one who brought him to your cabin?"

Kylie rolled her eyes in grand Sara fashion. "I wouldn't do that, Della." She stood to go check her e-mail on some off chance that her mom had answered her.

"You know what I heard?" Miranda leaned in as if she had a piece of juicy gossip to share. "I heard Fredericka's parents were rogue. Someone had to do some serious arm pulling to get her in here."

"What do you mean by rogue?" Kylie asked, remembering Burnett of the FRU suggesting her parents could be rogue, as well.

"People who refused to adhere to the rules. For werewolves, it mostly means they hunted food that wasn't on the approved list."

"By . . . not on the approved list, do you mean like . . . humans?" Kylie asked, getting a chill.

"Or other supernaturals and livestock. Even pets."

Kylie's mind shot straight to Lucas Parker and his parents. Was that why Lucas and Fredericka were buddies? Because their parents were rogue werewolves?

Della stood and went to the fridge. "Want something to drink?" She glanced back.

"A Diet Coke, please," Kylie said.

"Miranda?" Della asked.

"Diet Coke sounds good."

Kylie stared at the "No new mail" message. "I asked my mom what time she and my dad were born."

"And?" Della set a soda beside the computer.

Kylie picked up her Diet Coke and went back to the table. "Mom couldn't remember, so she said she'd check the birth certificates. She's supposed to e-mail me. When she gets around to it." Kylie dropped back into a chair. "Knowing her, that could be next year sometime."

"Yeah, that's like when they say 'maybe' and they really mean 'no.'" Miranda moved to the desk to check her own e-mail.

Della dropped back in her chair, popped the top of the soda, and took a long sip.

"You can have soda?" Kylie asked.

"Yeah." She frowned. "Why?"

Kylie shrugged. "I don't know. I mean, I saw you eating pepperoni, but I thought vampires could only drink . . . you know."

"Blood?" Della finished, sounding annoyed that Kylie couldn't say it.

"Yeah. Blood." She pushed the word out of her mouth and tried not to turn green.

"No, I can have other stuff. It doesn't supply my body

nourishment and nothing tastes as good as it used to taste. Oh, and some things have really bad effects on me. Like broccoli."

"What happens if you eat broccoli?" Kylie asked.

"Explosive, really bad gas."

Kylie made a face. "I think that happens to everyone."

"Nope." Miranda looked over her shoulder. "She's right. Nothing is worse than a vampire fart. Except . . ." She looked at the screen and started typing. "Except a witch's fart after she eats a bean burrito."

They all laughed. When the moment passed, silence rained down on them again. Della turned her soda can in her hands. "I did it."

"Gross, you farted?" Miranda covered her nose.

"No," Della said. "I had sex."

There was like this reverent pause.

"And?" Miranda finally asked, and turned in the chair.

"It was nice. Really nice. Lee and I had been dating for a year. I loved him. It felt right." Tears filled Della's eyes, but even without them, the pain rang in her voice. "But then I turned into a vampire."

"He couldn't accept you?" Kylie's chest ached for Della, and she remembered how hurt she'd been when Trey dumped her.

Della wiped her eyes. "I didn't actually tell him. I was going to, but . . ." She bit down on her lip. "I went to see him after I was turned, and when he kissed me, he pulled away. He said I was cold and that I must still be sick and he . . . didn't want to kiss me until . . . until I felt warm again."

"What a jerk," Miranda said.

Della inhaled. "How do you tell the guy you love that you'll never be warm again?" Della's chin trembled.

Kylie rested her hand on Della's. "Maybe you should have tried to tell him. Maybe he could have understood if he knew—"

"No." Della shook her head and her sleek black hair moved in a wave around her face. "I don't think so. He's a wonderful guy, but he's so straight-and-narrow second-generation Chinese—like his family and my dad's family. He almost broke up with me when he realized my mom was Euro-American."

"He doesn't sound so wonderful," Kylie said.

Della shook her head again. "It's not all his fault. It's his upbringing. We're raised to believe we're supposed to be perfect. Make the best grades, go to the best schools, get the best jobs. We're not . . ." She bit down on her lip. "We're not supposed to be monsters."

"You're not a monster," Kylie snapped, appalled that Della would say that. And yet deep down, hadn't Kylie considered Della that in the beginning? And even worse, wasn't Kylie afraid she might learn she was a freak of nature herself?

"She's right," Miranda said.

Kylie gave Della's cold hand a gentle squeeze. "If he doesn't love you, then you'll find someone else who will. You're young. You're beautiful. You've got the rest of your life ahead of you." The question formed in Kylie's head and before she could stop it, it spilled out. "Are you immortal? Or are you already . . ."

"Dead?" Della finished for her.

Kylie flushed with embarrassment. "Oh gosh, I'm so sorry. That was so rude. I'm trying to make you feel better and I . . . It just slipped out."

"It's fine," Della assured her. "I'm not dead. Vampires' bodies function differently, that's all. Don't believe everything you read in those teen novels. We're not immortal; we only live to about 150."

"That's a pretty good deal." Kylie looked over at Miranda. "How about witches?"

"Life expectancy is about the same," Miranda said, never looking away from the computer.

"And other supernaturals?" Kylie wondered if she discovered she too was a supernatural, if she'd have an expanded life expectancy.

"Fairies live the longest." Miranda talked while she typed something into the computer. "I think there's one old dude that's like five hundred or so."

"Are you hoping you're fairy, now?" Della asked.

Kylie put her right elbow on the table and dropped her chin in it. "No. Oh, hell, I don't know," she muttered, letting go of a pent-up sigh. "This just sucks. Why can't my mom just answer me for once in her life? I hate not knowing anything."

Kylie looked back at Miranda. "Can't you help me out?"

"How?" Miranda asked, her concentration still on her e-mail.

"You are brave," Della giggled, understanding what Kylie meant. "Don't you remember she screws up her spells?"

"A gift for you." Miranda shot Della a one-finger salute over her shoulder.

Della laughed harder. "At least it's not your pinky."

Kylie ignored Della and their gestures. "Can't you do a spell that makes my mom find the birth certificates and e-mail me the info? Seriously, if you can make a peanut butter and jelly sandwich appear from nowhere, why can't you do this?"

"Well . . ." Miranda continued to stare at the computer. "I tell you what. Touch your nose three times and say Miranda is a goddess."

Kylie stared at the back of Miranda's head. "Are you serious?"

"Serious." Miranda turned around and she didn't appear to be joking. "Come on, touch your nose three times and say Miranda is a goddess."

"And you won't turn my mom into a toad?" Kylie held her left index finger in front of her nose.

"I wouldn't do that if I were you," Della warned.

Miranda scowled at Della. "I pinky promise not to mess up." She held out her pinky.

"And if I do this, I'll get my mom's e-mail?" Kylie couldn't believe she was considering this, but . . .

"Yup." Miranda grinned. "Or you could just come check the computer. Because you just got an e-mail from her."

Kylie jumped up and literally pushed Miranda out of the chair. Holding her breath, Kylie reached for the mouse. She could be one click away from knowing for sure that she was a supernatural.

One click. God, she was so scared.

Chapter Twenty-eight

"Open it already," Della shouted from behind Kylie.

Kylie looked over her shoulder, from Della to her right to Miranda on her left. Taking a deep breath, Kylie looked back at the e-mail and clicked open.

Hey hon, I was wrong. I wasn't born at eleven o'clock, it was ten p.m. Ten twenty-three to be exact. Your dad was born at nine forty-six a.m. Did you call your . . .

Kylie stopped reading. Neither of her parents was born at midnight. Emotion did cartwheels inside her chest. Heavy emotion. Was this relief? It should be relief.

It meant she wasn't a supernatural.

"See, I told you guys. I'm not one of you." Her chest clutched with a heavy emotion that didn't feel like relief. She didn't want to be one of them, did she? Or maybe what she felt was just disappointment for not fitting in. Again. Wasn't that the story of her life?

Deep down, you've always known you were different. Holiday's words played in Kylie's head. And for the first time, she admitted to herself that Holiday was right. Kylie had always felt different. Always felt like the outsider. But she wasn't . . . different. Well, she might be different.

She just wasn't a supernatural.

This was the proof.

"I don't believe it." Della spoke up first.

Then Miranda piped in. "Holiday mentioned it does skip generations."

"Only in rare situations," Kylie said.

"Maybe your mom's lying," Della added.

Kylie looked back at the vampire. "Why would she lie?"

Della shrugged. "Maybe she's just in a pissy mood because she's getting a divorce. I don't know."

"Your parents are getting a divorce?" Miranda asked.

"Yeah," Kylie said, not even the tiniest bit upset at Della for mentioning it. She may have only known them for a few days but she trusted these two.

"Sucky." Miranda pressed a hand on Kylie's shoulder and squeezed.

"Yeah." Kylie stared back at the e-mail.

"Why are they divorcing?" Miranda asked.

"I don't know. Mom's so . . ."

"Bitchy." Della tossed out the word.

Kylie almost nodded, then stopped. "No. She's not really a bitch, she's just . . . cold, distant. About as warm as a popsicle. I actually heard my dad tell her that a while back."

"So your dad's having an affair," Della said matter-of-factly.

Kylie turned in her chair and stared at Della. "No."

Della made a face. "Believe me, if he accused your mom of being a popsicle, he's found some young 'warm' thing to screw."

"He's not like that," Kylie said with conviction. Right then she realized what she said about her mom being cold.

"And by cold, I meant . . . emotionally, not—"

"I know," Della said. "Don't go thinking you've got to tiptoe around my feelings." But her eyes said differently.

Kylie knew all about pretending to be tough. She'd had a crash course in it these last few weeks.

Kylie looked back at the screen. "Mom, she's just . . . hard to live with sometimes. I don't blame my dad for leaving her."

"So are you going to live with your dad?" Miranda asked.

The question took Kylie back to the day she'd stood in the driveway, begging her dad to take her with him. As much as it hurt to remember, she had to accept the truth—that day, it felt as though when he decided to leave her mom, he'd also decided to leave her.

"It's late and I'm tired." Kylie got up and went to the bedroom and unlike earlier, this time she was able to cry.

The next morning Kylie marched into her meeting with Holiday and placed a copy of her mother's e-mail on the table in front of the camp leader.

"See, I told you so," Kylie said. "Now maybe you can just call my shrink and have her tell my mom to bring me home."

The idea of going back home wasn't nearly as life-altering as it had felt a few days ago. There was even a part of her that didn't want to go—but considering she wasn't supernatural, she really didn't belong here, either.

"What's this?" Holiday glanced back at the note, and her eyes widened when she read it. Looking up, she met Kylie's gaze. "Okay, I admit I'm surprised, but it doesn't really change the facts."

"Why not? You told me that only in very rare circumstances would it skip a generation."

"What about the fact that you see ghosts? That you were born at midnight? Or that your brain doesn't read like a human?"

Kylie dropped into the chair across from Holiday. "I could be crazy. Or like you said the other day, just a freak of human nature and dealing with a super-charged ghost."

Holiday nodded and then leaned forward. "Or . . . maybe the people you think are your parents aren't really your parents."

Kylie's mouth dropped open. "Believe me, with the crap that is going on at home right now, I'd love to believe I was adopted, but I've seen pictures of my mom pregnant."

Holiday opened her mouth as if to argue and then shook her head. "Like I said earlier, this is your quest."

"*Was* my quest. I completed it. I found the answer. I'm just a human."

Holiday propped her right elbow on the table and rested her chin in her open palm. Kylie had begun to think of it as the camp leader's trademark mannerism because she always seemed to do it when she was launching into one of her "Is this how you really feel?" speeches.

It reminded her of her shrink, Ms. Day, who did pretty

much the same except hers was to lean back in her chair and nod.

The worst part was that tactic always worked on Kylie, too.

"Are you really sure of that?" Holiday asked. "Do you really want to leave Shadow Falls Camp?"

"Yes. No. I don't know." Kylie dropped her face into her hands for a second. "I mean . . . right now, everyone is with their own kind. Miranda's with the witches, Della's with the vampires. And I'm . . . well, I'm here with you because I don't belong." Kylie felt like a total outsider—a misfit.

"Is anyone making you feel unwelcome?" Holiday asked.

"It's not that," Kylie said.

Holiday let out a deep breath. "I saw Fredericka last night. If there's a problem—"

"No problem," Kylie said, not wanting the she-wolf to think Kylie had tattled. "This has nothing to do with her." And that much of it was completely true.

Holiday looked back at the paper. "Look, I'll make you a deal. Give me . . . no, give yourself two weeks to think this over, Kylie. If you still want to leave then, I'll personally talk to your mother."

Maybe because deep down Kylie wasn't looking forward to going back home to her mom—or, more likely, because she knew she'd miss Miranda and Della—she decided two weeks wasn't such a big deal.

"You got it," Kylie said.

"Great." Holiday stood up. "And since I may only have two weeks, I think it's time we get serious."

"Serious about what?" Kylie asked as Holiday pulled two yoga mats from the closet.

"Ghosts." Holiday spread out the mats on the floor and then motioned Kylie to sit down. "You have to learn to deal with your ghosts, Kylie."

"I just have one," Kylie said.

Holiday arched a brow. "It starts with one. But believe me when I say others will come. As a matter of fact, they already have come. You just don't remember."

Kylie's stomach began to twist into a knot. "What are you talking about?"

"I read in your files that you've been having night terrors."

Holiday's words sank in. "You're telling me that the night terrors are . . . ghosts?"

Holiday nodded. "Right now, they are coming to you when you're asleep. But eventually, if it happens with you the way it did with me, they'll start appearing when you're standing in line at the movie theater, sitting in a classroom, even out on a date."

Kylie recalled the nights she'd awakened feeling completely terrified, but clueless as to what had caused it. Chills crawled up her spine. "I just want to learn how to turn them off."

A frown appeared on Holiday's face. "That's your choice. But let me put it to you like this. To reach the cut-off switch, you have to pass through a place where spirits like to hang out."

"Is it like a one-time-only switch? Once I cut it off, I won't be bothered again?"

Holiday shrugged. "That depends."

"On what?"

"On how badly a spirit wants to talk to you." Holiday sat down on the mat. "Have you ever done any form of meditation?"

Kylie shook her head.

"Have you heard about out-of-body experiences?"

"No." And she preferred to stay in her body, thank you very much. "So are you saying ghosts can just keep turning my switch back on even if I don't want them to?"

"A powerful one can." Holiday motioned for Kylie to sit on the mat. "Or you can just hear them out and see what they want. The latter works best for me. Now, let's practice some meditation techniques."

The next four days passed in a blur. Kylie tried to talk Della and Miranda into taking a hike to the falls, but neither of them wanted any part of it. It appeared that if Kylie wanted to see the falls, she was going to have to go by herself. There was only one little problem—the thought of facing dancing death angels by herself scared the crap out of her. So she decided to stop fixating over seeing the waterfalls. It wasn't as if she didn't have other things to fixate about. Things like Della and Miranda's persistent bickering. They continued to fight at least once a day. And Kylie continued to break them up before one of them murdered the other.

Kylie spoke with her mom every morning and night, too. When Kylie didn't call her, her mom took it upon herself to call Kylie. The fact that her mom did call made Kylie more aware that her daddy didn't. She told herself it was simply a male thing, that most men didn't call unless they had something to say.

Besides, she'd see him Sunday, which was tomorrow. A fact her mother had been a tad upset about. But please, her mom had been the one who told her to ask if he was coming.

And Kylie was glad she had. She really wanted—needed—to see her dad. And for some reason, probably because she missed him so much, the closer Sunday came, the closer Kylie was to forgiving her dad. Hopefully, by tomorrow her dad would have missed her enough that he would agree to let Kylie live with him when her two weeks were done at camp.

Kylie ate up about sixty minutes talking and texting Sara, who amazingly had completely recovered from her pregnancy scare and was now back in full swing with her new boyfriend—a nineteen-year-old cousin of one of her neighbors.

If Kylie read Sara's innuendos correctly, the two of them would be having sex in the near future. Kylie had come so close to reminding her friend what she'd just gone through, but at the last minute, she lost her nerve. That or she simply decided that saying it would accomplish nothing other than to push her best friend further away.

Sara never excelled at taking advice.

Trey had called twice with the same song and dance. He loved her, he was sorry. If she'd just give him a chance he'd prove how much he loved her.

Kylie suspected his "proof" would include their getting na-ked. And the more she thought about it, the more inclined she was to keep her clothes on. She'd even asked Trey if he could just be her friend for the summer. But then he'd freaked out when she'd said another boy's name. What would he do if she decided to move on and go out with someone else? Go off the deep end, she suspected.

Why couldn't Trey be more like Derek? She'd asked the half Fae to be her friend, and other than telling her he had wanted her to kiss him, he had stopped coming on to her.

Oh, he was nice. Always spoke to her, even asked about her problems with her parents. They also talked about Holiday's resentment at both of them for wanting to turn off their gifts. Most days, he would even come and sit with her for at least one of their meals. Nevertheless, everything about his behavior spoke only of friendship.

No more hot lingering gazes up close where she could see the flecks of gold in his eyes.

No more special smiles.

No more feeling his breath on her cheek.

No more touching.

Even when he sat beside her, he always seemed to make sure there was a good six inches of space between them.

The fact that she'd see him sitting shoulder to shoulder with other girls stung like a fire ant.

She ignored the sting and told herself it was for the best. She was leaving in a little more than a week. And face it, the best things weren't always fun.

For example, learning how to meditate, trying to get to the off switch to cut off the ghosts, was turning into an all-time dreaded chore. Holiday had her hitting the mat three times a day. They'd tried burning incense, counting, music, and even visualization, but nothing seemed to help. Kylie's mind refused to find an altered state of any kind.

Holiday stayed forever hopeful, Kylie not so much. "It will happen, I promise," Holiday would say after each failed session.

For Kylie, it was just more proof that she wasn't one of them. Not that she really needed more proof, but still . . .

The only thing that left the slightest bit of a question in her mind was that Soldier Dude wouldn't quit showing up. Kylie told Holiday to send him a message to quit wasting her time. Holiday gave Kylie the pat answer of, "It doesn't work like that."

Kylie had learned to hate that saying.

Almost as much as she hated the daily visits with the ghost.

Thankfully, he hadn't gone spastic on her with the blood games again, but just seeing him was starting to give her the heebie jeebies. The way he looked at her, the way he stood, it was eerily familiar. Kylie convinced herself that Holiday had been right. Her night terrors had probably been filled with images of him, hence the reason seeing him gave her an odd sense of déjà vu.

Holiday had even suggested Kylie try talking to him, but that idea totally creeped Kylie out. She got this mental image of him opening his mouth only to have worms or blood ooze out. Nope, she'd keep her mouth closed and pray he did the same.

Thankfully, the last few days she'd pretty much managed to stay out of Lucas's and Fredericka's way. But every morning when she waited to see who drew her name in the Meet Your Campmates Hour, Kylie would hyperventilate, worrying one of them would get it.

And today was no different. If they did draw her name, Kylie had already decided to fake a bad headache and beg off.

Sure, Fredericka would probably accuse Kylie of being afraid of her. But best to have her accuse Kylie of it than to have her know it for certain. And if Kylie had to spend an hour alone with the she-wolf, Fredericka would for sure smell Kylie's fear.

Kylie stood between Miranda and Della watching as the campers drew names and announced their companions.

Kylie knew Miranda was praying that Chris, a really cute vampire, would draw her name. Della never seemed to care who got her name, but yesterday Kylie had seen the way the sneaky vampire kept eyeing Steve, one of the shape-shifters.

When Kylie asked Della about it, she denied it, but Kylie noticed Della's cheeks had actually gotten a little color in them. Who knew a vampire could blush?

Derek walked up beside Kylie. "Hey." She smiled. And yeah, maybe her smile was a little wider than normal.

"Hi," he said rather matter-of-factly, and then focused on the campers drawing names. With his attention not on her, Kylie let her gaze move over him. He wore a light green T-shirt that fit tight across his chest. Kylie remembered resting her head against him. She recalled with clarity how good it had felt, and how when she looked up, his lips had been so close to hers.

Blinking, trying not to let her mind go there, she shifted her gaze away from his chest. He wore khaki shorts that hit almost to the knee. His legs were a bit hairy but not at all skinny. She was moving her gaze up when she noticed the Band-Aid on the middle of his elbow joint.

She reached over and pulled his arm closer. "Is this . . . is that . . . You gave the blood?"

"Yeah." His eyes met hers and for the first time in days he

didn't instantly look away. They were having one of those moments that she'd missed.

She gently ran her finger over the Band-Aid. "I'm sorry."

"For what? You didn't do anything."

"Did it hurt?" she asked.

"No." He continued to gaze down at her and it felt like there was no one else in the world but them. She saw the gold flecks sparkle and darn if she didn't want to lean even closer.

"Derek!" a very hyper voice called out. "I got your name!"

Suddenly, Derek was yanked away. Kylie looked up and focused on the yanker—Mandy, a cute brunette fairy.

Kylie watched the girl wrap her arms around Derek's neck and pull him down for a fast kiss. At first, Kylie waited for Derek to look shocked at the girl's show of affection. Instead, he glanced at Kylie for a mere second and then refocused on Mandy, who then stepped up on her tiptoes and kissed the boy again.

And Derek didn't look surprised at all. He looked . . . he looked happy. Then he smiled at Mandy—the same "special" smile he shared with Kylie.

"Great. Are you ready?" Derek asked the too perky brunette.

"Tell me again where this spot is?" Mandy asked.

"How about I just show you instead," Derek answered.

Was he taking her to the creek? Kylie's chest grew heavy. At first, she didn't recognize the emotion and then she remembered feeling it when she saw Trey with his girlfriend at the party. Thankfully, she managed to stomp it down before Derek turned back around.

His soft green eyes met hers. "See you later. Okay?"

"Yeah." She forced a smile on her face that felt about as real as a smiley face. She and Derek were just friends; she had no right to be jealous. And yet . . . why did it hurt so much?

She bit down on her lip. See, this was why she didn't want to start having those feelings for Derek. Because it hurt. Then as if she wanted to punish herself even more, she turned and saw the two of them holding hands and walking away.

"Oh, crappers," Miranda snapped. Kylie turned to look at her, realizing she'd almost forgotten her roommates were even there. Well, Miranda was still there. Della had already left.

"What?" Kylie asked. "Who got your name?"

Miranda made a face. "Not me. *You.*" She gave Kylie an elbow in her ribs. "Or are you telling me you didn't hear who just got your name?"

Chapter Twenty-nine

Kylie swung around and touched her temple, thinking she might as well start faking the headache right now. "Who?"

"Me," came a familiar male voice beside her.

Kylie turned around and faced Perry and then removed her finger. Perry was *not* worth faking it.

"Promise you won't touch my ears," he said, but in his eyes she saw his apology.

"Fine, but don't go turning yourself into anything. It freaks me out."

"You're no fun," he answered, but Kylie noticed he stared mostly at Miranda.

"Yes," muttered Miranda, glancing back at Kylie. "Chris got my name. Wish me luck," she said, and then reached up and let her hair down.

"Good luck," Kylie said, and noticed the frown on Perry's face.

"So where do you want to go to talk?" Perry asked, his gaze

latched on Miranda and Chris as they walked away. Kylie had never seen such a sad-eyed shape-shifter.

"I don't care where we . . ." The idea hit with the subtleness of a dump truck. It was wrong. Oh, so wrong, but she couldn't help herself. "I know just the place by a creek bed."

The next day Kylie stood in the dining room at ten o'clock sharp, waiting on her dad. She had her spiel practiced, knew exactly how she was going to approach the subject of her moving in with him. And it was so much easier that she'd thought it would be.

Last night, her mom had announced that she'd been given a promotion, but it would require some travel. Hence, it simply made sense that Kylie would stay with her dad. Not that she'd told her mom. Nope, that could wait until later.

Derek walked through the dining hall doors. When he spotted her, he came over. Kylie felt her face flush remembering how she'd taken Perry to the rock expecting to find Derek and Mandy there, doing God only knew what. But nope, Derek hadn't been there. So Kylie had simply walked past the big rock and taken Perry into the woods another half mile before they stopped to visit.

Plain and simple, she hadn't wanted to taint the memories of where Derek and she had really gotten to know each other.

And while she'd felt loads better knowing he hadn't taken Mandy to their special place, Kylie wasn't stupid enough to think that it didn't mean he'd taken Mandy somewhere else to do . . . God only knew what. Nor was she stupid enough to blame him for it. How could she when Kylie herself had been the one who'd asked to be just friends? And yet . . .

"You're here early." Derek offered her a friendly smile.

Kylie couldn't help but wonder what kind of a smile he'd offered Mandy when they'd been alone. Had he kissed her? Had he ever taken her to the rock? "Dad said he'd be here ten o'clock sharp."

"So is your mom going to come later?" he asked.

"No," Kylie said. "Mom doesn't want to chance running into him. The world would end if they had to see each other."

"Sorry about that. That has to be tough." He said it with such concern that her heart dipped a bit. All last night she'd watched him and Mandy laughing, sitting shoulder to shoulder. She ached to go back in time and stop herself from telling him she just wanted to be friends. Then again, considering she was probably going home soon, maybe it was best.

"Is your mom coming?" Kylie asked, liking that he'd trusted her enough to tell her his past. *Had he told Mandy anything?*

"Afraid so," he said. "She's a tad overprotective. Has been since . . ."

"Your dad left?" Kylie asked, and lowered her voice.

He nodded and right then, the front doors opened and in came several sets of parents, along with some more campers.

"There she is," Derek said. "I'd better go."

"Good luck," Kylie said, and unable to stop herself she reached over and gave his hand a squeeze. Touching him felt right and . . . wrong. The tingles traveling up her arm were not those that should come from a friend. He stopped moving away and stared at her.

His smile seemed extra warm. "You, too."

Kylie watched him go and admitted that she was going to miss him. Heck, she was going to miss Miranda and Della, too. She wouldn't miss their bickering, but she'd miss them.

Shaking herself out of the melancholy, she tried to find her dad in another group of parents as they flooded in.

Kylie didn't see him, but she did see a set of parents that had to be Della's. A Euro-American woman stood with an Asian American man, scanning the crowd. Knowing that Della hadn't expected them for another hour and had stayed at the cabin, Kylie walked up to the couple.

"Hi, I'm Kylie. Are you Della's mom and dad?"

"Yes, where is she?" the woman asked.

"She wasn't expecting y'all so early. If you like, I can get someone to run to the cabin."

"Is she still in bed?" the dad asked. "My God, I thought this camp was supposed to straighten her out." He looked at his wife. "I'm going to ask for the results of the drug tests. If they don't have them, I'm taking her out of here and placing her in a better facility."

Kylie tried not to react to the harshness of the man's tone. But on the inside, she gave thanks for her dad. So what if he hadn't shown up at the police station, and maybe he should have come to see her before she was packed off to camp, but without a doubt, Kylie felt certain he was loads better than Della's grumpy dad.

"Oh, she's awake," Kylie said, knowing it was probably a lie, but wanting to protect Della from his demeanor.

Giving the room another check for her dad, she said, "I'll tell you what, I'll run and get her."

She walked slowly to the door and took off in a dead run to get Della up and dressed.

An hour later, Kylie sat at the back of the dining hall watching everyone else visit. She'd gotten Della up and to the dining hall in record time. And on the way Kylie had stopped in the office to see Holiday and warn her about Della's father wanting to see drug tests.

Kylie gazed at Della now, sitting and chatting with her sister, while her parents sat stiffly listening in. From the distance, the visit didn't appear to be going well. Della had been tied in knots about seeing them, and after hearing her father's temper, Kylie couldn't say she blamed her.

Miranda's mom and dad showed up about twenty minutes after Della's. Kylie had never seen Miranda appear so insecure as she did around her parents. She sat with her shoulders slumped over and not smiling. Miranda always smiled and her posture wasn't that of the browbeaten child, but that's how she appeared in their presence. Kylie wanted to march over and tell both Miranda's and Della's parents how happy she was to have them as roommates, but for some reason, it seemed hokey.

Derek and his mom had gotten up to go take a walk. He'd actually brought his mom over to meet her. Kylie had to bite back a laugh when his mom brushed a strand of his hair off his brow and Derek blushed. Guys never liked it when their moms made a fuss over them.

"Hey." Holiday came over to where Kylie sat. "Your dad's not here yet?"

"Not yet. He probably misjudged how long it takes to get here. Mom always was the one who figured out the maps and such. And you know men, they'll drive for hours before they stop and ask for directions."

Kylie knew she was close to babbling but she couldn't help it. Babbling was better than thinking about the possibility her dad simply wasn't going to come.

Holiday grinned. "Men. We can't live with them. And it's no fun living without them."

"Do you have . . . someone?" Kylie asked, even though she didn't know if it was too personal of a question to ask her camp leader. "I don't see a ring or anything."

Holiday shrugged. "Well, sometimes no fun is better than putting up with them."

"So you're divorced?" Kylie asked.

"No, we never made it to the altar. I had the ring, had the date, and even the wedding dress. An hour before the wedding, I realized I didn't have my fiancé."

"That must have sucked," Kylie said.

"Yeah, it did."

"Did he ever tell you why?" Kylie asked.

"He said he met someone more compatible. Another vampire."

"Oh goodness, it's not Burnett, is it?"

Holiday's eyes widened. "No. Why would you think . . ."

"He likes you," Kylie blurted out. "Everything time you aren't looking, he's looking at you."

"Please, that man's so arrogant, I'd never . . ."

"He's good-looking," Kylie said.

"I know, damn it." Holiday sighed. "I hate him for it, too."

They both laughed.

Holiday looked over at Della and her family. "Thanks for giving me the heads-up. Her father is a real handful."

"I know," Kylie said. "It made me realize how lucky I am. Wait till you meet my dad. He's not like that."

"I'm looking forward to it," Holiday said.

Kylie knew Holiday was hoping she could take a look at her dad and pronounce him supernatural. Not that Kylie believed it. Her dad wasn't gifted. Well, he was, but not that kind of gifted.

Kylie sighed and looked up at the door and wished he'd hurry up. She needed one of his hugs in the worst way.

Her gaze shifted back to Della and she wondered if her dad ever hugged her. "Do you think Della should go live with other vampires?" Kylie asked Holiday.

Holiday sighed. "It's really hard for a new vampire to coexist with normals. Especially if they live with someone who is controlling. But Della really cares about her family, and leaving them is going to be tough, too. I'm afraid either path she chooses is going to be really hard."

"I hate that," Kylie said, her heart hurting for her friend.

Right then the doors opened. Kylie held her breath waiting to see if it was her dad. Instead, in came Lucas Parker with an older woman. Kylie watched how Lucas caringly held the woman's arm. "Who is that?" Kylie asked.

Holiday looked up. "Lucas's grandmother."

Kylie hadn't considered the probability of running into

Lucas's parents. The last thing she wanted was for them to recognize her—especially since it was obvious that Lucas didn't. "His parents aren't coming, then?"

"Afraid not. His parents were killed right after he was born. His grandmother raised him."

"Not right after he was born," Kylie said, not thinking before she spoke.

"Yeah, it's terrible." Holiday said, misunderstanding Kylie's comment as heartfelt disbelief instead of an announcement of a fact. "I think the files state he was only a week or two old when it happened."

"Oh." Kylie looked away. Then she remembered what Miranda had said about kids born to rogues. Had Lucas lied about his parents because otherwise he'd have been judged? And was the saying true that if one was born rogue, they died rogue?

"Not again," Holiday said.

Kylie looked up and saw Burnett James walking into the room. He wore a huge frown on his face and she didn't have to be supernatural to know something was very wrong.

Holiday pulled out her phone and dialed a number. She frowned and then dropped it in her pocket. "Why is it half the time when he shows up, Sky manages to be unavailable and I have to deal with him by myself?"

Kylie didn't think Holiday was expecting an answer so she just shrugged and didn't say anything.

"Excuse me," Holiday said. "Looks as if I have another battle to win."

Seconds later, Kylie watched Holiday and Burnett walk out

of the room together. Checking her watch, Kylie considered giving her dad a call and making sure he hadn't had a flat tire or something. Of course, she knew her dad was completely capable of changing a tire, because he spent hours teaching Kylie how to do it.

My girl is never going to be stranded. Kylie smiled, remembering how they'd held a timed tire-changing contest. As the good memories played in her head, she decided she had to forgive him for his recent indiscretions. He'd been too good of a dad to hold a few slip-ups against him. She smiled again, knowing her father would totally agree that she should stay with him if her mom was going to be traveling.

Nevertheless, Kylie wasn't smiling an hour later when he still hadn't showed. With crazy thoughts like car accidents running though her head, she pulled out her phone and dialed his number.

He answered on the third ring. "Hello, Pumpkin," he said.

Her chest eased just hearing his voice. "Hi, Dad? How close are you?"

"How close am I to what?"

Kylie's throat tightened. She recalled his words. *I'll be there at ten o'clock sharp.* "Didn't you remember?"

"Remember what?"

The knot in her throat started crowding her tonsils and her sinuses stung. "It's parents day at the camp. You said . . ." She bit down on her lip and prayed he'd laugh and tell her he was right around the corner.

Only he didn't.

"Damn." She heard him inhale. "Honey, I can't come up there today. I'm up to my eyebrows in paperwork from the office. It's been a crazy week."

"But you said . . ." Kylie jumped up and started walking through the dining room before she completely lost it and broke down in the middle of a room filled with parents.

"I said what?" he asked.

"I gotta go." Kylie closed her phone and shot through the doors seeking a place to be alone. Only she wasn't alone. She felt the cold presence following her all the way to the cabin. Anger and hurt filled her chest so full, Kylie could hardly breathe. Hand on the doorknob, she paused. The cold seemed to press against her back, so she peered over her shoulder.

Not only was he there, but like her, he was crying. Only the tears rolling down his face were the color of blood.

Fear tried to find room in her chest, but her anger knocked it out of the way. "Go away!" she yelled at the ghost. "Leave! Me! Alone!"

Chapter Thirty

The next morning Kylie stepped out of her bedroom and was shocked to find Della typing at the computer. Della was never here in the mornings.

"You didn't have an early morning thing to attend?" Kylie asked.

"Not really," Della said. Her mood came off as somber. Actually, all three of them had been pretty somber since yesterday. They hadn't even participated in their usual before-bedtime-chat at the kitchen table. No doubt, after parents day, they all had demons to deal with, and demon-dealing was usually best done solo. Not that Kylie had been alone for a big part of the night.

Soldier Dude had popped in and out all night. She hadn't seen him exactly, but she'd felt his cold presence. She only hoped that she caught on to the whole meditation thing soon so she could put a stop to this.

Della's hands paused on the keyboard and she looked over at Kylie. "I'm sorry if my dad was rude to you. And thanks for coming and getting me like that."

"He wasn't really rude to me." It was you he was rude to, Kylie almost said, but decided Della probably already knew that about him and didn't need to be reminded.

"Yeah, well, he's hard to take sometimes. But believe it or not, he means well."

"At least your dad showed up." Kylie remembered how she'd walked a thin line between lying and changing the subject last night to avoid telling her mom that her dad hadn't come. Her mom would have had a fit if Kylie had told her about his no-show. And her mom's fits weren't pretty. Still, a part of Kylie almost wished she had.

After all, her dad had acted as though he'd never promised to be there.

"Do you want to check your e-mail?" Della asked. "I think you got one from your dad."

Kylie's chest gripped. "No. I'll . . . check it later. *Or not.* Right now she wasn't ready to hear any excuses. Kylie looked around. "Where's Miranda?"

"She's outside. She's hoping to catch a glimpse of Chris but she said she'd wait for us. You ready to go?"

Kylie nodded. "Sure."

Seconds later, she and Della stepped out the door to find Miranda standing at the side of the cabin.

Miranda glanced toward them. "Hey guys, there's a baby bird that looks like it fell from its nest. Oh crappers, I think its wing is broken, too. Poor thing."

Della and Kylie hurried over to join her. Miranda, palms outstretched, had the small bird held up to her face. One of the bird's wings was hanging at an odd angle.

"Can't you just zap it well?" Della asked.

"I wish. But I'm afraid I would . . . screw that up, too," Miranda said, her tone filled with a bit of self-loathing—no doubt a result of her visit with her mom.

Miranda looked at Kylie. "Do you think that girl . . . the one who scanned you for a tumor . . . might be able to heal it?"

"I don't know," Kylie said, and noticed how the bird's eye color had gone from black to blue. Then she noted how the bird stared at Miranda. Call Kylie suspicious if you want, but she'd seen that gaga-look before on a certain shape-shifter's face. She glanced at Della, who met her gaze and then rolled her eyes.

Oh, yeah. It was definitely Perry.

"I think the humane thing to do is break its neck," Kylie said.

"Oh, definitely," Della echoed.

Kylie edged closer. The bird turned his head to peer at her and actually flinched. *That's right, you little twerp, you'd better be afraid of me.*

"You're so cruel." Miranda brought the bird to her breasts, then tucked her chin down to talk to it. "Don't you worry, Miranda's gonna take care of you," she cooed.

"Why don't you check its sex to see if it's a boy or girl?" Kylie couldn't help but snicker.

Miranda's poor-thing expression twisted upside down as she finally caught on to what Kylie was saying.

Miranda glared suspiciously at the bird. "Perry, is that you?"

The sparkles started popping all around Miranda's hands. Miranda jerked her palms from beneath the bird. Landing right on his butt was a red-faced Perry.

"I was just flying by. I didn't . . . I didn't do anything wrong. I wasn't even looking in the windows." His gaze shot to Kylie. "And don't you touch my ears or my neck." He got up and ran off.

"I should turn him into the rat he really is," Miranda said, apparently embarrassed she'd been fooled.

Kylie completely understood Miranda's feelings, then she remembered seeing embarrassment on Perry's face, and she knew why, too. The last person he wanted to look bad in front of was the girl he had a crush on. "You know he likes you, don't you?"

Miranda's mouth dropped open. "No, he doesn't."

Della snorted but didn't say anything.

"Yes, he does," Kylie said. "You should have seen him the other day when you ran off with Chris for the Meet Your Campmates Hour. He looked like a whipped puppy. And the whole time we were together, he kept asking questions about you."

Miranda stood there, her mouth agape. "If he likes me why hasn't he said something? We were even here together last year."

Kylie glanced at Della. "You wanna help me out here?"

"Nah," she said with a grin. "I think you're doing okay on your own."

Kylie turned back to Miranda. "I wasn't here last year, but . . ."

"But what?" Miranda asked.

Kylie shrugged. "I don't think he knows how to tell you he likes you," she said.

"Oh, please. He's not shy."

"He's not shy being a class clown or the class smart-ass. But when you get him alone, he comes off pretty tongue-tied. Honestly, he wasn't half as annoying, either. I personally think the downside of being able to change into anything is the fear that you don't know who you really are."

Kylie stopped and considered her own words. "Gosh, I actually sounded smart right then. Didn't I?"

They all laughed and started walking to breakfast. They were halfway there when Miranda swung around to face Kylie. "You really think Perry likes me?"

Kylie chuckled. "Yes."

Della raised her chin up and sniffed. "I smell loooove in the air."

"I'm not . . ." She paused and then said, "Did you smell it on him?"

"No," Della admitted. "But that's because shape-shifters don't put out the same pheromones. I'm not attuned to what a horny bird smells like."

They all giggled and then started walking again.

"He's cute, though, isn't he?" Miranda asked.

"In a way," Kylie said.

"Maybe a little," Della offered, and then asked, "so, what are you going to do about him?" She placed her hand over her heart to add drama to the question.

Miranda shrugged. "Wait and see if he makes a move."

"Why wait? If you want him, go get him. Don't be a wuss."

"Right." Miranda flipped back her hair and put it up with the band she had on her wrist. "I don't see you putting the moves on any guy."

"That's because I'm not pining over anyone here."

"Liar," Kylie said.

"Please," Della said. "Who do you think I got the hots for?"

"Steve, the tall shape-shifter with sandy-colored hair," Kylie said matter-of-factly. "You couldn't stop looking at his butt the other day."

Della's mouth dropped open and she rolled her eyes. "You are so wrong." She fanned herself with her hand. "But the boy is eye candy to the max."

They all chuckled. "What about you?" Miranda asked Kylie.

"I don't have time to pursue anything."

"You got the same amount of time we do," Miranda said.

"No, I don't." Kylie stopped walking. She hadn't told them about her two-week deal with Holiday, and for good reason. They weren't going to like it. "I . . . Holiday agreed to talk to my mom about my going home after two weeks."

"Why?" both her friends asked at the same time.

"Because I don't belong here. I'm not one of you."

"Bullshit!" Della said. "You just don't want to be one of us. You still think we're freaks. I see it every time the word *blood* is mentioned."

Okay, she might have had a point about the blood.

Kylie still shook her head. "It's not—"

"You can't go," Miranda said, interrupting her. "Who's going to stop Della and me from killing each other?"

"Oh, screw it," Della said, frowning, and looked at Miranda. "Let her go back to her safe little world where the only thing she worries about is if her daddy loves her. If she doesn't want to be friends with us, I certainly don't want to be friends with her. Hell, I didn't like the bitch anyway."

Della shot off so fast Kylie didn't see her go. Miranda stood there staring. "She's just mad. She didn't mean that."

"I know." Kylie bit down on her lip, but Della's words still hurt.

Miranda twirled her ponytail. "I hate to say this, but I don't blame her. I'm mad at you, too." And then Miranda took off.

Just great, Kylie thought. On top of everything else, she'd managed to piss off her two new best friends.

When Kylie got to the dining hall, Miranda and Della were sitting at a different table from where they usually sat. Kylie got the message loud and clear. They didn't want to be near her.

Fine.

Picking up her food tray, Kylie moved to her normal table, feeling a tad self-conscious about being alone. The door opened and Kylie looked up just as Derek walked in. His lips spread into a warm smile, one of his special smiles, that made her heart swell with appreciation. He started walking toward her, and relief filled her chest. She could really use a friend right now.

She continued watching him, suddenly aware that his eyes and smile didn't seem fixed on her. Sure enough, he didn't stop at her table. Kylie counted to ten and tried to wipe the pain from her eyes before she turned to see where he'd gone.

Peeking over her shoulder, she spied Derek cozying up with Mandy, his shoulder fully against hers. Swinging back around, Kylie stared at her eggs and her emotions felt just as scrambled.

She liked him, she didn't like him. What the hell was wrong with her?

Trying to decide whether attempting to eat was a mistake, Kylie heard Della's I'm-pissed voice. Kylie looked up expecting to find Della and Miranda going at it, but she was wrong. Della had her nose in the face of another vampire chick. Then the girl pointed a finger in Della's face and said something in a low voice that Kylie couldn't hear.

Kylie's first instinct was to march over there just in case Della needed reinforcements. Della had stood up for her against the she-wolf, but before Kylie got to her feet, Della took off.

After managing to down at least a half piece of toast, Kylie went out front to find Della. No Della. Instead, some of the other campers were drawing names. She was so not in the mood to chat with someone for an hour, but neither was she in the mood to go back to the cabin where Soldier Dude might appear. Deep down, she sensed that her talking to him yesterday had somehow made him more determined than ever to make contact with her.

She spotted Miranda standing by herself and walked over, hoping she might have gotten over her anger. Unfortunately, Miranda cut her a cold look. Not giving up, Kylie leaned in and asked, "What was the problem between Della and the other vampire?"

Miranda shrugged. "Don't know, she wouldn't tell me. It appears that when she's mad at you, she's also mad at me." Miranda's name echoed from the front and she took off without another word.

Kylie was watching Miranda walk away when she felt someone step beside her.

"You ready?" The deep male voice made her stomach drop.

Kylie glanced up into Lucas's blue eyes. "Ready for what?"

"I got your name." He held up a piece of paper.

And I got a headache. Or PMS. Or bad cramps. Just been diagnosed with the flu. She had to come up with something to get out of this. But with his blue eyes focused on her, the words didn't come out. She looked around the crowd to see if the she-wolf was sizing Kylie up for a casket. Fredericka wasn't around.

"I know a place we can go," he said. His hand came around her back to nudge her along.

She took a step, trying to get the words *I can't* to slip out, but they wouldn't come. And just like that she knew why. She wanted to know if he remembered her. Why it mattered, she didn't know. But it did.

"You seemed interested in the dinosaur tracks." He met her gaze. "I know where there are some more. Why don't we go see them?" He guided her down the path that led toward the cabins, and she followed.

It wasn't until he turned to go down one of the wood trails that Kylie sensed something was different. Then she knew what the difference was. She wasn't afraid of him. When had she stopped being afraid of Lucas Parker? Maybe she was just getting immune to fearing supernaturals as a whole.

Questioning the logic behind her lack of fear, she recalled what she knew about him. He'd been raised by rogues. He'd killed her cat. Was it really smart of her to trust him?

She searched her instincts for anything resembling fear, and nope, it wasn't there. What she did find was the memory of how tenderly he'd helped his grandmother into the dining hall. And then Kylie remembered how he'd protected her from the neighborhood bullies.

"You do know that if your girlfriend sees us together she's going to be pissed, right?"

"What girlfriend?" he asked.

She rolled her eyes at him. "The one who is usually attached to your hip."

The muscle in his jaw tightened. "Fredericka is not my girlfriend."

"Oh, so she's just the girl you make out with behind the office, then," Kylie said before she could stop herself.

His frown deepened. "I figured that's what you thought that day."

"So I was wrong?" Kylie purposely allowed the sarcasm to play in her voice. "Do I look stupid to you?"

He stopped walking and swung around so fast that Kylie bumped right into his chest. He caught her shoulders and set her back. The feel of his hands on the shoulder straps of her white tank top sent heat flashing through her chest. But it faded the moment she saw his angry expression.

"No, you don't look stupid," he said in almost a growl. "But you are making assumptions without all the facts, and that's not a sign of intelligence."

Kylie's mouth dropped open at his insult. "So what was she doing, showing you her new bra? Come on. She was buttoning up her blouse when I stumbled on you guys."

He frowned and pushed a hand over his face. "You're right. I'm sorry I said that." He moved his hand and opened his eyes. "I admit you had a right to jump to that conclusion, but you're still wrong."

She offered him another eye roll.

"She wasn't showing me her bra; she was showing me her tattoo. On her shoulder. She got a wolf tattoo and wanted me to see it."

He started walking again and Kylie followed. "Well, she obviously has a serious crush on you."

"I know." He sounded frustrated. "She and I . . . we sort of hooked up last summer at the very end of camp."

"So she *was* your girlfriend." Kylie stopped moving and glanced at him.

He shook his head ever so slightly. "It wasn't even like that. We . . . met up on a full moon, and . . . it shouldn't have happened. But it did."

Kylie had visions in her mind of two wolves playing leap frog, but not quite leaping, and she felt her face flush.

"We haven't even spoken since camp last year. But she shows up here acting as if we're together. I tried discouraging her."

Kylie pretended to be interested in a bird singing in a tree so she wouldn't have to look at Lucas. "She obviously doesn't discourage very easily, or you've done a bad job of discouraging her."

"Probably both. I've even talked to Holiday about it, because she's driving me crazy."

Kylie started walking again. It wasn't her place to ask, but . . . "What did Holiday say?"

"That I'd probably have to be up front with her. But . . . I don't know, I guess I don't want to hurt her."

That or you just like having a girl hanging all over you and unbuttoning her shirt to show off her . . . tattoo. Kylie knew her last thought might be unfair, but it applied to most boys she knew. Heck, even her dad had warned her that teenage boys were generally after one thing.

Not that she was exactly listening to any of his advice right now.

"If you're that worried about hurting her, maybe you do care about her," Kylie said.

"No," he said adamantly, and then added, "okay, I feel sorry for her. She's had a rough time of things at home, and people judge her too harshly for it."

Kylie, knowing Lucas's past, read more into his statement than he knew. Or did he know? Did he realize she remembered him and that she knew he'd lied to Holiday about having lived with his grandmother all his life?

It suddenly occurred to her that when he'd jerked her aside to ask about what the FRU had wanted with her, maybe he'd been afraid she was tattling on him. Was he still afraid she'd tell?

The slightest hesitation about being alone in the woods with him wiggled through her mind, and that's when she realized they were deeper in the woods than she'd ever gone before.

Deep enough that nobody, not even her campmates with super hearing, could hear her scream.

She brushed a strand of hair behind her ear. "Exactly how far away are these dinosaur tracks?"

Chapter Thirty-one

"Not too far," Lucas said. If he was aware of her sudden insecurity, he hid it well.

"They're actually in a creek bed right outside the property line of our camp," he added without looking at her. "But there's this part of the fence that's been cut that we can slip through."

"I didn't think we were supposed to leave the campgrounds."

His focus shifted from the trail to her. "It's only a few feet off the property. Hey, it's up to you." He came to a complete stop. "You seemed interested the other day on the hike. I just thought . . ."

Kylie swallowed hard and glanced from side to side.

His nostrils suddenly flared as if trying to catch a scent. "You're afraid of me again? Damn, I thought you got over that."

"I have," she stammered, and wondered when he noticed her lack of fear. "I just . . . I'm remembering the snake the other day," she lied.

The suspicion in his gaze faded, and he almost looked

relieved. "Don't worry, I can smell those things a mile away, and I'm faster than any water moccasin." He started walking again.

She followed.

They walked without talking for a few minutes. The woods seemed to swallow their footsteps. His pace was fast, but not so fast she couldn't keep up.

"Have you figured out what you are yet?" he asked.

"No. But there's more than a good chance I'm just human."

He stopped abruptly and looked back at her.

Kylie held her hand up in front of her forehead. "Don't do it. And don't say it. I know I don't read like a human. But frankly, I'm tired of everyone checking out my head. It's as bad as guys staring at my boobs."

The moment the last sentence spilled from her mouth, she wished she could suck it back in, especially when she remembered him checking out her boobs the night she'd passed out.

"Sorry. I guess I can understand how that might get to you. Having us . . . stare at your pattern all the time." He grinned.

And damn if it wasn't the kind of smile that made a girl melt. They stood there studying each other and then it became downright awkward. He finally shook his head and started walking again.

They had walked another forth of a mile when she noticed a Band-Aid on his arm. "Did you . . . give blood?" She pointed to his arm.

"Oh, yeah." He looked at the Band-Aid as if he'd forgotten it was there, ripped it off, and tucked it inside his jeans pocket. "I helped Chris with his drive."

"Chris, the vampire?" she asked.

"Yeah," he said as if it was no big deal. And she recalled Derek acting the same way.

"You don't find it . . . strange?"

He arched a brow. "Strange?" He studied her as if he didn't get her question.

Kylie realized the stupidity of her question. Lucas turned into a wolf. Compared to that, drinking blood probably seemed like nothing.

Then he answered, "People donate blood all the time, Kylie."

"That's to save someone's life," she said, just to prevent the awkward silence.

"And vampires die if they don't drink blood."

Kylie wasn't sure if she'd known that, but hearing him say it had her head swimming. "Can't they survive on . . . ?"

"Animal blood?" he finished her question. "They can and do drink animal blood, but to maintain proper nourishment, they need some human blood in their diet. It's the same as donating to the Red Cross."

Without meaning to, she let her next thought slip out of her mouth. "Sick people don't drink it. It's injected into their veins."

"Does it really matter how it gets into their system? Personally, I don't see the difference."

She gave his analogy some thought and felt small and inconsiderate.

"Aren't you rooming with a vampire?" he asked.

"Yeah." But somehow in her mind she'd separated Della the friend from Della the vampire.

"And she hasn't asked you to donate yet?"

"No." And Kylie knew why, too. Della knew how Kylie and even Miranda felt about the whole blood issue. For some reason Della's angry retort from this morning rang in her head. *You still think we're freaks.*

"All the vampires are supposed to get someone to donate. If they fail, they don't participate in the rituals."

Kylie remembered Della hadn't gone to her regular early morning meeting today—then there was the argument Della had with another vampire. The memory of Della standing up to Fredericka flashed in Kylie head, then came the flash of how she'd protected Kylie from her cousin, Chan. Della had been willing to go the limit for Kylie, but Della hadn't even felt comfortable enough to ask Kylie for blood.

You still think we're freaks.

Della's accusation rang again in Kylie's mind.

Kylie didn't consider Della a freak, but in truth, she hadn't accepted her for who she really was, either. Sum it up and it meant Kylie hadn't been much of a friend.

The realization hurt like a punch to her stomach.

"Is it safe?" Kylie asked.

"What?" Lucas asked.

"Donating blood to the vampires. Is it safe?"

"Of course it is. Holiday wouldn't allow it if it wasn't."

Opening herself up to accepting Della took Kylie down other mental paths. "What's it like?"

He shrugged. "It's just like they do it at a doctor's office."

"Not that. I mean, changing into a wolf. I heard some others say it was . . ." She tried to think how to put it.

"Scary?" he asked, and arched a brow.

"And painful," she answered, deciding not to try to sugar-coat it.

"I think it looks worse than it is." He didn't talk for a few minutes and then started again. "It's sort of like a really sore muscle being massaged. It both hurts and feels good at the same time."

"So it's not like Perry when he changes?"

"No, it's not like that. A shape-shifter's body changes on a whole different cellular level and speed. When we change, you can see the process as the body takes on the new form."

"It doesn't sound fun."

"But it is. It's exhilarating." His eyes lit up and Kylie didn't doubt he was telling the truth.

"And what's it like afterward? When you're changed, do you . . . are you still you?"

"Am I still me?" he asked, not understanding.

"Do you think like a human, or do you think like a wolf?"

"I'm not human, Kylie," he answered. "I'm a werewolf."

She felt her face flush. "I just meant—"

"I know," he said, and let go of a deep breath. "When I turn, I have very heightened senses and instincts. To hunt. To mate. To protect what's mine. They could be called very humanlike instincts. However, in werewolf form the instincts are harder to deny."

So maybe his killing her cat hadn't been out of meanness, but more from his instinct to hunt. Until that thought hit, she hadn't realized she'd been trying to find a way to forgive him.

The silence grew awkward.

"And when you're not turned, what are your gifts?" she asked.

"Heightened hearing, smell, strength, and agility."

"So it's the same as a vampire?" She recalled Della pointing out that vampires were the more powerful species, not that Kylie honestly believed her. Della was biased. Then Kylie suddenly remembered one of Della's gifts. "Can you hear my heartbeat?" *Could he also tell if she was lying?*

"Depends. Our strength and senses increase the closer we get to a full moon. But for the most part, our hearing is tuned to listen for intruders moving in and not so much for things such as heartbeats."

She recalled he'd jumped out of the tree the night of the campfire. It struck her as odd that he could do that but a wolf couldn't. Then again, she supposed there were lots of benefits to having fingers and thumbs.

"The fence is right here." He pushed the loose edge of the barbed-wire fence back, and motioned for her to slip between him and the opening of the wire. "Be careful not to get your shoulders cut."

The gap was small. Kylie squeezed by him and her breasts brushed up against his chest. The warm and tingly sensations shot through her so fast that she started to jerk away.

Before she moved, he must have sensed her tension and he pulled her against him. "Careful." His head lowered and his gaze met hers. They were so close that his nose brushed up against hers. "You're going to cut yourself on the wire."

She nodded and slipped through. The fence could have been wired with electricity for the tingles running through her body.

As soon as she was clear, he stepped through and dropped the wire. Their gazes met again. Somehow, she knew he was thinking the same thing she was—about how close they had been to each other. She could still feel the blood flowing to her cheeks.

"It's this way." He motioned her along, but she saw him take in her face—no doubt she was blushing. In just a few minutes, they got to the creek bed. He studied the water. "The water's up a bit," he said. "Usually, it's only trickling down. The tracks are right across the stream. It's only a foot deep, but you might want to take your shoes off if you don't want them to get wet."

Kylie sat down and removed her tennis shoes and socks and rolled up her jeans. He stood over her and watched. She looked up. "You're not going to take yours off?"

"Wet shoes don't bother me."

She stuffed her socks in her shoes and set them away from the water. The splashing sound of water filled her senses. Looking toward the stream, she asked, "Is the waterfall close to here?"

"It's a mile, but on camp property."

"Have you ever been there?" she asked.

"Once," he said.

"Was it as scary as everyone makes it sound?"

"A little," he said. "But I didn't see any shadows." He chuckled.

Was that because he couldn't see ghosts?

"You ready?" he asked, when she sat there thinking.

"You bet." Standing up, she dipped her toes in the creek. "It's cold." She smiled.

"Yeah, but in the afternoon when the sun is at its hottest, it feels great. Up about a half a mile there's a place that's deep enough to swim in. I try to go there at least once a week."

She got a vision of him swimming, and remembered her dream.

He stepped into the water and reached back and took her right hand in his. She looked down at his fingers locked around hers, her mind still trying to push the image of the two of them standing in waist-deep water, her breasts pressed against his chest.

"The rocks are slippery," he said, following her gaze.

"I think I can handle it." She pulled her hand free.

"When you fall on your ass, you'll be sorry."

"I won't." She smirked at him. But on her very next step, her foot and her pride hit a slick spot and without warning her legs slid out and up and she landed on her butt with a big splash.

"Crap." The cold water soaked through her jeans to her butt. Laughter, very deep and very contagious, rang out. He stood over her, his arms crossed over his wide chest, his blue eyes dancing with humor.

"Stop it." Almost laughing herself, she cupped her hand, caught a handful of the water, and tossed it at him.

He laughed harder, but then offered her his hand. She took it this time.

She was on her feet and went to take another step when she slid again, only this time she didn't go down alone. She landed on top of him, her face buried in his shoulder. She raised her head, and watched the cold water rush over his shoulders. Then she saw him looking down at her, still smiling. And looking good doing it, too.

"That's what you get for laughing at me." She grinned.

His chest expanded beneath her as if he took in a deep breath. And suddenly she didn't even feel the chill of the water—all she felt was the warmth of his body against hers.

"And this is what you get for laughing at me." He pulled her up a few inches until his lips touched hers.

She didn't try to stop him. Oh no, she actually climbed up higher on his chest so the kiss wouldn't be awkward. His hand moved up to the back of her neck. He shifted her head slightly so her mouth was more accessible to his. The slightly rough texture of his shaven cheeks felt wonderful. His tongue moved inside. Slowly at first, then without hesitation. Warmth built inside her and she couldn't seem to get close enough to him. Everything felt different from the kisses and caresses she'd experienced with Trey.

More, her instincts seemed to scream. She wanted more.

She ran her fingers through his damp, dark hair, loving how the strands felt. Loving all the emotions swirling through her, over her, making her feel so alive, so new.

Her breasts pressed against his chest felt fuller, and maybe it was the dream driving her, but she wanted to feel him touch her. It wasn't until she heard voices nearby that she came to her senses. She pulled her mouth from his and pushed up a few inches off his chest. His eyes opened and he stared at her with a hooded gaze. She saw the wildness in his eyes, a hunger like she'd never seen before. More than anything, she wanted to be the one to feed his hunger and taste the wildness. Then the voices drew closer. And right then, everything she felt was just too much.

She moved off him, as unsure of these new emotions as she was of her ability to stand up on her own two feet. "We should . . . I heard . . ." She stood.

"They're not coming this way," he said. He sat up and glanced up at her through his dark lashes. Exhaling, he scrubbed his palm over his face. "Damn," he muttered, then looked back up at her. "I probably shouldn't have done that, should I?"

"Probably not," she agreed, even thought she wouldn't give the moment back for anything.

He slung back his wet hair, sending the drops of water reflecting off the sunlight spinning out. "Then forget it happened, okay? Just forget it ever happened."

"I don't think I can forget." She'd be remembering this kiss and this moment years from now. Because as much as she liked kissing Trey, it was as if this was her very first grown-up kiss. Her first real taste of passion. This kiss, the thing she'd felt was somehow more. And God help her, because while she wasn't ready for "more," she still wanted it. And that, she supposed, was the true meaning of passion.

Aware of the awkward silence building between them, she looked around. "Where are the tracks?"

"There." He pointed her to the edge of the creek.

She moved over there, slowly. Staring down at the prints, she pretended an interest in them. He suddenly stood beside her, casting a long shadow. When she looked up, she caught him staring at her chest.

She glanced down and saw that the water had made both her satin bra and white tank top practically invisible. Her nipples, still tight and tingling, pushed against the fabric.

She crossed her arms.

"You should wear my shirt." He tugged his wet blue T-shirt up. Kylie watched as his shirttail shifted upward, exposing a very hard abdomen. The hem of his shirt inched higher, and she took in the cutest inny belly button she'd ever seen. And then his chest. Solid. Hard. A few drops of water glistened against his skin. Her heart beat to the sound of passion again.

Realizing she stared, she turned away. "Maybe you should just promise not to look and keep your shirt on."

"I *might* be able to do that. But the six guys that are about to arrive in less than thirty seconds might not be so cooperative. Then I'll have to teach each of them a lesson."

"I thought they weren't coming this way?"

"They turned around." He started putting the shirt over her head. She raised her hands and helped him. With the shirt in place, he offered her half a smile. His gaze lowered to her chest.

"Much better." He reached out and brushed a wet strand of hair off her cheek. "You have no idea how beautiful you are, do you?"

The voices were at the bank of the creek now. Not that Kylie cared. Every instinct she had was zeroed in on the man standing in front of her and the compliment he'd just given her.

He made her feel beautiful. He made her feel sexy.

"You ready to head back?" Lucas asked.

She nodded, but right before she turned, she heard her name. "Kylie?"

Damn if she didn't recognize the voice, too.

She looked back to the bank and found herself staring at a very puzzled-looking Trey.

Chapter Thirty-two

"Do you know him?" Lucas asked, his bare arm brushing against hers in a protective manner.

Too stunned to speak, Kylie managed to nod. And then Trey started over, splashing through the water.

"Everything okay?" Trey asked.

He didn't look at her. Instead, he kept his gaze riveted on Lucas. Or rather, on Lucas's bare chest.

"Yes," she said, finally finding her voice. "We . . . we were just looking at the dinosaur fossils."

"Is this Derek?" Trey's tone was full of accusation. Not that he had a right to accuse her of anything, considering everything that had happened between them. But the hurt in his eyes was genuine and it tugged at her heart.

"Trey, this is my friend, Lucas. Lucas, this is Trey."

Both boys stared at each other. Instead of exchanging handshakes, they offered each other cold, unfriendly nods.

"We should go," Kylie said to Lucas, and nodded a good-bye to Trey.

She started walking across the stream. Lucas fell in step beside her. She almost slipped again, but Lucas caught her, bringing her fully against his chest as Trey watched from the other side of the stream.

"Boyfriend?" he asked, releasing his clasp on her waist.

"Ex." She got to the other side and sat down to put on her shoes, but she could still feel Trey watching her. She knew all too well how he felt. The same way she'd felt seeing him and that girl at the party. Poetic justice, just dues, turnabout was fair play—a bunch of emotional qualifiers skipped around her head, but truth was, she felt none of them.

"Why did he ask if I was Derek?" Lucas asked.

"It's a long story." And one she didn't want to share right now. As she tied her shoes, guilt tied knots in her chest. She shouldn't feel guilty.

But she did.

Shoes on, she stood up and started walking, never looking back. Her emotions ran like wild horses in her mind.

Lucas held out the fence again and she slipped through—without brushing up against him this time.

As soon as she knew Trey couldn't see her anymore, she stopping thinking about him and started thinking about the kiss. Needing to feel grounded, she started putting it into perspective. Yes, it had been a good kiss, but it hadn't been more than a kiss.

Right?

They hardly spoke on the walk back. And she hardly looked at him, because seeing him without his shirt was . . . making it hard to think. When they had almost gotten to the camp trail,

Kylie realized she hadn't gotten the one answer she wanted from him. Did Lucas remember her?

She tried to find a way to ask without it sounding as if she wanted him to remember her. As if she thought what they'd shared as children had connected them. It didn't.

How could it, when he'd even suggested she forget the kiss? Her chest began to tighten just a little. God, why did his saying that have to hurt so much?

She took a deep breath. Just add that question to the growing list she'd started since coming to Shadow Falls.

While the rest could probably wait, this one couldn't.

She wanted to know—needed to know—if he remembered her.

Just blurt it out. Just blurt it out. She saw the clearing in the woods ahead and knew her time with him was short. She might not talk to him again before she left.

"You know, you kind of remind me of someone," she said.

"Do I?" He didn't look at her.

"Yeah." She waited for him to ask who.

He didn't ask. Instead he said, "I get that a lot."

They came to the clearing and stepped out on the trail. His gaze met hers. "I have to go. I'm leading another hike." He turned to leave.

"Lucas?" she called after him, and he swung around. She pulled off his shirt and handed it to him. He took it.

She pulled her damp shirt away from her bra. It wasn't completely dry, but no longer as transparent.

She saw his gaze lower to her chest briefly, then he met her eyes.

Do you remember me? "Thanks for . . . showing me the dinosaur tracks."

He nodded. "You're welcome." He hesitated, and then said, "I'm sorry, Kylie."

She knew he was apologizing for the kiss. First, he tells her to forget it ever happened and now he apologizes for it. Her chest clutched.

Then he took off again and Kylie stood there with one thought running through her head. *She wasn't sorry. She wasn't thrilled Trey had stumbled upon them. But neither was she sorry.*

Kylie had just put on some dry clothes when she heard someone come into the cabin. Stepping out of her room, she spotted Della standing by the open fridge drinking . . . something.

Blood. Kylie forced herself to accept it. Her friend was a vampire and vampires drank blood, had to have it to live. It was time for Kylie to face things. "Hey."

"I'm not talking to you." Della screwed the top on the bottle and placed it in the vegetable bin as if to hide it.

"I don't blame you. I haven't been a very good friend."

Della turned around. "Is this your way of saying you're not going to leave?"

Kylie tried to think how to answer that. "I don't know yet. I told Holiday I'd give it two weeks. So I guess I shouldn't say one way or another until then."

Then, before she lost her nerve, Kylie moved in and stretched out her arm, rubbing a finger over her vein in the crease of her elbow. "Do you have the stuff to do it?"

Della's brow wrinkled. "To do what?"

"To draw blood. Derek said that you guys were trained."

"I didn't . . ." Her eyes widened. "I never asked . . ."

"I know, but you didn't ask because you knew I'd say no. Right?"

"That's part of it." Della continued to study her.

"And the other part?" Kylie asked.

"Because you just stopped being afraid of me. I didn't want you to look at me like a monster."

"You're not a monster," Kylie said. "You're just a vampire."

"And you don't see that as a monster?" Della asked.

"Not when I realize it's you."

Della hesitated. "My parents would think I was a monster. Lee would think I'm a monster."

"Screw what they would think," Kylie said. "You're not a monster." She held out her arm. "You need blood to live."

"I can survive just drinking animal blood for the summer," Della said.

"Why should you when I've got extra?"

"You'd really do it?" There was a catch in Della's voice.

"Well, I heard that once you agree to it, you can't take it back," she teased.

"I wouldn't hold you to it."

"I was joking. I want to do it."

"Do what?" Miranda asked, stepping into the cabin.

Kylie looked back. "I'm giving her some blood."

Miranda's eyes widened. "Seriously?"

Kylie nodded. "She offered to fight Fredericka for me. I owe her that much."

Miranda made a face. "Oh, hell, if you're gonna do it, then I've got to do it."

"No, you don't," Della said.

"Yes I do. Because we're a team. All of us."

Della's eyes grew moist. "I don't allow witches on my team."

"Tough titty, vamp," Miranda said. "Because you got one." Miranda held out her arm. "Let's do it. But it better not hurt. I hate needles."

"I can't do it until we get it cleared with Holiday or Sky."

"Then let's go get it cleared," Miranda and Kylie said at the same time.

Right then, a toad, aka Miranda's piano teacher, plopped down at her feet. "Not again," she seethed, and eyed the toad. "Won't you ever learn?" Miranda pointed her finger at the amphibian. "Keep this up and I swear, I'm reporting your butt to the police."

"Maybe you should," Kylie said.

Miranda looked at Kylie. "Yeah, but he never . . . All his offenses could be explained by accidents—trying to show me the right keys on the piano, that kind of thing. The only way I know he was really doing it was because of the spell."

"I'm telling you," Della said, "we should cook his horny ass. Or give him to the werewolves. I heard they love toads."

The toad jumped across the room and then faded into thin air. Kylie got curious. "When he pops in here, is he disappearing from wherever he is?"

"Yup," Miranda said. "But except for the first time, it's happened when he's alone. Or at least that's what I think when I peek into where he ends up when he goes back. I think he gave up teaching piano lessons."

"Well, at least that's good," Kylie said.

Miranda's eyes grew round as if she just remembered something. "Is it true that Lucas got your name this morning?"

"Yeah," Kylie admitted.

"Oh, shit." Della pushed Kylie into a kitchen chair. "Start talking. What happened?"

Miranda dropped into a chair. "Yeah, spill it."

Kylie did spill it. It all rolled off her tongue so fast she couldn't stop it. And not just about the kiss. She told them about Lucas living next to her, about her cat. She told them about the amazing kiss and about the whole mess with Derek and Trey—including her mixed-up feelings for Derek after he'd moved on without giving her so much as a second glance. When Kylie finally shut up, Della and Miranda sat there, their eyes wide and their mouths hung open in disbelief.

"Damn," Della said.

Miranda leaned back in her chair and sighed. "I wanna be kissed like that. I'm so ready to be swept off my feet."

"That's easy," Della said. "Why don't you go find Perry and lay one on him?"

Miranda shook her head. "Please, if the guy doesn't have the balls to even tell me he likes me, he's not going to have the balls to kiss me."

"Then put a spell on him to make him grow a pair," Della said.

They all laughed. And then Kylie's phone began to ring. She glanced at the caller ID and saw her dad's number on the screen. Her laughter faded into a frown. And then, just because she didn't want to let anything ruin the mood, she reached down and turned off the ringer and then slipped the phone back in her pocket.

The next day and a half flew by. It helped that there were no more bouts of drama—no surprise visits from Trey, no confrontations with Fredericka, not even any arguments between Miranda and Della. They had donated blood and it felt right.

And then night fell.

Kylie woke up in a cold sweat. She sat up in her bed, knowing the ghost was here. Then Kylie realized she wasn't in her bed. She wasn't even at camp.

Her heart raced as she tried to make sense of her surroundings. She knew she wasn't in Texas anymore. Not even in the United States, for that matter. It felt . . . foreign and yet somehow familiar, like images she'd seen in the Gulf War movies her mom loved.

Kylie stood outside of a small house on a plot of land devoid of trees and grass. It was hot. Not Texas hot, more dry desert heat. The sun had set and the time seemed caught between light and dark. The smell of burning rubber and wood, of devastation, filled her nose. Plus there was noise. So much noise. It was as if someone suddenly turned up the volume because the noise around her was deafening—there were screams and loud pops—bombs echoing off in the distance. Gunshots. Someone was yelling for her to follow them. "It's not our problem," the male voice screamed.

What's not my . . . She heard the wailing—a woman, Kylie realized. A woman screaming for help, screaming in pain.

Fear climbed up Kylie's spine and she knew whatever was happening to the woman was terrible. And unjust. Kylie didn't want to be a part of it. Didn't want to see it, didn't want to know about it. Too ugly. *Not my problem.*

What was not her problem? Confusion filled her mind.

It's a dream. Just a dream. Wake up. Wake up. She tried to remember how Dr. Day had taught her to stop the dreams, but she couldn't. She closed her eyes really tight and opened them, hoping she'd be back at her cabin.

She wasn't. Somehow she'd moved closer to the house and to the screams. The woman was in the house. Someone hurt her. Who? Why? What did it all mean? Why was Kylie here? Why was she stuck in a war movie? Or was it a movie? No, a dream.

Her mind tried to compute the questions. *No time,* a voice deep inside her demanded, *only time to feel, to understand.*

Why did she need to understand?

Her questions faded and she felt completely present in the dream again, in the havoc, in the ugliness of war. She felt an enormous guilt for not wanting to be involved with the woman. If she ran, if she ran right now, she knew she could catch up with the others and get away.

Choices ran through her head. She could live if she left now. But could she live knowing she'd allowed this to happen to the woman?

No. She couldn't. She glanced down at an assault rifle in her hand. Just like the ones from the war movies. She had to stop whoever was hurting that poor woman.

Kylie kicked in the door and aimed her gun at the man hunched over the woman. "Stop it!" Kylie screamed, but it wasn't her voice making the demand. It was a man's voice.

Kylie froze for a second, then she saw that the man had a knife. She saw the woman, her clothes ripped, and blood covering her face and hands, as she scrambled away from her assailant.

The man swung around to face Kylie. He rushed forward, his bloody knife held high. Her finger on the trigger tightened. She saw him fall and felt no remorse for shooting him. He was evil, she knew it.

A young boy came running in the front door. His dark hair and eyes seemed haunted and older than his years. "No!" he screamed when he saw the bleeding woman huddled against the wall. He fixed his eyes on Kylie.

He started yelling something in a language Kylie didn't understand. He pulled a gun from his pants pocket and aimed it. Aimed it right at Kylie.

Pop. Pop. Pop. She heard the shots. She didn't feel them, but she knew she'd been shot—she also knew when she fell to the floor she was dying.

Suddenly, she stood in the corner of the room looking at the boy and the woman. Her gaze shot to the body lying in a heap, the body she'd just left—the person she had been. Soldier Dude. Blood streamed down his face. He reached inside his uniform and pulled out a letter. He brought it to his lips and with his last breath, he kissed the envelope.

Kylie's heart ached for the loss. She didn't know him, but she cared. Cared that he had died. Cared that he had died trying to save someone.

The woman sat up, looked at the dead soldier, and started screaming again, and so did Kylie.

When she woke up, she was still screaming, standing with her back against the kitchen wall in her cabin. Miranda and Della, dressed in their pajamas, stood in front of her, staring.

Kylie let go of her tension and felt herself slide down the wall. Her throat felt raw, her heart raced.

"She's having a night terror," Miranda said from far away.

Kylie wanted to believe it, but no. She'd never remembered the others. This time she remembered. Somehow she knew that this had been more than just a dream. This was how Soldier Dude had died.

Kylie sat there for a good ten minutes, assuring Della and Miranda she was fine. When they finally went back to bed, Kylie returned to her bedroom. Realizing she couldn't sleep, she got dressed and went to see Holiday. The camp leader had told Kylie if she ever needed her, night or day, she could come to her cabin. Kylie was about to find out if Holiday really meant it.

Moving down the path toward Holiday's cabin, Kylie couldn't help but notice how the night seemed void of noise. Not a bird, not even the shuffle of a raccoon. In her mind, she heard the woman's screams again and saw the soldier take his last breath. Tears dampened Kylie's face. She brushed them away, not wanting to be crying when she got to Holiday's cabin.

Suddenly, the dark silence shattered. Kylie heard arguing in the woods. The voices were gone just as quick as they'd begun, though. The hairs rose on the back of her neck. She ignored the fear of the unknown and focused on what she knew. The soldier was dead. He'd died trying to save someone. She kept walking. Holiday's cabin was only another five minutes away.

She took another step, and that's when she felt someone move into place behind her.

That's when she felt the hand grab her arm and jerk her back.

"You shouldn't be out now," the eerily familiar voice snarled.

Chapter Thirty-three

Kylie swung around. It felt as if her heart jumped up and slammed against her tonsils. As soon as she saw it was Sky, Kylie breathed a sigh of relief.

"You scared me," she said.

When Sky's hold tightened, Kylie's relief started to vanish. "I . . . I need to speak to Holiday. She said if I needed her, I could come. It didn't matter what time."

Sky continued to stare, but her grip finally lightened. "What do you need to see her about?"

"I had another bad dream. Only I remembered this one. The ghost was there."

Sky dropped her hold and then stepped back as if she wanted no part of Kylie's ghost. "Do you know which cabin is hers?"

Kylie nodded. Sky motioned for Kylie to continue, and she did. Even so, Kylie felt Sky watching her as she took each step. Kylie wasn't sure why and then it finally hit her that Sky probably thought Kylie was going to or coming from a hookup with a boy.

Kylie stopped in front of Holiday's cabin door and knocked. A few seconds later, the camp leader, wearing a big night shirt, opened the door.

"Kylie?" Layers of concern filled Holiday's voice. "Is everything okay?"

The distress in Holiday's voice opened up Kylie's floodgates again. Tears formed in her eyes and her throat grew tighter. "No." Kylie shook her head side to side. "It's not okay."

Holiday pulled Kylie inside and wrapped her in a solid hug. Kylie allowed herself to be held by someone who seemed to understand. When the hug ended, Kylie told her, "I think I know what the ghost wants from me."

When the sun rose, Kylie still sat on Holiday's sofa, going over and over the dream. The camp leader confirmed what Kylie had suspected. It hadn't been a normal night terror, but an out-of-body experience. The ghost had brought Kylie into his last memories. Holiday agreed that Kylie could be right, that the ghost might have been accused of committing the crime he'd died trying to stop, and now he wanted someone to let the world know he wasn't the villain. Nevertheless, Holiday also said that it was seldom that easy.

"Do you think he's going to try to do this again?" Kylie asked, hugging her knees. While she wouldn't deny that she had a newfound respect for the man, even found her heart grieving for him, she didn't want to do this again. Every time she remembered that woman's screams, remembered pulling the trigger to kill the woman's attacker, she felt sick.

Holiday squeezed Kylie's hand. "I don't think ghosts realize it's as hard as it is on us. They can be relentless at times."

Kylie shook her head. "I can't do this, Holiday. I'm not brave enough." Her insides started shaking again.

Holiday sighed. "You're doing fine. And I'm here whenever you need me, Kylie. Why don't you go to your cabin and get some sleep? Take the day off and just rest."

"What if it happens again?"

Holiday reached for a pad of paper. "I'm giving you my cell number and if you need me, I'm just a phone call away."

Isn't that what her father had said? But another hug from Holiday and Kylie almost believed her.

Around noon, Miranda and Della brought Kylie some lunch. "You didn't have to do this," Kylie insisted, and picked at the pizza.

"You donated blood. I'm obligated to you for life," Della teased.

"What about me?" Miranda asked. "I gave blood, too." She held up her arm to show off the Band-Aid.

"Yours wasn't that good," Della teased, and then she looked at Kylie again. "Derek asked about you at breakfast this morning. He said he needed to talk to you about something."

Kylie sighed. With everything else, did she even have it in her to start thinking about Derek? "Did he say what it was about?"

"No, but he looked serious."

"Oh," Miranda added, "you missed the excitement, too. You know Chris, the vampire? He and that blond werewolf—I think his name is Nathan—they got in a fight. Sky had to break it up."

"There was blood all over the place," Della said. "And it smelled so good."

"Why were they fighting?" Kylie popped a piece of pepperoni into her mouth.

"A reason?" Miranda asked. "Everyone knows vamps and wolves don't get along. Especially the males." Miranda shot a glance at Della, who was already frowning.

"Not true," Kylie said. "Lucas even gave blood to Chris. They're roommates."

"And some of the vampires didn't want him to take it," Miranda said.

"Why not?" Kylie asked.

Miranda shrugged. "Stupid prejudices. One of them said they didn't want to be indebted to a dirty dog."

"That's just a stupid rumor," Della said. "I don't know if anybody really said that."

"Yeah, but that's what everybody's saying happened. Oh, and guess what else you missed?" Miranda started twisting in her chair. "Guess who sat at our table?"

Kylie saw the twinkle in Miranda's eyes. "A bird with a broken wing."

Miranda grinned. "How did you know?"

"Because you've got that goofy grin and started dancing, stupid." Della laughed.

"I don't have a goofy grin," Miranda snapped.

"No fighting. I'm trying to digest my food." A minute later Kylie asked, "Anything else happen?"

"The FRU showed up again," Della said, her voice more serious this time, and then she rose and walked to the computer. "I didn't hear anything, but that tall dark guy was all over Holiday, reading her the riot act about something."

Kylie took a drink of her diet soda and told Della and Miranda what she knew. "So, something is going on, guys. And whatever it is, it's serious. On the second day at camp, Burnett told Holiday that if 'something' didn't *stop* happening, they would close the camp down."

"Close it down?" Della swung around from the computer. "They can't do that. This is what keeps us sane and keeps us from killing each other."

The computer let out an e-mail-alert beep. Della glanced at the computer and then back at Kylie. "You got another e-mail from your dad."

Kylie dropped her pizza, suddenly not hungry anymore. She still hadn't spoken to him. Kylie knew she was wrong to keep dodging him, but so was he. He'd told her he would come to the parents day. Add the fact that Kylie felt he'd also stopped loving her, and the whole daddy subject was just another demon she needed to tame. And she intended to do it. Sometime later. When it didn't hurt so darn much to think about.

"Holiday didn't look happy," Della added. "Especially when they brought Lucas into the office."

Kylie's gut clenched. "They talked to Lucas? What did they say?"

"I don't know," Della said. "But he looked mad enough to kill."

When Miranda and Della left a short while later, Kylie lay back down. But sleep evaded her. And not just because she was afraid a certain ghost would snatch her up for another trip down memory lane. She thought about Holiday and wondered about the mess with the FRU. She wondered about Lucas. Did they find out his parents had been rogue? Did Lucas think she was the one who said something?

Her mind raced and she didn't know which problem to give herself over to, or how to stop thinking about it all.

She'd already logged in about forty minutes talking to Sara this morning, listening to her go on and on about Phillip, the new guy she was seeing. Then Kylie had spoken to her mom and lied like a big dog. *Everything at camp was just peachy.* When Kylie heard a knock on the cabin door, she was thrilled over the distraction.

But not so thrilled when she opened the door and found Lucas standing there. Okay, she was thrilled he was there, but why couldn't she have looked better? She looked like she'd just crawled out of bed, which she had, while he looked . . . great. He stood in her doorway, with one hand behind his back.

She opened her mouth to say something but couldn't even get out a normal greeting. It wasn't just lack of sleep, either. No, it was remembering their kiss.

And how he'd told her it had been a mistake.

"Hi." He grinned as if he knew she was tongue-tied. "Your roommate, the one with the tri-colored hair, said you weren't feeling good."

"Yeah, but I'm feeling better now," she managed to eke out, and then said, "I heard the FRU talked to you?"

He nodded. "It was nothing."

She sensed that was a lie.

"I got you something." He shot her his killer smile.

And darn it if she didn't just melt into a puddle. Holding on to the doorknob, she asked, "What did you get me?"

"I went to town to pick up some stuff for Holiday and . . . I found it." He suddenly looked guilty.

He pulled out his arm, and Kylie expected to see a bouquet of some inexpensive flowers. Not a wiggling, mewing black and white kitten.

Her breath caught.

"I think you should take it. It doesn't like me too much."

Kylie took the kitten and cuddled it against her chest. The thing was so small it almost fit in the palm of her hand. She stroked the feline's forehead and heard the tiny thing purr. Was she dreaming? She had to be, because the kitten had the exact markings of her cat, Socks. The cat he'd . . .

Her gaze shot up to his. "You remember?"

He nodded. "Of course I do." There was a minute of silence. "I should . . . go." He started to walk away and then turned back around and came back to the door. He leaned his arm against the frame and met her eyes. Something about his posture told Kylie whatever he was about to say was serious. "Kylie, I swear, I tried to stop him. It was the first and last time we fought."

"Stop who?" she asked.

"My dad. He was bigger and a heck of lot faster than I was then. But I tried." He took another step back and then pointed to the side of the porch. "The litter box supplies and cat chow are there."

Kylie just nodded. His admission about his dad having been the one who killed Socks had sent a shock through Kylie's system. All these years she'd assumed . . . "Do you want to come in? Help me set it up?"

For a second, she thought he was going to say yes. Then he looked deeper into her eyes and she saw some of the wildness of desire she remembered from the kiss. "I'd better not."

"Why?" she asked, knowing his refusal wasn't just about coming inside. He was saying no. No to the possibilities running through her mind each time she thought about him. No to the possibilities of more kisses, and their getting to know each other for real.

"It wouldn't work." he said. "There's some things going on in my life right now. It's not a good time, believe me."

She couldn't accept his dismissal, not without trying. "You know what they say about waiting for the perfect time, don't you?"

He closed his eyes. "I can't drag you into this, Kylie."

"Drag me into what?"

Opening his eyes, he reached out and passed a finger over her lips. "You are so innocent. And I am so tempted." He dropped his hand. "But I can't. Take care of yourself, Kylie Galen."

His final words sank in and they sounded a lot like goodbye. She reached out and grabbed his arm. "Are you leaving?"

His gaze met hers. He didn't answer her, he didn't have to. She saw it in his eyes.

"Is this about the FRU?" she asked.

He let go of a deep breath. "I can't . . ."

She dropped her hand. "I never said anything about you to them or Holiday. I swear it."

He smiled but it was the saddest smile she'd ever seen. "I know." Tucking both his hands into the tips of his jean pockets, he looked at her. "You know, I didn't think you could get any cuter than you were when you were six. But I was wrong." He leaned down and his lips lightly touched hers. It happened so fast, she barely felt it.

She wanted so much more than that quick compliment and chaste kiss. "Are you leaving?" she asked him again.

He didn't answer. He'd moved off the porch. Kylie stood by the door and watched him walk away. And although he never told her for sure, she knew. She knew Lucas Parker was going to disappear from her life again.

Less than an hour later, Kylie heard someone knock again, or make that pound, on the cabin door. She'd just made it into the living room when the cabin door swung opened with such force it slapped against the cabin wall.

Kylie saw Burnett first, followed by a very unhappy Holiday.

"You don't walk in uninvited," the camp leader seethed.

"He was here. I can smell him." Burnett glared down at Holiday.

"I don't care. You respect my wishes, or I'll take it up with your boss."

"You already have." The vampire's eyes tightened with anger.

"Well, I'll do it again," she said.

"I have to find that kid," Burnett growled. "I don't have time to play nice." The vampire focused his gaze on Kylie.

"Sorry we barged in," Holiday said.

"What's wrong?" Kylie asked. She didn't have to ask who they were looking for.

Burnett took a step toward her. Holiday grabbed him by the arm to yank him back, but he didn't budge.

"Where is he?" Burnett demanded.

"Kylie, have you seen Lucas Parker?" Holiday countered in a calmer voice.

Kylie swallowed. "He came to check on me about an hour ago. But he left."

Burnett leaned his head to the right as if listening to her heartbeat. "Did he tell you where he was going?"

"No," she said. And she was so glad he hadn't. "Why? Why are you looking for him?"

Burnett just stood there staring.

"He's not a bad guy," Kylie said.

Burnett swung around and walked out. Holiday took one step after him and then glanced back at her.

"He's not a bad guy," Kylie repeated to Holiday.

"I have to go," Holiday said. "I'll come by in a little bit."

Holiday shot out, trying to catch up with Burnett. Kylie stood there in the living room and remembered again the day Lucas had popped his head over the fence and told her to make sure she didn't leave her new kitten outside. All this time, she'd considered his words to be an admission of guilt. She'd blamed him unjustly, painted him as some evil individual.

And Kylie wasn't doing that again. In her heart, she knew whatever they were accusing Lucas Parker of, he hadn't done it. And if he had, there had been a damn good reason.

Chapter Thirty-four

"Change back or I'll neuter your ass right now!"

Miranda's warning jarred Kylie awake shortly before three that afternoon.

Not that Kylie wanted to wake up now. For all she cared, Miranda and Della could duke it out this time. Kylie pulled a pillow over her face when Miranda's threat repeated itself in her head.

Neuter? Della didn't have a pair of balls to remove. So who was Miranda threatening?

Oh, no. Socks, Jr.?

"Fine," Miranda's voice rose again. "You asked for it."

"Stop!" Kylie screamed, and shot out of bed just in time to see Miranda holding the kitten and wiggling her pinky at it.

"You were so wrong," Miranda snapped. "It's not me he likes. He was in bed with you."

"No, no." Kylie pushed her hair back and tried not to laugh. "That's not Perry."

"Then who is it?" she asked.

"It's not anyone. It's a real kitten."

"He fooled you again."

"No. He's not fooling me. That's a real kitten. Lucas gave it to me."

"Lucas?" Miranda's eyes widened. "That's what I came to tell you. He's missing. The FRU have been looking everywhere for him."

"I know," Kylie said.

"How do you know?" Della asked, popping into the bedroom.

The kitten let out a pathetic meow. Kylie took the scared feline from Miranda. "Holiday and Burnett came here looking for Lucas earlier today."

"Was he here?" Miranda asked.

"No, he'd already left." Kylie hesitated. "What do they think he did?"

"Beats me," Miranda answered.

Kylie hugged the kitten closer.

"Whatever it is, it must be pretty bad," Della said. "They even brought human cops out to talk to Holiday. He's up to his eyeballs in trouble."

After Della and Miranda left, Kylie sat in the living room floor playing with Socks, when Helen knocked on her door.

"Hey," Kylie said, and asked her to come inside.

"I heard you weren't feeling well."

"It's nothing," Kylie said, wondering if Helen had come to

offer her healing powers. And then she noticed something amiss in the girl's posture, as if the girl wanted to say something but couldn't spit it out. At first Kylie almost worried she'd had second thoughts about Kylie having a brain tumor.

"What's wrong?" Kylie asked.

"It's stupid, really." Helen said. "But . . . I needed some advice."

"From me?" Kylie asked.

Helen nodded. "You see, I kind of like Jonathon, but I don't think he knows I like him. And I've never been good at things with guys. I was hoping maybe you could . . . you know, tell me how to do it."

"Me?" Kylie said, and almost laughed. "Seriously, I'm not the person to come to with this."

Helen looked disappointed. "But I've never even had a boyfriend. And I don't know anyone else I could ask."

Kylie stared at Helen and remembered the girl had gone the extra mile to help her. "I've only had one real boyfriend. And because I'm not . . . flirty, I just went for honesty."

"Like what kind of honesty?" Helen asked. "Because I don't see myself as flirty either."

Kylie shrugged. "It sounds dorky, but I just asked him if he had a girlfriend. When he said no and asked why, I just said that I was sort of thinking that I liked him. I mean, I know so many girls who do the whole flipping hair, giggly thing, and maybe that works best. Then again, honesty worked for me once. Maybe it will work with Jonathon."

And maybe Kylie thought, if she could just figure out what she felt, maybe she would give honesty a try again.

• • •

The next few days were something of a blur. And not a good blur, either. Kylie and Holiday weren't getting anywhere with the meditation. Della and Miranda's bickering was at an all-time high. Trey was calling and leaving long messages on Kylie's phone. Kylie couldn't stop thinking about Lucas. Oh, and her dad had called her mom and told her that he hadn't visited Kylie the last week and that Kylie wasn't answering any of his e-mails or phone calls.

Her mom gave her hell for it, too.

"You lied to me," her mom had accused.

"No, I just let you believe he came."

"Same thing. And . . . and . . . you can't get mad at your dad," she insisted.

"Why?" Kylie asked. "You're always mad at him."

Then her mom got her panties in a wad because Kylie's dad insisted on coming out this weekend. At first, Mom had said she wouldn't come. Now she was back to being furious, and saying she was coming and that they were just going to take shifts visiting.

Guess who she expected to take care of all the scheduling?

Right. Mom expected Kylie to do it.

The only positive thing happening was that Soldier Dude hadn't returned. Kylie wanted to believe he was gone for good. Holiday wasn't convinced, though. Then again, Holiday wasn't in the best of moods lately. When Kylie asked what was going on, Holiday just shook her head and said it would work itself out.

Kylie had also asked Holiday about Lucas. The camp leader

let out a big sigh of frustration and said she couldn't talk about that. Kylie had to bite her tongue to keep from telling Holiday that trust was a two-way street. It would be nice if Holiday wouldn't be so secretive.

The tension Kylie saw in Holiday seemed even more pronounced in Sky, which struck Kylie as odd. Because so far, the werewolf leader seemed immune to the frustration brought on by the FRU's constant visits. Kylie got the impression that Holiday and Sky were having problems.

If that wasn't bad enough, the tension from the two leaders seemed to be having a bad influence on everyone else. There had been another fight, this one between a witch and a fairy.

"Told you witches and fairies don't get along," Miranda had said the day she, Kylie, and Della stumbled upon the fight being broken up by Holiday.

"What are you going to do if I discover I'm part fairy?" Kylie asked Miranda.

"Damn," Della said. "Did you just say what I think you said?"

"What?" Kylie asked, clueless.

"Are you finally admitting that you're not all human?"

With everything else going on, Kylie hadn't given the whole human or not human issue a lot of thought. And strangely enough, it didn't even seem to matter anymore. Okay, that wasn't true. She still wanted to know, but if she did find out she was supernatural it wasn't the end of the world. As a matter of fact, it was the idea that she might not be "special" that seemed to bother her more.

"So?" Miranda asked her.

"I am whatever I am," Kylie said.

Miranda started to say something and Della held up her hand. "Shh."

Kylie and Miranda paused and listened. All Kylie could hear was the background noise from the wildlife park.

"What do you hear?" Kylie asked, almost worried Chan had returned.

"The animals," Della said. "They are seriously pissed."

"At what?" Miranda asked.

"Like I would know," Della said. "But I've never heard them so . . . angry."

Right then, Helen came up beside Kylie and leaned in to whisper, "It worked. I asked if he had a girlfriend and it was just like you said happened to you. He asked me why and I told him I was thinking I might like him. And now, we're going to go on a picnic tomorrow, just to get to know each other better. Thanks."

Kylie gave Helen's arm a squeeze. "That's great. Come by before the date and Miranda can fix your makeup. Won't you, Miranda?" Kylie looked over at her friend.

"I'd love to," Miranda said.

"Thanks," Helen said, and ran off.

Saturday morning, Kylie stood back from the crowd waiting to hear who they'd be paired with for an hour and finished her conversation with her dad. She'd finally given in and called him on Friday. He'd acted like nothing was wrong, never even said anything about not coming last week, or about her not answering his calls or e-mails. He told her he was looking forward to seeing her on Sunday and then he started talking about a trip he was taking to Canada in a few weeks.

Kylie explained that her mom was also coming tomorrow and that they would have to take shifts. Kylie was positive that her dad would tell her that whole shift thing was stupid, that they could both just visit her.

Maybe deep down, a tiny part of her hoped they would both come at the same time, and then, miracles of miracles, maybe they would take one look at each other and decide they'd missed being together.

That's the thing about miracles. They didn't happen that often. Her dad didn't call the shift thing stupid. As a matter of fact, he seemed just as adamant not to see her mom as her mom was not to see him.

"How about I show up after lunch?" he asked. "And I'll call first to make sure she's not there."

Kylie bit her lip to keep from asking him where her real dad was. Every since a divorce had been mentioned, her father had changed. Completely, wholeheartedly. Parents weren't supposed to do that to their kids. She was certain it was written in the parents' rulebook.

"Fine," Kylie said. *And if you don't show up, don't worry. I don't think it will hurt as much the second time.* "Later, then," she said, and closed her phone.

"You ready?" a male voice said from behind her, leaning in close to her ear. "I got your name."

Kylie recognized Derek's voice. She'd managed to evade him all week. Not to be mean, but out of a basic need for sanity.

Her life was already a friggin' mess. She didn't need to add anything else to it. Besides, he had a girlfriend who was probably more than happy to spend time with him.

She turned around. "You already had my name," she said.

"I got lucky a second time." There was something about his voice, as if he worried she wouldn't believe him.

She didn't. "You did it again, didn't you?"

"Did what?" he asked, but she knew darn well that he understood exactly what she meant.

"You traded some more blood for my name, admit it."

He shrugged. "I wouldn't have to if you'd quit avoiding me."

"I haven't been—" She didn't want to lie to him, so she just shut up.

A couple of people walked past and he leaned in. "If you really don't want to go, you know I won't make you."

She looked up and saw the total honesty in his gaze. He hadn't touched her, so she didn't think he'd altered her emotions, and yet . . . everything inside her shifted. How could she have such strong feelings for Lucas and still be angry with Derek because he'd hooked up with another girl? It didn't add up.

Then again, why should it? Nothing in her life made a lick of sense lately.

"I've been worried about you," he said, and his voice sounded so concerned . . . and so warm.

"You mean when you weren't with Mandy?" she asked. And then she wanted to kick herself for acting as if she had a reason to be jealous.

He looked a little uncomfortable. "That's sort of what I wanted to talk to you about."

"I don't do relationship advice," Kylie said.

"I heard you do. Helen said she talked to you about her crush on Jonathon. Miranda mentioned talking to you about Perry. And what's that other vampire's name . . . ?"

Kylie let out a breath. "Fine, for some unknown reason people think I'm Cupid." But she didn't want to play Cupid for him and Mandy.

"Maybe you're related to him," he said, sounding serious for a moment.

Kylie's heart did a tight squeeze. "Could I be?"

"Some supernaturals are descendents of the gods," he said.

"Would my parents have to have been born at midnight? Or is that one of the instances that it could skip a generation?"

He shrugged. "I wouldn't know. But I bet Holiday would. You want us to go find her?" he asked, apparently willing to give up part of his hour to help her get an answer.

"That's okay. I'm meeting with her after lunch."

"So, my possible goddess." He did one of those old-timey bows. "Can I have the pleasure of your company for an hour?"

She grinned at his antics. "If you promise to behave." Or did she want him to?

"That takes all the fun out of it, but I promise." He shot her a sly look and she saw that his eyes were twinkling.

They started walking and he hesitated. "Same place? Or does the thought of the snake scare you?"

"Same place is fine." A nervous tickle did a slow dance down her spine. It wasn't about the snake, but about the memory of how close she'd come to kissing Derek that day.

They walked down the trail in silence. The sun did its

magical thing again of casting sprays of light through the trees. Kylie couldn't help but wonder what it was about being with Derek that made everything feel . . . enchanted.

"Is it you?" she asked as they got to their spot.

"Is what me?" he asked.

She eyed him with skepticism. "Are you the reason that everything feels . . . magical and so vivid? The colors, the smells, the way sun streams in."

"Oh, that's just my charm." His tone came off teasing.

"Seriously?" she asked. "Are you doing this?"

He laughed.

"Stop laughing," she insisted.

He stopped, but he didn't stop smiling. "Okay, seriously, I don't know what you mean. I'm not doing anything. It's just pretty back here."

He jumped up on the rock and held his hand down.

She hesitated and looked at his hand.

"I promised to behave," he said.

She took his hand and he lifted her up. She sat beside him, but not too close.

He pulled a knee up to his chest. His jeans looked well-worn but comfortable, and his T-shirt was a dusty green. It wasn't tight, but snug enough that it showed off the width of his shoulders. It might have been the shirt he'd been wearing when she met him. He looked really good then, and still did. Right then, Kylie wondered how she could have ever compared him to Trey. Derek was so much hotter than her ex-boyfriend.

"So you and your girl are having problems?" Kylie blurted out, trying to change the course of her thoughts.

"You could say that," he answered in a sly voice, and she watched him run a finger across his chin. Her gaze studied his lips and she wanted to taste him.

"What's wrong?" She blinked, ignored the slyness in his tone, and hoped hearing him talk about Mandy would chase off her thoughts of kissing him.

"Well, she thinks I have a thing for another girl."

Kylie felt her stomach tighten. "Do you?"

"No."

Okay, that hurt, but she tried to deny it. Oddly enough, the advice she'd been giving to everyone else, to be honest, seemed almost impossible for herself. Maybe in part because she wasn't even sure what she felt.

"But," he continued, "I think I sort of led her to think that."

"Why?" Kylie asked.

"I hoped she'd be jealous. Maybe appreciate me a little more."

"And how did that work for you?" Kylie asked, believing those kinds of games didn't end well.

"I don't know. Did you get jealous?"

Kylie looked up at him. "I . . . you mean, me?" She shook head. "But you and Mandy are—"

"Friends," he said.

It still wasn't fitting together. "But you . . . she kissed you."

"You obviously haven't ever noticed her in a crowd. She's a serial kisser. I think her parents are French."

Kylie tried to digest what he was saying. Harder yet was digesting what she felt. She liked Derek. Really liked him. And she was attracted to him. Maybe it wasn't the same intensity that she'd felt for Lucas at the creek, but it was real. And in some ways even more real than the explosive attraction she felt for Lucas.

And Derek hadn't left, the little voice in her head said.

"You okay?" he asked.

"Yes. No." She shook her head. "I'm just befuddled." Okay, there. She'd given honesty a shot.

"I know," he said.

She remembered he could read her emotions and really wished he wouldn't. The fact that he figured things out before her didn't feel right. A breeze stirred her hair and a strand got caught in her lips.

He gently brushed the stand back. "I'm just relieved you're not mad at me."

"Give me a few minutes," Kylie said. "It could change. My emotions are all over the place lately."

He grinned.

She felt herself being lured again by his smile. She shook her head. "Derek, I just—"

"Kylie, I didn't tell you this to pressure you. I'm telling you this because I realized how stupid it was trying to make you jealous. It occurred to me that it could totally backfire. What am I saying? It did backfire, because you wouldn't even get within ten feet of me."

She bit down on her lip. "I'm sorry. It's been a crazy week."

"You're going through a lot. That's another reason I wanted to see you. I sensed you're stressed."

What all could he sense? Kylie wondered. Did he sense her stress involved Lucas? Had he sensed she was jealous? Kylie remembered the day she'd seen Mandy kiss Derek.

"You're right. I was jealous of you and Mandy. But I still don't know if . . . I don't think—"

He held up his hand. "I'm fine with being your friend. But I'm not going to lie to you this time. I'm hoping it becomes more. But until it does, I'll respect your wishes."

She looked at him and found herself falling for him a little more. "You can do that?"

"You bet." He leaned back on the rock and put one hand behind his head. The position did wonders for his arms and chest. "Especially now that Lucas is gone," he said, and from his tone, Kylie somehow knew that Derek suspected a lot more than she wished he did.

Chapter Thirty-five

Oh, God. Did Derek somehow guess that she'd kissed Lucas? Could her emotions give that much away? Kylie didn't know. But neither did she want to ask.

So she lay back on the rock and looked up at the trees. The sound of the nearby waterfalls seemed to stir in the trees. Her mind went to the legend for a second, but then Derek's nearness was a much more intriguing thing to think about.

They didn't talk. Derek shifted his arm closer until the back of his hand brushed up against hers. That little touch sent tingles coursing through her body.

"Your mom coming tomorrow?" she asked.

"Of course. She never turns down an opportunity to embarrass me."

Kylie giggled, remembering how Derek had blushed when his mom had straightened his hair. "She loves you."

"She treats me like I'm three." He paused. "Your mom or dad coming?"

"Both," Kylie said. "Or so they say." Her dad had lied once.

"Did you know the world might end if they accidentally have to be in the same room together?"

"Is that what's got you so stressed?"

"Some of it."

He turned his arm over, slipped his hand into hers, and offered her a gentle squeeze. "I care about you. I don't like seeing you upset." His warm hold on her hand tightened again. He'd promised to behave, but she supposed he didn't see holding hands as misbehaving.

She wasn't sure she could call it that, either. She did know it felt good—sort of like a hug. His palm felt warm, not unnaturally warm, but just one person reaching out to another. "I care about you, too."

"Good," he said, and she could almost hear the smile in his voice. They didn't talk for the next few minutes, and then he asked, "Is the ghost another part of what's stressing you out?"

"Yup." Feeling safe with him, she told him about the dream she'd had of the ghost, and how she thought the ghost wanted her to help exonerate him of a war crime he didn't commit.

Derek listened as she rambled. Realizing she'd done most of the talking, she asked, "Do you still want to turn your back on your gift of communicating with the animals?"

"Yes. I'm getting really good at tuning them out. Holiday says if I keep this up, soon I won't even notice them. Of course, she says that as if it's a bad thing." He paused. "What about you? You still want to kick your gift back?"

The fact that Kylie had to stop and think about her answer left her a little surprised. "It scares me," Kylie said. "I don't think I'm brave enough to do it. But since the dream, I just keep thinking about the soldier. How brave he was. He knew when he went back to save the woman that he wouldn't live through it. I wish I knew his name so I could find out if he was accused of doing something he didn't do. And if he was, then I want to find a way to make it right." She closed her eyes for a second. "But you know what's weird?"

"What?" Derek's fingers wiggled in her hers.

"Every time I see him, he looks familiar. Like I know him from somewhere."

"Maybe you do."

"Maybe," Kylie said. "But I've even asked my mom if we had anyone in our family who ever served in the military and she said no."

Derek shifted beside her. "Did Holiday say how a ghost picks the person they attach themselves to?"

"She said it could be all kinds of ways. I could have passed by somewhere his spirit was, or it could be personal."

Derek raised his arm to check his watch. "I hate to be the bearer of bad news, but our hour was up thirty minutes ago."

"That is bad news." She closed her eyes. "Derek?"

"Yes."

"Thank you."

"For what?" he asked.

"For everything." She rolled over and looked at him. And heaven help her, but she wanted to kiss him so bad she could scream. And if the look in his eyes was any indication, she wasn't the only one wanting.

He moved in just an inch. She could feel his breath on the

corner of her mouth. He was so close, she could count his lashes, but it was his lips that tempted her.

"Kylie." The way he said her name made her melt a little more.

"Yes," she managed.

"You're making it hard for me to keep my promise."

"I'm sorry." She almost kissed him then. Almost. But knowing it wouldn't be fair to him, or herself, she didn't do it. Not yet.

The next morning Kylie sat with her mom and watched her check her watch for the tenth time. Kylie couldn't help but wonder if her mom hated being with Kylie so much, or if it was the thought of her dad showing up that made her mom so eager to leave. Probably both.

"I'm so glad it's working out here," her mom said, straightening her tan suit jacket. The color did nothing for her olive complexion and dark hair. It only enhanced what looked to be dark circles under her eyes.

"Your friends seem nice, too." Her mom glanced over to Della and her parents at the table in front of them.

Kylie had introduced her to both Miranda and Della when she arrived. Her mom leaned in. "The hair is a bit much on that one girl. But if you tell me she's not too wild, or doing drugs or anything, I guess I have to believe you."

"She's not wild, Mom," Kylie muttered. Silence followed, and Kylie knew what it would be like living with her mom, dealing with her mom's prejudices and awkward silences. Kylie could feel the chill from across the table. Not a ghostly chill, either.

Or was it?

Kylie shifted her gaze across the room and saw him standing in the corner, staring, crying more tears of blood. Her heart gripped and Kylie really wished she knew his name so she could help him.

"Are you sure we don't have any family in the military?" Kylie asked her mom again.

"Positive, dear." She looked at her watch again. "Your camp leader—what's her name? Holiday? She seems nice, too."

"Holiday is nice," Kylie said, remembering how she'd exchanged glances with Holiday after she'd met her mom and seeing the camp leader shake her head no, as if to say, her mom wasn't supernatural.

"Okay, I guess I should go," her mom said. "Do you want to walk me to my car?"

Kylie spied the clock on the wall. Her mom was leaving thirty minutes early. *So much for mother/daughter quality time.*

"Of course." Kylie got up. As they passed Della and Miranda with their parents, Kylie realized neither of them seemed particularly happy. Tonight's table chat, a nightly ritual, was going to be more like a whine session.

Kylie and her mom walked to the parking lot without talking. Thankfully, the ghost didn't join them. When her mom turned around to say her final good-byes, she reached out and gave Kylie's arm a squeeze.

Kylie's chest tightened as the memory of needing a hug at Nana's funeral came barreling back at her.

"You know, some moms hug their kids."

Shock crossed her mom's face. "Do you need me to hug you?"

"No," Kylie said. *Who wanted a hug you had to ask for?* It was like having to ask for an apology.

"Bye, Mom." Kylie turned around and went back to the dining hall to wait for her dad. She didn't look back and watch her mom drive away, even though she knew her mom would be waving and expecting Kylie to do the same. From now on, no hugs equaled no farewell waves.

Kylie almost didn't recognize him. First, where was the touch of gray lining his temples? Second, his hair was not naturally two-toned. And for sure, he didn't wear it in a spike cut. She wasn't even going to talk about the clothes he wore. Old men should never, ever wear tight jeans.

"Is that him?" Holiday asked.

Kylie wished she could lie and run out the back door, but her dad spotted her across the room and started over to her.

"Is he a supernatural?" Kylie asked, fighting the embarrassment and looking back at Holiday's twitching brows.

"No." She let out a big sigh. "But that doesn't mean—"

"I know," Kylie interrupted.

"How's my pumpkin?" Her dad pulled her into a tight hug. Kylie closed her eyes and tried to forget how he looked and just let herself soak up the comfort of having his loving arms around her. Tears filled her eyes and she swallowed hard, praying she could contain them.

"I'm okay," she muttered, and pulled back. Her sinuses stung, but the tears didn't fall.

"Is this one of your friends?" her father asked, motioning to Holiday.

Kylie looked at Holiday's camp-leader badge and wondered if her dad's dye job had fried his eyesight.

"I wish." Holiday held out her hand. "I'm Holiday Brandon, one of the camp leaders."

"You're kidding me," her dad said. "You can't be a day over twenty. And you don't look like any camp leader I've ever seen." His smile widened and his gaze shifted down Holiday's shapely form.

"No kidding." Holiday eased her hand from her dad's.

Kylie gawked at the man who had been her rock, who had been there through skinned knees, mom arguments, and even boy problems. The reality rolled over her like a dump truck. Her father was flirting. With Holiday. Holiday who was . . . well, at least fifteen years younger than her dad.

"What happened to the gray in your hair, Dad?" Kylie blurted out.

Her dad looked back at her. "I . . . I don't know."

"Well, excuse me," Holiday said, and Kylie could swear she saw a smile appear in the woman's eyes. "I'll let you two visit."

Or not, Kylie thought. She didn't know this man, and she wasn't all that sure she wanted to get to know him, either.

. . .

"He wasn't like that before," Kylie said a little over an hour later, still fighting the urge to cry.

Kylie's dad had stayed less than an hour. Holiday, as if sensing Kylie was upset, asked her to go with her on a run into town to buy some supplies.

"Divorce is hard on people," Holiday said. "Trust me, when my parents divorced, they went totally bonkers, too. Mom even got breast implants and started borrowing my clothes."

"How did you survive?" Kylie asked.

"You just do. Of course, large ice cream consumption helps." Holiday smiled as she pulled into the ice cream shop parking lot. "What do you say? Wanna feed our worries with creamy, sweet, cold stuff?"

Kylie nodded.

Holiday reached for the door. "Follow my lead. First we have to sample at least five flavors each, then we order a triple scoop."

Kylie laughed. "What worries are you feeding?"

"Are you kidding? Do you know how many hours I've been stuck with Mr. Big, Bad Vampire?"

"Burnett," Kylie said, understanding. "Why don't you just say yes?"

"Yes? Oh, no. Over my dead fairy body. He's as irritating, rude, and obnoxious as he is . . . hot."

"So you're in love, huh?" Kylie teased.

Holiday pointed a finger at her. "Keep this up, and you won't get any ice cream."

As Kylie and Holiday fed their faces with everything from

chocolate mint to banana chocolate fudge, Kylie, hyped up on sugar, let a question slip that she normally wouldn't ask. "How do you know you're in love?"

Holiday licked her spoon clean of her cotton candy–flavored ice cream. "You don't ask easy questions, do you?"

Kylie spooned up a bite of butter pecan. "Nope."

Holiday studied her ice cream. "I've thought I've been in love several times. A few times with my heart and even more times with my hormones."

Holiday's answer described Kylie's situation with Lucas and Derek perfectly. Kylie spooned up a bite of ice cream. "And none of those worked out?"

"Nope. That's the tricky thing about love. It walks like a duck, quacks like a duck, and smells like a duck. But after you sleep with it a month or so, or get dumped at the altar by it, it starts smelling more like a skunk."

Kylie leaned forward to ask. "Is this your fancy-dancy way of telling me I shouldn't sleep around?"

Holiday pointed her spoon at Kylie. "Nope, it's my fancy-dancy way of saying you gotta be careful." She leaned in. "Just because a guy rings your bell, doesn't mean you have to toot his horn."

Kylie laughed and so did Holiday.

Holiday stirred her ice cream. "If I could go back, I wouldn't have slept with three of the guys I did. But you can't go back. And the memories. Bad, bad memories are tattooed on my brain." She tapped her spoon against her forehead. "You can't even get them lasered off."

Kylie nodded. She had a few bad memories of her own that she couldn't shake, so she totally related.

When they finished their ice cream, they walked next door to the used bookstore. Kylie happened to catch the title of a book that had been left on a shelf. *Overcoming Dyslexia*. Picking up the book, she flipped through it and wondered if Miranda had ever read it.

She walked over to the counter and asked if they had any other books on this subject. The lady took her to a whole section of books about different disabilities. Kylie selected three more on coping with dyslexia and paid for them.

Holiday was still browsing, so Kylie stepped outside and took in the small town's main street. It was quaint. Antique stores, specialty shops, and even a candy store—the kind of place her parents used to drag her to when she was a kid.

A couple walked past holding hands and Kylie tried to remember if, on any of those trips, her mom and dad had ever acted like they were in love. She couldn't recall ever seeing them holding hands. They always did their own things when they were out. Her dad played golf. Her mom shopped.

Kylie had just moved over to Holiday's van when she spotted another couple step out of the bed-and-breakfast. They were kissing. Not the quick, touch of lips kind of kissing, but tongues moving in and out of each other's mouth like they were in heat or something. The kissing quickly progressed to the butt-grabbing stage. *Find a room,* Kylie thought, wondering if they knew they had an audience or if they even cared. Ahh, but wrong or right, Kylie couldn't look away.

Mostly because alarm bells were sounding in her brain.

There was something familiar about them.

She watched the woman's hands slip into the front of the man's jeans. Kylie's mouth dropped open. Gross. That was so lewd, yet Kylie, now hiding behind the van, still couldn't turn away. When the couple finally parted mouths and the guy turned forward, recognition hit.

Kylie gripped the side of the van, her knees suddenly feeling like jelly.

"Oh, my God."

Chapter Thirty-six

Dad?

Kylie grabbed the door handle to keep herself from falling face-first onto the street. What was her dad doing . . . doing with . . . Kylie's gaze shot to the woman, or she should say, shot to the "girl." Kylie recognized her dad's new assistant whom she'd met last month at a company picnic. The girl was in her third year of college.

Still leaning against the van, Kylie did the math. While math wasn't her best subject, she figured the girl to be about four years older than Kylie herself.

And just like that, Kylie figured out a bunch of things. Like how her father's six pairs of underwear ended up being grilled— how her mom's countless cold-shoulder moments toward her dad suddenly added up to be fair justice.

Realizing the couple had walked to where they might spot her, Kylie moved to the other side of the van. And the cold that followed her around the van told Kylie she wasn't alone. Yet, too emotionally distraught to think about the ghost, Kylie concentrated on not barfing up the triple scoop of ice cream she'd just consumed.

Holiday arrived shortly. "You okay?"

"Great," Kylie lied, too embarrassed, too horrified to give details. Bad enough her father had flirted with Holiday, but to see him with someone who probably still treated her skin for acne, well, it was just too much.

On the way back to the camp, Kylie looked at Holiday. "Do you know what qualifies as justifiable homicide?"

"No." The camp leader laughed. "But if I have to put up with Burnett much longer, I might become an expert. Who are you thinking of offing?"

"My parents." The vision of Kylie's dad groping his assistant filled her head and her chest ached. "Or maybe just my dad."

Kylie waited a few more minutes before she dropped the bomb. "Do you think . . . you could hold off a few more weeks before you talk to my mom about my going home?"

Holiday didn't look at her, but Kylie saw the smile of victory in her profile as she continued to watch the road. "You betcha."

Monday night, almost everyone hung out at the dining hall to watch movies. Kylie, Miranda, and Della had stayed up way too late Sunday night nursing the wounds inflicted by their respective parents. Then Kylie and Miranda went over the books Kylie had bought on dyslexia.

"This won't work," Miranda said, frustrated at just trying to read the first chapter.

"What if I read it to you?" Kylie said.

Miranda looked up at Kylie and her eyes went misty. "You'd do that?"

"You'd do it for me, wouldn't you?" Kylie asked.

"In a snap," Miranda said.

Hence, the two of them had stayed up way too late. So instead of hanging out to watch a movie, Kylie headed back to her cabin.

When she opened her cabin door, the smell hit her and she wrinkled her nose. She obviously needed to clean the litter box. Then Socks, the little ball of fur Lucas had given her as a farewell gift, stuck its head out from under the sofa and hissed.

"Come here, sweetie," she cooed, but dang it if the kitten didn't go deeper under the sofa. Her phone buzzed. Kylie pulled it out of her pocket, saw that it was her mom, and placed the phone on the coffee table and tried to coax the kitten out.

After several failed attempts, Kylie gave up. "Fine, sleep under the sofa." Frustrated and tired, Kylie started pulling her shirt off over her head and went to get her PJs on.

When she reached her dresser, she heel-kicked off her tennis shoes and pulled out her favorite nightshirt. Slipping off her bra, she dropped it on a chair. Then and only then did she raise her eyes to the mirror.

Her breath hitched. It took her mind a second to compute what she was looking at in the reflection. And another second to get friggin' mad.

"Get out of here, you twerp!" She hurried and slipped on her night shirt before turning her full fury on Perry, who had transformed himself into a lion and was stretched out and taking up her whole bed.

"Out!" Kylie seethed.

The lion roared.

Kylie grabbed her boobs beneath the nightshirt and raged, "You finally got a peek at your first set of boobs, didn't you? You are so . . . so pathetic. And don't you think for one minute that I won't tell Miranda about this, either."

She reached down and picked up her shoe and threw it at the beast. "Out!" The animal roared again. "I swear to God, Perry, if you don't sparkle your ass out of here, I'll pin both your ears behind your head and break your neck."

The room's temperature suddenly dropped a good fifty degrees.

"Don't scream," a male voice said. "And don't make any sudden moves."

Kylie's heart slammed against her ribs when she saw the soldier standing beside her night table. It wasn't so much that he was there that had her mentally stammering, it was that he'd spoken to her.

She took in a deep breath. A wisp of steam escaped her lips as she exhaled.

Goose bumps rose on her flesh. She crossed her arms to fight the chill. "The lion isn't real," she managed to say. "It's Perry. He's a shape-shifter."

The soldier wasn't bleeding this time. But the memory of the dream, of seeing him dying on that dirty floor came hurtling back. Her heart ached for him. Now that he was finally talking to her, would he tell her his name? Oddly enough, even mentally referring him as Soldier Dude didn't feel right. He deserved more respect.

"It is real, Kylie," he said as the lion roared again.

She reached for her other shoe and hurled it at Perry.

"Kylie, listen to me." The ghost's voice grew louder, firmer. "That isn't Perry. It's real. And it's dangerous. Don't provoke it. Move to the door. Get out, now."

His words sank in and she stared harder at the lion.

The lion who was not sparkling back into human form.

The lion who stood up and leapt from the bed.

The lion who moved in front of the door and prevented her from escaping.

The lion, who paced back and forth while sizing her up as if trying to decide what kind of sauce he wanted her served with.

Kylie didn't, couldn't, look away from the lion, but she spoke to the ghost. "Okay, the door thing didn't work. Got any other ideas?"

"Stay calm." His words rang the same time the animal roared, sounding angry. Hungry.

"That's kind of hard to do." She shivered, both from the cold and the thought of the lion's teeth ripping open her rib cage.

"He's waiting for you to run. If you stay calm, it will give us some time."

"Time to do what?" she asked. The lion dropped down on the floor and started cleaning his paws. Was he washing up before dinner?

"Time to think of something else," he answered.

Hearing her own teeth chatter, she glanced over at the ghost. "Can't you . . . make him leave?"

"If I could, he would already be gone." Sincerity added deepness to his voice. In spite of her panic, something about the ghost struck that chord of familiarity again. As if she knew him, or maybe as if she should know him.

"What's your name?" She tried to stop shaking, but couldn't.

"Daniel Brighten," he said.

She let the name bounce around her head, trying to find a connection. Nothing clicked. Blinking, she met his blue eyes again, watching as a strand of his blond hair fell across his brow. "Why?" she asked. "Why are you following me around? Is it about how you died?"

"No," he said. "I needed you to know that I didn't have a choice."

Why did he need me to know that? Kylie flipped her gaze from him to the lion every other second. "Do I need to tell someone? Did you get accused of hurting that woman?"

"No."

The lion stood back up and Kylie's breath caught. She looked around for something to defend herself with.

"Don't do that," the ghost said.

"Don't do what?"

"Don't grab the chair."

She gazed back to him. "Can you read my mind?"

"No, you were looking at it."

"I'm scared," she admitted.

"I know, but if you grab it, the lion might feel threatened."

"Yeah, well, I'm kind of feeling threatened, too. The beast is supposed to be next door at the refuge, not in my bedroom." Kylie suddenly remembered Della telling her that the animals sounded angry. Was the lion angry at her now? "How did it even get here?"

"I don't know, but let's worry about that later."

A deep rumble sounded from the lion's chest. Kylie wasn't sure if that was his angry noise, but from where she stood it sure as hell was his scary noise.

"Don't panic, Kylie. He can smell it."

Daniel was right, Kylie decided. Animals, like supernaturals, could smell things like fear. She inhaled slowly. *Think about something else. Think about something else.* Her mind found a topic and she looked at Daniel again.

"Is Nana, my grandmother, in heaven?"

"Of course she is."

"If you can visit me, why hasn't she?" The steam from her lips snaked up to the ceiling.

"I was here first."

"Where were you first?" Her teeth chattered again.

"Waiting until you were old enough to understand. They only allow one spirit to come to you at a time, until you are able to cope."

"Well, they were wrong." She looked back at the lion.

"Wrong about what?"

"I'm not ready to cope yet."

He smiled.

Kylie hadn't meant it to be funny. "So you've actually seen Nana?" New goose bumps started forming on top of the old goose bumps. Kylie knew she would feel warmer if the ghost left, but the idea of being alone with the lion didn't thrill her.

"She is not a woman who can be missed," he said. "Not even in spirit form."

Curiosity struck. "Did you meet her before . . . before she died?"

"A long time ago." His light blue eyes, combined with his blond hair, pulled her in for a second. She studied him. And then it happened.

She saw inside his head. She was doing what all the other supernaturals could do. Seeing his pattern. A tiny thrill ran through her.

Blinking, she continued to look at his pattern. He had vertical lines and then some odd kind of writing, like Chinese, or prehistoric symbols. "You are . . . were supernatural, weren't you?"

The lion let go of another roar. Kylie flinched as the beast stood. "I think he's hungry," she said. "I think I should get the chair now, don't you?"

The ghost didn't answer. Kylie noticed the temperature rising. Oh, shit. Even the ghost feared being eaten alive. Only he couldn't be since he was already dead.

Just as she might be soon if she didn't think of something quick.

Tears filled her eyes. She was alone. All alone. And then the lion tossed his head back and forth and lunged at her.

Chapter Thirty-seven

Kylie shot behind the chair, thinking about using it as a weapon, but when she looked up, the lion had backed up. He poked his face out the bedroom door as if something out there had caught his attention.

Then Kylie heard it, the kitten. The lion took a step out of the bedroom. She could go slam the door, push the bed against the wall.

And listen as the animal ate her kitten alive.

"No!" She rocked the chair back and forth to get the lion's attention. "Come here, you ugly foul-smelling monster."

The lion backed up, growled, exposing his teeth, and shook his mane at her.

For some reason, she thought about the soldier and his choice to die as he went back to save the woman.

I'm not going to die. I'm not going to die.

"Daniel, please come back," she called out, not wanting to be alone.

The cold brushed over her skin again. "Holiday is getting help."

The lion came closer to the chair. New tears filled her eyes. "Don't leave me again, okay?" she begged.

"I won't," he said. "I never wanted to."

"Kylie?" Holiday yelled out from the living room.

The lion charged at the door. "Don't come in," Kylie screamed, and shook the chair to keep the beast's attention in case Holiday didn't hear her.

Kylie heard retreating footsteps. "Burnett is on his way to get a sedative gun," Holiday called. "He's just a few minutes away. Are you safe?"

Safe? She had a lion in her bedroom. But if Burnett was on the way, maybe . . . Kylie started to answer when she heard more voices.

"No," Holiday said.

"No what?" Kylie asked.

"It's too dangerous," Holiday said as if talking to someone else.

Footsteps sounded from the cabin's living room. The lion growled. Derek appeared in the doorway. His soft green eyes met hers, and then shifted to the lion. Fear flickered in his eyes, and she felt the same fear as he did.

The thought she might have to watch the lion attack Derek sent her heart bouncing against her ribcage. "Leave, Derek," Kylie said, trying to sound calm even though she was a breath from screaming. "Listen to Holiday."

"I can do this," he said in a confident voice. "I have the gift, remember?"

Derek took a step into the room. The lion shook his mane and growled.

Derek didn't move. He stared at the beast. Then he started unbuttoning his shirt.

"What are you doing?" she asked, and while the idea of seeing him without his shirt tempted her, this was so not the time.

"He doesn't like how I smell."

"Then for God's sake keep it on so he doesn't eat you."

"It's okay." Derek tossed his shirt back into the living room. He looked even better than she imagined. Then, holding his palms out, he took another step forward. The lion roared, but didn't charge.

Derek took another step. This time, the lion lunged for him, almost taking Derek's arm in his mouth.

"No." Kylie started rocking the chair to get the animal's attention.

"Stop that," Derek ordered.

"It stops him from getting you."

"Kylie, you're making him mad. Trust me, okay? Stop!"

The firmness in his voice got her attention. Soldier Dude stood silent in the corner, so she couldn't stop shivering.

"I'm going to come over to you," Derek said. "I want you stand behind me. Then we're moving out the door. You go through first and I'll shut it. You understand?"

Almost as if the lion knew Derek's plan, he growled and faced Derek, but backed up closer to Kylie. Each step Derek took, the lion took another closer to Kylie.

A urine smell filled Kylie's nose. The big cat's backside hit the chair and knocked Kylie against the wall.

When she refocused, she saw Derek now stood inches from the lion. So close that the beast's mane brushed up against his bare abdomen. Derek's muscles tightened and his upper body appeared hard, almost chiseled.

"Now ease out from behind the chair, Kylie," Derek said.

"Do as he says," Daniel said, speaking up.

Kylie moved her foot and the lion slammed his head into Derek, and almost knocked him down.

Derek rebounded. "Slowly, Kylie," he said, as if he didn't realize the lion could open his mouth and use him for a chew toy. "Slow and easy."

She inched out, afraid to even breathe, and then Derek caught her arm and eased her behind him. She placed her hands on his bare sides. The palms of her hands pressed against his warm skin.

"That's good. Now we're going to do baby steps back until we're out the door. You're doing good. Keep going."

Kylie felt the door's threshold against her heel. Derek reached around to the left for the doorknob, and the lion lunged and swatted his claws at Derek.

Derek's hiss filled Kylie's ears, and she knew the beast's claws had ripped into his skin. "You okay?" she asked.

He didn't answer, just reached again for the knob. The lion roared, but didn't charge this time. Kylie continued to move backward into the living room as Derek slowly followed. As he closed the door, Kylie saw Daniel smile.

"You did it." Holiday rushed inside the cabin. Kylie stood there, hugging herself, her insides trembling, and feeling sick to her stomach.

"Help me move the sofa to the door in case he decides to charge it," Derek said.

As Derek and Holiday moved the sofa against the door, Kylie noticed blood dripping down his hard abdomen.

"You're . . . hurt." Her teeth chattered so hard she could barely talk. She pointed at him and felt a cold sweat drip from her forehead.

"Just scratched," he assured her.

She took the steps separating them and fell against him. She didn't care that she was getting blood all over her favorite nightshirt, either. She dropped her face against the warm wall of skin and muscle and continued to shake.

He wrapped his arms around her. Holiday moved in and placed a hand on her back.

Kylie didn't know which one of the fairies were doing it, or if it was both—she honestly didn't care—but the thousands of tiny pinpricks of panic started to fade. She felt safe and that was all that mattered.

She buried her face deeper into Derek's naked shoulder, loving how he smelled, how it felt to be this close to him.

"Put Kylie down in one of the other bedrooms," Holiday said.

"No. I'm fine." Kylie raised her head, but didn't want to leave the comfort of Derek's arms. She needed this for just a little longer. He was so warm and she was so . . . cold.

Kylie saw Daniel standing behind Holiday. He smiled at her and then faded. "Thank you," Kylie said, hoping he heard her.

"You're welcome," Derek answered.

Kylie looked back to offer Derek his own verbal gratitude, but a loud *whack* stopped her. The cabin door slammed open so hard it sounded like it had cracked. Burnett came barging into the cabin, his eyes glowed red, and he held a big rifle in his hands.

"You promised me that you wouldn't come up here," he seethed at Holiday.

"I changed my mind," she said, not sounding at all remorseful.

The lion roared on the other side of the door and Burnett roared with him. "I'll take care of that first, and then I'll deal with you."

"Yeah, well, good luck with that." Holiday smirked.

Burnett started toward the door. "Wait." Derek set Kylie back. "Let me calm him down so he won't think you are killing him."

At first Burnett appeared doubtful, but then Holiday nodded. "Fine," Burnett said.

Kylie couldn't say she'd offer the beast that much courtesy, but deep down, she admired Derek for doing it.

The two men eased the sofa away from the door. Burnett pressed his ear to the door and then said, "He's on the other side of the room." Then he reached for the knob.

"Be careful," Kylie said.

Derek looked back at her and smiled. "Piece of cake."

"You don't have to stay here," Kylie told Holiday, who pulled a chair beside Kylie's bed about an hour later. The camp leader had personally cleaned Kylie's room to remove the stench of the animal.

Holiday leaned in and whispered, "It's this or I'll get my ass chewed out by Mr. Big Bad and Handsome. So just pretend like you need me until he leaves. Now that they've taken the lion, I don't think he'll hang around longer than a few more minutes." Sitting back in her chair, she bit down on her lip. "Boy, am I glad Derek was around."

Something occurred to Kylie. "Couldn't one of the witches have stopped this?"

"If I could have found them," she said. "They were all out on a hike with Sky. I knew Burnett had just left here to go back to the wildlife park, so I called him."

"What was he doing at the wildlife park?" Kylie asked. Then she said, "What's going on, Holiday? How did the lion get here? Who put it in my room? And don't tell me that it's your job to worry, either."

It didn't appear as if Holiday was going to answer. Her expression turned grim, and she dropped her hands into her lap. "You're going to find out tomorrow, anyway."

"Find what out?"

"Someone is raiding the wildlife park. Killing the very animals the park is trying to save. Most of the animals killed have been on the endangered species list. Of course, the government didn't waste any time blaming us, either. Any strange crime happens anywhere and someone is pointing to the supernaturals."

"They think one of us is doing it?" Kylie asked.

Holiday bit down on her lip. "Not only do they believe it, but as of this afternoon they have proof. At least they think they do."

"So someone here is doing this?" Kylie asked.

"They found a blood trail leading back to our camp."

"But the lion wasn't killed," Kylie said.

"No, but the fact that it was here just makes things worse. Someone had to help that animal escape."

"And someone put it in my room," Kylie said.

"That or it could just be a coincidence," Holiday said. "He could have wandered into any cabin."

"But the cabin door was closed," Kylie said.

"Maybe one of you left it opened. Then he might have hit it and shut himself in."

"Or someone put him here," Kylie said.

Holiday reached out to touch her again, to calm her, and Kylie held up her hand. "I'm okay."

Falling deeper into her pillow, Kylie stared up at the ceiling. "Do they blame Lucas for this?"

Holiday was quiet for a moment. "He's being looked at as a possible suspect."

"I don't believe it," Kylie said. "He's not like that."

"I know, but . . . I can't convince them of that. Especially since Fredericka took off this afternoon."

"She did?" Kylie watched Holiday nod, and she felt the tiniest bit of jealousy. "Do you think she's with Lucas?"

"Knowing her, yes."

Kylie clutched her hands together, accepting she had to get past Lucas, but still refusing to believe he was guilty. "Are they going to try to shut down the camp?"

Holiday's frown deepened. "If they can't get to the bottom of this, they'll try. I'll fight it with every ounce of fairy dust I have in me, but . . . it may take more than me."

Silence filled the room and then Holiday said, "Burnett's going to hold a meeting tomorrow and probably interrogate everyone. I wish I could stop him, but damn it, with all the evidence, I can't even argue with him that it's not one of us. But throwing accusations around in a group of adolescent supernaturals is sure to backfire."

"Do you really believe someone here is doing it?"

"Yeah. Either that or someone is trying awfully hard to make it look like we're doing it."

The door to Kylie's bedroom opened and Burnett stuck his head in. "Are you going back up to the office?"

Holiday's expression changed to fake concern. She rested a hand on Kylie's shoulder. "I'm afraid she needs me. We'll talk tomorrow."

Burnett wasn't fooled, that was apparent by his expression, but he didn't argue, either. Well, as long as one didn't call slamming the door an argument.

"Jerk," Holiday muttered.

"I can hear you," he retorted from the other side of the wall.

Holiday frowned. "I swear, he's this close to me siccing a death angel on his ass." And she didn't try to say that quietly, either.

"I thought you didn't know if they really existed," Kylie whispered after a few minutes. If she'd thought they existed, she would have asked Daniel Brighten, the soldier, to go find one. Then she recalled what Holiday had said about all ghosts being angels. For sure, Daniel had been a big part of what saved Kylie.

She leaned close. "All I have to do is threaten and even big bad vampires usually piss in their pants."

They both laughed and then Kylie said, "He saved me, didn't he?"

"Derek?" Holiday asked. "Yeah, I would say he did."

"No. I mean, Derek did save me, but it was the ghost who told you, right?"

"Sort of," she said. "Because he's attached to you, he can't really communicate with me. But he found someone who could." Holiday reached down and squeezed Kylie's hand. "Nana said to tell you she loves you. But she wished you wouldn't have let them bury her wearing that purple lipstick."

Kylie got tears in her eyes and laughed at the same time. After a few minutes, she said, "I finally did it."

"Did what?"

"I saw into someone's mind." Kylie almost told her it was the ghost's mind that she'd been able to see, but for some reason she wasn't ready to talk about that. It was as if she needed to digest it all first. There were a lot of things she needed to digest.

Holiday grinned. "Welcome to our world, girl."

Kylie's smile was weak, but it was real. "Does that definitely mean . . . that I'm one of you guys?"

"Yup." Holiday brushed a strand of hair from Kylie's cheek.

"When you saw Nana, did you check if she had been a supernatural?"

"I did. She was human." Holiday gave Kylie's hand a squeeze. "How do you feel about this new development?"

Kylie let out a deep breath. "A little scared. A little relieved. Now I just want to figure out what I am."

"You will, Kylie. The answer is here. It always is."

Chapter Thirty-eight

Holiday was right.

Not about Kylie discovering what she was. It had been five days since Kylie had almost been a lion's dinner, and her identity crisis was still alive and thriving.

The thing Holiday had pegged right was Burnett's method of solving the wildlife crimes backfiring. As soon as he announced that someone at the camp was guilty everyone started pointing fingers. The vampires accused the werewolves because most of the animals killed had been from the feline family and everyone knew werewolves hated cats.

The werewolves accused the vampires of doing it because their blood supply was low. The fairies accused the witches because they sometimes used tiger blood in some of their spells. The witches accused the fairies because everyone knew fairies were sneaky little bastards. Someone pointed out that the shapeshifters were known to use wild animals as sport to hunt and conquer them.

Then, the finger-pointing stopped being species-directed and certain unlucky individuals got suspicion slapped on them. Lucas and Fredericka got voted to be the most likely guilty parties. Then Derek's name got thrown in the hat because he could communicate with animals, and everyone knew he didn't want the gift. Then because Kylie was still considered "the weird one" with a strange pattern and a closed mind, her name got tossed into the guilty hat as well.

Kylie had even forgotten herself and went to Della and accused her cousin Chan of being the culprit. Maybe he really was one of the Blood Brothers gang. Della did what Della always did. She got furious.

Tension at the camp was at an all-time high. People had stopped participating in the Meet Your Campmates Hour, and Holiday and Sky were having a hard time just keeping everyone from killing each other.

Then there was the tension between the two camp leaders.

Kylie had walked into the office and overheard them tossing verbal punches. Sky insisted it was time to throw in the towel and close down the camp. Holiday insisted right back that it would be over her cold fairy body before she let them close it down. Sky accused Holiday of being a martyr and unrealistic, and Holiday accused Sky of having lost her faith in the school and of half-assing her job this year.

Kylie didn't know Sky very well, but she knew enough to agree with Holiday. For some reason, Kylie had never warmed up to the werewolf camp leader. In some ways, the woman even reminded Kylie a bit of her mom. Cold, uncaring, and closed-off.

Not that Sky might not have reasons for joining the ranks of the Ice Queen Sorority. It appeared that Kylie's mom sure as hell did.

It was funny how all of a sudden Kylie saw the relationship between her mom and dad differently now. Yeah, her mom was cold, but her dad was a cheater. It sort of became a "what came first, the chicken or the egg" kind of question. A question Kylie didn't have the answer to.

While it still hurt something fierce to think about the divorce, Kylie had decided to try not to make it her problem. Face it, she had enough fires to put out in her own life. Heck, she'd almost become kitty chow. In the back of Kylie's mind, she still wondered who wanted her harmed badly enough to put the lion in her room. The only name that came to mind was Fredericka. But if she believed Fredericka guilty, did that not put more suspicion on to Lucas?

Thoughts of Lucas snuck into Kylie's mind more than she wanted. Now at least when they showed up, they had to compete with thoughts of Derek. He and Kylie hadn't been alone since the whole lion scene, but he sat with her and Miranda and Della sometimes during meals. Every now and then, she'd catch him looking at her with more than friendship, but good to his word, he never put any pressure on her.

Nope, the pressure she felt came from herself. One minute she'd make up her mind to just walk up to him and kiss him. The next she'd find herself thinking about her dad, about Trey, and she'd wonder if giving herself to a relationship was worth the heartbreak that seemed to follow.

And then there was the whole issue of trying to figure out

what she was. For some reason, she felt that once she got that solved, she'd be free to make other life choices.

Kylie walked back into her cabin, stopping to sniff the air for beast smells. Nose still up, she felt her foot being attacked by Socks. Scooping the little fellow up in her hands, she brought him to her face.

Whenever Socks was running amok, Kylie figured the cabin was free of beasts and ghosts. Daniel had only dropped by a few times—each of which would send Socks scrambling under the sofa. Not that Socks had to stay hidden long; Daniel was back to short visits and he'd stopped talking.

"So the coast is clear, huh?" Kylie asked Socks.

"Except for a very happy witch," Miranda said, barreling out of her bedroom to give Kylie and Socks a hug.

"Let me guess," Kylie said. "Perry finally grew a pair and kissed you."

"No," Miranda said. "I'm beginning to wonder if he ever will. But forget about him right now, because I finally did it. Well, with your help, of course."

"You did what?" Kylie asked.

"I got rid of Mr. Pepper."

"Of who?"

"My piano teacher."

"Oh gawd, tell me you didn't let Della cook him."

"No. I figured out what I messed up with the curse, and reversed it. I used those books to help me figure out what I could have gotten backwards—words, letters. It was like a puzzle, but I finally figured it out." She held her arms up in the air in victory. "I'm toad free."

Kylie laughed.

"And . . ." Miranda continued, "the best part is that Mr. Pepper checked himself into a mental hospital."

"Because he has a thing for young girls?"

"No, because he's been dreaming he's a toad, but . . . he confessed to the doctor that he was worried about his attraction to little girls." Miranda laughed. "I sort of dropped in on his first session. But what's important is maybe he'll get some help."

"You did good," Kylie said.

"No. We did good. I wouldn't have done it if not for you. And while I'm not sure I'll ever make High Priestess, I still might be in the running. You're my hero, Kylie Galen."

"And I'm not?" Della asked, walking out of her bedroom.

"Sorry," Miranda said. "You'll have to try harder next week."

Kylie put Socks down so he could attack Della. For some reason, the kitten loved her Donald Duck slippers.

Kylie watched the kitten take swats at Donald's bill and then reality wormed its way into her good mood. "We may not have next week. They really may shut the camp down if they don't find out who is terrorizing the wildlife park. We've got to stop pointing fingers and do something. I don't know about you guys, but I don't want to go home."

"Did something else happen?" Della asked.

Kylie told them what she'd learned when she'd stopped by Holiday's cabin. "They almost snagged the white tiger."

"How?" Della asked. "I thought that vamp from the FRU was guarding the place."

"He is, but someone broke into the lion's fences again, and

while Burnett was investigating that, someone cut the fence to the tiger's cage."

"Poor animals," Miranda said.

"Yeah," Kylie answered, remembering Derek saying the lion that had shown up in her cabin had been confused and scared. "Wait," Kylie said. "Why didn't I think of this before?"

"What?" Della and Miranda asked at the same time.

"I think I know how to get to the bottom of this."

Chapter Thirty-nine

"It doesn't work like that," Derek said ten minutes later, wearing his shirt completely unbuttoned. No doubt Kylie had banged on his cabin door after he was already undressed.

Kylie glanced at his chest and noticed that his scratches were healing. "What do you mean, it doesn't work like that? I thought you could communicate with animals."

Derek closed the cabin door and moved her off the porch as if he was afraid one of his roommates might be listening.

"It's not like I can ask them questions. I hear or, should say, sense their emotions. And not even all of them."

"You said the lion told you he didn't like how you smelled."

"He didn't tell me. He thought it." Derek shook his head. "It won't work, Kylie."

"But it has to." Her throat tightened. "They're going to close down the camp, Derek. I'm just getting a grip on the whole non-human stuff, I can't leave now."

He studied her face for a moment. "I know, but—"

"It's not just about me, either. You've seen what's been

happening at the camp. Everyone is turning on each other. Everyone says the camp is what helps keep peace among all of us. If they think the various supernatural gangs are bad now, think of—"

He put a finger to her lips and she fought the desire to slip her hands inside the opened shirt and hug him. "I'm not disagreeing with you. But I just don't think it will work."

Right then she remembered. For Derek to be able to turn off his gift, he had to continue to shut them out. Yet he'd saved her from the lion. She hadn't even considered his sacrifice until now. How could she have forgotten that?

"I'm sorry." She closed her eyes a second. "It's because of your gift, because you have to stop using it. I forgot—"

"No," he said. "Okay, yeah, maybe a little."

"It's okay, Derek," she said, seeing guilt in his eyes. She remembered that only a few weeks ago she would have eaten worms to send her gift packing. "It's not fair of me to ask you to do this." She turned to leave.

He grabbed her by her arm. "Wait." His gaze met hers. "I was serious when I said it was only a little part of why I'm hesitating. To be honest, I'm this close to saying the hell with it and playing the Tarzan role."

She saw from his expression that he told the truth. "Hey," she said. "That Tarzan role saved my life. Don't belittle it."

"I know, and that's why I'm thinking about accepting it. But this is . . . over the top. It's not like I can sit down and have a chat with the animals. It doesn't work that way."

"How do you know?" Kylie asked. "Have you tried?"

"No, but . . . others have this gift. And if I could actually do that, Holiday would have said something."

"Holiday has said a thousand times that everyone's gift is different. Look, I know you said that so far all you hear are their thoughts, but somehow you communicated with that lion not to make hamburger meat out of us."

"Okay, if by some miracle I can actually communicate with them, it still won't happen. That FRU James guy wouldn't let me near the animals. He had me in the office again today. He thinks I'm involved. He even accused me of doing it to impress you."

Kylie considered going to Holiday right then, but she knew Holiday would worry someone might get hurt and would say no. She tilted her chin back in defiance. "Then we don't ask him to let us in. We sneak in."

"Sneak by a vampire? That's like trying to fool Superman."

"Yeah, but I happen to know what his kryptonite is."

"He has a kryptonite?" Derek asked.

"Yup. And her name is Holiday."

Kylie admitted this might be a long shot, but when it was your only shot, you made the most of it. And that's what she and Derek had done. They had to acquire a little help to pull it off, but she was dang proud of her plan.

Kylie and Derek waited a few hundred yards away from the wildlife park gates, hidden behind some trees. According to Della, that distance would be far enough that Burnett couldn't smell them. Kylie clutched the maps of the park she'd printed off the Internet from the computer in Holiday's office.

Once Burnett was out of the way, getting into the camp was going to be a piece of cake. Well, it was when you had a certain eye-color-changing shape-shifter helping you out. And to make sure they didn't run into any unexpected surprises, Della would make a sweep of the park, and then stand as lookout.

Their biggest concern was if Derek's ability would allow him to learn anything from the animals. He was skeptical.

Kylie wanted to believe in miracles.

Her phone rang. "Done," Miranda said.

Which meant Miranda had managed to get Holiday's cell phone and send Burnett the 911 message, a ruse Kylie knew he would not be able to resist. Helen, gracious enough to help, was right now having a meltdown by the creek that required Holiday's help. The longer Burnett searched for Holiday, the more time Derek would have with the animals.

However, first they needed Burnett to leave. And he did a few minutes later, when he slammed the door to the office and disappeared into the night.

"Looks like he's in a hurry," Derek whispered.

"I think he really cares about Holiday." Kylie's heart pinched with guilt for scaring Burnett. To make up for it, if things calmed down, Kylie might help get the two of them together.

"Ready?" Derek asked.

She nodded. They ran toward the park, knowing the clock was ticking.

Perry had the gate open for them when they arrived. "See

ya." Because his presence might upset the animals, he took off, sparkles falling around him as he transformed into an eagle and disappeared into the dark sky.

"It still freaks me out to see that," Della said, stopping at Kylie's shoulder.

"What did you find?" Kylie asked, knowing their time was short.

"One guard, human—sleeping on the job—in the back office." Della paused. "Are you sure you don't want me to come, too?"

Kylie shook her head. "I think the less people involved, the more likely the animals will communicate with Derek. Go back to the camp and let us know when Burnett heads back. Hopefully in time for us to get out."

Having already studied the maps, Kylie and Derek took off to the section called the "lion's den" first. Lion's den? That so didn't have a good ring to it.

While there were some stars out, the moon, as if stingy with its light, only peered out from behind a cloud every now and then. Even the animal sounds seemed more ominous than usual, or maybe Kylie's perception was warped because she knew they were trespassing—basically breaking the law. Either way, she found herself moving closer to Derek.

"The lions are right around the bend here," he said.

She wasn't sure if it was cat urine or something else, but the stench hit her nose. "I can smell them." The odor took her back to being trapped in the room with the beast. Her emotions started jamming to the tune of panic.

"Relax," Derek said.

The fact that he could read her emotions still unnerved her. "I'm trying."

"There's something I need to know," he said at the same time as a lion's roar rang out.

"What?"

"What are you going to do if we learn that Lucas is behind this?"

"I'll do the same thing I'll do if we discover someone else is behind it. Tell Holiday." She paused. "But that's not what we're going to find."

"You seem really sure he's innocent."

She could feel Derek studying her. "And you seem really sure he's guilty."

"That's because the evidence says he is."

"It's all circumstantial."

"For someone who was scared shitless of the guy, you sure have changed your tune."

Kylie realized where this conversation could lead and she wanted to call it over. "I just want to find out who's doing this and pray it stops them from closing down the camp."

"Me, too," he said.

Feeling a blast of icy wind brush against her, she wrapped her arms around herself.

Derek studied her. "Is the ghost here?"

"Maybe." She looked around and didn't see him. "He's only come back a few times since the lion incident and he never stays but a few seconds."

"Maybe he'll help us out the way he did then."

"Maybe, but I'm hoping we don't need any help," she said, and the coldness left as quickly as it had appeared.

They stopped at the fence. "This is it." Derek peered through the chain-link fence.

"Are they here?" She couldn't see them.

"Yeah. Behind the tree and beside the pond over there."

"Do they know we're here?" Kylie asked.

"Hell, yeah."

She took a small step back from the fence. "How are you going to do this?"

He chuckled. "I was waiting for you to tell me."

"You're serious?" she asked.

"Partly," he said, sounding a tad insecure.

"Okay." She bit down on her lip. "Can you read them?"

"Right now, all I'm getting is that they see us as a threat."

"Why?" Kylie asked at the same time as another wild animal noise—maybe an elephant?—filled the night. "Surely that's not all they're feeling."

"They're males." He snickered. "We don't elaborate on feelings."

"Real cute," she muttered.

"I thought so." He grinned.

"This is serious." She nudged him with her elbow.

"I know." His smiled faded. "I told you I didn't know if this would work."

"Just concentrate," Kylie said. "Ask them what they're afraid of in your mind."

He leaned his head on the fence and closed his eyes. She

watched him. Time crept by, one minute, two. She had to bite her lip to keep from asking him if it was working.

Then thinking if she concentrated, too, maybe it would be better, she moved against his back and placed her hands on his sides. *Why do we scare you? Why do we scare you?* She repeated the question in her mind.

"Kylie?" Derek whispered.

"You getting something?" she asked, hoping.

"I was until . . ."

"Until what?" she asked.

"Until you pressed your breasts against me. And thinking about them beats lion chatter hands down." He chuckled. "You're going to have move back."

She stepped back and gave him a swat on his back.

He laughed, but then went back to concentrating.

She heard a rustle behind the fence. "I think one of them is coming."

"Shh," he said.

She hushed, but when the lion pounced on the fence, she let go of a scream as loud as his roar. Jumping back, heart pounding, she landed on her butt.

"That's the same lion, isn't it?" she asked, staring at the creature who stared at her. She would never forget his eyes, golden and hungry.

Derek didn't answer. He didn't even turn around to offer her a hand up. Then she noticed how he stood frozen, eyes open, staring at the beast as if . . . as if they were having a mental chat.

Staying where she was on the ground, so as not to disturb them, she lifted her hands to dust off the gravel. She hadn't given her hands one dusting when she felt herself being lifted off the ground.

She screamed, and another hand slapped over her mouth.

Derek swung around but before he could even take a step forward, a blond guy had him by the throat, pressing him into the fence. The lion roared behind him.

"Not so loud." The voice didn't sound even slightly familiar. From the coldness of the touch, Kylie knew the person who had her was a vampire, or something equally cold-blooded.

Derek struggled to free himself. The lion's roar grew more threatening.

"What do we have here?" her attacker asked.

Kylie managed to look at him. Auburn colored hair. Red glowing eyes matched his hair. Definitely vampire, she decided, noting his fangs that hung slightly over his bottom lip.

"Looks as if someone is hungry," said Red, the vamp holding her against him. "Bet the kitty would like to eat a young tender thing like you. Problem is, so would I."

"What the hell?" The blond guy who had Derek by the neck yelled out, and then he dropped in a dead faint to the ground.

Kylie noticed the intense look on Derek's face, and she knew he'd done something to the blond. Then Derek's gaze shot to her and Red.

"Get your hands off her," Derek said, his voice hoarse.

Kylie saw him lunge forward, but out of the sky two more guys dropped, each grabbing one of Derek's arms. He struggled.

"Excuse me," Kylie's attacker said. "I think I'll go have a snack." He jumped back at least twenty-five feet, taking her with him. They landed with a thud. Kylie's whole body jarred and she bit the edge of her tongue.

Hard.

She tasted blood as it pooled onto her tongue.

She tried to pull away but the vampire's strength made her feel as capable as a bug against a fast-approaching windshield.

"Oh man, you smell good." The vampire raised her off the ground and turned Kylie's head toward his. "Pretty, too." He studied her for a second as if reading her pattern and then his mouth came down on hers.

She knew he drank her blood and wasn't kissing her, but she wanted no part of it. No part of him.

Fight. Fight dirty. She remembered dating lesson number one that her father had taught her. Pulling back her leg, she let go with everything she had and kneed that bastard in the balls.

She hadn't even considered if vampires had the same weak spot. But the vamp's scream proved they did. However, she could have foregone being tossed through the air like a rag doll. Her back slammed against the fence and she slid down to land with a clunk on the ground.

Everything in her said she needed to stand up, get ready to fight. But unable to breathe, it took everything she had just to open her eyes.

She saw the two vampires who had been holding Derek had fallen to the ground like the one earlier.

"Kylie, you okay?" Derek suddenly appeared standing over her.

"She's mine," said a gravelly voice.

Helpless, Kylie watched the vampire who kissed her snatch

Derek up by the neck, and throw him across the fence and in with the lions.

Kylie heard the lions roaring and envisioned them ripping Derek apart. "No!" she screamed.

The vamp looked at her as if she were the prize in the box of cereal. "What are you?" he asked, and reached down to pick her up.

An enormous cold showered her. Colder than anything she'd ever felt. Icy needles touched her skin, cut through her human tissue, and found its way to her bones. For a second, her arms and legs felt paralyzed.

Then suddenly Kylie was standing. The vamp held someone in his arms. Then Kylie realized he had *her* in his arms. His eyes now glowed an even hotter red.

Oddly enough, she wasn't afraid. She waited for him to get closer, sensing she could deal with him. But not knowing how.

From the corner of her eye, she saw Derek pull himself over the top of the fence.

"I said don't touch her." Derek jumped off the fence at Red.

Red dropped her body and knocked Derek back against the fence. "You don't know when to die, do you?" he growled.

Another dark figure dropped out of the sky and hit Red so hard he fell to the ground. Kylie recognized Della instantly.

Derek turned back to check on Kylie's body, but another dark figure slammed him against the fence again.

Without thinking, Kylie moved forward. She grabbed the vamp holding Derek and slung him away. She watched in a kind of daze as the vamp's body flew thirty or forty feet in the air to land in a patch of woods.

When she looked back, Derek stared right through her.

"Wow, did you see that?" she asked Derek, but he didn't answer.

He joined Della in sparring with the vamp she'd kneed in the balls. The taste of the guy's mouth still lingered on her tongue and she wanted to spit. But first she moved in, found an open spot, tightened her fist, and swung. The vamp flew backwards and landed in a crumbled heap.

Both Derek and Della swung around and stared at each other as if confused.

"Kylie?" Derek screamed.

"Yeah," Kylie answered, but then she watched Derek run over to her body on the ground. He turned her over and for the first time she felt the shock run through her system. If she wasn't in her body, where was she?

Derek screamed her name and then said, "Breathe, damn it. For God's sake, Kylie, breathe." He shook her.

Oh, crap. Was she dead?

Chapter Forty

Looking down at her clothes, Kylie realized she wore army fatigues. She was . . . she was in Daniel Brighten's spirit body again—just like in the dream. *Did that mean she wasn't dead?*

She looked back at her own body and saw that Derek was fighting off two more vamps to keep them away from her. Della swooped in to help.

Remembering she could help them as Daniel's ghost, Kylie took a step toward them. But just like that, she realized she was back in her own body. She pushed herself off the ground, determined not to just lie there. Moving, however, caused her a ton of pain.

Someone else suddenly appeared and fought beside Derek and Della. Kylie squinted at their newest ally.

Sky?

Floodlights flared to life. The night's darkness, along with several of their attackers, scurried away like rats.

Burnett, along with a few other FRU-looking people, seemed to come at them from all sides. They grabbed a couple of the vamps and locked them in handcuffs at both their wrists and ankles.

Derek rushed over to Kylie. "Are you okay?"

She nodded, although her body was hurting in places she didn't know could hurt.

"What the hell happened?" Burnett demanded of Derek. He reached for Derek as if prepared to slap a pair of cuffs on him.

"It's my fault," Kylie insisted. "I made him do this."

"She did not," Derek insisted.

"No, it was my idea." Della surged forward.

"No, they're all lying. It's not their fault." Sky moved in.

Everything seemed to go silent for a long moment, and then Derek spoke up. "Sky planted the blood that you guys found that led back to the camp. She helped those rogues take the animals. But she came to our defense in the end."

Kylie knew Derek had learned this from his mind meld with the lions. The lions had talked to him, just as she'd hoped they would. A tiny bit of happiness about being right swiveled through the chaos of the moment, and she let herself savor it.

"He's telling the truth." Sky held out her arms to be cuffed.

Burnett put the cuffs on her. "Why?" he asked, staring at her as if disgusted.

"They . . ." she said looking at the captives, "have my sister. Threatened to kill her if I didn't help them get the camp shut down." Sky glanced at Kylie. "I could do it when that was all they wanted, but this . . . They promised no one would be hurt. I don't know how the lion got in your cabin, Kylie, I swear. I was told to take the witches out for a hike. I knew they were planning something, but hadn't thought . . . They said no one would be hurt." She shook her head and looked back at Burnett. "I was only trying to save my sister."

"They? Who are 'they'?" Burnett growled, and looked at the two vamps cuffed on the ground. One of them growled at Burnett and fought against the handcuffs. Two of the other FRU men subdued him.

Kylie suddenly realized the red-haired vampire, the one who'd first grabbed her, had gotten away. And for some reason that thought sent chills down her back.

"The Blood Brothers," Sky answered. "The vampire gang."

"And why did they want the camp shut down?" Burnett asked.

"They feel as if the camp is corrupting potential members," Sky answered. "And from what they said, they aren't the only ones thinking it. Most of all the rogue gangs are starting to rebel against the camp."

"Do you know where they're keeping your sister?" Burnett asked, and Kylie heard the slightest hint of sympathy in his voice for Sky's dilemma.

"No. But my father's hired someone to find her."

Holiday came rushing forward. Her gaze shot to Sky wearing cuffs. "What are you doing?" she asked Burnett.

"My job," he answered, and started walking Sky away.

Holiday shot forward. "You let her go—"

"He can't, Holiday," Sky said. "He's right. I screwed up. I'm sorry."

"What are you sorry for?" Holiday asked.

Sky looked back at Derek. "Tell her," she said.

Burnett looked at Holiday almost as if to say something, and then he nudged Sky to start walking.

Holiday looked back at Kylie, Della, and Derek. "Someone better start talking. And fast."

Holiday had a doctor rush to the camp and go over everyone inch by inch. Other than a few scrapes and deep bruises, they were pronounced fine. It was after two in the morning at that point and Kylie's muscles ached like a bad devil and she wanted nothing more than to go to bed. But apparently Burnett had other plans.

Kylie and her partners in crime—for some reason, Helen, Perry, and Miranda had all confessed to being part of Kylie's plan—were told to wait in the dining hall. Holiday and Burnett walked in. Kylie saw the shadows of pain in the camp leader's eyes; no doubt Sky's betrayal had cut deep.

Burnett started the dialogue, or you could call it the chewing down. He referred to what they'd done as stupid and foolish. He told them they were lucky that none of them had been killed. Yada yada yada.

And he was right.

But Kylie would have done it again in a heartbeat.

She sat there and took her punishment like the rest of them. Yes, she knew sneaking into the park hadn't been without some risk, but she hadn't planned on going to war with a vampire gang. All she'd wanted to do was get Derek to the animals so he could possibly get some answers.

Which, by the way, had worked. Not that Burnett mentioned that in his ass-chewing.

"Did you even realize that they had outnumbered you by five? I can't believe . . ." He continued his rant, reminding them they were supernaturals and they were supposed to be smarter than that.

A question popped into Kylie's mind and before she could stop herself, it slipped out of her mouth. "Are you still going to close down the camp?"

Burnett, not happy about being interrupted, frowned. "If this is the kind of behavior we can expect, we have no choice."

Enough. Enough. Enough.

When the word scraped across Kylie's mind the third time, she stood up. "We did the only thing we knew to help."

She hadn't a clue where her assertiveness came from, perhaps exhaustion, but she couldn't seem to stop herself.

"You seem to have forgotten that we didn't plan to get into an out-and-out brawl with a vampire gang. All we wanted was to get Derek close enough to communicate with the animals and find out what the hell had been going on."

"You should have come to us," Holiday said.

While her heart went out to the camp leader, Kylie had a point to make. Since she'd already pissed Burnett off, she might as well keep going.

"Why should we come to you?" Kylie asked. "You didn't trust us enough to tell us what was going on. Yes, we know you're the camp leader, but we're not in kindergarten here. You say we're here to learn how to cope in the outside world but then you try to shield us from anything that might be the least bit unpleasant. And let's say if we did come to you with this, I don't think you'd let us do it because you'd be worried it could be dangerous. And then there's you." Kylie pointed to Burnett.

"That'll be enough," Burnett snapped.

Not hardly. "Even if Holiday had agreed to let us do it, there's no way you would have let Derek in the park because you thought we were all suspects."

"Ditto," Derek said.

"Amen," Della said.

"You go, Kylie," Miranda snapped.

Everyone else in the room nodded their heads in agreement.

"That's not important," Burnett charged.

"Yes, it is." Holiday held up a hand to silence the tall, dark, and menacing vampire. "Kylie's right. I don't like it, but she's right."

Holiday took a deep breath. "I have the tendency to be a tad overprotective." She looked at Burnett. "And you have a tendency to be . . . well, a jerk."

Burnett's expression was a cross between shock and anger.

"I'm just being honest." Holiday glanced back at Kylie and the rest of them. "And to answer your question, Kylie, Burnett has already informed me that thankfully the camp will not be closed down."

Everyone in the room let out a yelp of victory.

"As a matter of fact . . ." Holiday glanced at Burnett as if almost asking permission to continue. He frowned but nodded. "As a matter of fact, Burnett has also just informed me that my request to turn Shadow Falls Camp into Shadow Falls Camp Academy has been granted."

"Like a full-time school?" Kylie asked.

Holiday nodded and Kylie saw her gaze seek out Della. "We're hoping this will help alleviate some of the strain of the newly turned supernaturals who find living with normal parents impossible. It will allow them to maintain contact and hopefully prevent these families from completely severing relationships."

Kylie grinned and glanced back at Della, who appeared as if she might start crying.

"And," Holiday continued, "while it's true, I did just call Mr. James here a jerk, and true, he is one, I'd also like to point out that tonight his boss informed me that . . . contrary to what I thought, he's been a supporter of the school. His boss said he's been our advocate all along. So like it or not—and for the record, I don't like it—he is deserving of our respect."

Burnett had his arms crossed over his chest, staring holes at Holiday. Kylie suspected the camp leader didn't glance at him just to piss him off.

"That said," Holiday motioned for the door, "it's very late and since tomorrow is parents day, we have to be up and at our best in the morning, even if we have to fake it."

Miranda, Della, and Kylie walked out together. "Chan wasn't there," Della said. "I would have smelled him."

"I know," Kylie said.

"Who's Chan?" Miranda asked.

"I'll explain it later," Della said, and then she looked back at Kylie. "When Sky said that she didn't put the lion in your room, she was telling the truth."

"I thought she was," Kylie said. But something about that whole incident still didn't read true. Not that she'd ever really find out.

They started toward their cabin when Kylie saw Derek. "You two go," Kylie said. "I want to say good night to Derek."

"Do you smell those hormones?" Della asked Miranda.

Kylie frowned at Della as they walked away and then she turned to find Derek.

"Hey, wait up," Kylie called to Derek.

He turned around and started moving toward her. When they met in the middle, he was smiling. "I liked how you stood up to Burnett and Holiday," he said.

Kylie shrugged, unsure where she'd gotten the courage to do it, but lately she found herself speaking her mind. She didn't think it was altogether a bad thing, either.

"And I liked how you stood up to the vampires earlier. What did you do? They kept dropping."

He grinned. "Apparently, I have the ability to shock their systems with emotional overload. It was pretty cool, wasn't it?"

"Yeah, it was," she said.

He studied her. "Your ghost was there, too. Wasn't he?"

"Yeah," Kylie said, not really ready to share the whole out-of-body experience thing.

Their gazes met, held. "It worked didn't it?" Kylie said. "You communicated with the animals. That's how you knew about Sky, right?"

He nodded. "Yeah. You were right."

She thought she heard something in his voice—like regret. "Are you upset that it happened?" Like flies on a bad banana, guilt buzzed around her chest. He'd done it for her. "If you are . . . I mean, I'm sorry that—"

He reached out to put a finger over her lips. "You don't need to apologize. I'm glad I did it. To be honest, it felt right. Tonight felt right." He pushed a strand of her hair behind her ear and left his hand there. "We did good. We make a good team."

"You've saved my life twice now. Three if you count the snake." She looked up at him, at his soft smile. His hand touching her neck felt so good. So right. Without thinking, she moved up on her tiptoes and pressed her lips to his.

He wasn't the one who started the kiss.

Nope. She did that.

He wasn't the one who deepened the kiss.

Nope. She did that, too.

He wasn't even the one who moved in closer.

Nope. That would be her.

Not that he seemed to mind.

But he was the one who moved his tongue inside her mouth. Deep inside her, she heard a little voice say, "Oops."

She pulled back. They were both breathing hard. She wasn't sure either of them had breathed this hard when they'd been fighting rogue vampires.

He opened his eyes and looked at her. "Wow."

Kylie inhaled, still trying to catch her breath, trying to clear her head. She stared down at her shoes, because looking him in the eyes right now seemed too much. She hadn't meant that to happen. Or had she?

He ran his finger under her chin and tilted her head up. Damn. He was going to make her look at him. Then he'd probably ask the question she couldn't answer.

"What was that, Kylie? Just a thank-you for saving your life . . . or was it more?"

Yup, that was the question she was afraid he'd ask. "I don't know," she answered honestly. "Maybe just a weak moment."

He laughed. "Do me a favor." He leaned closer.

"What?"

"Whenever you're feeling weak, come see me."

She went to give him a thump in the chest, but he stopped her. He brought her hand up to his lips, his green gaze never shifting from her eyes, and he gently kissed the top of her hand. The moisture of his lips sent a shiver, a wonderful kind of shiver, all the way down her spine.

For some unknown reason, that second kiss wreaked more emotional havoc than the first had. And that's when she noticed how beautiful the sky was. It appeared . . . enchanted. The stars twinkled like something out of a Disney movie. Was Derek doing this? Was he using his gifts and making her see things differently? And did it matter if he was? She didn't have the answer. "I should . . . should probably go. Tomorrow is parents day."

"I'll walk you to your cabin." He arched a brow.

"I'm not kissing you again," she blurted out, before she thought about it.

He laughed. "I bet you will."

She knew he was right, but . . . "Not tonight."

"I figured that. Good thing I'm patient."

Derek's kiss and maybe everything that came before it had helped Kylie not think about seeing her mom—about what she would or wouldn't say about seeing her dad making out in the middle of town. Then there was the other question she had to ask. The question that made Kylie's entire insides twitch.

The question Kylie hadn't let herself think about.

But now, standing in the dining hall, waiting for her mom to arrive, Kylie wondered if she shouldn't have been thinking about it. Face it, some things just weren't meant to be blurted out.

Her mom walked in and Kylie saw her scanning the room for her. Kylie took the second to just notice her mom. Like her brown hair, her brown eyes. Like how Kylie didn't look anything like her. Except for the nose. She'd for certain gotten her mom's little ski-lift nose.

"I almost didn't find you," her mom said as they sat down at one of the least crowded tables. Her mom's butt wasn't on the seat when she said, "You haven't been getting enough sleep, have you, Kylie?"

Was it some kind of mother radar or something that made a mom know these things? "Just restless," Kylie lied.

Her mom leaned over the table and whispered, "You aren't having those dreams again, are you?"

"No," Kylie said.

Her mom cut her eyes in that don't-lie-to-me stare.

"I swear."

"Okay," she said.

"Hello, everyone," Holiday said at the front of the hall. "I know I don't normally address you on these visits but I've got some news I'd love to share. First, I'm sorry to have to tell you that due to family issues, Sky Peacemaker, my co-leader of the camp, has to take an unplanned leave of absence."

Kylie had to admit, Holiday managed to explain it without really lying.

"However," Holiday continued, "we are in the process of looking for a replacement. Until then, we have a temporary—just temporary—replacement. And I'd like you to meet Mr. Burnett James. He comes highly recommended."

Kylie wondered if Holiday knew how telling the second "just temporary" was? The fact that she was going to have to work with Burnett was no doubt eating her alive.

"My second news . . ." Holiday then went into her spiel about the camp becoming a boarding school.

Kylie watched her mom as Holiday did her dog and pony show. She half expected her mom to stand up and applaud and scream out, *Freedom at last, freedom at last.*

Oddly enough, her mom was able to hide her excitement. Kylie felt a shot of guilt scratch across her conscience. How unfair was it that Kylie wanted to sign on full-time to the school, and yet she was going to be pissed at her mom for wanting the same.

After Holiday finished, Kylie looked back at her mom and said, "You want to take a walk? There are some paths through the woods that are nice."

Her mom looked down at her feet. "Sure. Luckily I wore tennis shoes."

Kylie decided to take her mom to a less woodsy trail that ended by the creek. It wasn't as nice as her and Derek's spot, but still pretty. She went by the cabin to get a blanket for them to sit on.

Her mom meandered around the cabin. "This is sparse, but nice."

Socks came running out of her bedroom and attacked her mom's shoelaces. "Oh, it's sooo cute."

Her mom picked up Socks, Jr., and held it up to her face. "Whose kitten is it?"

"Uh, mine."

Her mom looked surprised. "Okay, but don't you think you should have cleared that with me first?"

"I . . . yeah, I guess I should have," Kylie said.

Her mom continued to stare at the feline. "Do you know what cat this reminds me of?"

"Socks?" Kylie said.

"Yeah. Do you remember her? We had that cat when you were born. Your dad got it for me the day we had our first sonogram. He was so excited, he . . ." Her mom stopped talking and blinked as if to chase the memory from her mind. "Yeah, cute kitten." She put the feline down as if she half blamed the kitten for bringing on a painful memory.

Kylie saw the emotion in her mom's eyes, and she wished she could punch her dad. She swallowed the knot forming in her throat and went to grab a blanket.

They walked in silence, and then her mom asked, "You are calling your dad now, aren't you?"

Kylie almost lied, but then said, "The phone works both ways, Mom. If he wants to talk to me, he can call."

"Honey, men aren't always good at—"

"It's not men we're talking about. It's Dad."

"I'm sure he didn't intentionally forget about coming to see you. His work sometimes can be challenging."

"Really?" Kylie asked. "Is that why you barbecued his shorts on the grill?"

Chapter Forty-one

Her mom continued alongside Kylie, walking through the path in the woods. "I'm not very proud of doing that."

"You should be," Kylie said. "I think it was very fitting."

Her mom looked at her before speaking. "He's just going through something right now, Kylie. That's all."

The fact that her mom would defend him pushed Kylie over the edge. "Yeah, he's going through his super-young assistant."

Her mom stopped and grabbed Kylie's arm. Tears filled her mom's eyes. "Oh, baby. I'm so sorry."

Kylie shook her head. "Why are you apologizing? Are you having an affair, too? I swear, if you're seeing someone my age, I'm divorcing both of you."

"No. I would never . . . I didn't want . . . you to find out. You were always so close." Her mom held a hand over her trembling lips for a second. "How did you find out?"

Kylie sensed it would hurt her mom to know that her dad brought the bimbo with him last weekend, so she lied. "I caught him in a lie."

She shook her head. "He never was good at lying."

Right then, Kylie wondered how good her mother was at lying. Did her dad even know the truth? She stopped moving and closed her eyes and considered the question she needed to ask.

"My, this is pretty," her mom said.

Kylie opened her eyes and found her mom looking over at the stream. "Yeah." Kylie moved closer to the stream and stretched out the blanket for them to sit.

Her mom sat down and stared at the water. "Is there really a waterfall here?"

"I'm told there is," Kylie said, hoping to keep the frustration about never having seen the falls from her voice. And right then, she decided even if she had to go alone, she was going to see that falls—for some crazy reason, it seemed important that she went. "I've never seen it, though."

"Why not?"

Kylie shrugged. "Supposedly, there's a legend about there being ghosts there. Most everyone is afraid to go there." Me included, Kylie thought, but didn't say it—not that it would stop her next time.

"Really?" Her mom looked intrigued. "I love ghost stories, don't you?"

"Sometimes," Kylie answered honestly, and glanced away so her mom couldn't read anything in her expression.

"Well, it's peaceful here," her mom said. "I like it." She leaned over and patted Kylie's hand. "Thanks for bringing me here."

Call Kylie a coward, but she shelved the question she didn't want to ask, and went for the less explosive topic. One her mom should be happy about. "What do you think about the camp turning into a boarding school?"

"Your camp leader sounded happy about it," her mom said, still staring at the water.

"What do you think about me signing up?"

Her mom's head snapped around. "What? Hon, that's a boarding school. That means you live here."

"I know," Kylie said, honestly surprised at her mom's reaction. "Just think, you wouldn't have to put up with me." Kylie tried to go for a teasing tone. But if her mom's expression was any indication, Kylie missed by a long shot.

"No," her mom said. "Let me make this clear. Hell, no. You have a home and it's with me."

Two things, two huge emotional realizations hit Kylie at once. One, she really wanted—no, make that needed—to stay at Shadow Falls Camp. Somehow, some way, she had to convince her mom to let her do this. And the second realization was that her mom didn't want to get rid of her. Kylie had been so sure, so certain that given the choice her mom would have packed Kylie a little knapsack and had her out the door in no time.

With her emotions playing bumper cars in her heart, Kylie didn't know what to say. "I . . . I really like it here, Mom."

"You like it at home, too," she said.

Not anymore, was her true answer, but that suddenly seemed cruel. "But . . ."

"If this is retaliation for the divorce—"

"It's not," Kylie said. "I promise. I just . . . It feels right here. I'm getting to know who I really am. Remember how you used to tell me that I had 'belonging issues' because I didn't want to join any of the clubs or teams at school? Well, here, I belong . . . I belong here, Mom."

"You have Sara. You two are as close as sisters."

"I love Sara. I always will, but we're not . . . as alike as we used to be. We don't even talk every day now. She's found some other girls to hang with and honestly, I don't fit in with them."

Her mom's eyes grew worried. "But—"

"Mom, please . . ." Kylie saw she'd made headway because her mom wasn't arguing nearly as adamantly as she normally did. Then Kylie remembered another trump card. "You said your new job would require lots of travel. What do you think you're going to do with me when you're gone?"

"Well, your dad will take over."

Kylie cocked her head. "Do you think I want to go over to his place while his girlfriend, who is practically my age, flaunts herself all over him?"

"Then I'll turn down the promotion," her mom said. "You are more important to me than . . . than any job." Tears filled her mother's eyes.

Tears filled Kylie's eyes at the same time. She couldn't help herself. Then because it just felt right, she reached over and wrapped her arms around her mother.

"I love you," Kylie said, and held on. She held on tighter than she had ever held on before.

Her mom didn't pull away. She patted Kylie's shoulder. It wasn't the warmest embrace, but it had potential. Then, not wanting to push her luck, Kylie pulled back.

"I'm sorry," Kylie said.

"For what?" her mom asked, and Kylie noticed her mom's

face was a splotchy mess. Another thing they had in common that Kylie hadn't realized.

"I'm sorry," Kylie said. "I really don't want to hurt you. And it's not as if you have to make a decision today. I'm here all summer, but I really do like it here. And Holiday said the students could come home on the weekends. There would be all kinds of vacation days. And I'm only three hours away. Heck, you work out of your home so you could even move closer."

Her mom sighed. "But you're my daughter, baby." She ran her hand over Kylie's cheek. "I don't want other people raising you."

"Mom, would you get real? I'll be seventeen in a few months. You've already raised me." Kylie hesitated and then added, "Besides, you should be dating and stuff."

Her mom's eyes widened. "I don't think I'm that brave."

"Why not? You're beautiful and with a new wardrobe, you could be . . . hot." Her mom was much prettier than the tramp her father was involved with right now.

Her mom sighed. "When did my little girl grow up?"

"I don't know." Kylie grinned and lay back on the blanket. Her mom followed her lead and lay back. They listened to the creek water flow and stared up at the blue sky peeking out through the white cotton-ball clouds. Maybe it was Kylie's imagination, but she could almost hear the falls even from here.

Finally, Kylie sat up. Her mom did the same. "Mom, can I ask you something?"

"Sure, hon."

Kylie looked at her mom and just blurted out the question. "Who is my real dad?"

Chapter Forty-two

Kylie saw her mom flinch. She didn't look at Kylie, almost as if trying to decide what lie to tell.

"The truth, Mom," Kylie said. "I need to know the truth."

Her mom finally looked at her. Both tears and panic filled her big brown eyes. "Who? Did your dad . . . tell you?"

Which dad, Kylie thought, but didn't say it. She knew the one her mom meant.

Relief flowed through her. Her dad knew. Kylie hadn't wanted to believe her mom could have lied to him all these years. Then Kylie's relief vanished and she wondered if this was what the divorce was really about. Had her dad just discovered he wasn't Kylie's biological father? Her heart tightened at the thought that the divorce was her fault.

"No, Mom, I promise. He didn't tell me. It was just . . . a feeling." That much was true. She didn't have proof, she hadn't even asked Daniel. But the odd feeling that Daniel looked like someone she knew had finally made sense.

He looked like the girl she saw in the mirror every morning when she brushed her teeth—the same blue eyes, the same blond hair, the same bone structure. They even walked like each other.

And then there was his brain pattern. She kept seeing it in her head and then she remembered how Helen had described Kylie's pattern.

But she couldn't tell her mom any of this.

"Plus, I don't look like Dad at all," Kylie said instead.

Tears dampened her mom's cheeks. "Oh, baby. I'm so sorry, baby. I'm so sorry."

"What happened?" Kylie asked. "Please tell me the divorce isn't about this."

"No, baby." Her mom wiped her tears, and started talking. "I met him, Daniel Brighten, at the gym. He worked there. He was . . . I don't even know how to explain it, but to say he was charming. Almost magical. I fell in love with him the moment I laid eyes on him."

Her mom stared off at nothing as if remembering. "He asked me out. On the first date, he told me that in three weeks he was set to ship out for the Gulf War. Three weeks was all we had. I know it sounds so wrong, and I'll lock you in your room if you ever do this, but . . . after that first date I knew he was the one. By the third, I was . . . There was nothing I wouldn't do for him. We were inseparable.

"When he left, he told me that when he came back, he was going to marry me. That he'd introduce me to his family. They lived in Dallas, so I'd never even met them."

Her mom's breath hitched. "Two weeks after he was deployed, I realized I was pregnant. In my next letter, I told him." She bit down on her lips, and more tears flowed. "He stopped writing. I thought . . ." Tears rolled down her cheeks. "At first I thought it was because he didn't want the baby." Drawing in a deep breath, her mom wiped her face. "About two weeks later, I saw his obituary in the paper. Now I don't even know if he got the letter."

Kylie's heart clutched and she remembered seeing Daniel pull the letter from his pocket to his lips. Tears filled her own eyes and she fought the need to tell her mom about her dreams, about Daniel coming to see her.

Her mom wrapped her arms around her knees as if she was cold. Kylie knew he was here. He stood beside her mom, looking at her with so much love in his eyes that Kylie's own tears came faster.

"I was . . . only eighteen years old," her mom went on. "My mom might have understood, but my dad, he was . . . it would have killed him. Your dad—I mean your stepdad—we had dated off and on through high school. He . . . always claimed he loved me."

She held her head up. "He called me right after all this happened. I told him it wasn't a good time. He didn't take no very easily. He showed up at work and I went out and had coffee. I told him. I don't know why I did. But I needed a friend."

Her mom turned and looked right at Kylie. "He did what most men wouldn't do. He got down on his knees and asked me to marry him, right then."

Kylie thought about her dad, how much he must have loved

her mom to have done that. But what happened to that man now? How could he be the same man who . . .

Her mom continued. "He asked for one thing, one promise. He never wanted anyone to know that you weren't his." She pressed her hands against her lips again. "Your real father was gone. I was desperate. I never . . . never realized how hard that promise would be to keep."

Kylie reached for her mom's hand.

"The day you were born, it was like seeing your dad all over again. You are so much like him."

I know, Kylie thought, and gave her mom's hand a squeeze. Then she looked up at Daniel Brighten.

"I know, if he'd lived, he would have loved you so much."

Kylie closed her eyes and then the words popped out. "I think he does love me. I think he loves you, too."

Her mom did it then. She wrapped her arms around Kylie and hugged her. It wasn't quick, and not even awkward. It was just right.

They stayed there by the creek for another couple of hours. Talking about everything. She told Kylie about the whirlwind love affair she'd had with Daniel. They even talked about Nana.

"You know," her mom said. "The day of the funeral. It took everything I had not to find me a tissue and remove that God-awful purple lipstick they put on her."

Kylie laughed. "I'll bet Nana would have appreciated it." And right then Kylie felt another breeze whisk by. It was cold, but it wasn't the same cold as Daniel's. Kylie smiled and knew Nana's spirit was close.

"Nana was special," Kylie said.

A while later, they started back through the woods. Their shoulders brushed up against each other as they walked. Her mom reached over and squeezed Kylie's hand. "Your dad," her mom said. "The man who raised you . . . he loves you. I know you're mad at him."

"I have a right to be mad," Kylie said.

"I know," her mom answered. "I'm mad at him, too." She hesitated. "No, I'm furious. But I don't think he could have loved you more if you were his own. This is just . . . a midlife crisis." She stopped walking. "Or maybe the truth is something I don't even want to admit."

"What?" Kylie asked.

"He loved me, Kylie. In the beginning, he loved me so much. And I . . . never loved him like I loved Daniel. I never told him, but he knew it. And in time, I . . . God help me, but I resented the promise he asked me to make. Every time I looked at you, I saw your real father and I felt as if I was lying to you. Lying to myself. The marriage suffered. Our relationship suffered." Her mom waved a hand between them. "It was easy to blame him, but honestly, I'm just as much at fault. I didn't have to make that promise."

Her mom reached over and brushed Kylie's hair back. "He was a good father. For years, most of those sixteen years, he was a good husband. He deserved a woman who loved him as much as he loved her. He never had that. How unfair was that to him? Maybe after all that time, he just couldn't handle it anymore."

Kylie knew her mom had made valid points. Things she

should consider when she reevaluated her relationship with her dad. "He could have just asked for a divorce. He didn't have to start cheating with someone practically my age."

"I'm not saying he's right. Or that he's perfect. But he loves you, baby. He loved you even when he didn't have to."

Before her mom left, she made Kylie promise to call her dad again soon. It was a promise Kylie intended to keep, but not today. Probably not even tomorrow.

"Why does romance have to be so complicated?" Kylie blurted out as she barged into Holiday's office later that night.

Kylie had been in her room since her mom left, thinking about her dad and mom and Daniel and comparing all that to what she felt for Lucas and Derek. It wasn't the same thing, but in some small way, it almost felt like it was.

Holiday looked up from the paper on her desk. If the woman's expression was any indication, she was in about the same mood as Kylie. Confused and hurting. No doubt, Holiday and Burnett had butted heads again.

"Good question," Holiday answered. "I personally think the gods did it just to piss us off."

Kylie dropped down in the chair across from her desk.

Leaning back in her chair, Holiday studied her. "You've been quiet all day. Did the visit with your mom go okay?"

Kylie decided to spill the beans. "Daniel Brighten, the ghost, is my real father."

Holiday nodded. Not the reaction Kylie expected.

Kylie felt her gut tighten. "If you tell me you knew this all along, I'm gonna be so pissed."

"I didn't know." Holiday held up her hand. "I suspected. There's a difference."

"You should have told me."

"It doesn't work like that."

"Well, I don't like how it works," Kylie barked.

Holiday let go of a sigh. "Sometimes I don't, either."

They got quiet. Music from the dining hall wafted into the room. A party was going on. A celebration of sorts for not having to close down the camp and for the decision to make the camp a boarding school. For many of the campers, it would be a lifesaver.

"Everything else okay?" Holiday asked.

"Yes." Then Kylie felt that if she didn't get it all out she would burst. "No, it's not okay. I like two guys. One left so that should make it easy, right? Especially since the one who left is probably off having kinky sex with his she-wolf. But no, I've got my mom, my dad, and Daniel's story in my head telling me how it's not fair to care for someone if you care for someone else." She stopped talking just so she could breathe.

"I'm sure that not's easy," Holiday said.

"Oh, I'm not finished yet. It gets better, because this guy, the one I like, has the power to toy with my emotions. And when I'm with him, I feel as if it's too good to be true. That makes me wonder if maybe what I'm feeling is real. Maybe he's just using his power to make me think I really like him."

Holiday frowned. "I don't think Derek would do that."

Okay, Kylie knew Holiday would figure out who the boys were, but hearing his name made Kylie's chest clutch.

"Then again," Holiday said. "Derek is male. Their logic isn't the same as ours."

"So you agree; he could be doing this, couldn't he?" Kylie asked.

Holiday looked as if she'd been put on the spot. "He could, but again I don't think Derek is that type."

"I don't think he is either, but . . ." She closed her eyes. "I'm just feeling so confused."

Holiday sighed again. "I wish I could tell you it gets easier when you're older. But where men are involved, there always seems to be some bafflement."

"And then there's Daniel," Kylie seethed. "Now that I need for him to show back up so I can ask him what the hell I am, he's not cooperating. He's off playing golf or poker with St. Peter or whatever men do in heaven. Or heck, maybe he's found himself some hot too-young girlfriend like my dad has and decided to drop me in the grease, too."

Holiday laughed. "Have you considered that maybe Daniel wants you to find this out for yourself?"

"Oh, that's so not fair," Kylie said. "Your parents didn't die or anything and leave you to go scrambling around to find out what you were. You were born knowing it."

Holiday shook her head. "Everyone's journey is different. Why don't you make that your next quest?"

Kylie slammed back in the chair. "I don't want another quest. Why can't it just be easy?"

Holiday grinned. "Easy is no fun." She sighed. "As much as I hate admitting it, if men were easy to figure out, they probably wouldn't be as much fun as they are."

"Yeah, but feeling as if your life is raining chaos isn't fun. And that's what I've felt for the last two months."

Holiday frowned and reached over and patted Kylie's hand. "And I'm about to make some things even more difficult for you."

"What?" Kylie pulled her hand away from Holiday.

The camp leader frowned and pulled a letter from her desk drawer. "I wasn't going to give you this, but then . . . I remembered what you said about me being too protective."

A wiggle of concern shot through Kylie. "You know, being protective is good sometimes."

"No. You were right," Holiday said.

"Is it from Daniel?" Kylie stared at the envelope.

"No. It's from Lucas."

"Just shoot me now." Kylie banged her head on the desk.

Holiday giggled. "It can't be that bad." She reached over and gave Kylie's hand another squeeze. "You are a special girl, Kylie. If I had to guess, I'd say these two aren't going to be the only ones who will jump through fire to get your attention." She stood up. "I think I'm going to go sit in on the party for a while. Stay in here as long as you want."

"Holiday?" Kylie said her name without turning around.

"What?"

Kylie looked back. "Did Lucas write to you, too?"

Holiday nodded.

"Do you know if . . . if Fredericka is with him?"

Holiday's eyes shifted. "Yes."

"Thanks." Kylie turned around. Holiday's footsteps faded into the sound of the music from next door. Kylie pulled the letter closer. She remembered how it had felt to kiss Derek—hot, safe, except for the little doubt that her emotions were being manipulated.

Her kiss with Lucas had been . . . hotter, but nothing about it had felt safe. Maybe that was even why it had been hotter. Risk and passion seemed to go hand in hand.

Kylie stared at the letter. Was there anything that Lucas could say in that letter that would change the fact that he'd left, that he was with Fredericka—a girl he admitted to having sex with? A girl he'd even admitted caring about.

No, Kylie thought. There was nothing Lucas could say to change that. Any more than her dad could change what he did to her mom. Or what Trey had done to her.

The music seemed to call out to her. There was a party going on and she should be there. She folded the letter and put it in her pocket. She deserved to just enjoy tonight. Later, she'd find out what Lucas had to say.

She stood up, turned to leave. The cold hit her so fast, her breath caught, then, the room filled with a thick fog.

Okay, this was different.

The thought no more went through her head when Kylie knew how different. This wasn't Daniel.

She tried to relax. But face it, this ghost business was going to take some getting used to. "Daniel?" She said his name almost hoping she was wrong.

A section of fog slowly lifted. A woman, no more than thirty, with long dark hair, stood there. She wore a beautiful white gown, or it had been beautiful at one time.

Kylie's heart thudded against her chest bone as she took in the bloodstains. The woman looked at Kylie with dead eyes, eyes filled with so much hopelessness that Kylie wanted to cry.

"Stop him," the woman said. "Stop him, or he'll do it again."

"Who?" Kylie asked. "Who did this?" Kylie gripped her hands together and wished Holiday hadn't left. "Are you looking for Holiday?"

The woman didn't answer. Instead, she faded into the fog. Kylie stood there, hugging herself against the cold, as the fog rose and disappeared into the ceiling. Slowly, the temperature crept back up.

"That is so unfair," Kylie muttered.

"What's unfair?"

Kylie swung around. Derek stood in the doorway. Dressed in faded jeans and a light blue shirt, he looked . . . good. Safe. She met his eyes and she saw the affection he held for her.

Right then, she decided that for tonight she was going to forget.

Forget about the letter in her pocket.

Forget about not knowing what she was.

Forget a certain woman wearing a blood-soaked gown.

Forget that she still hadn't made the trip up to the falls.

Even forget that her mom still hadn't agreed to let Kylie stay at the school.

Tonight, she just wanted to listen to some music, and sit next to Derek—shoulders touching.

"You going to the party?" she asked.

"I've been there. Waiting on you."

"Then let's go."

Kylie started moving toward the dining hall, and Derek followed her. She paused at the threshold, and he bumped into her. Hit with déjà vu, she remembered almost the same thing happening the first time she'd walked through these doors.

She'd been so scared, so certain that she would hate it here. Then again, she'd also sensed that her life was going to change. And yeah, she had been right about that.

"Are we going inside?" Derek asked, brushing up against her. His breath felt warm against her neck.

She nodded, but she just stood there wanting to take it all in. She saw Miranda chatting with Perry. The shape-shifter had yet to admit he liked Miranda, but Miranda was patient. Helen sat with Jonathon who played a game of chess with another vampire.

Della, sipping a glass of blood, stood watching the game. Since learning about the Shadow Falls Camp turning into a boarding school, Della had seemed to lose some of her pent-up anger. Not all of it, but some.

"You okay?" Derek asked, leaning even closer to her ear. He felt solid and so warm standing behind her and right now that was what she needed.

"Yeah." Kylie spotted Holiday sitting with Chris, listening to him play his guitar.

Looking across the room, Kylie found Burnett leaning against a wall, his attention so locked on Holiday that the world could end and he wouldn't notice. Yup, Holiday was his kryptonite, all right.

A sense of belonging filled Kylie's chest. She looked back at Derek and smiled. "Yeah," she repeated. "I'm okay."

Awake at Dawn

To my husband, Steve Craig—my partner, my best friend, and my hero. Your love, support, and willingness to do laundry helped me take my dreams and make them our reality. Thank you for being a part of my dreams. I love you.

Acknowledgments

To my fabulous critique partners, who laughed with me during lunches, gave me endless support when my characters were misbehaving, and drank chocolate martinis with me to celebrate every good moment of life. To the amazing and supportive booksellers at Katy Budget Books. You guys rock. To my daddy, Pete Hunt, and my mother, Ginger Curtis, who taught me the value of laughter and love. And to my daughter, Nina Makepeace, and my son, Steve Craig, Jr. By far, you two are the best things I've ever done in my life. And last but certainly not least, to my wonderful editor and agent, whose belief in me is the springboard of my inspiration.

Chapter One

"You have to stop it, Kylie. You have to. Or this will happen to some-one you love."

The spirit's ominous words flowed from behind Kylie Galen and mingled with the crackle and pop of the huge bonfire about fifty feet to her right. The frigid pocket of air announced the spirit's presence loud and clear, even if the words were only for Kylie's ears and not for the thirty other Shadow Falls campers standing in the ceremonial circle.

Miranda stood by Kylie in the people chain, completely un-aware of the ghost, and gripped Kylie's hand tighter. "This is so cool," Miranda muttered, and looked across the circle at Della.

Miranda and Della were not only Kylie's closest friends, but also her cabin mates.

"We give thanks for this offering." Chris, or Christopher as he referred to himself tonight, stood in the middle of the circle and raised the sacred goblet up to the dark sky as he blessed its contents.

"You have to stop it," the spirit whispered over Kylie's shoulder again, hindering her concentration on the ritual.

Closing her eyes, Kylie envisioned the spirit the way she had appeared to her several times now—mid-thirties, long dark hair and wearing a white gown—a gown covered in blood.

Frustration bounced around Kylie's already tightened gut. How many times had she pleaded with this spirit to explain, to tell her who, what, when, where, and why? Only to have the dead woman repeat the same warning.

Long story short, ghosts just coming out of the closet sucked at communication. Probably as bad as beginner ghost whisperers sucked at getting them to communicate. Kylie's only option was to wait until the ghost could somehow explain her warning. Now, however, wasn't the optimal time.

I'm kind of busy right now. So unless you can explain in detail, can we chat later? The words formed in Kylie's mind, hoping the ghost could read her thoughts. Thankfully, the chill running down Kylie's spine evaporated and the night's heat returned—Texas heat, muggy, thick, and hot, even without the bonfire.

Thank you. Kylie tried to relax, but the tension in her shoulders remained knotted. And for a good reason. Tonight's ceremonial event, sort of a show-and-tell, was another first in her life.

A life that was so much simpler before she knew she wasn't all human. Of course, it would help if she could identify her non-human side. Unfortunately the only person who knew the answer was Daniel Brighten, her real dad. She hadn't known he existed until he'd paid a visit to her a little over a month ago. And he'd obviously decided to let Kylie deal with her identity crisis all on her own.

He seldom visited anymore, bringing a whole new meaning to the term *deadbeat dad.* Yup, Daniel was dead—died before she was born. Kylie wasn't sure if they offered parenting classes in the here-after, but she was tempted to suggest he find out. Because now, when he did drop by, she would catch him watching her and just when she started to ask him a question, he'd fade away, leaving only a cold chill and her unanswered questions.

"Okay," Chris said. "Release your hands, clear your mind, but whatever you do, do not break the circle."

Kylie, along with the crowd, followed his directions. Yet as she released her hands, Kylie's mind refused to clear. A whisper of wind picked up a few strands of her long, blond hair and scattered it across her face. She brushed it behind her ear.

Was her deadbeat dad afraid she was going to ask for sex advice or something? That always had her mom disappearing from a room—running around in search of another give-this-to-your-teen pamphlet. Not that Kylie had actually asked her mom for sex advice. Honestly, she was the last person Kylie would go to for *that* kind of advice.

Why, the mere mention of her being interested in a boy sent her mom into a panic as the letters S-E-X practically flashed in her mom's eyes. Thankfully, since Kylie had been shipped off to Shadow Falls Camp, the supply of sex-related pamphlets had declined.

Who knew what she'd missed this last month? There might have been a few STDs discovered that she didn't know about. No doubt her mom was stockpiling them for when Kylie went home for a visit in three weeks. A visit she wasn't looking forward to, either. Sure, she and her mom had sort of mended their not-so-good relationship since her mom had confessed about Daniel being her real dad. But the new mother-daughter bond felt so fragile.

Kylie couldn't help but wonder if their relationship wasn't too delicate to actually spend more than a few hours together. What if she went home and found things really hadn't changed? What if the distance between her and her mom still existed? And what about things with Tom Galen, the man Kylie had perceived to be her real dad all her life, the man who had walked out on her mom and her for a girl only a few years older than Kylie? Kylie had been mortified at seeing him sucking face with his way-too-young assistant. So much so, she hadn't even told him.

A late-night breeze brought the smoke from the roaring bonfire into her face. She blinked the sting from her eyes, but didn't dare step out of the circle. As Della had explained, to do that would have shown a lack of respect to the vampire culture.

"Clear your mind," Chris repeated, and handed the goblet to a camper on the other side of the circle.

Closing her eyes, Kylie tried again to follow Chris's directions, but then heard the sound of falling water. Jerking her eyes open, she looked toward the woods. Was the waterfall that close? Ever since Kylie had learned about the legend of the death angels at the falls, she felt driven to go there. Not that she longed to come face-to-face with any death angels. She had her hands full dealing with ghosts. But she couldn't kick the feeling that the falls called her.

"Are you ready?" Miranda leaned in and whispered, "It's getting closer."

Ready for what? was Kylie's first thought. Then she remembered. Was Miranda freaking kidding?

Kylie stared at the communal goblet being passed around the circle. Her breath caught when she realized it was only ten people away from being placed in her hand. Drawing in a deep smoke-scented gulp of air, she tried not to look disgusted.

Tried. But the thought of taking a sip from a container after everyone had smacked their lips on the rim landed somewhere between gross and nauseating in her mind, but for sure the biggest yuck factor was the blood.

Watching Della consume her daily nutrition had gotten easier this last month. Heck, Kylie had even donated a pint to the cause—

supernaturals did that sort of thing for their vampire friends. But having to taste the life-sustaining substance was a different matter altogether.

"I know it's sickening. Just pretend it's tomato juice," Miranda whispered to their friend Helen standing on the other side of her. Not that whispering helped in this crowd.

Kylie looked across the circle of supernatural campers, their faces cast in firelit shadows from the bonfire. She spotted Della, frowning in their direction and her eyes glowing a pissed-off gold color. Her acute hearing was only one of her gifts. No doubt Della would call Miranda on her "sickening" remark later. Which basically meant Kylie would have to convince the two of them not to murder each other. How two people could be friends and fight so much was beyond her. Playing peacemaker between the two was a full-time job.

She watched another camper raise the goblet to her lips. Knowing how much this meant to Della, Kylie mentally prepared herself to accept the glass and take a sip of blood without barfing. Not that it stopped Kylie's stomach from wanting to rebel.

Gotta do this. Gotta do this. For Della's sake.

Maybe you'll even like how blood tastes, Della had said earlier. *Wouldn't it be cool if you turned out to be vampire?*

Not, Kylie had thought, but wouldn't dare say it. She supposed being vampire wouldn't be any worse than being werewolf or shapeshifter. Then again, she remembered Della practically crying when she talked about her ex-boyfriend's repulsion to her cold body temperature. Kylie preferred to stay at her own temperature, thank you very much. And the thought of existing on a diet that mainly consisted of blood . . . ? Well, Kylie seldom even ate red meat, and when she did . . . cook that cow, please.

While Holiday, the camp leader and Kylie's mentor, had said it was unlikely for Kylie to start exhibiting any huge metaphysical changes, Holiday had also said anything was possible. Truth was, Holiday—who was full fairy—couldn't tell Kylie what her future held, because Kylie was an anomaly.

And Kylie hated being an anomaly.

She'd never fit in the human world, and damn it if she wasn't a misfit here, as well. Not that the other campers didn't accept her. Nope, she felt closer to these supernaturals than she did human teens. Well, she did as soon as she learned that no one here was dying to have her for lunch. Why, Della and Miranda were now her two major best friends—there wasn't anything she couldn't or wouldn't share with them. The blood donation pretty much proved that fact.

Okay, there was one thing Kylie couldn't share with her two best friends. Ghosts. Most supernaturals had a thing about ghosts. Not that Kylie herself didn't have a thing about them. But it didn't stop the pesky phantoms from regularly popping in for visits.

Nevertheless, whatever type of supernatural she was, being a ghost magnet was her gift. Or . . . one of them. Holiday believed that ghost whispering was probably one of many of Kylie's gifts and that others would manifest over time. Kylie just hoped any future gifts were easier to deal with than the indecisive and communication-challenged dead people.

"It's coming," Miranda said.

Kylie watched someone pass the glass to Helen. Kylie's throat tightened again. Her gaze shifted to Derek, the brown-haired half fairy, standing three campers past Helen. Kylie had missed him drinking the blood. Not that she was sorry. The next time they kissed, she didn't want to think about him drinking blood.

He smiled tenderly and Kylie knew Derek could sense her emotional turmoil. As crazy as it seemed, his ability to read her emotions was both what attracted her to him and kept her from getting closer.

Well, it wasn't so much his ability to read her that kept her from allowing their relationship to deepen, it was his ability to control those emotions. Being half Fae, Derek not only could read her emotions, but with a simple touch, he could alter her emotions, turn fear into fascination, anger into calm. Was it at all surprising that she stayed in awe of the sexy-as-sin boy?

Call her paranoid, but after seeing how her dad—make that her stepdad—had cheated on her mom and then how Trey, her ex-boyfriend, had dropped her in the grease when she'd been hesitant to go all the way, trusting the male gender was difficult. Trusting one who had the power to manipulate her emotions was even harder.

Not that it stopped her from liking Derek or from wishing she could throw caution to the wind. Even now—her stomach clenched as she thought of drinking blood, surrounded by the entire camp—she felt herself being lured to him. Felt herself wanting to lean up against his chest, to get close enough to see the gold flecks in his pupils melt and mesh into the vivid green of his eyes. She wanted to feel his lips on hers again. To taste his kiss. She learned these last few weeks how good he could kiss.

A clearing of Miranda's throat brought Kylie back to the moment. When she saw Derek's caught-you smile, she knew he'd read her turned-on emotions, and her cheeks warmed and she shifted her gaze away from Derek to Miranda.

Oh crap. Miranda held out the glass for Kylie to take. It was showtime.

She took the goblet. It felt warm against her palm, almost as if the liquid inside had just been drained from its life source. Her stomach knotted and her throat followed course. She didn't know if the blood was animal or human.

Don't think about it.

She inhaled and the coppery smell, like old pennies, filled her nose, and before the glass touched her lips, her gag reflex prepared to bounce.

Just do it. Show Della that you respect her culture.

She swallowed hard, tilted the glass up a notch higher, and hoped like hell Della appreciated this. Telling herself she only had to taste, not drink, she waited for the moisture to dampen her mouth.

The second the warm liquid wet her lips, she went to pull the glass back, but somehow the thick red blood snuck through her tightened lips. Her gag reflex jumped but then the taste exploded on the tip of her tongue. Almost like black cherries but better, sort of like ripe strawberries but tangier and sweeter, the exotic flavor had her mouth opening and greedily swallowing. As the liquid slid down her throat, the smell of old pennies vanished, replaced with a spicy fruity scent.

She had almost downed the whole glass when she remembered what she was drinking. She yanked the glass from her lips, but couldn't stop her tongue from dipping out the corner of her mouth to catch a drop that tried to escape.

Immediately, the intensity of everyone's gaze on her pressed against her awareness and a deeper reality sank in. Murmurs filled her ears . . .

At least now we know what she is.

How come she's not cold?

Looks as if we're going to up our blood drive.

Della's victory yelp followed.

Kylie's hands started to shake. The smoke from the bonfire filled her nose and throat and made it hard to breathe.

Crap! Crap! Crap! What did this mean? Was she . . . a vampire?

She scanned the wide-eyed faces to find Holiday, wanting to see her reassuring smile that said it was okay, that said this . . . this meant nothing. But when she found the camp leader, her expression mirrored that of the others—shock.

Blinking, hoping to wash away the start of tears, she shoved the almost empty glass into the hands of the person beside her. No longer caring about showing respect, she took off at a dead run.

Five minutes later Kylie was still running. Running faster than she knew she could move. But was it vampire fast? The hot, muggy summer air filled her lungs and came out in gasps. Even with the night temperature clinging to the high eighties, a chill ran down her spine. Was she at this moment morphing into a vampire? Was she growing cold? Hadn't Della said it was painful? More like excruciatingly painful.

Was she in pain? Emotionally yes. But physically? Not yet.

She kept moving. The sound of her feet hitting the ground filled her ears, and the sound of the thorny vines snagging her jeans and then ripping away seemed too loud. Her consciousness throbbed right along with the beating of her heart. *Thump. Thump. Thump.*

How many times had she told Della she wasn't a monster? And yet the mere idea that Kylie might be a vampire seemed . . . too much.

The smell of the bonfire smoke clung to her clothes and filled her nose. Yet the taste of the sweet blood lingered on her tongue. She ran harder. Faster. Did her speed mean she was a vampire?

She didn't want to think about that.

Didn't want to accept it.

Her lungs finally gave out, declined the air she tried to force down. The muscles in her legs cramped and her knees shook. She stopped, her legs refusing to support her weight, and collapsed in the middle of a thorn-infested field. Pulling her legs to her chest, she hugged her shins and dropped her head on her knees.

She drew hot air into her lungs that now begged for oxygen. One breath, then two. Physically exhausted, she went still as the realization finally stuck. If she were a vampire, would she not have Della's stamina? Maybe that came with the change of body temperature. The dampness on her cheeks told her she'd been crying.

The air suddenly chilled. Turned cold.

Not vampire cold.

Dead cold.

She wasn't alone—another spirit had joined her. But who was it this time? Holiday had explained that in time, her abilities would increase and she would have to deal with more than one ghost at a time. But right now, there was only one ghost she wanted to see. Only one thing she wanted.

She wanted answers. "Daniel?" she called her father's name. And then louder. "Daniel Brighten. What am I?"

When he didn't appear, she screamed his name again and again. Her throat became sore, but she didn't stop. "You come here now. You give me answers or I swear to you, I'll never, *NEVER* acknowledge your presence again. I will shut you off, eradicate you from my mind, and refuse to see, talk, or even think of you again."

As the threat fell from her lips, she didn't even know if she had the ability to do it, but something inside her said she could. She dropped her head against her knees and tried to breathe.

Suddenly the cold grew nearer. She felt it surround her. Felt it wrap around her in a tight embrace. It wasn't just any cold, it was Daniel's cold.

She raised her face and saw his spirit kneel beside her. His blue eyes, the same light color as her own, met hers. His eyes, and most everything else about his facial features, from the oval-shaped face to the slightly turned-up nose, were so much like hers that it was a bit disturbing. When his arm curled around her shoulders, the knot in her throat doubled.

"Don't cry." He brushed a tear from her cheek. "My little girl should never cry." The icy touch shouldn't have been comforting, but it was.

"I drank blood and it was good." She spit out the words like a confession.

"And you see this as wrong?" he asked.

"I . . . It scares me."

"I know," he said. "I remember feeling much the same the way."

"Did you drink blood? Are we . . . vampires?" The word almost wouldn't come.

"I never tried blood." His expression filled with empathy. "But, Kylie, you didn't do anything wrong." His voice came out soft, his words soothing. The cold, his cold, lessened her fear of the unknown and she felt . . . loved.

Right then, she knew love had no boundaries, not even death. Love had no temperature. Maybe being cold wasn't altogether a bad thing. She leaned into him and drew comfort from his nearness.

Minutes passed. She blinked away her tears and sat up. He shifted from his kneeling position and sat beside her. Wiping her face, she stared at the father she'd never known in life. Yet, even separated by death, she felt the bond. "Tell me. Please tell me what I am."

The smile in his eyes faded. "I wish I could give you what you want, but I don't have the answers. I was older than you when I realized I was different from everyone else. But it wasn't until I was eighteen and away at college that things started happening."

"What kind of things?" she asked, and then somehow she knew. "You saw ghosts?"

He nodded and cupped his hands together. "I thought I had lost my mind. Then one day I met an old man fishing. He told me he was fairy."

"Did he tell you what you were?" she asked.

"No, just that I wasn't human and, of course, I thought *he* was crazy. It took me months before I believed him. When I went back to find him again, he was gone."

"But what about your parents?" Kylie asked. "Didn't they tell you?"

"No. And when my ability to recognize other supernaturals made sense to me, I realized they were both human. At that time, I didn't know that I couldn't have been their child. Since my death, I learned I was adopted. Not that it made them any less my parents. They loved me. And they would love you, too."

"They never told you that you were adopted? How could they lie to you like that?"

"Back then it was considered best to keep adoption a secret, even from the child. I have yet to find out who or what my real parents are. So you see, the answers you seek were the same answers I sought right before my death. Maybe you can discover them for us both."

"But . . ."

"But what?" he asked.

"I thought ghosts were all-seeing. They are in the movies, anyway. Isn't there someone on the other side who could tell you?"

He smiled. "You would think so. But no, even here, they want you to find your own answers."

"That freaking sucks," Kylie said. "Being dead should have some benefits."

He laughed. The sound echoed with familiarity. It was another thing she had gotten from him—the tenor of her laugh. Her thoughts went to her stepdad, the man whom she had loved so much and yet who had turned his back on her and her mom. She still didn't know if she could forgive him. If she wanted to forgive him. And then the strangest thought hit: she had loved the wrong father.

Her throat felt tight again. "I missed you all my life," Kylie said. "I didn't know I missed you, but I know it now. You were supposed to be there."

He placed a hand on her cheek. "I was there. I saw you take your first step. The day you fell off your bike and broke your arm I tried to catch you. You went right though my arms. And remember the day you flunked that algebra test and you got so upset that you ran off and smoked a cigarette?"

She frowned. "I hate algebra. But I hated the cigarette, too."

"Me, too," he chuckled. "I've been here, Kylie, but I can't stay here much longer."

His words bounced around her head and hit her heart with a thump. "That's not fair. I just got to know you."

"My time in this realm is limited. I've used much of it watching you grow to be the woman you are."

"Then ask for more time." Her throat tightened. She had lost one father already; she didn't want to lose another one. Not now. Not before she even got to know him.

"I'll try, but it may not happen. I don't regret spending my time with you then." The corners of his eyes crinkled into another smile. "I see in you the best of your mother and the best of me. And while I know you don't want to hear this right now, I see the best of Tom Galen. He is not all bad, Kylie."

She wanted to tell Daniel he was wrong, to insist she wasn't like Tom Galen, but her thoughts were interrupted by the whisk of wind. It came on so fast, as if something had shot past, something so fast that her human eye hadn't detected it. Something not human.

The dark silence that followed told Kylie she was right. "I'll bet that's Della." Kylie looked around. "Looking for me." But even as Kylie finished the sentence, she felt the cold of her father's presence fade. "No, please don't . . . go." Her last word rang out in the warm yet eerie and lonely silence.

Gone. He was gone.

Her chest tightened, then she came to the realization that even though he'd come to her, he didn't have the answers she wanted. Her surefire plan of solving her identity crisis had been squashed.

Biting her lip, she pushed away her thoughts of her father and prepared herself to face Della. Could she explain to her friend her reservations about being vampire without hurting her? Would Della be totally furious that she'd broken the circle and disrespected the vampire culture? Knowing Della, the answer would be a *hell yes*.

Della had a lot of unresolved anger and it didn't take much to infuriate her. Some of her angst could be blamed on being vampire—vampires weren't known for their loving dispositions, but most of Della's issues were from her family. Apparently, her super-strict father had noted the changes in his daughter since she'd been turned, and he didn't like them. Not being able to tell her dad about being vampire, Della had remained silent, which made her dad accuse Della of everything from drugs to just being lazy. The sad part was, Della loved her father so much that disappointing him was breaking her heart.

Kylie waited for Della to return, to come to a whizzing stop. She didn't. Had her ghost-fearing friend sensed her father's presence and kept going? The lack of sound suddenly seemed menacing.

"Della?" Kylie called out.

No answer came. Not unless you considered the dead silence

an answer. Kylie recalled Della's cousin, Chan, and the uninvited visit he'd paid to Della and her after she'd only been here a few days. His presence had brought on this kind of dead silence as well.

The memory of that night filled Kylie's head. Della had assured Kylie that he'd only been joking about her being a snack, but after Kylie's little run-in with the Blood Brothers gang of rogue vampires, when she'd nearly become a snack for real, trusting an unknown vampire took a little effort.

When the night's stillness continued, Kylie forced herself to speak. "I know someone is here." She stood up, hoping her false bravado would become real. The whisk of speeding wind passed again. "If that's you, Della, this isn't funny."

No one answered. Kylie stood there, trying to think of what to do next. Then she heard it. Very slight, but still the definite rustle of some bushes—someone was behind her. Breath held, she swung around to face the music.

Chapter Two

At first Kylie didn't see anything, then her gaze shifted lower to the ground and locked on to a pair of eyes—eyes that glowed golden in the night's obscurity. They weren't vampire eyes. Nope, they weren't Della's golden hue that expressed her anger. These weren't even human.

Canine?

No.

Wolf.

She nearly tripped taking a step back, as her heart screamed *run*. But the one word that whispered though her head next stopped her from attempting escape. *Lucas?*

Her chest clutched tighter but no longer from fear. Something akin to longing warmed her heart. Then the warm, gooey feeling slipped right into the feeling of betrayal. The hot-looking werewolf had kissed her senseless, made her want him, and then run off with Fredericka.

Kylie's gaze shot up to the cloud-covered moon. Even through the gray mist, she could tell it wasn't full. That didn't happen until next week, when the werewolves at the camp were planning their own ceremonial event.

Which meant the wolf staring at her couldn't be Lucas. Which meant it was a real wolf. A real wild-animal kind of wolf. Which meant she should be trying to get the hell away before it decided to attack.

Her gaze shot back to the wild animal, and while her mind created images of the creature snarling, ready to pounce, what she saw wasn't anywhere near as frightening. The gold eyes held hers. The cloud shrouding the moonlight must have shifted, and Kylie was able to make out the medium-size wolf in detail. Its coat looked thick and coarse, and it held a mix of colors from gray to red. She wouldn't call it beautiful, not exactly, but it sure as heck didn't appear threatening.

Lowering its snout, it slowly moved forward. Even though the thing still didn't look hostile, Kylie took a step back. As if sensing her fear, it crouched lower to the ground in a submissive position.

"What are you—someone's pet wolf?" Another thought hit. A real wolf couldn't have made the supersonic blast of air. But a real shape-shifter could.

She slammed both her hands on her hips and gave the beast a hard cold look. "Damn it, Perry, is that you?"

Perry, the powerful shape-shifter of the camp, loved to play jokes. But Kylie had had it up to her eyeballs with his tricks. Enough was enough.

"Game's over or I'm going for your ears." Kylie waited for the diamond-like sparkles to fill the air around the wolf as it changed back into human form. "Now!"

No sparkles.

The creature, down on all fours, inched forward.

"No," Kylie insisted, accepting that this was truly a wolf. "You stay there." She held out her hand and the animal seemed to listen. "Nothing personal, but I'm more of a cat person." Her voice rang loud and brought her awareness again to the lack of night noises.

No crickets. No birds. Not even the wind dared to blow. She looked up at the tops of the trees, which held so still they looked photographed. Even the Texas vegetation appeared frozen with fear.

She fought the sense of danger stirring in her chest and looked back at the wolf, more certain than ever that the danger didn't stem from the creature's presence. No, whatever was here was much more evil than a wild animal. Chills tap-danced up her spine, sending all her barely-there hair on the back of her neck standing at attention.

The wolf lunged up on all fours, sniffed the air, and snarled. It took a step away, then turned back around. Its golden eyes met hers almost as if to warn her of danger.

Not that she needed to be further warned. Her heart skipped a beat. The brush of cold wind passed again, only closer this time, and it left a foul odor that carried the stench of death. The wolf's snarl grew more intense.

"Kylie?" Her name echoed from the distance, the sound leaking from the thicket of trees. She brought her head around and the whisk of air shot past her again. Only this time, Kylie got the feeling that it kept going. Whoever, whatever it was, wanted her alone. She folded her arms over her middle and tried not to shiver from the thought.

The wolf made a soft whine and she turned her head and made eye contact again. It moved its head slightly, as though giving her a farewell greeting, then it turned and, causing only a slight rustle of vegetation, it disappeared.

"Kylie." Her name came again, carried with a slight whisk of wind. This time she recognized Derek's voice.

"I'm here," Kylie yelled, and, not wanting to be alone a second longer, she took off running.

• • •

She ran toward the sound of Derek's voice. Her heart pounded as she dodged trees and jumped over patches of thorns. She kept running. As if she could escape the fear she'd just felt, as if she could run away from her problems. Oh, yes, she so wanted to leave her problems behind. With each thump her foot made against the hard earth, she felt her fear slip farther away, but the problems not so much. They hung on, but exertion of energy still felt good. Good until she smacked right into something, or rather . . . someone.

Derek.

His muscled body let out a gush of air and he hit the ground with a thud. Kylie, thrown off balance, toppled down on top of him. His clean, spicy scent filled her nose at the same time his arms wrapped protectively around her.

"You sent the wolf," she muttered, still short of breath, as she just now recalled his ability to communicate with animals.

"What wolf?" His gaze shifted left then right. "Are you okay?" He rolled her over onto the ground. One of his legs still rested on top of hers and his left arm lay across her middle, while his palm fit right into the curve of her waist. Warmth and comfort pulsated from his touch. He pushed the curtain of hair from her face with his other hand. His gaze, filled with concern, met hers and she fought the lump of emotion crawling up her throat.

"Kylie, talk to me." His tone echoed the same caring she saw in his eyes, and that warm feeling she always got when he touched her spread inside her chest.

"Damn it, are you okay?"

She blinked up at him and she meant to say yes, but the truth came out. "No. I'm not okay."

"What happened?" His arm tightened around her waist.

All her problems came raining down on her like pitchforks and one made a direct hit to her heart. "I drank blood."

"We all drank blood. It was part of the ceremony," he said, and she got the feeling he was trying hard to say the right thing.

"But I enjoyed drinking it," she answered.

"I know," he admitted. "Your emotions were skipping all over the place when you drank it—passion, euphoria, joy."

She raised her head off the ground an inch. "What does that mean? Seriously, what does that mean?"

"Maybe you just like it," he answered with a cautious tone.

"Or maybe I'm vampire?" she countered, then she dropped her head on the ground and closed her eyes.

He didn't say anything for a minute, and then spoke up. "You saw a wolf? You said something about a wolf?"

"Yeah," she answered. "He was acting strange, almost friendly."

"He's not here anymore," Derek said as if his gift allowed him to check the nearby woods for animals. "It was probably just a stray dog."

"He looked like a wolf."

"Then he was probably a hybrid."

"Probably," she admitted, realizing she might be overreacting.

Neither spoke for a few minutes. Closing her eyes, she savored the feel of Derek's body next to hers and slowly relaxed. When she opened her eyes, the stars above sparkled with a fairy-tale radiance. The tall grass around them danced in the wind. Derek was doing it again, making the world around her appear utopian, too perfect. Even the air became fragranced with the spicy scent of plants, hinted with the floral aroma of wildflowers. She closed her eyes again, afraid to let herself be completely pulled into the world he created.

"Do you think you're a vampire?" he asked.

His question brought back some reality. She looked at him. "I don't know. I'm so friggin' confused."

He ran his hand over her cheek. "Does it really matter what you are, Kylie? It sure as hell doesn't matter to me."

"Of course it matters." She propped herself up on one elbow. "You don't understand because you know what you are. You've always known what you are. Everything about what I perceived about myself, who I am, what I am, who my father is, it's all been ripped away. All I'm left with is a bunch of questions. Nothing is like I thought."

Tears filled her eyes. "And—"

Derek's mouth met hers. Her eyes fluttered closed. The sweetness of the kiss sent all her emotional havoc out of her mental window. She let herself enjoy the moment. Let herself be pulled into the sensations of just feeling and not thinking. And, oh goodness, it felt good.

When he drew back she wasn't ready for it to end. She opened her eyes. No longer under the sweet sensations of his kiss, she wasn't sure how she felt about him shutting her up. She sat up. "Why did you do that?"

"Do what?" he asked.

"Kiss me when I was trying to talk."

A smile formed in his eyes. "You don't like me to use my gift to calm you down, so I thought I'd use my charm instead."

"If it is just your charm, and not your gift, how do you make everything so much like a fantasy world?"

He shook his head, and his brown hair brushed against his brow. "I told you, I'm not doing that."

She cocked her head to the side and sent him an accusing look.

"If I am doing it, I'm not doing it on purpose. I swear. Being with you makes me happy and maybe being happy ups my charm." His smile was contagious and any emotions taking up residence in her chest similar to anger or distrust vanished.

She thumped his shoulder with her palm. "You think you're that charming, huh?"

His smile widened. "I think you like my kisses." His gaze lowered to her mouth where she could still taste the moisture of his kiss.

"Really?" she teased. "You're that sure of yourself?"

"I'm sure that you're not feeling upset anymore. And that's what matters, isn't it?" He passed a finger over her lips. "Because I really hate seeing you upset."

Her heart squeezed and she wondered if that was a confession that he was indeed manipulating her emotions. Then again, was it wrong to want to make someone happy, to chase away their fears? Oh heck, what was she waiting for? What kept her from saying yes to everything Derek wanted? Yes to agreeing to go out with him. Yes to . . . to more kisses and to wherever those kisses led. She leaned in closer, wanting to taste his kiss again.

"See," he said playfully, and arched his eyebrows. "Admit it." He moved in. His mouth came so close to hers that she could practically feel it moving when he spoke.

"Admit what?" She put a little tease in her own voice, hoping she drove him as crazy as he drove her.

"Admit that you like my kisses. And then say yes to going out with me."

She cut her eyes up at him and grinned. "I'll admit I like your kisses, but do you like mine?"

"More than anything." He closed the tiniest bit of distance between them. "Go out with me." He kissed her again. Softly at first and then deeper. She felt his tongue slip inside her mouth. She felt herself gently being lowered back to the ground. Felt his hand slip up under her shirt and touch her bare skin at her waist. He'd touched her like that before but she got the feeling he wouldn't take that touch higher; he wouldn't push the intimacy any further until he had her approval.

And just knowing that made her want to approve. Knowing it was her choice and he would respect whatever she chose meant so much. But was it enough to take that leap?

She reached for his hand, seriously considering moving it higher, giving him permission to . . .

"You two need to go back to the camp." The deep voice penetrated Kylie's sensual haze.

Both Kylie and Derek jerked apart. Burnett, the temporary camp leader and a member of the Fallen Research Unit, a supernatural unit of the FBI, stood over them. Kylie's face grew hot with embarrassment at her and Derek being caught making out in the grass.

Derek didn't seem to be bothered. He shot to his feet and looked around. "What is it?"

Kylie stood up. Only then did Kylie recall Burnett's dark tone and notice that his eyes glowed red. A sign that he was on the defensive. Obviously danger lurked close by.

"What's happened?" Derek asked.

"Someone else was here earlier," Burnett said.

"Who?" Kylie managed to ask.

"I don't know. But they're vampire and not one of us. Now get back to the camp."

"Maybe I should come with you?" Derek offered.

"And leave her alone?" Burnett asked firmly, his frown deepening.

Derek cut his gaze back to Kylie and then back to Burnett. "You're right. I'll make sure she gets back safe. Do you want me to come back?"

"No," Burnett insisted. "I'll be fine. Just keep an eye on the camp. Let everyone know to be on the lookout. Stay together."

And leave her alone? Burnett's question kept playing in Kylie's head and with each repetition, she felt more annoyed. She wanted to insist she could take care of herself. God knew Della would be having conniption fits at being treated like she needed to be protected. Then Kylie recalled how frightened she'd felt before she'd started to run, before she'd found Derek. Obviously, Kylie wasn't Della.

Did that mean she wasn't vampire? Or did it mean she was just a vampire lacking anything that resembled courage? Did yellow-bellied vampires even exist?

Burnett continued, "Don't let Holiday leave either. Tie her down if you have to. Got it?"

"Got it." Derek reached for Kylie's elbow and started walking.

Kylie didn't budge. "I felt it earlier," she blurted out. "It moved past me several times. Almost as if teasing or testing me." She recalled how it kept flying past, making its presence known without letting her see it.

"That's odd. Vampires don't normally tease. Or test," Burnett said. "They see prey and attack to kill. Now go back to the camp."

Chills ran up and down her legs. Derek sensed her fear because he reached for her hand and offered her palm a warm emotion-quieting squeeze. Her fear lessened.

"Come on. Let's get back." Derek took her by the elbow. The sound of his voice helped her brain connect to her limbs, and she started moving.

They walked at a fast pace and without talking. The sounds of an occasional owl and crickets sang out into the darkness. Not that she minded their music. Music was good. Music meant intruders weren't near.

"Why didn't you tell me a vampire came at you?" Derek asked, frustration adding a new layer of intensity to his voice.

"I . . . at first I thought it was Della and then . . ." Then she had thought it was Chan, but she couldn't tell Derek about Chan. She'd promised Della. "Then I heard you calling. And I started running and I wasn't so afraid anymore." She looked at the frown etched on his face. "I told you about the wolf."

"I think the vampire was a bigger deal."

"Yeah and I would have . . . told you, but you started kissing me."

"So that makes it my fault?" His tone came out harsher than before.

"Sort of," she said, not liking it that he was annoyed with her when only a few minutes ago they'd been kissing. She started walking faster.

They continued moving in tense silence for another five minutes. With each step, she realized how silly their argument was. "I probably should have told you right away. I wasn't thinking." She stared away from him, afraid he wouldn't accept her offer for a truce.

She heard him inhale. "I'm sorry. I shouldn't have been grumpy." He reached for her hand again. His palm felt good against hers. "It just scares me thinking that . . . that you could have been hurt." He sounded older. His voice deepened and his need to protect gave his tone a new quality. In spite of still feeling a bit annoyed at his thinking that she couldn't protect herself, she liked the new quality. It made her feel safer.

Yes, with Derek she felt safe, but it didn't stop her from looking at the trees and praying the wind didn't stop blowing, that the night didn't go silent again.

Chapter Three

"What happened?" Miranda cornered her in the dining hall twenty minutes later.

As soon as Derek had told Holiday about the rogue vampire on the prowl, she called everyone and told them to gather here.

Deep down, Kylie still trembled. Be it from fear, or perhaps Della's icy mood, Kylie couldn't say for sure. Della's cold shoulder could be felt from clear across the room.

"Come on, spill it," Miranda said. "And then I've got something to tell you."

Kylie looked at Della again. "How mad is she at me?"

Miranda glanced across the room. "On a scale of one to ten, ten being totally vampire pissed off, I'd say she's about a fifteen . . . and climbing."

"Great," Kylie muttered.

Miranda shrugged. "She'll get over it. You know how she is. Now tell me what happened."

Kylie shook her head. "I ran off and . . ."

"But why did you run off? Why did you . . . drink the blood like it was a cold beer on a hot Friday night?"

Kylie looked down at her shoes. She didn't want to talk about this, not now. "I don't know."

"You liked how it tasted, didn't you?" Miranda sounded offended.

The most Kylie could do was nod.

"Okay, then what happened?" A frown marred Miranda's expression.

Kylie swallowed the tightness down her throat.

"Come on, give it up," Miranda snapped.

"I ran and then I felt someone there—a vampire someone. And then I heard Derek. I think he scared off whoever was there. I took off running and found Derek and then we just . . ."

"You what?" Miranda asked, hanging on to her every word.

Started making out. "Nothing. Burnett showed up."

A whisk of air blasted them as Della came to a sudden stop beside Kylie. "And you told him you thought it was Chan, didn't you?" Della obviously had been listening the whole time.

Kylie looked at Della. "No. I didn't."

"Who's Chan?" Miranda asked.

"Nobody," Della snapped at Miranda. "Mind your own business." Obviously, Della didn't want anyone to know her vampire and scoundrel cousin had broken one of the biggest Shadow Falls rules: no visitors without permission passes. That especially went for those who were against the FRU's attempts to govern the supernaturals.

Miranda, unhappy, glared right back at Della.

"Was it Chan?" Kylie asked, not caring if Miranda overheard. Kylie understood Della's loyalty to Chan. He'd been the one who'd helped Della get through the painful change. However, it made sense that if Chan had broken the rule once, he very well might break it again.

"I told you he wouldn't come back," Della snapped.

"But how can you be so sure?" Suddenly Kylie remembered how frightened she'd been in the woods when she'd met Della's smug cousin. She folded her arms over her middle and took on a defensive posture. Just because Della believed Chan wasn't a threat, didn't mean crap. He could be a part of the Blood Brothers gang as far as Kylie knew.

"Because I trust him, unlike other people. I thought you and Miranda were friends. All I asked was that you respect the fact that tonight was important to me. That—"

Kylie's frustration level peaked. "Damn it, Della. Why does everything always have to be about you?" The words hadn't fully left Kylie's mouth when she spotted the look in Della's eyes. The same look her friend got every time her parents came to visit. The look that told Kylie that Della felt like an outcast.

Kylie dropped her attitude. "I didn't mean to show disrespect. I just freaked out, okay?"

"Why?" Della's anger sounded in her voice, but it was hurt that colored her eyes.

"Why what?" Kylie asked, but deep down she knew what Della was asking her. She just needed a few seconds to figure out how to word it so it wouldn't sound so bad.

Della moved an inch closer. "You freaked out because you don't want to be a vampire, right? You think I'm a monster, don't you? You're scared to death that you might become like me. That's why you freaked out, wasn't it?"

Kylie opened her mouth to answer but no words came out. Probably because she couldn't lie to Della. The vampire would know the truth. Della turned to leave. Kylie reached out to stop her, but Della was gone.

"Where did she go?" Kylie searched the dining room twice and still couldn't find her. The room was filled with excited campers milling around.

"Just let her go cool off," Miranda said.

"I can't." Kylie knew how much this hurt Della.

Finally Kylie spotted Della's midnight-colored straight hair behind a group of shape-shifters. Kylie started walking over.

Miranda followed her. "Seriously, why don't you just give her some time?"

"Go away," Della growled before Kylie came to a complete stop.

"No." Kylie stood her ground.

Della's eyes glowed gold with anger. Then her top lip raised just enough to show her extended canines. There was a time when seeing Della like that would have scared the bejeebies out of Kylie, but not anymore. She wasn't afraid of Della.

"I don't think you're a monster," Kylie said. "But that doesn't mean I wasn't scared."

"Liar," Della growled.

"I'm not lying. Check my heartbeat if you want," Kylie said. "Listen to my heart, see if I'm lying."

Della turned to walk away, and Kylie caught her elbow this time. "Don't you dare walk away," Kylie insisted.

"Let me go," Della rumbled in a low voice. When Kylie didn't let go, the vampire swung around, her eyes brighter, her teeth fully exposed.

Kylie heard a few murmurs in the crowd. The argument had obviously drawn attention. Della heard it, too, because she looked around and hissed. The few people standing close by scattered like scared mice.

Kylie still wasn't afraid.

"Uh, we should leave, too." Miranda bumped Kylie with her elbow. "She's really pissed off now."

Kylie didn't look at Miranda. She continued to stare at Della, letting her know that she wasn't afraid. "I'm not leaving until she hears me out."

"I don't have to hear you out. I know what you think." Della's angry glare, filled with so much hurt, slapped against Kylie.

"That's unfair." Kylie glared right back at the pissed-off vampire.

"What's unfair is that I thought you were my friend." The hurt in Della's eyes shined brighter through the golden hue.

"I am your friend. I gave you my blood," Kylie said.

"Me, too," added Miranda, sounding nervous.

When Della's expression didn't change, Kylie continued. "And I also remember you telling me how scared you were when you found out you were turning. You said you were so afraid of what was happening. You said you didn't want to change."

Della turned to leave again. But Kylie kept talking and didn't let go of her elbow. "Are you the only one allowed to be afraid?" Kylie felt the emotion swell in her chest, and tears filled her eyes. "Are you so special that no one else can feel that?"

Kylie half expected Della to zip off. Maybe even pull her arm out of her socket when she did.

She didn't. But neither did her friend turn around. She just stood there for several long seconds. One. Two. Three. Kylie counted and waited, hoping this meant—

"Fine," Della bit out in frustration, and finally turned around. Her eyes were no longer gold. She looked down, then up again. "You're right." She looked away and then back at Kylie. "I'm sorry."

"Damn," Miranda said a little loud. "I didn't know vampires could or would *ever* apologize."

Della shot Miranda a cold look. "I didn't apologize to you. So why don't you go find your broomstick and fly to Timbuktu. That is if your dyslexic, screwed-up sense of direction will get you there. And don't bother coming back, either."

Miranda took an offensive step toward Della. "You are so mean—"

Della bared her teeth and growled. "I heard you when you told Helen that blood was disgusting. You promised you would respect—"

"Is it disrespectful to be honest?" Miranda asked.

Kylie moved between them. "You two can sling insults, call each other names, and even kill each other later. But right now . . ." She looked at Miranda. "I need a minute alone with Della. Please."

Miranda's chin notched up a few inches. She didn't like it, but she walked away. That was the thing about Miranda. She might get pissed in a flicker of a heartbeat, almost as fast as Della, but Miranda got unpissed just as quickly. Della on the other hand—that girl knew how to hold a grudge. And while she pretended nothing could hurt her, Kylie saw her vulnerable streak and it ran even wider than Miranda's.

Finally alone, Della and Kylie stood there staring at each other. Kylie spoke first. "I'm sorry, too. I didn't mean to disrespect your culture. I really just freaked out."

Della nodded. "I get it. Didn't get it at first but . . . I do now." Della sighed and a smile touched her lips. "You loved it, didn't you? The blood. It was good."

Kylie wasn't proud of it, but she admitted the truth. "It was awesome."

Della touched Kylie's arm. "But you're still warm."

Kylie nodded. "And if I am vampire, wouldn't I already be cold?"

"I don't know," Della said honestly. "Maybe you just haven't changed yet. But you're about to."

Kylie remembered Della telling her that turning had felt like boiling water running through her veins.

"I'll be here for you," Della said as if she'd read Kylie's mind. "To help you through it. If it happens. You won't have to be alone. I think I remember most of what Chan did to help me."

"I know you will." Kylie tried to smile. Right then, she spotted Miranda staring at them from across the room, looking like a lost puppy. Kylie felt bad asking her to leave. "So will Miranda. She will be there for me. And she'd be there for you, too. I really . . . really wish you two would stop fighting."

Della shrugged. "She's just so good at pissing me off."

"And you her," Kylie defended Miranda.

"Yeah, but she's not like you. You seem to know what I'm feeling, always manage to say the right thing." Della's brow crinkled as if in thought. "It's almost as if you're an empath. You know, like Derek and Holiday and you can read emotions?"

"No," Kylie said, but deep down she couldn't help wonder. Hadn't she always been good at reading people? Like with her mom, she'd always sensed the distance her mother kept between them, knew there was something keeping her mom from bonding with her completely.

"Is everything okay?" The familiar female voice came from behind Kylie.

Kylie and Della looked over at Holiday.

"Yeah," Kylie and Della said at the same time.

Holiday gave Kylie's arm a squeeze. "We need to talk about what happened tonight, and we will just as soon as things calm down."

Kylie nodded and while Holiday's touch offered a small amount of comfort, she couldn't help but wonder if Holiday hadn't touched her just to check her temperature—to find out if she'd changed into a vampire.

"Later, okay?" Holiday asked.

"Yeah." Kylie did want to talk to Holiday, yet she sensed the camp leader would tell Kylie the same thing she always did. *I don't have the answers. I think this is something you must find out for yourself.*

But how was Kylie supposed to find the answers? Her plan of getting information from Daniel had been flushed down the toilet. Where did that leave her?

The chirp of Holiday's cell phone brought Kylie back to the present.

Holiday yanked the phone to her ear. "Burnett?" Holiday's expression hardened. "No. You have the wrong number."

Kylie heard the frustration in Holiday's tone. No doubt the camp leader was worried about Burnett. A little of that worry wiggled into Kylie. She'd been the one to run off from the vampire event—if anything happened to Burnett it would be Kylie's fault. Looking off at the log walls of the dining room, she tried to deal with the guilt.

Then Kylie remembered that Burnett was probably the last person in the world who couldn't take care of himself. The man was six foot three of hard muscle and his vamp powers were some of the strongest. Or so Della had said. Since Burnett had stepped in as a temporary assistant, Della had become a bit of a Burnett fan.

"I'm sure he's fine," Kylie offered, and leaned into a dining chair.

"No one stands a chance against him," Della insisted.

But neither Kylie's nor Della's comments helped. Holiday's brow remained pinched with worry. And it was more than normal concern, too. Kylie sensed the attraction between the two of them the first time she saw them together. Just because Holiday didn't want to get involved, didn't mean she didn't care.

Holiday dialed a number and then snapped her phone closed.

"Why would he turn off his phone?" Holiday's eyes tightened. "He has to have known I would want to talk to him."

"I can answer that," Della said. "You see, when you're out in the woods looking for someone, hoping to find them before they find you, nothing takes away your advantage more than a ringing phone."

The truth of Della's words only brought a deep frown to Holiday lips. "He could have called before he left. He's just being . . . difficult. I swear, I can't wait until they hire someone else. I simply cannot work with that man."

Della grinned. "You can't work with him, you say you don't like him, but look how worried you are about him."

"I'm not worried . . . I mean, I am worried, but not . . . It's not like . . ."

"Like you really care about him," Della finished off Holiday's sentence, and then continued. "Like you have the hots for him? Or do you have the hots for him? You know one might assume—"

"You got the hots for me?" Burnett's deep voice rang out as he moved to stand behind Holiday.

Holiday's face blushed—from anger or embarrassment, Kylie wasn't sure. Then Holiday swung around and confronted the tall, dark vampire. Burnett's eyes briefly met Kylie's and he nodded.

Kylie recalled what she'd been doing the last time Burnett's presence had startled her, and was sure her face reddened right along with Holiday's.

"So you're alive," Holiday snapped. While her voice expressed anger, her expression told another story—genuine, heartfelt relief. Seeing the emotion, Kylie forgot about her own embarrassment. No doubt about it. Holiday cared a lot about Burnett. Probably more than she wanted to admit.

"You never answered," he said. "You got the hots for me, or not?" His dark eyes lit up with a smile.

Squaring her shoulders, Holiday started talking. "Della assumed I might have the hots for you. And you know what they say about assuming, right?"

"It makes an ass out of you and me," Della answered, and gave Kylie the elbow. "Get it. A. S. S. U. M. E."

Holiday cut her eyes to Della in visual reprimand, then started walking away. She got three steps and swung back around. "Are you coming?" she snapped at Burnett.

"You didn't ask me to," he answered.

"Well, I assumed you would know I needed to discuss what happened."

He arched one dark brow upward. "And what did you just say about assuming?"

Della grinned and appeared totally entertained by Holiday and Burnett, but Kylie's thoughts went in another direction. She cleared her throat. "Didn't you guys agree to be forthcoming with all of us from now on? So why do you have to leave? Why can't we all hear this?"

Holiday frowned.

"She's right." Burnett held out both his hands. "You did say that at the meeting. I believe it was the same one at which you called me a jerk," he added.

Holiday's eyes brightened with frustration. Obviously the man didn't know when to keep his mouth shut.

"Fine," Holiday said between her closed teeth. The two of them stared at each other, and neither of them blinked. When the silence became long, Holiday let go of a deep breath. "Why don't you address everyone then?" She waved at the front of the room. "The floor is all yours."

"I think I could do that," Burnett answered, but his expression said he didn't really like addressing the group. Kylie also got the feeling that Holiday knew it.

Holiday shot off, and Burnett watched her go. "I don't know which is worse, talking to everyone or talking to her alone." He looked up at Kylie and flinched as if he hadn't meant to say that aloud. Then before he moved to the front, he looked at Della. Kylie could swear she saw him mouth the words "Thank you."

When he left, Kylie studied Della. "How long did you know Burnett was in the room?"

"Pretty much from the time Holiday walked over here." Della grinned. "Hey, we vampires have got to stick together." She nudged Kylie with her elbow as if saying Kylie was one of them. Kylie wasn't so sure she was. Then again, she wasn't sure she wasn't, either.

The door to the dining room swished open. Kylie looked that way. Derek walked into the dining room, and his gaze went straight to her. The sweet smile he sent her reminded her of the kisses they'd shared earlier. A warmth brought on by the memory filled her abdomen at the same time an unnatural coldness brushed her skin.

Goose bumps popped up on her arms when she heard the words again. *"You have to stop it. You have to. Or this will happen to someone you love. Soon. Soon. It will happen soon."*

"Who? How soon?" Kylie muttered under her breath. The spirit materialized only a foot from Kylie's face. She still wore the blood-soaked gown, only this time the blood dripped from the hem of her gown and pooled around her feet. Kylie's breath caught, and while it was the last thing Kylie wanted to think, her mind took her there. To the sweet, addictive flavor of blood.

"Soon what?" Della asked. Kylie looked from the ever-growing puddle of blood to Della's slightly slanted eyes that hinted at her Asian heritage. Then she watched those eyes widen with fear. Della shivered and took a step back. "You've got company again, don't you?"

Della ran off. At the same time several other campers standing close by started backing away as if they had figured out what was happening as well. Feeling ostracized, Kylie's throat tightened and her sinuses stung.

She fought to keep the tears from filling her eyes. When she looked back to the spirit, it had faded and the air had lost its chill.

Kylie's lungs swelled with frustration. Frustration, no doubt, brought on by all her unanswered questions. Her whole freaking life was one big unanswered question.

"Excuse me." Burnett's deep authoritative voice filled the room. "Can everyone give me your attention? I know you're all curious as to what happened tonight. And since Kylie reminded Holiday and me that we said we'd be more forthcoming with situations, I figure I'd best explain."

Chapter Four

Hearing Burnett speak lessened the emotional lump in Kylie's throat. Everyone looked toward the front.

"We had an uninvited visitor to the camp this evening," Burnett explained. "A vampire."

"Was it from that gang? The ones who attacked you guys at the wildlife park?" Helen asked, and glanced over at Kylie.

Kylie moved a little closer to the front, not wanting to miss Burnett's answer.

"I don't know for sure." He looked around the room as if searching for someone. A second later, his gaze settled on Holiday and his expression softened.

"But," Burnett continued, "I don't think they were here to hunt. If he or she were here to kill, he had a chance at easy prey and didn't take it." His gaze shifted to Kylie, making it clear, at least to Kylie, that she was the "easy prey."

Easy prey. Prey maybe, but *easy*? That annoyed Kylie more than she wanted to admit. Okay, sure, she wasn't exactly Superwoman, but she'd held her own fighting the Blood Brothers that night at the wildlife park. Granted, she'd had some help from Daniel, but nevertheless, she'd kicked ass right alongside everyone else. Didn't she get any credit for that?

Burnett cleared his throat. "Chances are it was just someone curious about the camp."

Kylie recalled how threatened she'd felt those few minutes back in the woods when she'd felt the vampire's presence. It had felt like more than just curiosity. It felt menacing. If Derek hadn't shown up, Kylie didn't know what would have happened, but she suspected it wouldn't have been good.

"Or it could be the gang just wanting to let us know they haven't run scared. It could have also have been just a friend or relative looking for someone, and they didn't want to go through our visitor check. And if any of you have a vampire friend who might try this, please let it be known loud and clear that entering this camp without getting a visitor's pass is considered a serious offense. If I find them, I'll treat them like a hostile. And that goes for all species, even humans."

Kylie hoped Della was listening. Personally, Kylie didn't care too much for Chan, but she knew Della did, and for her sake, Kylie would hate for something to happen to him.

Burnett's gaze grew cold with his warning before he continued. "While I don't see this as an out-and-out threat, neither do I think we should totally let our guards down. The Blood Brothers gang was stupid enough to try something once. They might be stupid enough to try again."

"I still don't understand what it is they have against us," one of Miranda's witch buddies said.

"I'll take that question," Holiday said, and made her way up front. "If you'll notice, we have more vampires here than any other species. The reason is clear. The virus can be passed down so many generations and therefore parents of a newly turned vampire may not even be aware that supernaturals exist. This makes living at home extremely difficult, which leads many of them to joining the gangs. But since the camp opened, we've saved more than four hundred newly turned vampires from following that dark path. We've obviously cut into their membership immensely. They see Shadow Falls as standing between them and their gangs' growth potential."

She paused. "Any other questions?" When no one spoke up, Holiday added, "Now, it's almost two in the morning, so why don't you all go back to your cabins and try to get some rest? But remember what Burnett said. Don't let your guard down."

As the crowd started to leave, Kylie went to join Miranda, who stood by herself in a corner and played a video game on her phone. When she saw Kylie, she cocked her head to the side and smirked. Which reminded Kylie of a cute but pissed-off puppy.

"Oh, so when everyone else abandons you, now you want to be around me," Miranda said.

Kylie frowned. "I hurt Della's feelings and I just needed to apologize." *And I couldn't do it with you two verbally scratching each other's eyes out.*

"But you don't care if you hurt my feelings," Miranda said. "It's good to know where I rate."

"You don't believe that," Kylie said.

"I don't?" She shook her head, her multicolored hair—pink, black, and green—shimmering around her shoulders. "Is this the way it's going to be from here on out? Because you're both vampire, you don't want me around."

"No. It's not like that. And . . . we don't know if I'm vampire."

"You liked the taste of blood."

"That doesn't make me a vampire." Frustration built in Kylie's chest. But when she met Miranda's eyes and saw the insecurity lingering in her friend's eyes, Kylie stopped thinking about her own fears. "And for the record, I'm sorry I hurt your feelings. I didn't mean to do that."

"And for the record, neither did I," Della added, joining them in the corner.

"Wow," Miranda looked at Della. "That's almost an apology. And to a dyslexic witch."

"Don't push it," Della said.

"Fine." A smile lit up Miranda's eyes. "Let's make a pact that no matter what Kylie ends up being, no matter what happens, we'll always stick together."

Della snorted. "What planet have you been on? We already made that pact."

They started moving toward the door but stopped when Holiday called out Kylie's name.

"Can I see you a minute?" the camp leader asked.

Della and Miranda said they'd wait outside. Kylie walked over to Holiday.

"I know you want to talk about what happened tonight, but I'd like to get my talk with Burnett out of the way first. Is it okay if I stop by your cabin and we can chat in your room?"

Kylie remembered Holiday's comment about it being late. "If you'd like to wait and talk to me in the morning, we . . ."

"No." Holiday's brow wrinkled. "Don't you want to talk about this tonight?"

Kylie stopped trying to be polite. "Yeah, I would like to talk."

Holiday gave her a quick hug. "It's going to be okay."

While Kylie realized she wasn't as scared as she was earlier about the whole vampire possibility, there was still a whole heck of a lot of ambivalence bouncing around her insides. "I know." She smiled and hoped she sounded more confident than she felt.

When Kylie got back outside, everyone had disappeared except Miranda and Della, who sat in the big white rocking chairs on the office cabin's porch.

"What did she want?" Miranda asked.

"To tell me she's going to drop by the cabin in a few minutes to talk."

"To talk about what?" Della asked.

"Stuff." She didn't want to open up the whole vampire thing for another discussion with Della.

Miranda hopped up from her chair. "You guys ready?"

They walked down the trail to their cabin. Between the stars and moon, it wasn't too dark. The night sang out its song, of which Kylie was more than grateful. It was when the night music stopped that Kylie worried.

"I got kissed tonight," Miranda blurted out.

"Wow," Kylie said. "Perry finally made a move, huh?"

"About time that guy grew a pair of balls." Della giggled.

"It wasn't Perry." Miranda kicked at the dirt-worn path.

"Not Perry?" Kylie grabbed Miranda by the elbow. "Who was it?"

"Yeah, who was it?" Della studied Miranda really hard. "If you say it's Steve, I'm kicking your little witch's ass. You know I have a thing for him."

"It wasn't your shape-shifter Steve." Miranda frowned. "It was Kevin."

Kylie's mouth dropped open. "Not Kevin, Perry's roommate and good friend? Please tell me it wasn't *that* Kevin."

"Okay, I won't tell you." Miranda dropped her face in her hands. "What am I going to do?" She peered at them through her fingers.

"This is not good," Kylie said.

Miranda still stared at them through the mask of fingers. "I didn't mean for it to happen." She dropped her hands. "I . . . I was coming back to the cabin thinking you might be here and I ran into Kevin. I was worried about you. We started walking together and talking and then . . . then, he just kissed me and . . ."

"And what?" Della asked.

"And I didn't stop him."

"But was it yummy?" Della asked.

"Sort of. A little bit. I don't know. Why do I feel so guilty?"

Kylie stared at Miranda. "Because you've been acting like you like Perry."

"But Perry's not acting like he likes me. Sure, he sits with me sometimes at lunch and dinner, but don't you think if he liked me he'd have kissed me or something?"

"I think he's just nervous," Kylie said.

"I think he doesn't have a pair of balls," Della added.

"Stop it!" Miranda's face grew red.

"Stop what?" Della asked.

"Stop talking about Perry's genitalia. It's crude and I don't like it."

Della grinned. "Ooh-la-la, somebody likes Perry enough to defend his boys."

"So what if I like him. What's it to you?" Miranda placed her hands on her hips.

"It's nothing to me." Della's tone now sounded annoyed. "But it might be something to Kevin since you sucked face with him earlier tonight."

"Stop it," Kylie said. "I swear. Can you two not go fifteen minutes without getting pissy with each other?"

"She started it," both Della and Miranda said at the same time.

Kylie looked from one girl to the other. "Both of you started it. And both of you need to stop it. I'm up to here with it." Kylie put her hand on her forehead. "Seriously, I mean—"

"Shh." Della put a finger over Kylie's lips.

"What is it?" Miranda whispered.

"Do you not know what *shh* means?" Della asked.

Kylie pushed Della's finger from her lips and listened. A silence filled the night. Not the total kind of silence as it was back in the woods, because in the distance, sounding almost like background music, she could hear the insects and birds, but close by, everything had grown quiet.

Kylie leaned in and whispered, "Is it another vampire?"

Chapter Five

Della raised her nose in the air. "Not vampire. It's a wolf. It's been following us for a few minutes. I got a whiff of it a few minutes ago, and I thought it was just passing by. But it's not." She pointed toward the woods.

"What's a wolf doing this close to the camp?" Miranda asked.

Just like that, Kylie remembered the wolf from tonight. Derek hadn't made a big deal of it, so neither had Kylie.

"You wanna see me kick some wolf butt?" Della's eyes lit up as if the thought thrilled her.

Kylie remembered the wolf and its submissive posture. It hadn't been threatening. "No, I don't want to see you kick wolf butt." She grabbed Della's elbow.

"Why not?" Della asked. "It's not a werewolf. It's just an animal."

"Yeah, a real live animal. It's not hurting us," Kylie said. "So why would you hurt it?"

"It's following us. And that's creepy," Della answered.

Miranda leaned in. "I hate to say this but I agree with Della. It's creepy."

Kylie stared into the woods, and between the collage of trees she spotted the golden eyes staring back at her. A shiver ran up her spine. Creepy? Maybe, but it still hadn't hurt anyone. Then Kylie couldn't help but wonder if the wolf's presence wasn't some sort of message, or a piece of a puzzle. Or was it like Derek had said, just a hybrid animal wanting company?

"Oh man. Is that its eyes?" Miranda pointed into the woods.

"Yeah," Della snapped. "And I don't like it. I'm really in the mood to kick wolf butt."

Realizing Della was serious, Kylie snatched up a small rock and slung it in the direction of the wolf. "Go away," she yelled.

The rustle of underbrush filled the silence as the animal shot off. Then she looked up at Miranda and Della. "There, it's gone. Happy now?"

The sound of the insects started chiming again.

"Not really," Della said. "It would have been more fun if I'd done it my way. I could have used a snack."

"Tell me you wouldn't have killed it," Kylie insisted.

"Just a little bit." Della grinned.

Kylie rolled her eyes and hoped like heck Della was joking.

"Is it really gone?" Miranda looked down the line of the woods.

"Yeah," Della said, and they started walking again. But Kylie couldn't help but look back and question just exactly why the wolf was here. Then a thought hit and it felt as if Kylie's heart bounced around her ribs for a second. Could Lucas be trying to send her a message?

"Back to my problem," Miranda said as they approached their cabin. "What am I going to do about Kevin?"

"That's simple." Della jumped up onto the cabin porch. She turned around and looked back at Miranda. "You have to make up your mind." She held out her right palm. "Do you want Kevin?" She held out her left palm. "Or do you want Perry? It's not really that hard. Kevin?" She lifted her right hand. "Or Perry." She moved her left hand up higher.

"What if I choose Perry, but he never chooses me? Never makes a move. Never even kisses me. What if I end up being the oldest witch virgin alive?"

"Then you'll know you screwed up." Della shrugged.

"You're not a lot of help." Miranda looked at Kylie. "What do you think?"

"I think . . ." Kylie remembered kissing Derek tonight, wanting things to be different, but feeling as if something was always stopping her from taking that leap. Then she remembered feeling torn between Derek and Lucas.

"I think you shouldn't come to me for relationship advice. I suck at it." Kylie shot up the steps and went into the cabin.

Thirty minutes later, Kylie snuggled in her bed with her kitten, the kitten Lucas had given her. Outside her door, she heard Miranda and Della talking to Holiday. When the camp leader had knocked on the cabin door, Kylie pulled the blanket over her face and closed her eyes. She felt her kitten climb on top and paw at the blanket. It wasn't that she no longer wanted to talk to Holiday. It was more like she doubted this chat would help.

How many times did she have to hear Holiday say "I don't know, Kylie, this is something you'll have to figure out for yourself"? Why did Kylie think this talk would be any different? Wasn't that the definition of insanity? To do the same thing over and over again and expect different results?

"Kylie?" Holiday's voice penetrated the blanket as she tapped on the door.

Leaving the blanket over her head, Kylie called out, "Come in."

Kylie heard the door open into her tiny room, she heard it shut, and she heard Holiday come to a stop. "That wasn't a very enthusiastic welcome," the camp leader said.

"You want me to fake it?" Kylie moved the blanket off her head and sat up. Socks moved to snuggle in beside her.

Holiday smiled and sat down at the foot of Kylie's bed. "I know it's tough."

"You don't know the half of it." Kylie pulled her knees to her chest and watched Socks move over to the camp leader and rub his face against her arm. "I had a plan to figure it all out. All I needed to do was get Daniel to hang around long enough to tell me what he was, so I'd know what I am. He finally shows up tonight, but he doesn't have any answers." Kylie's throat tightened.

Holiday looked genuinely puzzled. "How could he not have the answers?"

"Because he was adopted. He didn't realize he wasn't human until he was eighteen. And I don't even know where to start to find the answers now."

"You'll figure it out," Holiday said, stroking Socks from his head to his tail. "I believe that with all my heart."

Kylie's eyes started to sting, which basically meant that the tears were on their way. "Does liking the taste of blood make me a vampire?"

Holiday hesitated.

"Wait. Let me guess. You don't know, do you? And then you're going to tell me that this is probably something I just need to find out for myself." Kylie wiped the first of the tears from her eyes.

Holiday let go of a deep sigh, then reached over and took Kylie's hand. "You're only partially right. Right in the fact that I don't know if you are vampire. But I think I can honestly say that liking the taste of blood doesn't make you one. I know of humans who enjoy drinking blood and that doesn't make them vampire. Even if some of them are freaks and they think it does."

"So this whole thing could be insignificant." Kylie pulled her hand away from Holiday.

"Yeah, it could be insignificant." Holiday's tone left a lot of doubt.

"But you don't believe that."

"I think it probably means something. I just don't know if it means you're vampire."

"But what else could it mean?"

Holiday gazed at Kylie with a ton of sympathy shimmering in her green eyes. "I don't know. But . . . I do believe that if you keep searching, all the answers you *really* need will be answered."

"*Really* need?" Kylie repeated Holiday's words. "As if I don't need *all* of the answers?"

Holiday raised her right eyebrow. "We never figure it all out, Kylie. Some things are meant to be a mystery."

"Maybe some things," Kylie said. "But not this. Not about what I am. I feel as if everything in my life is on hold until I have this answer."

"Then keep searching," Holiday said.

Kylie dropped her head on her knees and moaned. "See, I knew you would say that." Socks came running over as if to check on her.

Holiday put her hand on top of Kylie's head. "When one door closes, find another."

Kylie gazed back up. "And what if there isn't another door?"

"Then you try the window."

"And if there's not a window?" Kylie asked.

"Then you find a sledgehammer and make a window. Life isn't supposed to be easy. Generally speaking, the harder something is the more rewarding the results will be."

"But what if I fail?" Kylie asked. "What if someone is stabbed to death because I wasn't smart enough to find the right answers? I've done what you said and asked specific questions and all the ghost ever does is repeat the warning. She just keeps saying, 'This will happen to someone else,' if I don't stop it. She won't tell me who, when, or where. How the heck am I supposed to find those answers?"

"How do you know someone will be stabbed?" Holiday asked.

"Because she's bleeding profusely and it looks like her gown has been sliced and diced. Bullet holes are round."

"You've seen a bullet hole?" Holiday asked.

"On television."

Holiday bit back a grin. "Okay, I see where you might think it's about a stabbing, and she could be trying to tell you that, but remember when Daniel first came to you, you thought he'd been wrongly accused of a war crime."

Kylie slumped back on her pillow. "I suck at this."

"At what?" Holiday asked. "Communicating with ghosts? I told you, they're the ones who need a refresher course in getting their messages across."

"Not just the ghosts," Kylie said. "Everything. I suck at *not* being human."

"Not true." Holiday bumped Kylie with her shoulder. "You've done better than I ever thought you would."

Kylie cut her eyes up to the camp leader. "Is that supposed to be a compliment?"

Holiday chuckled. "Yeah, it is." She paused. "Hey, if it makes you feel any better, sometimes I'm pretty sure I suck at everything, too."

Kylie stared at Holiday and saw a touch of regret flickering in the depth of her eyes. "Do any of those things involve Burnett?"

"That is a subject I think I'll pass on right now." Holiday let go of a deep breath that hinted at frustration and Kylie felt certain it was all about Burnett.

Kylie remembered telling Miranda she shouldn't ask her about relationships, but for some reason Kylie couldn't stop herself from speaking up now. "Della was right tonight when she said you seemed to care about him."

Holiday twisted her ponytail in a tight knot. "I care about world peace. I care about the mangled moral compasses of today's politicians. I care about all the innocent creatures pancaked on that stretch of road two miles past our camp. Point is, I care about a lot of things, and my caring isn't going to change a thing—especially not a relationship between myself and that stubborn, egotistical, macho vampire."

"You're attracted to him," Kylie said. "And don't try to deny it. You've even admitted that much to me."

"Okay, I won't deny that. He's got that whole hard body, vampire magnetism going for him. But when I was young, I had a crush on Big Bird. That wouldn't have worked out either."

"Big Bird. Really?" Kylie asked. "It was the Cookie Monster for me." They both laughed, and then Kylie added in a serious tone, "It could work if you wanted it bad enough."

"I haven't got that much patience."

"Hmm," Kylie said. "Some very smart person just told me that the harder something is the more rewarding the results will be."

Holiday studied Kylie. "Do you really not have enough worries of your own to chew on that you want to take on my issues, too?"

"Everyone else's seems easier than mine." Kylie smiled.

"Ever heard that saying about the grass always looks greener on the other side? Well, it's the same way with problems. We all have our hurdles to overcome. So why don't you solve yours and let me take care of mine?" Holiday brushed a lock of Kylie's hair behind her ear. "But thank you for caring."

Holiday smiled and Kylie once again felt the bond between them inch closer. Kylie had long wondered what it would be like to have an older sister. She couldn't help but think this was as close as she'd ever get to that type of relationship.

Holiday studied Kylie and her eyebrows twitched. Kylie knew Holiday was testing to see if Kylie had opened up the doors of her mind. The first day at camp, Kylie had learned that supernaturals had the ability to read brain patterns. Supernaturals also allowed other supernaturals to read deeper, to get a glimpse of who and what they were.

Not Kylie, of course. The only brain pattern she'd been able to see had been that of the ghost of her real dad. And while other supernaturals could see Kylie's brain pattern, she had yet to learn to open up to let anyone get a deeper glimpse.

"Are you doing the mental exercises I told you to do?" Holiday asked.

"Yes," Kylie said, and watched the camp leader's brow crease. At least twenty minutes a day, Kylie was supposed to meditate. But so far it hadn't helped, or at least if it had, no one had told her.

"Anything?" Kylie asked, not wanting to be the odd duck anymore.

"No. You're still tight as a drum. Any luck reading anyone?"

"No. Maybe I'm a supernatural retard."

Holiday rolled her eyes. "If anything I think it's just the opposite. I think your brain is holding off giving you your powers until it thinks you're capable and mature enough to deal with them."

"Are you calling me immature?" Kylie made her point and stuck out her tongue.

"Not immature." Holiday chuckled. "I think you're wiser than a lot of girls your age." Her expression went serious again. "But that doesn't mean that you haven't got a lot to learn." Holiday stood up. "Do you think you can sleep now?"

"Maybe," Kylie said, but deep down, she doubted it.

Holiday got to the door, then turned back. "Oh, about the ghost problems. If she doesn't give you anything to work with the next time she shows up, tell her you're going to shut her out until she offers something more concrete. Then do it. If she doesn't give you something different, change channels on her. Nothing ticks off a ghost more than being ignored. That usually makes them figure out a better approach."

"How do I change channels?" Kylie asked.

"Concentrate on something else. It has to be something you want to think about." Holiday's brow rose as if she'd just remembered something. "Like making out with Derek."

Kylie saw something in the camp leader's eyes and she knew. "Burnett told you."

Holiday nodded. "And I'm not going to get involved with that, but just promise me you're not doing anything you'll regret."

"Nothing happened," Kylie said.

"This time." Holiday let go of another of her deep sighs.

Kylie sat up a little straighter. "Derek would never try to pressure me into . . . anything."

Holiday's chin lowered and her gaze zeroed in on Kylie with startling effect. "It's not Derek I'm worried about, Kylie."

Kylie looked down at her hands, feeling exposed. How did Holiday know how close Kylie was to giving in? Then Kylie remembered Holiday was just like Derek—she could read people's emotions. Obviously, just being around Derek had Kylie putting out turned-on vibrations. Good grief, she might as well just put a sign around her neck that said I'M HORNY. And wasn't that just lovely?

"Kylie . . . it's nothing to be embarrassed about. And I'm not asking you not to . . . What I'm asking is that when you do make that decision, it's a decision you make rationally and not one you just let happen. You understand the difference?"

Kylie nodded.

"Good." Holiday walked out.

Even after the door closed, Kylie's chest filled with even more emotion—embarrassment, uncertainty, and a touch of resentment. She didn't want Holiday or anyone knowing her deepest emotions or desires.

Then she recalled the sister-like bond she'd found with Holiday, the one Kylie totally valued. She supposed there was a downside to every good bond. She supposed a real older sister, even an all-human one, would have felt compelled to talk to her about sex.

As Kylie dropped her head back on the pillow, she remembered how it had felt to kiss Derek and wondered if she could ever make a rational decision where he was concerned. Especially when he had the ability to control her emotions.

Socks leapt up on the mattress, and Kylie was totally caught off guard when her thoughts went from kissing Derek to kissing Lucas.

Great. Just freaking great. She grabbed her pillow so tight that if it had a life, she'd killed it. Socks let out a pathetic meow and scurried back to the foot of the bed. Kylie moaned into the foam stuffing beneath the pillow case. She was already going to have a hard enough time sleeping and now she had the whole Derek versus Lucas thing to mull over.

Chapter Six

An hour later and she hadn't hit a lick of sleep yet. Well, not more than a few seconds. Every time she'd almost be there, she'd get this strange kind of sensation as if she was floating, or maybe flying, and the odd feeling would yank her from the light slumber. Once, right before she'd awoken, she'd spotted Lucas, as if she was about to dream of him.

He'd been surrounded with what looked like clouds, and a cool breeze stirred the foggy atmosphere. Just when she'd get a good look at him another cloud would float by, hiding him from her. He'd been wearing a button-down shirt, left unbuttoned, and that breeze would pick up the ends of the shirt, showing off his chest and flat stomach. That's when the cloudy atmosphere started moving faster and the sensation of flying grew stronger and yanked her awake.

Catching her breath, she sat up and pushed her hair from her face. Disappointment started to build, but she chased it away. She couldn't even think about the other "Lucas" dream—them in the water, only partially clothed—without blushing. She certainly didn't need to add a second dream to her couldn't-think-about list.

Rolling over, she punched her pillow as if the bag of foam

could be the blame. Then sitting all the way up, she turned on her light and without even knowing what she planned to do, she pulled out the letter. The letter from Lucas. The one Holiday had given her weeks ago but she hadn't read.

Hi Kylie,

I've started writing this letter a dozen times and crumpled it up and tossed it away. Maybe it's because I don't know what to say, when there is so little I can say at this point and time. Maybe it's because I just shouldn't write you, because . . . it's wrong. There are so many reasons why I shouldn't think about you all the time, reasons that have nothing to do with you and everything to do with me. I know I'm not making sense and if I could, I would explain it to you. Hell, maybe if things turn out the way I hope, I can explain it to you. Not sure that would change anything, but damn if I don't hope.

Do you see why I keep tearing this letter up? It doesn't make sense, does it?

What should make sense is this. You are so special, Kylie. And I'm sorry I didn't say this to your face. I'm sorry I didn't tell you right away that I remembered you. But I was so shocked to see you that first day at camp. Shocked and thrilled. You knew things about me that I'd tried to keep hidden—hidden from everyone including myself. My parents did some very bad things, and while I was young and didn't know better, I participated in much of it. You have no idea how hard I've tried to forget about that time of my life.

Actually, you were the only thing I didn't want to forget about. The little blond neighbor girl who looked like an angel, and who was a mystery. What were you? Who were you? You both scared and intrigued me even back then. I didn't understand how you made me feel inside. I wanted to kill the boys who threw those rocks at you,

I wanted to touch your hair to see if it was as soft as it looked. On full moons, I would watch you, hoping that you would turn. That you would end up being a were.

I think I just figured out why I have to write this letter. To tell you what you meant to me, just in case I never get to tell you that in person. Now if I can just put this in an envelope before I decide this is stupid and toss it in the trash.

Thinking of you.

Lucas

P.S. Dream of me.

His last line seemed to echo in her head. *Dream of me.* If only he knew . . .

Then all her other emotions were chased away by the residual anger. Just exactly what did he mean, dream of him? Dream of him doing what? Playing leap frog with Fredericka?

Kylie stuffed the letter back into its envelope and dropped it back in the drawer. Did he think his letter was supposed to make her feel better? If she was so special, why had he run off with Fredericka? Why hadn't he even tried to explain that to Kylie in the letter? Why was he being so secretive?

Did he think she wouldn't know that Fredericka was with him? Did he think it wouldn't matter? Duh, he'd admitted having had sex with the girl. He admitted that she thought they were a couple. And now he took off with her. How could he think Kylie wouldn't be upset about that? Were all men just dogs? No, wait . . . make that wolves?

No, she really needed to completely get over Lucas. Move on. And that was exactly what she intended to do. Cutting off her light, she dropped back on the pillow. Then she got a vision of

Lucas and the she-wolf making out and she gave the pillow one last punch.

The next morning Kylie had to drag herself out of bed to get dressed and comb her hair. She'd tried to go back to sleep after waking up at dawn with the icy chill of a spirit's visit. It hadn't worked. Now, with only an hour or two of sleep, she really would have loved to have buried her head under the pillow and ignored the daily grind. Who needed a thing like breakfast or nutrition? She dropped her butt back down on the bed.

She'd almost fallen back asleep when a thought jarred her fully awake again. Was she not hungry because she'd drunk the blood last night? Was she already losing her appetite for human food?

"You coming?" Miranda called out.

"Yeah, I'm coming." She fell back on her pillow, stared at the ceiling, and tried to decipher how she felt about all this in the morning light. So okay, the idea of becoming a vampire didn't feel like the end of the world anymore, but it still felt like a major calamity. Plus, she needed to know. Had a right to know what she was.

"You coming in the next century?" Della yelled out about three minutes later.

Calling Della a name under her breath, she started to sit up.

"Right back at you," Della yelled in return.

Yelled. Della yelled it back. Kylie tilted her head and tuned into the noises around her to see if her hearing had become supercharged overnight. But nope, she couldn't hear any better than she had last night. Which could mean Holiday was right. Her liking blood didn't mean Kylie was vampire.

Or at least not yet.

Forcing herself to get up, she ran a hand through her hair and went to face her roommates and the day.

"Good morning to you, too," Miranda said when Kylie stepped out of her room and didn't say a word.

Kylie shot her a mock smile. Then she did what she did every morning. She studied Miranda, twitched her eyebrows, and stared really hard at her campmate's forehead in hopes of seeing her pattern. But nothing. Just a tiny pimple near her hairline. Not that Kylie would inform Miranda of it. The girl would likely freak.

"You sure are perky this morning," Della said, joining them from her room.

"Didn't sleep well," Kylie said.

"Me, either," Miranda chimed in, and sighed pathetically. "What am I going to do if Perry finds out that Kevin kissed me?"

Della chuckled. "Run and hide before he turns into a fire-breathing dragon and scorches your ass."

"I'm serious," Miranda snapped back.

"And you think I'm not?"

Miranda glared at her.

Della shrugged as if conceding and started for the door. "First, you need to decide what you want to do."

"What do you mean?" Miranda asked as they walked out of the cabin. Then while waiting to hear Della answer, Miranda turned around and waved her hand up and then down at the door, putting a protective charm in place.

Miranda had started doing it last week, saying she felt an uninvited presence trying to come in. Part of Kylie wondered if it were the ghosts that Miranda wanted to keep out. Not that it was working. Every morning at the first sign of dawn, Kylie was awakened by the cold.

"I mean," Della answered, "are you going to start liking Kevin, or are you planning to hang in there with the shape-shifter in hopes that Perry will . . ."

"Don't say it. Leave his testicles out of your dialogue." Miranda pointed a finger at Della.

Della jumped the rest of the way off the steps then looked back up at Miranda with mock innocence. "I wasn't going to mention his testicles."

From the grin on Della's face, Kylie knew the vampire was lying. Nevertheless, she had a good point.

"She's right." Kylie put in her two cents' worth. "You need to make a decision."

Miranda frowned and pulled back her hair. They walked a few minutes without talking. Miranda seemed to be contemplating something.

"But I don't have to make it like . . . right now," Miranda said. "Do I? I mean, there's a chance that Kevin will just forget it happened. It wasn't really even that good of a kiss."

"Hey, Miranda." The voice came from about fifty feet behind them.

All three girls turned around and confronted the mediocre kisser moving down the walking path.

"Fat chance that he forgot," Della said and sniffed the air. "You don't even want to know about his hormones right now. The guy's got it bad for you."

"Really?" Miranda asked. "I thought you said you couldn't read the hormones and pheromones of a shape-shifter? When Perry was a bird, you said—"

"I said I didn't know what horny birds smelled like. But in their natural states, shape-shifters pollute the air with their lust just like everyone else does." She waved a hand in front of her face.

Miranda looked from Della to Kevin, who was closing in on them.

"Hi." He stopped right in front of the three of them. Kylie had never really noticed Kevin before, but she supposed he was kind of hot in his own way. Not anywhere near Derek's status, but he had some boy charm. And if you asked Kylie, he was even cuter than Perry, not that Kylie disliked Perry. The shape-shifter had sort of grown on Kylie these last few weeks.

"Did you sleep well?" Kevin asked Miranda, and dropped his hands inside the pocket of his khaki shorts. Kylie noted the navy T-shirt he wore hung a bit loose on his medium-size frame. His hair, a brownish blond, hung a little on the long side. He grinned, his blue-eyed gaze zeroing in on Miranda with obvious romantic interest.

"Yeah," Miranda answered, which was a lie, and Kylie noted Della rolling her eyes.

"I thought maybe we could walk together to breakfast," Kevin said.

"Okay. I guess."

Miranda looked to Kylie as if to ask if she thought her answer had been a mistake.

Kylie didn't know what to think, so she just smiled nonchalantly. No doubt, if Perry found out Miranda and Kevin were hooking up, he would be hurt. While Kylie wasn't afraid of Perry, a lot of other campers feared his powers. So hurting Perry could be a bad thing. But then Kylie saw the blush rise in Miranda cheeks and she also noticed how the girl stood a little straighter. Right or wrong, Kevin's interest in her was doing wonders for her friend's confidence.

When Miranda and Kevin took off ahead, Kylie and Della hung back. They stood there without talking until Miranda and Kevin took the turn in the trail that offered them some privacy.

"Whatcha think?" Kylie asked Della as they both started walking at a slow pace so as not to catch up with the two ahead of them.

Della rolled her eyes. "I think sooner or later some serious shit is going to hit the fan."

"Yeah, but did you see how her eyes lit up?" Kylie asked. "Everyone wants to think a guy likes her. Maybe Perry will see it and realize he needs to make a move."

"That's when the shit will hit the fan. You do not play with a shape-shifter's emotions, especially not one as powerful as he is. I'm telling you, the fact that Perry didn't turn himself into a wild boar and gore your ass the night you bobbed his ear is a miracle. It was the first thing Chan explained about the supernatural world to me. Beware of shape-shifters, they are one badass species."

Della tilted her head to the side as if listening. "Oh, shit. Make that sooner."

"What?" Kylie asked, not that Della answered.

Della had disappeared. Kylie didn't understand until she heard Miranda scream and some serious animal roaring punctuated the morning air.

Running with everything she had, which was amazingly fast compared to the speed she could run a month ago, Kylie got to the V in the trail just in time to see two huge black bears swinging claws at one another.

Della was holding Miranda, who fought to get away, as if she wanted to break up the fighting animals. It took Kylie about half a second to realize that these weren't your average giant bears. Nope. They had to be Perry and Kevin.

When the larger bear raked its claw across the other bear's shoulder and blood squirted onto the dirt path, Kylie screamed out, "Stop it!"

She would have gotten more attention from a brick wall. The

two angry animals continued to swing at each other. Suddenly, a few sparkles filled the air, and one bear transformed into a lion, a lion about the size of a minivan. Its roar rang so loud, it hurt Kylie's ears. Within a few more seconds, the other bear transformed into a lion—only larger. The sound of clashing teeth could be heard between the piercing roars, and more blood moistened the dry earth beneath their paws.

Kylie didn't know if the damage the two shape-shifters did to each other was permanent or if when they transformed they came back in one piece. When one lion grabbed the other by the throat, Kylie realized she couldn't just stand by and watch these two possibly kill each other. Not thinking about the consequences, she flung herself into the mix, grabbed the larger lion by its mane, and yanked as hard as she could.

"Don't do that," Della yelled out, and while Kylie couldn't see her, she suspected Della was talking to her. And just when Kylie actually considered listening to Della's advice, the huge cat stood up on his back paws, bringing Kylie up with him. With her two fists knotted in the orange hair of the lion's mane, Kylie's feet swung in the air. The beast opened its mouth, blood dripped from his teeth, and it roared with fury unlike anything Kylie had ever heard. The feline's angry eyes cut back at Kylie. She saw the eyes turn from a deep gold to purple. And somehow she knew this was Perry.

"Put me down and stop fighting!" she yelled.

Right then the other lion rammed Perry in the side. The hit jolted Perry back and Kylie almost lost her hold on the mane. She looked to the ground a good six feet below. The fall would no doubt hurt, might break a bone, but she would survive. However, the fall would also put her right in the path of Kevin's angry swipes and snapping jaws. Surviving that might be a little harder, so she tightened her hold on the mane and hung on for dear life.

Perry started shaking his head as if to rid himself of her presence. She swung from the right to the left like a not-so-loved stuffed animal in the hands of an angry child. Kylie's fingers started to slip. She glanced back down, trying to figure out an escape route, but her thoughts shifted when she saw Kevin's jaws sink into Perry's soft lion underbelly. Tightening her hold on the thick mane, she raised her foot and kicked the attacking lion right in the eye to stop him from killing Perry. Kevin let go, but when he retreated, Kylie saw blood dripping from his mouth.

Perry roared, from pain or fury Kylie wasn't sure. Maybe both.

Kylie heard Della yelling something. Next, Kylie felt her friend flying past as if in an attempt to rescue her, but each time she passed, Perry would shift direction, moving Kylie out of Della's reach.

"Enough!" Kylie screamed at the lions. "Both of you, stop it! Stop it or I'll get the death angels here."

The words no more than left her mouth when Kylie felt the temperature drop around her. The air in her throat felt icy. Her idle threat rang in her ears. But then she couldn't help but wonder . . . Did she have the power to call forth the death angels or was this just Daniel or another ghost making their presence known at an inopportune time?

Or maybe an appropriate time.

Hadn't Daniel helped her in the past? Suddenly it didn't matter, because she saw bright orange sparkles appearing around Kevin. Perry drew back his right paw as if to attack Kevin during his morphing stage.

"Don't do it, Perry," Kylie demanded.

Perry roared as if complaining, but he came back down on his four paws. Kylie let go of his mane and dropped. Still a couple feet off the ground, she landed off balance on her feet and then fell flat on her butt. When she looked up, there were sparkles appearing around Perry and she saw his human form take shape. With clothes, thank goodness.

He looked down at her, his eyes glowing bright yellow, and fury still filled his expression. But he wasn't bleeding. "That was stupid of you. Never, never ever get in the middle of a fight with shape-shifters. You could die."

"You're scolding me?" Kylie asked, flabbergasted that he had the nerve to reprimand her. "I wasn't the one trying to maul a fellow campmate. And I was trying to protect you." She leaned on one hip and rubbed her bruised backside.

"I didn't need protecting." His voice boomed and his gaze shot to Miranda.

Glancing back at Kevin, Kylie realized his changing process took longer than Perry's. As soon as Kevin appeared, he stepped away from Perry.

"This isn't over. We'll finish this later," Perry said to Kevin, his voice sounding more like a roar.

"Fine." Kevin stared Perry right in the eyes, and Kylie almost thought they were going to start again, but Kevin turned and walked off.

Kylie realized it took nerve to turn your back on Perry when you'd just taken a chunk out of his belly. But somehow the fact that Kevin was the one to walk away, that he never once looked at Miranda, left Kylie with little doubt which of the two held more power.

When Kevin disappeared into the woods, Kylie waited for Perry to say something to Miranda. But no one spoke. The birds in the distance started back on their song.

"Are you okay?" Miranda asked.

Kylie looked up to assure Miranda that she was fine, but then she realized that Miranda wasn't talking to her, but to Perry. Kylie shifted her gaze to him. He looked fine. Not a scratch on him. Which meant that when shape-shifters changed back into human form they healed from any injuries they'd received. And that meant Kylie had thrown herself in the middle of the fight and gotten a bruised ass for no good reason at all. She could have let them rip each other to shreds. She should have.

Just friggin' great. Still sitting on the ground, propped up on one side of her hip, she gave her backside another rub and watched as Miranda moved closer to Perry.

"Why did you do that?" Miranda sounded half honored he'd fought for her and half pissed because, well, he'd fought for her. "Tell me." She took another step toward the source of her anger.

"I felt like it," Perry growled back. Indeed, his anger became apparent in the way his body changed the moment she stepped closer. His posture hardened as if he was unable to bend. His blond hair hung scattered over his sweaty brow. His eyes were blue for a second, then changed to bright green.

He still personified the fierce appearance of an angry lion—gone was the jokester, the guy who always had something funny or sarcastic to say. And for the first time, Kylie understood why everyone was a little frightened of him.

"You didn't do it because of me?" Miranda asked, obviously not picking up on the fury he wore like an outer skin. "Because you were jealous?"

Perry didn't answer Miranda. He just stared at her and asked his own question. "So it's true?"

"What's true?" Miranda said.

"You kissed him," Perry said. "I didn't believe him when he

told me. I thought he was just trying to piss me off, but he wasn't making it up, was he? You really did it. You kissed him."

Miranda's eyes grew a tad larger. "Yes."

Silence hung in the hot morning air.

"No," she blurted out, and shook her head, sending the streaks of pink, black, and green in her hair intermingling with each movement. "I didn't kiss him. He kissed me."

"But you kissed him back," he accused.

Kylie held her breath. Della came to stand beside Kylie and extended her hand. Kylie accepted Della's help and, once upright, she reached back and gave her rear end another rub.

"Answer me," Perry demanded.

Kylie's gaze shot back to Miranda and Perry. The tension radiating from the couple seemed to suck all the oxygen from the air and made it hard to look away.

"This could get nasty," Della said.

Chapter Seven

Kylie crossed her fingers that this whole mess could somehow have a good ending to it—that the only thing nasty to come out of it would be her sore ass.

"Be honest," Perry demanded.

Miranda hesitated before answering. "I . . . I didn't kiss him back."

Della shifted her head closer to Kylie's ear and whispered, "She's lying."

Perry took a step closer to Miranda and studied her as if trying to figure out if he believed her. "Why don't I believe you?" He paused. "And even if you didn't kiss him back, you didn't stop him."

Miranda hesitated and then her shoulders dropped as if in defeat, and Kylie knew Miranda had decided to come clean.

"No. I didn't stop him. And yeah, maybe I did kiss him back just a little. But—"

"That's all I need to know." Raw and bitter pain filled Perry's color-changing eyes and for a second all Kylie could think about was feeling that same hurt when she'd seen Trey with his new girlfriend plastered at his side. Then there was the pain of seeing Mandy kiss Derek. And don't forget when she learned that Lucas had run off with Fredericka.

"That's not fair," Miranda said.

"Oh, it's not fair, but that's just too bad," Perry said. "It could have been good between us." He turned around and walked away.

He got about ten feet down the path when Miranda called out to him. "Aren't you curious about why I didn't stop him?"

Perry turned around and faced her. "I'm more curious as to why you think I should care."

Miranda's breath seemed to catch at Perry's words. She took several steps closer to him. "I didn't stop Kevin because . . . because I was tired of waiting for you to kiss me."

"Really?" Perry's feet ate up the few feet between him and Miranda. His right arm swept around her and pulled her against him. He didn't pause or even hesitate. He kissed her—not just a light peck, either. It looked to Kylie like the good kind of kiss, the kind Derek had given her last night. The kind of kiss a girl could feel all the way to her toes. And from the way Miranda leaned into Perry, Kylie could guess that Miranda's toes were feeling it all.

"Wow," Kylie muttered, and grinned.

"Yeah, wow." Della leaned in closer. "I think Perry just grew a pair."

Kylie bit down on her lip to keep from laughing. "If this was a movie, there would be some music playing in the background."

"I could sing," Della chuckled.

"And ruin it," Kylie teased back. "I've heard you singing in the shower." Both grinning, they looked back at the kissing couple.

Perry dropped his arms and stepped back. The abruptness with which the kiss ended seemed wrong. And it wasn't just Kylie who thought so. Miranda barely managed to catch herself.

Perry stared at Miranda, his expression not exactly one a person expected to see on a guy's face who'd just kissed a girl silly. The anger and hurt Kylie had noted earlier in Perry's eyes hadn't been wiped away with the kiss. If anything, he looked even angrier now.

"That," Perry said, his tone mirroring the emotion in his eyes. "That was just to show you that I would have been worth waiting for."

"Would have?" Miranda asked, her voice shaky.

"Yeah, would have." Perry turned and started walking away. But he stuck his right hand back and shot her the bird.

"What's that supposed to mean?"

"Figure it out," he said, but didn't look back.

Miranda swung back toward Kylie and Della. She put a hand to her lips and her eyes grew bright with moisture.

"Oh, crap." Kylie's heart clutched for her friend.

"Jerk," Della called out at Perry.

Holiday came running around the trail. She stopped and looked at the three of them and the departing Perry. "What just happened?" Holiday asked.

"Nothing," Della said.

Holiday glanced from Della to a teary-eyed Miranda who stood frozen watching Perry leave. Then the camp leader looked back at Della. "I heard it."

"Okay . . . almost nothing," Della said, and shrugged.

Holiday, as if reading Miranda's emotional havoc, walked over and wrapped an arm around Miranda. "Come on, let's go talk?"

"What are you doing?" Della asked, stumbling into the kitchen at two a.m.

Kylie looked up from the computer screen. "Using a sledge-hammer to make another window."

Della took a step back. "Are you having one of those funky dreams again?"

Kylie smiled. "No. I'm looking to see how many Brightens there are in the Dallas area."

"How many what?" Della dropped down at the kitchen table.

"Brightens. My dad's name was Brighten and Mom told me that his parents were in Dallas when they met. Since Daniel can't tell me what I am, I've got to find it out myself."

"But I thought . . . Didn't you tell me he was adopted?"

"Yeah." Kylie looked back at the screen and frowned. "Damn, there are over a hundred Brightens in the metropolitan Dallas area. Who knew that was such a popular name?"

"If he was adopted then how is this going to help you figure out what you are?" Della leaned over to peer at the screen.

"Maybe they will help me find his real parents."

"I'd love to be a fly on the wall for that conversation. 'Hey, Grandma and Grandpa, I'm your granddaughter you never knew you had, but not really since I know you adopted my dad who died before I was born and I really don't care about you guys, I just want to know my real grandparents.'"

Kylie frowned at Della. "You are not helping me any."

"I'm just calling it like I see it."

"Well, I wish you wouldn't." Kylie closed her eyes and tried to hold on to the tiniest bit of hope she had. But deep down she was afraid Della was right. The chances of actually finding the Bright-ens were near impossible. Getting them to tell her about his birth parents when she shouldn't even know he was adopted, well, it was probably going to take more than a sledgehammer to open that window.

"Hey," Della said, and nudged her shoulder. "Print up those numbers and Miranda and I can help you call them."

Kylie looked back at Della. "You would do that?"

"You gave me blood," Della said.

"Yeah, I did," Kylie said, and looked back at the computer screen. Then mentally she picked back up the sledgehammer and hit the print button.

"Let me go! Let me go!"

Two mornings later, something startled Kylie awake. Confused as to why she struggled in her own bed, she snapped open her eyes. The steam of her own breath floated above her face in snake-like patterns. The frigid air in the room told the time. Dawn.

She pulled the covers up to her neck and closed her eyes. And *bam*. The dream she'd just lived came crashing down on her.

Let me go! Let me go!

She heard her own scream like an echo, as if it was just now bouncing back from the dark corners of her bedroom. Her heart raced, pounded against her chest bone like a trapped animal. *Thump. Thump. Thump.*

She wadded fistfuls of blanket in her hands and mentally fought being pulled back into the nightmare. Her efforts were futile. The dream became her reality.

Cloth ties cut into her arms as someone attempted to tie her down. Blinking, she tried to focus, but her vision seemed impaired. Everything seemed impaired. Her head swam. She counted one, two, maybe three smeared and blurry figures standing over her. She kicked her legs, but an overwhelming sluggishness hampered her strength.

She pulled at the restraints, but the figures looming above multiplied. Their hands caught her limbs faster than she could move them. The ties around her wrists grew tighter. Unable to move, she watched in horror as another blurred figure came at her with a knife.

"No!" Her own scream jarred her from the nightmare. Snapping her eyes open, she clutched her fist and stared at the ceiling, afraid if she even blinked she'd be taken back.

"Just a dream. Just a dream." She repeated the words over and over. Rolling to her side, she tried to stand, but the dizziness from the dream now plagued her body for real. She fell back to the bed.

"Just a dream. Just a dream." She counted her breaths in and out, and only when the room's temperature dropped did she try to get up again. The wave of dizziness had passed, but the panic hung on. Her mind flashed through the frightening images, sending volts of fear coursing through her veins. Then she realized with horror that in the dream she had been the woman. She had been the ghost.

Grabbing her jeans, she slipped them on under her nightshirt. Not bothering to put on shoes or a bra, she scurried out of her room and out of her cabin. Her heart hadn't stopped racing when she came to the foot of the cabin steps. In spite of the hour, darkness hung like a cloak over the sky, only a glimmer of light clawing at the eastern horizon.

She started down the trail that led to Holiday's cabin, but remembered Holiday saying that she went to the office at first light.

Swinging around, Kylie ran down the path to the office. The ease and speed with which she moved should have been comforting, but it just served as a reminder that everything in her life was changing. And she didn't have a clue where those changes would lead her.

She'd gotten halfway to the office when her lungs finally demanded more oxygen. Drawing in deep breaths, she bent her knees slightly and rested her palms on her lower thighs. Staring down at her bare feet, she fought to keep images of the dreams from playing like a bad video in her head.

"Just a dream," she whispered into the dark silence.

And that's when she noticed it. The stillness. The dark dead silence.

The kind of silence that meant she wasn't alone. The lack of cold told her this wasn't a spirit. She remembered the vampire who'd dared to enter the camp. The one Burnett insisted could have fed on her if that had been its intent. Was it back to finish the job?

She stood erect. Her first instinct was to run.

Her second was to scream.

Her third instinct, not nearly as strong as the first two, was to pull up her big girl panties and face whoever—or whatever—it was.

Before she actually fully embraced option number three, the world around her came back to life. Finding comfort in the frogs, an occasional bird, and the chirp of insects, she pushed back the panic from her chest. No doubt the last few days had made her a bit suspicious. A second of silence in dawn's symphony didn't mean she was being followed.

Or at least not by a vampire. For some reason she remembered . . . She cut her eyes to the edge of the path, where the trees loomed as if guarding the woods. No golden wolf eyes peered out at her from the darkness. No creatures of the night either. Obviously, the only thing following her right now was her own paranoia. Brought on stronger by the nightmare.

Letting go of another deep gulp of held-in oxygen, she started back down the path. She got a few more feet when she heard it. Before she could react, the whish of early morning air blasted past her.

Prepared to fight for her life, thinking only of rogue vampires, determined to prove she was not easy prey, she raised her arms.

Then she saw it.

Not a vampire.

The huge bird—a cross between a large blue heron and something that might have existed in prehistoric ages—parked its feathered ass in front of her. It flapped wings that had a seven- or eight-foot span. Shocked, and still not quite believing her eyes, Kylie gasped. The thing towered over her by a good two feet. Unsure what to do, she took one step back. The sparkles started forming immediately.

Crossing her arms over her chest, she felt stupid for not guessing right away. "That wasn't funny," she hissed when Perry appeared.

"What wasn't funny?" he asked, in a serious tone that she'd seldom heard leave Perry's lips.

"You scared the crap out of me, that's what. I'm really sick and tired of—"

"Sorry. I didn't mean to scare you. I saw you running. I wanted to make sure everything was okay."

She didn't know if it was his tone or his expression, but she knew he'd told the truth. He hadn't been pulling a joke. He'd been concerned.

"Everything's fine." Yet when she got a better look into his eyes, she realized nothing was fine.

Perry, the practical jokester, was in a world of pain. Almost a mirror reflection of the pain she saw in Miranda's eyes. And it was so stupid. If they both cared so much why didn't they just move past the whole Kevin thing?

"She really likes you, Perry," Kylie said before she could stop herself.

"She likes Kevin, too."

"She doesn't like Kevin. He kissed her, that's all. And you two weren't even going out."

"She knew I liked her," he said. "I sat with her almost every day at lunch."

"Yeah, but a boyfriend is supposed to do more than just sit with you at lunch."

"I know that," he smarted back. "And I would have . . . I was just waiting for the right time."

"And why isn't now the right time?"

"It's too late," he said.

She shook her head. "You're really going to let a kiss come between you and someone you really care about? Are you that—"

"Stubborn?" he finished. "Yeah, it's part of being a shape-shifter. Which, obviously, you know nothing about because you almost got yourself killed."

"But if you care about her then—"

"Cared," he said. "I cared about her. Miranda's history." Little flickers of light started forming around him. "Oh," he said. "Thanks for trying to protect me the other morning. But seriously, don't ever do it again." The giant bird reappeared. The flap of its wings moving past sent Kylie's hair up in the air and at the same time a deep ache fluttered to the pit of her stomach.

The golden hue of light filling the office window met Kylie as she took that last turn. She stopped and let herself just stare at the window, remembering the somber look in Perry's eyes and wishing she could change that.

Moving up the steps, she opened the door and called out Holiday's name so she wouldn't be worried about who visited at this ungodly hour.

"In my office," Holiday called back, and Kylie moved into the room.

Holiday motioned for Kylie to sit down. Dropping into the chair, Kylie slumped back in the seat.

"Are you okay?" Holiday asked, sorting through a stack of mail.

Kylie sighed. "Miranda's still depressed. I just ran into Perry, and I tried to talk to him but he's not listening. Not that he doesn't look as miserable as Miranda. He's not even making any jokes. Della is PMSing and therefore is losing her patience with Miranda because all Miranda wants to do is eat ice cream and whimper over losing Perry."

Kylie stopped to breathe for one second, then continued. She was babbling, but she couldn't stop. "Not that it's really Miranda or the PMS making Della so difficult. It's the idea of going home for parents weekend and spending it with her family. But Miranda, even when she's not depressed, has never liked dealing with Della's mood swings. So now, Della and Miranda are threatening to rip each other's hearts out and feed them to my cat. Actually, I think Della wanted Miranda's liver, it was Miranda who's going for Della's heart. So to answer your question . . . No, nothing is okay."

Holiday looked up from the mail and offered one word. "Interesting."

"What's interesting?" Kylie had a vague flashback of being in Dr. Day's office and being psychoanalyzed.

Holiday's gaze shifted back to the mail. "Several things actually." She set a piece of mail apart from the others before looking up again. "But let's start with the fact that I didn't ask about Miranda, or Della, or Perry. I asked how *you* were doing."

"So I'm a freak because I care about my friends?" Kylie asked, suddenly feeling annoyed. And yeah, she was about to start her period, too, so it might be a bit of PMS. Or it could just be the hundred other problems sitting on her shoulders like an unhappy gorilla.

"I didn't mean to imply you were a freak." Holiday's soft, caring tone aggravated Kylie more than the psychoanalytical one. Probably because it made Kylie feel less like a freak and more like a bitch.

Holiday dropped her chin in her hands, a gesture so Holiday-like, that in Kylie's mind the camp leader's chin was permanently in her hand. "I was implying that I think you hide your own problems from yourself by concentrating on the problems of everyone else."

Kylie recalled that her reasons for her early morning jaunt to the office were not exactly about Perry or Miranda. So okay, maybe Holiday had a point. Not that Kylie really felt up to admitting it right now.

"Then again, maybe I'm just a nice person." Kylie sank deeper in the chair and regretted getting pissy. None of Kylie's problems could be blamed on Holiday, and if anything, Holiday and their growing relationship was one of the few things that felt right in Kylie's life right now. For that reason, she offered an apologetic smile at the end of the sentence.

"Nice? Oh, I don't doubt that." Holiday grinned. "So, let's try this one more time. How are *you* doing, Kylie?"

Kylie sat up and propped both her elbows on the desk. "How much time do you have?"

"However much time you need." Holiday let a few silent seconds pass and then asked, "What's going on with you and Derek?"

"Nothing. Why?" Kylie asked.

Holiday arched a suspicious brow. "I saw you skip out of the dining hall yesterday when he walked in, and the same thing happened at dinner."

"I just didn't want to talk to him." It was the truth. Part of it. Neither did she want anyone with the ability to read her emotions or smell her hormones to know how turned on she got by just looking at him. Until she could get her wayward thoughts in check, best not to be close to him in a crowd. Or alone, she admitted. And yeah, sooner or later she was going to have to explain that to Derek. Later being her first choice.

"So something is wrong?" Holiday asked.

Kylie crossed her arms over her chest. "Am I imagining things, or didn't you just tell me to be careful not to . . ." She didn't want to say it out loud. "You warned me to be careful around him? And now that I'm being careful, you act as if that's wrong. What is it you want me to do?"

Holiday pursed her lips to the side in thought. "Careful, yes. But I didn't mean for you to avoid him."

"You might not have meant that, but right now this is my way of being careful. My way of dealing with it."

Holiday held up her hand. "Fine. You deal with it your way." She paused, then let go of another deep sigh that told Kylie she didn't approve. "Have you spoken with your stepdad yet?"

Kylie rolled her eyes. "Did my mom call you again? I swear. I don't get why she thinks it's such a great idea that I forgive the man, when she doesn't have plans to forgive him anytime in the next century."

Holiday's mouth did another one of those twists to the right as if she was considering the words before she released them. "He's divorcing your mom, not you."

Yeah, Kylie's mom had sort of said the same thing, but Kylie didn't buy it. "It sure as heck doesn't feel that way." She could still remember begging him to let her go live with him. But no, he hadn't wanted her, and why? She looked up at Holiday again. "Did my mom also tell you he's screwing a girl who's only a couple years older than I am?"

"No," Holiday said. "But you told me. The day we went for ice cream." Sympathy filled her eyes. "Look, Kylie, I'm not saying he hasn't done something wrong. But this still isn't about you and him. If I let the relationship between my father and mother affect how I felt about them, I'd hate them both."

"I'm sorry, but I totally disagree. It might not be about him and me, but what he's done affected me," Kylie said. "It affected me in so many ways. For example, my mom called me yesterday and told me she's considering selling our house. The house I grew up in, the place I've called home all my life."

Holiday leaned back in her chair. "That's tough. I can still remember how upset I got when my mom sold our house. But . . ."

"No buts," Kylie said. "My mom shouldn't push me to do something that she can't even do. She can't forgive him. Maybe I can't forgive him, either. So just tell her *that* the next time she calls. Or maybe I'll tell her myself."

Holiday frowned. "It wasn't your mom who called. It was your stepdad. And he said he's—"

"Oh, crap. He called you?" Kylie remembered how embarrassing it had been when her dad had hit on Holiday, gawking at her as if she was candy and he had a sweet tooth. "Please don't tell me he asked you out or anything?"

"No. He sounded genuinely worried. He said he keeps e-mailing and calling you but you don't answer."

"If he was so worried he could just show up for parents day. But does he do that? No. And you know why? I'll bet it's because his girlfriend doesn't want him to come. Her parents probably won't give her permission to leave town."

"Or maybe he doesn't show up because he thinks you don't want to see him." Holiday shook her head. "I just think . . . maybe you should try talking to him." She bit down on her lip and then her mouth tightened to the right again. "Oh, hell. I've already tossed my two cents in. I might as well go for the quarter. I also think that you are using avoidance as a way of dealing with everything that's going wrong in your life right now. Your dad and now Derek. And frankly, I should add that avoidance is a poor excuse for a coping method. I know because I've tried it a time or two."

"Yeah," Kylie said, back to feeling pretty bitchy again, yet unable to stop. "But until another coping method magically appears in my bag of tricks, this one is going to have to do." She almost wanted to defend herself and tell Holiday that she wasn't avoiding everything. She'd spent the last day and a half calling Dallas area Brightens, trying to find her dad's adoptive parents, so she might find his real parents, so she might find out what she was.

Holiday frowned. "We all have to learn lessons the hard way, don't we?"

"I guess so," Kylie said, not sure it could get any harder. "I'm just not ready to deal with my dad . . . stepdad . . . or with what I'm feeling about Derek. Is it too much to ask to just be given a reprieve?"

"No, it isn't too much to ask. But generally speaking, the longer you put off dealing with something, the harder it is to solve. Sometimes, you just have to face things head-on. My dad used to say that you should look trouble right in the face and spit in its eye."

"I never mastered the art of spitting," Kylie said.

Holiday smiled then glanced at the mail again. Sighing, she raised her gaze. "Do you want to avoid this as well?" She pushed a letter across the desk.

"What?" Kylie stared at the envelope and saw her name scribbled in a familiar script.

Lucas's script. He had written her another letter.

Chapter Eight

A part of Kylie wanted to push the letter back across the desk. Hadn't she promised to get over him? She knew Holiday wouldn't force her to take it. Didn't Kylie have enough on her plate right now? Why willingly take on more crap?

Holiday pulled the letter back to her side of the desk.

Looking up at Holiday, Kylie expected to see some disapproval in the camp leader's eyes because, once again, Kylie wasn't so eager to confront her problems head-on. But all she saw in Holiday's expression was empathy.

"I'm not sure I want to read it," Kylie confessed.

"Why?" Holiday asked.

"He ran off with another girl."

"I don't think he thinks of Fredericka as—"

"But she thinks of him like that. And if she throws herself at him . . . well, he's a guy."

"I know," Holiday said. "However, not all guys—"

"But some are. And telling the difference is like math—it's hard. You think you understand it and then you get the answer wrong. And don't even try to disagree because it's the reason you won't give Burnett a shot."

Holiday dropped her chin back into her palm and didn't argue with Kylie's assessment. After several beats of silence, she said, "I could just stick it back in a drawer and if you decide you want to read it later, you can."

Yes, Holiday could do that, but could Kylie? Could she really walk out of here and not take that letter with her? Could she pretend that she didn't care about Lucas? That she hadn't worried about him since he'd left—worried about what it was that he couldn't tell her, and worried that some of what he couldn't tell her involved Fredericka?

Oh, and if she still cared about Lucas, what did she really feel about Derek? Or was her feeling about Derek even her own feeling, or was he messing with her emotions?

Oh, hell. Could her life get any more messed up?

Might as well take the letter and let the chips fall where they may.

Kylie reached out and pulled the letter out from under Holiday's palm. After staring at it for a few seconds, Kylie folded it and stuffed it in the pocket of her jeans. Later, alone, when she felt like spitting that problem in the eye, she'd deal with it.

When she looked up, Holiday nodded as if somehow telling Kylie she'd done the right thing. Not that Kylie was sure about that. Very little in life felt like a sure thing right now.

The room went back to the awkward kind of silence and Holiday shifted to another subject that was just as disturbing. "Has the ghost given you anything new?"

"New, yes. Helpful, no." Kylie frowned and wished she could avoid this problem like she did her stepdad and Derek. But the violence and the threat issued by the ghost didn't leave Kylie any option. "I think she was tortured by her abductors."

"Ouch," Holiday said. "And you really think this happened, or do you think it's just her trying to communicate something to you?"

"I think it happened." Kylie bit down on her lip, her thoughts going to the warning that this would happen to someone she loved if she couldn't stop it. "It felt too real, sort of like the dream I had where Daniel got shot. I was her in the dream. And they were coming at me with weird knives. I felt drugged and when I tried to fight back they tied me down." Remembering the terror, Kylie felt her heart rate quicken. Panic once again started building in her chest.

Holiday reached over and touched Kylie's hand. Her touch sent calming warmth up Kylie's arm. The fear collecting in Kylie's heart ran away like scared mice. And just like that, the panic faded into something less overwhelming.

Kylie looked up at the camp leader. "Thanks, but that's not going to fix anything. It's like a Band-Aid on a bullet wound."

"I know." Holiday frowned. "But when all you have to offer someone is a comforting touch, you want to offer it."

Kylie released a deep breath. "What's going to happen if I don't figure this out?"

Holiday's hand, resting on Kylie's wrist, grew warmer as if she sensed Kylie would need another shot of calm. "You accept that you did everything you could in your power to try to stop it and move on."

The enormity of exactly what Holiday was saying, coupled with the responsibility that rested on Kylie's shoulders, suddenly felt like too much. Kylie jerked her hand from under Holiday's palm. "No. I couldn't . . . I couldn't live with myself. I mean, if I understand this right, someone is going to die. Actually die and it's not going to be an easy death, either." All the problems in Kylie's life started bouncing around her head like ping-pong balls. Tears filled her eyes. It still hurt to think about her grandmother's funeral—she couldn't lose someone else. "Failure isn't an option."

Kylie's mind started racing, trying to figure out who she loved that could be in danger. Was it her mom? Was it someone from back home? Someone here at camp? It could even be Holiday. Oh lord, what if it was Lucas or Derek? She glanced at the door and fought the overwhelming desire to leave.

Holiday cleared her throat. "As much as we don't ever want to fail, our gift isn't a guarantee that we can help everyone. Sometimes we have to accept that we can't fix things."

Kylie shook her head. "You might be able to accept that, but I can't." She bit down on her lip until it hurt. "I should have refused this gift. I can't do it. I should have sent it back with a big note that said thanks, but hell no." The knot grew larger in her throat, crowding out her tonsils. "Is it too late to refuse it now?"

"I'm afraid so," Holiday answered. "You opened yourself up when—"

Kylie jumped up so fast that the wooden chair shot out from beneath her and hit the floor, filling the small office with a loud crack.

"Kylie, wait." Holiday's voice chased Kylie as she hurried out the door, but she didn't pay it any heed. Damn it. She had to figure out a way to decipher the ghost's message. Had to, because if not, someone she loved would die and Kylie couldn't live with herself if that happened.

With her throat still tight with emotion, Kylie moved up the steps of her cabin right about the time the sun finally crawled out of the corner of the eastern sky. The golden spray of light hit her back and cast her elongated shadow on the porch. As she took the next step, the sun must have risen higher because her shadow seemed to dance on the porch planks. Dancing shadows reminded her of . . . the falls.

Kylie's breath caught. She needed to go to the falls. As crazy as it seemed, it was as if something was telling her that she'd find the answers there. She let the idea sink into her tired brain. And like the sun against her back, the first glimmer of hope started to grow.

Taking in a big gulp of air through her nose, she suddenly felt refreshed, energized.

She could do this. She just didn't want to do it alone. Her gaze returned to the cabin's front door. Why should she have to do it alone? She had friends. Ghost or no ghosts, they would help her if she asked.

Okay, sure, she'd asked them to go before and they'd turned her down flat, but this time was different. This time, she'd beg. They would do it, wouldn't they? There was only one way to find out.

She hurried through the front door, zipped past the ankle-chasing Socks, and yanked open Della's door. "I need you. Wake up." She watched Della raise her head and study her through sleepy, nocturnal eyes. Morning just wasn't Della's best time.

Next, Kylie rushed over to Miranda's door and slung it open. "Miranda. Wake up. I need you guys."

Miranda rose up on her elbow. Her eyes were puffy—crying puffy, as if she'd stayed awake half the night sobbing into her pillow—which, knowing Miranda, she probably had. Kylie's heart squeezed for her friend and she almost said, *Never mind.* But then Kylie batted back the desire to give in because she really wanted both Miranda and Della with her. And maybe Della was right—it was time Miranda stopped moping and started moving past the pain.

"Please," Kylie said before Miranda had a chance to whine.

• • •

Kylie went to the kitchen table to wait, but she felt too anxious to sit. So she paced around the kitchen, waiting for her two best friends to get up so she could commence her begging.

"This better be important," Della said, and stumbled into the kitchen and dropped down in a chair. "Do you know what time it is? It's not even six yet. This is when I get my best sleep."

Miranda stepped out of her bedroom only seconds later, wearing a T-shirt, shorts, and bunny slippers. Kylie stared at Miranda's slippers; the ears bounced with each step as the sleepy girl shuffled over to an empty chair. Once she settled in, she looked up. "What is it?" she muttered.

"We're a team, right?" Kylie asked. "We're there for each other. Isn't that we've said?"

"Why is it that I think this is a setup?" Della dropped her head on the oak table, and her forehead thudded against the wood. If anyone else would have dropped her head that hard, it probably would have knocked her out, or at least left a goose egg of a knot. But not a vampire.

"Just tell us what it is." Miranda folded her arms on the table and rested her chin on top of her wrist. Her multicolored hair feathered out onto the table.

Kylie glanced from Miranda to Della, still facedown on the table, and her heart picked up a notch. If they said no, it was going to sting.

Della must have heard the thumping of Kylie's heart, because she raised her head and stared. "Spill it, ghost girl. How bad could it be?"

Swallowing, Kylie did it. Just spilled it. "I need you both to come with me to the falls. I just want—"

"Oh, hell no," Della said.

"Not happening," added Miranda at the same time, and sat up.

"But I have to go," Kylie said.

"Then go." Della waved her hand toward the door.

Kylie swallowed the knot down her throat. "I don't want to go alone."

"So you want us to sacrifice ourselves, too," Della bit back.

"Nothing is going to happen," Kylie insisted.

"Then why do we have to go?" Miranda asked, a frown marring her lips.

"Nothing bad is going to happen." Kylie dropped into a chair, losing hope due to their attitude.

"Says who?" Della asked.

"Says me," Kylie answered. "I just . . . I don't want to go alone."

"Because you're scared," Della insisted. "And for a damn good reason. Don't you know what death angels do?"

Kylie hesitated. "They are the ones who stand judgment of supernaturals." She repeated what she had heard, but truth was, she didn't completely understand death angels. How could she when no one really wanted to talk about them? Well, no one but Holiday, and most of what she would say was that she had never met one face-to-face.

"Yeah, they are the ones who stand judgment of us and sometimes they dish out the punishment, too," Miranda said. "I knew a girl, Becca. She was . . . toying around with spells on people who pissed her off. People who really didn't deserve it. So maybe she was being bad, but damn, her spells were more an annoyance than anything else. Then two days later, she walked outside and her clothes caught fire. Poof, just like that, she went up in smoke. She's disfigured now, scarred like crazy, and everyone says it was the death angels teaching her a lesson."

"Or maybe it was someone she'd cast a spell on getting even with her," Kylie said.

"They were all questioned by the witches council. Proven innocent."

Kylie shook her head. "We don't even know if death angels really exist. Chances are, they are just powerful ghosts," Kylie said, repeating another thing Holiday had said. If Della and Miranda had heard even half of what Daniel had done by pulling her into his dreams, and pulling her out of her own body and into his so she could relive his death, well, they'd probably think he was a death angel.

Della leaned her chair back on two legs. "If you don't believe they exist, then why do you even want to go?"

"Because if there's even the slightest chance that they exist, and are more powerful than regular ghosts, then they might be able to help me save someone I love." She'd never explained any of this to Della or Miranda. How could she when the moment either of them heard the word *ghost* they freaked?

"Save who?" Della, balancing the chair on two legs, started looking around the room as if they had company.

"I don't know. It could be you." Kylie stared right into Della's black eyes. "Or you." She pointed at Miranda. "There's a ghost who just keeps telling me someone I love is going to die. And it's up to me—"

"I hope it's not one of us," Miranda said.

Della snorted. "Maybe it *is* one of us and we die because you take us and offer us up as a sacrifice to the death angels."

"You know I wouldn't do that." Frustration buzzed around her gut even stronger than before. She tapped her left bare foot on the tile floor, trying to be patient, but her patience seemed to be in short supply lately.

Della shook her head. "I mean, it's bad enough that we have to accept that you have ghosts popping in all the time, but to actually go looking for the death angels . . ." She dropped the chair down with a whack. "I don't want to wind up with scars all over this face. Nope."

Kylie glared from one friend to the other. "Okay, even if they exist, what have either of you two done that is so bad that . . . that they would set you on fire?" She glanced at Miranda. "You aren't casting spells on anyone." She looked back to Della. "And you don't—"

"You don't know what I've done," Della snapped, her eyes glowed brighter. "Hell, *I* don't even know what I've done. There's a time when you turn vampire that you lose it completely, and I lost it. I don't know what happened for a whole two days. I don't want to know. Which is why I don't live in a glass house. Why I don't waste a heck of a lot of time judging others. And why I don't go to places where death angels are said to hang out. Maybe you haven't ever sinned, but I'm not perfect."

Kylie heard the undercurrent of guilt in Della's voice. "I don't think you would have done anything that bad."

"I wouldn't bet on it." Miranda made a face. "Look how mean she's to me," Miranda mouthed off.

Della glared at Miranda. "Oh, please, I haven't ever been mean to you."

"Bull crappie," Miranda said. "That's all you've been to me these last few days. I'm hurting and all you've done is poke fun at me."

"Yeah, but I do it out of love. Hoping to make you see what a dumbass you're being. Grieving over a guy who gets his shorts in a wad just because one of his friends kissed you. You should be out kissing all his other friends just to show him that you don't care. Not whining—"

"I'm not a dumbass." Miranda held out her pinky finger.

"I told you never to point that damn pinky at me." Della

jumped up and started screaming something about how all witches should be doomed to hell.

Kylie sat there, listening to them sling insults. Then frustrated and completely out of patience, she got up, collected her shoes by the door, and walked out. She stopped outside on the porch to put on her Reeboks.

Dropping her butt down on the porch, she slipped on her right shoe. Her toes felt cramped, just like her chest, and she loosened her laces before she tied them. Did Della or Miranda even realize she'd walked out? That's when she realized that frustration and impatience weren't the only emotions fighting for a spot in her chest. This hurt.

Didn't they realize how badly she needed them right now? Then taking her time to lace up her shoes, she hoped they'd have a change of heart.

That they'd decide their friendship meant enough to trust her on this.

Right shoe tied, Kylie slipped on the left and commenced the process. She could still hear them yelling at each other. They still hadn't realized she'd left. Or maybe they had and didn't care. That really hurt, too.

If either one of them had needed her, she'd have been there.

She stood, realized that she still wore her nightshirt over her jeans and was without a bra, but she didn't care. She jumped off the porch.

Taking off down the trail in a solid run, she wasn't even sure how to get to the falls. But something in her gut said she'd find it. She'd do this. And she'd do it alone.

Kylie came to quick stop at the edge of the woods, unsure which way to go. She recalled hearing the falls at the rock where she and

Derek had gone. She also recalled hearing it at the creek where the dinosaur tracks were. The falls had to be between the two, so she took off down the trail. She'd only moved a few feet beneath the thick umbrella of trees when the dusty dawn light faded to a foggy shade of purplish gray. She could feel the mist on her face.

The early morning heat chased away the night's coolness, forcing it to leave in the form of fog. But the cloudy haze clung to the trees and hung a few feet off the ground. Apprehension prickled the back of her neck. Believing she was slightly paranoid, she ignored the sensation and kept going. Going faster.

After about a quarter of a mile on the trail, she ventured off the cleared path, hoping the sound of the falls would call out to her as it had seemed to do before. She listened and she continued to sprint. No falls. Only the sound of the soles of her tennis shoes hitting the earth accompanied by the normal sounds of nature.

She kept moving between the trees, finding a path or making one as she went. The thorns in the thick brush snagged on to her jeans, as if trying to stop her from going any farther. She didn't slow down. Occasionally, a low-hanging branch would seemingly just appear in her way, but she either ducked in time or brushed it back with her arms.

She recalled trying to keep up with Della through a patch of woods very similar to this one on the night of the first campfire. She'd barely been able to walk it. That wasn't the case anymore. Her legs moved one after the other in succinct, effortless strides.

The thought hit again: change. Everything was changing. She felt it in how she moved, the speed with which she moved, she felt it in how her mouth pulled oxygen into her lungs. What else would change?

Not important, not right now, she told herself. The only thing that mattered was her understanding the ghost's message. Saving someone's life took priority. Then she could worry about herself.

She blinked, and then knocked a low-hanging cluster of leaves from her face. A loud crack sounded, and she could swear it was the limb breaking, but she didn't believe it. The deeper she moved into the woods, the thicker the brush was and the faster she ran. The faster her heart pumped with a mixture of fear and anticipation. Her whole body tingled with adrenaline.

Was she crazy for going to the falls? What if Miranda and Della were right? What if death angels looked at her sins and chose to punish her?

Her mind searched for the wrongs she'd accumulated though her life: lying to her mom, standing by and watching some girl bully another kid in school, hitting a squirrel during driver's education. The more she thought the longer her list of sins seemed to be.

Was she asking for trouble by going to the falls? Or saving someone she loved from something terrible?

Then she heard it. Or rather, she didn't hear it. The only noises bouncing off the trees were the sound of her shoes and the thread-ripping sound of the vines catching and being torn from her jeans as she ran. She stopped, folding her arms over her middle. Winded, she bent over at the waist. As she drew in shaky breaths, a stillness invaded the woods. The soundless air hung heavy, even heavier than the fog that had risen a few more feet and now snaked through the trees. And just like that she knew. She had company.

Chapter Nine

The sound of twigs being crushed underfoot told Kylie her company stood behind her. She froze, air caught in her lungs, fear sank into the pit of her stomach. Had the death angels found her?

She hadn't decided her next move when she heard, "Holy crappers, that was fun."

Kylie recognized the singsong voice. She fought back the panic and turned around. She couldn't believe what she saw. Miranda clung to Della's back and her legs wrapped around the vampire's waist. "Ride's over. Open your eyes. We found her." Della unlocked Miranda's ankles and nudged Miranda off her back, but her gaze never left Kylie.

"You okay?" Della asked Kylie. "Your heart's really racing. Is something wrong?"

Even with raw panic still running through her veins, Kylie couldn't help but smile. They'd come. Emotion filled her chest and shot upward and knotted in her throat. Unwanted tears filled her eyes.

"You let her ride on your back?" Kylie asked, hoping they wouldn't notice her watery weakness.

"It was that or wait on her. She's slower than a three-legged turtle using a broken walker."

"Am not," Miranda said.

"Are too," Della countered.

Kylie tried to swallow the lump in her throat.

"What is it?" Miranda and Della asked at the same time, dashing Kylie's hopes that her emotion would go unnoticed. Not that it really mattered. They'd seen her cry before.

"We're sorry we told you no," Miranda piped up again, elbowing Della. "Aren't we?"

"Yeah," Della said. "Are you really okay?" she asked. "Your heart's running super fast. Really fast. Not human fast."

Kylie blinked again. She did feel weird, but not completely a bad weird. "I'm fine. Actually, I'm better than fine now that you two are here. Thank you." The words came with sentiment and more tears formed in her eyes.

Della shrugged. "Yeah, well, if I die or something, I'm coming back and haunting your ass."

"Don't worry," Miranda said to Kylie and half smiled. "If she starts haunting you, I've got a spell that will lock her in purgatory for at least a dozen years."

Della shot Miranda a mock frown and then she reached out and latched on to Kylie's elbow. "Come on, let's go track us down some death angels."

"Can I climb on your back again?" Miranda asked, and rubbed her hands together.

"No. And if you tell anyone I gave you a ride, I'll break your kneecaps. I'm not going to become everyone's joyride."

"Unless it's a boy, right?" Miranda giggled.

"That's gross," Della said, and Miranda giggled harder.

Kylie looked at her friends and realized it was the first time in days she'd heard Miranda laugh. "I love you guys."

"Yeah, we know," Miranda said, and they all three started walking. The humorous mood slowly faded in the dark shade of the trees.

They walked without talking. A bird chirped above, the wind rustled the leaves. Kylie assumed she was going the right direction because Della never spoke up and she'd told Kylie earlier that she could find the falls just by listening to it.

As they moved, trampling over and sometimes through the thick brush, Kylie noticed her pace matched that of Della's. It was Miranda who seemed to be struggling to keep up.

They made about a hundred feet, and Kylie noticed Della eyeing her under her lashes. Had she noticed Kylie's newfound energy as well?

"What is it?" Kylie asked.

"Nothing," Della said. "It's just . . . your heart's still racing really fast and you look . . . different."

"Different?" Kylie asked, and looked from Della to Miranda and back. "How do I look different?"

Della continued walking but held her hands out in front of her boobs. "The girls."

Kylie looked down at her chest. "You've seen me without my bra before."

Della stopped. "It's not that your girls aren't supported. It's that they're bigger."

"They are not." Kylie stopped walking and protectively cupped her full size Bs in her palms. And the craziest thing happened. They didn't feel right. They felt . . . "Oh, damn." They felt bigger.

"She's right." Miranda cupped her own boobs as if checking them.

"Oh, God," muttered Kylie, staring down at herself.

"Hey, if you don't want them, pass me a cup or two over here."
Della laughed.

Kylie recalled thinking that everything was changing. She just
hadn't expected that to mean her boobs.

"That's not all," Miranda added. "You're taller, too. You must
have had a growth spurt overnight."

"A growth spurt?" Kylie stood straight and visually measured
herself against both Della and Miranda. She did appear to be a bit
taller. Right then, her shoes felt tight, too. What was happening to
her?

"My aunt Faye used to tell me every other week, 'You've just
grown like a weed. Must have had a growth spurt.'"

Kylie wanted to believe that this was just a normal—human
normal—growth spurt, but she didn't believe it. Her gaze shot to
Della. "Did you . . . did you, like, get bigger right before you turned?"

Della looked down at her chest. "Do I look like I got bigger? I
wish."

Kylie looked back down at her boobs. "What if it doesn't stop?
What if I just keep getting bigger?"

"Then you'll have boys lining up for miles." Miranda snickered.
"Hey, you know how they feel about boobs. The more, the merrier."

"You could always change your name to Barbie," Della said,
grinning. "My mom wouldn't even let us play with Barbie because
she said it was an unhealthy body image. I think it was because she
knew that with us being part Asian, we would probably suffer from
the no butt, no boobs syndrome. And she didn't want us to get our
body image from a stacked piece of plastic."

"You've got a butt," Miranda said.

"Yeah, thank God. I at least got that from my mom. She's not
short on bootie." She looked down at her chest. "Unfortunately, I
took my dad's boobs."

Kylie tried to appreciate their lighthearted reactions to her situation, but it didn't dampen her concern. Okay, she'd admit that she'd occasionally wished she had a wee bit more up top. Especially when she compared herself to Sara, her best friend back home who no longer called, whose boobs were an eye magnet for guys. And sure, another few inches of height meant Kylie would look thinner.

None of that made her feel better. The idea that all this stemmed from some unknown, inhuman DNA she had coursing through her body made her nervous. Nervous because she didn't know how far it would go, or what would come next.

Would she end up having to have her size F bras custom-made like Sara's great-aunt did? Dear God, the woman nearly smothered Kylie when she hugged her at Sara's family's picnic.

Kylie still had her boobs in her hand when the chill ran down her back and up her arms, and her lips felt frosted from breathing in the icy air.

Company had arrived.

Standing right in front of her was the ghost. Only she looked even worse than before. She was emaciated, too thin. Even her cheekbones protruded from the sides of her face, giving her the appearance of a skeleton.

"You have to do something. Soon. You have to do something. They killed me. Killed me and they will kill her, too." Then the ghost folded over and barfed all over Kylie's too-tight tennis shoes and Della's pretty white running shoes.

"Gross." Kylie jumped back and slammed into Miranda.

"Gross what?" Della said, and looked down, and then Miranda moved in to see what was happening.

Kylie couldn't answer. She knew they wouldn't see the barf, she knew it wasn't really there, that as soon as the ghost left so would the vision, but Kylie was a bit of a sympathy puker, and real or not, right now it looked pretty damn real. Her gag reflex started to jump up and down in her throat. She looked away from her shoes.

"Do something," the ghost repeated.

"Oh, shit," blurted out Della. "They're here, aren't they?" Della started turning in circles, talking to things that weren't there. "I swear, I swear I'm sorry for everything I've ever done."

"Me, too," Miranda said, her eyes shifting from left to right.

Kylie stared at the ghost and, not wanting to freak out Della or Miranda any more than they were, she spoke to the spirit in her mind. *I'm trying to do something. But you have to tell me who it is. I need more information.*

"Killing me," said the ghost. Then she and her puke disappeared into the thin, icy air.

Kylie, realizing she still held her magically growing boobs in her hands, dropped her arms to her side. While she gave her chest one last look, her new boob size no longer seemed important. She had to get to the falls and see if the death angels could help her.

Glancing at Della and Miranda, Kylie said, "Let's go."

"I didn't catch on fire," Della said, sounding surprised. She elbowed Kylie. "Does that mean I didn't do anything that bad those days right after I turned?"

"Maybe." Kylie didn't have the heart to tell her that it hadn't been the death angels, so she just started walking. In a few seconds, she heard the almost hypnotic sound of the cascading water. She wasn't sure if it was real or from some mystical calling, but she kept walking.

They traveled another five minutes in silence. Then Miranda tucked a strand of her straight multicolored hair behind her ear and looked at Kylie. "Do you really think someone you love is going to die?"

"The ghost seems to think so," Kylie said, trying not to sound frustrated.

"And she won't tell you who?"

"According to Holiday, some ghosts have a hard time communicating."

"That sucks."

"Yeah." The overwhelming responsibility to save someone filled Kylie's chest with a heavy ache. If someone died because she couldn't figure this out, she wasn't sure she could forgive herself.

"Do you really think that the death angels might help you?"

Kylie considered Miranda's question. "I don't know for sure, but yeah, for some reason I believe they will."

"You really aren't afraid of them?" Della asked.

"Sure I am," Kylie said, but when she saw the fear appear in Della's eyes, she qualified it. "But I don't think they're evil."

Miranda piped up. "Do you think maybe you could ask them to . . . to make Perry forgive me?"

"Oh, please," Della said. "Perry just needs to pull his head out of his ass. You don't need forgiving."

"Not true," Miranda said. "I'd have been mad if he kissed someone else."

"Mad, yes. But to totally drop you because of it is ridiculous. I mean, it's not like you slept with Kevin or like you even gave the guy a blow job. He kissed you . . . big friggin' deal."

Kylie's mind shot to kisses. To both Derek's and Lucas's. They had felt like big deals to her. *Don't go there,* she told herself. But even as she tried to chase all thoughts of kissing from her mind, she remembered the letter she had in her pocket. Lucas's letter.

One thing at a time, first save someone's life, then worry about boys. And magically growing boobs. And the fact that she still didn't know what type of DNA she had coursing through her non-human veins.

"If you are going to be asking favors," Della said, "ask if they can get me out of going to see my parents for parents weekend. My parents are going to be watching my every move, trying to find the signs that I'm doing drugs. I'll probably be peeing in a cup every two hours so they can see if I'm using. I swear, if I make one wrong move, they'll yank me out of the camp and put me in a detox center with the washed-up child stars."

"I just want Perry to give me another chance. I . . ." Miranda continued talking, but Kylie tuned her out. Della grew quiet, as if lost in worry about spending time with her parents.

Kylie hated to let both her friends down, but right now she couldn't worry about their problems, not when it might even be one of their lives on the line. "I'm not going to be asking for favors. I just need to see if they can help the ghost communicate better with me. I've got to figure this out."

Miranda hurried her steps, still struggling to keep up. "Do you really believe it could be one of us that the ghost is trying to warn you about?"

"I don't know." The words the ghost had said replayed in Kylie's head. *"You have to do something. Soon. You have to do something. They killed me. Killed me and they will kill her, too."* That's when Kylie realized that for the first time, the ghost had referred to the person with a pronoun. She said *her.* Hope that more answers would soon be revealed began to build in her chest as she continued toward the falls.

"Okay, this place is totally freaking me out," Della spouted the moment they stepped through the clearing and got their first glimpse of the falls.

"I agree." Miranda took a step back. "I don't think we should be here. I feel it."

Kylie kept moving, her gaze moving left and right, trying to soak it all in. It was . . . beautiful. No, more than beautiful. It looked picturesque. It looked photoshopped, as if someone had spent hours adding details. All those tiny details added up and created an ambience. The emotional essence of this place seemed as alive as the trees. As Kylie took in the fragrant air, it took her a minute to define what she felt. But she finally got it. The place breathed reverence—like an old temple or church.

Maybe it was the way the sun streamed through the trees as if spotlights from heaven. Maybe it was how the cascade of water tossed out tiny droplets of water that danced in the air and turned silver in the rays of light. Or how the verdant plant life glistened with all the pinpoints of dew. Or perhaps it was the noise. The rush of water filled her ears until she felt the same vibration in her blood. Or it could be the way the moist air tickled her throat and filled her chest with warm emotion. Not bad emotion. Acceptance.

"Okay, we said we'd come here with you. We did. Now let's go." Miranda took a step back.

"Not yet," Kylie said, unable to move her eyes from the rush of water falling from fifty feet above. Then, without thinking, as if she were being lured, she stepped into the creek bed. Just walked in, didn't even stop and think about removing her shoes, or rolling up her jeans.

"Whoa. I'm not following you," Della called out. "Really, we need to get back for breakfast. Let's leave, okay?"

"Just wait on me. A few minutes." Kylie didn't look back. Her shoes and jeans soaked up the shin-deep water like a sponge. She took another step and then another.

"Are you sure you should go in there?" Miranda's voice tightened with concern. "Come on, Kylie. Let's go, okay?"

"If you go in there, you might not be able to come out," Della warned.

Kylie didn't answer, not when she could swear she saw someone or something move behind the spray of glistening water. The figure shifted again. Someone was definitely there. She just hoped that it was someone with answers. And not someone ready to make her spontaneously catch fire for any past sins. But just to be sure, as she took her next step, she sent up a prayer for forgiveness for anything bad she'd done.

The tiny droplets of moisture sprayed on her face as she drew closer. She took the final step. The gush of water splattered on her head and shoulders.

Walking through the falls into the cavern-like darkness, she wiped a hand over her face, waiting for her eyes to adjust. Her skin pickled with goose bumps, not the kind of goose bumps that came from ghosts; no, they were the kind that came from fear. She stood completely still and hoped with the return of her vision came a bit more courage.

The sound of the falls echoed and closed off any noise from the outside world. When she blinked, the darkness suddenly didn't seem so blinding. She realized that the mouth of the falls was really a cave. Just when her eyes seemed to distinguish shapes, she saw someone dip behind a rock wall.

"Hello?" Her voice seemed lost in the rush of the water. When no one answered, Kylie continued, "I know someone is here."

"Then I guess I'll just come out," a voice boomed from behind the rock. It took Kylie a few minutes to recognize the voice, and she did recognize it, but she still couldn't believe it when she saw him step forward.

Chapter Ten

"What are you doing here?" Kylie asked.

His tall masculine figure kept moving toward her and Kylie actually took a step back. She wasn't so much frightened as she was surprised. And perhaps still awestruck at everything she felt. The whole reverent ambience felt even stronger in here.

"Probably the same thing you're doing here," Burnett answered. "Curiosity."

It wasn't her reason. She'd come for help, but she didn't correct him—and not because she didn't trust him. She met his gaze. If she were being completely honest with herself, she knew she hadn't gotten over being intimidated by him, but she'd grown to respect him as had most everyone else in the camp. She respected him enough that she wished Holiday would reconsider her no-vamp rule where men were concerned. The two of them would make a great couple. His dark side to her light. His seriousness to her teasing manner.

She felt him watching her and knew he was expecting an answer.

But she had her own questions. She took a deep breath. "Curious about what?" she asked.

"The whole ghosts thing. The legend." He tucked his hands into his jean pockets and looked around.

"That's strange," Kylie said.

"What's strange?" He turned and looked back at the cave as if checking his surroundings for safety. Oddly enough, Kylie wasn't worried about her own. The warm, good feeling filling her chest convinced her not to worry. She was safe here.

"Your being curious about ghosts. I thought . . . I mean . . . most supernaturals prefer to sort of stay in the dark about it all."

"Yeah, but Holiday's so fixated on them, I just thought . . ." His words faltered.

"That maybe understanding ghosts would help you understand her?" Kylie asked, somehow certain that she'd read him right. Again, she got a feeling that Burnett really cared about Holiday.

He nodded as if admitting it out loud might ding his macho ego. "Personally, I think she talks about it so much just to scare me."

"Probably hoping to scare you off." Kylie bit her lip when she realized she'd said that aloud.

He looked at her. "That, too." He paused a few seconds and then asked, "You wouldn't be willing to enlighten me on any of the reasons why she'd be doing that, would you?" Apparently he'd decided his macho ego could be damned.

Okay, now Kylie was up crap creek without a paddle and a huge leak in her canoe. Telling Burnett about Holiday's past felt almost like betrayal. "I . . . uh . . . I . . ."

He held up his hand. "Say no more. I get it." Shuffling his feet, he looked around again and then focused back at her. "So you're like Holiday, right? You feel spirits, and see them?"

She nodded.

"Do you feel the death angels?"

She started to deny that she sensed a strong presence of someone or someones, but considering the whole church-like ambience,
she decided against lying. "I feel something. Don't know exactly
how to describe it. It's like—"

"Really?" he asked.

"Really." She looked around and wondered if whatever she felt
would give her the answers she needed. "You don't feel anything?"

"If I did, I wouldn't be here now." He chuckled, but Kylie
could swear she heard a tad of nervousness in his tone.

"Doesn't the legend say that they come here at dusk?" He ran his
hand through his dark hair that looked a shade darker than normal.
Her gaze went back to the falls and she realized his hair was wet. She
felt her own hair then, hanging damp on her shoulders and shifting
back and forth on her back.

He took a few steps closer to one of the large boulders. His
shoulders and arms shifted with corded muscle and appeared almost as hard as the rock walls. Once again, Kylie couldn't help but
admire how attractive he was. Not that he made her body tingle
the way Derek did, but she could appreciate the way he was put
together. Holiday really should let herself fall for him.

"It says you can see them dancing on the walls at dusk. It
doesn't mean they're not here at other times," Kylie answered honestly, hoping she was right. Hoping the presence she felt here was
real and could give her answers.

He nodded and looked around again. "Why is it that the place
wasn't so scary until you showed up?"

Kylie laughed. "It must be my magnetic personality."

He smiled. "Probably. You and Holiday." Just the way he said
Holiday's name tugged at Kylie's heartstrings.

"It was another vampire," Kylie blurted out. "He hurt her a lot."

Burnett looked confused for a second, and then understanding filled his eyes. "So she's prejudiced against all vampires?" He sounded hurt.

"I would call it protective," she said. "And not all vampires. She doesn't seem to have a problem with any vampire but you."

He tilted his head to the side and looked at her. "You say that as if it's a good thing."

"It might be," Kylie said. "There has to be a reason you get on her bad side so quickly."

He seemed to consider her analogy. "I see what you mean." His gaze shifted to the wall of water again. "Why don't I walk back to the camp with you? Make sure—"

"Actually, I was hoping to stay here for a few minutes. Alone," she said before he offered to stay with her.

A frown pulled at his mouth. "I'm not sure you should be alone in the woods. Not after what happened the other night."

"I'm not alone," Kylie said. "Della and Miranda are right outside, waiting on me."

She thought he was going to say something completely macho, like tell her she should have brought a boy with her.

Instead he said, "Okay. Good."

Yeah, good, Kylie thought. Della would have had a conniption fit if she knew he considered her less capable than the opposite sex.

He tilted his head to the side as if to listen. "That's really strange. I can't hear them. Or smell them in here." His brow creased. "Then again, I didn't hear you until you spoke." His gaze cut around their surroundings. "Maybe this place is haunted." A grin pulled at his mouth. "And on that note, I think I'll head back to the camp." He took two steps and then turned back. "Don't be long. And make sure you guys stay together."

"Got it," she said.

He nodded and again tilted his head to the side and studied her. "Are you okay? Your heart . . . it's beating really fast."

She shuffled her wet tennis shoes on the rock. "Della said the same thing. I think I'm okay," Kylie said, not wanting to share her recent and unexpected all-natural but definitely not human boob job.

He studied her for a few minutes and Kylie got the craziest feeling he'd noticed more than her heartbeat, but he was careful not to make her feel uncomfortable. She appreciated that.

He started to walk out and then turned around. "Thank you for—"

"You're welcome," she said, not wanting to hear or think about how angry Holiday would be when she found out Kylie had told Burnett even the least bit about her past. And Holiday would find out, because Kylie had every intention of telling her. Keeping it a secret would make it feel like even more of a sin. And right now, right here, she especially didn't want to up her quotient of sins.

Five minutes after Burnett left, Kylie stood in the same spot. "Look, I got a ghost who is saying someone I love is going to die. I'm supposed to save this person, but the ghost isn't giving me a lot to work on. I'm getting scared. Really scared."

And she should feel sort of stupid talking to herself. Yet she didn't. While she couldn't see anyone here, she felt them.

"Can you . . . like, help me out here?" She waited. She listened with her ears. With her heart.

No answer echoed back, not in her mind, her ears, or her heart. Unless you considered the sensation of calm and rightness that made her chest feel lighter, her problem less urgent, and her ability to deal with everything almost manageable.

Was this the answer? That everything was going to be okay? Or was this like Holiday's and Derek's touch—just a quick fix to the emotional havoc living and breathing inside her? Doubt tried to sweep away the calm.

She dropped down on the uneven earth beneath her, a mix of rock and moist dirt, and rested her palms behind her for support. Tilting her head back, she felt her damp hair sway slightly and tickle her back through her nightshirt. Low on her back. Lower than ever before. Sitting up again, she reached back to touch the ends of her hair. Her hair, like her boobs, must have undergone a growth spurt. What did all this mean?

Trying to embrace the soothing emotion this place produced, she stared at the wall of water not five feet from her and felt the tiny droplets moisten her skin. *Don't worry, dear. Life is gonna be okay. One foot in front of the other.* She heard her grandmother's words echo in her mind.

"You really here, Nana? Or am I just remembering?" She posed the questions aloud.

The lack of cold told her she was alone. A tiny part of her wanted to rebel, to demand an answer, not just to her ghost's problem but to all her issues. Just as she was about to open her mouth, a bit of wisdom seemed to wiggle through the frustration. This, whatever "this" was making the falls feel special, wasn't open to demands or rebellion. In addition to the calm, Kylie sensed a power.

Not evil, but firm.

Not uncaring, but unyielding.

Unyielding enough to set a girl aflame and scar her for life? Kylie didn't know that answer, and for her own sanity she wasn't sure she wanted to know.

Then, realizing she was probably pushing Della's and Miranda's limit for waiting, she stood up. When she did, she felt the folded envelope in her pocket. Lucas's letter. Another thing she'd have to deal with soon. And while none of her issues had changed, she did somehow feel more confident about handling them. And maybe, Kylie thought, that was as much help as she was going to get.

The morning passed in a mind-numbing haze. Either due to her lack of sleep or the residuals from her growth spurt, Kylie wasn't sure. She dropped her lunch tray down beside Della and gave the dining hall a quick search for Derek.

His before-lunch group often got caught up in hiking and missed the meal. As her gaze swept the other side of the dining hall she realized how much she wanted to see him.

And how much she didn't want to see him.

God, she was so wishy-washy. If she was having a hard time dealing with her back-and-forth emotions, she could only wonder how Derek felt. He probably thought she was a few French fries short of a Happy Meal. And he'd be right, wouldn't he?

Without a doubt, the calm and confidence she'd gotten from this morning's trip to the falls was beginning to wane. When another visual sweep around the room didn't find Derek, she dropped in a chair and focused on Della, who sat there sipping her blood with very little interest. Then Kylie noted the empty seat next to Della.

"Where's Miranda?" Kylie asked.

"Don't know," Della muttered, and turned her glass in her hand.

Kylie tried not to stare at the blood in the glass for fear she'd recall how good it tasted. Instead, she picked up her ham sandwich and took a big bite. "You okay?" Kylie shifted the lump of bread in her mouth so she could speak.

"Yeah. Just mulling things over," Della said.

"About going home in three weeks?"

"Actually, I wasn't worrying about that, but now that you re- minded me, I can add that to my worry agenda. Thanks." Sarcasm laced Della's voice.

"Sorry." Kylie stared at the sandwich with disinterest. "So what are you worrying about?"

"Just stuff," Della snapped.

"Ooookay," Kylie said, letting Della know her mood wasn't appreciated. Hey, Kylie got the whole vampire bad attitude, but at times—

"Sorry," Della said. "It's just that talk of death angels this morn- ing got me worrying about . . . things."

"You mean about the time when you turned and can't remem- ber the details."

"Yeah." Della sounded relieved that Kylie remembered, and she looked at Kylie as if seeking help. "What if I did something re- ally terrible?"

How terrible? Kylie almost asked. Was Della actually worried that she might have hurt someone? Then she remembered who she was talking about. "First, I don't think you would do something really terrible. I mean, even the fact that you are worried you did something terrible means you're not a terrible person."

Della didn't look convinced. "But when you turn, it's so crazy."

"But you're not crazy," Kylie said. "And you're a good person."

Della nodded and looked as if she wanted to say something else, but then she looked away. Kylie had a sneaking suspicion that there was more to Della's concerns than met the eye. Did she remember more than she was saying? Whatever it was, Kylie wished she knew how to help.

"I wonder what's up with Miranda?" Della said in an obvious attempt to change the subject. "God, I hope she hasn't gone back into mourning over little boy wonder."

"She seemed okay earlier." Kylie looked to the table where most of the witches ate lunch to see if Miranda was there. She wasn't.

While the camp was supposed to encourage intermingling between the species, and it did, there seemed to be something about mealtime that encouraged the "birds of a feather flock together" mentality, the exception being a few interspecies couples and a few cabin friends. Helen and Jonathon took turns sitting with the vampires and the fairies. Until recently, it hadn't been unusual for Perry to join Miranda at their table. And a couple times a week, Derek would sit with Kylie during meals.

At least once a week, and never on the same days, even Della and Miranda would opt out of sitting with her and sit with their kind. Kylie told them they didn't have to sit with her. She understood if they wanted to sit with their same-feathered friends. They didn't listen.

Whether it was out of loyalty or because they felt bad for her, Kylie didn't know. But deep down, she appreciated it to no end. Who wanted to eat lunch alone? That would remind her too much of her old high school when Sara was sick or skipping school.

Thinking of Sara, Kylie pulled out her phone and checked to see if she had any messages from her best friend. It had been almost a week since Kylie had sent her several texts asking how things were going and telling her she would be home in three weeks for the weekend. It kind of hurt that Sara hadn't even gotten back in touch. Did that mean Sara didn't want to see her?

Sure, Kylie would be the first to admit that they no longer seemed to have a lot in common—Kylie not being human being at the top of the list—but what they had was a ten-year friendship, years of being each other's best friend. Didn't that merit her taking a few hours out of her weekend to at least pretend she still cared?

Kylie's phone rang. Thinking it would be eerie cool, almost psychic, if it was Sara, Kylie waited for the number to come across the screen. Not Sara. She cut off her phone and set it on the table.

"Don't tell me, either Trey or your stepdad," Della said.

"Two points for being right." Kylie grabbed her sandwich again.

"Which one?" Della asked.

"Dad. Stepdad." Even after meeting and learning to love Daniel, she sometimes forgot that Tom Galen wasn't her real father. Kylie sank her teeth into the soft bread, but didn't taste anything.

"Is he still banging his intern?"

Kylie swallowed. "Don't know. Don't care."

"Liar," Della said.

"Okay, how about . . . don't know, wish like hell I didn't care?"

"Now you're telling the truth." She studied Kylie and passed her glass of blood under Kylie's nose. "Do you want a sip?"

Kylie frowned and pushed the glass away. "No."

"You're lying again." Della arched a brow.

"Fine!" Kylie snapped, and even to her own ears, she sounded like Della had earlier. "I want it, but I don't want it. And don't go thinking it's because I think something's wrong with being vampire. I think it's fine. It's just that I . . . I'm a bit overwhelmed with trying to figure out what I am."

"Believe it or not, I understand." Della continued to study her. "You know, your heart is still beating faster than normal."

"I know." Kylie pulled her hair over her shoulder. "And look.

My hair grew, too." She sighed when she remembered how she'd only found one bra that allowed her to squeeze her size-bigger boobs into it.

"Damn." Della reached out and touched her hair. "Have you talked to Holiday about all this yet?" She glanced at Kylie's chest again. "I don't want to scare you or anything, but it's kind of weird."

Oh, great. Just when she'd almost convinced herself it was no big deal, Della was telling her differently. Kylie let out a deep breath. "No, I haven't told her yet. I have a meeting with her at two o'clock."

"You don't sound very happy about it," Della said.

"I'm not."

Della looked shocked. "What happened? You usually sing her praises. You pissed at her for something?"

"No. But she's gonna be pissed at me."

"For what? Going to the falls?"

"No. I don't think she'll be upset about me going to falls." At least Kylie didn't think she would. "It's what I did while I was there that's going to tick her off."

"What did you do?" Della looked confused as she sipped her blood.

"I kind of told Burnett about Holiday having had her heart broken by another vampire."

"Really? What happened?"

"He asked me about her and then—"

"Not that," Della said. "I mean with the other vampire?"

"I . . . don't know it all." Kylie realized she shouldn't have told Della, either.

"Okay, so what's wrong with telling Burnett that?" Della asked.

Kylie rolled her eyes. "It wasn't my place to tell him. Or you. So don't say anything."

"My mouth is sealed." Della reached over to Kylie's plate and stole a chip. "You know why you told him, don't you?" She studied the chip she held with the edge of her fingertips.

"Because I'm stupid," Kylie answered.

"No, because it's clear to you and everyone else that those two need to go bump uglies." She popped the chip into her mouth and made a face. "I used to love potato chips and now . . . ugg, they taste like toad ass."

Kylie completely ignored the potato chip/toad ass commentary while she tried to understand. "To do what? Bump what?"

"Bump uglies, bang each other, burn off some of those flaming hormones they put out when they're in the same room together."

"Uglies?" Kylie still couldn't wrap her head around it.

Della snickered. "I heard a comedian call it that. She was giving all the different names for doing the deed. Funny, isn't it?"

"Maybe," Kylie said, but couldn't be sure. Her sense of humor had taken a day off and so had her appetite. She stared at her sandwich, missing only a few bites. Was her loss of appetite a sign? Would she someday think potato chips tasted like toad ass?

"Speak of the horny little devils," Della said.

Kylie looked up. Holiday and Burnett walked into the dining hall. Holiday led the way, and Burnett studied her from behind. For a second, Kylie feared Burnett had told Holiday what Kylie had said. She envisioned an angry and hurt Holiday giving her a good talking-to, and Kylie's chest tightened. Oh, God, why had she said anything to Burnett? It had been wrong. So wrong.

Then Holiday met Kylie's gaze—no anger or hurt lingered in her green eyes, only a residual concern. Probably still worried about her and how she walked out of her office this morning. Holiday mouthed the words, "Two o'clock," and pointed to her watch.

Kylie nodded.

Holiday smiled and then walked up to the front of the dining hall and took a lunch plate. Burnett continued to follow her, his gaze taking in her every move, as if trying to memorize every inch of her body.

"Wait a minute," Kylie said. "If vampires can smell those hormones, how come Burnett doesn't seem to know Holiday feels that way about him? I mean, when I hinted that Holiday might be feeling something other than just annoyance, he seriously acted surprised."

"That's simple. We can't smell our own hormones and most of the time we can't smell the hormones of the people we're attracted to. I never smelled my boyfriend's." A sad smiled touched her lips as if some memory had tiptoed across her mind. "And I know Lee felt them."

Kylie sensed that Della still cared about Lee, but she also got the feeling that her friend wasn't about to admit it, nor did she want to talk about it. "That's weird how that works."

"Yeah. It's as if when we're attracted to someone, the emotion triggers the off button of our hormone sensor. Now, if you aren't attracted to someone and they've got the hots for you—oh yeah, we can smell that like a bad fart."

Kylie chewed on that information for a few seconds and then said, "But then how come Derek can tell when I'm thinking about . . ." Okay, Kylie wasn't sure she wanted to say that aloud, but curiosity provoked her to continue. "Are you saying he's not attracted to me?"

"No." Della grinned. "He's not vampire. He's not even smelling anything. He's reading emotion. That's a completely different thing."

"Oh." Kylie looked back down at her plate and forced herself to eat a chip but her mind continued to churn. Once she swallowed, she forced herself to ask the question, in a very low voice, of course.

"Do Derek and I . . . do we really spill hormones all over the place? I mean, is it so bad that it's embarrassing?"

Della's eyes widened, but she didn't answer. Which was so unlike Della. She never hesitated to tell you like it was.

"Oh, crap. Is it that bad?" Kylie asked.

Della cut her eyes upward. Kylie was just about to figure out what that eye shift meant when a warm breath whispered across her neck.

"Is what bad?" Derek asked.

Chapter Eleven

"Nothing is bad," Kylie answered Derek, and desperately tried not to emit any hormones or emotions that might have gone sailing in the air when her gaze locked on him. Problem was, she didn't have a clue how to stop them. Where the hell was her sensor button?

Off! Off! Off! She mentally jabbed at the off button in her mind.

Derek shifted and dropped down in the chair beside her. She didn't want to look at him, afraid that her doing so would increase the leakage of hormones, but not looking at a person was exceptionally rude. Or so said her mom.

"Everything okay?" Derek asked, probably aware she still hadn't looked at him.

"Don't be rude," she could almost hear her mom say. "It's fine." She looked at him. And because she'd been avoiding him for the last few days, she practically gobbled up his image. Her breath caught. Holy moly, did he look good.

Oh, yeah, she was so gonna blame this on her mom!

He was a tad sweaty, not yucky sweaty, but yummy sweaty. His skin glowed a bit, and he smelled a little like sunshine, as if he'd soaked up all the good scents from his hike. She figured his skin would taste a little like salty sunshine if she pressed her lips against it. His brown hair curled up on the tips and looked windblown. He wore a dark green T-shirt that hugged his torso. And the jeans he wore were his favorite. Or at least, it was the pair he wore more than others. She recognized them both because the knees were faded and they fit him snugger than most. And snug looked really, *really* good on him.

Della's snicker drew Kylie's attention away from Derek. The vampire grinned and waved a hand in front of her nose. Realizing what she meant, Kylie felt her face turn red.

When she stole another glace at Derek, his gaze had shifted and was now glued to her boobs. Which probably meant that he was at this second polluting the air with all kinds of pheromones as he tried to figure out how the girls had grown overnight.

"I . . . I gotta go find Miranda." Kylie popped up from her chair and shot out of the dining room like someone wearing white and in desperate need of a tampon.

"Miranda, you here?" Kylie called out as she entered the cabin five minutes later.

Her friend came scurrying out of Kylie's bedroom. She had panic plastered on her face and tears filled her eyes. Tears in Miranda's lovesick eyes had pretty much been the norm these last few days, but something appeared different. Kylie sensed it right away. And yeah, it had a little something to do with the fact that she'd stormed out of *Kylie's* bedroom immersed in a cloud of guilt.

"I'm so sorry," Miranda said, and hiccupped. "Really, really sorry."

"Really, really sorry about what?" Had Miranda found Lucas's letters and read them? Purposely invaded her privacy?

"I didn't mean to do it."

"Didn't mean to do what?" Kylie insisted, feeling her patience seep out like a balloon with a pinhole. Those letters were private. Heck, she hadn't even read the second one. When she'd returned from the falls, she'd stuffed it in her drawer with the other one. Told herself she'd read it tonight, or maybe tomorrow, or maybe even never. She wasn't sure her heart could handle dealing with whatever Lucas might say on top of everything else she had on her plate.

"I've done it dozens of times before, and I never had a problem undoing it until now. Please, please don't be mad at me."

Kylie suddenly got the feeling this wasn't about Lucas's letter. "What did you do?"

Miranda's gaze shot back to Kylie's bedroom, but when Kylie took a step, Miranda moved in front of her. "I'll fix it. I swear I will. I'll figure it out. I won't sleep or eat until I fix this."

"Fix what?"

"Please don't be mad."

Kylie physically moved Miranda. Then she walked into her bedroom to find out what Miranda didn't want her to see and swore she would fix.

Kylie's gaze shot first to the bedside table where she stored her most private things. The drawer was closed. No letters were strewn on the nightstand. A movement on her bed caught her eye. She shifted her gaze.

She blinked.

She screamed.

Then she hauled ass out of her bedroom in less than a flicker of a second.

She ran right into Miranda, who caught her by her forearms. "I'm sorry. So sorry."

Kylie caught her breath. "Why . . . ?" She inhaled. "Why is there a skunk in my bed?"

Kylie felt a familiar brush against her ankle. She looked down expecting to see Socks. But nope. No Socks.

Kylie screamed again and jumped clear across the room.

The skunk raised its pointed little head in the air, meowed, and came scurrying after her.

"I'm so sorry," Miranda cried.

Kylie looked up at Miranda and then down at the skunk quickly approaching her. Its paws pranced up in the air in a very familiar and very cute feline kind of way.

Socks?

"No," Kylie said. "Tell me that's not . . . Oh crap, you didn't!"

"I'll fix it. I will," Miranda said.

Kylie had just returned from art hour with Helen and Jonathon. Pacing, she stood in front of the office, waiting for her two o'clock appointment with Holiday. How was Kylie going to tell the camp leader that she'd ratted out her past romance with a vampire?

By the way, did you know that Burnett didn't know you used to date a vampire? Nope, that wouldn't do.

Hey, Burnett and I were talking and I happened to mention how you had your heart chewed up by one of his kind. That didn't sound like it would go over too well, either.

"Kylie?" Derek called out to her.

Oh, crappers!

She saw him walk though a crowd of campers waiting to sign up for kayak classes and she resigned herself to facing him. However, she did take several steps away from the crowd.

"Hey." He stopped in front of her and studied her carefully.

"Hey." She moved in backward steps, continued to motion him to follow her another ten feet away from the crowd.

His gaze stayed glued to her eyes as she continued to move in reverse. "Have I done something wrong?"

"No." She shook her head.

"Then have you been smoking something? Because you're acting really weird."

She completely understood why he thought she'd lost track of reality. However, in her defense, her reality for the last six weeks was completely different from the one she'd grown up believing in.

"It's not . . . it's . . ." She glanced around to make sure no one with super-hearing powers was in close range. "I'm embarrassed, okay?"

"Embarrassed about what?" His gaze lowered to her breasts. "That?"

She reached out, put her finger under his chin, and brought his face up. At least he had the decency to blush.

"Sorry. It's just they . . . you're . . ."

"Bigger. I know."

He reached out and caught a handful of her hair. "And your hair is longer."

"I'm taller, too," she said.

He took a visual measure of her and his eyes widened. "What happened?"

"I wish I knew." She attempted to keep the frustration from her voice. It wasn't his fault. "I woke up growing out of everything."

He grinned and his gaze lowered for a nanosecond before glancing up. "It looks nice."

"And why am I not surprised you feel that way?" She frowned.

His smile faded and he just stood there staring at her face. She wondered if it really took that much effort not to gawk at her breasts or if he had something else on his mind.

"Look, if I haven't done anything, then why have you been running away from me for the last two days?"

She shuffled her feet, painfully aware that her shoes were pinching her toes at this moment. "I told you. I'm embarrassed."

"Embarrassed . . . about getting bigger?"

"No. Well, yeah, that's embarrassing, too. But that's not why . . . why . . ."

"Why you've been avoiding me. Just say it. Because that's what you've been doing." He now sounded half mad, or at least half annoyed. But what she really heard in the tenor of his voice was insecurity. And honestly, she couldn't blame him. She'd feel all those things if he'd been dodging her the way she'd been doing him.

She bit down on her lip. "I'm sorry. It's not what you think."

"So what is it? Because I'm lost here. I mean, your emotions mostly seem okay when I'm around you, they actually seem really great at times, but then you run off."

"And . . . that's sort of why I'm running off," she said.

His brow creased. "And . . . I still don't understand."

Okay, she was going to spell it out for him. Her face flushed just thinking about it. "When I'm around you all I can think about is kissing and making out." *And going further than I've ever gone with anyone.*

His brow creased deeper, but at least some of the chip he seemed to carry appeared to fall off his shoulders with his new posture. "Okay." He tucked a hand into his jeans pocket. "Now can you explain to me why that's a bad thing?"

"It's not so much a bad thing, but it's . . . a private thing. I don't even want you to know what's going on inside my head. Much less all the vampires and other fairies wandering around the camp."

His shoulders tightened as if the chip had returned. "So you're embarrassed because other people know you like me."

"No. I mean . . . liking you is one thing. Wanting to . . . make out is another."

"You want to make out with me?" He almost grinned, and then ran a hand through his hair. "You know, I didn't think it was possible to feel complimented and insulted at the same time. But you've managed to make me feel both."

"I didn't insult you," she said.

"You did if you mean that you're embarrassed for people to know that you like me."

"I told you it's not about liking you."

"Okay, you just don't want people to know you're attracted to me."

She opened her mouth to speak, but wasn't sure what to say. "Yeah. Sort of. I mean, it's just private."

"Private?" He hesitated as if trying to figure out what she meant. "It's never all that private."

"It is for humans," she said. "And I may not be a hundred percent human, but . . . I mean, let's face it. I've had sixteen years of living as a human, and less than two months of trying to cope with being . . . Oh wait, I don't even know what I am yet." She shook her head, feeling her frustration level rise. "But yeah, I kind of like how humans do this."

"How they do what?" he asked, as if he wasn't following her.

Not that she could totally blame him, because she wasn't so certain she was following herself. "I like how humans keep their personal thoughts and feelings to themselves."

He stood there chewing on what she said. She could tell that her argument wasn't making sense to him.

"No," he said. "You're wrong."

"Wrong about what?" Now she was confused.

"It's not private for humans, either. They don't keep everything to themselves."

"Only if they chose to tell someone," Kylie said.

"Bullshit!" he said. "Look at Helen and Jonathon over there. Are you going to tell me that you, the human part of you, can't see that these two people are attracted to each other? And what about Burnett? You knew he was lovesick for Holiday before I did. You can see it."

Okay, he had a point. But she didn't like him jabbing her with it. "See it, yes. But I can't feel their emotions or smell the pheromones they put out because they want to . . ." *bump uglies* ". . . get it on. And knowing other people can . . . do that with me, well, it freaks me out a little, okay?"

He shook his head. "Are you sure it's other people knowing it that's freaking you out? Or is it you knowing what you feel for me that's freaking you out?"

She stared at him. "I don't know what you mean."

"I mean, that I'm not so sure you want this." He waved a hand between them.

"Want what?" Just like that, she got flashbacks. Flashbacks of having a similar argument with Trey. Oh, please. Not again.

"You and I. Us. You don't want us to become an 'us.' Every time I feel as if we get a little closer, you end up pushing me away. I've asked you to go out with me at least six times and you never answer me. What's up with this?"

Yup, she'd had almost this very conversation with Trey. "It's always about sex, isn't it?"

"What?" His mouth dropped open. "No. I wasn't talking about that."

"So you don't want sex?" she asked, getting angrier by the second.

He stood there staring at her as if she'd grown two heads and a tail. And God help her, considering everything that had happened to her lately, she almost wanted to check the mirror to make sure she hadn't sprouted a second head. Ditto for the tail.

"Where the hell is this coming from?" he asked.

Suddenly, she became aware that the crowd had gotten closer to them and several of the people in that crowd had the hearing of a gossip-hungry bat. She glanced at her watch and saw it was after two. "Sorry, I'm late."

Kylie stormed into Holiday's office. She dropped down in the seat across from the desk and looked her friend and camp leader right in the eyes. "I hate boys. I'm seriously considering going lesbian."

Holiday's expression was part grin, part groan. "If it was that easy, ninety percent of the women in the world would be gay." She made a funny little face and then asked, "So . . . boy problems?" She reached for a can of soda and took a sip.

"More like boys, skunk, and ghosts."

Holiday choked on the diet drink. "Skunk?"

Kylie sank into the chair, feeling defeated and frazzled from her argument with Derek.

"Miranda turned Socks into a skunk. And she can't figure out how to turn him back." No sooner had the words left her lips than Kylie realized it sounded as if she was tattling. "Not that I want you to say anything."

Holiday tried not to smile, but the edges of her mouth twisted up. "She was probably practicing for the show that her mom entered her into when she's back home."

"She explained why she did it. And I don't want her to get in any trouble . . . but what if she can't figure out how to change him back? I'm going to be stuck with a skunk for a pet."

Another smile threatened to appear on Holiday's lips. "I'm sure she'll figure it out."

Kylie shook her head and then dropped her hands into her lap. "You have no idea how much I wish my life could just go back to normal. Like human normal? Nobody trying to read my thoughts, change my feelings, or making it my job to save someone's life."

Holiday leaned back in her chair and stretched her arms up as if she'd sat too long in the same position. Hands still up in the air, she gave the papers scattered on her desk a frown. "Don't know about human, but normal does sound good sometimes, doesn't it?"

Something about Holiday's mood had Kylie's own concerns shifting. "Is everything okay?"

"Me? Oh, I'm fine." She dropped her hands and sat up a little straighter as if to put up a front. "It's you I'm worried about, Kylie. You seemed very upset this morning."

Kylie recalled how she'd stormed out of here. "I'm sorry. It sometimes . . . it just feels as if it's too much."

"I know it feels like that. But it will work out," Holiday said.

Kylie frowned. "You sound like my mom. She always says, 'God won't give you more than you can handle.' "

Holiday chuckled. "And we just wish He didn't trust us so much, right?"

"Yeah." Kylie saw the concern flare up in Holiday's eyes again. "What about your problems?" She motioned to the desk, sensing Holiday was upset.

"It'll be fine . . . just have a lot of financial crap to figure out with us going full-time here at the camp. There are teachers to be hired. Heating units to put into the cabins. And I don't have a clue how we're going to manage it."

"I thought the government, I mean the FRU, funded the camp."

"They do to some degree, but when they agreed to let me open the boarding school, they put us on a tight budget. These days even government programs are cutting back." She looked at the desk again. "It's probably not as bad as I think it is. It's just . . . Sky used to do all the financial work, and now I'm stuck with it."

"Burnett's not good with doing that kind of stuff?" Kylie asked, hoping to ease into a conversation about him.

"I don't know. But since he shouldn't be helping out here for more than another month, I don't see any reason for him to get involved with this side of the business."

Take the sugarcoating off what Holiday said and it basically meant she didn't trust Burnett. Was that because he was vampire, or could it be because she'd trusted Sky, her last co-camp leader, and Sky had let her down? Holiday never talked about Sky much, but Kylie sensed her friend's betrayal had hurt her more than she wanted to admit.

"Have they hired a new camp leader?" Kylie asked.

Now Holiday's expression turned into a full groan. "No. But they've promised by the end of summer I should have someone. And that can't come soon enough."

"Is he really that unpleasant to work with?" Kylie sensed Holiday's frustration came from Burnett, which only made Kylie worry about how Holiday would take Kylie's confession.

"We're just too different." Holiday's gaze lowered to Kylie's chest and stayed there for a fraction of a second too long. Which meant Holiday had noticed the growth spurt.

Kylie's thoughts shot away from her confession and turned on her own issues. "Can you explain this?"

"Explain what?" Holiday asked innocently enough, but it didn't convince Kylie.

Kylie held out her hands in front of her boobs.

Holiday's brows wrinkled. "I was hoping you'd just gotten a new Wonderbra."

"Afraid not. There's my hair, too." Kylie pulled it over her shoulder. "Plus, my shoes are almost too tight and I'm pretty sure I'm a whole inch taller."

"Mmm." Holiday almost appeared as if she worked at keeping her expression unreadable.

"Mmm, what?" Kylie leaned forward, pressing her hands on the desk.

"Mmm, it's odd." Holiday said, but something about the way the camp leader glanced back to her papers hinted that she wasn't being one hundred percent up front with Kylie.

"Please don't do this now," Kylie insisted.

Holiday looked up. "Do what?"

"Hide something. It's happening to me. I have the right to know what the hell is going on."

"I'm not hiding . . ." Holiday stopped talking and sighed. "I don't consider it hiding anything when I'm surmising, guessing. I'm not sure if it's fair to give you information when I'm not sure."

"What's not fair is to leave me completely in the dark. Because believe me, whatever you have to tell me isn't going to be half as bad as what I'm imagining."

Holiday nodded. "Okay, but just remember . . . it's speculation. Even Burnett said he didn't see it being a sure sign."

Kylie had suspected that Burnett had noted her boob increase. To his credit he'd dealt with it well, but to think he and the others were discussing it, well, it felt like overkill. Really dead stinky overkill. "You two discussed my boobs?"

"No. Well, yes, but not . . . Look, he said he noticed some changes in you when he ran into you at the falls. I insisted he tell me what they were."

The mere mention of Kylie seeing Burnett at the falls had Kylie remembering she needed to come clean, but first she had to know. "What's the speculation?"

"Some female werewolves—"

"Werewolf? Oh, damn! Not werewolf. Anything but werewolf."

Chapter Twelve

"Hey!" Holiday's hand came to rest on Kylie's arm. "You see, this is why I didn't want to tell you. I knew you'd jump to conclusions."

Kylie blinked. "What is it that some female werewolves do? Grow super boobs?"

"No. Well, sort of." Holiday bit back a smile. "When they reach a certain level in maturity, when they are close to mating age, they'll fill out rather quickly."

Kylie's heart pounded and all she could remember was what Miranda had said about seeing a werewolf change into wolf form, about how painful it appeared. "But that sounds just like what is happening to me. So how is this speculation or jumping to conclusions?"

Holiday shook her head. "Unless a werewolf had been turned, most start shifting into wolves when they are four or five. It would be very rare that it would happen to you at this age. And then there's the fact that werewolves undergo some rather strong mood swings a few days before and after a full moon. Dr. Day reported that she saw you during a full moon and saw none of these signs. And I watched you on the last full moon just to see if perhaps she missed something. I didn't note *any* changes in your behavior."

"Maybe I'm just a late bloomer," Kylie said, not that she was hoping it was true. "And I've never been one to let my emotions out too much. So maybe you just didn't see me being moody."

"There's also . . . your cat," Holiday continued. "All felines have an aversion toward weres. Not so with you."

Kylie recalled how, years ago, her cat had reacted to Lucas. She remembered how the kitten had reacted to Lucas the day he'd dropped it off. But then suddenly Kylie remembered something that might be important. "Oh crap. The wolf."

"What . . . wolf?"

"The other night . . . when I ran off after I tasted blood. I ran into a wolf. He hung around me. Even showed up again later that night, but—"

"It wasn't a full moon," Holiday said. "It couldn't have been a werewolf."

"I know that's why I didn't think . . . I mean, I just thought that it was someone's half-tame wolf. He knelt down in front of me and tried to crawl forward, like he wanted me to touch him or something." She had to remind herself to breathe. "Do you think that could mean something? Is it some kind of ritual that wolves hang out with werewolves before they turn for the first time?"

Holiday stared back at Kylie as if trying to think. "I've never heard of it. But I'm . . . Sky was always the one who took care of counseling the weres. So I don't have all the knowledge of it. But I'll ask around. Burnett will know."

"He's not a werewolf." Kylie wished Lucas were here. Here to advise her, to help her make sense of all this. But no, he'd run off with another she-wolf. And Kylie still hadn't read his letter because she was so pissed that he'd done it.

"Burnett's not were, but his job with FRU requires extensive research on all supernaturals. Believe it or not, he's as smart as he is

arrogant. And I hope you don't think . . . I mean, when he spoke to me about your increase in size, there was nothing in his tone but concern about how you were dealing with these changes."

Even distraught about the idea of being werewolf, Kylie realized that Holiday was defending Burnett. Like it or not, Holiday had found some respect for the vampire. Not that this excused Kylie from the fact that she shared Holiday's private information. But couldn't Holiday see that she and Burnett should give the romance a shot? Just how mad was she going to be about Kylie telling him about her past relationship with another vampire?

"About the falls . . ."

"I understand," Holiday said.

"Understand what?" Kylie asked, hoping it could be that easy. That Burnett had told Holiday about his and Kylie's conversation and she wasn't upset.

"I understand why you went there," Holiday started, straightening some papers. "I go at least once a week myself. It's the best place to go to . . . think, to try to figure out things. Did you get any answers about the ghost this morning?"

Kylie shook her head. "Just a sense of rightness."

"Then you have to have faith that you're doing all you can," Holiday said.

Kylie suddenly remembered. "You told me you hadn't ever seen a death angel."

"I haven't," Holiday said.

"But you said you weren't even sure they were real."

"I don't think the version of the legends that everyone believes is real," Holiday said.

"Then what makes the falls so . . . special?"

Holiday hesitated as if trying to find the right words. "I think it's a holy place. I think the Big Cheese running everything up there in the heavens created it for those of us who have to deal with spirits. It's a place we can find some peace. And sometimes even answers."

"Like a church?" Kylie asked, recalling the reverence she'd felt there.

"Yeah, sort of like a church. There's a lot of spiritual power there. You felt it, right?" Holiday placed her hand over Kylie's.

Kylie pulled her hand back. "Yeah. But . . . why didn't you tell me? I asked you about the falls and you didn't say anything. I mean, I could have . . . I could have been going there all along. Maybe I would have figured out more what the ghost is trying to tell me by now."

Holiday dropped her hands on the desk, and empathy filled her green eyes. "You don't tell someone about the falls, Kylie. The falls has to call you to it. And I'm assuming it called you or you wouldn't have gone there."

Kylie couldn't deny she had felt the calling to go. Yet she still resented the fact that she had to figure everything out herself. What was wrong with a little direction, a little helping hand?

"I'm somewhat shocked that Burnett went there," Holiday said. "The only supernaturals who get called to the falls are those with ghost-whispering powers. The other supernaturals find it too emotionally stimulating . . . or I guess I could call it intimidating."

Kylie recalled how Della and Miranda had reacted. Yeah, intimidating was about right.

"Even Sky wouldn't go there." Holiday looked up at Kylie. "Did Burnett actually go behind the falls?"

"He was there when I went in." She hesitated. "He went there because of you," Kylie said, using this as her opening. If she didn't take it now, she might back out. Then her breach of confidence would be even worse.

"Me?"

"He wanted to understand you better. And I think he thought if he . . . could understand the whole ghost thing, then—"

"He said that?" Surprise widened Holiday's eyes.

"Yeah." Kylie hesitated and then just blurted it out. "I told him that you had your heart broken by another vampire. That it was why you . . . don't want to get involved with him."

Holiday's brow furrowed instantly and her eyes grew tight. It wasn't a look Kylie noted on Holiday's face very often. "You told him what?"

"I know I shouldn't have done it. But . . . he asked and at first I didn't tell him, but—"

"Why would he . . . No, why would you tell him anything?"

"He really likes you, Holiday."

"How he feels doesn't matter. I didn't share that with you to tell anyone else." She stopped talking, but the frustration flared in her eyes.

"I'm sorry. I am. And I know it was wrong, but I think . . . I mean, it's almost as if you're letting what your fiancé did to you stop you from seeing the possibilities with Burnett. You're punishing him for something that he didn't do."

Holiday's expression didn't soften. She swallowed a deep breath. "Kylie, what happens between Burnett and me isn't . . ." She closed her mouth and the muscles in her jaw clenched. "Why don't we stop this talk right now and we'll take this up later. I need some time."

Kylie felt a huge hole open up in her chest. "Please don't . . . don't be mad at me."

Holiday held up her hand. "I'm not exactly mad. I'm . . . disappointed."

"That's even worse," Kylie said, and her chest grew tighter. "Really, I'm sorry."

Holiday stood up and motioned for the door. "I'll see you to-morrow."

Tears prickled Kylie's eyes, and more than anything she wanted to argue, to beg Holiday to forgive her. To plead with her not to let her slip-up change the relationship they'd found. But something deep inside told Kylie it could be too late.

At almost nine that night Kylie lay in her bed staring at the ceiling with a dad-blasted skunk sharing her pillow. She'd opted out of going down to the dining hall and participating in pizza and basketball night. Burnett had put up a basketball court and all the guys had formed teams. With as little sleep as she'd gotten these last few days, you'd think she'd have been out like a blown bulb. Not.

She cut her eyes to the drawer where she'd placed Lucas's letter and for a flicker of a second her mind switched from her Holiday problems to her Lucas problems, and then it went to her Derek problems. Next her mind came against the idea of being werewolf. Oh, joy!

When her mind slapped against the whole issue of someone she loved being in danger, Kylie instantly recalled the feeling she'd gotten from the falls, that if she stayed on course, at least that problem would be okay.

Too bad all her other issues didn't seem so manageable.

The ring of her phone brought a moan to her lips—not that she couldn't use a mental break from juggling her problems. And maybe if she was lucky, it was Sara, finally calling her back. Sure they weren't as close as they once had been, but she still cared about Sara, and she'd been thinking about her a lot lately. But was she up to talking with her former best friend?

"Don't want to startle you," she told Socks, who may or may

not have the whole spraying thing down. "I need to reach for my phone." The animal opened one beady eye and looked at her and then let out a poor excuse for a meow.

Miranda had spent all day attempting to change Socks back to his ol' self. Kylie had finally told her to give it a rest. She even told her not to be so hard on herself, that this was just a hiccup. A huge, freaking hiccup, but Kylie didn't tell her that.

The phone stopped ringing and Kylie wasn't even compelled to check to see who'd called. She glanced at Socks again. "A really huge freaking hiccup," Kylie muttered. But considering she hoped that Holiday would forgive her, she decided it might be best to practice what she preached, or at least practice what she prayed for . . . forgiveness. And she had prayed. Remembering how Holiday had looked so betrayed brought a wave of pain to Kylie's heart.

How could telling Burnett about Holiday have felt almost right at the time? And now feel so wrong? And yes, telling Burnett the truth had felt right. She'd been compelled to do it, as if her gut had given her the push. So much for listening to her gut!

Her phone rang again. Pulling her cell over, not certain she wanted to talk to anyone, Kylie studied the number . . . and a sudden knot swelled in her chest.

Chapter Thirteen

Mom. The realization hit and hit hard, too. She never thought she'd feel this, but she missed her mom. Wished she were here to . . . to just be here. And it wasn't just because they'd sort of found new ground with their relationship. Kylie even appreciated the old ground they'd had.

As much as Kylie had sworn her mom had never loved her, the longer Kylie was away from her the more she began to see things differently. Sure her mom had been emotionally distant, and sure Kylie wasn't really *anything* like her. But for some reason now, Kylie saw all the other ways her mom had shown love. The pancakes every Saturday morning. The loaning her the credit card anytime Kylie mentioned she needing anything. Even the stinkin' sex pamphlets showed her mom cared—not that Kylie wouldn't be happy if the pamphlets stopped, but still . . .

Hitting the talk button, she fought back a wave of nostalgia. "Hi, Mom." Kylie swore she wasn't going to cry, and with effort she managed to keep her voice from shaking.

"Sweetheart?" The immediate concern in her mom's voice had the knot in Kylie's throat growing, and emotion stung her sinuses. "Are you okay?"

How could her mom know something was wrong when all Kylie had said was two words? Was her mom psychic? *No, she was only human.* It had to be maternal instinct. And her mom had never lacked that.

"I'm okay." Kylie bit the inside her cheek to keep from weeping.

"What happened, baby?"

Tears formed in Kylie's eyes. "It's nothing." She watched Socks reposition himself on the pillow and she prayed he wasn't about to spray her. Getting skunked by her skunk-cat would be the absolute last straw. "Just a hard day, is all."

"What kind of hard day? Do you want to come home? All you have to say is the word and I'll drive up there tonight and pick you up."

"No, Mom. I love it here." Kylie recalled her mom hadn't given her an absolute yes on signing her up for boarding school. Which meant Kylie shouldn't be talking about anything negative concerning Shadow Falls right now. She really had to get her mom to agree—especially if . . . if Kylie ended up being werewolf. How in the hell did one explain that to a human parent? "I just . . . I made a mistake today and someone I really care about is upset with me."

"We all make mistakes," Mom said. "You just need to apologize."

"I did."

"And they didn't forgive you? Are they still mad at you?" her mom asked.

"Not so much mad. Just disappointed in me." Kylie's chest swelled with regret as she recalled Holiday saying those words to her. Kylie knew what it felt like to be disappointed and hurt by someone you trusted. It was worse than being mad. Like her dad. Okay, with him she was both mad and hurt, but the "hurt" feelings had her heart breaking. While being mad and angry almost felt good, no good feelings came from feeling hurt. None.

"Do you want to tell me what happened?" her mom asked, sounding as if she didn't want to pry, but felt it was her maternal obligation to do so. Amazingly, Kylie wanted to answer. She couldn't and wouldn't tell her mother everything, but she could tell her some.

"Someone told me something in confidence. And I . . . told someone else. At the time, I really thought telling it might help . . . fix a problem. But . . ."

"But it didn't help?" her mom asked.

"No," Kylie said. "I mean, not that I can see yet."

"Kylie, it sounds as if you were trying to do the right thing. I wouldn't be so hard on yourself. This is just a little hiccup, girl." Kylie almost laughed at her mother's chosen words. Wasn't that exactly what she'd told Miranda? Maybe Kylie was more like her mom than she knew. Tightness gripped her chest.

"I love you, Mom," Kylie said without thinking.

"Oh, baby," her mom said, now sounding as if she was going to cry. "I love you, too. Is there anything I can do to help? I'll come there and kick ass if I have to."

A tear rolled down Kylie's check. "You'd kick ass for me?"

"In a New York minute."

Kylie chuckled and sniffled at the same time.

"Are you ready for a change of subject? Something fun?" her mom asked, sounding excited. "It's the reason I called."

"Yes." Kylie wiped her eyes. She really could use some good news.

"You'll never guess what I signed us up for that Friday night when you're back."

"What?" Kylie asked, and realized she didn't really dread going home anymore. It would be good to spend some time with Mom, to hopefully get away from the problems pressing down on her at the camp.

"You were the one who got me thinking about it."

"Thinking about what, Mom?" Kylie asked, sensing her mom's excitement.

"A ghost hunt. Remember, you mentioned the falls being haunted at the camp?"

"A ghost hunt?" Kylie couldn't believe her ears.

"It's a dinner at a reputedly haunted B&B and then they take us on a tour. Isn't that totally cool?"

Kylie dropped back on her pillow and now she really wanted to cry. "Yeah. Totally . . ." *not* ". . . cool."

Thirty minutes after Kylie had hung up, she started counting sheep, inviting sleep to come take her away. While sheep number one hundred took a flying leap across her bed, Kylie's mind started replaying her argument with Holiday.

"How he feels doesn't matter. I didn't share that with you to tell anyone else," Holiday had said.

"I'm sorry. I am," Kylie had said. *"And I know it was wrong, but I think . . . I mean, it's almost as if you're letting what your fiancé did to you stop you from seeing the possibilities with Burnett. You're punishing him for something that he didn't do."*

You're punishing him for something that he didn't do.

You're punishing him for something that he didn't do.

Then her mind completely skipped to the argument she'd had with Derek.

"It's always about sex, isn't it?" she had said.

"No. I wasn't talking about that," he had countered.

Kylie recalled all the anger welling up inside at that moment. Bottled-up anger, leftover anger. Anger she'd felt toward . . . Trey.

You're punishing him for something that he didn't do.

"Oh, shit!" She sat up. Had she done the same thing she'd accused Holiday of doing? The more she thought about it, the more she realized that Derek had never, not even once, pressured her about sex. His statement about her pulling away had everything to do with her dodging him. Not about her getting naked.

Then a bit of her mom's dialogue came into play. *"We all make mistakes. You just need to apologize."*

Mom was right. Which Kylie realized was another thing she never thought she'd ever catch herself thinking where her mom was concerned. But damn it, her mom was right. Kylie needed to apologize. Standing up, she shucked off her nightshirt and slipped back into her too-short jeans, her too-tight bra, too-tight tennis shoes, and a T-shirt, then went to find Derek.

The moment Kylie stepped outside, the humid hot air surrounded her. She started to head toward the dining hall and then stopped. Derek generally left the nighttime events early to call his mom. Not that he told everyone what he was doing. But he'd confided in her.

Warmth filled her chest. She liked that he'd confided in her. Oh, heck, she really, really liked Derek, and with all her heart, she hoped he'd accept her apology. Because she didn't want to go into what she had to say around super-hearing individuals, she headed toward his cabin. She set her pace at a slow run, which only a couple of weeks ago would have been amazingly fast for her. As she moved, she felt the trees hovering above. She felt the wind stir her hair. She caught a glimpse of the bright stars, but she didn't care too much about the scenery. Instead she concentrated on what she would tell Derek when she saw him.

Halfway there, the feeling hit. The feeling as if someone was watching her. She slowed her pace and listened. The night was still chirping, there was no dead or unnatural silence, but she still felt it. Glancing from right to left to the edges of the woods, she checked to see if the wolf was back. There were no golden eyes peering back at her from the brush. She tried to convince herself it was nothing, but she picked up her pace, eager to find Derek—eager to have Derek's solid, bigger frame beside her.

His arms around her.

Her head on his shoulder.

Maybe his mouth melting against hers.

Oh yeah, thinking about Derek chased away her fears.

She made that last turn down the trail and saw there were lights on in his cabin. Someone was there. "Please let it be him."

She made it another hundred feet when she noticed that his cabin's front door was open. That was a little odd. When she got up the porch steps, she noted the smell. The ripe berry scent. She hadn't yet defined the aroma when her tennis shoe hit a slick spot and she went down.

Plopping down on her butt, she pressed her palm against the porch to lift up. But the sensation of something wet and thick beneath her palm gave her pause.

That's when she recognized the sweet berry scent.

Blood.

Her gaze shot to the porch.

A lot of blood.

The rectangle of light pouring from the doorway caught her attention and Kylie saw it. Dark red droplets led the way into the cabin like breadcrumbs in the forest.

Her heart stopped.

Oh, God. "Derek!" she screamed his name, but no answer
bounced back.

She lunged to her feet and ran into the cabin, screaming his name
over and over.

Chapter Fourteen

"Derek?" Her heart pounded. She followed the trail of blood, through the living room, down the hall. It led to a closed door. She grabbed the knob. Locked.

She heard a noise on the other side. "Derek?" she yelled. Again no answer.

Not thinking, driven by raw panic, she took a couple of steps back and rammed the door with her shoulder. Part of the door ripped off with the hinges; the other part splintered into two or three pieces and crashed on the bathroom floor. She crashed on top of it. Face-down.

That's when she realized the noise she'd heard behind the closed door had been the shower. That's when she saw a very naked and very wet Derek yank back the shower curtain.

His body was hard, corded with muscle. Defensiveness glinted in his eyes and his posture. He looked prepared to take on an intruder.

Which would be her, by the way.

He stared at her sprawled on top of the splintered piece of his bathroom door. She stared at him . . . naked with the shower curtain still clutched in his fist.

"Uh, I . . . I saw blood and thought . . ." *What had she thought?* Rogue vampire, ax murderer, serial killer on the loose. She hadn't put a villain in her fears. Her concern had just been for Derek's safety.

"You knocked the door down." Disbelief rang in his matter-of-fact tone.

"I know," she answered, unable to say anything else. Unable to look away from his body.

"But it's solid oak."

"I know." She felt the solid oak beneath her and was a little shocked that she'd done it, too. If it mattered at all, her shoulder felt a little bruised. And it was the slight pain that brought some reality back into the moment.

"You don't have any clothes on." Oh, God, did she really say that?

"I know. I usually shower that way."

Her face began to burn.

When he didn't seem to worry about his lack of clothes, Kylie decided that maybe it was her place to worry. After all, she had been the one to storm into his bathroom and break down his door while he'd been showering.

She turned her back on him. A totally useless, unproductive move. It didn't stop her from seeing him. The mirror hung over the low counter, which she now faced, offered her the same view.

A really awesome view, too. She'd seen naked men in the movies. Well, almost naked. And she'd seen naked statues. Beautifully posed, carved-in-stone statues that left nothing to the imagination. In person was definitely better. Oh, goodness, he looked good wet and without his clothes on.

Then she realized that while she'd been enjoying the view, he'd been watching her enjoying it. His gaze from the mirror locked with hers. That rush of blood returned to her face. She glanced away from his reflection in the mirror to her shoes just as he grabbed for a towel.

That's when she decided to explain again. "I . . . I saw blood and I panicked."

"Yeah," he answered. "Chris gave me a bloody nose when he elbowed me in the face playing basketball."

She looked up to the mirror to check out his face. "How bad was it?"

"Just a bloody nose." Holding the towel around his waist, he reached for his jeans on the floor, and then he met her gaze back in the mirror. "I'm gonna put on some pants. So you might want to look down again."

She did, and she blushed again, too. Only when she heard the zipper did she look up. He stood closer, right over her in fact, holding out his hand to help her up. She took it.

"Are you okay?" he asked as soon as she came to her feet.

She rubbed her shoulder. "Just a little bruised."

"I would imagine."

She saw him look back at the door. "I'll tell Holiday I did it," she said.

"It's okay." He picked up a piece of the wood and tried to bend it. When it didn't move, he looked back at her. Then he reached out and touched her arm and his touch shifted slowly up to her elbow.

His touch felt warm and moist, much like the air in the bathroom. Tingles climbed up her arm and filled her chest. Her gaze went to his broad shoulders and she wanted to kiss him there, in the place where she had rested her head so often.

"You're still warm," he said. "Normally, a vampire doesn't gain strength until after they've turned."

Disappointment shattered the mood. His reason for touching her had been to check her body temperature, not because . . . because he just felt compelled to do it, the way she felt compelled to touch him.

"I think that's the problem," she said. "I'm not normal." She bit down on her lip and then decided to just tell him. "Holiday said . . . she said some female werewolves have"—she glanced down at her breasts—"growth spurts around this age."

"So she thinks you're werewolf?" he asked.

"No, not really. She said that . . . nothing else seems to point to werewolf. So we're back at square one."

"Sorry," he said. "I know you want to figure it out." He ran a hand up her elbow again, and this time she knew it wasn't to check for temperature. The tingles and mood came back.

Letting go of a deep sigh, she met his beautiful green eyes. "That's why I came here."

"What's why you came here?" he asked. He moved out of the bathroom and to the first door on the right. She followed him and stopped when she realized it was his bedroom. She watched him grab a shirt from his closet. He held it to his flat stomach but didn't put it on. She had the craziest feeling that he'd left it off because he knew she enjoyed looking at him. He stepped closer to her. "Why did you come here?"

Focus. Focus. Quit thinking about his body. "To tell you I'm sorry. For being such a bitch this afternoon. I was . . . confused. I mean, Trey . . . He did me wrong and when you said what you did, I just jumped back to what Trey did. What he did really hurt me, and I think I just projected it all on to you."

He pulled her against him and pressed his lips to hers. The kiss was hot, passionate, and she didn't want it to end. And when it did, he was the one who pulled away, not her. She was happy, however, to see his breath was as uneven as hers.

"The answer is yes." Derek's lips were moist and still so close to hers that she felt the words whisper across her cheek.

"I'm . . . I'm not sure what the question is," Kylie said, thinking she'd missed something because she was drunk off his kisses.

"The last thing you asked me this afternoon was if I wanted sex. I want to make myself clear. I want you. I want you so badly that sometimes it's all I can think about. Some nights I wake up and I'm so . . ." He bit back his words and let go of another deep breath. "What I'm trying to say is while I want you really badly, the last thing I'd try to do is pressure you into doing something that doesn't feel right."

"It does feel right." She placed her hand on his chest. And oh my, did it feel right to touch his bare chest. The temptation to ask him to do it, to pull her over to the bed and teach her all about sex, was almost overpowering. However, there was still something that held her back.

"Or at least mostly right." She pulled her hand from his bare skin. "I think I just need to figure out who I am first." She stared at his chest, afraid if she looked him in the eyes, she'd turned candy apple red again. Unfortunately, he raised his hand and tilted her head back and forced her to look at him.

"I know who you are, Kylie. You're warm, funny, and beautiful. You are so good to everyone, everyone likes you. And you've got tons of spunk. I really like spunk."

"I mean *what* I am," she corrected, feeling his fingers brushing against her neck.

"*What* you are doesn't matter. Because what you are isn't going to change *who* you are." He dropped his hand from her chin. "And

I'm not saying this to rush you to have sex. I just want you . . . I wish you could see yourself through my eyes. I wish you could see how special you are. And I don't care what you turn out to be."

Tears prickled her eyes and she wrapped her arm around his naked torso and pressed her cheek against his warm wall of chest that smelled clean, soapy, and moist. "You're the one who's special," she whispered.

"Nope," he answered, and chuckled. "If I was special I wouldn't be thinking about how I could change your mind about having sex right now. So let's get out of this room before I decide to tackle you on my bed."

She laughed and looked up into his eyes.

He smiled and ran his hand up under her shirt and to her bare back where he cupped his hand in the curve of her naked waist. "That whole breaking the door down was really a turn-on."

"And not the fact that you were naked?" Had she said that? Instantly, she wished the floor would swallow her up.

"Nope, it was definitely the door thing. Now if you'd been naked . . ." He let go of a deep gulp of air. "Okay, we'd better quit talking about this." He pulled away from her, caught her hand, and tugged her out of his bedroom.

She let him lead her out into the living room. He eyed the couch and then looked back at her. His eyes looked heavy, sleepy, and hot. "Almost as bad as the bed."

She grinned and he pulled her out onto the front porch. He slipped on his shirt, then dropped down and leaned against the cabin on the blood-free end of the porch. Once settled, he looked up and patted the spot on the porch beside him. She lowered herself beside him, and scooted over so her arm was against his. Leaning her head on his shoulder, she said, "Thanks."

He shifted and lifted his hand around her shoulder and pulled her a tad closer. "You're welcome."

Neither of them said anything for several minutes. She just sat there, close and absorbing the feel of him beside her. Questions tumbled around her head like a pair of tennis shoes in the dryer. But embarrassment kept her from voicing them.

"Go ahead and ask it," he said, almost as though he was reading her thoughts.

She raised her head off his shoulder. "Ask what?"

"Whatever it is that's making you feel embarrassed and curious. I can read your emotions, remember?"

She frowned. "And I hate that, too. I don't want you reading me."

"But I can't help it. I don't know how to not read you." He chuckled and looked down at her. And just like all the other times they were together, the night had a fairy-tale feel about it. The stars twinkled like diamonds in the sky. The trees looked too full. The moon, less than a week from being full, gave off enough light that she could see his face. "I think you're going to have a bruise." She touched the side of his nose.

He caught her hand in his and kissed the inside of her hand. "So, what is it that's making you embarrassed and curious?"

"I'm just . . ." If she didn't tell him now, he'd probably envision the worst. Then again, what she was curious about might be the worst.

"Just ask me." He nudged her with his shoulder.

She hesitated and then just blurted it out. "I'm curious about how many girls you've been with. I know you're almost eighteen and . . ." Her words faltered. Kylie knew he wasn't a virgin, and not just because he'd said something that led her to believe it, but just how . . . he kissed.

His brow crinkled and she could tell he wished he hadn't pushed her to ask.

"Oh," he said.

"Oh?" she repeated. And now more than ever she wanted an answer. "You made me ask, now you have to answer."

He hesitated. "A few."

"That's vague." She pulled her fingers from his.

He breathed in and then out. "Okay, four."

"That's more than a few."

"Sorry." He didn't deny that he'd been lying. "It just feels awkward talking about it with you."

"Yeah, it does," she said, realizing she didn't like knowing. Didn't like thinking about him being with someone else. "Sorry I asked."

"Don't be." He leaned back against the cabin wall and went back to listening to the night. "Can I ask you something?"

"Sure." A nervous flutter tickled her stomach. But considering how personal her own question had been, she couldn't tell him no.

"If Lucas were still here, would you still be sitting next to me?"

Chapter Fifteen

His question ran across all sorts of nerves and not the good ones, either. "What kind of question is that?"

"Obviously a hard one." He pulled his knee up to his chest and stared down at his toes.

Something told her he was reading her right now—trying to understand her emotions. But how could he when she didn't understand them herself? "He's not here," Kylie said.

He looked over at her. "Rumor has it that he's coming back."

She felt her breath catch in her throat. "Doesn't matter," she forced herself to say. "He's with Fredericka."

"He'd drop her for you like this." Derek snapped his fingers. "He's not blind or stupid."

She shook her head. "Well, maybe I don't want anyone who'd run off with someone else."

He arched an eyebrow. "It's the 'maybe' in your answer that worries me more than the confusion you're feeling right now." He leaned his forehead down to hers. "Please don't break my heart, Kylie."

Her own heart almost broke right then. "It's the last thing I want to do."

He kissed her softly, then pulled back. "I should get you back to your cabin before everyone gets back here."

She nodded and accepted his hand to help pull her up. They started to walk off the porch when he stopped. "Oh, I forgot. I got something to give you." He ran back inside and returned after a few short seconds holding a piece of paper.

"What's this?" she asked when he put it in her hands.

"It's a telephone number of a private investigator."

When he didn't continue, she asked, "And I need it for . . . ?"

"You said you were trying to find your real grandparents. This guy is good at finding people. If anyone can find them, he can."

Kylie looked up from the paper. "Do you really think he could find them after all this time? I mean, I've been trying to just find Daniel's adoptive parents, but I can't even find them."

"He's that good," Derek said.

Her heart started to sink. "And probably that expensive. I can't afford him." She started to give him back the paper.

He caught her hand. "He's not charging you, Kylie. Call him."

"Why wouldn't he charge me? You said he was a PI."

"Because he's a friend of mine. And I used to do some work for him on the side."

"You worked for a PI?"

"Yeah. I went to him to see if . . . if he could help me locate my dad."

That piece of news also surprised her. She didn't think Derek wanted anything to do with his dad. "Did he find him?"

"Yeah," Derek said. "You missed a great pizza tonight," he added, making it clear he didn't really want to talk about his dad.

But Kylie couldn't stop herself from asking. "And did you see him?"

"No. I just wanted to know where the bastard was."

Kylie sensed Derek's pain. "So how did you end up working for the PI?"

"He found my skill of reading emotions very helpful."

Still wanting to soothe away the look of hurt from Derek's eyes, she reached up and planted another kiss on his lips. A good one. She pulled him close, so close that her one-cup-size-larger breasts were pressed against his chest. Derek's hands came down to hold her around her waist. One of his palms slid up under her shirt and slowly shifted upward. He caressed her upper back, stopping right below her bra strap as if not wanting to cross a line. A line she almost wanted him to cross.

When she pulled away, her breathing came faster. "Thank you, for this." She held up the paper.

"Wow," he said, smiling, and touched her lips. "If he actually finds them, what do I get?"

She elbowed him in the ribs. He laughed and then wrapped his arm around her shoulders as they started back to her cabin.

At eight a.m. sharp the next morning, Kylie had one roommate out of the cabin—Della had left for her vampire rituals—and Kylie was working on getting rid of the other. She told Miranda to go on to breakfast without her. Kylie would catch up later. Miranda had stepped out the door but she'd stayed there for five minutes or so performing some kind of ritual. Kylie finally poked her head out the door to ask, "What are you doing?"

"I told you earlier, I'm just trying to protect our cabin."

Kylie remembered her roommate claiming that an unwelcome presence lurked nearby, although Kylie hadn't really felt anything. Other than when she'd been alone in the woods or paths.

"Protect it from what . . . exactly?"

Miranda tossed up some kind of herbs in the air. They crackled and popped on their downward descent, telling Kylie they weren't just regular herbs. "I don't know . . . exactly."

"Didn't you already do something to get rid of it?"

"Yup, but the bad boy is still here. Just won't go away."

Kylie didn't want to ask, but she figured she had to. "Could it be a ghost?" Because if it was, Kylie wasn't so sure Miranda should attempt to keep it away. Like it or not, dealing with ghosts was sort of Kylie's job. Not that so far Miranda's rituals had prevented the ghosts from visiting. However, if Miranda's herbs were in any way keeping Daniel away, well, Kylie couldn't have that. She really needed to talk to Daniel.

"No, it's not like one of your spirits," Miranda said.

"Then what is it like?" Kylie felt a tad apprehensive and remembering the unwelcomed vampire visitor from the other night. "I mean, wouldn't Della know if it was like something rogue?"

"Yeah, but this isn't . . . normal. It's involving magic. I can't put my finger on it yet, but I'm working on it," she said.

Working on it like she was working on changing Socks back to feline form? Kylie didn't say it, because that would have hurt Miranda, but Kylie couldn't help thinking it.

"Have you mentioned it to Holiday?" Kylie asked.

"Not yet. Let me try to deal with it first."

Kylie nodded, but she wasn't too sure.

"You ready to go yet?" Miranda asked after tossing up one more sprinkling of herbs.

"No." Kylie brushed a few of the tiny crackling herbs from her hair. "I . . . got a few phone calls to make."

"Okay, but don't be too late. After Campmate Hour, we've got cooking together, and today we're supposed to bake brownies, and you're supposed to decorate them. And they won't let us eat them until after you've done your thing. And I love, love brownies. And don't want to have to wait."

"I won't be that late." Kylie was actually enjoying the food art lessons she'd signed up for last week. Who knew she'd get off on decorating cupcakes and such? Drawing with pen and paper had never been her thing, but working with icing was kind of cool. Then again, she'd always kind of enjoyed watching those cake-decorating shows on cable.

Miranda started to walk away and then turned back. "Who are you calling?"

Holding the phone number of the private detective in her hand, she almost told Miranda the truth, but decided she wasn't ready to share. "I'll explain later."

"Trey?" Miranda asked.

"No way," Kylie answered.

"Sara?" Miranda asked.

"I'll explain later." Kylie frowned, remembering Sara still hadn't tried to call her back.

"A secret admirer," Miranda continued as if were a game. "A hot stud muffin who kisses like no tomorrow that you haven't told us about? Oh, I want to meet him."

Kylie groaned. "I don't have a stud muffin."

"Really? The way you blushed when you talked about Derek naked, I thought he was your stud muffin."

"Go to breakfast." Kylie waved her off.

"Oookay," Miranda said, and started off.

Kylie shut the door and looked at the scrap of paper she held in her hand. She finally felt as if she might be closer to finding answers. She hadn't had any luck finding Daniel's adoptive parents, or even knew if they were still alive, and she didn't have a clue how to go about looking for his real ones. But if Derek was right . . . if this guy was that good, then maybe he could find them. And because they were supernaturals, or at least one of them had to be, and considering they had a longer life expectancy, then there was a good chance they could be alive.

And if she found them, she would find her answers. She would finally know what she was. God, she really, really hoped this guy was as good as Derek believed.

Just thinking Derek's name, or maybe it was Miranda's whole stud muffin talk, either way, Kylie got flashbacks to last night. To the whole shower scene and to the hot kisses they'd shared.

"Wow. If he actually finds them, what do I get?"

Derek's question played in her head. She knew he was joking, he didn't expect payment of any kind for helping her. And perhaps that was part of the reason she wanted to reward him. Or not exactly reward him. She just wanted . . .

Don't go there, she told herself. It was way too early to start thinking about those kinds of things. Think about decorating cupcakes. Or think about making the call.

Grabbing her phone off the kitchen counter, she sat down at the computer desk. Taking a deep breath, she dialed the PI's number.

"Brit Smith Agency," he answered.

"Hi." She didn't exactly know where to start. "Uh, my name is Kylie Galen."

"Derek's girl?" the man said.

Kylie felt her stomach wiggle at being called "Derek's girl." It sounded really nice, even though Kylie wasn't officially his girl. Then again, seeing him naked . . . *Don't go there.*

"Derek said that you might be able to help me find someone."

"Yeah, something about your dad being adopted. Let me get to my computer and I'll take notes."

"Sure." While Kylie waited, she looked up at her computer and decided to check her e-mail. She moved the mouse to wake up the computer.

Seconds later, a *Springville Times* newspaper article appeared on the screen. When Kylie started reading, she realized it wasn't just any article. It was the *Springville Times* obituaries. Springville? Wasn't Della from Springville, Texas? But why was she . . .

"Ready," Mr. Smith said. "What's your father's name?"

Kylie looked away from the computer. "Daniel Brighten."

"Parents' names?"

"I don't have their first names," Kylie said.

"Okay," he said. "What county was he born in?"

"I . . . don't know."

"But it was Texas, right?"

Kylie started feeling less and less hopeful that this would lead her anywhere. "I'm not really sure."

"Okay," he said, and this time his okay sounded less enthusiastic. "Maybe we should start by you telling me what you do know."

Her mind started gathering information. "His parents lived in Dallas when my mom met him. I've been . . . calling all the Brightens in the Dallas area. So far I haven't found anyone who claims they knew my father." She went on and told him about how Daniel had died in the Gulf War. And even told him a little about how her mom and Daniel had first met. It wasn't a lot to go on and she knew it.

"That's not a lot to go on," Mr. Smith said, just proving her point and making her even less enthusiastic. "But I'll see what I can dig up. I'm working a big case right now, and it might take a while before I start on this, but when I have something I'll let you know. Meanwhile you keep on asking questions."

"Questions to who?" Kylie asked.

"Your mom, of course."

"I think she's told me everything she knows," Kylie said.

"Maybe," Mr. Smith said. "But parents are funny about divulging info about relationships and things like this."

Kylie bit down on her lip and wondered if he could be right. For certain her mom wasn't the most open-book type of person. "I guess you could be right."

"Yeah, and even if she's not keeping something from you on purpose, she might not see something as important. She does know you're looking into finding his family, doesn't she?"

"Uhh. Not really."

There was a silence. And she supposed Mr. Smith was wondering if he could get in trouble doing work for an underage kid.

"I plan to tell her," Kylie said. "I just haven't really had the chance." *Or decided how to do it.*

"Good. Believe me when I say that these kinds of things work out best if you're up front about them."

"Yeah," Kylie said, and tried to figure out how that conversation would go with her mom. How could she explain that she wanted to meet Daniel's real parents, not just his adoptive parents, because she needed to know what species of supernatural she was?

Hanging up from the PI, Kylie sat there feeling let down. The PI thing didn't sound like the answer anymore. And if that didn't work, what would? If only she could get some more information from Daniel.

She looked up at the ceiling. "You wouldn't be able to come for a visit, would you?"

No spiritual cold filled the room. Kylie was about to get up when her gaze went back to the computer screen and the obituaries. She noticed that the dates on the deaths were back eight months ago.

A terrible thought hit. Was Della looking at obituaries because . . .

she thought she might have killed someone during those blackout days when she turned?

Kylie's gaze went back to the screen to faces of the people who had died. Only a few obituaries listed cause of death, and none said, "drained of blood." While her heart knew that she should feel bad for the deceased, she couldn't help but think of Della. How hard would it be to even think you might have killed someone?

The next few days passed in an uneventful blur. Kylie had tried to talk to Della about what she found on the computer, but Della refused to talk about it. She'd tried to ease into a conversation about Daniel with her mom, but her mom had brushed her off.

While every morning she woke up right at dawn to a blast of icy temperature, the spirit left without any visual or verbal contact. Nothing from Daniel either. So it appeared even everyone in the spirit world was giving Kylie the brush-off.

Kylie wasn't sure what that meant. She got Daniel's absence. He had said his time on earth was now very limited, but what about the female spirit who insisted that someone Kylie loved was about to die?

Holiday told Kylie not to worry, that when the spirit needed to talk, she would speak up. Holiday even tried assuring her that, more likely than not, the ghost's lack of presence was more good news than bad. Either she'd realized things weren't as imminent as she had first thought, or the situation had been handled. Kylie hoped it was the latter. But her gut told her not to get her hopes up.

While Holiday and Kylie had met twice since she'd confessed her mistake of passing info on to Burnett, Holiday had remained almost distant, very matter-of-fact. Kylie had tried apologizing again, but Holiday had stopped her and said it was forgotten.

Forgotten maybe, forgiven not so much. Kylie sensed it when she looked into the camp leader's eyes. And the pain of knowing that her mistake had altered their relationship left an empty spot in Kylie's chest. To make matters worse, there seemed to be even more tension between Holiday and Burnett. Obviously, Kylie's interference not only hadn't helped, but it had made the rift between them even wider.

"You ready?" Kylie heard Miranda call out from the living room. Socks raised his little skunk face off the mattress and hissed. No doubt the kitten/skunk was tired of Miranda following him around and trying to undo her screw-up. Kylie wouldn't be surprised if Socks didn't end up spraying her. If he could spray, that is.

"No. I haven't even touched my hair," Kylie called back, and looked around for her hairbrush. "Why don't you go down to breakfast and meet up with Della and I'll meet you as soon as I can?"

"Got it!" Miranda called. "But hurry, I can't wait to head off. It feels like years since I've gotten to go shopping. And hey, when you leave, make sure you shut the door and don't just break it down."

Kylie frowned and wished she hadn't told Miranda and Della about the whole shower scene at Derek's. But not sharing didn't feel right, even if they teased her about it.

"Did Holiday say we had to be back at a certain time?" Miranda called out again.

"No," Kylie said.

Holiday, in spite of her emotional distance, had agreed to let Kylie, Della, and Miranda take one of the school vehicles into town and do some clothes shopping. It was either that or Kylie was going to have to borrow someone's shoes and bras. Thankfully, the growth spurt appeared to have come to an end. Not that it stopped Kylie from worrying. What did it all mean? And when would she know for sure what to expect next? The full moon would be here on Monday. The weres of the group had planned their show-and-tell event for that night, planning on allowing the group to actually watch one of them turn.

Every now and then, whenever Kylie let her mind go there, she worried she might be doing some show-and-telling that night, too. If her body's change was because she was werewolf, didn't that mean she might do a little morphing herself? Her heart raced at the thought. Would she know what to do? Would she remember who she was?

Kylie heard the cabin door shut and she reached for her phone to make sure she hadn't missed a call from Mr. Smith the PI. Looking at the phone, she realized she did have some messages. Her hope rose that it was him with good news.

But nope. No call from the PI. Two more messages from her stepdad and one from Trey. Great. Just friggin' great! She deleted all three messages without listening to them.

When she reached inside her drawer to find her brush, her eyes landed on Lucas's letter. Curiosity ate at her to open it, but another emotion—one Kylie could best describe as guilt—kept the letter sealed and unread.

Please don't break my heart, Kylie.

Derek's words played across her mind. She had no intention of breaking Derek's heart. She had no intention of getting involved with Lucas. So would someone please explain why she felt guilty about reading his letter?

Maybe because she kept dreaming about him. Almost dreamed about him. Oddly enough, the dreams always stopped before they really got started. However, Kylie had a feeling that was best. She somehow sensed that they would be all too similar to the dream she'd had about him before. Dreams that involved kissing and touching where clothes were considered optional.

Why did she keep almost dreaming of him?

Because you have unresolved feelings for him, a voice from within answered.

A voice Kylie really wished would keep her mouth shut. Kylie didn't want to have any feelings for Lucas. He was off with Fredericka. And Kylie was now with . . . well, almost with Derek. They hadn't even kissed since the night she'd seen him naked. A memory that never ventured too far from her mind. However, since that night, he'd sort of kept his distance from her. Kylie didn't know if it was because he sensed she still felt embarrassed about everyone picking up on her uncontrollable desires for him, or if it was something else.

It could be his way of trying to show how it felt to be avoided. Though Derek didn't seem the type to play head games.

Maybe it was simply because she still hadn't made any verbal commitment to being a couple, to going out with him. Not that this had anything to do with Lucas or his letter. Nope. Not at all. Lucas was history. Even if he came back. He'd made his choice when he took off with Fredericka.

Not that she would be rude to Lucas if he did come back. They could even be . . . friends. If his little she-wolf allowed it.

Thinking of Fredericka shot Kylie back to the night she'd been trapped in the bedroom with the lion. The Blood Brothers, a rogue vampire gang, had started terrorizing and killing the wildlife at the animal preserve next door hoping the FRU would blame the camp and then close it down. They had sent the lion into the camp as part of the setup. However, Kylie couldn't help but think that someone had made sure that lion had gotten in her bedroom. That someone would be Fredericka. Was she wrong to suspect her? Kylie didn't think so.

Oh, heck, this trip down memory lane was stupid. So was the fact that she hadn't opened Lucas's letter. She snatched up the envelope, opened the seal, and was just about to pull the letter out when her phone rang.

Dropping the letter on the bed and checking the number, she took the call. "Hi, Mom."

"Hi, sweetheart." Her mom sighed. "I'm afraid I have some bad news."

"What is it?" Right then, the room's temperature dropped. Kylie felt her stomach twist into a tight knot. Had someone she loved been hurt, like the ghost had warned? "Are you okay, Mom?" Kylie asked as panic began to pull at her heartstrings.

"No. I'm not okay."

Oh, God! The temperature in the room dropped another ten degrees. "What is it? What's wrong?"

"I just received an e-mail and my company is insisting I fly out today to a meeting in New York. It's with a big client and . . . I'm going to miss seeing you on parents day. I checked to see if there was a red-eye flight back and it's already booked."

The chill hung on, even as Kylie's panic lessened. "It's okay." Kylie looked around to see if the ghost had materialized. She hadn't. Kylie reached over and petted Socks, who looked around with nervous, beady skunk eyes. Socks always knew when a spirit was here.

"I wanted to see you. I feel as if I haven't seen you in months."

"It hasn't been months," Kylie said. "Just two weeks." Yet deep down, Kylie realized she was going to miss seeing her mom, too. "I'll be coming home in a couple of weeks for the weekend, anyway. We'll have plenty of time to catch up then."

"And we have the haunted B&B dinner and tour," her mom added, sounding so thrilled.

"Yeah. That, too." Kylie tried not to let her dread leak out in her tone.

They talked a few minutes about her mom's schedule and about her mom's cousin who wanted to come down for a visit. Kylie almost brought up Daniel again, but couldn't figure out how to turn the conversation that way.

As they talked, Kylie pulled the blanket up closer. The cold from the spirit lingered and even grew colder, but she still didn't materialize.

"Oh, guess who I saw at the grocery store?" her mom asked.

"Who?" God, it was getting even colder.

"Sara."

Kylie's heartstrings gave her emotions another tug. "How's she doing?"

"Actually, she didn't look good at all."

"What did she do, dye her hair or get a nose ring?" Kylie asked, knowing how Mom felt about such things. She might have suddenly found common ground with her mom, but that didn't make the woman perfect or change the fact that she was judgmental.

"Not that," her mom said. "Sara's not that kind of girl."

Her mom would be surprised at some of the things Sara had done with drinking and boys—not that it made Sara a bad person. She was just . . . going through something.

"She just didn't look . . . good," her mom continued. "She's thinner than she should be. I hate it that you girls feel as if you have to be size zero to look good. I hope you aren't losing weight."

"Nope, if anything, I think I'm growing." Frowning, Kylie looked down at her boobs, a tad worried what her mom would say when she saw her.

"Which reminds me, have you gone shopping yet?" her mom asked. "Your camp leader called and confirmed it was okay if you drove to town. I told her I'd already given you permission."

"Actually, we're going today." Kylie shivered again from the ghostly cold.

"Well, have fun. And keep it reasonable." The maternal tone filled her voice.

"I will," Kylie promised. "Under a hundred dollars. I remember what you said."

"Okay, go up to a hundred and fifty. But no higher."

"Mom, I didn't ask—"

"I know." Her mom chuckled. "But I'm offering." She grew quiet a second. "Ahh, my baby is growing up." Her mom let go of a deep, heartfelt sigh. "Oh, I forgot to mention it, I told Sara you were coming down. She said you'd texted her and told her and that she owed you a text. And she'd probably be in touch in the next few days."

Sara owed her about four text messages, not including the phone calls and e-mails, Kylie thought.

She and her mom chatted a few more minutes. Mostly about her selling the house—another subject Kylie had to bite her tongue on. "I'll still do my best to come see you on Saturday. Maybe I can get a flight out first thing in the morning. If I get in by ten, I might be able to make it. Even if I'm a little late."

"Mom, it's okay. Don't worry. And they're pretty strict about visiting hours here." *As in if you come in without a pass, you might be taken down by a vampire.* "So really, don't worry, okay?"

"I just miss you," her mom whimpered.

"I miss you, too."

When Kylie hung up, the spirit's chill still lingered in the air. Kylie got the crazy sensation she'd been listening in on the conversation. But why?

"Do you have something to say?" Kylie asked. "Something to show me?" she muttered with less enthusiasm. Kylie really didn't like the freaky visions or dreams, but if that was what it took to solve this and protect someone she loved, she'd do that and more.

No answer filled the cold air and a few seconds later, the chill faded. She looked at her clock on the bedside table and moaned. She was late, which meant Della and Miranda were probably already pissed.

She grabbed her brush, phone, and purse and headed out. Right before she shut the door, she looked back at Lucas's letter on her bed.

"No time now," she muttered, and shut the door and left, but as she took off in a run down the trail she could almost hear Holiday: *"Avoidance isn't a very good coping method."*

Yeah, yeah, yeah, Kylie thought. One thing at a time.

"Hey," Miranda called from the dressing room three hours later. "You two still out there?"

Kylie and Della, both checking out some tops on a nearby rack, walked back to the dressing room area. "Yeah, we're here," Kylie answered.

They were two hours into their shopping spree, and were having a great day so far. The only negative blemish had been seeing the sidewalk where she'd watched her dad and his slutty intern getting it on.

Miranda stepped out of the dressing room modeling a pair of jeans. "Okay, tell the truth. Do these make my butt look good?"

"Turn around," Kylie said.

"Did you say good or big?" Della asked, and grinned.

Kylie would admit the few downtown Fallen stores didn't offer the same experience that shopping at her mall back home did, but it hadn't stopped them from having a blast. Kylie would even admit the town had a certain quaint charm about it. Obviously, she had really needed some time away from the camp.

"Is that a slam because I don't have much of an ass?" Miranda looked over her shoulder as if to see her butt.

"They look great," Kylie interjected.

"Hey," Della said. "Considering I'm lacking in one department," she glanced down at her chest, "I don't pick on body parts. Unless they're really bloody and then—"

"Shh," Kylie said, realizing a couple of other teens were lurking nearby.

Della, not appreciating being hushed, frowned. The frown added to the overall intimidating don't-screw-with-me air she carried on her shoulders all day. Not that the air was intended for her and Miranda. Nope. Rumor had it that the homegrown teens, as well as some of the campers in the area, had it out for all the Shadow Falls teens. Kylie hadn't experienced it the few times she'd come into town, but Holiday had mentioned it at their last camp meeting, so Kylie knew the stories had merit.

"Shh, why?" Della asked.

Kylie cut her eyes to the two girls. Della's frown deepened to a full-blown scowl.

Kylie wondered if Della hadn't picked her all-black outfit on purpose, as if dressing like trouble would keep trouble away. In truth, Kylie wasn't sure the outfit didn't do more harm than good, but arguing with Della was useless, so Kylie hadn't said a thing.

One of the girls started moving closer, and Kylie sent up a quick prayer that this wasn't going to spoil their day.

"Hi, my name's Amber Logan," the cute redhead said, looking at Kylie. "Are you new in town or here with one of the . . . camps?"

The way she said *camps* led Kylie to believe this wasn't going to end well.

"A camp." Kylie put a bit of extra nice into her voice, hoping to ward off any trouble.

"Which one?" the tall blonde standing behind Amber asked, and she cut Della a cold look.

Nope, this wasn't going to end well.

"Shadow Falls," Della answered with attitude, and her dark eyes grew a little golden. Kylie just hoped the girls didn't notice

"Boners," the blonde whispered to Amber.

"What did you say?" asked Della, her shoulders coming back as she took a defensive step forward.

Blondie grinned. "The camp used to be named Bone Creek Camp. So they call you guys . . . boners. It's not personal."

"It feels personal," Della growled.

Both Amber and Blondie took a step back.

Kylie saw Miranda stick out her little pinky as if ready to cast a spell. Kylie shot her a warning glance, but it wasn't Miranda who Kylie worried about.

"Nice to meet you," Kylie told the girls, and latched a hand on Della's elbow, hoping the touch would help her see reason. She couldn't go vampire badass on these girls. She couldn't even threaten to kill them without stirring up a whole big pot of trouble.

"'Bye," Kylie added, and motioned for them to leave with her free hand.

Amber shot Della another calculating look. From the spark of fear in her eyes, Kylie figured the girl wasn't all that stupid. She turned around, nudged her blond friend, and the two went their own way.

"You better tuck your tails and run," Della muttered, pulling away from Kylie.

"I could have given them the worse case of pimples you've ever seen," Miranda snapped.

"Oh, I could have done much worse," Della snarled.

"But you didn't." Kylie latched a hand around each girl's arm, just in case they changed their minds. "You both showed an amazing amount of restraint. I'm very proud of you."

Della shot Kylie a huge frown. "Don't you ever just lose it? I mean, don't you ever just wanna rip somebody's heart out and beat them over the head with it?"

"I get mad, yes," Kylie said, and grinned. "Don't know if I've ever wanted to bludgeon someone to death with their own heart, but I have my moments."

"Yeah, what do you do when you're really pissed? Frown at someone?" Della chuckled.

"Yeah," Miranda piped in. "But have you seen her frown? It's very effective."

They all laughed.

An hour later, after shoe shopping and trying on a few more pairs of jeans, they moved to the lingerie section. Because she'd already spent close to a hundred dollars, Kylie headed to the clearance rack. They all dropped their packages and browsed through the array of underwear.

"Do either of you wear thongs?" Miranda held up a red stringy pair of panties.

"Not me," Kylie said. "I like regular bikini."

"Personally for me, wearing a thong is like flossing your ass," Della said, and all three of them burst out laughing.

After the giggles subsided, they went back to checking out bras.

A store attendant walked up. "Would you like me to measure you to make sure what size you are?" she asked Kylie.

Kylie looked up at the store clerk and back at the four bras she held in her hands. "Uhh, no . . . thank you. I think I can figure it out."

"Okay, but it's very important you get the right size."

Kylie nodded. "I will."

"It will only take a minute," the attendant said, a tad more insistent that time.

"I know . . . but I'm fine. Thank you," Kylie added.

The woman's expression said Kylie was making a mistake, but she walked off.

"Ugg, no way would I let a stranger handle my girls," Miranda whispered. "These are virgin girls." She giggled.

"I think the ol' biddy just wanted to see your boobs." Della growled at the clerk's back.

Kylie elbowed Della and tried not to snicker. "She was just doing her job."

"Duh, she was like eyeing your boobs like they were candy, and I'm standing here holding a bra and she didn't even ask to measure me!"

"I think there might be a reason for that." Miranda snickered again.

"Bitch!" Della said it with a smile.

Relief swept through Kylie when she saw Della's smile. The last thing Kylie wanted now was for Miranda and Della to start smacking each other around verbally.

Della cupped her A-cup boobs. "At least these puppies aren't virgin. And believe me, Lee didn't complain."

Miranda laughed. "I'm surprised you didn't tell me that I didn't have an ass."

"I'm saving that insult for next time," Della said.

"I'm going to try on these." Kylie studied the bras she held.

"Can you hold these?" Kylie handed Miranda her bags containing two pairs of jeans and two pairs of shoes.

"Here, try this one on, too." Della held a bra out.

"I don't like black bras," Kylie said.

"Yeah, but I'll bet Derek does." She grinned and wiggled her brows.

Kylie rolled her eyes. But she snatched the bra from Della and headed off to the dressing room. Behind her, she heard Della and Miranda laughing.

Trying on bras reminded Kylie of the Goldilocks fairy tale. One felt a bit too big. One was a bit too lacy, and one, the black one, was a bit too . . . sexy.

Now to decide which ones to take home. Kylie glanced down at the pile of bras and had just slipped the strap of her old bra up onto her shoulder, when she heard:

"I like the black one best."

The deep male voice that came from behind her had her heart leaping into her throat. Her eyes shot to the mirror.

Before she saw his face, she saw the blood.

He stood right behind her. Big splotches of red color stained his shirt. Even his auburn-colored hair was soaked in it.

His eyes flashed a vivid red color. He shot her an evil smile and his elongated canines showed at the edges of his mouth. Recognition hit—Blood Brothers.

Chapter Sixteen

Kylie opened her mouth to scream, but neither air nor words came out. Panic gripped her throat and blocked off all oxygen and verbal communication. She swung around, not certain if it was to fight or to run.

He wasn't there. Her gaze shot back to the mirror as if only his reflection had been real. He wasn't there, either.

Her gaze shot to the open door to the dressing room. It had been closed. He'd really been here.

She slammed the door. Sucked a bit of oxygen into her lungs. Tried to scream again, but stopped when the dressing room door swung open and whacked against the wall.

Every muscle in her body clenched. *Fight.* The one-word command echoed inside her. Then Della appeared behind the door that now hung half off the hinges.

"Was someone here?" Della asked. Her eyes shined bright amber. Her canines appeared sharp and threatening under her raised upper lip.

Still unable to speak, Kylie nodded.

Della careened forward when Miranda rammed into her back.

"What happened?" Miranda peered over Della's shoulder. "Why did you take off like that?"

Tears stung Kylie's eyes. She sometimes cried when she was scared, and she had been scared—mortified, actually—but these weren't frightened tears. These were tears of anger. No, make that fury. Fury from feeling violated. *I like the black one best.*

His words rang in her ears. How long had that slimeball been watching her try on bras?

"Is someone here?" Miranda asked. "Ghost? Non-ghost?"

"Vampire," Della snapped at Miranda, and looked back at Kylie. "You okay?"

Kylie nodded again. "Is he gone?"

"For now." Della snatched up Kylie's purse and bras and handed them to Miranda. "Go pay for these while she gets dressed."

Miranda took off. Della looked back at Kylie. "You really okay?"

"I think I'm mad enough to rip out someone's heart and beat him with it." She bit down on her lip to keep from crying. "How long was he here playing Peeping Tom?"

"Just seconds." Della's color grew paler. "It wasn't Chan, was it? I mean, it didn't smell like him, but . . . all I could mostly smell was blood."

"No." Kylie grabbed her shirt and yanked it over her head. Her mind flashed the image of the blood dripping from the guy's hair.

"So you did see him?" Della asked.

Kylie poked her head through her T-shirt and met Della's eyes. "It was . . . it was that creep that we fought at the wildlife park. The one who grabbed me."

Della lifted her nose in the air. "Oh, shit!"

"Is he coming back?"

"Somebody is." She grabbed Kylie by the arm and hurried her out.

When they walked out of the dressing room, Miranda was taking the package from the woman at the checkout counter. Della motioned her to follow and she did without questioning. Obviously, Miranda could see panic in both of their eyes.

"What's going on?" Miranda asked.

"We have to get back to camp," Della said.

"Is he here again?"

"Let's just go," Della snapped.

The moment they stepped out of the door, a black SUV came to a screeching stop in front of the store. Della growled and then pushed Kylie and Miranda behind her.

The window lowered and Burnett stared out. His own eyes were a fierce golden color. "Get in."

"What about the car we drove?" Kylie asked, though she didn't know how she could even think, let alone drive responsibly with the panic still bouncing around her gut.

"Get in!" Burnett's tone demanded obedience.

And they complied.

"What's going on?" Della asked Burnett once they'd all piled into the backseat.

Burnett didn't answer. He focused on driving. The SUV took off before Kylie realized someone was sitting in the front seat with him. It was a dark-haired woman around Burnett's age. She looked familiar and Kylie realized she'd been among the crowd of FRU the night of the fight at the wildlife park.

"Toss them the scrubs," Burnett told the woman.

Three plastic bags with what looked like a pair of hospital scrubs tucked inside each were thrown in the backseat. "What are these for?" Kylie asked.

"Take your clothes off," Burnett ordered. "Put all your clothes back in the bag. Shoes, socks, underwear. Everything. Then put the scrubs on."

"Do . . . what?" Kylie asked.

"You heard me," he snapped.

"Why?" Kylie and Della asked the same question.

"Do it," the woman ordered.

Della and Miranda started to undress, but Kylie grabbed their hands and stopped them.

"No. We're not taking our clothes off until you explain why. And it better be a damn good reason because I don't take my clothes off just because someone tells me to. Just ask my ex-boyfriend!"

The woman turned in her seat and glared. Her eyebrows twitched as if trying to get a reading on Kylie. Too bad it wouldn't work.

Not that the woman gave up immediately. She continued to stare. Her amber-colored eyes grew a bit brighter, and somehow Kylie suspected that she was werewolf. Pissed-off werewolf. "Do it," the woman insisted.

"No." Amazingly, Kylie didn't feel intimidated. She glared right back. She even did her own twitching and tried to see the woman's brain pattern. It didn't work, but the were didn't know that.

"Do as he said! Or I'll do it for you," she ordered.

Burnett caught the woman by the shoulder. "Selynn, let me handle this." His gaze shot to the mirror and Kylie met his golden reflection. "Kylie, please . . ."

"No!" Kylie honestly didn't know where her newfound gumption stemmed from, but it felt good. It gave her some small sense of control. She really needed to feel in control to help combat the feeling of being victimized.

"Do you realize what you're asking?" Kylie continued to hold both Della's and Miranda's hands. "For us to take our clothes off in a car with a man sitting in the front seat with a rearview mirror. And you aren't going to explain why?"

Burnett reached up and ripped the mirror from the car's window.

"Damn!" Miranda said.

"Two girls were killed in town," Burnett said.

"Shit," Della said.

"Oh, hell," Miranda said.

The only thing that came out of Kylie's mouth was a gasp.

Burnett continued, "I need your clothes to prove that you three weren't involved with their murders. The FBI and FRU will demand it. So, please, do as I say."

Kylie let go of their hands and started undressing. In a few minutes, all three of them sat in green scrubs, looking like surgical doctors. No one said a word during the process.

Miranda collected the three bags and handed them to Selynn. "Here."

"Do you really think anyone will think we had anything to do with this?" Kylie asked, remembering the blood all over the rogue vampire's head and shirt.

"No," Della said. "But they'll believe I did." She sounded hurt. "It was a vampire kill, wasn't it?"

"Yes," Burnett said. "But I don't believe you did this. I'm just taking precautions until we know who did."

"We already know who did it," Della said. "Kylie saw him."

"Saw who?" Both Selynn and Burnett swung around.

"It was the rogue vampire," Kylie said. "The one who attacked me at the wildlife park."

"Damn it!" After almost running off the road, Burnett pulled over and rammed the car into park. He twisted in his seat again and met Kylie's eyes. "You aren't hurt, are you?" His eyes shot to her neck as if . . .

"No. I'm not hurt." A big wave of I-wanna-cry, I-wanna-cry-right-now filled her chest.

"Did he say anything?" Burnett asked.

I like the black one best. "No," she said.

Burnett's stare deepened. "Now isn't the time to be lying."

Kylie swallowed. "He didn't say anything that would be helpful."

"Let us be the judge of that?" Ms. Badass Werewolf sitting in the front seat said.

Kylie frowned. "He said he liked the black bra best. I was in the dressing room." The feeling of being violated hit strong again and the anger accompanying it welled up in her chest.

Burnett's expression changed from demanding to empathetic in a split second. "Are you sure you're okay? He didn't . . ."

"I'm fine," she managed to say, but she felt the tears fill her eyes and looked away from Burnett's concerned expression.

"He came and left so fast that by the time I sensed he was there he was gone," Della said.

The memory of his reflection in the mirror filled Kylie's head. "He had blood . . . all over him. His shirt. His hair."

Miranda slipped her hand into Kylie's and gave it a squeeze as if offering moral support.

Burnett's frown deepened and he turned back around and started the car. He looked over at Selynn sitting in the seat beside him. "Make the call. Tell them it's a Code Red."

"You sure you want to attempt that?" Selynn asked.

"What's a Code Red?" Della asked right before Kylie posed the question.

Burnett answered hesitantly. "Right now, the only ones who

know about this are the FRU. Code Red means we'll fix it so it looks like a car accident."

"You're going to let him get away with it?" Kylie asked.

"No," Burnett said. "But neither can we let something like this leak out. Any rumors start floating around, making higher-ups nervous, and they'll close down the school."

Selynn held up her hand as if to silence everyone. Then she spoke into the phone. "It's a Code Red." She paused. "I know." She cut her eyes to Burnett. "He gave the order, I'm just the messenger."

Burnett frowned and Kylie got the impression that whatever Burnett was doing, he was doing it for the school and maybe even Holiday. But she couldn't help but wonder about the good of the townspeople—the human people who would never know that a murderer had come and taken two of their own.

When they walked into Holiday's office thirty minutes later, Holiday practically leapt out of her chair and ran over to them. "Thank you, God," she yelped, and wrapped her arms around all of them in a group hug. Della was the first to pull away.

"We're fine," Della said.

Speak for yourself, Kylie thought. She could have used a few more seconds of a hug. It was the closest she'd felt to Holiday since the whole Burnett issue.

"Look." Della pointed to the television screen mounted on the wall.

Kylie glanced up and her breath caught. The screen showed a wrecked car and then two pictures of girls. *It couldn't be.* She felt suddenly nauseous.

Holiday grabbed the remote and turned up the volume.

"Two girls were killed today in an automobile accident. It appeared . . ." the reporter continued.

"We met them in town," Kylie blurted out, her chest filled with heaviness. "We talked to them." For some crazy reason, that short encounter made their deaths even more personal. "The redhead is named Amber. I don't know the blonde's name."

"They weren't very nice." Della voice sounded tight. "But they didn't deserve to die."

"No, they didn't." Miranda put her hand over her lips and just stared at the screen.

Kylie would have verbally agreed, but she couldn't. She recalled with clarity the blood on the rogue vampire's shirt and emotion closed her voice box. It had been their blood she'd seen. When the tears prickled Kylie eyes, she felt like a crybaby, but then she noticed both Della and Miranda had a wet sheen to their eyes, too.

"I feel . . ." Kylie forced the words out. "I feel as if it's somehow my fault."

Holiday stabbed at the remote and turned it off. "It's a terrible thing. But the only person responsible for this is the rogue who did it." Then she just stared at each of them as if needing to visually memorize them. "When I heard two girls were found . . . I thought . . ." Holiday's eyes pooled with tears. And that pretty much made it a cry fest. Even Della joined in the tear party.

Right then, Burnett walked into the office. His gaze went from one female to the other. Kylie could almost hear him groaning inwardly.

"I . . . I'll be . . . right out here." Obviously even a hard-bodied vampire trained by the FRU wasn't capable of dealing with four crying women.

Fifteen minutes later, Burnett poked his head back in the room, and when he saw they were no longer in tears, he walked in. On his heels came Selynn, the werewolf who'd been with him in the car. She stood so close to Burnett's side that her shoulders brushed up against his forearm. Burnett stepped to the side and started explaining that he needed to interview them separately. He opened the door and told Kylie and Miranda to wait outside of Holiday's office.

As the two of them started out, Selynn looked over at Holiday. "You should leave as well." Selynn's voice held such a condescending tone that Kylie decided right there and then that she really didn't like her. Not even a little bit.

Holiday shot the woman a look that Kylie could only describe as fiercely protective. "Sorry, but I don't take orders from anyone when it involves my campers. Or has Burnett not informed you of this?"

"She can stay," Burnett interjected.

Selynn placed a palm on Burnett's forearm. "I really don't think that's wise."

"The girls will feel more comfortable with her here." He stepped away from her touch. But Kylie noticed Holiday's gaze take in the familiar way the woman treated Burnett.

Jealousy flashed in Holiday's eyes. Not that it lingered more than a second. One blink and the emotion vanished. And probably for a reason, too. Selynn glanced at Holiday as if looking for a reaction. Which led Kylie to assume that Selynn had feelings for Burnett. Not that Kylie sensed that Burnett returned any of the feelings.

Then again, he might just be good at hiding his emotions. Could this be part of the reason Holiday refused to get too close to Burnett, because she knew he was already involved with someone? Instant distrust for Burnett stirred inside Kylie.

Burnett motioned for Kylie and Miranda to leave. Kylie, suspicious of Burnett for Holiday's sake, didn't move until Holiday confirmed the order.

"Who do they think is in charge?" Selynn asked, annoyed at Kylie's show of authority for Holiday.

"Can we please just get started?" Burnett said.

Kylie and Miranda walked out into the front room of the office.

"He's checking to see if we're lying. That's why he wants to talk to us separately," Miranda whispered.

"I don't think he thinks we're guilty." Kylie defended him, though she wasn't so sure she could say the same about Selynn. Then Kylie wondered again about the relationship between Burnett and the rude were.

"God, it sucks." Emotion gave Miranda's voice a raspy tone. "I can't believe we actually met the girls who were killed."

"I know," Kylie said but, honestly, she didn't want to think about it. She still had this overwhelming feeling that it was her fault. She dropped down onto one of the two desk chairs filling the small entry room and stared at her hands. Was this the bad thing that the ghosts had been talking about? No, the ghost had insisted it was someone Kylie loved. That thought sent another wave of sorrow sloshing in her gut. She hadn't loved those girls, but someone had. They had mothers, friends . . . Closing her eyes, Kylie tried to reconnect to the calm she'd found at the falls. How long could she hang on to that feeling when bad shit just kept happening?

"It could have been us." Miranda pulled at a thread attached to her light green scrubs.

"I know." Kylie gripped her hands together.

It was only a few minutes before Selynn and Della walked out. Kylie stood up. Selynn motioned at Miranda to follow her. Then she turned to Kylie and Della. "We prefer if you don't speak. And

Burnett can hear you if you do." She practically smirked before following Miranda into the office.

Della snarled at the werewolf's back. "Bitch," she mouthed the word. And when the werewolf was in the other room, Della said it out loud. "Bitch." She glanced at the office door. "I don't care if you can hear me, Burnett. She's a bitch. You know it. I know it. And Holiday knows it."

Footsteps sounded on the office's front porch. Kylie glanced toward the door just as it opened and Derek rushed in. "Thank God." He stopped and just stared at her as if noting the hospital scrubs. Right behind him followed Perry, looking just as worried.

Perry's gaze shot around the room. "Where's Miranda?" Fear and some other deep emotion filled his now copper-colored eyes.

Kylie didn't have a chance to answer because Derek swooped her into a big hug. She let him hold her, even rested her head on his chest and sighed at how good it felt to be this close to him.

"Why do you want to know?" Della mouthed off. "You don't like her, remember?"

"Is she okay?" Perry demanded, his voice a deep rumble of emotions. Kylie didn't bother to pull away to see, but she imagined his eyes were changing colors as he spoke. She'd noticed his eyes shifted with his emotions.

"Don't go all T. rex on me." Della lost her smartass tone. Whether out of fear of Perry or if she heard the emotion in his voice, Kylie didn't know.

"You okay?" Derek whispered in her ear.

"Yeah." *Hell, no.* Kylie pulled back to look in his eyes and she saw the same concern flashing there that she noted in Perry's. A rush of calm flowed from Derek into her. She didn't argue this time. She really needed it.

The door to Holiday's office opened. Miranda walked out. Perry met her eyes, then he turned and left the building. Miranda watched him go. "What did he want?" she asked.

"To make sure you were okay," Derek answered, and slipped a hand around Kylie's waist. "I saw him right after I heard what happened and I told him. He was worried about you."

"But not worried enough to even speak to me, huh?" The look on Miranda's face was half sad and half angry. She met Kylie's gaze again. "Your turn." She pointed to the office door. "Watch out, the she-wolf bites."

Kylie gave Derek's hand a tight squeeze and then walked into the room to face Burnett and the she-wolf. Kylie was no longer as intimidated by Burnett as she was the first time she'd been interrogated by him, but a nervous tickle still fluttered in her chest.

Chapter Seventeen

Burnett made Kylie go over what happened several times. Then he asked specific questions. "You said the rogue vampire was bloody. Did it look like fresh blood? How much time passed from when you saw the girls to when he appeared?"

Then Burnett asked the same questions in a slightly different way. At one time she'd have thought he was trying to catch her in a lie, but now she suspected his intent was to make sure she wasn't forgetting something and hoping a slightly different question might lead her to remember some minor detail that could be useful. Problem was, Kylie didn't want to remember. She longed to forget, to wipe it from her memory forever. And seriously, what else could she tell him that might be helpful?

"Could you describe the blood to me?" Burnett straddled a straight-backed chair in front of Kylie, reminding her of their first interrogation. Only this time she sat on the sofa with Holiday beside her.

"I already did." She felt her patience being pulled like a tight rubber band.

"One more time." His tone demanded obedience.

It was the tone that finally made Kylie snap. "You know who

did this. You know who his victims were. So is any of this *really* necessary?" She gritted her teeth and tried not to start crying again.

"We decide what's necessary," Selynn answered in her haughty tone, moving in behind Burnett.

Kylie glared up at the werewolf, not trying to hide her contempt. Selynn's tone annoyed Kylie even more than Burnett's harsh tenor. At least with Burnett, she heard real concern. With Selynn, it seemed to be all about power. She liked having it and enjoyed using it.

"You think we did this, don't you?" Kylie asked Selynn.

"I think—"

"Stop." Burnett frowned at Selynn, then glanced back at Kylie. "Kylie, I know you didn't do this. And I know this isn't easy. However, blood patterns might tell us if he was killing for sport or for food."

His statement made her stomach churn. "And why does that make a difference? Those girls are dead no matter what his reasons were for killing them."

"I think she's had enough questions." Holiday placed her hand on Kylie's wrist, offering moral support and a strong surge of calm. The rush of peaceful energy slowed Kylie's heartbeat and lessened the tightness in her chest. Not that it could make it all go away. Kylie didn't think that power existed.

Burnett looked at Holiday, then at Kylie. "It won't change what happened. But right now, we need all the information we can get on this creep to be able to catch him. To stop him before he does this again."

Burnett's words shifted around inside her head and pulled at her conscience. Two girls had died. Violently died. Was it too much to ask for Kylie to suffer through a few more minutes of questions? No, it wasn't. Taking in a breath, she sat up straighter.

Holiday stiffened. "For a vampire, your hearing is really bad. I said she's had enough."

"It's okay." Kylie turned her palm over and gave the camp leader's hand a squeeze. "If it helps stop this guy, I can do it." But she didn't let go of Holiday's hand.

Ten minutes later, apparently when Burnett felt he'd drawn every detail about the incident he could out of her, he stood up and looked down at her. "Thank you, Kylie. I know this wasn't easy."

She nodded and after she let herself breathe in and out a couple of times, she decided it was her turn to ask the questions. "Do you think he wanted it to look as if we'd killed these girls? Like they tried to frame someone at the camp for killing the animals?"

Burnett shook his head. "No. There's nothing to lead us to conclude that."

"Do you think . . . do you think he followed us into town?"

He considered her question for a second. "No, I don't. I think it was a coincidence that he ran across you."

Holiday squeezed Kylie's hand. "I told you, this isn't your fault."

"No, it isn't," Burnett said. "This has nothing to do with you, Kylie."

"Then how come it feels so . . . personal?" Kylie asked. "I mean, he keeps showing back up. At the park and then last Friday. I didn't actually see him then, but I'm assuming it was him. And even after that I . . . I've felt as if someone was following me."

"When did you feel this?" Burnett asked.

"Yesterday morning when I came to the office before breakfast. At first, I thought it was the wolf but—"

"Wolf?" both Burnett and Selynn said at the same time. While Burnett looked concerned, Selynn immediately started twitching, trying to read Kylie again. It took everything Kylie had not to reach up and cover her forehead. Maybe even give the woman the finger.

"When was this?" Burnett asked.

"A couple of days ago," Holiday answered. "It wasn't a were-wolf. Kylie said it appeared to be semi-tame. Nonthreatening."

"Was it a shifter?" Burnett asked.

"I'm . . . not sure. But I know it wasn't Perry." Kylie hesitated and then recalled what this conversation was really about. "But the wolf isn't important. Two girls are dead and I . . . I feel as if it's somehow my fault. I think he was after me, not them."

Burnett dropped back down in the chair facing her. "I can understand how you might feel that way. But if he was out to hurt you, he could have done so the other night in the woods. I don't think this is personal. Not toward you. To the camp as a whole . . . maybe."

"Then why does he keep coming to see me? It doesn't sound like a coincidence."

Burnett frowned. "It's not a coincidence. You put yourself in situations that offered him the best opportunity with the least of amount of risk. And the first time, he didn't come to you. You had gone to the wildlife park where the Blood Brothers were. And if he was here the other night, and we're not sure it was him, then he probably spotted you when you ran off in the woods and saw it as an opportunity. And today, he was probably . . . hunting when he sensed other supernaturals in town. Again, you were the one alone in the dressing room. He took advantage of it."

And got himself an eyeful, Kylie thought. "But you even said that if he'd wanted to kill me the other night, he could have but he didn't even try. So what did he want with me then?"

Burnett hesitated. "I think he wanted to send a message to the camp. To let us know that the gang hasn't moved on. I'm sure the arrest of several of their gang members has dented their egos. If they pulled out right away, it would appear as if they lacked courage. If they stay around, they at least save face. I'm sure he realized that killing you would have brought too much trouble down on the gang."

Kylie tried to grasp exactly what Burnett was saying. "But he killed those girls. Are you saying that didn't cause trouble? That doesn't make sense."

Burnett looked at Holiday as if asking for her help.

Holiday squeezed Kylie's hand. "When a supernatural kills another supernatural, it's easier to deal with the offense. We have our own justice system."

"And when they kill a human? What happens?" Don't let them say "nothing," Kylie thought. Please God, don't let them say "nothing." She might be part supernatural, but she was still part human.

"That's part of the FRU's job," Burnett said. "But as you might guess, it can make getting justice tricky."

Kylie felt her shoulders getting tighter. "Are you telling me that he's actually going to get away with this?"

"No." Burnett said in a deeper tone. "You have my word, Kylie, I will do everything I can to make sure this guy pays for this."

Exactly how Burnett intended to make him pay wasn't clear. Nor was Kylie sure she even wanted to know. But something about the way he said those words told her this wasn't a promise he made lightly. And for that, she was grateful.

That night, the camp leaders held a meeting of all the campers at the dining hall and served up both pizza and sage advice. Burnett spoke about being extra careful. "Stay on the main paths and trails and don't go through the woods without having someone with you," he explained. "Depending on how dense the trees are or how the wind is blowing, an intruder's scent could go undetected."

Della shot a grin at Kylie and then turned back to Burnett. "Maybe you should cancel parents weekend," she suggested.

Burnett looked at Della. "That's over two weeks away. I hope to have this problem resolved by then."

"Hey, can't blame a girl for trying," Della muttered.

"I have a meeting with the High Council next week," Burnett said. "I'm hoping I'll get some assistance to deal with what happened here."

Kylie leaned in closer to Della. "Who are the High Council?"

"Sort of like the Senate, made up of a bunch of elders from the different species." Della smiled. "I just learned about it this afternoon. Chris did a talk about it in our vamp meeting."

"A Senate? I didn't think all the species got along," Kylie said.

"They don't. But neither do the Democrats and Republicans and they still meet."

"I guess so," Kylie said, and then another question popped up. "What kind of assistance will they offer us?"

"Depends. Chris said the council has to vote to even look into the case."

"Vote? Two girls murdered, how can they say no?"

Della shrugged. "You have to remember that not all the elders are in line with the government's way of thinking. "

"You mean some of them are rogue?"

Della nodded. "According to Chris, most of the elders respect the government, but don't want to be controlled by it. So they follow some of the rules, but not all of them." One of Della's eyebrows rose upward.

Kylie shook her head. She had enough trouble trying to understand human politics—did she really have it in her to grasp this, too? "If they take the case, then what?"

"They either allow the council of the accused species to do the punishing and deal with things or they turn the guy over to the FRU. And I don't want to think about what happens to them then."

"Me, either," Kylie admitted.

Della glanced over to the door and her mood seemed to have changed. "I'm going to head on back to the cabin. I've got some stuff I want to do."

"What kind of stuff?" Kylie remembered the obituaries she'd found on the computer screen.

"Just stuff," Della snapped.

Kylie leaned in. "You could never do anything like this."

Della glared at her. "I'll see you later."

"Do you want me to walk with you?" Kylie asked, remembering Burnett's caution to stay together whenever possible.

"Are you kidding me?" Della asked. "If something attacked, I'd just end up having to protect both of us."

"Hey . . . I'm not so helpless anymore." After thinking about what those girls might have gone through, Kylie wasn't so upset about her new found strength, either.

"Just because you broke one door in, and don't lag behind when hiking through the woods, doesn't mean crap." She grinned, letting Kylie know she was mostly teasing. "I'm fine. I'll see you later."

Della took off, and Kylie watched her go. Her heart ached for Della. Then she saw her vampire friend turn and give a couple of boys the finger. No doubt they'd probably said something rude and crude.

"Hey." Holiday stopped beside Kylie. "Is Della okay?"

"I hope so." Kylie realized that ever since they'd returned from town, the distance that had seemed to come between her and Holiday because of the whole Burnett issue had vanished. Had they bridged a gap, and could Kylie keep it from reappearing?

"Are you doing okay?" Holiday asked.

"I've been better," Kylie said honestly. "I just keep thinking about those girls."

"Maybe Sunday we can take a walk to the falls," Holiday said.

"That sounds good." The thought of going there with someone who could feel the same thing Kylie did seemed nice.

Right then, Burnett looked over at them and Kylie saw Holiday notice it, too. Kylie cringed, worrying that Holiday would remember she was mad at her.

"I should apologize," Holiday said, obviously reading Kylie's emotions again. "I . . . I overreacted about the whole thing with Burnett."

Shocked, Kylie looked at her. "No you didn't. I was wrong to say anything to him."

"Maybe, but your heart was in the right place. When we care about people, we sometimes overstep our grounds. I of all people should know that. I'm a famous overstepper." Holiday's voice tightened. "Today when Burnett first came to me and said they had two teens down and I thought . . . Well, let's just say our issue really felt stupid." Holiday put her arm around Kylie and gave her a sweet, sisterly hug.

"Thank you." Kylie fought the swell of emotion in her throat. "But you are going to make me cry."

Holiday looked up toward Burnett. "Hey, if you cry, maybe it will send him running again. If I knew all it took were a few tears to get him to leave, I'd have been crying for the last seven weeks. "

Kylie grinned and when she looked up at Burnett, she saw Selynn walk up to him and say something. "What's she still doing here?"

"Don't know for sure," Holiday said in a whisper. "I'm sure she wants something. And I bet it starts with a B and is tall, dark, and good-looking."

Burnett listened to something Selynn said and then walked out the door with her. "And she may have just got it," Holiday said, her voice revealing rejection.

Kylie hesitated to ask, but then it just popped out. "Are those two . . . you know?"

"Dirtying up the sheets?" Holiday said.

"Yeah." Kylie mentally added that to Della's list of ways to say getting it on.

"This afternoon he came into my office and made the announcement, 'I know how things looked between Selynn and me. And it's not that way. Or at least not anymore.'"

"So they were together and they broke up?" Kylie asked.

"He said they ended it two months ago. That they were never serious."

Kylie raised her eyebrows. "And how long ago was it that you met him?"

"Two months," she said.

"Hmm," Kylie said.

"Hmm, what?" Holiday asked.

"Just a meaningless hmm," Kylie lied. "So what did you tell him?"

"I told him that I didn't have a clue why he felt as if he needed to tell me about Selynn."

"Could he tell you were lying?" Kylie asked.

"Yup," Holiday chuckled. They just stood there for a minute looking out at the crowd. "Any more info from the ghost lately?"

"Nothing," Kylie said. "It scares me that . . . I've messed up somehow."

"I don't think that's it at all. She's probably trying to figure out how to tell you what she needs you to know."

"I hope so," Kylie said.

Angry sounds exploded from across the room. "What did you call me?" a loud voice boomed. Kylie and Holiday looked up. Two werewolves stood nose-to-nose, about to go fist-to-fist.

"My work is never done," Holiday said, and took off to break up the fight.

Kylie watched her go—watched her calm the tempers of two very high-spirited boys. After a few minutes of feeling a bit like a lone ranger, she spotted Miranda hanging with her witch sisters. She knew Miranda wouldn't mind if she joined them, but Kylie decided against it. Helen and Jonathon sat at a table playing chess. She could go watch Helen embarrass Jonathon again with her natural talent for chess, but for some the reason, the two seemed to be enjoying being alone.

Another sweep of the room and Kylie found Derek. He leaned against a wall, arms crossed, watching her. A slow smile widened his lips. Something in his smile told her he could really use some company.

She gave the room a quick check to see how many individuals could either smell her hormones or read her emotions. They were everywhere. What to do? What to do?

She glanced back at Derek, remembered how good it had felt when he'd held her those few minutes in the office, and she thought . . . *what the hell*. She started walking toward him.

"Wanna go eat pizza in the moonlight?" Derek whispered in her ear when she stopped in front of him.

Standing this close, she could smell his freshly showered skin. A vision of what he'd looked like standing in the buff wearing only a few water droplets filled her mind. She blinked the vision away.

"Is that like dancing in the moonlight? It's supposed to be

seductive." She smiled and then bit her tongue. Why was it when she got within three feet of him, all she could think about was . . . him?

He grinned. "It could be. With the right person. And the right pizza." He laughed. "Hey, I'm hungry."

They got themselves two slices each of pizza and a couple of drinks and walked out of the dining hall.

"I know the perfect place," he said as they left the chatter of voices and the air-conditioning behind in the dining hall. The night air was warm and smooth. He pointed to the two large, white rocking chairs at the front of the office. She followed him. She was just about to sit down when the phone in her pocket chimed.

Sitting her drink down, she balanced her plate in one hand and pulled out her phone to check the number. She frowned when she saw her dad's number and she hit the off button.

"Who was it?" Derek moved the second rocker over so they faced each other.

"My dad . . . I mean, my stepdad," she corrected herself.

"You still aren't talking to him?" Derek sat down and picked up a piece of pepperoni pizza and took a big bite.

"Nooooo." She stuffed her phone back in her pocket and dropped down in her rocker. Their knees touched and it felt nice.

"Why not?" Derek asked between bites of pizza.

Kylie stared at him. "Why would I want to talk to him?" She positioned the plate in her lap.

He finished chewing and swallowed. "Because you care about him. Because up until the shit hit the fan with your parents' marriage, he was a pretty good dad." He held up his finger. "You're the one that told me that."

"Yeah, but I didn't tell you to use it against me." She picked up the slice of pizza and stared down at the oozing cheese. Her mouth watered and her stomach grumbled. Thankfully, she was finally hungry. For a while there, she thought the blood had ruined her for eating regular food.

"I'm not using it against you." He took a sip of his drink. "I'm just . . . trying to help. Because when you saw it was his number, your emotions went all lonely and sad. I felt them all the way to my gut. Maybe if you talked to him, you wouldn't have to feel that anymore."

"He cheated on my mom." She fought back the slight annoyance she felt toward Derek and took a small bite of pizza. The spicy sauce along with the gooey cheese made her taste buds jump up and down.

"That's just it," Derek said, taking another bite of his slice. "He cheated on your mom. Not you."

Kylie swallowed the pizza and frowned. "Why does everyone keep saying that as if his infidelity didn't affect me? It broke their marriage up. Nothing is the same for me anymore."

Derek studied her over the rim of his drink and started his rocker moving. "Maybe if you spoke with him, some of it would be the same. The relationship between you and him could be the same."

She dropped her pizza back on her plate, frustration chasing away her first sign of hunger in days. "You know, for a guy who won't even think about talking to his dad, you're a fine one to talk. I mean, you had a detective find your dad, and you still won't even contact him."

His jaw tightened. "And your point?"

She narrowed her own eyes and steadied her stare at him. "My point is, back off, okay?"

Derek scraped his feet on the porch, brought his rocker to a fast halt, and stared at her. "How far back do you want me to go? I'm already scared to even talk to you in public. Isn't that far enough?"

Frustration filled his voice, but it was the hurt in his eyes that made her see reason.

Why was she being such a B with an itch?

"I'm sorry." Kylie said. "I shouldn't have snapped at you. And I don't mean that you can't ever talk to me in public. I just . . . I'm just . . . I'm so moody." Kylie remembered what Holiday had said about the mood swings in werewolves before the full moon. Was that why she was acting this way? She looked up at the dark navy sky and focused on what almost appeared to be a full moon. Come Monday she'd know, wouldn't she?

When she glanced back at Derek, he'd continued eating. Not that he looked all that happy. He wouldn't even look at her. Her thoughts shifted from what might happen on Monday to the anger that had just passed between them.

"Hey," she said to get his attention.

When he looked up, his discontent showed more on his face.

"I'm really sorry," she said again.

He dropped what was left of his pizza back on his plate. "You shouldn't be," he muttered, and used the back of his hand to wipe his mouth. He closed his eyes for a second. "You're right. I wouldn't want you trying to tell me I needed to call my father. It's just . . ."

"Just what?" she asked.

"I feel everything you feel and it can be a tad overwhelming."

"Bad overwhelming?" she asked.

"Not really," he said, and glanced away.

"So we're okay? I'm forgiven for being a bitch?" she said in a soft, pleading voice.

"I don't think you've hit the bitch mark yet." He smiled. "But yeah, you're forgiven for being grumpy." He set his plate on the porch and stood up. Bracketing his palms on the arms of the rocking chair, he leaned down and kissed her. The kiss wasn't overly sexy, but the soft way his lips brushed against hers had her heart swelling with emotion. Emotion that was as gooey as the cheese pizza she'd abandoned.

"Mm." He pulled back, smiling. "I don't know if it's you, or the pizza, but something tastes good."

She touched his cheek. "Will you still like me if I'm werewolf?"

"What do you think?" His lips met hers again. This kiss came with a touch of his tongue and had her pulse racing even faster than its abnormally fast pace.

But when he pulled back this time, he wasn't smiling. He didn't look happy.

"What is it?" she asked.

"Nothing." He sat back down in his rocking chair.

She looked at his expression through the moonlight. "I hate it when people do that."

"Do what?" he asked.

"Say nothing, when it's sooo obvious that it's something."

He let go of a sigh. "Okay, if you must know. It just occurred to me that maybe I wouldn't be so thrilled if you turn out to be werewolf."

"Because I'll get all hairy?" Kylie asked.

"No." His expression darkened. "Because . . . because Lucas is werewolf."

Chapter Eighteen

Later, after Derek walked her back to her cabin in an uncomfortable silence, Kylie decided to go to bed early. She'd only been in bed a few hours when she felt herself having a dream. She knew it had to be a dream from the moment she became aware of the floating sensation. She rolled over and tried to force herself awake, but then she saw . . .

Him.

Again.

Lucas.

He looked at her and smiled. His bright blue eyes looked heavy, sleepy. She realized that she was no longer above him, but stood beside him. He wore jeans and a light blue button-down shirt that wasn't buttoned. Her gaze went to his chest and then up again. All the way up, away from his open shirt. His black hair looked mussed, as if he'd just gotten out of bed himself, and the dark strands appeared to be a tad longer. It even had a bit of waviness to it.

"You came," he said.

"Came where?" she asked, feeling out of her comfort zone.

He didn't answer her, instead he said, "Come on, let's go for walk." He held out his hand as if wanting her to take it.

She hesitated. The idea of touching him tempted her, but she remembered she was angry at him, although she couldn't quite recall why.

"I don't bite." He smiled again.

It was just a dream, she told herself, and slipped her hand into his, forgetting about the hint of anger she felt inside. His palm felt so warm against hers that it made her giddy.

"I missed you," he said.

She didn't know what to say, so she didn't say anything. Or at least not about missing him. But she had, she knew she had.

"Where are we going?" she asked when he started walking.

He stopped. "Where would you like to go?"

All of a sudden, Kylie realized they were standing in a patch of woods; large trees with sweet-smelling flowers hung overhead.

"Paris? The mall?" He looked around as if just noticing the scenery. "Or would you like to go back to the lake, like in the last dream?" His voice grew deeper, huskier. "Is that where we're going?"

Blood rushed to her face. *How did he know about that dream?* Then she remembered this was just a dream. Nothing had to make sense. Right? Yet this dream seemed even stranger. Different.

He laced his fingers through hers. "We could go anywhere, as long as I'm with you." His irises appeared to darken and his eyelids looked heavier.

She recognized the emotion. Desire. Hunger. Passion. She'd seen it in his eyes the day they'd kissed at the creek by the dinosaur footprints. But that wasn't the first time she'd seen that look. She'd seen it first in her dream. The dream of them swimming—of him touching her.

"We can even do anything . . . because . . ."—he moved in closer—"because this is just a dream. It's not real. Just like the first one. But it's your choice. You're the one in the driver's seat."

His head dipped down an inch, and his face felt lightly scratchy against hers. Then his lips brushed across her cheeks until he found her lips. She let him kiss her. At first, she didn't respond. At least not until his tongue slipped between her lips.

Unable to think of anything else, she gave in and started kissing him back. It was hot. It was wonderful. It was just a dream. His hands were on her back, and then shifted to her front. Her breasts felt swollen when he brushed his palm across them.

Then . . . she remembered Derek. Strong, kind, beautiful Derek. And then she remembered Fredericka. Yeah, that was why she was mad at Lucas.

She jerked back. She was breathing hard. He was breathing hard, too.

She started floating away.

"Don't go, Kylie," he said. "Come back. Please."

Kylie suddenly became fully awake. She jackknifed into a sitting position. Her heart raced as if she'd run a marathon. Her palms felt sweaty. Her body tingled in front. It tingled darn near everywhere.

Socks, still in skunk form, meowed from the foot of the bed.

"Weird dream," she said aloud, and it felt good to hear her own voice. "A very weird dream."

Then she remembered Lucas's letter. His first letter.

Dream of me, he'd signed it.

Was it a coincidence?

Crazy possibilities started forming in her head. What if . . . ? What if werewolves had the power to get inside one's dreams? What if these weren't just dreams, but something more? Did that kind of power even exist?

The more she thought about it, the more she started to believe it, and the angrier she got. How dare he just come into her dreams and . . . kiss her. Touch her. Wasn't Fredericka enough for him? Did the she-wolf know Lucas was skipping out on her to come visit Kylie in her dreams?

So many questions and no answers. She realized one place she could look for answers.

Turning on the light, she yanked open the drawer and pulled out his letter. She'd already unsealed it and it slipped from the envelope easily enough. She blinked to adjust her eyes.

> Hi Kylie,
>
> Another letter from me. For all I know I'm the last person in the world you want to hear from. But it doesn't stop me from writing you. Or from thinking about you. But damn, I think about you all the time—wonder if you have discovered what you are and the many talents that you have. I've spoken to Burnett and when I asked about you, he only said you were fine. I think he knew I wanted details but for some reason, he wasn't willing to give them. It makes me wonder what you're doing that Burnett won't share. I don't want to think about it too much, because I'll start worrying.
>
> You could say that I feel very possessive of you. I'm not saying it's right, but I did meet you first.
>
> Do you remember when we met? You were in your front yard, lying on the ground, staring up at the sky. When I came over, you didn't even say hello. You looked at me with your big, curious eyes and asked if I saw the elephant. At first I thought you were crazy, but then you pointed to the clouds.

Kylie stopped reading as the tiny piece of memory started floating around her head. She did . . . remember. Taking a deep breath, she went back to reading.

I remember I told you I didn't see the elephant in the clouds. But I did. I don't know why I lied, probably because you made me nervous. I could see you weren't human, but I couldn't tell what you were and it seemed strange. Not really a bad strange. You were just like a puzzle I wanted to figure out. Ha! It's been ten years, and here I'm still trying to figure you out. Part of me wonders if it's because you are a female, girls are always a mystery, or if you are really that big of a puzzle.

Anyway, I hope you'll think this is good news, but I may be able to come back to the camp. I've spoken with Burnett about it and he said he has to get clearance from a couple other people and if they say it's okay, I'll be back. Hopefully, I'll be able to explain more then.

Okay, I hope to see you soon, but until then . . . dream of me.

Your admirer and friend forever,

Lucas

Kylie dropped the letter and just stared at those three words. *Dream of me.*

Exactly what did he mean by "dream of me"?

Did it mean anything? It had to, didn't it? Kylie folded the letter and stuffed it back in her drawer. Her emotions ran all over the place. Then she realized a second place she could look for answers. The place she always went for answers. Holiday.

Kylie looked at the red glowing numbers on her clock. Still too early. It wasn't quite . . . five.

But what happened to the regular cold that always came at dawn?

She looked at the window and saw the vaguest sign of sunrise. For some reason, her mind moved away from ghosts and to the two girls who'd died yesterday. They would never see another sunrise.

Never experience another day. Or have another dream. She clutched two handfuls of blanket and fought back the emotion.

She'd just gotten her breathing back to normal when the cold crept into her bedroom like a bad omen.

"Okay," Kylie said, searching for patience that she seemed in short supply of lately. "How about let's have a talk? What can you tell me that I don't know? Give me something. You gotta give me something so I can help whoever it is that needs help."

"You can save her." The ghost's words filled the frigid air and her spirit appeared. Her long dark hair flowed over her shoulders. She didn't appear as thin or sick this time. And there was something about her, something that looked vaguely familiar. Kylie wondered if that meant anything.

"You can save her. You don't know you can, but you have the ability," the ghost said.

"How am I going to save her?" Kylie asked, hoping this might lead her to understand the identity of the person. She needed something, damn it—something to help her figure this out. "Who do I need to save?"

"She's scared. She needs you."

"Who?" Kylie gritted her teeth. "Just tell me who, and I promise I'll do everything I can to save her. Can you understand that I can't save anyone until I know . . ." The ghost vanished.

"Damn it!" Kylie dropped back on the bed. She breathed in and out and tried not to think about her frustration with the ghost. Tried not to think about the frustration with Lucas and the so-called dream. Tried not to think about the girls who'd lost their lives yesterday.

With so many limitations on what she could think about, she found one she could. Today was parents day.

That sent a whole new wave of frustration over her. Her mother wouldn't be here. Her dad . . . her stepdad . . . was off bumping uglies with a girl practically Kylie's own age, and Kylie would probably be the only one whose parents didn't show up.

Didn't that make her feel special?

"Daniel?" she said her father's name aloud. "Could you maybe drop in a minute?" *For moral support. Maybe answer a few questions about your parents?* "Please." No answer came. She counted to ten. Said a prayer. And waited another minute before she lost her patience.

She pounded her fists on the mattress. It felt like a juvenile and stupid thing to do, but in her mood, it also felt good. So good, she continued to do it for a few more minutes.

Socks let out a frightened cry and Kylie felt him take a flying leap off the bed. She might have felt sorry for him if she wasn't in such a piss-poor mood. And that's when she remembered what the whole mood swings problem could possibly mean. She, Kylie Galen, might be morphing into a wolf in two days. Could life get any more friggin', fraggin' messed up?

Chapter Nineteen

After Kylie had given her mattress a good beating, she got dressed, apologized to Socks for acting silly, and left her cabin in search of Holiday.

The mornings were getting hotter and muggier. Welcome to July in Texas, Kylie thought as she made her way to the office to ask questions. The frustration buzzing in Kylie's gut encouraged her to run, but as eager as she was to find answers about the dreams, she was equally uneager to ask the questions. Holiday, with her emotion meter, would probably read what kind of dreams Kylie was talking about.

However, her need for answers obviously weighed in more than her need to avoid embarrassment, because she kept walking.

The moment Kylie stepped onto the office cabin porch, she heard angry voices coming from inside. She stopped by the white rockers where she and Derek had eaten pizza last night and listened. Not to eavesdrop, but to make sure Holiday was okay.

"What the hell is wrong with my money?" a male voice boomed, and Kylie immediately recognized it as Burnett.

"Nothing is wrong with it," Holiday answered. *"I didn't say I wasn't going to accept it. I said give me a few weeks to decide."*

"A few weeks to try to find another investor, you mean. Tell me that isn't what you're doing."

"Fine," Holiday answered back. *"That's what I'm doing, but—"*

"Do you hate me and vampires so much that you'd risk having Shadows Falls shut down?"

Kylie flinched when she realized she had shifted from concern for Holiday to . . . eavesdropping. Not wanting to infringe on Holiday's privacy any more than she already had, Kylie stepped off the porch and moved a good fifteen feet out of hearing range.

"I'm not going to let Shadow Falls close down!" Holiday's voice still reached Kylie's ears. Wincing, Kylie turned and moved another twenty feet back.

"But you won't deny hating me, will you?" Burnett snapped.

"Hate is pretty powerful word," Holiday said.

Kylie looked at the office in the distance, frowned, and moved another ten feet back.

"Damn it," Burnett said, his voice, loud and clear, still reaching Kylie's ears. It was as if . . . as if he stood right next to her.

"Not good," Kylie muttered, realizing she shouldn't still be able to hear Burnett and Holiday. They were inside. She was outside. And a good—she measured her distance—a good fifty feet from the office.

Oh crappers! Things must be changing . . . again. Kylie grabbed her boobs to make sure they hadn't grown another cup size. Thankfully, they felt the same.

"I just want to help," Burnett continued, and so did Kylie. She continued to move back. Back. Back. Back far enough so the conversation wouldn't reach her ears.

"Then help me by trying to understand," Holiday countered.

"What the hell am I'm supposed to understand? That you'll do anything to get rid of me? That's why you're doing it, isn't it?"

"I don't . . ." Holiday's voice wavered.

"Because you're afraid if you take my money you'll have to put up with me. Are you so attracted to me that it's that difficult to be around me? Hell, let's just have sex and get it out of your system. Maybe then you can stand being with me!"

"You are so arrogant," Holiday snapped. *"Having sex with you is the last thing I want."*

"Ahh, finally. Now, I know you're lying," he said. *"You are attracted to me."*

"La, la, la, la." Kylie started singing and covered her ears. She didn't want to hear this. Nope. Not even a little bit. She turned away and started back to the trail that led to her cabin.

Seconds later, she heard a door slam shut. Felt a whish of air. She blinked and when her eyes opened Burnett stood there raking a hand through his hair. "That woman is the most difficult, the most stubborn redhead I've ever had the displeasure of meeting."

He shot off, leaving only a blurry streak in his wake.

"And you're falling in love with her," Kylie whispered. She didn't know how she knew it, but she did. And somehow she realized she'd sensed it back at the falls, too. The genuine emotion she'd heard in Burnett's voice and seen in his eyes had been what encouraged Kylie to tell him the truth about Holiday's past. Not that it nullified the fact that it wasn't her place to tell. Still . . .

Kylie looked back at the office and remembered her questions about her dream, remembered her newly discovered hearing abilities, too. Was this a werewolf talent? She recalled asking Lucas if he could hear her heart beating and he'd told her that weres' hearing wasn't really set to do that, but to hear enemies approaching. What kind of hearing ability had Kylie just experienced? Was it werewolf or vampire?

Turning her head to the side, she listened to see what else she could hear. Nothing. Sure, she heard the normal noises, but nothing seemed too loud or out of the ordinary. Della had said she could hear the animals at the wildlife park. Kylie couldn't hear that. So why had she been able to hear Holiday and Burnett's fight? What did this mean?

Staring up at the sky soaked with pale early morning colors, she tried to accept all the things about herself that were changing. Problem was, to completely understand, she needed to know what the hell she was! With a chest full of emotion, she started walking back to the office, praying Holiday might have the answers.

"Holiday, it's me." Kylie called out when she stepped inside the main office ten seconds later.

"In my office," Holiday answered.

When Kylie stopped at the door, Holiday swept her palms over her cheeks. She was crying. Or she had been.

Her eyes were still washed with wet sadness, and her face looked red. Angst and sorrow filled Kylie's chest. "Are you okay?"

"It's nothing." Holiday waved a hand in the air. "Burnett and I just had . . . words."

"I know," Kylie said, deciding the best approach was to come clean. "I heard."

A frown appeared on Holiday's lips and Kylie wasn't sure if it was because she thought Kylie had been intruding or if the expression stemmed from her lingering frustration with Burnett.

"I didn't mean to eavesdrop," Kylie said quickly. "When I stepped up on the porch and heard arguing, I wanted to see if you were okay, but then I moved off the porch, but I could still . . . hear. So I moved farther. And I could still hear." A little of her panic crept in Kylie's voice.

Holiday's frown deepened. "Were we that loud?"

"No. And that's what's so freaky. I shouldn't have been able to hear you. I kept getting farther back and I . . ."

Holiday's eyes widened. "And you could still hear us? Are you sure we weren't just loud?"

"Positive," Kylie said. "I was at the beginning of the trail."

"Wow," Holiday said.

"Yeah, wow!" Kylie dropped down into a chair. Her gaze shifted to the bills strewn out over the desk. Holiday's emotion and frustration still filled the room. Kylie looked at Holiday. "Are we really in financial trouble?"

Holiday eyed the stacks of bills. "A little bit. But it'll work out in the wash."

"Are you going to take Burnett's money?"

Holiday's eyes tightened in worry. "I will before I let Shadow Falls suffer. But this issue isn't important right now. You're important. Are you okay with . . . this?" She studied Kylie. "I mean your sensitive hearing."

"Do I have a choice?" Kylie batted back a bad mood. "If I say I'm not okay with it, will it just stop?"

Holiday shot her a sympathetic smile. "I can only guess how hard this must be on you. I mean, I grew up knowing certain things would happen and expecting there to be some surprises, but I'm sure for you, it's really a shock. These last few weeks have been a real eye-opener for you, haven't they?"

"Just a little bit," Kylie said sarcastically, and pushed her palms into her eye sockets. When she looked up, Holiday studied her. "I just want to know what I am. If I knew that, then . . . I think I could deal with it. I'm so tired of thinking I'm this, and thinking I'm that." She gripped her hands together. "I've been . . . so moody lately. A real bitch. I grew a cup size, half a shoe size, and added an inch to my height overnight, and now I'm hearing things I shouldn't be hearing. Do you think this means I'm werewolf?"

Holiday chewed on her bottom lip as if considering. "Sensitive hearing is one of the gifts of being werewolf, but it's also part of being vampire—though I'm told they each have different types of hearing."

Kylie hung on Holiday's every word, hoping she would tell her something Kylie didn't know. But some of it she already knew.

"Like I told you," Holiday continued, "when you mix human with supernaturals, or different species mix, sometimes the offspring are born with different abilities, but they always inherit the DNA and the main gifts from the dominant parent. And they fit into one pattern of a species. I'm sure your pattern will emerge soon. With all the changes happening to you so quickly, it's bound to become apparent any time."

Kylie struggled to understand. "But you also said if I was werewolf or vampire you thought I'd already have experienced some of the basic transitions."

"I did say that," Holiday admitted. "But I also said I've never seen a case like yours."

"I'm just a freak."

"No. You are unique."

"I don't want to be unique." Kylie sighed. "Do fairies ever have sensitive hearing?" She looked at Holiday.

A smile whispered across Holiday's lips. "Not commonly." She continued to study Kylie as if reading her disappointment. "You want to be fairy?"

"Yeah. I mean, if I have a choice, I'd go with that or a witch. Something that doesn't . . . you know . . . change me or my body temperature." Kylie thought of Della and how she'd feel if she knew Kylie felt this way.

"Am I terrible for wanting that?" Kylie asked. "I love Della and I don't want to hurt her feelings, but I just . . . I'd rather be witch or fairy. I mean, most of the gifts they get are not so complicated, not so hard to live with."

Holiday chuckled. "Are you forgetting about the ghosts? That's mainly seen in fairies or elves. And believe me, most supernaturals would die before wanting to deal with spirits."

"True." Kylie blinked. "I did sort of forget about that. And yeah, it's a royal pain in the ass. At first, it terrified me, but now that I've had some time to deal with it . . ." She paused and remembered the ghost's little visit this morning and the nightmare from the other morning. "Okay, it sometimes still terrifies me and frustrates me. But at least now I'm almost used to it."

Holiday leaned her elbows on her desk. "Whatever you are, whatever gifts you end up getting, you'll find that time will make those changes less scary as well. Whatever happens on Monday, I know—"

"Monday? Because it's a full moon. You think I'm werewolf now?"

Holiday held up her hand. "I don't know. I do know that you are an amazing young lady and no matter how things end up, you're going to be okay."

Kylie leaned her head back in the chair, stared at Holiday, and moaned. "I hate this. I really, really hate this." Then she remembered the reason she'd come here this morning. She sat up again and took a deep breath.

Then she nipped at her bottom lip, trying to remember how she'd planned to ask about it. Hadn't she come up with a less embarrassing way to approach the dreams? "One more thing . . ."

Holiday sat there, patiently waiting.

"Dreams . . . ?" Kylie only got out the one word.

"What about them?" Her expression grew concerned. "Has the ghost been giving you more dreams?"

"No."

"Night terrors?" Holiday asked.

"No." Oddly enough, Kylie hadn't had one of those in a long time. That is, if you didn't call the vision dreams with the ghost night terrors.

"Are you sleepwalking again?" Holiday asked.

Okay, it was going to get weirder if she didn't start talking. "I've been having strange dreams. I know I'm dreaming in the dream. And in the dream the people I'm dreaming about know it's a dream, too. I almost feel as if . . . as if he's breaking into my dreams."

"He?" Holiday asked.

"Lucas." Kylie felt her face flush. "Is it possible for someone, for Lucas, to actually come into my dreams? To actually . . . visit me? It feels so real. And I . . . if it is real, I want him to stop doing it. I mean, in both letters he mentioned dreams. And if it's real, he needs to stop it."

Holiday's eyes widened, but she didn't say anything.

"What is it?" Kylie asked.

"I . . ." Holiday stumbled as if trying to decide what to say.

"Don't lie to me, or keep something from me, even if you're just guessing. Just tell me what you think is the truth." She reached across the desk and placed her hand on top of Holiday's. "Please."

Holiday's brow creased in concern. "Okay, but you probably aren't going to like this."

Oh, great. That was not what she wanted to hear.

Chapter Twenty

"He's really doing it, isn't he? He's breaking into my dreams." Kylie's heart filled with resentment.

Holiday slowly shook her head. "I don't think . . . I mean. I'm only guessing, but it's probably not him."

"Oh, it's him. I saw him." She put her hand in front of her face about an inch away from her nose. "He was this close to me." *And closer.* She recalled how he'd kissed her.

"No, I didn't mean it wasn't him in the dream. I mean, it's not him coming into your dreams."

Kylie tried to wrap her head around what Holiday was saying to her.

Holiday continued. "What you're talking about is what we call dreamscaping, and I've never heard of a werewolf with this gift."

"Well, you've heard of one now." Kylie felt herself getting angrier, remembering the dream with them swimming. "And the thing he's doing . . . he shouldn't be doing."

Holiday held up her hand. "However, it is a very common gift with those of us who share the gift of ghost whispering."

Kylie sat there, staring at Holiday, not wanting to believe the camp leader. "Are you saying that . . . I'm . . . I'm doing this?"

Okay, Kylie had put her foot in her mouth before, but she'd never had it in there so deep she felt her toes wiggling against her tonsils.

Holiday leaned in, her expression almost one of apology. "Yeah, that's exactly what I'm saying, Kylie."

Kylie nearly choked on a big breath of air. "So the person I'm dreaming about, do they . . . I mean, can they remember the dreams?" Her heart stopped as she recalled the first dream, the one of them swimming, the one where she'd practically flashed the girls at him.

Okay, so she'd totally flashed the girls at him.

"Some do," Holiday said. "Some don't."

Thank you, Jeeessus! She was definitely going with the "some don't."

Holiday continued, "However, supernaturals would remember."

Okay, I take back that thank-you.

Kylie really wanted to die now. Then she recalled Lucas saying, *You're the one in the driver's seat.*

"So . . . whatever happens in these dreams . . . Am I, like, in charge of it? Am I responsible for what happens in the dream?"

From Holiday's expression, she must have just realized what kinds of things Kylie was eluding to. "Our emotions often guide our dreamscapes just as they do our dreams."

"Our?" Kylie asked. "Do you . . . do this, too?" Hey, misery loved company.

Holiday held out her right hand, her thumb and index finger pinched close together. "I'm slightly gifted in this area, but yes, I've experienced it some." She waited a few seconds before continuing. "Ultimately, you are the one in control—if you are in control of your emotions."

Well, that pretty much left Kylie in the dark. How many times had she admitted feeling no control when it came to boys and kissing, let alone . . .

Holiday continued, "The dreamscaper sort of sets the stage for the dream. You offer a script to the person you are dreaming about and, depending on the strength of your abilities, and the person you are dreaming about, he or she can either refuse the script or attempt to alter it."

Kylie's head started to throb. No doubt from stress. "But it feels so real."

"It is real, but it's not." Holiday reached over and took her hand. A lot of Kylie's stress began to fade. "Think of it as going to see a movie. If you go see a movie with someone, you both share the experience. You live through the emotions, but it didn't actually happen."

Holiday released Kylie's hand, and then leaned back in her chair. "I'm impressed by this new ability of yours, Kylie. Really. If someone is highly skilled in dreamscaping, it's considered a very powerful gift. You can learn a lot from it and even teach others through the use of dreamscapes. And very few of us are lucky to have it."

"Lucky me," Kylie said with zero enthusiasm. "I don't suppose it's one of those returnable gifts?" she asked, feeling overwhelmed.

"Not returnable. I'm afraid the time has already passed to refuse your gifts. When you accepted your role as a ghost whisperer, you pretty much accepted it all." Holiday smiled. "But believe me, in time you will probably feel more in control of it. Seriously, Kylie, this is a very special gift."

Kylie crossed her arms over her special extra-size breasts and tried to take it all in. Holiday's words replayed in her head. *I've never heard of a werewolf with this gift.* "So . . . if I am gifted with this, does it mean I'm not going to be morphing into a werewolf this Monday?"

Holiday didn't say anything, but Kylie saw that look on the camp leader's face again. The one that said she was either trying to figure out if she should say something, and if she did, how to say it in a way to soften the blow.

"Just spill it," Kylie told her. At this point, she might as well hear everything.

Holiday wrinkled her brows. "You are good at reading me," she said. "Really, too good," she said as if that could mean something, too.

But Kylie was too focused on the werewolf issue to care what other things Holiday was thinking. "What are you telling me now?"

Holiday shook her head. "I was going to talk to you about this later. But first, I want to say up-front that it's still surmising." She paused.

"Okay . . ." Kylie waved her hand to hurry Holiday along.

"After our talk yesterday where you mentioned the wolf . . . Well, Selynn and Burnett told me that . . . there's an old legend about real wolves being drawn to weres who are supposed to be in the hierarchy of the pack."

"So, I'm like an important werewolf?" Damn, she didn't even want to be a regular werewolf—she for sure didn't want to be an important one.

"I said it was just surmising on our part. Because frankly, Kylie, all the other stuff, the fact that you've never turned, that your other gifts aren't those common with weres, it doesn't line up. Especially when you realize that most all hierarchies in a were group are full-blooded. No human blood. So, you see, I don't want you to start thinking this really means anything. Because frankly, I'm not sure it does."

"Or it could mean a really big something," Kylie said, and wondered if she'd ever figure it all out. Or if she was destined to go through her life not knowing who or what she really was.

Before Kylie left Holiday's office, the camp leader asked Kylie to help her greet the visitors, deliver cold water and hot coffee, and keep peace in the dining hall during parents day. She got the feeling Holiday didn't need her help as much as she worried Kylie would go back to her cabin, fall into bed, and crawl into a deep state of insurmountable depression. Since Holiday could actually read Kylie's emotions, that was a big possibility.

Now, prepared to play the part of a greeter, the door to the dining hall opened and several parents came rushing in and looking around for their kids.

Kylie realized a problem with Holiday's no-depression plan. Seeing eager parents walk in and embrace their kids wasn't exactly cheering her up. Remembering the call with her mom and how upset her mom was about having to miss the visitation helped chase away some of her melancholy. But then her mind shot to her stepdad and the reasons he wasn't going to show up. Too busy bumping uglies with his skanky girlfriend!

Kylie turned around and went to the table to start pouring glasses of iced water.

Ten minutes later, the noise in the dining hall rose as more parents arrived. Kylie looked around and her thoughts went to her mom again. Not that her mind lingered on Mom too long. Nope. She had better things to knock around in the batting cage of her mind. Like the realization that Kylie had been barging into Lucas's dreams and handing him a dream script that read: let's get naked, go for a swim, and make out.

Not that he'd exactly been complaining about it.

Oh, and the best part, according to Holiday, was that Lucas would remember these dreams, too. So when he came back to the camp—if he came back—she'd have to face him.

Nope. She definitely didn't want to think about that.

She grabbed another tray and started lining up glasses to fill with water.

"It's Kylie, right?" A soft voice spoke beside her.

Kylie glanced up from the tray. The woman appeared to be in her early fifties. She wore her dark hair short in a classic older lady cut, and her soft green eyes studied Kylie with a smile.

"Yes, it's Kylie." She forced herself to smile back and she was glad she did. It took her only another second after noticing the eye color to recognize the woman. "Hi, Mrs. Lakes."

Kylie looked around to see if she could find Derek, thinking his mom was obviously looking for him. "I haven't seen him, but I'm sure—"

"Oh, he's right over there." She pointed in the opposite direction from where Kylie looked. Kylie was tempted to turn around and find him, but something kept her from it. She recognized the emotion right off the bat. Guilt. Guilt about her dreams.

Please don't break my heart. Derek's words echoed in her head and she realized it would break her heart if she knew Derek was skinny-dipping in his dreams with some other girl.

Staring back down at the plastic glasses lined up like dominos on the tray, she hoped Derek wasn't close enough to read her emotions.

The woman put a hand on Kylie's arm and leaned in. "I told him I wanted to snag a glass of water."

"Oh, here," Kylie reached down and picked up a glass.

"Thank you, dear," Mrs. Lakes said, but she winked. "Actually,

I just wanted to say hello and tell you . . ." She leaned in again. "You are practically all he ever talks about."

The guilt in Kylie's chest doubled, but this time she couldn't stop herself from looking over the woman's shoulder at Derek. He made a face at her as if he was worried about what his mom might be saying.

"I think my son is sweet on you," Mrs. Lakes said.

Kylie shifted her focus back to Mrs. Lakes but she didn't know how to answer. "I . . ."

The woman smiled. "I'm so glad he found nice friends here." She looked down at her glass. "Now, I'll leave and stop embarrassing you. Thank you for the water."

As Kylie watched the woman walk away, she muttered, "I'm sweet on him, too." And she was. What wasn't to like about Derek? She liked him for his easygoing ways, she liked the way he was nice to everyone and didn't think he was better than anyone else. She liked him in other ways, too.

The vision of him standing naked in the shower filled her mind. She was really, really sweet on Derek.

So, why hadn't she barged into *his* dreams? Why wasn't Derek the one whom her subconscious went to for fulfilling some kind of naughty fantasy? Feeling her face heat up just thinking about this in public, she looked back down at the glasses of ice water.

"Hi, Pumpkin."

Thoughts of fantasies immediately took flight. *Hi, Pumpkin. Hi, Pumpkin.* Realizing who stood right behind her, she froze. Even if she hadn't recognized the voice, only one person called her pumpkin.

She turned and lifted her eyes to her dad . . . stepdad. "What are you doing here?" she blurted out, and damn it if she didn't want to drop to the floor, curl up in a ball, and start to cry.

"What do you think I'm doing? I came to see my girl." He

smiled and looked at her the way he used to when she did something cute, or when she showed him a good report card.

Yup, she wanted to cry all right. The tightness in her throat made that crystal clear. "You didn't tell me you were coming." Was that enough of a reason to walk away? "You should have told me."

The loving father look on his face quickly changed to an unhappy father look. "I would have told you if you'd taken my calls," he said in a disgruntled voice. It was a voice he didn't use a lot, because her mom had always been the heavy.

"I've been busy," she answered.

His eyes tightened. "We both know I left you about seven voicemails, two texts, and a couple of e-mails. And I don't think you've been so busy that you couldn't have returned just one of them. I even called your camp leader."

The tears she didn't want to come started filling her eyes just as anger started filling her chest. But she welcomed the anger, because it crowded out the hurt. She looked into his eyes. He had no right getting angry at her. No right to tell her what she'd done wrong when his wrongs had totally ruined her life. Ruined her mother's life, too.

"Do you really want to talk about right and wrong?" she asked.

To his credit, his expression went from annoyed to ashamed in zero flat. "I guess your mom's been talking to you. Damn it! She really shouldn't have told you about our problems."

"What? Are you kidding me? Are you seriously going to stand here and blame this on Mom?"

He blinked. "I just . . . I don't think she should have said any—"

"Stop." Kylie gripped her hands to keep them from trembling . . . or from punching him in the nose. Right then, she wasn't sure which was more likely to happen. "Mom didn't tell me anything." Tears spilled down her face. "Mom didn't have to tell me anything.

You told me. No, wait. I misspoke. You didn't *tell* me anything. You showed me."

"What are talking about, Kylie?" He leaned in and lowered his voice as if hinting she should do the same.

But she was too mad, too hurt to care who heard their argument. He'd left her. He'd left her and her mom for some bimbo. The vision of him and his slutty little intern making out in front of the downtown B&B filled her head.

"Well, first you hit on Holiday when you came to visit me," she said. "That was embarrassing enough, but then I saw you in town later that day. You hadn't come alone. And I saw you and your intern standing in the middle of downtown Fallen. You want to know why I remember it so well, Dad?"

He opened his mouth as if to say something, but nothing came out.

So she continued, "Because you had your *tongue* shoved down her throat while she had her *hand* jammed down your pants." Kylie blinked and felt more tears spilling over onto her cheeks. "Lovely," she seethed. "It was such a lovely sight, seeing your dad practically get a hand job in public."

Instantly, she realized that the entire room had gone deadly silent. *Damn!* Had she really screamed that out in the middle of the entire camp and their parents?

She glanced out at the crowd. Staring at her and her father. And from the look on everyone's face, yeah, she had.

Okay, now she really, *really* wished she'd taken her dad's hint about lowering her voice. Turning around, not looking at her dad, not looking at the crowd, she walked out of the dining room, hoping she could get outside before she started crying in earnest.

She would have run, but exhibiting her superfast supernatural running skills would have caused even more of a scene.

So she walked slowly toward the exit and pretended she didn't feel the tears gliding down her cheeks.

She pretended her heart wasn't breaking.

She pretended that she didn't know that about one hundred pairs of eyes were watching her go.

But pretending could only take her so far.

This . . . this was too damn real, and it hurt her too much.

Chapter Twenty-one

The knock sounded on her bedroom door not three minutes after she crawled into her bed and pulled the covers over her face and continued to cry. "Go away," Kylie called out.

The door opened. She yanked the cover from her face, expecting to see Holiday. But nope, Derek stood there with a heck of a lot concern for her shimmering in his eyes.

Seeing it only made her start crying harder. She cried because of her dad, and she cried because she felt bad about the dreams she'd had about Lucas. Derek rushed over to the bed and pulled her against him. If he read any of her emotions about guilt, he didn't say it. He just held her. And she loved him for doing that, too.

She buried her head on his shoulder and continued to sob in his arms. She didn't care that she was getting tears and snot all over his shirt. His arms felt so good wrapped around her and while he didn't say it, the way he held her said he didn't care about his shirt, either. Good thing, because when she got through crying, it was really going to be a mess.

"Hey?" Another voice came from the open door.

Kylie pulled away and saw Della and Miranda standing there.

"I could turn him into a toad if you want," Miranda said, waving her pinky. "Or maybe a skunk. I could use the practice."

Socks, who'd been sleeping at the foot of the bed, raised his head, meowed loudly as if in agreement, and then shot off to hide under the bed.

Della snarled. "I could pick him up and drag him up a tree and then drop him on his head a few times until he comes to his senses."

Kylie cried harder and then for some reason she started laughing. She wiped her eyes and looked at three of the most beautiful people in her world right now. "Did I really say that in front of all your parents?"

"Yup. I think my dad had a stroke," Della said, grinning from ear to ear. "It came just at the right time, too. He'd been grilling me about drugs again."

"My mom passed out cold," Derek teased.

Then they all started laughing. Kylie collapsed against Derek again. When she pulled back, she wiped her face and looked up.

And that's when it happened. That's when Kylie's whole world opened up in a way it never had opened up before.

She blinked. At first, she thought there was just something wrong with her eyes. But nope. There was no mistaking it. She could see inside their foreheads. She could see into them the way she'd seen into Daniel's head in the vision. She, Kylie Galen, could finally see supernatural patterns.

"I'm doing it, guys! I'm finally doing it!" She started bouncing up and down on the bed. "Holy crap, I'm really doing it."

"Doing what?" a familiar voice asked from the doorway.

He didn't call her pumpkin this time, but she recognized her dad's voice. He stood beside Holiday, who glanced at Kylie with a huge apology in her eyes. Obviously, her father had demanded she bring him here.

"Can I have a word with my daughter alone?" He stepped inside her bedroom.

"Only if that's what she wants," Derek said, sounding defensive and older.

Kylie rested her hand on Derek's arm. "It's okay."

Derek stood from the bed, but he didn't stop glaring at her dad for one minute. To her dad's credit, he just stood there and took Derek's angry stare as if he knew he deserved it. Della actually growled, and Miranda twitched her little finger at him.

Kylie hoped she remembered to give each of them a big hug later.

"Come on, guys," Holiday said, and motioned for them to leave. They all stepped out of the room. Then Holiday reached in, her concerned gaze meeting Kylie's eyes right before she closed the door.

Kylie pulled her knees up to her chest and wrapped her arms around her shins. Her heart must have dropped to her stomach because she could feel it pound in the pit of her gut. She stared at the top of her jeans-covered knees and not at him, because looking at him hurt too much.

Besides, if she looked at him, she might start crying again, and she didn't want to do that.

He sat down beside her on the twin bed. From the corner of her eye, she saw him fold his hands together in his lap. She heard him breathe. She heard herself breathe, too.

She closed her eyes.

Sooner or later, one of them had to talk. But for once Kylie decided not to be the bigger person here. Let him do all the work.

"I screwed up," he finally said. "I never dreamed I could screw up so badly."

Opening her eyes, she forced herself to look at him. The first thing she noticed was that he looked like her dad again. He wasn't wearing those tight jeans. His hair was combed like it should be and not spiked. He still had the highlights in his hair, but alone, they weren't so bad.

"I don't blame you for being furious at me, but I do love you, Pumpkin." He rested his hand on her knee and his touch sent tiny pinpricks of pain rushing to her heart. Tears filled her eyes.

She blinked, but didn't trust her voice to say anything just yet. And even if she did trust it, she wasn't sure what to say.

"I never wanted to hurt you," he continued. "I never dreamed that you'd be in town that day." He shook his head, closed his eyes, and when he opened them back up, she saw something she'd never seen before. Her dad was crying. Real live tears, too. The ache in her chest doubled.

"I don't know what got into me, Kylie. I lost my head. I turned forty and then your grandmother got sick and she died." He inhaled. "All I could think about was getting old. Then Amy—the girl at the office—she started flirting and it made me forget everything for a little while." His breath caught. "It made me forget that the most important people in the world to me are you and your mom."

Kylie knew it was her turn to talk, but she still didn't know what to say. She couldn't say she forgave him, because she didn't. Then a thought struck.

"Did your girlfriend break up with you?" Was that the only reason he was here now?

"Yeah." He looked embarrassed. Kylie was surprised he hadn't tried to deny it. "But that's not why . . . I'd already realized how badly I'd screwed up before we broke up."

She remembered her mom telling her how her dad had deserved someone to love him as much he had loved her all those years. That's when Kylie felt a small part of herself give in. She couldn't stay mad at him forever. She just couldn't. Maybe she *was* ready to forgive.

He reached over and ran his hand over her head, the way he'd done all her life. "I love you, Kylie. You're my daughter."

No, I'm not. She remembered that he'd made her mother promise not to tell her about her real father and her anger returned.

She batted at her cheeks to remove her tears. Then she offered him the only thing she could. "I'm hurt and I'm really mad at you right now. As soon as it stops hurting so much, I might be able to forgive you. But not now."

He nodded. She watched a tear slip from his lashes. He wiped it away. Then he leaned in and pressed a soft kiss on her forehead. "I love you, Pumpkin. Just remember that."

As Kylie watched him get up to leave, she realized that just because you couldn't forgive someone didn't mean you stopped loving them. She bounced off her bed and wrapped her arms around her daddy. He hugged her back. He hugged her so tight. And it felt so good, she wept on his shoulder. Big tears. Dinosaur tears he'd called them when she was young.

She knew that in just a second she was going to have to let go, and that she still wouldn't tell him he was forgiven, because he wasn't. But for just a few seconds she wanted to feel that her daddy loved her. And while she wasn't up to saying it yet, she hoped he understood she still loved him, too.

A few minutes after her dad left, Kylie was still stretched out on her bed when Holiday knocked on her door.

"You okay?" Holiday poked her head in the door.

"I'm working on it." Kylie had stopped crying. Something about her daddy's hug had eased some of the ache.

"You mind company, or would you like to be alone?"

"Company would be nice." She tried to see around Holiday. "Is everyone still out there?"

Holiday stepped into the room. "Just me. I made them go back and visit with their parents for a while."

"Good," Kylie said, and then recalled the scene she'd caused in the dining room. "I'm sorry about everything. I just lost it."

"Please." Holiday dropped onto the bed beside Kylie. "We needed a little excitement. I mean, if something crazy doesn't happen every fifteen minutes, it just doesn't feel right." She giggled.

Kylie grinned and then she remembered, excitement buzzing in her chest. "I did it. I . . ." She twitched her eyebrows and looked at Holiday. "I'm doing it now. I can see your pattern. You've got some horizontal lines and then . . . and then triangle shapes on the left."

"That's great!" Holiday hugged her. "I knew it would happen for you. Congratulations."

"But does this mean I'm opening up, too? That people can read me now and I won't come across like a snooty bitch anymore? And can . . . oh, man!" Hope started to build. "Can you see what I am? Look and tell me."

Holiday stared at Kylie's forehead. Her expression told Kylie the answer before Holiday spoke.

"Sorry. You're still a snooty bitch." Holiday grinned. "But it will happen any time now. Opening up takes more practice. Are you still doing your visualization exercises?"

"Not as often as I should," Kylie admitted. "But I'll start being better, I promise."

"Have you experienced any more of the sensitive hearing?"

"No. Why? Does that mean anything?" Did Holiday know

something she wasn't saying? Did she think Kylie was back to being a werewolf now?

"No. I was just curious." Holiday reached up and tucked a strand of Kylie's hair behind her ear. "Are you really okay? You've had a rough few days."

"Tell me about it." Kylie's thoughts went back to the girls who were killed. She looked at Holiday. "What if . . . What do I do if those girls from town—their ghosts, I mean—come to me to help them?"

Holiday gripped Kylie's hand. "That won't happen."

"How can you be so sure? If their spirits are still here and—"

"It won't happen," Holiday said with more certainty this time. And that's when Kylie understood. "They came to you?"

She nodded. "I'm helping them cross over." Then Holiday gave Kylie a feel-better hug. Its soothing effects did wonders.

"Now, let's go back to you," Holiday said. "Are you okay?"

"Not completely okay," Kylie said, and then admitted a piece of truth that Holiday deserved to hear. "You were right. I feel a little better after seeing my dad. I didn't let him off the hook, either. I'm still furious at him, but . . . I know he loves me. And I love him and sooner or later, I'm sure we'll be back to something that is almost normal."

Holiday leaned back on Kylie's pillow. "Normal is overrated, anyway."

"I'm beginning to wonder if I'd even recognize normal now." Kylie raised her thumb to her mouth and nipped at the corner of her nail.

"Well, if you did recognize it, you probably wouldn't like it anymore," Holiday teased.

"I just want to figure out this whole mystery with the ghost, if someone really needs me or doesn't need me. Do these ghosts have a clue what they put us through?"

"I don't think so." Holiday touched Kylie's arm again. "But I really believe everything is going to be okay."

For the next few minutes, only silence filled the room. Kylie looked down at Holiday resting on the bed. "Can I ask you something?"

Holiday cocked an eyebrow at her. "It doesn't involve Burnett, does it?"

"No," Kylie said. "But it's about boys."

"Okay, shoot." Holiday sat up.

"Is it . . . normal if you really like one guy to still be infatuated with another?"

"The whole Derek and Lucas issue, huh?"

"Yeah." Kylie frowned. "But I liked it better when I didn't name them."

"Okay, no names. Two guys." She held out one finger. "First, we can't always control our attractions to other people. Take my aunt Stella, for example. She's been married to my uncle for fifty years, but the woman is goo-goo over Tom Selleck. Owns every movie and TV show he ever made, she spends hours every week watching him strut across her fifty-two-inch flat screen." Holiday gave Kylie a soft look as if she realized the whole Tom Selleck talk wasn't working. "I think I've said this to you before. You are too young to worry about things like this."

"You're wrong," Kylie said. "Why wouldn't I worry? Just because a person is young doesn't mean that being loyal to someone isn't important. And it still hurts if someone isn't loyal to you. It hurt like hell when Trey hooked up with another girl. It hurt Perry when Miranda kissed another guy, and they weren't even going out yet. Okay, I admit that at this age, it might not bring about the same disastrous outcome as . . . as my dad cheating on my mom, but it still hurts. So I have to worry, because I don't want to hurt anyone."

"Wow." Holiday frowned and sat back up. "When you put it like that, you are so right, and I am so wrong. I'm sorry."

Kylie stared at the camp leader for a moment. "I appreciate your admitting you were wrong," Kylie said. *Adults don't always do that.*

"Is it okay if I try again to offer some advice?" Holiday asked.

Kylie nodded.

Holiday paused in thought for a second. "Can I guess that this is all about the dream you had with Lucas?"

"You could guess," Kylie said. "But I won't confirm or deny it."

Holiday smiled. "Kylie, you didn't intentionally seek out the dream. You didn't even know you could do it. So you really aren't to blame. And the fact that you find yourself attracted to more than one guy is completely normal. I've got three guys right now that all I have to do is think about and I start tingling all over."

Kylie gave Holiday's words serious thought. "But did you feel that when you thought you really cared about someone else?"

"Yeah. Even when I was engaged, I still could appreciate a good-looking guy." She paused. "Being committed or loyal to someone doesn't mean you won't ever be attracted to someone else. It means you won't physically act upon the attraction." She grinned. "My aunt Stella, she used to tell my uncle he'd better pray Tom Selleck didn't show up on her doorstep asking her to run away with him. But the truth is, I know she'd turn Tom down flat. She loves my uncle Harry."

Holiday made a face. "Don't ask me why, though—he's bald, has a gut, and snores." She chuckled. "That said, I'll bet that woman has had some really hot fantasies about Tom."

Kylie laughed and then they both reclined back on the bed.

The twin-size mattress offered just enough room for them both to stretch out with their shoulders pressed against each other. For a second they didn't talk. Kylie stared at the ceiling and finally posed another question. "Is Burnett one of the guys who makes you tingle all over?"

"No Burnett questions, remember?"

"Okay," Kylie said. "But if I was older, he'd make me tingle."

Holiday laughed. "You and half the world. Including Selynn." The humor in her voice faded.

Silence reigned again. Maybe it was thinking about Selynn and Burnett that brought on Kylie's next question. "Lucas told me in his letters that he was trying to get permission to come back to the camp. Do you know if he's coming back?"

Holiday hesitated. "He'll be here either tomorrow or Tuesday."

"Is Fredericka coming with him?"

"Yeah," Holiday said.

"Great," Kylie muttered. So if she did morph into a werewolf, Fredericka, who would also be in wolf form, would probably chase her down and rip her wolf ass to shreds.

Her day was just getting better and better.

Chapter Twenty-two

That afternoon, Kylie decided to skip the picnic dinner at the swimming hole. First, she didn't have a bathing suit that would fit; second, she really wanted to make a few calls to see if she could locate any Brightens who might know something about her real dad. And third, well, she hoped the ghost would drop by again. Something about the way she'd shown up when Kylie had been talking to her mom felt odd.

Kylie knew she couldn't start fixating on trying to guess who the ghost was talking about being in danger. But deep down, the fixating had bit. Could the ghost be talking about her mom? Could her mom be in danger?

Worried that it might be true, Kylie had called her mom. Twice. But her phone was turned off. Probably because she was in mid-flight. Kylie sat down at the computer desk, telling herself everything was fine, and pulled out the printed list of phone numbers. Her cell rang. Hoping it was her mom, she took the call without checking the caller ID.

"Mom?" Kylie asked.

"Not Mom. It's Sara."

"Oh, hi," Kylie said, trying to figure out which one of the

multitude of emotions about Sara she should let control the conversation. There was the hurt she felt that Sara—whom she'd considered her best friend for years—hadn't returned any of her calls in almost a month. There was the concern she felt knowing that Sara was . . . going through something. And then there was the melancholy she felt because she knew her friendship with Sara would never be the same again.

When the silence seemed awkward, Kylie jumped in. "My mom said she saw you in the grocery store the other day."

"Yeah, she did. She's looking good, too. I like her new look and hairstyle. She said you talked her into getting a makeover."

"Did she do it?" Kylie asked. "She hasn't told me she did it."

"Oh, I hope I didn't ruin her surprise."

"Nah, I appreciate the warning. Does she look good? Or dumb?"

"Good. She looks . . . younger, I guess. You know, kind of like she might be about to start dating."

"Dating?" Kylie knew this was a possibility, she'd even suggested it, but for some reason now the idea hit her stomach like a bad piece of chicken. "Did she *say* that or are you just guessing?"

"No, she didn't say it. She just looked, you know, like a woman who wanted to be noticed by a man. Tighter jeans and a fitted top that showed off her girls. I almost didn't recognize her."

Was Sara saying her mom was dressing like a ho? That wasn't the makeover Kylie had suggested. Realizing the conversation had gone quiet again, Kylie started talking to fill the silence. "Mom said you looked . . ." Kylie had almost lied and said good, but at the last minute decided not to do it. ". . . thinner. Are you on some new diet again?"

Sara was the first to try every new diet endorsed by Hollywood: low carbs, no carbs, all fruit on Tuesday, all brown rice on Wednesday, the crazier the better.

Not that she ever stayed on any of them.

"Not really," Sara said. "I think it's the birth control pills. I heard they'd cause me to gain weight, but they seem to be doing the opposite with me."

Sara was on the pill? It struck Kylie again how much things had changed between them. The old Sara would have certainly told Kylie something as big as getting on the pill.

But then, Kylie hadn't exactly been in a sharing mood with Sara lately, either. Of course, trying to explain to a normal about being a still unidentified supernatural was a little—well, a lot— more difficult than discussing birth control pills.

"Did your mom agree to you taking them?" Kylie asked, knowing Sara's mom was a bit of a religious fanatic and constantly preached against premarital sex.

"Are you kidding? She'd die if she found out. I went to the clinic and I faked her signature."

Kylie had heard about some other girls doing the same thing to get around the Texas law that required a parent's signature before dispensing the pills.

Another long pause followed.

"So, who are you dating?" Kylie asked.

"A couple of different guys." Sara sounded purposely vague. Kylie couldn't help but wonder if Sara was having sex with the couple of different guys, too. Once upon a time, she might have asked.

"So," Sara said. "You're still coming home in a couple of weeks, aren't you? Camp from hell is almost over? No more being a boner, huh?"

Annoyance chomped down on Kylie's stomach. Obviously, Trey had told Sara about the whole boner reference, because Kylie couldn't remember mentioning it.

"Actually, I'm only coming home for the weekend. And I really like it here." Kylie didn't tell her about the whole boarding school possibility just because she didn't want to go into it. But she sent up a silent prayer that her mom agreed to it. The thought of going back to her old school and not having the old Sara at her side was just too much.

"Really, you like it? You hated it at first. Camp Freaky, isn't that what you called it?" Sara sounded shocked.

That was before I actually realized I was a freak, too. Well, not a freak, but not all human, either. "I guess things change." Kylie meant her relationship with her one-time best friend, as well as her feeling about the camp.

"Yeah, I guess so." Another pause. "Well, text me when you get in town and hopefully we can meet up."

She wasn't even going to get a definite "Yes, I'll see you" from Sara. That hurt like a paper cut to the lip. Pushing away the feeling, she answered, "Yeah, I'll do that." But she wasn't so sure she would. Seeing Sara might just be too weird to deal with right now.

"Okay, my mom is calling me to help with the dishes," Sara said.

Kylie couldn't hear anyone calling in the background. Not that she wasn't eager to end the call as well. This had been hard. Really hard.

"Okay, bye," Kylie said. *Have a good life. Nice knowing you.*

As soon as Kylie hung up, the phone rang again. This time, she looked at the caller's phone number.

Derek?

He didn't normally call her. "What's up?" she asked with a touch of worry.

A ghostly cold invaded the room as she waited for Derek to speak. A wave of dizziness had Kylie grabbing the computer desk.

She had experienced this enough to know that it meant a vision was about to occur.

Or was occurring, she corrected when she saw the casket sitting where the kitchen table had been seconds earlier. The woman in the casket was the ghost. A few people moved around the casket with tears in their eyes.

"Kylie?" Derek's voice came on the line.

"Yeah." She stared at the casket and the people and wondered what she was supposed to learn from this vision. That was why they happened, right? The ghost was trying to tell Kylie something. But what?

I'm scared, Mama. From the back, Kylie saw the little girl reach up and take her mom's hand.

It's just Grandma. The couple walked up to the casket.

"Kylie, are you there?" Derek's voice sounded upset . . . or something.

She recalled her concern about Derek calling her. It was so out of character for him.

"Yeah. I'm here. Is everything okay?" Kylie asked, and her concentration on Derek made the vision fade like an old photograph. It lost its color and went into black and white mode as if dating the scene as something that happened a long time ago. Then the vision grew weaker, almost transparent. "Don't go," she said.

"Go where?" Derek asked.

"Not you," she said, but it was too late, only a vague outline remained of the scene. The woman holding the little girl's hand turned around. Kylie got only glimpse of her face, but something about her looked familiar.

Shaking her head, and remembering Derek was still on the phone, she asked, "Is everything okay?"

"No," he said. "It's not okay."

"What's wrong?" she asked.

"You're not here."

She rolled her eyes. "I thought you were serious."

"I am. I've been looking forward to this afternoon all day, thinking you'd be here."

"But I wanted—"

"Please," he said. "I . . ." His voice lowered. "I haven't ever seen you in a bathing suit."

"And you still wouldn't. I've grown out of my bikini top, remember?"

"Don't remind me," he said with a tease in his voice.

"You're terrible," she reprimanded, but she wasn't all serious. She liked the fact that he was attracted to her.

"Just put on a pair of shorts and a T-shirt and come down."

Kylie bit down on her lip. She looked at the computer screen, which displayed the list of the Dallas Brightens she hadn't called yet. Della and Miranda had been helping, but so far nothing.

"Please," Derek said.

His plea echoed in his voice and she felt herself giving in. On top of just wanting to make Derek happy, she remembered that she could read everyone's brain patterns and realized seeing everyone all together would be fun. She could compare one brain pattern to another.

"You had a rough day," Derek said. "You deserve some fun in the sun."

I've had a rough few months. "I'll be there in a few minutes."

"Really?" he asked, almost shocked that she'd given in. Didn't he know how much he meant to her?

"Really," she said, and smiled. The smile warmed Kylie inside and out. The memory of how he'd stood up for her even to her dad played in her mind. And that's when she knew that the next time Derek asked her to go out with him, she'd say yes.

It took her fifteen minutes to decide which pair of shorts and T-shirt to wear. She wanted to look good. Extra good. Maybe she and Derek could sneak off together and . . . and hopefully he would ask her to go out with him. Heck, maybe she might even ask him.

When she realized how much time had passed, she tore out the door. The shortest route to the swimming hole was through the woods, so she took it. The speed with which she moved shocked even her. Her foot-eye coordination of where to step and how to miss the trees flabbergasted her.

While speed and agility had never been something she longed for, she found herself feeling a sense of pride at her new talents. If only she knew from what species these new talents stemmed.

She was over halfway to the swimming hole when she felt it. Felt that sensation of being followed. The hair on the back of her neck stood up. And wouldn't you know that's when she recalled Burnett's warning about staying on the paths and out of the woods.

Listening, hoping to hear something other than the sound of feet pounding against the earth, she felt better when the normal sounds of the woods filled her ears. Whatever presence loomed close by wasn't so ominous that birds and insects stopped their songs.

Not that she should stake her life on the wisdom of the birds and insects. The feeling hit stronger . . . someone was here. What should she do?

Logic said for her to keep going; turning back would only put her farther away from the help of the others if trouble struck. Her mind went to the girls who'd been killed in town and amazingly, she found herself running even faster.

The clearing in the woods appeared in less than a minute. The bright sun hit her eyes and she could hear the other campers laughing and splashing in the water. When nothing attacked her, when no evil presence appeared wearing a bloody shirt and tried to yank her back into the woods, she wondered if this feeling of being watched wasn't all in her head. Could she be that paranoid?

She stopped in the clearing beside a tree and tried to catch her breath, feeling completely winded from her run. She almost had her breathing back to normal when she saw Derek coming toward her. He wore only a pair of swim trunks. His chest was bare and wet like the other night in the shower. The trunks were regular boy trunks, a little loose on him, even hung a little low on the waist, but they were wet so they molded against his form. Since she knew what he looked like without them, she found herself feeling breathless again.

"Hey," he said, and when his gaze fell to her mouth, she could tell he wanted to kiss her. He looked around and saw that they had an audience. So instead of kissing, he reached out and took her hand. "Come on, the water feels great."

It did feel great. And for the next hour, Kylie played water volleyball, splashed around, studied everyone's brain pattern, and completely forgot about the problems pressing on her shoulders. The only downside was watching Perry watch Miranda. She looked really good in her bathing suit and Kylie wasn't the only one who noticed, either. The guys were all stealing glances, even Derek, and then Perry would cut them glances, and not the friendly kind of glances either. His eyes would turn jet black, reminding Kylie of some kind of serpent.

Nevertheless, between the water and the laughter, Kylie hadn't had so much fun in . . . well, forever.

Then all the fun came to a jarring halt when she spotted Holiday running out of the woods in a panic and heading straight for the lake.

Her expression grew tighter with each hurried step. What was wrong? Holiday's gaze found Kylie's and suddenly she knew that whatever was wrong involved her.

Kylie started moving out of the water, but her toes sank into the mud at the lake's bottom the closer she got to shore. All the stresses in her life lined up like dominos in her mind, and she wondered which one this new problem involved.

Selynn appeared behind Holiday and her gaze shot to Kylie, as well. This wasn't going to be good.

Kylie met Holiday at the edge of the water and purposely ignored Selynn. "What's wrong?"

"We have a problem." Holiday's gaze shot back to the water and she waved someone else in. Kylie turned and saw Derek swimming in to join them.

"What is it?" Kylie asked again, still ignoring Selynn, who had moved in.

"You're coming with us," the werewolf spouted out. Her hand clamped down on Kylie's wrist. "Now."

Chapter Twenty-three

Kylie frowned and shook Selynn loose.

"I'm not going anywhere until you tell me what's going on." Kylie's gaze went back to Holiday who watched Derek step up on-shore. "Will somebody please tell me what is wrong?"

Holiday glanced back. The line of stress furrowing the camp leader's brow told Kylie this was serious. "It's your mom."

"My mom?" Kylie took a deep breath. Bits and pieces of her mom's conversation filled Kylie's mind. Then the ghost's warning echoed like a bad song in her head. *"You have to stop it. You have to stop it or someone you love will die."*

Oh, God, no.

"What's wrong with my mom?" The words barely spilled from her lips. She remembered her mom was flying home sometime to-day. Kylie's heart clutched as she envisioned a plane crash. Oh God, was her mom . . . ?

"She must have come to see you." Holiday said. "Late. For some reason, the new security alarm on the gate didn't work. And she got in without anyone knowing."

"She's here?" More than Kylie wanted air, she wanted to know her mom was alive and well. That her plane hadn't crashed. That some freak hadn't kidnapped her and was torturing her the way the dreams seemed to imply.

"Yes. She's here," Selynn said in her haughty tone. "Against school policy. Visiting hours were over hours ago."

Kylie's gaze went to Selynn. What was the she-wolf saying? Was her mom okay or not? Kylie looked back at Holiday.

"What happened?" Kylie repeated her question. "Is she okay?"

"She's . . . upset." Holiday's frown deepened. "She was trying to find your cabin and got turned around. She . . . she saw some things she shouldn't have."

"What?" Kylie remembered how stunned she'd been when she first saw Perry change into a unicorn. "What did she see?"

"She needs to be erased," Selynn snapped. "And quickly."

Erased? "What . . . is that supposed to mean?"

The she-wolf grabbed Kylie by the arm and started pulling her toward the woods.

Kylie put on the brakes.

"What does erase mean?" she asked again, not anywhere close to understanding, but miles from liking how it all sounded. She yanked her arm away from Selynn and then took a step closer, so close Kylie could count the woman's eyelashes.

"You better not lay a finger on my mother!" Kylie growled, and the sound of her voice seemed unnatural to her own ears. It was deeper. Coarser.

"Kylie, listen to me." Holiday's hand came down on Kylie's back, sending a surge of calm into her tense shoulders. Kylie might have listened, might have even accepted the calm emotion from Holiday if Selynn hadn't been there.

"We don't have time for this," Selynn snapped. She grabbed

Kylie by both arms, her fingers digging into Kylie's biceps hard enough to bruise. When Kylie tried to pull away again, Selynn tightened her hold.

"She's human," Selynn said. "She has to be dealt with. Now."

"Dealt with?" Fury, anger, and fear for her mother's safety threatened to overwhelm Kylie. "Damn you, where's my mother?" Kylie's voice sounded deeper than before.

"Stop it, Selynn!" Holiday said. "You're upsetting her. She doesn't understand what is going on."

"Yeah, stop it!" Derek's voice rang out.

Kylie felt Holiday's touch come against her shoulder again. The fairy attempted to fill Kylie with a peace-inducing emotion, to curb her fury, but Kylie somehow rejected the flow from moving inside her.

"Your mom is going to be okay," Holiday said, her voice seeming to echo from some other place. "She's at Helen's cabin right now. She—"

Once Kylie heard her mom's location, she again tried to pull away from Selynn's grip. But the she-wolf tightened her hold, her fingernails cutting into Kylie arms. Kylie recognized the pain, but it felt as if it was happening to someone else.

"Let go!" Kylie hissed in Selynn's face.

When the woman didn't release her. Kylie, acting on some instinct she didn't even recognize, grabbed the woman by her shirt and slung her out of the way.

Several gasps echoed around her. One might have even been from Kylie when she saw Selynn flying like a rag doll through the air before she landed in the water with a loud splash. The werewolf came up covered in mud and spitting mad. She roared and started swimming back to shore, and once on dry land, she locked gazes with Kylie, slung her head back, growled, and charged.

Holiday jumped in front of Kylie and held out her hand. "One step closer and I will summon the wrath of the death angels. And if you think I'm joking about that, you don't know me very well."

But Selynn didn't stop. She kept coming.

Then Derek and Della tackled her, sending the she-wolf tumbling to the ground with a grunt.

Kylie didn't stick around to hear or see what happened next. She took off through the woods, her blood pumping through her veins as she ran with everything she had to reach her mother.

As she moved with inhuman speed, she felt a blast of air pass by her and she spotted a blur of movement. The sudden silence of the woods told her it was vampire. Not that she cared.

She only wanted to reach her mother before anyone touched her. If anyone hurt one hair on her head . . .

Kylie heard her mother's screams right before she exited the woods near the path that led to Helen's cabin. Panic clawed at Kylie's chest like a wild animal seeking escape. She cut through the last of the trees, flew over the path, and arrived at Helen's porch.

Burnett, with a windblown Holiday at his side, stood there blocking the door. And Kylie knew Burnett had brought Holiday here.

"Let me out of here!" Her mom's scream reached Kylie's ears.

The rich berry scent that she now knew as blood filled her nose. She stared at Burnett. "Move!"

"Kylie." Holiday jumped in front of Burnett. "Listen to me, okay? Your mom is fine. She's very upset and we're going to have to calm her down."

"She's hurt." Kylie struggled to breathe and fought the desire to break through Burnett and the door to get to her mom.

"She's not hurt," Burnett insisted.

"I smell blood," Kylie seethed.

"That's not her blood," Burnett answered, his eyes turning a burnt orange color.

"I swear," Holiday said, and attempted to touch Kylie, but Kylie jumped back. Holiday lowered her hand. "Your mom isn't hurt, Kylie. I promise you. Please calm down. We're going to fix this. But we need your help."

"Trust them, Kylie," a voice said at the same time a familiar coldness invaded her breathing room.

Kylie turned to see Daniel standing next to her. "Trust them," he repeated.

Tears filled Kylie's eyes as Daniel wrapped her in his cold embrace. "It's okay." His icy breath came at her ear, as comforting warmth filled her chest.

An awesome sense of peacefulness flowed though her body. The same kind of peacefulness she'd felt at the falls. The kind that said things weren't as bad as she thought. The kind that said she should have faith.

She raised her head to look at Daniel, but he was gone. Feeling overwhelmed, her legs wobbled and she dropped to her knees on the porch.

Holiday crouched beside her. "She's going to be fine, Kylie. I promise."

Kylie looked at Holiday. "What . . . what did my mom see? Perry . . . ?"

"No." Holiday brushed Kylie's hair from her face. "I had given permission for Helen to donate a pint of blood to Jonathon. He was bleeding her, and against my rule he was . . ." Holiday paused and then firmly added, "He was drinking from the tube when your mom stepped in. I'm sure it looked really bad to her. She panicked."

Kylie dropped her face into her hands. "Oh, God." How the hell was she going to explain this to her mom?

"Jonathon was startled," Holiday continued. "He grabbed her and pushed her into Helen's bathroom, shoved the dresser against the door, and sent Helen after me. I got Burnett here as quickly as I could."

"I didn't hurt her," Jonathon said, stepping up on the porch. "I probably should have handled it differently, but I swear, I didn't hurt her. I'm sorry this happened."

Kylie looked at Jonathon. His shirt had stains of blood, Helen's blood, she told herself, not her mom's blood. Following him up the steps was Derek.

"Here's what we have to do," Burnett said. "It's called erasing."

"No," Kylie said, instantly being reminded of her emotions and her fight with Selynn.

"It's not a bad thing," Holiday said. "Erasing means that the memory is removed from her mind. It won't hurt her. But the calmer she is, the easier it is and the more successful it will be. And right now she's not calm. I think if you talk to her, you can calm her down."

"Talk to her? She saw someone drinking blood from an IV tube. What am I supposed to tell her that will calm her down?" Kylie asked. "Oh, don't worry, Mom, they're just vampires?"

Holiday looked Kylie right in the eyes. "She's worried about you now more than she's scared," Holiday assured her. "Just let her know you're fine and then Derek will come in—"

"Derek?" Kylie swung back to look at Derek. "Why Derek?" Something that looked like guilt clouded his eyes.

"We've recently discovered that Derek has the gift of erasing," Holiday said.

Derek nodded and for a fraction of second, Kylie wondered why Derek hadn't told her about his new gift. She thought they shared everything. Then her thoughts went back to her mom. "But if he's new at this, then . . . what if he messes up?"

"He won't mess up," Burnett said. "He's practiced on me numerous times."

Kylie looked back at Derek. She didn't know what all went into erasing someone's memory, but the idea scared her. "Don't you have someone with more experience?" Much to Derek's credit, he didn't appear offended by her request.

"He's on another case right now," Burnett said. "And the sooner we take care of this, the better it is. If we wait too long, he might have to remove more data from her mind. It could require he remove hours before what happened. Obviously, the less memory time that we have to remove the better."

"Is it at all dangerous?" Kylie looked at Holiday for the answer.

Holiday shook her head. "When it's done soon enough, the biggest side effect is a headache and confusion at the loss of time."

Kylie looked back at Derek. "Promise me you won't mess this up."

"I won't," he said. But was that doubt in his voice?

"What do you have to do?" Kylie asked.

"Just touch her," he answered.

Kylie nodded. She remembered Daniel's assurance that she should trust them, and she stood up. "Okay. I guess." Then she heard her mom start screaming again. She looked at Burnett. "Nothing better go wrong."

"Mom," Kylie called to her mom five minutes later from behind the large dresser that Jonathon had moved in front of the door.

"Kylie?" her mom screamed. "Oh, baby, are you okay? Tell me you're not hurt. Tell me these crazy people—"

"I'm fine. I'm going to get you out, okay?"

"Hurry, baby," her mom said. The rawness in her mother's voice told Kylie her mom had been screaming and crying for way too long. "We've got to get out of here. There are some very bad people here."

"It's okay, Mom," Kylie said.

"Hurry, baby. Hurry before they come back."

Burnett motioned that he planned to move the dresser and then leave. Derek nodded. Then Burnett, with one hand, pushed the heavy piece of furniture out the way and, in a flash, was gone.

Her mom yanked open the door and flew out, wrapping her arms protectively around Kylie. "We gotta get out of here!" She spotted Derek and pushed Kylie behind her. "Stay away," her mom yelled.

Derek looked at Kylie as if he was unsure how to proceed.

"It's okay, Mom." Kylie's heart broke when she saw her mom's tear-streaked face. "This is Derek. He's a nice guy."

"I don't trust him," her mom said. "We can't trust anyone here. I just want us to leave. Now." Clutching Kylie's arm, she started moving toward the door, keeping herself between Derek and Kylie as if in protection.

Unsure what to do, Kylie stopped moving. She couldn't let her mom walk outside. If her mom was freaking out with just Derek, she would surely lose it if she saw Jonathon and Burnett.

"Mom, Derek is a good guy. He's going to help us leave," she lied. "Aren't you, Derek?" Kylie looked at him.

"Yes . . . Mrs. Galen. I'm going to help you and Kylie get away."

Her mom looked at Derek and back at Kylie. Panic shone in her eyes, but she didn't jump back when Derek took a step closer.

"Let me get the door," Derek said. He moved in and when he did, he reached out and touched her mom's arm.

Kylie hadn't known what to expect when a person's memory was erased, but when her mom's eyes rolled back in her head and she collapsed in a dead heap on the floor, Kylie screamed.

Shaking, and still in mid-scream, she dropped down beside her mom to make sure she was still breathing.

"It's okay." Derek dropped beside Kylie and touched Kylie's elbow. "She's just unconscious. I promise, Kylie," he said, as if reading her fear.

Burnett appeared and scooped her mom up in his arms. "I'm putting her in her car. You come with me," he said to Kylie. "We'll need you there when she wakes up."

His gaze held Kylie's for a second. "It's all going to be okay," he told her. "Follow me. It's almost over now."

Burnett disappeared. Kylie took off, too. She wasn't anywhere near as fast as he was, but with luck, and considering he had her mother in his arms, he could bet she wouldn't be far behind him.

"Mom, you okay?" Kylie tapped on her mom's car window only five minutes later.

When her mother didn't instantly wake up, it took everything Kylie had not to yank open the door to see if she needed CPR. But Burnett's list of don'ts still echoed in her head.

- Don't show panic, because she might pick up on it and it will make her even more nervous.
- Don't try to explain too much; let her come up with her own conclusions of what happened.
- Don't start crying for no reason.

And as he'd said that one, he'd pointed to Kylie's tears.

It was the "crying for no reason" part of number three that Kylie would have argued about if she hadn't been so damn worried about her mom.

Kylie tapped again on the window. "Mom?" She fought to keep her voice calm.

The way Kylie saw it, she deserved to go on a crying jag that lasted for a good two weeks. The emotional trauma she'd endured this last half hour would go down as one of the top worst half hours of her life. Even the fight at the wildlife preserve hadn't kicked her in the gut so hard.

She glanced down at her arms, expecting to see bruises and nail marks from where Selynn had grabbed her. Oddly enough, her skin was smooth and unmarked. Weird. Had she just acquired a new quick healing gift, too?

Her mom's eyes fluttered open and Kylie refocused on the situation before her. Her mom sat up and looked around, obviously startled. Kylie's first thought was that the erasure hadn't worked.

Then her mom turned her head and her confused eyes met Kylie's.

Kylie plastered a smile on her lips, hoping to appear as if everything in the world was just peachy. "When did you get here, Mom?"

Her mom's brow creased and she raised her wrist to see her watch and then opened the door. She turned and put her feet on the pavement, but didn't climb out of the car. "I . . ." She blinked. "I rushed over here from the airport." She ran a hand through her dark hair, which now had highlights of red running through it.

"You must have fallen asleep after you got here." Kylie bit her lip, realizing she'd broken one of Burnett's rules.

"Yeah." Her mom pressed a hand to her temple, a sure sign of the headache Holiday had said might come. "I was up all night at the airport hoping to get a flight on standby."

"You must be really tired," Kylie offered.

"Yeah. Gosh." She looked back at her watch and then stood from the car seat. "I hardly even remember arriving here. I must have parked and zonked out. Which is a good lesson for both of us. Don't drive while under the influence of exhaustion." Her mom reached over and gave Kylie a hug. "It feels so good to see you."

Damn it, if Kylie didn't feel herself breaking another rule. Tears filled her eyes and she hugged her mom really hard. Ahh, but her tears weren't just because of the last thirty minutes. No, they were because of Kylie's last sixteen years and the rarity of hugs from her mom. And because it brought to mind the hug she'd given her dad . . . stepdad, before he'd left a few hours ago.

When her mom pulled back, she looked at Kylie. "Are you okay?"

"Yeah." Kylie batted at her tears. "It's just . . . you don't hug me a whole lot."

"Something I guess we need to work on, huh?" her mom said, and touched her temple again.

"Yeah, we need to work on that," Kylie said. "But we're off to a good start." And they were. Kylie could feel it.

Her mom looked at her watch again. "I must have slept for an hour."

"You probably needed it," Kylie said, and started walking back through the gates.

"Yeah. I was going to call and let your camp leader know I was going to be here a little late. I remember what a big deal they made over visiting hours, but wouldn't you know it that my battery died in my phone. It's completely dead."

"Yeah. Luckily I walked by and saw your car and told Holiday you were here. But they are very strict about visiting hours." *Please God, don't let me have to go through this again.*

"Which I think is silly," her mom said. "It's like they are trying to hide something."

"Nope." Kylie lied through her teeth and almost felt bad doing it. "Not trying to hide anything." Except things like: people drinking blood, changing into any kind of creature imaginable like super-size bears or unicorns or wolves. Or girls who accidentally turn kittens into skunks. In other words, the usual stuff that happened at Shadow Falls.

"But they're still strict," Kylie said. "They say it's for our safety. Besides, you know, like you used to tell me. Rules are rules."

"I know and I'll try to follow the rules from now on."

Thank you, Jeezus! "Would you like to go sit in the dining hall?" Kylie asked.

"Or your cabin," her mom said.

"Sure." And then Kylie remembered Socks—her little skunk. "Uhh, I forgot that . . . Della and Miranda invited a few girls over. The dining hall might work better."

"That's fine," her mom said. "Maybe I could grab something to drink so I could swallow a couple of aspirins. My head is pounding like I'm going to have an aneurysm."

An icy coldness suddenly settled around Kylie again. For a moment, she thought the ghost was back.

She looked at her mom. "Don't say that."

"Don't say what?" she asked.

"The aneurysm crap." It had been one of the many unsaid possibilities Kylie had considered happening with someone messing with your mind, and erasing your memories, and it still freaked her out.

Her mom smiled. "I'm just being a drama queen. I'm fine."

"Good," Kylie said. And when she looked at her mom, she recalled how frightened she'd been that she might never see her again. Another wash of emotion filled her chest. Kylie almost reached out to steal another hug. She didn't. Not just because it might make her mom suspicious, but because where her mom was concerned, she'd probably handed out her quota of hugs for the month.

Amazingly, thirty minutes later, they hadn't run out of things to talk about. Of course, they'd talked a good fifteen minutes about her mom's new makeover. All of which Kylie admitted liking. Sure, Kylie was still a little hesitant about the thought of her mom dating, but Kylie decided to cross that bridge when she came to it.

Then her mom noticed Kylie's "growth spurt."

"Tell me that's one of those Wonderbras making you look so big."

"'Fraid not," Kylie said. "I'm a growing girl."

That conversation led to her mom asking about Kylie's shopping trip. But Kylie didn't want to talk about shopping, or anything that occurred during her recent trip downtown. So she told her mom that her dad had come to visit. They talked a good five minutes about him. Kylie hadn't given any details about the embarrassing scene she'd caused. She'd never even told her mom that she'd seen her dad in town.

She also opted out of telling her mom that her dad had broken up with his little girlfriend. For some reason, she didn't want to remind her mom about that.

"I'm glad you two talked," her mom said. "No matter what mistakes he's made recently, he is a good father."

"Yeah," Kylie agreed.

Then Kylie spent another five minutes telling her how much

she loved camp and her interest in the cake decorating class, all prep work for getting a commitment from her mom about signing her up for the boarding school in the fall. Not that she planned to ask about it today. Face it, whether her mom remembered it or not, she'd had a pretty lousy day.

"Seriously, you really enjoy decorating cakes?" her mom asked. "I do, too. Do you remember that I took that class when you were younger and made you the Cinderella cake?"

"Yeah," Kylie said. "I loved it." Another big freaking lie. She'd been fourteen and embarrassed out of her mind when her mom had served a fairy-tale cake at her soccer meet, but hey, what did one more little white lie count compared to the others she'd told today?

Lies aside, this whole new direction in their relationship was really going well. So well, Kylie decided to chance asking for more info about her real dad.

Picking up her soda, Kylie twirled the can in her hand. "Mom, can you tell me a bit more about Daniel?"

Her mom's eyes widened. "Sure. I guess. But I think I pretty much covered everything the last time you asked."

"You hardly told me anything. Like . . . where were his parents from?"

She smiled. "I remember him telling me that they were originally from Ireland."

"They're Irish?" Kylie asked, not sure it would help, but not sure it wouldn't. "When did they come to America?"

"I don't know."

"Was Daniel born in the States?"

"I'm guessing he was. He didn't have an accent."

"But you don't know for sure, right?" Her hope started to wane. If he was adopted in Ireland, wouldn't that make it almost impossible to trace him?

"I think he would have told me if he was born somewhere else."

Kylie nodded. "You said his parents were in Dallas, right?"

"Close to Dallas. You know, somewhere up there."

"Where?" Kylie couldn't believe she'd spent this last two weeks calling Dallas numbers only to learn they didn't even live there.

"I can't remember." Her mom studied Kylie. "You're not thinking of trying to find them, are you?"

Okay, decision time. Kylie had told the PI that she would eventually tell her mom about her quest. Maybe this was showtime. "Would it upset you if I was?" Kylie asked, not wanting to add any more stress to her mom's day.

Her mom frowned. "I . . . I just . . . We don't even know if they're still alive."

"They could be," Kylie said, and couldn't tell her mom that her real interest was in finding them so they might be able to lead her to Daniel's real parents. Soon, her mom might find that out, but one thing at a time. Besides, she didn't have a clue as to how she could explain that she knew Daniel was adopted. Well, not a clue without going through the whole ghost thing, and that was totally a conversation she didn't want to have with her mom.

"Seriously, would you mind if I tried to find them?"

Her mom let go of a deep breath. "I don't mind, Kylie. I guess I'm just worried they will be very angry at me if you did. There have been so many times that I felt guilty for not letting them know about you." There was something in her mom's voice that drew Kylie's attention.

She suddenly realized if her mom felt guilty about not telling them, then she had to know where they were.

"Do you know where they are, Mom? Do you know how I could find them?"

Chapter Twenty-four

Her mom looked down. "I . . ."

"Please, Mom," Kylie said. "Please. If you know anything, tell me."

Her mom seemed preoccupied with her soda as if fascinated by the condensation running down the can. "I couldn't bring myself to throw away his obituary," she said finally. "I put it in the back of the frame of your baby picture hanging on the wall. It has their names and the town they lived in."

Hope flared anew in Kylie's chest. "When you get home, can you scan and e-mail it to me? Please."

Her mom nodded. "If they are still alive, they are going to hate me."

"I don't think so, Mom. They'll probably just be happy to meet me now."

Her mom touched Kylie's cheek. "I'm sorry, baby. I did what I thought was best at the time, but now . . . it looks as if I didn't make the best decisions."

"You did fine," Kylie said. And without thinking, she gave her non-hugging mom another hug.

. . .

An hour later, Kylie watched her mom's car move down the road until it was a tiny blue dot that finally faded from view. Both Burnett and Holiday were waiting on her at the gated entrance when she returned.

"I think my mom is going to be fine," she told them, assuming that's why they were there.

Then she realized Burnett had probably been listening to their conversation the whole time. That's when she got a feeling they weren't here just about her mom.

"Am I in trouble for fighting with Selynn?" she asked. The thought had crossed her mind during her conversation with her mom. Like it or not, Selynn was FRU.

Holiday shook her head. "No. Selynn deserved what she got. She handled the situation all wrong. Terribly wrong."

Holiday glanced up at Burnett as if she was saying this to him as much as to Kylie. "If anyone says one thing about what went down out at the swimming hole, I'll be the first to tell them how the cow ate the cabbage."

When Kylie was about to ask Holiday what she meant about the cows and the cabbage, Burnett shrugged. "I don't think anyone will be saying anything," he said, humor dancing in his eyes. "I never have understood that saying. How does a cow eating cabbage translate into giving someone hell for something?"

"I have no idea." Holiday looked back at Kylie. Burnett's gaze followed Holiday's, and they both returned to that weird kind of staring. And Kylie went back to wondering what the heck was going on.

"If it's not Selynn, then what is it?" Kylie asked.

Burnett stuck his hands into his jeans pockets. "I think we just wanted to make sure you're okay."

She started to answer him, but realized they both were staring at her again. "If that's all, why are you two gawking at me as if I'm about to grow a tail?"

"Do you think you might grow a tail?" Concern filled his voice.

Oh, shit! He was serious.

Kylie swiped her hand over her butt to make sure nothing had suddenly appeared. When nothing was there, she frowned at them. "What is it that you're not telling me?"

"You showcased some new talents today," Burnett said.

"You mean running fast?" Kylie asked.

"And taking on Selynn," Holiday said. "A were this close to a full moon is . . . pretty hard to take on."

"So you're back to thinking I'm a werewolf now?"

Holiday glanced at Burnett and then they both looked back at Kylie.

"We're still not sure." He started studying Kylie anew.

"What is it?" she demanded.

"It's your brain pattern," Holiday said, her tone making it sound like a confession.

"What about it?" She touched her forehead. "Have I opened up? Can you tell what I am?"

"No," Holiday said. "It's just . . . your pattern is shifting."

"Shifting? You mean, it's changing?"

Burnett and Holiday both nodded.

"What does that mean?" Kylie asked.

Holiday's expression went from curiosity to sympathy in a flash. "It's just . . ."

"Surmising, I know. Just tell me." She motioned with her hands for the camp leader to hurry up.

"The only brain pattern that shifts and changes is a shape-shifter," Holiday said.

"So, you now think I'm a shape-shifter?" Kylie tried to wrap her head around being a shape-shifter. Turning into giant lions and . . .

"It's not changing like a shape-shifter," Burnett corrected. "A shape-shifter only changes when they change forms."

Kylie looked down at her chest and lower, almost to make sure she hadn't morphed into anything, and to make sure her boobs hadn't taken on another cup size. Then she gave her butt another swipe, praying again that she hadn't grown a tail. "I'm not changing."

"We know," Burnett said.

Then, as if sensing Kylie had about had her quota of crap for the day, Holiday came over and dropped an arm around her. "Come on, why don't we take a walk to the falls?"

Kylie nodded. She'd been thinking about going back to the cabin and having a good long cry, but a trip to the falls sounded even better.

"I'll come with you," Burnett said.

"I think we'll go alone," Holiday replied.

"I don't think you two should be that deep in the woods alone," he countered. "We still don't know why the security gate wasn't working."

"I don't think we're exactly vulnerable." Holiday nodded her head to Kylie.

"I would feel better if I went with you." He frowned. "You won't even know I'm there. I'll stay at a distance."

Holiday rolled her eyes, as if to say "whatever," then she guided Kylie to turn around and they started walking toward the trail that led near the falls. "I might be happy with a fifty-mile distance."

"When are you going to remember I can hear you?" Burnett said from about fifteen feet back.

"When did you ever think I forgot?" she countered in a low voice.

. . .

Monday morning Kylie woke up to the chill of the ghost. She opened her eyes, but the spirit hadn't materialized yet. "You do know just coming here and waking me up isn't going to help me, don't you? You need to give me something, find a way to show me who it is I need to help."

No answer came back and Kylie pulled the covers over her chin and just stared at her breath making little clouds of mist rising above her nose. The visit to the falls with Holiday had been both amazing and amazingly disheartening. She and Holiday hadn't even talked; they just sat beside each other, staring at the wall of water cascading down in front of them. The same ambience Kylie had found existed there last time seemed even stronger this visit. That was the amazing part.

And the amazingly disheartening part? The message she took away from the visit wasn't so much everything was going to be fine. Nope. It was more like: stay focused and keep the faith.

And if Kylie had thought she could argue with the presence at the falls, she would have looked up at the rock ceiling and roared, "Really? That's all you're going to give me?"

Honestly, how was she supposed to stay focused when she didn't know what to focus on? Sort of hard to focus on ghosts when they wouldn't even appear, wasn't it?

The temperature dropped another few degrees.

"Yeah, I'm talking about you," Kylie said aloud to the spirit.

Keeping the faith was almost equally impossible. Having faith meant believing nothing bad was going to happen. Didn't two girls being killed by a rogue vampire qualify as bad? Who could consider having your mom's memory erased to be a good thing? Add her changing brain pattern that had everyone staring at her as if she were a freak—and let's not forget her uncontrollable desire to barge into people's dreams—and, well, her faith could use a pack of steroids to build it back up again.

Kylie let go of a big gasp of frustration when the cold of the spirit started to fade. Great! Just another day of being shocked awake at dawn with nothing to show for it. Rolling over, she punched her pillow and felt her mood grow darker by the second.

Oh, it wasn't just a general Monday blues kind of mood, either. Nope, this was more. Tonight was the full moon. Who knew what was going to happen? But the fact she'd awoken in such a piss-poor mood was even more of a sign that she might be werewolf.

Not that morphing into a wolf was the only bad-mood trigger. After finally making up her mind to say yes to going out with Derek, she hadn't had a chance to get him alone and give him her answer. There was also the particular werewolf coming back to the camp today or tomorrow. Make that two weres coming back. She wasn't exactly looking forward to getting reacquainted with Fredericka. And facing Lucas after the whole dream fiasco? Oh yeah, that was going to be so much fun. Not!

Kylie let out a groan, punched her pillow, and pulled the covers over her head.

Five minutes after Kylie was up, and two minutes after checking and realizing her mom still hadn't sent her the scan of Daniel's obituary, Kylie managed to piss off both Della and Miranda. After they both managed to piss her off. So Kylie made up her mind— she was taking a day off. A complete day off from people. And that included all the supernatural varieties, too.

Today, it was just her and her skunk.

Snatching a bottle of soda from the fridge, she scooped up Socks, told her roommates to tell Holiday she was taking a vacation day, and went back into her bedroom where she slammed the door just because she felt like it.

At nine o'clock, Holiday tapped at her bedroom door. "Just checking on you."

"I just want to be alone," Kylie said, hearing the door open, but not moving from the facedown position she'd landed on her bed an hour ago.

"Bad mood?" There was a bunch of meaning to Holiday's question that Kylie didn't want to think about.

"Yeah, a real piss-poor bad mood." Kylie rolled over.

"Okay." Holiday bit down on her lip. "Just remember, I'm here if you need me."

"I know," Kylie said.

At ten o'clock, there was another knock. This time, the knock sounded at her cabin front door.

"Go away," she yelled out.

A minute later, Derek walked into her bedroom without being invited. That pissed her off even more. Then, she remembered something else that had pissed her off that she hadn't spoken with him about yet.

"Why didn't you tell me about the whole erasing thing?" she blurted out.

He dropped down on her bed. "Burnett kind of said I shouldn't tell everyone."

"Am I everyone?" she asked, and sat up, pulling her knees to her chest.

Whether it was her tone, her question, or if her mood was contagious, she didn't know, but she recognized pissed off when she saw it. And Derek was pissed off. "Maybe if you'd been more accessible to me, instead of worrying that someone might figure out you liked me, we could have spent more time talking."

"I think I've apologized for that." She hugged her shins. "Not that it means you've forgiven me," she said with a touch of sarcasm.

He shook his head. "Okay fine, so maybe I don't have a right to be mad about *that*."

His inflection on the word *that* led to her next question. "But you're mad about something, right?"

He frowned. "I shouldn't be." He ran a hand through his hair and looked at her. The deep emotional hurt that Kylie saw in his eyes chased away her own bad mood and she started to worry about him.

"What is it that you shouldn't be mad about?"

He stood up from the bed and paced across the room. "You never lied to me. Not really. And I could see you still had feelings for him. You'd feel guilty and I knew you were probably thinking about him. I knew it, because I felt it. Yet like an idiot, I kept on pursuing you, even when you refused to go out with me."

She shook her head. "You're not making sense."

He stopped walking and let go of a deep breath. Then his beautiful, warm, and still-hurting eyes met her gaze again. "I can only be mad at myself."

"For what?" she asked again, her bad mood trying to move back in.

"But what I can't get over is that you didn't tell me."

"What didn't I tell you?" She felt confused and yet . . . not really. She sensed he was talking about Lucas. Not that it really mattered, because she and Lucas were history. She'd made up her mind.

Yeah, there were the dreams. And she felt the guilt creep around her again.

He waved a hand in the air. "You see, this is how you feel half the time I'm with you. Guilty." He shook his head. "Tell me it's not true. Tell me that you haven't been getting letters from him this whole time."

His question bounced around her head. "I . . . I never wrote him back." She wanted to assure Derek that she hadn't done anything wrong. But the truth hit and it hung on like a big mean dog to a bone he considered his own. If he'd been getting letters from some girl who'd kissed him, she would have been jealous. She wouldn't have liked it. Certainly not if he'd been having sexy dreams about her, too.

"Derek," she said softly, "I swear to God, I didn't mean—"

"To hurt me," he finished her sentence. "I believe you. I know you didn't do this to hurt me. You aren't cruel or mean. You don't have a devious bone in your body. You're just . . . confused."

She stood and walked over to him and tried to take his hand in hers, but he pulled away. His withdrawal hurt. Meeting his eyes, she tried to find a way to explain it. "You're right. I'm confused about a lot of stuff. But I'm not confused about what I feel about you. I care about you. A lot. When I'm with you, I feel safe and when you kiss me I feel everything. Everything looks so beautiful and . . . and I don't even care if you're doing it anymore. I just want that feeling, okay? I want to go out with you."

"If you'd really wanted that, you'd have said something earlier."

"I did want to, I was . . . just confused. Like you said."

"Because of Lucas?"

"No." She offered him the answer she'd offered herself. "Because I'm still trying to figure out what I am."

"But I told you that what you are isn't important."

"It is to me," she said. But deep down, deeper than she wanted to look, she knew what he said was true. Not knowing what she was, was only part of the reason she hadn't agreed to go out with him earlier. The other part was Lucas.

But that didn't change how she felt about Derek, she insisted to herself. It was just like Holiday's aunt Stella. She might feel an attraction for Lucas, but she wouldn't act on it. She tried again to take his hand, but he wouldn't let her.

"You have to decide, Kylie, because I can't stand living in this limbo. I have too much limbo in my life with my father and I just can't deal with it anymore."

"I've already decided," she said. "It's you. I was going to tell you yesterday and then . . . everything happened."

He stepped closer and her heart sighed with relief. She leaned in for a kiss. She wanted him to kiss her so badly; she wanted to make him see how much she cared about him.

He touched her cheek. "Until you're sure about what you feel about him, then you can't trust how you feel about me."

"That's not true." She tried to kiss him, but he put a finger over her lips, stopping her.

"No. No more. Until you've made up your mind, we're just friends. Just friends." Pain and hurt echoed in his voice and took a flying leap, landing right in her heart.

She didn't want to just be his friend. She wanted more. "Please don't do this, Derek. I never meant—"

He put his finger over her lips again. "I know you didn't mean to hurt me, Kylie. But it does hurt. I feel . . . everything. That's what makes this so hard." He took a step back. "I'd better go."

Pain welled up inside her. Tears filled her eyes. She was going to lose him. She knew it as well as she knew her own name.

He got to her bedroom door and turned back. "As your friend, I'm telling you this. Fredericka is back. She wants to hurt you. And

I don't think she'll stop with just telling me about the letters. Be careful. Especially until after tonight. Weres are hyper-aggressive before they turn."

Kylie felt her own aggression boil up inside her and she swiped at the tears sliding down her face. Until he mentioned it, she hadn't stopped to guess how he knew about the letters Lucas had sent her. And now that she knew, she didn't like it one iota. Fredericka had told Derek about the letters.

And in doing so, she hadn't just hurt Kylie, she'd also hurt Derek.

Kylie closed her hand into a fist. "Don't worry," she said. "I'm not as helpless as I used to be."

"Helpless, no," he said. "But she's got meanness on you hands down. You don't want to tangle with her."

An hour later, heart still breaking, Kylie checked her e-mail and found her mother had finally sent her the scan of Daniel's obituary. Maybe her emotions were already primed and ready to go because of her already sucky day, but when she read about her father's death, Kylie dropped her head on the desk and wept. She wept for Derek and she wept for Daniel.

She recalled the dream/vision she'd had about his death. He'd been leaving a war-torn village and had returned to save a woman from some insurgents. He had not only given his life for his country, he had given it to save a stranger.

"I love you, Daniel." She wished he would drop in for a visit.

She noted his parents' names and that they lived in some place called Gladlock, Texas. A search on the Internet showed it was a small city about seventy-five miles outside of Dallas. With her heart still hurting, she did a search for a phone number for

Kent B. Brighten. The computer hadn't completed the search when the door to the cabin swung open.

Kylie glanced up, expecting to see Miranda or Della. But nope. Fredericka had come a'calling. And she'd bypassed the proper etiquette of knocking before entering, too.

Chapter Twenty-five

"Well, if it isn't the ghost girl." Fredericka's smartass tone hit Kylie the wrong way.

"She's got meanness on you hands down. You don't want to tangle with her." Derek's words rang in Kylie's head.

Okay, so Derek was right. She didn't want to tangle with Fredericka, but Kylie wasn't sure she had an option now considering the werewolf stood less than six feet away. Kylie had no way out. Too late to run and hide under the bed.

Kylie stood, staring at the girl's dark eyes and hoping the she-wolf wouldn't see Kylie's streak of insecurity.

Yesterday with Selynn, Kylie hadn't felt fear. Nope. She'd been acting on instinct to protect her mother. Now the only one needing protection was Kylie herself; the kick-ass instinct had a taken mini-vacation.

"Gosh, I didn't hear you knock." Kylie tried to imitate Fredericka's curt tone and defensive posture, hoping to bluff her way through this.

The glimmer of a smile danced over Fredericka's lips as if Kylie's bluff had fallen short.

"I thought it best if we got this little talk over with." Fredericka glanced around the cabin as if taking in the furnishings. Not that it was much to look at or different from the other cabins. The over-stuffed brown sofa was paired with an overstuffed gold chair that almost matched. Kylie's mom had brought her a few throw pillows that added splashes of color to the room. The end tables had utilitarian lamps with plain white shades, and Miranda had added a few crystals around the room.

Behind Fredericka, Kylie saw Socks freeze in a panic at seeing a stranger in the cabin, and the skunk unfroze long enough to bury himself under a red and gold sofa pillow.

Kylie didn't blame him, either.

"What talk is that?" she asked. "The one where I explain it's rude to walk into someone's home without knocking?" Her snarky comment might set Fredericka off, but Kylie sensed this was a test, and to show fear felt more dangerous than provoking the she-wolf.

Fredericka released a low growl, and her eyes brightened. When her uninvited guest's gaze shifted up and down Kylie's stance, it took everything Kylie had not to crawl under the pillow with Socks.

Fredericka's brows twitched. Kylie, never prouder of her new talent, twitched back. The she-wolf's pattern looked much like those of the other weres she'd noted at the river yesterday, but the darkened edges appeared ominous. Did that mean anything? Kylie really needed to sign up for Brain Pattern Reading 101.

"I hear you might be one of my own kind." Fredericka's eyes tightened.

The idea of sharing a bloodline with this bully made Kylie feel sick. Her gaze went back to the trembling pillow on the sofa. She recalled what Holiday had said about her not being were because felines had an abhorrence of werewolves. Kylie hoped Holiday was right about that. Even drinking blood for the rest of her life felt like a better option than bring a were.

Kylie held her defensive stance. "I wouldn't believe everything you hear."

"And if I were you, I wouldn't forget that if you do turn, we'll likely meet. And on full moons the emotions are always generally out of control, resulting in high casualty rates."

"Then I'm sure you will be watching your back," Kylie said, really bluffing now.

Fredericka's brows pinched. "Especially when a female feels another is making advances toward her mate."

"So, you still having a hard time holding on to your man?" Kylie fought back her fear.

The gold in Fredericka's eyes grew brighter. "What's that smell?" Fredericka held her nose up in the air.

Kylie didn't dare glance at the pillow hiding Socks. "Wouldn't know, but if it's offensive, the door is right behind you."

"It smells sort of like . . . I don't know, lion, maybe?" Fredericka's left eyebrow arched.

Kylie didn't blink. "I knew you did it."

"Did what?" Fredericka's smile turned into more of a smirk. Then she shifted back a couple of steps and dropped down on the sofa with an exaggerated plop, as if she planned on hanging around a while.

The sound of the sofa giving up air was quickly followed by a half-hiss and half-meow. The pillow fell away and a black and white tail sprang up into the air. Fredericka turned just in time to take the full spray directly in the face.

Twenty feet away, the stench had Kylie covering her nose, but she couldn't stop smiling.

The she-wolf screamed and dove at the animal. While Socks had gotten in touch with his skunk side, he obviously hadn't forgotten his feline roots. He flew off the sofa in full frightened-cat mode. His ascent into midair sent the lamp on the end table crashing to the floor.

Wiping her eyes with her palms and howling, Fredericka shot off the sofa after Socks. Socks, now perched on top of the overstuffed chair, reacted accordingly and flew in midair, bouncing off the walls as he ran for his life.

The thought of what the she-wolf would do to her kitten had Kylie giving chase. Wooden chairs cracked against the floor, the microwave flew across the room, the computer desk nearly fell over, and a few dishes left on the counter shattered beside the chairs. Everything spun in circles with one kitten-turned-skunk, one she-wolf, and one unidentifiable supernatural chasing each other around the living room/kitchen, each with their own agenda.

Socks to live.

Fredericka to kill.

Kylie to protect.

Unfortunately, Socks was no match for the angry she-wolf, and in seconds Fredericka had Socks cornered by the refrigerator. A loud roar filled the cabin. A wash of adrenaline shot through Kylie as Fredericka dove for the poor animal.

Just before Fredericka latched her paws on to Socks, Kylie latched on to the girl's forearms. Picking her up in the air, she hauled the struggling Fredericka over to the front door and tossed her out.

She landed about eight feet from the porch with a loud thud. Her eyes, now a bright gold, stared up in horror at Kylie. The she-wolf rose off the ground on all fours, her knees bent, shifting back and forth, as if revving up to pounce again.

Kylie didn't flinch.

She breathed in.

She breathed out.

She welcomed another round.

"You bitch!" Fredericka growled, and tossed her head back.

"You hurt my cat and you'll see how big of a bitch I can be!" Kylie voice sounded as animal-like as the she-wolf's. Then, suddenly frightened, not of Fredericka, but at what Kylie would do if the girl came at her again, she stepped back and slammed the front door. The whole cabin shook from the impact. And right then a cold presence filled the room.

Company.

Great. The cabin smelled of skunk, she had a majorly pissed-off she-wolf outside, and *now* the spirit wanted to drop by.

Five minutes later, Kylie still stood with her back to the refrigerator, breathing through her mouth so she wouldn't gag at the pungent odor, and trying to calm herself and a very scared skunk-kitten. Socks, seconds after Kylie had come inside, had climbed up her leg, cuddled into her arms, and buried its little pointed nose in her armpit. Kylie wondered if the nose in the armpit wasn't so much his need to escape the smell as it was to hide.

The ghost paced the tiny living room as though she was trying to think. Kylie watched the spirit walk in circles before realizing the ghost's wardrobe.

"Why are you wearing a hospital gown?" Kylie asked, but the spirit didn't answer. And when the ghost faded, relief flowed over Kylie. She closed her eyes and tried to recall the calm she'd gathered at the falls about the whole "Someone you love is dying" situation.

Then the door to the cabin swung open. Thinking it could be Fredericka again, Kylie tensed and then un-tensed when she saw Holiday and Miranda.

"Are you okay?" Holiday asked.

Kylie nodded and Socks, hearing more commotion, snuggled

tighter into Kylie's armpit. Miranda and Holiday both covered their noses and their wide-eyed gazes moved around the ransacked cabin.

"What happened?" Holiday asked.

Fredericka happened, Kylie almost answered, but then bit back the words. She'd never been much of a tattler and didn't want to start now. "Socks got startled." It wasn't altogether a lie.

Holiday, her hand still plastered over her nose, squinted at Kylie. "I know Fredericka was here." Her voice came out muffled behind her palm.

"She told you?" Kylie asked.

"Didn't have to," Miranda piped in. "We smelled her when she walked past the office."

"What happened?" Holiday repeated her question from behind her fingers.

Miranda took a step closer. "She was spitting mad," Miranda broke in again, humor in her voice. "Seriously spitting. Did Socks get her in the face?" The witch laughed and wrinkled her nose at the smell again and waved her hands around the air as if to perform a bit of magic.

Kylie's next intake of air didn't include the skunk stench. "Thanks," she said to Miranda, surprised that her roommate had removed the smell without any goofs.

"Welcome," Miranda said with a sense of pride. "Odor removal is a piece of cake. Learned in the potty-training stage."

Holiday dropped her hand. "Miranda, can I have a minute alone with Kylie?"

Miranda rolled her eyes. "Why is it that everyone is always sending me away?" She stomped off into her bedroom, but flashed Kylie a smile before shutting the door.

Holiday met Kylie's gaze. "Now, what happened?"

Fredericka just stopped by to remind me that she tried to kill me once by putting a lion in my room and once might not be enough for her.

When Kylie didn't answer, Holiday studied Kylie suspiciously. "My job here is to show everyone that we can all get along without incident." She sighed. "I agreed to her coming back because . . . I know she doesn't have anywhere else to go. I'm afraid she'd be pulled into a gang, but if she's starting trouble, Kylie, I'll show her the gate."

Kylie knew Holiday meant what she said and she appreciated her loyalty to no end. While the temptation to tell the truth bubbled up inside Kylie, her own sense of loyalty bit down. She knew how important it was to Holiday to save every one of her campers from the dark side of the supernatural world. Even Fredericka.

Kylie wasn't sure the she-wolf was worth saving or even if she was salvageable. But Kylie didn't want to be the one to make that call. Besides, she didn't want Holiday having to solve Kylie's problems. She got a mental image of how she'd managed to toss Fredericka out the door. Maybe, just maybe she was capable of taking care of herself.

Giving the still-scared Socks a good scratch behind his ears, Kylie said, "It's not a big deal. Socks didn't like Fredericka and Fredericka didn't like Socks. No one was hurt." *Yet,* a little voice echoed inside Kylie, but she ignored it. "I'm sure we can work it out."

When Kylie looked up, she spotted Della standing behind the camp leader in the doorway mouthing the word "Liar."

Holiday looked at Della and then faced Kylie again. "You're sure?"

Kylie nodded. It felt less like a lie.

Holiday gave Kylie a hug and then took off. Miranda came out of her room, and Kylie dropped Socks to the floor and started picking up the mess. Miranda and Della did the same.

"You don't have to help," Kylie said.

"Please," Miranda said, and they continued to straighten chairs. Della lifted the microwave back on the counter. She plugged it back in and when the light came on, she said, "Good as new."

When the room was put back together, they all sat down at the kitchen table. "Okay," Miranda said. "Give us the details and don't leave out the good parts. And by good parts, I mean when little Miss She-wolf got sprayed in the face. Something tells me that that is going to be my favorite part. Heck, I'll bet you're even glad I turned Socks into a skunk now, right?"

Kylie leaned back in her chair and told them the whole story, including the part about Fredericka telling Derek about Lucas's letters and even the part about Fredericka halfway admitting she'd been the one to put the lion in Kylie's bedroom.

"Why the crap didn't you tell Holiday?" Miranda asked.

When Kylie didn't answer right away, Della piped up. "Because she's too damn nice."

"It's not that," Kylie said. She bit down on her lip. "Okay, maybe that's part of it, but it's Holiday I'm worried about—not Fredericka. Plus, I want to deal with this myself."

"Now, that part of it I can respect." Della crossed her arms over her chest. "Then there's the saying about how you should keep your friends close, and your enemies closer."

Miranda frowned. "Fredericka's meaner than a rattlesnake. Are you sure you can handle her?"

"If she can't, I'm always up for kicking a little werewolf ass," Della said.

Emotion swelled in Kylie's throat and she barely managed to

swallow it. "Is Lucas here, too?" Kylie recalled the hurt in Derek's eyes. The emotion in her throat doubled.

"Not yet," Della said. "I heard Fredericka say he was showing up tomorrow."

Kylie blinked, hoping to contain her tears. Then she recalled the dreams and how hard facing Lucas would be.

Miranda leaned in. "Do you think Derek's serious about breaking up?"

"He didn't break up with her," Della corrected in a harsh tone. "They weren't going out."

But he might as well have, Kylie thought, and that's when a couple of tears slipped out. Standing up, she said. "Thanks guys, but I'm . . . I just want to—"

"You still feeling pissy?" Della asked.

"Yeah," Kylie answered. Her gaze shifted to the computer showing her grandparents' phone number. She was even too distraught to deal with that right now. Tomorrow. Kylie got to her bedroom, shut the door, and dropped facedown on the blue-and-white bedspread. She had just closed her eyes when she heard Miranda sigh. A sigh Kylie shouldn't have been able to hear through her closed bedroom door.

"Do you think she's werewolf?" Miranda asked.

Kylie grabbed a pillow and covered her head, but it didn't stop Della's answer from filtering through the foam to reach Kylie's supercharged hearing.

"Probably," Della answered. *"But I'm not going to hold it against her. She'll be the nicest werewolf that ever existed."*

"Me, either," Miranda said. *"Not all weres are bad. Not that I've ever been close to any of them."*

Great, Kylie thought. Her friends seemed certain she was doomed to a life of nasty moods and howling at the moon. Kylie tried to imagine what it would be like to morph into a wolf. Then she remembered that Fredericka was going to be waiting with bated wolf breath for a chance to get even with her when—okay, if—she did turn.

And then she recalled Derek saying that he didn't want her to be a werewolf because she'd have that in common with Lucas. Was that why he'd pulled away? Gawd, why did life have to be so damn hard?

Kylie stayed in her room the next few hours. Feeling an emotional storm rage inside her, she tried to think of anything that could take the edge off. She'd napped, actually fallen asleep, but had awoken when the temperature dropped in the room. She looked around for the ghost, but the spirit didn't materialize. Remembering the ghost's appearance after Fredericka left, Kylie asked, "Do you have something to say?"

Her question vibrated in the still coldness of the room. Kylie hadn't expected an answer, but asking was her job, right? Staring at the ceiling, she jumped when something crashed to the floor. Turning around, she saw her phone had fallen from the nightstand. When she picked it up, she heard someone on the line.

"Hello?" Kylie recognized Sara's voice.

"Hey," Kylie said.

"What's up?" Sara asked.

Kylie huddled under the covers to ward off the cold. "Nothing. Did you call me?"

"No. You called me," Sara answered.

"Oh." Kylie glanced at her cell. "My phone fell off the nightstand. It must have dialed you accidentally."

"Oh." The awkwardness rang louder than Sara's voice.

"Where are you?" Kylie asked, just to chase away the uncomfortable silence because just hanging up felt too rude. It wasn't as if Kylie could say what's on her mind like, *Hey guess what? I just tossed a werewolf out of my cabin for trying to kill my kitten that's now a skunk, and tonight, I might turn into a wolf myself.* Right then Kylie realized she'd been blaming Sara for the distance in their relationship, claiming Sara had changed. Well, hell, now look who had undergone the most change.

"At the mall with Tina," Sara answered, her voice sounding strangely tight.

"Tina?" Kylie asked, hoping to show interest in Sara's life.

"Tina Dalton. She just moved here."

"Is she nice?" Was Tina Sara's new best friend?

Sarah chuckled. "Not really, but her brother is hot."

"Hmm," Kylie teased. "Good thing I didn't have a brother or I'd think you were just interested in him all these years."

Sara laughed and Kylie joined in. A little of the awkwardness faded.

"It was strange that you called," Sara said. "I was just thinking about you. Do you remember when we were thirteen and you did that backward flip and knocked both of us off the trampoline? Our moms took us to the emergency clinic by our neighborhood because they thought you had broken an arm and I had a goose egg on my head."

"Yeah," Kylie said. "What made you think about that?"

"Who knows," Sara answered with the same tight voice.

Kylie leaned back on her pillow. "You thought the doctor was cute."

"He was cute." Sara sounded normal again. "Any hot guys at the camp?"

"Yeah." Kylie took in a deep breath and when she released it, it came out as a fog. Strange. She'd thought the spirit had left but she was moving closer.

"You hooked up with any of them?" Sara asked.

Kylie's heart tugged. "Kind of, but . . . we sort of . . . called it quits." *Or he called it quits.* A shiver ran down Kylie's back and she looked around again for the ghost. She still hadn't materialized, but her chill filled the room.

"That sucks," Sara said, and in the background Kylie heard someone call out Sara's name. "Hold on a sec."

The line went silent as if Sara had covered the receiver. But Kylie's ears picked up Sara's intake of air. Whether Sara had moved her hand, or if it was Kylie's hearing abilities, she wasn't sure. She still didn't grasp how this whole gifted hearing thing worked. It came and went. Just like her strength.

"No, I'm not using my insurance." Sara's voice filled the line. "I'm paying cash. Of course my mom knows. Look, is the doctor going to see me or not?"

Kylie frowned when she realized that Sara had lied about being at the mall. The reasons for the lie filled Kylie's head. Had she run out of birth control pills? Or did she think she was pregnant again? Tightening her grip on the phone, Kylie was reminded of how different they were. How sad was it that they couldn't share things—neither werewolves or sex?

"Kylie," Sara said. "I need to go."

"Okay. Bye." Kylie put her phone back on the nightstand. When she looked up, the ghost sat at the foot of her bed, appearing incredibly sad. Kylie started to speak but the spirit faded.

"Great," Kylie muttered. "Communicating with spirits is almost as bad as communicating with old friends."

• • •

At eleven thirty that night, Kylie walked with Della and Miranda to the campfire. Her heart swelled with the fear of what would or wouldn't happen to her tonight, but she refused to show it. Of course, Della pretty much knew what she was feeling because she kept studying Kylie with an enormous amount of sympathy.

The moment the three of them cut through the clearing, Kylie spotted Derek standing in a group of four other fairies. He glanced at her. The full moon offered enough light for her to see the soft concern in his eyes.

No doubt he could read her fear. Stopping, she muttered to Della and Miranda to go ahead and let her talk to Derek. Her two roommates walked off.

Kylie waited for Derek to come and offer her his comforting touch—just a touch to ebb the fear from her heart. She could really use a little of his calm right now, not to mention his touch. His gaze met hers, but instead of moving over, he glanced back at his circle of friends. That's when Kylie got the first hint of how things would be between them from now on.

Obviously, being *just* friends meant no more kisses and touches.

Kylie's first impulse was to beg him to stop this nonsense. Her second impulse didn't involve begging. Anger crowded out some of her fear. Even though she knew Derek was partially right—in the beginning, there was some truth to her confusion with Lucas stopping her from going out with him—didn't Derek trust her enough to know she wouldn't cheat on him? His lack of faith in her just plain ol' made her mad. Really, really mad.

Sure, it might be her uncontrollable werewolf-related aggression bringing on the fury, but she felt it all the same. And once again, being mad felt better than being hurt, even better than being frightened, so she clung to the anger and hoped Derek would read it. She even stepped closer, giving him ample opportunity.

She knew it worked when he turned back around and his green eyes met hers. She didn't blink, didn't attempt to look away, wanting to make sure he read every bit of her anger. A frown tightened his brows and he walked away, probably wanting to get out of emotion-reading range. While tempted to follow him and cloak him in her emotional state, she didn't.

Just go. Her chest tightened as the hurt crowded out the anger. *Just remember, I wasn't the one who called it quits.*

Taking a deep breath, she looked around until she spotted another lone soul who looked almost as miserable as she felt. Perry stood by himself, leaning against a tree and watching Miranda chatting cheerfully with a group of guys—one of whom was Kevin. Knowing misery loved company, Kylie went to join Perry.

Perry snarled at her when she walked up. "What? Are you going to tell me how much she likes me again?"

"Nope," Kylie said. "I've come to the conclusion that anything to do with the opposite sex should be banned and considered illegal."

Perry studied her through his brown eyes. "Trouble in paradise?"

"Yup."

He sighed. "Maybe we should hook up and teach a few people some lessons."

"In your dreams," Kylie said.

"Not even there." He frowned. "The only girl appearing in my dreams lately is the girl who is too busy flirting with everyone to even say hello to me."

Kylie gaped at Perry. "I can't believe you." Where did he get off thinking Miranda should talk to him when he'd been the one to call it quits? Like Derek.

Before she voiced her opinion, Luis, the were in charge, called for everyone's attention. Kylie's anger with Perry and over Derek dissolved and she fell right into the lap of fear again.

Her heart thudded. She felt the moon's rays on her as if it were the sun. Her skin actually stung and it took everything she had not to stop and stare up at the huge orb in the sky and scream for it to stop.

"It's not as scary as you think," Perry said.

Kylie met his gaze. "Does everyone know what's going on with me?"

"Pretty much." His eyes, now a bright blue, studied her. "It's not bad."

They moved closer to where the ceremony was taking place and she looked up at Perry and gave him credit for his sincere concern for her "I didn't think shape-shifters and werewolves were the same thing."

"We're not," he said. "But we both shift and I've spent a lot of time talking about it with others. They all say the same thing, 'It's not a big deal. Like a muscle cramp.'"

She bit the inside of her cheek and recalled Lucas describing it the same way. Unfortunately, she'd never been fond of muscle cramps. A thousand questions started stirring in her head. Why hadn't she found more answers? She felt her heart stop, start, then flutter like a trapped butterfly.

Swallowing fear, she searched the crowd for Fredericka. "Will I know who I am?" she asked Perry. Her lungs felt too tight to breathe even though she didn't spot the she-wolf.

"Sure you will." His gaze shot over Kylie's shoulder. Kylie feared he saw Fredericka behind her.

"You okay?" Holiday's comforting voice came to her ear.

Kylie turned just as Holiday motioned for Perry to move on.

Kylie leaned in and her voice caught as she confessed the truth. "I'm scared out of my gourd. I'm not ready for this." Her eyes stung with the new urge to cry.

"You're going to be fine. I don't even think . . ." Holiday didn't finish her sentence. Instead, she placed a hand on Kylie's shoulder and the majority of her panic faded. "Come on, I'll stand beside you."

They walked to the crowd and formed another circle much like they had at the vampire ceremony. Luis stood in the middle and in his hands he carried a skull. Not a human skull, it looked to be a wolf. He held up the skull. It seemed to catch the moonlight and glow. He started recounting the story of the first werewolf, and then telling about his kind's many gifts, but Kylie couldn't listen. Nothing felt right. Her gaze shot to the moon, and she could swear she saw the man in the round silver circle wink at her.

Then Kylie noticed that many of the campers were walking off. The werewolves. Kylie glanced at Holiday with questions in her eyes.

"Most prefer not to transform in front of an audience," the camp leader explained.

Kylie didn't blame them. She didn't want to do it, either. Would her clothes fall off? Would they see the hair growing on her skin?

Her only thought was to run, but Luis stopped talking and the sound that came out of his mouth was one of sheer terror. In the background, Kylie could hear what sounded like the screams of the others as they, too, turned. Air caught in her throat again. Her feet felt nailed to the ground. She didn't want to hear this, didn't want to see it, but like an accident on the side of the road, she couldn't look away.

Luis dropped to the ground, his back arched, and the sounds— half growl, half moan—continued. It was like something out of a horror movie. Kylie watched his body contort in ways no human body should ever twist. He arched his neck back so far it looked as if it would surely break. His jawbone grew, his cheeks became elongated, and where the face of a young man had once been the snout of a wolf appeared. And then came the hair.

Kylie's heart jolted. Her skin started to crawl. Her stomach knotted.

Oh, God! Something was happening to her.

Chapter Twenty-six

Kylie felt as if seltzer ran through her veins. She watched Luis, now a complete wolf, run off into the woods. Then everyone there turned and stared at her.

Watching.

Waiting.

She looked at Holiday. "I need to . . . be alone." She walked away. She didn't run—didn't want to draw any more attention to herself than she already had—but she walked fast, afraid the sounds of terror would any minute begin to flow from her own throat.

She made it to the woods before the urge to run overtook her. She moved at amazing speeds, dodging trees, jumping over stumps, and ducking under branches. How long she ran, she didn't know. But out of breath, out of energy, she finally collapsed in a heap of trembling muscles.

Stilling gasping, she stared at her hands. She touched her face to make sure she hadn't started the change.

Nothing. No change. She closed her eyes and tried to stop the feeling of her crawling skin. That's when she heard it.

A low, very ominous growl.

Opening her eyes, she saw the wolf lurching toward her. Mostly white with hints of gray and tan, its eyes glowed a bright golden. Its lips curled under and its sharp teeth were bared. This was no ordinary wolf. It was a werewolf.

Kylie tried to stand, but her muscles trembled and refused the command. The wolf seemed to notice her weakness. Its posture became more aggressive. The coarse hair on its back stood up and when Kylie looked it in the eyes, she knew. Knew with certainty the wolf was Fredericka. The she-wolf's growl deepened and then she charged.

Kylie found the strength to bounce to her feet, ready to run, when another wolf, even larger, crashed between two trees. Fredericka stopped. At first, Kylie thought she was about to be attacked by two beasts instead of one. But the second wolf, a dark gray in color with eyes that glowed a lighter gold, whipped around and growled at the oncoming wolf.

Kylie heard the competing growls and saw the two converge upon each other. She heard the sound of teeth clicking, and then, recognizing this as a chance to escape, she tore off through the woods. She ran, not as fast as before, for her energy had been spent, but she forced herself forward and didn't stop until she reached her cabin.

Collapsing on the porch steps, she forced air into her lungs. When she looked out at the woods, a pair of light golden eyes stared back Her next intake of air brought recognition. She wasn't sure how she knew, but it came with such clarity that she didn't question it.

Lucas was back.

The next morning, Kylie got her daily wake-up call with the dropping of the room's temperature. She groaned, rolled over, and glared

290 C. C. HUNTER

at the clock, not wanting to believe it was dawn. But yep. It was 4:59 a.m. The spirit was right on time.

It didn't seem fair, and not just because she didn't want to face Lucas yet. Hadn't she just put her head on the pillow? She'd never had three hours pass so quickly. It had been two a.m. when she'd collapsed in her own bed.

When Kylie ran inside her cabin after seeing Lucas, Holiday had been waiting on her to make sure she was okay. Della and Miranda were waiting with the camp leader at the kitchen table, all of them looking somber. Her two cabin mates looked shocked when Kylie arrived. No doubt they seriously thought she'd made the change into werewolf. But Holiday hadn't seemed so surprised.

After thinking about it, Kylie couldn't help but be suspicious. Did Holiday know something she wasn't telling Kylie? She loved Holiday, but her belief in the self-discovery crap, the idea that a person needed to find their own answers, was chewing on Kylie's last nerve.

The cold filling the room brought her back to the present.

"You have to save her."

Speaking of last nerves . . .

Kylie groaned and sat up. The ghost stood at the foot of her bed. The sweet smell of blood assaulted Kylie before she saw the ghost had donned her bloody gown again. The spirit met Kylie's gaze and clutched her abdomen as if she was going to be sick.

"If you're going to throw up," Kylie said, "would you mind stepping away from the bed?"

The cold, uncaring sound of her own voice hit Kylie like a slap across the face. "I'm sorry," she whispered. "I'm just . . . I want to figure it out and it's frustrating not to be able to."

The ghost rested a hand on Kylie's foot. Even beneath the blanket, the icy chill took hold. *"You have the ability to stop it. Please make it stop."*

"Make what stop? Has it already started?" Kylie asked, her chest tightening. Was someone she loved already suffering? Kidnapped and being tortured by the Blood Brothers, or something even worse?

"Damn it, answer me!" Kylie yelled. "Or at least give me a vision I can understand. I don't even care how scary it is, just do it."

The one of the funeral still made no sense.

The ghost faded and so did the coldness of her touch. But then Kylie felt tingly warmth spread down the tendons to her toes and up the arches to her ankle. Kylie pressed a hand against her foot. She'd never felt that before with Daniel. Was that supposed to mean something?

Frustration welled inside Kylie, but the sound of cascading water filled her head. Was this the death angels way of saying it would be okay?

Kylie's phone beeped, announcing she had messages. There were three: one from the private investigator, one from Sara, and one from her mom.

Recalling the fear that whatever might happen could already be happening, and not caring about the hour, Kylie dialed her mom's number.

Later, at eight o'clock that morning, Kylie dropped her breakfast tray on the table and sat down beside Della and Miranda, purposely not looking around because she was afraid she might see him. Or both hims. She wasn't any more eager to see Derek right now than she was to see Lucas. Derek's avoidance of her last night still stung.

Oh, she knew she'd avoided him only a couple of weeks ago, but it had been different. She hadn't avoided him because she didn't want to be with him; she'd done it because she'd wanted to be with him too much.

Staring down at her runny eggs, which were about as appetizing as roadkill, Kylie recalled her conversation she'd had with her mom. Frankly, Kylie didn't know if her mom believed the whole "I woke from a bad dream and didn't realize the time" spiel. But when her mom confessed she'd been having some really bad dreams lately, too, Kylie couldn't help but wonder if this was because of the erasing. Were her mom's nightmares about what she'd seen at Shadow Falls?

Suddenly, Kylie felt the hair on the back of her neck start to stand up. Without even looking back, Kylie knew someone had her locked in a serious stare. Unable to resist, she glanced over her shoulder. She should have known.

Fredericka.

Turning back around, her gaze shot across the room and she found herself staring right at Derek. His eyes expressed concern, caring, but not so much that he'd come over. Could he not sense how much she needed him? She looked away, but only found herself caught in the snare of a pair of blue eyes. Beautiful blue eyes that took her back to her childhood and trying to find elephants hidden in the clouds.

Lucas glanced over at the door and nodded as if asking her to meet him outside.

Kylie had to reach deep to find the courage to do what came next.

She picked up her fork and started heaping food into her mouth as if she were too hungry to leave. Yup, she'd rather eat cold roadkill, runny scrambled eggs than talk with Lucas. Plain and simple, she wasn't ready to face him, or the dreams. Then came the fact that walking out of this dining hall to be with Lucas would no doubt hurt Derek. She didn't want to hurt Derek. It didn't even matter that he didn't seem to mind hurting her.

It was after art when Kylie arrived back to the cabin to make her two phone calls. Sitting at the computer desk, she reached for the mouse to pull up her grandparents' number again. She'd debated who to call first. The PI or her grandparents. She opted for the grandparents. Though for the life of her, she didn't have a clue what she was going to say. How did you go about telling someone you were their long-lost grandchild—but not really theirs because you happened to know their dead son had been adopted?

Oh, yeah, this was going to be easy.

When the computer woke up, the screen brought up a list of car accidents for the Springville area, Della's home. Kylie chest grew heavy when she realized Della was still suspicious of what she might have done during her changing stage.

Kylie glanced at Della's shut bedroom door. She often came back to the cabin and napped after lunch.

Opening another screen, Kylie searched for the telephone number for Kent B. Brighten in Gladlock, Texas. Unsure what she would say, she punched in the number before she lost her nerve.

The phone rang once.

Twice.

Three times.

An answering machine picked up. "Hello, you have reached Kent and Becky Brighten. We aren't home right now, but if you'll leave . . ." The voice continued.

They were still alive.

Her heart quivered. The line beeped.

Decision time. Leave a message? Not leave a message?

She hit the end button.

Ten breaths and thirty seconds later, she called the PI. Another message machine. But she left a voice message, letting him know she'd gotten a name and number of Daniel's adoptive parents.

Trying to let her mind wrap around the possibility of actually meeting the Brightens, Kylie realized she wanted to meet them for reasons other than just finding Daniel's birth parents. It would be nice to learn more about her dad. She closed the screen and another one popped up. It was a double screen of two newspaper articles about two different car accidents, each with casualties.

Kylie started to read. One was about a man in his late forties and the other was . . . Kylie's heart tugged. A woman and her six-month-old little girl.

How could Della think she could have done something like that?

A knock filled the cabin and panic filled her chest. Was it Lucas? Or Fredericka again? She cut her eyes around the room, hoping Socks was hiding. The knock came louder.

"Kylie?" Burnett's deep voice boomed through the door.

Knowing he could hear her, Kylie called, "Come in."

He opened the door and walked to the kitchen table. She grew instantly worried about the reason he was here. Surely he hadn't come back to try to pull more information out of her about Holiday. If so, he'd leave disappointed.

He nodded to a chair. "Mind if I sit down?"

"No." Then, unable to stop herself, she blurted out, "If this is about Holiday, I—"

He held up his hand. "It's not about . . . Holiday." He frowned. "Though I have to admit she still puzzles the hell out of me."

"Maybe if Selynn wasn't hanging around, then . . ." Kylie shut her mouth, realizing she was doing it again.

"Selynn's on orders of the FRU, so I couldn't send her away. But as of today, she'll be leaving."

While Kylie hadn't seen the were since the lake incident, she'd heard she was still at Shadow Falls. Someone had said she was here due to the incident with the rogue vampire. And if she was leaving, did that mean they'd caught . . .

"Has something happened? Did you catch him?" She envisioned the two girls who'd been killed, and the vision left painful footprints on her heart.

Burnett leaned back in his chair. "That's what I came to tell you. I just got word that the Vampire Council has the guy. They are going to . . . handle the situation."

"What do you mean by . . . handle?" she asked.

"Just that. They will handle it."

"Will there be a trial . . . or something like that?" Would Kylie have to testify?

Burnett looked right at her, as if remembering his promise that the guy wouldn't go unpunished. "Not really a trial. The Vampire Council basically decide his fate, but . . . they have assured me that they don't take lightly the killing of normals."

She didn't want to think too hard about what his fate would be. That might remove some of the relief of knowing that she would never have to face that rogue vampire again. But how relieved could she be? Was this incident tied to the ghost's warning? Was someone she loved still in danger?

She stared down at her hands to try and digest the information and sort out her questions. When she looked up, she saw Burnett's eyes locked on the computer screen.

"What's that?" he asked in a dark voice.

Not wanting him to suspect Della of such a horrific crime, she grabbed the mouse and hit the red X. "Nothing." Too late she remembered he could tell when she was lying. And even if he hadn't, her clumsy attempt to get the screen cleared would have told him the truth.

His gaze shot back to her eyes. "Kylie, don't do this."

"Do what?" she asked, unsure what he thought she was doing.

"Tell me you aren't investigating car accidents looking for Code-Red incidents."

Code Red. Kylie remembered that was what the FRU called a staged car accident to mask a death at the hands of a supernatural. Kylie looked back at the blank screen. "So . . . one of those accidents was a Code-Red case?" Maybe to cover up a vampire kill? Like Della had feared may have happened when she turned?

He turned his head and studied her, reading her. "If you're not investigating it, who is?"

Oh crap, Kylie thought. *What to say? What to say? It couldn't be a lie or he'd know.*

"Della?" he asked.

"No," Kylie lied again without thinking.

He closed his eyes.

"Please," Kylie said, not even sure for what she was pleading.

His dark eyes opened and he looked at her.

"She couldn't have done that," Kylie said. "She's a good person."

Burnett glanced toward Della's bedroom door. He placed a hand on Kylie's shoulder and gave it a squeeze, then he walked out without saying another word.

Two seconds after he left, Della walked out of the bedroom. Kylie had tears of guilt in her eyes.

"It's okay," Della said, but she looked scared. "I was going tell him about it anyway." She started to leave as if to find Burnett.

"You couldn't have done that," Kylie said.

Della looked back over her shoulder. Tears brightened her eyes. "I hope you're right."

Kylie sat there for about thirty minutes, numb with guilt. If she hadn't been reading the screen when Burnett came in, this would not have happened. That's when she realized she couldn't just sit here. She had to do something. She tore out of the cabin, running with everything she had to the office where she expected Burnett would have Della.

Because everyone was either in a class or a meeting, the trail was empty. Kylie hadn't gone too far when she felt it—that feeling of being watched—but her heart and mind weighed too heavy on Della to care.

Kylie made it to the opening of the trail when she saw Burnett's car, with Della in it, pull out of the front parking lot. "No."

"It's okay," Holiday said from behind her.

Kylie looked back, and because the same worry she felt was etched on Holiday's face, she knew that Holiday had been informed about what happened. "It's my fault." Guilt filled her lungs, making it hard to breathe.

Holiday guided her to the office where she gave Kylie a hug. "It's okay," she repeated, sending a surge of calm into Kylie.

"Where's he taking her?" Kylie swallowed a lump of emotion.

"To the FRU office to do some tests. DNA and bite-mark imprints."

"So one of the accidents was a Code Red?" Kylie asked.

"Both," Holiday confessed.

Kylie's heart felt like it folded over onto itself.

"Is everything okay?" a male voice spoke from the doorway.

Lucas leaned on the door frame. Worry filled his eyes.

"It's fine." Holiday waved him out.

He didn't move. "You okay?" he asked Kylie as if he needed to hear it from her.

She had yet to speak to Lucas since he'd been back and for some reason, her voice box refused to work now. All she could manage was a nod. He walked away, leaving a wake of genuine concern.

Holiday pulled Kylie over to the sofa and they sat down. "It's really going to be okay." She pressed a hand on Kylie's back and sent comforting warmth washing through her.

But the image of Della with fear in her eyes filled Kylie's mind. Della and fear didn't mix. Della was strong, and bold, and way too kind to hurt someone. "She didn't do this," Kylie told Holiday. "It's stupid to put her through the tests."

"Della wanted to do this. She needs to know."

"But she didn't do it," Kylie said again, realizing Holiday hadn't agreed with her.

"That's what we're hoping, Kylie. But if she did, there are extenuating circumstances. She was undergoing the change. The FRU will overlook it, I'm sure."

Kylie inwardly flinched at Holiday's words. She didn't know what bothered her more—that Holiday could believe Della could do this, or that new vampires could kill innocent humans and not be held accountable.

Holiday called three hours later and told Kylie that Della would be returning. She gave permission for Kylie and Miranda to take the rest of the afternoon off and wait for her. And that's just what Kylie and Miranda did. They sat at the kitchen table waiting. Kylie turned a Diet Coke around in her hands. Miranda didn't even move.

"She didn't do this," Kylie kept saying. "How can they think it's possible?"

Miranda groaned as if tired of Kylie's litany. "This isn't the same world you used to live in. Shit happens here. Bad shit. Teenage girls die. Cats get turned into skunks. Werewolves come into your cabin and try to kill you. And when a vampire turns for the first time, they can . . . do things that they wouldn't do in their right minds."

"You think she did it!" Kylie accused.

"I don't know," Miranda said. "But if she did, it wasn't her fault and I won't stop loving her. And damn it, Kylie, you shouldn't, either. She thinks you walk on water. If you turn your back on her, it'll kill her."

Tears filled Kylie eyes at even the suggestion that Della could've done something so terrible. But deep down she knew, even if it was true, she wouldn't turn her back on her friend.

Ten minutes later Della, eyes red, walked into the cabin and dropped into a chair. "The bite marks weren't mine. None of the fingerprints, either."

A smile spread across Kylie's face and her heart. "I told you."

Tears slipped from Della's dark eyes and rolled down her pale cheeks. "They think Chan did it."

Miranda looked from Della to Kylie. "Who's Chan?"

"My cousin," Della told her, no longer caring about keeping the secret. "He helped me through my change. He didn't have to do it. But he did."

"Oh," Miranda said.

"Now they want to me to find out if he did it," Della went on. "To go undercover and get the proof of his guilt." She hiccupped. "But he was there for me when no one else was, and now I have to—"

"Just tell them no," Kylie said.

"You don't tell the FRU no." Della took in a deep breath. "Besides . . . they showed me the pictures." Sorrow filled Della's dark's eyes. "There was a baby. It was awful. If he did do this, he has to be stopped before he does it to someone else. I don't think I could live with myself if I let that happen."

That night Kylie attended a mandatory camp meeting because somebody had tampered with the security alarm again. According to Burnett, the alarm was being shut off—what he didn't know was if it was by someone on the inside or outside, but he was determined to find out.

Kylie wondered if her feeling of being watched coincided with the security alarm being turned off. Because now that the alarm was guarded, she didn't feel a thing, except safer.

After the meeting, she had headed back to the cabin alone and had taken the first step up onto her porch when a noise startled her.

So much for feeling safe. Her heart pounded and she turned. Her thoughts shot to Fredericka.

"How long do you think you can avoid talking to me?" Lucas leapt up on her porch.

Kylie shifted a bit closer to the light fixture above the front door, where insects buzzed, and looked at her watch.

"Obviously only about twelve hours," she said, noting it was nine o'clock on the dot. Today when she'd seen him in the office, she'd been too concerned about Della to worry about her Lucas issues with the dreams. But not tonight. She stepped out of the light, hoping he wouldn't see embarrassment color her cheeks.

"So you admit you've been avoiding me?" Humor laced his deep voice.

Humor she didn't appreciate. She met his eyes before looking away. "I'd deny it, but you wouldn't believe me." *Besides, avoiding things that make me uncomfortable is my specialty.*

Instantly, she recalled confessing to Holiday about how confronting her dad had made her feel better. Was it too much to hope that confronting Lucas would have the same effect?

One more peek at her cabin door and she knew she had to do this. Face him and get it over with.

"So, if you're not going to deny it, dare I hope you'll explain the reason you're doing it?"

She raised her gaze again and while she wanted more than anything to believe he didn't know about the dreams, she couldn't believe it. Obviously, she was much better at avoidance than denial.

"Reasons," she said.

"What?" He stepped closer and his scent, woodsy and rich, invaded her air.

"I have more than one reason."

"Okay." He caught the end of a strand of her blond hair and rubbed it between his fingertips. "Tell me the reasons."

She pulled her hair from his hand and took a step back. "Tell you? And take all the fun out of your trying to figure it out yourself?" She had meant for the words to sound curt, but she must have missed her mark because he chuckled.

She frowned.

His humor faded. "Okay, my first guess is that you're beginning to realize at least some of your gifts. Dreamscaping, for example?"

She flushed but didn't look away this time. "Now that I understand it, it won't be a problem." She prayed she was right. Holiday had said Kylie would get more control over it, hadn't she? Surely that meant she could shut it down. God, she hoped it was true.

He studied her. "That's a shame." His tone came out flirty again.

She glanced back at the door. She'd said what she needed to, hadn't she?

When she reached for the doorknob, he caught her arm. His touch wasn't rough, not even a little bit. It was tender and that gave her more pause. She'd had a hell of a day and could still recall how he'd seemed genuinely concerned for her in the office.

"Give me a few more minutes. Please."

She continued to stare at the door, so aware that he didn't drop his hand from her arm. So aware that his touch sent feel-good tingles down her arm.

"So what are the other reasons?" he asked. When she didn't answer, he continued. "Why are you so angry with me, Kylie? And don't deny it. I might not be able to feel your emotions like . . . some people . . . but I see it in your eyes."

Kylie didn't question who he meant by "some people." He must have heard about her and Derek. Good, she thought. But then, whatever he'd heard was history. Derek had ended it.

His hold on her arm tightened slightly. "Tell me what you're upset about so we can get past it."

One word sat on the tip of her tongue. *Fredericka.* But admitting she was upset about his being with Fredericka meant she cared about him in a boy-girl kind of way. She didn't want to admit that to Lucas. She hadn't liked admitting it to herself. And it wasn't even really true. She was just confused.

"I'm tired." She risked looking at him.

His blue eyes looked brighter in the golden hue of the porch light. He still had his hand around her arm and his thumb started brushing against her skin. "You got my letters, right?"

"Yeah."

"Is it the dreams that have got you upset, because I didn't—"

"I know—it was me, not you." She pulled her arm away.

He raised his eyebrows as if contemplating. "It wasn't all you," he said as if it cost him a lot to confess it. "Not the first dream. I mean . . ."

When he hesitated, her mind took over. "So you were doing it? You came into my dream?"

"No, I don't have that ability. But when you came into my dream the first time, I was already dreaming about you." He shrugged as if to knock some of the guilt off his shoulders. "At first, I didn't realize you were really there. Not until it became so vivid and real. And I didn't say anything later because I could tell you didn't understand what had happened. If that's what you're upset about. I probably should have stopped it but . . . It was a dream. And oh, hell, I didn't want it to stop."

Even if she had to give him credit for being honest, she was still upset. He should have stopped it. Or at least told her so she wouldn't have gone back the second time. Then again, she didn't know how she'd have reacted if he'd told her this then. A lot had happened in these past weeks. She'd accepted things now that she probably wouldn't have been able to accept then.

"The second dream, however, that was all you." His eyebrows rose as if the thought made him happy.

Caught off guard by the blue twinkle in his eyes, she said the first thing that came to her mind. "I bet Aunt Stella dreamed about Tom Selleck, too."

Chapter Twenty-seven

Confusion filled his expression. "What? Tom Selleck?"

Embarrassment filled her chest. Had she really said that? "What I'm trying to say is I don't think it will happen again. So let's forget it, okay?"

"Why won't it happen again?" His gaze became heavy, and he lowered his face an inch closer from hers. "It's obvious that you feel the same about me as—"

"As you do for Fredericka?" She wished she could snatch the question from the air before it reached his ears.

His brow creased and he leaned back on his heels. "So that's what you're angry about."

She didn't deny it. Not because she didn't want to, but because she didn't think she could pull it off.

"Look, Fredericka and I—"

"It's not important."

"It is to me. I never touched her while we were away. Not once."

"It doesn't matter because . . . what you two are, or what you do, is your business. Because you and I . . . we're just friends."

"We could be more," he countered. "It feels like more already."

"No." She looked him directly in the eyes, hoping he'd understand she meant it.

He pushed a strand of her hair behind her ear, and his thumb brushed over her cheek. "The last time we stood on the porch, you invited me inside and I think that invitation included more than just . . . being friends."

She remembered standing here, almost begging him to come inside, wanting . . . so much more than his company. But that was then—before her feelings deepened for Derek.

She caught Lucas's hand and moved it from her face. "But you said no. And you were right."

"You really believe that?" He tenderly folded his fingers around her hand.

Yeah, she did, because he'd run off with Fredericka.

"She followed me, Kylie. I didn't ask her to come. I would have sent her home, but it turned out I needed her."

Kylie tried to pull her hand from his, but his hold tightened.

"I didn't mean need her like . . . like that. I left to help someone." He paused. "I didn't tell you in the letters because if Holiday found out she'd have had a fit. I have a half sister. She'd been pulled into one of the gangs. I had to get her out, Kylie. She didn't deserve to . . . I should have been there for her earlier. She called and asked for help a few months before, but I didn't do it because I would have had to face my father. It was my fault it happened and I had to help. Then Fredericka helped me."

Kylie tilted her head back. "She helped you. She tried to kill me."

He shook his head. "She wouldn't have killed you last night."

It *had* been him. She'd known, but hearing him say it made it more real.

"She just wanted to scare you," he continued. "She doesn't like you because she knows how I feel about you."

"You had to fight her to stop her from charging me."

"That doesn't mean anything. That's the way we deal with things when we're changed. We don't stand around and use psychology when we're in our natural state."

"But last night wasn't the first time she tried to put me six feet under. She put a lion in my room before you left."

His expression darkened. "She did what?"

"She put a lion in my room. One from the wildlife preserve. If it hadn't been for Derek I could have died."

Disbelief filled his expression. "She wouldn't have done that."

Kylie yanked her hand from his. She couldn't believe he was defending Fredericka. But why was that unbelievable? He'd admitted to having sex with her. Then he ran off with her.

He raked a hand through his hair. "She's not like that, Kylie. I know she's harsh but . . . you don't know her like I do."

"You're right," Kylie said. "I don't know her like you do. And since you two have so much in common, why don't you go find her right now and . . . and be with her? That's where you belong."

"She's not the one I want." His words came out terse. "It's you. It's been you since . . . since the minute I first saw you."

Kylie closed her eyes and shook her head. This was all happening so fast. She'd finally gotten used to him being gone, and now here he was shaking up her life all over again.

"Tell me you didn't feel it," he whispered. "Tell me that you didn't feel the bond we had when we first met."

She had felt it, but she'd been five years old. She met his gaze again. "I don't know what to think, Lucas. You're telling me that there's nothing between you and Fredericka, but she obviously has other ideas. Maybe you should sort things out with her before you start something up with me." Her heart clutched when she realized this was basically the same thing Derek had told her.

"You make it sound as if I haven't already tried to do that."

She shrugged. "My life's really complicated right now. If you'd been around these past weeks, you'd know that. So for now, we can be friends. That's all."

Kylie heard voices on the trail. When she looked up, Derek and a few of his friends walked past. Derek didn't even look her way. She suspected it was because he'd already seen them. Seen them and assumed the worst.

Guilt filled her, but she pushed the emotion back, hoping Derek hadn't been close enough to sense it. She hadn't been doing anything wrong. Breath held, she watched the group of guys walk out of eyeshot.

When she looked back, Lucas studied her. "Is he why? Are you two serious?"

"That's not even important. You and I are just friends, Lucas. Just friends."

She turned and opened her door. Right after she shut it in his face, she heard him say, "Not if I can change your mind, Kylie Galen."

The next morning, Della had an early morning ritual and would be a no-show for breakfast. Miranda announced she'd be skipping as well. Kylie got a feeling the witch was up to something. Probably trying to reverse the spell on Socks. Kylie had almost asked but she'd fought sleep most of the night for fear she'd lapse into a dream with Lucas, and she didn't have the stamina for a long conversation about possible curse reversals.

Walking into the dining hall alone, Kylie felt everyone's stares and knew they were all twitching like crazy checking out her brain pattern. After she grabbed her tray of a Danish and fruit, she hesitated in the back of the room, searching for a seat. Today everyone had chosen to sit with their own kind. Since Kylie didn't have a kind, or at least know what kind she belonged to, she marched over to an empty table.

For the life of her, she didn't know why it was so hard to sit alone. She should have more self-esteem than to let something so silly make her feel uncomfortable. But calling it silly didn't change how she felt. She stared at her Danish and tried not to look as pathetic as she felt.

Hearing familiar laughter, Kylie glanced up and saw the fairy table all in chuckles. Everyone there looked content in their cozy circle of friends. Everyone but Derek. Hurt filled his eyes, but what was she supposed to do? She hadn't done this. He had. And she had a distinct feeling if she went to him, he'd walk away from her. That would hurt too much.

Picking up her pastry, she took a bite. It was her favorite kind with raspberry and cream cheese, but she barely tasted it. She swallowed another flavorless bite and felt as if everyone in the room stared at her. Her new shifting brain pattern hadn't stopped being the topic of conversation from what she'd heard.

Suddenly, a tray dropped down on the table beside her. Thinking it was Della back early from her morning event, Kylie sighed the words, "Thank you," and turned with a smile.

Not Della.

Lucas smiled. "Thanks for what?"

"Nothing," she said, and almost asked him to leave. But damn it, hadn't she told him they were friends? And as friends, there was no good reason why he couldn't sit at a table with her. Well, aside from a certain she-wolf who would want to kill her because of it.

His blue eyes twinkled with humor. "You've got jelly." He brushed his finger across her lip. Then he popped the digit into his mouth.

"That's what napkins are for," she said, reaching for one and giving her tingling lips a good swipe.

He chuckled.

Realizing Derek might be watching, Kylie cut her eyes to his table. He was gone. Which meant he'd seen them and taken off. Great. She let herself feel guilty for a second and then she got mad. She wouldn't be in this situation if he would have come over and sat with her. Nope.

Taking a deep breath, she reached for her milk and took a long sip. Then she looked at Lucas who was watching her.

"You are so damn beautiful," he said.

She rolled her eyes and put down her milk. "Just friends," she insisted.

"Okay. But you're still beautiful." His grin widened. "Even with a milk mustache." He handed her a napkin and chuckled. Then he grew serious. "Burnett told me about what happened with Della. Is she going to be okay?"

"I think so." She didn't go into any detail, or mention Chan. She didn't know how much Burnett had said, or how much even Della was supposed to be telling anyone about the Code-Red incidents.

"I heard about what happened in town and then with your mom," he added. "It sounds like you've had a crappy time since I've been away."

"Yeah, pretty crappy."

He picked up his pastry and took a bite without getting anything on himself, of course. "I also heard . . ." His eyes brightened in humor. "About what your skunk did to Fredericka. I'm sure she deserved it."

"She did." Was this his way of showing loyalty to Kylie over Fredericka? Not that he had to choose between them. Kylie and Lucas were just friends. And if she could just stop remembering how good it had felt to kiss him, she really thought they could be friends, too. "Your last few weeks didn't sound too great, either. Is your sister going to be okay?"

He nodded. "I think so. I've got her staying with some friends. I'm going to talk to Holiday about her enrolling here for school. You are signing up, right?"

Kylie pinched off a piece of pastry. "I'm hoping so. My mom said she's thinking about it."

The thought of what Kylie would do if her mom really said no caused her stomach to knot. She belonged here, with the others. Her gaze shifted around the different tables hosting what looked like families of supernaturals. Hopefully, soon she'd even discover what table she belonged to.

This isn't the same world you used to live in. Kylie heard Miranda's words from last night echo in her head. No, it wasn't the same world. It was dark and sometimes very dangerous, but it was her world now.

Chapter Twenty-eight

"How do I make it stop?" Kylie, exhausted from lack of sleep, asked the question as she dropped into a chair across from Holiday's desk at the start of their two o'clock appointment. "I don't want to do this whole dream crap anymore."

Holiday sat back and pursed her lips. "This gift is too special to call crap. And you can't stop it, but you can control it with practice."

"Okay, how do I control this shit then?"

Holiday chuckled. "Haven't you sensed yourself moving in the dream world?"

"You mean, like flying?"

"Yeah, like flying."

"Sure, but sometimes I don't wake up until I'm already in the dream."

"Okay, here's what you do. Before you go to bed . . ." Holiday rattled off a series of techniques to train herself to wake up from a dream. It wasn't a guarantee Kylie could control it but Holiday thought it was a first step.

They had moved on to the subject of the ghost when Holiday's cell rang. She picked it up from the desk and glanced at the caller's number. Her eyes lit up. "I . . . need to take this call. Can you give me a few minutes?"

Kylie started to get up, but Holiday sprang from her chair first and started toward the door. "Hello, Mr. Eastman."

Holiday shut the door behind her with a firm *click* and Kylie settled back and closed her eyes.

"Yes, I'm so excited that you're considering my offer." Holiday's words filled Kylie's ear.

Kylie snapped her eyes open. Not again with the sensitive hearing!

"I can't tell you how much Shadow Falls needs someone like yourself on our board."

Kylie put her hands over her ears, not wanting to eavesdrop.

"Yes, a hundred thousand should cover it."

Kylie frowned when the voice continued to sneak through her palms. Then she realized what this meant. Holiday had found another investor for Shadow Falls, which meant Burnett would be leaving.

Kylie's chest filled with a strange kind of achiness, a sense that this was all wrong. Not that there was a damn thing she could do about it.

After a few minutes, she heard Holiday tell Mr. Eastman that she'd be in touch soon and send him the papers to sign. She heard Holiday hang up and Kylie quickly started debating whether she should tell Holiday that she'd heard her phone conversation.

Several long minutes passed and Kylie came to the conclusion that she didn't need to tell. When Holiday didn't come back into the office, Kylie went to find her.

Holiday stood in the back room staring out the window at the basketball court. When Kylie joined her, she noticed that Burnett was shooting hoops with a group of boys. Kylie's gaze shot to

Derek, but she suspected it wasn't Derek who intrigued Holiday. No doubt the camp leader was having second thoughts. Hopefully even some third ones about turning down Burnett's offer.

Right then, Derek turned. His gaze found the window and she knew he'd sensed her. He didn't smile or wave. He turned back to the game and ignored her. Just like that, Kylie made up her mind. Enough was enough. She and Derek needed to talk.

The next morning, Kylie woke up refreshed. When the cold at dawn hit, Kylie had slept for about five straight hours. Holiday's tips on how to wake up before the dreams started had worked. She'd woken up twice to the sensation of flying. Once, she'd even seen Lucas, but she'd been able to pull back before he'd noticed her. She felt certain he hadn't even known she'd been there. Or at least she hoped that was the case.

Pulling the covers up to her chin, she looked around. No ghost appeared, but the cold hung on so Kylie knew the ghost hung with it. When Kylie's phone fell off the nightstand—again—she remembered how it had done the same thing the other day.

"Are you doing that?" she asked the spirit. "Wanna tell me something?"

No answer came back. Reaching for her phone, wondering if she'd find someone on the line again, she was relieved when there wasn't. Then seeing her blinking message light, she remembered she hadn't deleted her old messages.

She'd spoken to the PI and given him the new information she'd discovered about her grandparents. He said he would try to contact the Brightens. Not that it stopped Kylie from also calling them. She'd made a dozen calls to the number yesterday afternoon, but each time she'd only gotten the message machine.

Kylie went to delete the messages and realized she had one from Sara that she hadn't played. Remembering the mixed emotions she'd felt the last time they'd spoken, she put the phone down and gave herself permission to avoid it until later. Besides, she needed to get her speech straight to get Derek to come to his senses. She hoped her plan worked.

Kylie waited out in the dining hall before breakfast, looking for Chris. Don't let him walk up with Derek, she prayed.

When she spotted Chris walking up with Jonathon, she relaxed. When he got closer, she motioned him over. He said something to Jonathon and then started walking her way. Kylie could see curiosity spark in his eyes about why she wanted to speak to him.

It wasn't a secret that Chris, one of the head vampires, thought he was a total stud muffin. And Kylie would admit, with his blond hair and light eyes, he had sort of a California-beach-cute-guy look going for him. His body wasn't all that bad, either. But if he was thinking Kylie had a thing for him, he was about to be disappointed.

"What's up?" He smiled.

Kylie hadn't given much thought about how to approach this, so she just blurted it out. "I need a favor." Chris was in charge of Campmates Hour, where names were put in a pot and drawn and you would spend an hour getting to know this person better.

"What kind of favor?" His gaze shot to her breasts.

She almost called him on it, but considering she needed him, she let it pass. "I heard that if someone wanted to make sure they drew a certain name, you could arrange it."

"Oh." He looked disappointed, which told her he'd thought

she'd called him over for different reasons. He recovered quickly, though. "Did you also hear there's a price for doing it?"

"A pint, right?"

"Yep."

"Fine. I'll tell Holiday I'm donating." She started to walk away, but he caught her arm.

"You forgot to tell me who it is." He wrinkled his brow. "Let me guess. Lucas?"

Kylie frowned. "Derek."

Derek wasn't around when the names were called, so she went in search of him. He stood in the dining hall talking with Steve and Luis. Derek frowned when he saw her step beside him. That hurt. Forcing a smile, she leaned over and whispered, "Guess what?" She waved the slip of paper with his name in the air.

He said good-bye to the guys and motioned for her to follow. They walked outside past the crowd. She wondered if he just planned to go to their spot at the rock, but he stopped.

His green eyes studied her. "Did you rig this?"

"Rig what?" She feigned innocence.

He caught her arm and turned it over. She knew he looked for a bandage, or a needle mark, but his touch sent tiny pain-like currents running through her. "Did you buy my name with blood?" He dropped her arm.

She squared her shoulders. "So? You did it for me. Twice."

So much emotion filled his eyes that her breath caught.

"We have to talk, Derek. This . . ." She moved a hand between them. "It isn't right."

He raked a hand through his brown hair. "What isn't right is that I care about you while you care about someone else."

"Fine!" Kylie felt herself growing angry and losing hope. "Do I care about Lucas? Yes. But I don't care about him the way I care about you."

He shook his head. "You can't lie to me, Kylie. I can read your emotions and when you're around him you're . . . attracted to him."

"Okay, I'll even admit I'm attracted to him. But that doesn't mean anything."

"The hell it doesn't!" He started to walk away.

Kylie grabbed his arm. "You're no different."

"What?" His eyes brightened with anger and hurt.

"I saw you looking at Miranda when we were swimming."

"I didn't—"

"Yes, you did!"

"This is stupid." He started walking away again.

Kylie almost let him go, but she remembered that she was going to have to pay a pint for this. Damn it. She wanted her blood's worth.

She caught up with him. "Perry even noticed because he started giving you the evil eye."

He continued walking and so did she.

"Did I get bent out of shape about it? No, I didn't because I know that while you might have thought she was pretty in her bathing suit, it didn't mean you didn't like me."

He stopped and turned to face her. "That is different."

"How is it different? If I could read your emotions, like you can read mine, I would have read lust loud and clear."

"Yeah, but . . . but I'm a guy."

Her mouth dropped open. "So only guys can be attracted to someone? Please! What century are you living in?"

His eyes tightened. "I didn't mean it like that."

"Then what did you mean?"

"I meant . . ." He clenched his jaw. "Christ. I don't know, but it's still different."

"It's not, Derek! Don't you see? You're getting all bent out of shape because you're jealous and you have no reason to be."

"It's more than that," he said. "You just said you care about him. This isn't just—"

"Yeah, I care about him. We met a long time ago. And maybe that bonds us somehow. And yes, he's nice looking. But . . . I want to be with you."

She thought she was getting through to him, but he looked away. "I can't do it, Kylie. Until you can prove to me that he doesn't mean anything to you, I can't do this." He walked away again.

"Derek?" she called.

He turned around. "What?"

Her chest grew heavy. "You lied to me."

"About what?" Frustration colored his voice.

"You said we'd be friends. This isn't how you treat a friend."

He looked up at the sky before he met her eyes. "You're right. I'm sorry. I guess I can't be your friend." He walked off.

This time she let him go.

It was hard to get through the day. Kylie wanted to ask Holiday to let her skip the scheduled events, but she'd begged off too much. So she went to art, took a hike, and lost herself in cake decorating.

Every time she started to think about Derek, she'd mentally snap a rubber band around her heart. She was so focused on decorating her cupcakes that half the class was over before she realized Miranda wasn't there.

As soon as it was over, she ditched music class and found Della walking to the lake for kayak lessons. Della had been pretty low-key lately, still recovering from the whole FRU visit and testing. And she dreaded having to go undercover to try to help catch her cousin for murder. Of course, worrying about that meant she wasn't worrying about parents weekend. Hey, you had to find the silver linings where you could.

"Have you seen Miranda?" Kylie asked.

"No. Is something wrong?"

"She just wasn't in cake decorating. I was going to see if she was at the cabin."

"You want me to come with you?"

"No," Kylie said, remembering that Della had been looking forward to kayaking. "If I can't find her, I'll find you. I'm sure it's nothing."

Unfortunately, right before Kylie reached her cabin, she was certain she'd been wrong in her assessment. Her first clue? The high-pitched scream coming from inside.

Taking off at a dead run, Kylie reached the front door before she realized that the screams weren't Miranda's. Not that this realization slowed her down. Someone was in her cabin and screaming bloody murder. And Miranda was missing.

Jerking the door open, Kylie ran inside. "Miranda?"

"In here," Miranda called from her bedroom, her words barely heard over the shrieking.

Pushing open the bedroom door, Kylie thought she was prepared to face anything. She couldn't have been more wrong.

Chapter Twenty-nine

Kylie gaped at the screaming redheaded girl locked in the big purple cage in the middle of Miranda's room. Then her gaze shot to Miranda, reclining in the middle of her bed, painting her toenails as if it were a lazy Sunday morning.

"Let me out of here, you bitch!" The girl shook the cage.

Miranda finished spreading fuchsia pink on her pinky toenail before she glanced up. "What's up?" She smiled extra wide at Kylie.

"Bitch!" the girl screamed at Miranda then glared at Kylie. "Make her let me go!"

"I think I should be asking you what's up," Kylie said to Miranda, and then she looked back at the girl. A quick sniff of the air said there hadn't been any blood lost.

Yet, anyway.

"Release me!" the prisoner snarled.

Kylie glanced back at Miranda and raised an eyebrow.

"See what I caught." Miranda giggled. "Remember I've been telling you that someone was lurking around our cabin? I set a trap. And damn if I didn't catch Tabitha Evans."

"Do you know her?" Kylie asked.

"Yup, she's one of the witches I'm competing against in two weeks."

Tabitha shook the bars so hard that the cage rocked. "I'm the witch that is going to put a hex on you if you don't let me out!"

"Don't worry," Miranda said. "Her powers don't work as long as she's kept in my special cage. And I put a silencer about a hundred feet away, so no one can hear her yell."

"What's she doing here?" Kylie asked, concerned for the prisoner.

"Trying to undermine my confidence so I'd drop out of the competition."

"And if I'd known you were such a screw-up I wouldn't have wasted my time," the girl screamed.

Okay, so Tabitha deserved to be caged. "Do you think she's the one who's been cutting off the security alarm?" Kylie asked.

"No, this was done with magic. Pathetic, barely excusable magic, of course." Miranda glanced at the caged girl.

Tabitha hissed. "You're the one who's pathetic."

Miranda raised an eyebrow at her prisoner. "And you're the one in the cage."

The girl returned to shrieking. Miranda beamed with pride.

No doubt, catching Tabitha was good for Miranda's ego. Kylie hated to pop Miranda's bubble, but . . . "As cute as she looks in the cage, you do know you can't keep her."

"I don't plan on it," Miranda said. "I told her that as soon as she turns Socks back into a kitten, she can leave."

"And I've told you that I didn't do that! That was your screw-up! All you!"

"Please," Miranda said. "For weeks almost everything I tried to do came out wrong."

Miranda swung her feet off the bed and leaned close to the cage. "Change the skunk back into a kitten and you can go."

"And for the millionth time, I didn't do that!"

Miranda glanced back to Kylie. "Do you want me to paint your toenails?" Doubt filled Miranda's eyes.

"Look," Tabitha snapped. "If it wasn't you who did it, then maybe it was that old guy."

"I've got some nice reds," Miranda told Kylie, ignoring Tabitha.

Kylie wasn't so good at ignoring. "What old guy?"

"Don't believe anything she says," Miranda said.

"I don't know who he is, but he's vampire. But he has some other powers, too, because he was here using a similar spell as I was. Scary old guy."

"Please," Miranda said. "Tell me something I can believe."

"I'm telling the truth," Tabitha snapped.

Miranda rolled her eyes. Then she wiggled her pinky.

"Wait," Kylie said, but too late, the cage and Tabitha disappeared.

"Wait for what?" Miranda asked.

"Where did she go?"

"You said I couldn't keep her."

Kylie frowned. "What if she was telling the truth about the weird old guy?"

"Please, she's making up crap. Della would have smelled a vampire. Tabitha's crazy."

Kylie had to admit Miranda had a point. Della could sniff out vampires a mile away.

Miranda dropped back on the bed. "Can you believe I caught Tabitha Evans. I'm good."

Socks came slinking into the room cautiously. His puffy black and white tail pointed in the air as if ready to blow and go if needed. Kylie looked back at Miranda. She might be good at setting traps, but she hadn't quite gotten the spell down to turn Socks back into a kitten.

Then Kylie remembered her conversation with Derek. She mentally reached for the rubber band to snap herself out of thinking about him, but the dang rubber band wasn't there. All she could feel was a big empty hole in her chest where her heart used to be.

"I'm gonna lay down." Before she went into her bedroom, she stopped at the fridge. Yanking opening the freezer, she grabbed one of the many quarts of ice cream Miranda had bought to nurse her broken heart.

Snatching a spoon out of the drawer, Kylie wondered if there was enough ice cream in the universe to make her feel better.

She really didn't believe so.

The next week passed in a haze of heartbreak. Kylie gave her pint of blood and ate at least ten pints of ice cream. Derek continued to avoid her; Lucas continued to show up. Not that she could even get mad at him. He never made any passes. He was just being a friend. With her heart on the mend, she could use another friend.

Of course, they never discussed Fredericka or the dreams—and thankfully she'd managed to keep the dreams at bay. He had asked about Derek, though, and Kylie told him it was a sore subject. The only thing Lucas said was that Derek was an idiot. For some reason, Kylie appreciated Lucas saying it.

She also appreciated the fact that Fredericka had stayed out of her way. Kylie wasn't sure, but she suspected Lucas had something to do with that, too.

The ghost showed up every morning. Sometimes she'd speak, but she never offered anything that helped Kylie figure out who was in danger. Whenever Kylie would start to worry about the ghost's warning, Holiday would take her to the falls. They'd gone three times. Kylie kept leaving with the same message: stay focused and keep the faith.

Holiday hadn't mentioned anything about Burnett in all this time. Kylie wondered if she'd told him she'd found another investor, or if she was reconsidering his offer. Kylie caught Holiday spying out the window and watching Burnett and the others play ball at least six times. Two or three of those times Kylie had even stood with her, just so she could watch Derek. Not that he didn't know she looked on. He would always glance at the window.

Their eyes would meet. Kylie would remember how much she missed him while he appeared annoyed.

"You want to talk about it?" Holiday had asked the last time it happened.

Kylie had agreed to spill her guts, but only over ice cream. She'd eaten all of Miranda's stash and needed more. So Kylie and Holiday took the afternoon off and went back to the ice cream parlor where they ate their weight in cold creamy scoops of bliss.

"Why does ice cream go with a broken heart?" Kylie asked.

"Because if you eat enough of it, it freezes the heart and numbs the pain for a bit," Holiday answered, and they both laughed.

Daniel hadn't visited since the day her mom had broken into the camp and had to be erased, but her stepdad had called twice. Kylie had taken his second call. They talked about his job, about the weather, and then he mentioned the possibility of Kylie attending the Shadow Falls boarding school. He hadn't been positive or negative and said it was up to her mom.

When she hung up, she realized that her mom and dad must be talking for him to know about the boarding school. Kylie wasn't sure how she felt about that. Was her mom ready to forgive him? Kylie almost called her mom and asked, but with parents weekend less than one week away, Kylie figured she should wait and do it in person.

Miranda seldom mentioned Perry anymore. Not that it stopped Perry from watching Miranda. Anytime he was within a hundred feet of her, he had his gaze locked on her. Kylie knew that Miranda noticed it. She chose to ignore it. Not too hard considering her stress about the upcoming competition that her mother had entered her in during parents weekend. If she wasn't practicing for the event, she was attempting to solve the puzzle of what happened to Socks.

After two weeks, Socks didn't seem to mind being a skunk. He seemed to understand the power of his tail, and he'd raise it up in a threat at the least provocation. He even had Della walking a line. Thankfully, he hadn't sprayed again.

Della dreaded going home. And now she dreaded coming back to the FRU job waiting on her. Going undercover to find out if her cousin was responsible for the murders wasn't going to be easy for Della. A grumpy Della and a stressed-out Miranda meant the two were at each other's throats. Kylie often wondered if she didn't intervene if the two would really kill each other. But she loved the two of them too much to chance it.

The PI had finally discovered that Kent and Betty Brighten had taken a long vacation in Ireland. So Kylie's quest to discover what she was had been temporarily put on hold. Wasn't that just lovely?

The one good thing that happened lately was Kylie no longer felt that strange sense of being watched. She wondered if Tabitha had been the cause of it. But when she'd recall Tabitha, Kylie would remember what the girl said about an old vampire hanging around.

For some reason, that bothered Kylie. Not enough to mention it to Holiday, because in doing so she might get Miranda in trouble. And after the Burnett incident with Della, getting friends in trouble was the last thing Kylie wanted to do.

On Tuesday morning, Kylie woke up with what felt like an extra chill in the air. Either the ghost was trying to send a message or Kylie had more than one spirit hanging around. Great. That's all she needed, another ghost.

"What do you want?" Kylie trembled beneath the covers.

Her phone started croaking. Either her phone's ringtone had gotten changed or Miranda had managed to turn it into a frog. Kylie grabbed her phone. It stopped making the hideous sound and went directly to her voicemail messages.

First it played the one her dad had left, then one the PI left a few days ago. Next it played one that Kylie hadn't heard. From Trey, her boyfriend from the past. How had she missed this call? He asked her to return his call, saying it was important.

"Yeah, right," she muttered. "What, did you find out my breasts got bigger and you want to see them?" She shut the phone off, but not before deleting his message.

She had no sooner laid it back on the nightstand when the cell commenced croaking.

Grabbing it, she looked at the dang thing to make sure it was off. It was. So how did it make noise? She hit the off button again. The croaking continued.

"Are you doing this?" she asked the spirit. "If so, stop. Because it's not funny. And it's not telling me crap about what I need to know."

The phone went silent. The ghost appeared at the foot of her bed. *You have to do something soon. She's dying.*

Just like before, the spirit didn't offer a freaking clue as to who the mysterious "she" was.

Kylie got dressed and decided to visit Holiday. She doubted if hearing Holiday say she thought everything was going to be okay would take the edge off the fear, but she had to try.

She hadn't even gotten to the office porch when she heard the voices ringing in her ears.

"Tell me it isn't dangerous?" Holiday insisted, sounding furious.

"I can't tell you that," Burnett said. *"This work is always dangerous."*

"Then no. He can't go."

"I didn't come to ask you," Burnett said, sounding equally annoyed. *"He's gotten permission from his mother. He'll be leaving today around noon."*

Kylie turned and started walking in the opposite direction. She would have covered her ears, but that had never worked before, so she just kept walking, hoping the voices would fade.

"It's wrong," Holiday said. *"First, you involve Lucas, and now Derek. I have to put my foot down."*

Kylie stopped. *First Lucas and now Derek . . . what?*

"They are both exceptional boys," Burnett said.

"And that's my point. They are boys, Burnett."

"I was sixteen when I went to work for the FRU. Lucas is eighteen. Derek is only a few months shy of that. And he's an eraser, Holiday. Do you know how few there are of those?"

"I don't care about that. I care about him."

"He'll only be gone a month or less. Back in time for the school year to begin."

"Assuming he's not killed trying to do the government's work," Holiday snapped.

"I'm sorry," Burnett said, and there was regret in his voice.

Kylie heard a door slam. Burnett had left but she didn't move. She stood there on the trail, digesting what she'd just heard. Derek was leaving. He was going to work for the FRU. He wouldn't be back for a month.

Assuming he's not killed trying to do the government's work. Holiday's words played in Kylie's mind. Her heart froze. She took off down the trail toward Derek's cabin.

Chapter Thirty

Kylie got to Derek's cabin a minute later. She spotted Chris walking out of the cabin, dressed for his morning jog, and stopped. She would have jumped into the woods and hidden, but Chris was vampire, which meant he'd probably already heard her. So she started jogging and hoped he wouldn't stop and ask any questions.

When they ran past each other, she waved. He smiled and kept going. She continued down the trail past the cabin until she felt he wouldn't be in hearing range. Then she spun around, ran into the cabin, and went straight into Derek's room.

He was in bed, still asleep. His wide chest was bare. The sheet came low around his waist and Kylie wasn't sure if he had anything on beneath the sheet. She'd heard rumors that most boys slept in the buff. But she'd seen him naked and that didn't scare her away.

"Derek?"

He dropped his hand over his face.

She moved over to the bed and touched his shoulder. "Derek?"

His eyes popped open and he shot up. He stared at her but didn't look awake. "You've got your clothes on, so this isn't a dream." He flinched as if he realized he'd said that aloud and then he dropped back on the bed and stared up at the ceiling.

"It's not a dream." She sat beside him. "I heard what you're planning to do and I don't want you to go. Please, don't go."

He looked over at her with heavy-lidded eyes, but she could tell he was awake. "How did you find out?"

He hadn't answered her question, so she didn't answer his. "Were you not even going to say good-bye?" Tears filled her eyes.

He sat up and pulled the sheet around his waist. "I was going to say good-bye."

She blinked away the emotion. "You're doing this because of me, aren't you?"

"No. Not completely." He touched her arm and the floodgates of emotion really started pouring.

"Please, don't go," she said in tears.

"I have to. I need to get my head on straight." He blinked. "You were right. Well, partially right. I still think you have issues you need to resolve about Lucas. But . . . you were right about me being jealous. My ability to read emotions is getting stronger. And I don't know why, but with you, it's as if I feel everything you feel but . . . more. I don't know if it's because I care about you so much or what. But when you feel something I don't like, an attraction for another guy, anger, or even disappointment at someone, I . . . I go crazy inside. It's like someone is shooting me up with emotional adrenaline." He raked a hand over his face. "I've either got to learn to deal with this or . . ."

"Or what?" she asked. He didn't answer, but Kylie knew what he meant. He either had to learn to deal with the emotions she unleashed inside him, or walk away from her. But wasn't that what he was doing? Walking away?

"And you've got to deal with Lucas and . . ." He paused. "I'm also going to confront my dad. And when I come back in a month, we'll see how things stand. You may have fallen in love with Lucas by then. And if that happens, I'll have to accept it."

"Would it be that easy to accept?"

"No. But I don't see what other choice I have."

"But you do have a choice. Stay. Give us a chance. We'll work through this."

He shook his head. "I can't, Kylie. I just can't."

She looked at him and as hard as it was to accept, she finally did. Derek was leaving. He had made his choice, and it wasn't her.

Chin high, vowing that she'd done everything she could, she turned and walked out. He might have broken her heart, but he wasn't going to break her spirit. She would get over him. She would.

A week later, Kylie sat on a blanket out by the river where she and her mother had sat and talked about Daniel. Kylie just wanted to be alone to think, to try and wrap her head around how she was going to get her mom to sign her up for Shadow Falls' boarding school. And maybe, just maybe, Daniel would drop by while she was here.

She lay back on the blanket and stared up at the blue sky, and then she heard someone approach.

"See any elephants?" a familiar male voice asked.

She smiled at Lucas. "No, but I just saw a giraffe."

He looked up in the sky. "Where?"

"Over there." She pointed to the left. "Its neck is no longer con-nected to its body, but you can still see it if you squint."

He dropped down beside her. She thought he looked up at the clouds, but when she glanced back, she found him looking at her. He smiled. "You just get prettier every day, Kylie Galen."

She rolled her eyes. "Don't start."

"Okay, can I say I'll miss you?"

She sat up. "Are you going to your grandmother's house?"

"Yeah. We're in Houston."

She studied the tip of her tennis shoe, and decided to just ask. "Lucas, are you working with FRU?"

His eyes widened. "Who told you?"

"I overheard Burnett and Holiday talking about it."

"After I got inside the gang that had my sister, I got with Burnett to help me bring down a few really bad guys. So yeah, I sort of worked with them. And I told them if they needed me for anything else, I would be available."

"Isn't it dangerous?"

He studied her. "Are you asking out of concern for me or for Derek?"

"Both." She had accepted that Derek had left. She hadn't completely gotten over the heartbreak, but she would.

"It's not that dangerous. If you follow the game plan, things generally go okay."

He brushed a long stand of hair from her cheek. "You know I want to be more than your friend, right?"

She went to studying her tennis shoe again.

"I don't expect you to answer. I just wanted you to know before some other guy tries to move in." He leaned closer. "I'm patient, Kylie. I've waited eleven years for you. I can wait until you're ready." He pressed a kiss to her cheek. It wasn't anything like the kisses they'd shared, especially those in her dreams. But his nearness—his woodsy scent, the feel of his lips against her skin—sent a hundred butterflies into full flutter mode.

When she looked over at him, he was gone.

And obviously so were Kylie's wits. Because for the life of her, she didn't know what she'd planned to do, reprimand him for kissing her . . . or kiss him back.

And maybe it was better if she didn't answer her own question, too.

Friday morning, Kylie, Miranda, and Della, each carting suitcases, walked the trail to meet up with their parents. They walked slowly, like condemned prisoners moving to their executions.

"I'm going to be peeing on a drug test stick every hour," Della muttered.

Miranda sighed. "I'm going to screw up at my competition and my mom is going to give me up for adoption."

"I'm going to a ghost hunt," Kylie added. Both girls looked at her. "Don't ask."

Holiday met them at the end of the trail, channeling her normal, peppy self. "Smile, guys. It's only for a few days."

They all turned and looked at each other again. Kylie dropped her suitcase and hugged them both. "I expect a phone call from each of you twice a day."

"Twice a day," Della said. "I hope you don't mind if I call when I'm peeing on a drug test stick, because that's what I'm gonna be doing the whole time."

"Just don't flush," Miranda said. "I hate it when people flush when they're talking to me."

Five minutes later, over in the dining hall, Kylie gave Holiday a big hug. "Take care of Socks," she told her.

"I'm planning on bringing him over to my place," Holiday said.

When Kylie and her mom started out of the dining hall, Perry came over and gave her a nudge with his elbow. For Perry, that was equivalent to a hug. Kylie gave him a warm smile.

"It seems like you've made good friends here," her mom said.

"Yeah, I have, Mom. They're special."

Kylie almost ran out the door when Lucas stepped in front of her. "Hello, Mrs. Galen," he said. "My name is Lucas. I just wanted to say good-bye to your daughter."

Kylie's heart raced as she worried her mom might recognize him.

"Nice to meet you, Lucas," her mom said, and stepped away to give them some privacy.

He smiled. "Take care."

"I will."

He leaned in. "Dream of me," he whispered.

She rolled her eyes, but he just grinned and walked off. Kylie headed over to her mom.

"He's kind of cute," her mom said, but she had that tone—the tone she got before she started handing out the sex pamphlets. They walked out of the dining hall and headed for the car.

"Yeah," Kylie agreed, and for the umpteenth time, she hoped that the weekend went okay. No unexpected surprises, no long, uncomfortable silences with her and her mom.

When her mom started the car, the cold that filled the interior was more powerful than any car air-conditioning.

"Wow. I've never had this car get cool so fast." When her mom pulled out, Kylie glanced in the backseat to stare at the ghost in her bloody nightgown. Suddenly the ghost lurched forward and threw up all over Kylie's shoulder. The stench was awful.

Kylie fought to keep her gag reflex from bouncing up and down her throat.

"So," her mom said, oblivious to it all. "Where would you like to go for an early lunch? I'm starving."

Chapter Thirty-one

Kylie wasn't sure who it was who said you couldn't go home again. But he had it partly right. Oh, you could go home. It was just going to be awkward as hell. Amazingly, it didn't stem from her mom. They'd actually had a good three-hour drive home, phantom puke aside. The problem was the house. It felt cold, not just because the ghost had decided to tag along, but because of her dad. Or lack of dad. There was nothing, not one thing here that reminded Kylie that he'd ever lived here. Even the pictures of their father-daughter trips were gone, replaced now with pictures of just Kylie.

She couldn't blame her mom, but damn. For the first time since it all happened, Kylie worried about how her mom might really feel with her going away to boarding school. And maybe she even understood her mom wanting to sell the house.

"Doesn't it feel so good to be back?" Her mom hugged her.

Being back? Not so good. The hug felt nice, though. So nice it even made the house feel less awkward.

When Kylie went into her room, she couldn't help but laugh. On her nightstand was a whole set of pamphlets on all the sex-related topics Kylie had missed while away. The one on top, obviously the one Kylie's mom thought most important, covered info on safe oral sex. Oh yeah, crucial need-to-know information. Kylie was planning on running out tonight and having oral sex.

Her mom had the entire weekend scheduled with items from her We Gotta List. We gotta bake your favorite cookies. We gotta go eat at a new pizza place. We gotta be at the haunted house at six.

When, Kylie wondered, was she going to have time to run out and have "safe" oral sex?

Kylie added a big Gotta to the list. *Gotta convince Mom to sign me up for boarding school.* Even with her reservations about leaving her mom, Kylie was a supernatural and felt like a fish out of water back at home.

At six that evening, after baking cookies and enjoying some together time with her mom, Kylie crawled her fish-out-of-water butt into the car to go to the ghost hunt. And she seriously hoped that the B&B owner didn't mind if she brought a visitor along because sitting in the backseat—still bloody, still puking—was Kylie's ghost, who wasn't any more communicative here than she'd been back at Shadow Falls.

And to prove the point, the ghost disappeared before they arrived at the B&B.

Once they'd all gathered in the lobby of the B&B, the owner, a tall, heavyset woman in her late fifties, with dyed red hair, waved them into a semicircle. "Welcome. Welcome to Anderson's B&B. My name is Celeste Bell. Some of you may remember me from my many television appearances."

Kylie didn't but several of the other guests nodded their heads. Celeste was a professed ghost whisperer who had appeared on some cable show as an expert on haunting. She wore a long white gown, as if dressing spooky would help intensify the experience.

"The house was built in the late eighteen hundreds by Joshua Anderson, but tragedy struck before he ever moved in when his young bride was killed on their wedding day in a carriage accident. Joshua took his own life in the master bedroom. The place was subsequently sold and reopened as a saloon. More tragedy soon followed. Now, before we get started, let's talk about the rules."

The rules were simple. Stay together. No unnecessary chitchat. Celeste also insisted they turn off their cell phones because that kind of energy could chase away ghosts.

Funny, Kylie thought, her experience said ghosts really liked tinkering with her cell.

Kylie actually checked Celeste's brain pattern to see if maybe she was supernatural, but nope. The ten attendees, with the exception of Kylie and her mom, were all card-carrying senior citizens who no longer had to show their IDs to get their free coffees at their neighborhood Chick-fil-A. Moving slowly as a group, half of them using walkers, they followed the woman through the first floor of the house. In each room, Celeste stopped to tell another haunting tale, most from the house's days as a saloon.

Thus far, the place looked ghost-free.

While Celeste may have sucked as a ghost whisper, she was a good storyteller and she had everyone on pins and needles listening to the spooky tales.

"Now, we're going to have dinner. And I'll tell you about what happened in the early nineteen hundreds. Go ahead and sit down." Celeste motioned to the dining room table, with plates already filled with spaghetti. "For some reason," she whispered, "this room is always a bit colder than the rest of the house."

As if on cue, the temperature in the old parlor dropped a good forty degrees. Kylie's ghost materialized next to her. The patrons all huddled together, hugging themselves, as steam rose from their lips. The look on Celeste's face would have made attending the ghost hunt worth it if Kylie hadn't seen the look of sheer terror on her mom's face.

"It's okay, Mom," Kylie whispered.

"It's so friggin' damn spooky." Her mom never said *friggin'* or *damn*.

"Probably just a trick," Kylie lied.

"It's time. Time for you to do something!" the ghost screamed.

Show me what I have to do, Kylie said in her mind.

Right then, every cell phone in the room started ringing. Well, all of them except Kylie's. Her phone croaked like some demented frog. And since they had all been turned off, that brought some serious gasps.

But not as serious as when the chandelier crashed down on top of the table, sending plates of spaghetti shooting across the room.

Celeste, the professed ghost whisperer and cable TV "celebrity," fainted. Kylie didn't know people using walkers could move so fast. But not fast enough for her mom. Kylie thought for a second that her mom was going to knock a couple of them out of the way to take the lead spot heading out of the dining room.

Kylie knelt beside Celeste. As the last of the guests fought their way out the door, Kylie heard one of them say, "Who is Trey Cannon?"

Kylie looked up at the elderly man.

"Don't know," said another lady. "But that's who called me, too."

Kylie grabbed her phone, and sure as hell, she had a voice message from Trey.

Why would the ghost send Trey's message to everyone in the room?

Kylie looked up at the ghost who stood in the middle of the room wearing spaghetti all over her blood-soaked nightgown, which definitely would be putting Kylie off pasta for a long time. "It's Trey? I'm supposed to help Trey? But you said . . . 'she' needed help."

The ghost started to fade.

"Don't you dare leave!" Kylie screeched.

"I'm so sorry, baby. I thought you were right behind me," her mom called from the other room. Seconds later, she ran back in and dropped beside Kylie. "Oh, God, is she dead?"

The woman's eyes shot open and she screamed.

Twenty minutes later, while Kylie's mom spoke to the ambulance driver who was about to cart off Celeste and one of the guests who was now complaining of chest pains, Kylie got her mom's phone and deleted Trey's message. The last thing Kylie wanted was her mom getting suspicious. She hoped her mom hadn't heard Trey's name mentioned in the mix of things.

Kylie listened to his message. All he'd said was to call him. She did. It went to his voicemail. Just freaking great!

When Kylie woke up the next morning at nine o'clock, she had two startling realizations.

First: She hadn't been woken up at dawn by the ghost. Did this mean anything? Was it a good thing? A bad thing?

Second: And this was the shocker. She wasn't alone. Nope. Completely covered under the blanket next to Kylie was a body. Dead or alive, she wasn't sure.

Biting back a scream, she touched it. More like poked it. It wasn't cold. It even made a *oomph* sound. Her mom's head popped out from under the covers. When she saw Kylie's expression, she bolted upright. "What is it?"

Kylie blinked. "What are you doing in my bed?"

"Oh." She ran a hand through her newly styled hair that really looked good on her. "I came to check in on you. I guess I . . . dropped off."

Kylie giggled. "You were scared."

Her mom did an eye roll that would put Sara to shame. "Nooo." She broke down and laughed. "Okay, yes. It was freaky. I was shocked you could sleep."

"It was just a ghost." Kylie grinned.

"You say that as if you see them all the time." Her mom touched Kylie's cheek. "I'm so happy you're home. See how much fun we can have? You don't need to go to boarding school."

Kylie's breath caught. "But I really want to go, Mom."

The spark in her mom's eyes dimmed. "Let's not talk about this now. We have a wonderful day planned."

In spite of the anti–boarding school talk, and the fact that Kylie still was unable to get in touch with Trey, her mood remained positive. The ghost had apparently decided to give Kylie a reprieve. That or she decided she'd just caused enough trouble after last night's scene. A call to the B&B informed them that both Celeste and the old man who'd complained of chest pains had been released from the hospital.

They decided to do pizza for lunch and were primed to leave when Kylie's phone rang. When she saw it was Miranda, she asked for a few minutes. Her mom took off to check her e-mail.

"Hey," Miranda said. "I got us on three-way. Say hello, Della."

"A verbal ménage à trois," Della said.

"Gross," Miranda said.

"You wanna hear gross?" Della asked. "I just peed on my hand trying to piss on this damned drug stick while talking on the phone to you."

Kylie laughed. "I miss you guys." The sound of a toilet flushing filled the line.

"Oh, double gross," Miranda snapped. "I told you not to flush while I was on the phone."

Kylie dropped on the sofa. "Miranda, have you gone to your competition yet?"

"I'm not on until four." She sounded desperate.

"You'll do fine," Kylie said.

"You will," Della added. "How was the ghost hunt, Kylie?"

Kylie checked to make sure her mom wasn't near. "You aren't freaking going to believe this." She gave them the lowdown. They all had a good laugh and then the conversation switched to how much they all wished they were back at Shadow Falls. When Kylie realized she'd been talking for almost ten minutes, she told them good-bye. They agreed to talk this afternoon.

"I'm ready, Mom." The doorbell rang. Kylie ran to the door while her mom called that she was shutting off her computer. When Kylie swung open the door all the awkwardness from the night before came hurling at her. Funny how last night's unease had stemmed from her dad not being present and now it stemmed because he was here.

"Hi, Pumpkin."

The question popping around Kylie's head was if her mom knew Dad was coming.

"Are you ready to—" Mom's tennis shoes stopped so fast at the opening to the entryway. The skid marks on the marble floor and the shock on her mom's face answered Kylie's question.

Mom didn't know. Even more apparent, Mom wasn't happy.

Her dad's gaze went to her mom. "Hi, hon." His smile wavered.

The nervousness of his grin sent a desperate flutter to Kylie's gut. Okay, her dad deserved to be nervous. But it still felt downright wrong to open the door to her dad when this had been his home. His castle. Now he was unsure if he was welcome. And if her mom's expression was any indication, he wasn't.

"I thought maybe I could take you girls to lunch," he said.

Her mom took a step back. "I . . . I should have known you'd want to see her." She waved a hand toward the door. "You two go."

"Why don't you come, too?" her dad insisted.

"I think not," her mom countered.

"Kylie wants you to come." His father's gaze shot to her. "Don't you, Pumpkin? Like ol' times, the three of us."

Her mother frowned. Kylie frowned. Her dad grew more nervous. The tension in the room grew terse.

Her mom notched up her chin. "Why not make it four? Your whore can come, too."

"Oh! This is a bad time, isn't it?" Trey's voice came right behind her dad.

Kylie's mom shot up the stairs. Her dad looked stunned. Trey looked embarrassed.

Then her dad frowned at Kylie. "Didn't you tell her it was over?"

Had she heard him right? "Huh?"

"You didn't tell her that it was over with Amy?"

"Should I leave?" Trey asked.

"Yes," her dad answered.

Kylie's head reeled. She watched Trey go. She heard her mom crying. Kylie stared at her dad—stepdad. The idea that he'd actually attempted to use her to get her mom gnawed on some very raw nerves. The fact that he'd expected her to update her mom about his relationship status pretty much nuked those nerves.

She pointed at her dad. "Don't you ever try to use me to get to my mom!"

"I thought—"

"Then stop thinking!" She slammed the door. The house shook. The small glass window in the doorframe shattered. She saw her dad's startled expression through the broken window before he took off.

She breathed in.

She breathed out.

Then she took the stairs two at a time to check on her mom.

It took Kylie an hour to convince her mom to go out for pizza again. She'd tried calling Trey hoping to see what was so important that the ghost had sent his message to everyone in the room, but she got no answer. They were in the middle of lunch at the pizza parlor, still not back to their prior jovial mood, when her phone started croaking.

"Oh, honey," her mom said. "Change that ringtone." She hugged herself and called out to the waiter, "Can you turn down the air?"

Kylie grabbed her cell. There was no call, but an old voice message played.

"Hi, Kylie. It's Sara. I'm sorry I had to hang up like that. I . . . had something I had to take care of. Listen, I really want to see you when you're home. Please make sure to call me?"

"Who was it?" her mom asked, then lowered her voice. "Your dad?"

"No. A message from Sara."

Kylie stared at her pizza and got the strangest feeling. "Mom, would you mind if I went to see Sara after lunch?"

"Hi, Kylie," Mrs. Jetton said an hour later. "Sara will be thrilled to see you."

Kylie studied Sara's mom's expression. Her eyes looked red and her face pale. The somber mood filling the air ratcheted up Kylie's concern for her former best friend.

"She's in her room," Mrs. Jetton said.

Kylie almost asked what was wrong, but the chill running down her spine prevented her from talking. That short walk from the living room to Sara's door filled Kylie's head with dozens of memories. And for some odd reason, those memories brought tears to her eyes.

"You have to save her. You have to save her." The ghost's words vibrated in Kylie's head. She swallowed and told herself she was overreacting, that everything was fine.

Sara's door stood ajar and when Kylie saw Sara, Kylie gasped.

Sara looked . . . awful. So pale that Kylie watched her chest to make sure she was breathing.

Sara opened her eyes. "She told you, didn't she?"

Kylie used both hands to wipe the tears from her cheeks. "Told me what?"

"What the doctor . . . If she didn't . . . why are you crying?"

"Happy to see you." She tried to smile.

"You always were a lousy liar." Sara pulled the covers up. "Mom, can you please turn down the air? I'm freezing in here."

"Honey, I already did," her mom called from the living room. "I phoned the electrician. Something's wrong with the AC again."

A photo album on Sara's bedside table plopped to the floor.

Kylie picked it up. She wasn't surprised when she saw the face staring up from the album. Then she looked at the foot of Sara's bed at the same spirit of the woman. She'd lost the spaghetti and the bloodstained gown, but her expression was just as dire as before.

"Who is this?" Kylie passed her finger over the face. Sara leaned over to see. It appeared to hurt her to move. "My grandma. She died when I was four. Of the same kind of cancer. Isn't that freaky?"

Cancer. The word brought another gasp to Kylie's lungs and she had to work to keep her lips from trembling. She looked at the spirit. "I can't fix this."

"Yes, you can!"

"Can't fix what?" Sara looked at the album as if Kylie had broken something.

"Nothing." Kylie sat down beside Sara. The memories of them on this bed, sharing secrets, laughing at the stupidest things, filled Kylie's head.

She swallowed emotions that threatened to overpower her. "Do you remember when we laid here and practiced kissing mirrors before the sixth-grade dance?"

Sara smiled. "Yeah." She leaned on the pillow and closed her eyes. Her long brown hair looked thinner and it lacked its normal luster. The silence grew longer. Sadder.

Kylie stroked Sara's arm. "What did the doctor say?"

Chapter Thirty-two

Sara opened her eyes. "The oncologist said he'd try to get me into experimental trials, but . . . he thinks it's too late." A sheen of tears filled Sara's eyes. "Mom says I'm doing it, but . . ." Sara swallowed. "I don't want to die." Her lips trembled. "But I can still hear my mom saying dozens of times that if *she* ever got cancer, she'd rather die than go through what they put her mama through. She said they butchered her mom. I don't want to deal with that. The one surgery was bad enough."

Kylie recalled the dreams of knives coming at her. She looked at Sara's abdomen. "When did you have surgery?"

"Last week," Sara answered. "I'd missed so many periods. The clinic doctor felt a mass when she was checking me. Two days later, I was in the hospital."

"Why didn't you call me?"

Sara bit down on her lip. "I did. I didn't tell you that I thought I had cancer, but . . ."

Guilt filled Kylie's chest. The ghost, Sara's grandmother, had been trying to get her to listen to the message. The same message she had played earlier.

"Couldn't they take it out?"

Sara shook her head. "There's too much. It's everywhere."

The ache in Kylie's heart doubled. She recalled Trey's message that had been sent to everyone at the B&B. Why had the ghost sent Trey's message? "Trey?"

Sara looked down at her hands. "I'm sorry. I swear I didn't mean it to happen. I'd drunk too much. He'd drunk too much."

"What?" Kylie asked.

Sara looked up. "Shit. He hasn't told you, has he?"

It took only a second to digest what Sara said—it took less time for Kylie to know it wasn't important.

"I asked him to tell you because I couldn't stand it. He promised he would."

"He tried. I didn't take his calls. But I don't care, Sara." She took Sara's hand in hers and squeezed. "Trey and I are . . . so over. You're what's important."

Another tear crawled down Sara's pale cheek. "You're not just saying that because I'm dying, are you?" Sara tried to make it a joke.

Kylie didn't laugh. "No."

Sara pulled her hand out of Kylie's. "You're hot."

"You can do it." The ghost's voice came right behind Kylie's ear. *"It's your touch."*

Kylie looked back at the spirit. "Do you mean . . . like Helen?"

"What?" Sara asked.

Kylie continued to stare at the ghost.

"Do it," the ghost said. *"Please. Heal her. Before it's too late."*

"I don't know how," Kylie muttered.

"Am I hallucinating or are you talking to yourself?" Sara asked. "I mean, I am on some pretty good drugs right now."

Kylie looked back at Sara. "No." She felt the cold of the ghost inch closer.

"No, I'm not hallucinating or no, you're not talking to your-self?"

"No to both." Kylie tried to think. Could she really do this?

She looked down at Sara's grandmother's picture. "What's her name?"

"Fanny Mildred Bogart." Sara laughed. "I'm glad Mama didn't name me after her." It obviously hurt Sara to laugh because she moaned and dropped back on the pillow. When she opened her eyes, she stared at the photograph. "Do you want to hear something crazy?"

"What?" Kylie asked, but she thought she already knew what Sara was going to say.

"Sometimes I think she's here."

"She *is* here." Kylie took Sara's hand again and struggled to know how much to tell Sara.

Sara chuckled. "Now you believe in ghosts, huh?"

"Yup." Kylie inhaled. "You'd be surprised what I believe in now."

"Like what?" Sara asked.

"Like miracles." Kylie looked at Fanny.

"I could use a miracle." Sara smiled and tried to pull her hand away. "Why is your hand so hot?"

"How do I do this?" Kylie asked the spirit, holding on to Sara's hand.

"Do what?" Sara asked, her voice sounding as tired as her eyes looked.

"I don't know how, I just know that you have the power."

"That's not helpful," Kylie responded.

"You're talking to yourself again," Sara said, but she'd stopped trying to pull her hand away.

"I know," Kylie told Sara. Then Kylie remembered how Helen, the fairy who had the ability to heal, had touched Kylie's head when she'd checked her for tumors. And Helen had said that's what she'd done when she had healed her sister's cancer.

Dropping Sara's hand, Kylie scooted up to the head of Sara's bed. She brushed Sara's bangs from her brow. Then she reached over with her other hand and touched both of Sara's temples.

"What are you doing?" Sara asked, looking at Kylie and making a funny face.

"Trying to help you relax," Kylie said, knowing it sounded lame.

"Okay, this camp has turned you weird," Sara said, and started to reach up to move Kylie's hands.

"Tell her that your mom did this for you when you weren't feeling good," Fanny said.

Good idea. "My mom used to do this to me, and it really made me feel good."

Sara dropped her hands down. "Okay, but if you try to kiss me, I'm screaming for my mom." Sara giggled.

"What? I'm not your type?" Kylie asked, and giggled, and then she tried to concentrate on positive healing thoughts.

It was after nine that night when Kylie left Sara's house. When she'd been there for about an hour, Kylie had slipped into the bathroom and called her mom. She cried when she told her mom about Sara's cancer. Her mom said she'd call Mrs. Jetton tomorrow and that Kylie should stay with Sara as long as she wanted but to call before she started home.

Kylie didn't leave until Sara went to sleep. She had forgotten to call her mom, but since she lived close, she didn't worry.

Her neighborhood was dark, no streetlights—no lights on in

the houses, either. A power outage, Kylie told herself as she fought an urgent sense of unease.

And that's when it happened.

Something large hit the windshield of her car.

Chapter Thirty-three

Kylie's heart stopped when she saw the body against her windshield. She slammed her foot on the brakes. Oh, my God. She must have hit someone.

Then she saw the face staring through the windshield at her. The rogue, the vampire who'd killed those girls in Fallen. But how? Hadn't he been "dealt" with?

She accelerated and swerved, hoping to throw him off the car. It didn't work. Clinging to the car like a spider, he inched over, smiled, and punched his fist through her car window. Glass shards went everywhere. She screamed and pushed the accelerator harder. He reached for her. His fist wrapped around her neck and squeezed. She couldn't breathe. Couldn't move. Fireworks exploded before her eyes. Her last thought was of Sara. She hoped she'd healed her. One of them should live.

When Kylie woke up, she sat up on a cold, heavy wooden chair. Her head and throat throbbed. She went to rub her temple, but her hands wouldn't move. She heard a clinking noise, metal against metal. Chains?

She pried open her eyes but saw nothing. Pitch-blackness surrounded her.

Shuffling her feet, she heard chains rattling again. Aware of cold metal bracelets against her ankles and wrists, her mind started rationalizing. Her arms and legs were bound with some kind of metal chain. She attempted to shift her limbs to test her theory.

Yup. Chains.

She hated being right, too. The memory of the rogue filled her head. A scream lodged in her throat.

She blinked and hoped to see something but only blackness invaded her senses. She inhaled. The scent of dirt and concrete filled her nose.

The lightest intake of air reached her ears. "Is someone here?"

No answer came. "I know someone's here," she said. Trying to test her strength, she pulled at the chains.

She was barely able to move.

"So the rumors of your strength were just rumors." A raspy male voice echoed in the darkness.

"Release me!" Panicked even more, she fought against the chains that bound her, but she couldn't free herself.

"You shouldn't struggle, Kylie. You'll spend your energy uselessly. Save your strength to think. To make wise choices."

Forcing herself to calm down, she listened. The voice echoed in the room. She didn't recognize it. She remembered the rogue vampire who had crashed through her windshield. Panic clawed at her raw, dry throat. She tried to remember what his voice had sounded like. She could hear him in her head, but it hadn't been the same. Had it?

"What kind of choices?" she asked.

"We have much to talk about." Definitely not the rogue and not a voice she'd heard before. It sounded . . . rusty, almost . . . old.

From the way the voice bounced around the room, Kylie sensed she was in a tunnel.

"Where am I? Who are you?" She would have asked what he wanted, but she was too scared to know. Face it, when you find yourself in chains in a pitch-black room, tea and scones weren't usually going to be offered.

The only noise she heard was the sound of her own breathing and the lighter short breaths from the man with the rusty voice. Her mind shot to the visions with the ghosts and she wondered if she had misread them. Was Kylie the person who would be tortured?

Taking a deep breath, she pulled against the chains. She couldn't free herself. Where was her strength? "What do we have to talk about?" she asked.

The light flickered on with blinding brightness. She blinked and on the second rise of her eyelids she saw him. He wore a strange robe, like a monk. His skin was wrinkled, leathered. She tightened her eyebrows and saw his brain pattern. As she suspected, vampire.

An old, weird vampire like Miranda's enemy Tabitha had described. Kylie's gut had tried to tell her not to ignore it. She hoped this didn't turn out to be her fatal and final flaw.

"You were watching me."

"You have keen instincts." He stepped closer, frighteningly closer. His eyes were cold and gray. Dead gray. "Do you purposely keep your mind closed?" he asked.

She wondered how much she should tell him, or if she should tell him anything at all. Then again, if he thought she was blocking him on purpose, he might get angry. And she had to remember not to lie.

"I don't know how to open up."

The sound of metal scraping concrete rang out. Kylie looked behind the old man to a door being pushed open. Her heart stopped and her throat ached as she remembered the newcomer's hand cutting off her airway.

"I told you to wait," the old man scolded.

"But, Gramps, I'm just eager to see my new bride." The rogue moved closer.

Bride? Kylie yanked at the chains, repulsed by the idea of being his bride.

"Leave now!" the old man roared. His voice might be rusty and worn, but his tone demanded obedience. Frightening obedience.

The rogue stopped two feet from her. His auburn hair wasn't soaked in blood this time, but she could still see it in her mind. She knew the minute she looked into his cold, gray eyes, he was the same vampire who'd slipped into her dressing room—and the one who'd crashed through her windshield. "She's so pretty. Don't keep her from me too long."

He shot off. The sound of the iron door slamming shut echoed throughout the room.

Kylie glared at the old man. "He murdered two young girls."

"Yes." He hung his head as if ashamed. "My grandson made many mistakes. But he will grow wiser."

"The Vampire Council was supposed to . . ." Kylie remembered something Della had said about the Council, namely that they were all old, and just like that, she knew. "You are part of the Council. You lied to them."

He looked up. "I did not lie. I said I would deal with this. You are part of my plan."

"He kidnapped me." Could she shame the old man into letting her go?

"On my orders."

So much for that hope.

He moved closer. A sense of power moved with him. "In my

day, when our young men acted out, only one thing could tame them. A woman strong enough, pretty enough, to give them a reason to settle down."

"He can't be saved." Her pulse raced as the old man inched closer.

"He's wild now, but you fascinate him. Do you have any idea how many hours he spent in those woods by your camp, risking being caught, and for nothing more than a chance to see you?"

She shivered with disgust, knowing it had been him all those times.

"I was curious about who had stolen my grandson's heart and I followed him. Once I saw you, I could understand what drove him. You are very fascinating." He leaned down, his face inches from hers. His breath came against her cheek and she felt sick that they shared the same airspace. "What are you, Kylie Galen? Do you even know? Is there vampire in your blood?"

"He's a murderer. I would rather die than let him lay a finger on me."

His right eyebrow arched. "Death is always an option. Not one I recommend, though."

The panic started to claw anew in her chest.

"I saw you drink the blood." His cold touch on her arm made her skin crawl. "But you are still warm. I saw the strange wolf befriend you, but you did not turn on the day of the moon. Normally, I would seek a vampire as his mate, but you . . . my grandson is right. You are special."

She pulled again at her chains. "Let me go."

"You seek a family, Kylie Galen. We shall be that to you. You will bear me great-grandchildren, and with my genes and yours, they will be even more powerful. And you will teach my grandson to be a man."

"Not happening," Kylie sneered.

"We will convince you."

"I'm not easily convinced. And if your grandson isn't a man, maybe it's because he's lacked a role model."

The old man's eyes tightened. "I will tolerate much, but I demand your respect."

"You have to earn respect." It was her mom's favorite saying, and it never rang so true as it did now.

He shook his head. "In our world, respect is won by the person who has more power. Right now, my dear child, I hold all the power."

He disappeared. Vanished. Kylie didn't even see him turn into a blur. What was he? She remembered Tabitha, the witch who Miranda caught snooping around the cabin, saying he was more than vampire, and Kylie feared the girl was right.

He might have power, Kylie thought, but she still didn't respect him. And by God, she wouldn't bear his great-grandchildren either.

She yanked at her chains again, sought the strength within herself to get free. The strength didn't come. She considered screaming but something inside her said it would be a waste of energy. She needed to think. She needed to use her brain to get out of this.

She called out for Daniel. He was a no-show. Would the death angels or whatever it was at the falls come to her aid?

She closed her eyes and asked for help. Begged, actually. The thought of being touched by the rogue meant she wasn't above begging.

In the deep corners of her mind, a voice whispered, "You have the power within you."

"Please, that sounds like an old *Star Wars* movie!" When only silence answered, she continued, "This isn't any time for self-discovery." She yanked again at the chains, thinking the power she had was to break loose. She struggled until she felt her wrists and ankles bruise.

"He wants me to bear his great-grandchildren. I could use some help here!"

Trying to remember to breathe, she considered what power the death angels meant. She was a ghost whisperer, she could run fast, and occasionally found unknown strength to toss werewolves long distances. And she had special hearing that came and went. There was also a possibility that she could heal—she hoped so for Sara's sake—and she could dreamscape.

I can dreamscape! Wasn't that as good as a cell phone? If she could get Lucas, Lucas could get Burnett. Burnett would get her out of this. He would. He'd bring the whole FRU down on this old dude's ass.

She counted sheep. One hundred, then two. Every noise and sometimes the lack of noise kept her awake. Her eyes grew tired. She eventually grew tired. Finally, the floating sensation pulled at her subconscious. Then she flew, whooshed through the clouds. She saw him.

"You came." Lucas sat up on a king-size bed. He wore a sexy smile and no shirt. Not that now was the time to notice such things.

"The rogue has me. Get Burnett." She spoke quickly, afraid she'd wake up.

"What?"

"You heard me."

"Where are you?"

"Don't know. A tunnel. There's a lot of concrete. Iron doors, too."

He looked at her in panic. "I have to know where you are."

"I was unconscious when they brought me here."

"They?"

"The rogue's grandfather. He's one of the Vampire Council."

Lucas pushed both hands through his dark hair. "Listen, Kylie. The way dreamscaping works, you can fly. You're going to have to fly back to your body, but slowly. Look down and see landmarks. Then come back and tell me where you are. I have to know where you are or I can't help you."

"What if I can't come back? What if I wake up and can't tell you?" The panic made her feel heavy and it sounded in her voice. She didn't want to leave Lucas. Although she knew it was a dream, she felt safer here.

"You can do this, Kylie. Go!" He waved her away. "Hurry."

Kylie did what Lucas told her to do. She started flying back. Too fast. She concentrated until she found how to reduce her speed. Then she looked down. She saw a skyline. Houston skyline. She dropped lower until she saw a large building, the Toyota Center, she recognized it. Then she remembered her father had taken her downtown into the Houston tunnels.

Flying through the tunnel, unstopped by the walls, Kylie didn't slow down until she saw herself. Her heart hammered against her ribs. Seeing oneself slumped over in a chair, chained like a scene in a horror movie, freaked her out. She heard a noise. The iron door began to open. She felt herself falling into her body.

"No!" She had to get back to Lucas. She had to give him directions on how to find her.

Chapter Thirty-four

Fighting the pull to move back into her body, Kylie swung around and flew back the way she'd come. The speed prevented her from breathing.

Someone called her name. Not Lucas. It was the old vampire.

The clouds were thick. Wasn't Lucas just through the layer of fog? She felt herself being yanked back. She was about to wake up. "Lucas, I'm in the Houston Tunnel System. Under the Toyota building. Can you hear me?"

"What are you doing?" the dark, rusty voice growled.

Kylie jerked her eyes open. The old vampire stared at her. She remembered she couldn't lie. "Dreaming."

"What kind of dream? I felt the energy."

"A disturbing one. I . . . used to have night terrors when I was younger." No lie there.

He appeared resigned to believe her, but remained suspicious. Was there something for him to be suspicious about? Had Lucas heard her?

"I have some old friends interested in meeting you. For your own well-being, I hope you will be on your best behavior."

"Who are they? And why do they want to meet me?"

"I think, Kylie Galen, that you are even more special than you know."

"How am I special?"

He didn't answer. "If you can tell me that you will not try to escape, I will release the chains."

The thought of having the heavy metal bracelets removed sounded like heaven. The words were on the tip of her tongue, but they would have been a lie.

"We both know that if there is a way to escape I will take it. Your job is to make sure there isn't a way."

He laughed. "I appreciate your honesty."

"Enough to unchain me?"

"Not that much," he said.

She met his aged gray eyes. "I see no way to escape the room. Unless you believe I have the power to overtake you when the door is open. And since I can't break these chains, are you saying that your powers are weaker than this metal?"

He studied her. "You are very intelligent, my child. Dare I worry that you are as cunning as you are smart?"

"If I was that smart and cunning, would I be here?"

"Let's compromise." He closed his eyes and the metal bracelets around her arms and one from one ankle disappeared. Her right ankle was now attached to a long heavy chain.

Shocked at his ability, she stared at him. "What are you?"

He smiled. "See, I am already winning your respect."

"You misread curiosity for respect," she countered.

His eyes tightened, but a slight smile crept from behind his anger.

"What are you?" she asked again.

He folded his aged arms over his chest. "What's wrong, dear? Are the similarities frightening?" With that, he disappeared into the thin, cold air.

"What's that supposed to mean?" she yelled, and stood to see how far she could get with the chain attached to her ankle.

No nearly far enough.

Kylie tried to fall back asleep, to get back to Lucas, but she couldn't. She could only hope her message had gotten through and that he'd already phoned Burnett and they were on the way here now. How long would it take?

What if they didn't come? What if her message never got through? She attempted to pull the chain free, but her strength wasn't there. What was it with her strength? Why did it come and go?

Kylie started pacing, dragging the chain as she went. She couldn't reach the thick door, though it wouldn't have mattered if she had. When the vampire had disappeared, so had the doorknob. Opening it would have been impossible. Still she paced and tried to come up with a way out, with or without any help from Burnett. She glanced back at the door with its missing knob. What the hell was he? And what had he meant by that whole similarity crap?

The chain clattered against the concrete floor. She remembered she hadn't phoned her mom before she left Sara's house and she hoped like heck that she wasn't worried. Turning again, pacing toward the right wall this time, Kylie was surprised to hear voices. Was the old man back with his friends? She stopped moving and listened.

It wasn't the old dude's voice, but that of the rogue. Oh, great, was he planning on visiting again? Her body tensed and she looked around for anything that could be used as a weapon. Before her gaze swept the room, she heard the rogue's voice clearer.

"Who are you and what are doing snooping around here?"

Where were the voices coming from? She hesitated and moved closer to the wall. Suddenly, a loud thump sounded as if something heavy had been tossed across the room.

Or someone?

Her heart stopped. She moved even closer to the wall trying to see if the voices were coming from behind the wall. Another clatter echoed and she felt almost certain that it was.

"You will tell me!" the rogue hissed.

Fear filled her gut. Who was the rogue talking to? Was it . . . was it someone who'd come looking for her? Her thoughts and heart shot to Lucas.

"Unchain me and fight like a man!" Lucas's voice roared.

Her chest swelled with regret. She'd gone to him for help and . . .

"Why? You would only fight like the dog you are." A loud thud followed, and Kylie knew Lucas had taken a blow.

Her muscles tightened. A surge of energy shot through her. She grabbed the chain with one hand and yanked it out of the concrete. Then, turning to the wall, she charged at it with her shoulder. Only a flicker of a second before she hit did she consider how it might hurt.

Oddly, she felt nothing. Chucks of concrete fell around her. She knocked the big pieces from her face and then, realizing she stood on the other side of the room, she stared through the cloud of dust. Lucas lay on his side, still chained to a chair, much like the one she'd been in moments earlier. She saw his face, a bloody mess, and his eyes were closed as if he was unconscious.

Or dead.

She breathed in raw fury and looked around for the rogue. When she saw him, the shock on his face didn't surprise her. She charged him, but right before she had her hands on him, he disappeared.

"So you are not so powerless." The old vampire's voice boomed around her although she could not see him. The concrete wall behind her reformed and she sensed it grew thicker this time.

"What are you?" she hissed, knowing no ordinary vampire could build a wall back up.

"Did I not ask you the same thing?" he answered.

She ran to Lucas. A hand to his chest told her he was still alive. She yanked his chains off and dropped beside him on her knees. The gravel on the concrete floor bit into her skin.

Remembering she possibly had the power to heal, she moved her hands over him, then remembering what she'd done for Sara, Kylie pressed her palms around his head.

"Talk to me, Lucas. Please." The memory of him saving her from the bullies and of him looking up at the sky for elephants filled her mind and tears filled her eyes. "Please be okay."

She tried to think positively, tried to think about her hands sending warmth into his body. She didn't know if this was how it worked, but for Lucas's and Sara's sake, she prayed it was. Her heart filled with hope when the swelling on his face disappeared.

"Now talk to me," she whispered, and she began to lean down.

His eyes shot open, panic marred his expression, and he swung his fist.

She tried to catch it but whatever power she'd had was gone.

She did manage to avoid the punch to the face. Instead, his fist slammed against her shoulder. Pain exploded. The blow knocked her clear across the room.

"Christ!" He lunged to his feet. "I'm sorry." He picked her up and cradled her tenderly against his chest. "Are you okay?"

She nodded. Thankful he wasn't vampire and wouldn't know she lied. Her shoulder throbbed like a bad toothache. "Down," she managed to say.

He complied but her knees buckled and he had to catch her. "I'm sorry."

She looked into his blue eyes. "It's okay." He hadn't meant to hit her. "I don't think it's broken."

"Did you get . . ." She stopped talking, remembering the old vampire was probably listening.

"Burnett?" she mouthed the name, and looked up at him with a question in her eyes.

He nodded and she prayed he'd read her lips correctly and this meant Burnett and the FRU were coming.

Her shoulder pounded. Her legs shook. She leaned against the wall and slid down to sit on the cold concrete floor. Lucas sat down beside her. She shivered and he must have felt it because he put his arm around her. His body oozed heat. She leaned into him to soak up his warmth.

"You are so hot," she said.

"It's about time you noticed," he teased.

She would have smiled if her energy hadn't felt spent. In spite of the pain, she felt safe.

"It's a werewolf thing," he said. "Our body temperatures run hotter."

"What time is it?"

"After midnight," he answered.

She remembered her mom who must be panicking by now. Then feeling too exhausted to think, Kylie closed her eyes and leaned closer into his chest, careful not to move her shoulder.

He shifted her into his lap. His warmth surrounded her. She felt him moving a hand through her hair. "You've got something in your hair," he said.

"Probably concrete, from when I . . . came through the wall," she said.

"What wall?" he asked.

She recalled he'd been unconscious then. Did he even know she'd healed him?

"That one." She nodded. "He put it back together, though."

"I think I hit you harder than I thought."

She didn't have the strength to argue. "So tired."

"Rest." He pulled her closer. "Soon," he whispered.

Was he saying that it would be over soon? God, she hoped so.

"Kylie. It's time."

Lucas's words stirred her awake some time later.

She felt Lucas jump up with her in his arms and she became instantly alert. Loud noises came from behind the wall and, in one easy leap, he had them against the back of the room, away from the noise. Before she could insist Lucas put her down, the front wall collapsed and Burnett and several other FRU personnel hurtled though the cascading concrete.

Burnett rushed forward. "Is she okay?"

"Fine," she said, embarrassed that Lucas held her like a child. "Put me down."

"Her shoulder," Lucas said. "I think it's broken. My fault. I did it . . . accidentally."

"I'm fine." She went to move her shoulder to prove her point, and winced.

"They're here!" someone screamed from down the hall. Lucas, Burnett, and the other men ran through the rubble that had once been a wall. She stood alone in the cloud of dust their hasty departure had created. The sound of men fighting in the distance reached her ears. Feeling useless, she started to follow, hoping her strength would return, but she hadn't taken one step when she felt the rush of air move past her.

The young, evil-eyed rogue stopped beside her and before Kylie could do more than scream, he had her in his arms. Forgetting about her shoulder, she struggled. Pain exploded in her arm, but she continued to fight. But his hold was strong, and her own strength spent.

"No!" the deep rumble of Lucas's voice filled her ears.

"Put her down," Lucas demanded.

"She's mine," the rogue hissed.

"Over my dead body," Lucas roared, and his eyes deepened to a burnt orange.

"That will be my pleasure," the vampire roared back, his gray eyes now glowing red.

Realizing her opportunity, Kylie jabbed the palm of her hand into the rogue's throat. He dropped her, and she had no more than hit the ground when she saw Lucas attack. The sound of fist pounding into bone filled the room. In horror, she watched as Lucas was thrown across the room. She felt her own strength returning, but before she got to her feet, Lucas was back, holding the vampire by the throat. The sound coming from the vampire's throat left Kylie with no doubt that Lucas's hold was crushing his airway.

"Drop him!" The voice of the old vampire filled the room and made the air heavy. "Drop him or she dies."

While Kylie could see no one, she felt a hand close around her throat. She clawed at the invisible force that choked her and tried to pull air into her lungs. None came.

She saw Lucas's gaze shoot to her. Dark sparkles started filling her vision, and right before everything went black, she saw Lucas drop the rogue, who then disappeared. No wind, no air. Obviously the old man's magic had taken him away.

Still attempting to gasp air into her lungs, she collapsed to her knees. Lucas pulled her up.

Burnett suddenly appeared at their side.

"He came back for her," Lucas said.

"We need to get her away," Burnett said, and reached out and took her in his arms. "The FRU are following them."

"I'm going with them," Lucas said.

"No," Kylie said, forcing the words out of her bruised throat. But she wasn't in the room anymore. The wind hit her face so fast she couldn't breathe. Burnett readjusted her, and buried her face against his chest, a chest that wasn't near as warm or comforting as the one she'd just been sleeping against.

When he came to a stop outside a single-story building, Kylie raised her head. "Where are we?" She touched her neck.

"A clinic," he said, and moved her hand to check her neck.

"I'm fine. Put me down."

"Not yet. You might be fine, but Holiday would have my ass if I didn't have a doctor check you out."

She remembered Lucas. "You should have stopped Lucas from going after the rogues . . ."

"Couldn't have stopped him," he said. "Werewolves are too damn stubborn. But Lucas can take care of himself."

"He got captured," she said.

"Only to get inside to you," he said.

The realization made her gut clench. "He could have been killed."

"He wasn't." The lights came on in the building and Burnett moved in.

Kylie read the sign on the door as he carried her inside: PRO-TECT YOUR PETS AGAINST HEARTWORMS. "Wait. You're taking me to a vet?" Kylie looked around the small office with pet pictures posted on the walls and noticed the smell of animals.

"A vet and supernatural doctor," he said.

A man walked out of the door from the back. "In here," he said.

Burnett introduced her to Dr. Whitman as he carried her though the door. A big orange cat followed them into the back. When Bur-nett placed her on an examining table, the cat jumped up beside her. "I'm fine," she told Burnett and Dr. Whitman.

"Her shoulder," Burnett said. "And her neck."

When the doctor reached for Kylie's shoulder, she flinched. "I'm just bruised." She looked back at Burnett. "I've got to get back to my mom's. She's probably already at the police station."

Burnett picked up the phone and walked to the other side of the room.

Dr. Whitman moved Kylie's shoulder and studied her. Kylie flinched a bit, but she knew it wasn't broken. His eyebrows twitched as he looked at her forehead. "What are you?"

"Beats me," she said, and looked at his brain pattern. He was part fairy. The cat walked across Kylie to rub against the doc's side. She suspected he could communicate with animals the way Derek did, too. The thought of Derek had her heart remembering how much she missed him, but she pushed it away.

"Well, the girl's right. Her shoulder isn't broken," Dr. Whitman said as Burnett moved back over.

"Told you so," Kylie couldn't resist saying. "Now, would you please drop me off at my mom's house?"

"Thank you," Burnett said to Dr. Whitman, and motioned for him to leave the room. Once they were alone, Burnett turned back to Kylie. "I'm going to get you home. But first I need to know what happened tonight."

Kylie told him everything she remembered from the time the rogue had landed on her car, to right before Burnett burst through the concrete walls. She informed him that the rogue who'd killed the girls in Fallen was the grandson of one of the Vampire Council members. As well as the fact that it had been the vamps who'd been watching the campgrounds off and on all summer. Most of what Kylie had to say turned the vampire's eyes bright with fury.

"So, what's the deal with him wanting me to marry his grandson?" she asked when she was done.

Burnett shrugged. "In the past, our grandparents chose our mates."

"Even if the mate wasn't willing?"

"Afraid so." Burnett's expression filled with remorse. "You were right, Kylie. This was about you. I should have listened. I won't make that mistake again."

She nodded, sensing how hard it was for him to admit he'd made a mistake. "The old man, he's weird. His brain pattern says he's a vampire, but he's more than that."

"I know the man you are talking about. I've met him during my visits with the Council. He's vampire, but you're right, he's strange."

"He's more than vampire," Kylie said. "He put the wall back together after I broke it down."

"Maybe he had help from someone with other powers."

"I think it's more," she said.

"Maybe," he said, but Kylie could tell he didn't agree. "Okay, I'll get you home. And I'll have someone watching your house so you'll be safe."

He picked Kylie back up. "Hold on." She knew this time to bury her head against his chest.

In seconds, Burnett set her down in front of her house. "What do I tell her?" she asked.

"Don't know. I've never been good dealing with parents," he said. "But be creative."

"You're not a lot of help." She bit down on her lip. "Oh, crap, my car."

"We found it when we were looking for you. Someone will get the window replaced and have it back here before daybreak."

"Thanks."

He nodded. "I'm glad you're okay, Kylie. We'll go over everything again tomorrow evening when you come back to the camp. And call Holiday the first chance you get. She won't sleep until she talks to you."

Kylie reached up and hugged him. He looked unprepared for the show of affection. "Thank you," she said.

"You're welcome," he answered, obviously uncomfortable with the conversation as much as the hug.

She looked around at the darkness. The silence didn't even scare her because she knew Burnett was the one who caused it.

"I've got two men watching the house," he said as if he'd misread her expression.

"I believe you." She watched him leave. Then she went to the door. When she realized she didn't have her keys, she found the spare her mom kept inside the fake dog poop behind the azalea bushes.

She barely got the door open when her mom flew at her and wrapped her arms around her.

"Oh, God. I was just about to call the police. Where have you been, young lady?"

Her mom's hug squeezed her shoulder and made it hard to breathe. Pulling back and trying to mask the pain in her voice, Kylie said, "I forgot to call. And then . . . I was so upset over Sara that I just needed to think."

Tears filled her mom's eyes. "Oh, baby, I'm so sorry. The power went out. I fell asleep on the sofa waiting on you to get home. I woke up fifteen minutes ago and when I realized you weren't here, I called Sara's house. Her mom said you'd left, but she didn't know when."

Luckily Sara's mom had already gone to bed when Kylie left so she couldn't have known what time Kylie really left. "Well, I'm fine."

"I didn't hear the car pull in," her mom said.

Think quick. "I parked it on the street." She hoped Burnett was right and the car would be returned by daybreak.

Kylie faked a yawn. "You know, Mom, sleep sounds really good right now," she said, wanting to get to her room and call Holiday. But she'd have to use the home phone because her cell was back in the car.

"Okay, but we'll talk about Sara tomorrow."

Yeah, Kylie thought. They also needed to talk about her going to Shadow Falls for the next school year. But she decided to worry about that later, too. She hurried to her room and dialed Holiday's number.

"Have you heard from Lucas?" she asked when the camp leader answered the phone.

"Yes," Holiday said. "He's fine. But . . . last I heard, the people responsible for taking you weren't captured. Burnett is watching you, though. Don't worry."

"I know," Kylie said.

"Are you okay? I wish I could I touch you and calm you down."

"I'm fine," she lied.

"If you close your eyes and imagine the falls, it will help push away the panic."

"I will," Kylie said, and this time she wasn't lying.

Sunday morning, the ringing telephone woke Kylie at almost ten. She sat up, reached for the phone, and actually looked around, hoping she'd see the ghost. Hey . . . after over a month of seeing her first thing in the morning, she sort of missed her.

Pushing the talk button, she recalled her conversation with Holiday from last night. It had worked; imagining the falls had taken the edge off her panic.

"Hello," Kylie answered.

"Are you okay?" Della and Miranda's voices exploded at the same time over the line.

"I'm fine." Kylie leaned back on the pillow. "How did you find out?"

"When you didn't answer the damn phone all night, I called Holiday," Della said.

"Spill it," Miranda said.

Kylie gave them the short version and promised she'd tell them all the gory details later. Then she asked about their weekend. Miranda moaned and groaned about the event, but ended by telling them that she'd taken second in the competition.

"And the bitch Tabitha took fourth," Miranda said with pride.

"How are you, Della?" Kylie asked.

"What does this tell you?" The sound of a toilet flushing filled the line.

"Gross," Miranda said.

"I think my parents are shocked that I haven't shown positive yet."

After a few more minutes of chatting, they said good-bye. Remembering the car, Kylie scrambled out of bed and looked out the window. Burnett had been true to his word. The car sat on the street outside the house, looking as good as new.

If only everything else in her life could be fixed as easily.

"You're up," her mom said as Kylie walked out of her bedroom a few minutes later. Her mom had a towel wrapped around her head and wore her bathrobe as through she'd just gotten out of the shower. "Give me a minute and I'll fix us breakfast."

Thirty minutes later, Kylie was having pancakes and eggs with her mom. They talked about a lot of things but mostly about Sara. Kylie's mom told her that Sara's mom had called to make sure Kylie had gotten home okay.

Her mom picked up her plate and carried it to the sink. "Sara's mom said that Sara's was feeling good today, too. She's supposed to go to the doctor tomorrow to talk about her options. I sure hope it works out."

Kylie stood and helped clear the table.

"She doesn't need options," a voice whispered behind Kylie. *"You did it."* The temperature in the room dropped a good twenty degrees.

"I swear that air-conditioner has been acting up for a month now." Her mom shivered and went to check the thermostat. Kylie wondered if her mom's AC was really out, or if it had been Daniel causing the cold.

Kylie turned and saw the ghost. She looked healthy and young.

Beautiful. Kylie suspected that Sara would look just like her when she hit her thirties.

"Thank you. I knew you could do it."

"You don't have to thank me. She's my friend."

"Did you say something?" Her mom stood in the kitchen doorway.

The ghost smiled and faded.

"Yeah," Kylie said. "I said we need to talk about school." Kylie went and gave her mom a big hug. Her shoulder hardly hurt now. When she pulled back she just spouted out the words before she lost her nerve. "I know it's hard for you. I know you love me. But I need this right now. I really need this."

He mom touched Kylie's face. Then tears filled her mom's eyes.

She breathed in.

Then out.

"Baby, I'm sorry. But I just can't let you go."

Chapter Thirty-five

Kylie's heart squeezed. The room went cold again. Daniel appeared. He smiled. "Remind her . . ." he said, but before he could finish, he disappeared. Somehow Kylie knew what he'd meant.

"Mom," she said. "Remember how you told me that when you met Daniel, you just knew he was right for you?"

Her mom looked shocked that Kylie had brought up Daniel. "Yes, but—"

"This school is my Daniel, Mom. I know it's right for me. I know it in my heart. Please, don't take that away from me. Don't take this away from me, like Daniel was taken away from you."

"Don't I even get to walk you inside?" her mom asked, after she pulled to a stop in the parking lot outside the gates at Shadow Falls later that afternoon.

"It's not visitation day," Kylie said, and barely glanced back at the new spirit who'd hitched a ride with them as they passed the cemetery in Fallen. The dark-haired woman, wearing a pink fuzzy housecoat, appeared to be in her late twenties. She also looked completely confused and kept staring at Kylie and asking where she was. Kylie had tried talking to her in her mind, but the woman didn't hear. Plus, Kylie's mom had bitched the entire way about how the car's air-conditioner must be broken, too.

Scooting over, Kylie gave her mom a big hug. "Thank you," she said. Her mom had reluctantly agreed to sign the papers for Kylie to go to school that fall at Shadow Falls.

Sighing, her mom pulled back and rested her hand against Kylie's cheek. "I still don't like it."

"I know."

"Remember the condition," her mom said.

Kylie hadn't meant to argue, but the words slipped out. "I don't get it. You won't forgive him. You don't even want to see him, but you expect me to call him twice a week."

"He's your father," her mom said.

"Daniel's my father."

Her mom winced. "Yes, but Tom loved you like his own."

"I know. And I plan on forgiving him, but . . . it still hurts. And when he tried to use me to get to you, well . . ."

"I know," her mom said. "He was wrong. He's not perfect. Neither am I. I'm sorry I caused a scene when he showed up."

Kylie looked into her eyes. "Do you still love him?"

"I don't know. When it stops hurting so bad, I might figure it out."

They hugged again and a few minutes later Kylie watched her mom pull away. The ghost had decided to stick with Kylie and now stood beside her. She opened her housecoat and looked down at a big gaping hole in her abdomen. Why the heck couldn't Kylie get haunted by a ghost who died peacefully in her sleep?

"What happened to me?" the ghost asked.

"I don't know." Kylie watched the spirit fade. But Kylie had a feeling she'd be back. And she'd expect Kylie to help her figure everything out, too. That in itself frustrated Kylie to no end. How could she figure out the ghost's problems when she couldn't figure out her own? She checked her phone to see if the PI had returned her call she'd made to him right after she'd collected her phone from her car this morning. He'd left a text and said he had news, but didn't even hint at what the news might be.

When Kylie got to the gate, the feeling of being home made her heart race. This really was where she belonged. Holiday and Burnett were waiting for her as soon as she walked inside.

Holiday gave her a big, soulful hug. Burnett took her bag and motioned for her to follow him.

As they passed the dining hall, Kylie saw that several campers had also arrived early. Holiday had called Kylie and asked her to come back an hour early to talk. They walked into the office cabin and Kylie was stunned when Lucas stood right on the other side of the door.

His blue eyes met hers. "The shoulder okay?"

Kylie got a feeling he wanted to touch her, but he waited for her to make the first move. As tempting as it was to wrap her arms around him, it didn't feel a hundred percent right. Last night it had felt as natural as breathing, but now she wasn't so sure. "Only a little sore. Thanks."

"If you ever hit her again, accident or not, I'm going to come after you with a pitchfork," Holiday said. From the tightness in her eyes, Kylie knew the camp leader meant it, too.

"It wasn't his fault." Kylie stepped closer to Lucas and obviously he took that as the sign he'd wanted earlier. He moved his hand ever so slightly and touched her wrist. A simple touch, but it sent sweet warmth through her.

"Yes, it was." Lucas met her eyes. Guilt rang in his voice. "I have to learn to think before I swing." He looked at Burnett and

Kylie got a feeling Holiday wasn't the only one who'd given Lucas a talking-to.

Slowly, Lucas's hand slipped into hers and gave her palm a light squeeze. Ambivalence bounced around Kylie's stomach. She wasn't sure she was ready to give herself to the possibilities of where that touch could lead them, but neither was she willing to pull away. He'd risked his own life to save her. Remembering she should focus on something other than Lucas, she looked at Burnett. "Any luck on finding them?"

"No." His eyes brightened with anger.

"But we will," Burnett and Lucas said at the same time.

"The others in the Vampire Council have been told about what happened. I imagine there will be consequences."

In a few minutes, Lucas was asked to leave and then Burnett and Holiday took Kylie into Holiday's office. Burnett made Kylie go over everything three or four times. While it felt about as easy as eating rocks, she didn't complain about his drilling. Holiday's eyes filled with pride when Kylie told them about healing Lucas and possibly also Sara.

Finally, the question that had been brewing in her mind came out. "The thing I don't understand is why I couldn't use the strength to save myself."

Holiday gasped as if she'd come to a sudden realization. "You're a protector. I should have guessed after the incident with Selynn. When we were at the lake, you only gained strength when you thought your mother was in danger. It also explains why your real father, Daniel, wasn't able to save himself the day he died."

"Does that . . . tell you what I am? What he was?"

"I'm afraid not, but . . ." Holiday's gaze went to Burnett who looked equally surprised and amazed. "Being a protector is very rare and only is bestowed on the extremely gifted."

"Really gifted," Burnett said, and he sounded a little awed. "I've only met one other protector in my life."

A protector? Kylie didn't know what all it meant. "So, I have other gifts beside the ones I have now?"

"Probably." Holiday smiled. "I knew you were special, Kylie. I knew it from the moment I saw you."

"Could one of these gifts perhaps be the gift of figuring out what the hell I am!" Frustration colored her voice.

After a minute of being told the same thing: *It would eventually happen. She needed to be patient, make it her quest . . . bla . . . bla . . . bla . . .* Burnett went back to asking questions. "Did Mario say who these friends were that he wanted you to meet?"

"Mario?" Kylie asked.

"Mario Esparza is the old vampire's name."

She closed her eyes, not sure if she liked knowing his name. "No." Kylie shivered, imagining the kind of friends he probably kept. "What do you think he meant about the similarities he said we had? Do you think he believes I'm somehow like him? Could he be a protector or . . ."

"I don't know what he meant," Burnett said. "But I don't think he's a protector."

"You're not like him, Kylie," Holiday insisted. "He wasn't born at midnight."

"So he's evil?" Kylie asked.

Burnett looked at Holiday as if he wasn't sure what he should say. Holiday nodded as if giving the okay.

"Yes, he's evil. He's been a thorn in the FRU's side for years. We tried to get him thrown out of the Council, but we never had enough proof."

Kylie took a deep breath. "Do you think he'll come for me again?"

Again, Burnett glanced at Holiday before continuing. "I wish I could tell you that I thought it was over. He doesn't like to lose, but you have my personal guarantee he won't win this one. I will stop him, no matter what it takes."

Holiday reached for Kylie's hand and squeezed. "We need to wrap this up," she told Burnett. "I think most of the campers are in the dining room."

He didn't look happy. "Okay, but I may want to ask you some questions later."

Kylie nodded. They all stood. Burnett started out.

"Burnett?" Holiday said, her tone filled with uncertainty.

He turned around and for a second his expression was one of a puppy who sought affection and acceptance.

Kylie watched Holiday pull a piece of paper from her desk drawer. "You might want to take this. Read it over carefully before you sign."

"What is it?" he asked.

Holiday hesitated. "It's the paperwork. I thought you wanted to be an investor in Shadow Falls."

He glanced down at the paper and then back at Holiday. "So, you couldn't find any other investors?"

Her right eyebrow arched. "I suppose the school isn't considered the best of investments."

Kylie had to bite back a smile when she recognized Holiday's method of avoiding a lie for the purpose of hiding a different truth. She didn't want Burnett to know she'd had other offers, and Kylie knew why, too. To admit that she chose him over the others was admitting she didn't want to lose him.

"I will insist on having more of a say in how things are run around here," Burnett warned.

"And I'm sure I'll fight you on most of it," Holiday countered.

A slight smile whispered across his lips. "Fair enough."

Holiday nodded. "Most of my conditions are listed."

Burnett went to Holiday's desk and signed the paper.

"Don't you think you should have read it first?" Holiday asked.

"Let's just say that I look forward to fighting with you." He handed her the paper and walked out, leaving a sweet kind of tension in his place.

Kylie waited until she was sure Burnett was out of super-hearing earshot. "I know you had another investor lined up."

Holiday rolled her eyes. "And you know not to say anything about it, too, right?"

Kylie grinned. "You didn't want to lose him, Holiday."

"He's growing on me," she said. "But that doesn't mean—"

"Right." Kylie laughed.

Holiday frowned. "I'll bet Della and Miranda are waiting for you."

Kylie hugged Holiday before leaving. When she walked out of the office, Kylie looked toward the dining room and suddenly she wasn't so sure she was ready to face everyone. So much had happened and she hadn't even had time to adjust. Right then, she felt a hand slip inside hers.

She jumped and started to pull away, but stopped when she recognized the warmth of the palm in hers.

"Hey," Lucas said, and gave her a tug. "Let's take a walk."

She let him lead her behind the cabin that housed the office. The moment they stepped in the secluded spot beneath the trees, he stopped and turned and faced her.

"I'm really sorry I hit you." His hold on her hand tightened.

She shook her head. "You didn't mean to do it."

"But I still did it." He gave her hand another light tug and drew her closer. "Burnett said you . . . you healed me."

"Yeah," she said, feeling the warmth of his chest even though she wasn't pressed against him. She inhaled and realized that Lucas smelled like the woods. The scent of the trees and the moist earth clung to him.

"You might have even saved my life," he said.

"Yeah, but I was the reason you got hurt in the first place."

"Doesn't matter." He shot her a sly smile. "You know there's an old vampire legend that says if someone saves your life, you must stay with them forever."

She cut her gaze up at him. "You're not vampire."

He leaned down. His lips were so close to hers that she could taste them. "And for the first time in my life, I wish I were." He inhaled. "But since I'm not vampire, I think the least I can do is give you a thank-you kiss."

"The least you can do," she said, and then his lips touched hers. It wasn't overtly sexy like the kiss they'd shared at the falls, or the ones they shared in the dreams, but it didn't make it any less special. Or any less harder for her to pull away from. But she did pull away. It was just . . . too soon. But later, maybe . . . yes, maybe.

"We . . . we should probably go join the others."

"Yeah." And they walked in silence and he didn't let her hand go until they walked into the dining hall.

Kylie was nearly overwhelmed by everyone wanting to make sure she was okay. She wasn't sure who had spilled the beans about what had happened but it was clear they all knew.

Della, Miranda, Perry, Helen, and Jonathon all gathered around her. Lucas stood back as if giving her space. But he'd meet her eyes every few minutes. Once she even waved him over, but he shook his head, as if somehow he knew she'd been unsure about offering him the invitation. Or maybe it was because he was werewolf and his kind just always seemed to stay together. Nevertheless, she got an odd kind of feeling as if he was guarding her. She remembered how he'd protected her from the bullies when she'd been six and again she felt the bond that connected them. Now what Kylie needed to figure out was just exactly what that bond meant.

An hour later, Kylie's closest friends were all still eating pizza and chatting about how their home visits went. "Oh," Miranda said in her usual peppy voice. "I think I figured out what I did wrong with Socks. I'll have the little stinker back to his old self in no time."

"So, Miranda, your competition went okay?" Perry blurted the question out, sounding nervous. It was the first time he'd spoken to Miranda. Kylie knew this was his way of saying he wanted to start over with her, and Kylie would have hugged him if she hadn't been afraid Miranda might zap her with her award-winning pinky.

"It went fine," she said, but Kylie couldn't read Miranda's expression.

"Why don't you two just kiss and make up already?" Della said. "And then you can go somewhere alone and really suck face."

Miranda shot Della a huge frown that for sure meant an argument would follow later. Perry's eyes went black as he stared at Della, and then he walked off, looking a little rejected. Kylie just leaned back in her chair and wondered if things would ever change.

But then . . . some things had already changed, hadn't they? She found herself looking around for another face. While she tried really hard not to admit it, she missed Derek. More than that, she worried if he was okay. She decided to go find Burnett and ask, but her phone beeped with an incoming text.

She glanced at the caller ID. It was from the PI. Then Kylie saw she had a text from Sara. It read, "What did you do? Don't lie. I know you did it."

Kylie's heart lurched. Great. What was she going to tell Sara?

Her phone beeped again. When Kylie read the message from the PI, she gasped. "Grandparents back. Spoke yesterday. They want to see you ASAP."

Hope stirred inside her heart. Would this lead to the answer about who she was?

"Kylie?" Mandy called her name from the door.

Kylie turned around. "Yeah?"

"Holiday said for you to come to the office. Someone is here to see you."

"Who is it?" Kylie asked, feeling panicked at the thought of it actually being them. Was she really ready to do this? Was she ready to meet Daniel's adoptive parents? Her grandparents?

"I don't know, but there was an old couple knocking on the gate a few minutes ago."

And just like that Kylie heard the sound of cascading water. Something caught her attention out of the corner of her eye, and she looked toward the log wall where a mixture of light and shadows swirled in soft, almost hypnotic patterns. Dancing death angels.

She glanced at Della and Miranda. Neither reacted. Apparently, Kylie was the only one to see the show playing on the other side of the room. And then,

"Go and uncover your past so you may discover your destiny."

"Is everything okay?" Della asked, looking concerned.

Kylie took a deep breath. "Yeah. Fine."

And she hoped she was right about that, too.